Sword of
Honour

To Chris Patten, a man of honour,
in admiration

Sail forth – steer for the deep waters only,
Reckless O soul, exploring, I with thee, and thou with me,
For we are bound where mariner has not yet dared to go,
And we will risk the ship, ourselves and all.

– *Whitman*

CONTENTS

1

Decisions

Vice-Admiral Sir Graham Bethune put down his pen and waited for the elderly Admiralty clerk to gather up the letters and despatches he had signed. As the tall double doors closed behind him, Bethune stood up and glanced at the nearest windows. Bright sunshine; he could even feel the warmth across the room, with a sky so clear that it was almost colourless.

He heard a clock chime, and wondered how the meeting was progressing along the passageway. Senior officers, lords of Admiralty, and civilian advisers who had been called here to discuss the state of the dockyards and the needs of the medical services. At the Admiralty, it was another ordinary day.

He moved restlessly to the window and opened it, and the sounds of London rose to greet him. The clatter of carriages and the jingle of harness, the cry of a street pedlar risking the wrath of Admiralty porters to sell his wares to the passing throng.

Bethune caught his own reflection in the window, and smiled. Once he had thought he would never hold such an appointment; now he could hardly imagine anything else. After ships and the sea, it had seemed like something foreign. He touched the front of his waistcoat. Graham Bethune, Vice-Admiral of the Blue, one of the youngest flag officers on the Navy List. Like the uniform, the appointment fitted him perfectly.

He leaned over the sill and watched the procession of people. Many of the carriages were open to the sunshine, revealing women in colourful hats and fine gowns. It was April of the year 1814, but the war was still a brutal fact.

Like most serving officers, Bethune had become accustomed to the exaggerated assurances and the promises of final victory.

Reports arrived daily with news that Wellington's armies were breaking through one French strongpoint after another; the invincible Napoleon was claimed to be on the run, deserted by all but his faithful marshals and his Old Guard.

What did all those people down there really believe, he wondered. After so many years of war with the familiar enemy, was the prospect of peace still only a dream? He moved back into the room and stared at the painting on one wall, a frigate in action, sails pitted with shot, a full broadside spitting fire at the enemy. It was Bethune's last command. He had confronted two big Spanish frigates, unfortunate odds even for a captain as eager as he had been. After a brisk engagement, he had run one Spaniard ashore and captured the other. Flag rank had followed almost immediately.

He looked at the ornate clock with its simpering cherubs and thought of the one man he admired, perhaps envied, more than any other.

Sir Richard Bolitho was back in England, fresh from that other war with the United States; Bethune had seen the letter the First Lord of the Admiralty had sent to him in Cornwall, recalling him to London. Bolitho had been his captain all those years ago in the sloop-of-war *Sparrow*. Another war, but they had been fighting Americans even then, a new nation born of revolution.

No reason for the recall had been offered. Surely Sir Richard Bolitho deserved a rest after all he had done? He thought, too, of the lovely Catherine Somervell, who had come to this very office to see him. He often thought of them, together.

And when the impossible had come to pass, and there was peace again, permanent or not, what would happen to Bolitho, and to all the men he had known on his way up the ladder from midshipman's berth to Admiralty? *What will happen to me?* It was the only life he knew. It was his world.

The streets and seaports were full of crippled and tattered remnants of war, rejected by a life which had all but destroyed them. Bethune was sometimes surprised that he could still be sensitive about such matters. Perhaps he had inherited that trait, too, from *Sparrow*'s youthful captain.

He heard voices in the adjoining room, where his clerk held unwanted visitors at bay. He looked at the clock again. Too early for a glass. Bethune did not drink heavily or overeat; he had seen too many of his contemporaries deteriorate because they did not heed such things. He took exercise when he could, a luxury after a ship's restricted quarters, and he enjoyed the company of women, as much as they enjoyed his. But he was discreet, or tried to be, and he told himself it was for the sake of his wife and his two young children.

His servant was standing in the doorway.

Bethune sighed. 'What is it, Tolan?'

'Captain McCleod is here to see you, sir.'

Bethune looked away. 'Ask him to come in.'

What had made him so nervous? Guilt? Thinking perhaps of Bolitho's mistress, who had faced the scandal and had triumphed?

The tall captain entered the room. He had an impassive, melancholy face; Bethune could not imagine him at sea, fighting a gale or the enemy.

'More despatches?'

The captain shook his head. Even that seemed mournful. 'From Portsmouth, sir. By telegraph, just received.' He glanced at the ceiling as if to see through it to the device which could link the Admiralty building to the south coast more swiftly than any courier, faster than any horse, provided the weather was perfect, as it was today.

Bethune opened it, and then hesitated. It was round, school-boy writing, but afterwards he thought it was as though each word had been written in fire. Or blood.

He strode past his servant and the clerk at his desk, his steps seeming unusually loud in the deserted corridor. Great paintings watched him pass, sea battles: courage and heroism, without the human agony which was so seldom shown.

A lieutenant jumped to his feet. 'I'm sorry, sir, but the meeting is still in progress!'

Bethune did not even see him. He thrust open the door, and watched the mingled expressions of surprise, irritation, perhaps alarm.

The First Lord frowned. 'Is it so urgent, Graham?'

Bethune wanted to lick his lips, to laugh, to weep. He had felt nothing like it before.

'From the admiral commanding at Portsmouth, my lord. A despatch has just been received.'

The admiral said evenly, 'Take your time.'

3

Bethune tried again. It was a great moment, and he was a part of it, and yet all he could feel was sadness. 'Marshal Soult's army was defeated by the Duke of Wellington at Toulouse. Totally. Napoleon has abdicated, surrendered to the Allies, four days ago.'

The admiral stood, very slowly, and looked around the table. 'Victory, gentlemen.' The word seemed to hang in the air. 'If only brave Nelson could have seen it.'

Then he turned to Bethune. 'I shall see the Prince Regent immediately. Attend to it for me.' He dropped his voice to exclude the others. 'It could mean Paris for you, Graham. I would feel more secure with you there.'

Bethune found himself back in his spacious office again, without remembering the return.

When he looked out of the window once more, nothing had changed, not the people nor the horses and carriages. Even the pedlar was still standing with his tray of wares.

The elderly clerk was hovering by the desk. 'Sir?'

'Pass the word to the Officer-of-the-Guard for the First Lord's carriage and escort.'

'At once, sir.' He hesitated. 'Difficult to accept, sir. To believe . . . .'

Bethune smiled and touched his arm, even as Bolitho might have done.

Difficult to accept? It was impossible.

Lieutenant George Avery reined his hired mount to a halt and leaned back in the saddle to admire the view. The house was beautifully designed; magnificent was the only description, he thought, and probably larger than the one where he had spent the night.

It had been a pleasant ride from central London to this place on the bank of the Thames, and it had given him time to think, to prepare for this meeting with his uncle, Lord Sillitoe of Chiswick. He had sensed the jubilant mood of the people all around him, had seen their smiles and waves when he had passed; apparently it was unusual to sight a naval officer on horseback.

But it was more than that, so much more. The impossible had become a fact, and it seemed as if every man and woman in the city was in the streets to make certain that the news was not just another cruel rumour. Napoleon, the tyrant, the oppressor who had sought to enslave a continent, was beaten, a prisoner of the victorious Allies.

This morning she had watched him while he dressed and readied himself for this meeting. He could still feel the power and the passion of their intimacy. Could this relationship, too, be more than a passing dream?

He glanced at a church clock. He was five minutes early. His uncle would expect it, even though it was said that he made a deliberate point of being late for his own appointments.

And yet, Avery scarcely knew him. His uncle, Sir Paul Sillitoe as he had been then, had suggested that he should apply for the appointment of flag lieutenant to Sir Richard Bolitho. As the date for that first meeting had drawn near, he had almost withdrawn the application, knowing that it would only end in another disappointment. He had been wounded, and had been a prisoner of war. Upon his exchange, he had been required to face a court-martial for the loss of his ship, even though she had been lost through the captain's recklessness, and his own wound had rendered him helpless and unable to prevent his men striking to a superior enemy.

The memory of his first meeting with Bolitho, the hero and the legend, was very vivid; it would never leave him, and their association had restored him, had perhaps even made him something he might otherwise never have been.

But his uncle? A man of enormous power and influence; and now that Sillitoe had also become a personal adviser to the Prince Regent, that power was greatly feared, if not respected.

He patted the horse's flank, and spoke to the stable-hand who had come running to take his rein.

'See to her, will you. I doubt that I shall be here very long.'

Doors opened before he reached them, the sun streaming in to greet him from windows that faced the Thames, and the slow-moving masts of local traders making use of the tide. A fine staircase, elegant pillars, but also a spartan lack of ornaments and paintings, which his uncle would doubtless find flippant, and obtrusive.

A hard-faced servant in gilt-buttoned livery confronted him in the spacious hallway. Avery had heard it said that most of Sillitoe's servants resembled prize-fighters, and now he saw that it was true.

'If you will wait in the library, sir.' He did not drop his eyes, again, like a fighter wary of a treacherous attack.

Avery nodded in acknowledgement. The man did not ask for his name; he would know. Otherwise, he would not be here.

He walked into the library and stared out across the river. *Peace*. He felt the pain in his wounded shoulder, always a reminder, should he need one. He thought of her body arched against his; she had insisted on seeing the deep scar, and had kissed it with such gentleness that he had been both surprised and moved.

He caught sight of himself in a tall mirror; like a stranger, he thought. He still could not get used to the single epaulette on his shoulder.

They had all endured so much together. But when he tried to imagine the future, beyond the day or the week, it was like being lost, in a fog.

The war was over. Hostilities continued along the border of Canada and the United States, but that could not last much longer. *And what of us?* 'We Happy Few', as Bolitho had often called them. Adam Bolitho was still in Halifax as flag captain to Rear-Admiral Keen; Captain James Tyacke would be waiting for a new appointment, with the frigate *Indomitable* paid off to await her own fate.

He stared at his reflection. Still only a lieutenant, with streaks of grey in his dark hair to show what the war had cost him. Thirty-five years old. He grinned, surprised that he was able to consider a future without prospects, once Sir Richard Bolitho came ashore for good. In his heart, it was what Bolitho wanted, and Avery felt very privileged to know the inner, private man. Brave in his decisions, unwavering in their execution, but after the cannon had fallen silent and the enemy's flag had come down through the smoke, Avery had seen the other man, sensitive, grieving for those who had fallen, because he had required it of them.

What then for himself? A command of his own? Perhaps a little schooner like the lost *Jolie*, although that was unlikely. The navy would begin ridding itself of ships and men as soon as the terms for peace were settled amongst the Allies. Countless soldiers and sailors would be paid off, unwanted, left to fend for themselves. It had happened before. It would always be so.

'If you will come this way, sir.'

Avery left the library, very conscious of the silence; it made him realise how empty the place was. After a noisy, lively ship, it was to be expected. All sailors were like fish out of water when they came ashore. But compared with Bolitho's house in Cornwall, with its endless comings and goings of people from the farm and the estate, neighbours or well-wishers, this splendid residence echoed like a tomb.

His uncle rose from his desk as he entered, closing a large file which he had apparently been studying, although Avery sensed that he had been sitting facing the door for some while. To compose himself? That seemed unlikely. *To get it over quickly, duty done*, was that it?

They shook hands, and Sillitoe said, 'That will be all, Marlow.' A small man whom Avery had not noticed got up from another desk and scurried away. It must be his uncle's secretary but, typically, Sillitoe did not introduce him.

He said, 'I have some claret. I think you will approve of it.' He faced him again and Avery was very aware of the dark, compelling eyes, the hooded lids, the gaze which took in every detail. He could well imagine people fearing him.

'I am glad you are here. It becomes ever more difficult to find the time.' He frowned slightly as another servant entered with the claret and glasses. 'It is fortunate you were in London, and that you received my note.' The stare was impassive, no hint of triumph or contempt. He added calmly, 'How is Lady Mildmay, by the way?'

'She is well, sir. It seems there are few secrets left in London.'

Sillitoe gave a faint smile. 'Quite so. But then, you have not exactly taken pains to conceal your . . . how shall we describe it? Your liaison with this lady, who, I gather, was the wife of your last captain? Of course I *knew* of it. And I am not certain that I approve, not that I expect you would care.'

Avery sat down. What did it matter? *I owe this man nothing.*

He thought suddenly of Bolitho. *I owe him everything.*

'You will not have heard.' Sillitoe took a glass and regarded it severely. 'Sir Richard is recalled to London. He is needed.'

Avery sipped the claret without tasting it. 'I thought he was to be released from active duty, sir.'

Sillitoe gazed at him over the rim of his glass, a little startled by the force of the words. He liked his nephew, and had felt moved to act on his behalf after he had been released from a French prison, only to face a court-martial. A wretched and unnecessary affair, he had thought. But then, he had little time for the navy and its strictures and traditions. His elder brother had been a captain and had been killed in action; it had been that captain who had inspired the young Avery to enter the navy, and it had been that same man who had sponsored him as a midshipman. But Avery's outburst had taken him by surprise, and he did not like surprises unless they were his own.

Avery said, as though to himself, 'Then he will still need me after all.'

Sillitoe frowned. 'I have a deal of influence. I am also a wealthy man, some might say very wealthy. I have business interests in this country, and in Jamaica and the Indies. I need someone of integrity.' He smiled briefly. 'And, if you like, honour.'

Avery put down his empty glass. 'Are you offering me an appointment, sir?'

Sillitoe paced to the window and back. 'A new life, would be a fairer description.'

Avery watched him, suddenly aware of Sillitoe's discomfort. He was ill at ease, and because it was a state unknown to him, he was unable to contain it.

'Why me, sir?'

Sillitoe turned on him angrily. 'Because you should have something to show for your sacrifices, and your treatment, which I thought unfair.' He shook his head as if to silence some hidden voice. 'And because I intend that you should be my heir.' He faced him again. 'My half-brother is dying of fever and a self-indulgence which would have sickened his father, hard man though he was.'

The door opened a few inches.

'The carriage will be in attendance in fifteen minutes, m'lord!'

Sillitoe said, 'I must see His Royal Highness. Louis of France is passing through London, *en route* to claim his throne.' He grimaced. 'There will be much to do.'

Avery found himself on his feet and at the door, his hat again in his hand.

Sillitoe shaded his eyes to watch the river. 'Enjoy your freedom with the beautiful Susanna.' He reached out and took Avery's wrist in a grip of steel. 'Then come back, and tell me your decision.'

Avery heard the horses stamping impatiently.

Surprising that he should be so calm. Like that last day, when *Indomitable* had fought gun to gun with the enemy and men had died within inches of him. And Bolitho had been with him, depending upon him.

And suppose Sillitoe was wrong about Susanna, and that there might be something deeper than the mere fire of sexual excitement?

He said, 'I thank you, sir, but I fear I do not deserve your offer.' He thrust a coin into the groom's hand. 'My loyalty is to Sir Richard.'

Sillitoe watched him without expression. 'Then you are a fool.'

Avery settled in the saddle and gazed down at him. 'Very likely, sir.' He would have said more, but as he dragged at the reins he saw his uncle perhaps for the first time. The man of power and influence.

A man completely alone.

Bryan Ferguson vaulted down from his two-wheeled trap and made sure that the pony was within reach of water.

'You bide here, Poppy.' He glanced at the feed-bag, but decided against it; the pony was getting plump enough as it was.

Then he turned and looked at the low, white-painted inn, The Old Hyperion. Its sign, with the ship heeling to wind and sea, was barely moving. A warm April evening, but the inn would be empty with all the men working late on the farms. He could see the glint of water through the trees, the Helford river; it was a pleasant place. And being the only inn on the edge of Fallowfield village, it could capture what trade there was.

Earlier in the day he had been in Falmouth, and had been very aware of the changes brought about by the news of Napoleon's surrender. There had been more young men in the streets than usual, a sure sign that the dreaded press gangs had been stood down. It would take some getting used to. He flexed his one arm grimly. These days he hardly noticed that he was lacking an arm; it was equally hard to believe that he himself had been pressed into the fleet, along with John Allday.

Fate played strange tricks. Now Allday was coxswain and friend to Sir Richard Bolitho, and Ferguson was steward to the Bolitho estate. And Bolitho had been the captain of that ship, which had snatched them from the beach to serve the King.

He sighed. It was better to get it over with. They had doubtless seen or heard the trap rattle into the yard.

Unis, Allday's wife, was waiting to greet him.

'Why, Bryan, this is a surprise. You're allus at the market today!'

Ferguson walked through the doorway and glanced at the scrubbed tables, the flowers and the polished brasses. Welcoming and neat, like the woman who had greeted him.

'John's out the back, doing something or other.' She smiled. '*My* John, that is.'

The other John was Unis's brother, a one-legged soldier of the line, without whom she could never have managed with Allday at sea much of the time. Then she asked, 'You want to see him? Nothing wrong up at the house, is there?'

He said, 'A messenger came today, Unis.' It was pointless to try and make light of it. 'From the Admiralty.'

She sat on a bench and stared at her arms, which were dusted with flour. 'I thought . . . with the surrender an' that . . . it was all behind us. Will Sir Richard be needed again?' She touched the flour on her skin. 'My John?'

'It may be so.' He thought of Catherine Somervell's face after the messenger had departed. He had heard her exclaim, 'It's so unfair! *So wrong!*'

Just weeks since his return from the war across the Atlantic. Maybe they wanted to honour him in some way.

He heard Allday scraping his shoes at the parlour door and said, 'John would not be forced to go, Unis. Sir Richard would not do it.'

She was quite calm again, her breathing steady. 'I know that, Bryan. But you don't *think* like John, not about the sea an' Sir Richard.'

Allday strode into the room. 'Kate's asleep again, I see.' He shook his friend's hand. 'Going to be as smart as paint when she grows up, just like her mother!'

Unis said, 'I'll fetch a wet for you, Bryan.' She touched the

10

big man's shoulder, and Ferguson saw the pain in her eyes. 'You too, of course!'

Allday looked steadily at him. 'She's left us alone. So what is it, bad news?'

'Sir Richard's called to London. The Admiralty.' He shrugged. 'Same old story, eh?'

'They didn't waste much time. When do we leave?'

Ferguson was both moved and troubled. Like the last time, and all the times before that.

'He'll not expect you to go to London, you know that, man. You've responsibilities here now, Unis and that bonny little mite sleeping in the parlour. The fighting's over, with the French anyhow, and the Yankees will never come this far!' It was no good. What had he expected?

Allday said, 'My place is with him, you knows that. He needs me more than ever now. That eye of his is no better.'

Ferguson said nothing. Allday trusted him with the secret, knowing he would tell nobody else, not even his wife. Especially not Grace. He loved her with all his heart, but he had to admit that she loved gossip.

Allday looked at his hands, strong hands, with scars to mark the years at sea. 'Is Sir Richard put aback by the news?'

'It's hard to say. I watch him and his lady together – like you, I feel proud to be a part of it, but his thoughts he keeps to himself.'

Unis returned with two sweating tankards. 'When my brother gets back I must tell him to set up some more ale. I think we shall be busy this evening.' She looked at Ferguson. 'You told him, then?'

'Aye.'

Allday stared at the tankard between his hands, as if he wanted to crush it. 'Can you see Sir Richard taking on somebody else? It's hard, but we don't expect things to change, not overnight.'

She touched his shoulder again. 'You'll *never* change. I'd not want you to. I'd know you were pretending, putting up with it, just for me an' Kate. She's taken a real shine to you since you got back.'

She turned away, remembering the surprise and hurt he had shown when the child had gone to her brother John, as if he, her own father, was a stranger. It took time. But

11

now he would be going away again. And she must face it.

She thought of Lady Catherine, that day when she had seen her waiting on the harbour quay at Falmouth, watching the little fleet schooner *Pickle* picking up her moorings, Bolitho coming home. And her own man had been with him, as always. Catherine, so brave, so defiant in the face of all the scandal and the cruel gossip. She would take it badly.

There were voices in the yard, and she said brightly, 'The fish man. I asked him to stop by.' She wiped her hands on her apron. 'I'll deal with him.'

Alone again with Allday, Ferguson said, 'She's a marvel, John.'

'I knows it.' He looked around as if he were searching for something. 'I'll go and put up some ale. It'll not take a minute. You sit there and finish your wet. I needs to think awhile.'

Ferguson sighed. Next thing, Allday would be up at the house on some pretext or other, just to speak with Sir Richard, to tell him he would be ready.

He looked round, startled by a thud and something like a cough. He went quickly into the adjoining room, a cool place where the casks were stowed, ready to be tapped and moved to their trestles. One cask, a four-and-a-half-gallon pin, was lying against the wall. Allday sat with his back to it, his hands to his chest, his breathing loud and uneven, like a man dragged from the sea.

Ferguson knelt and put his arm around him.

'Easy, John! That damned wound again!' He watched his friend struggle for breath and wondered how long it had been like this. When Allday turned his head, he was shocked to see that his face was quite pale, grey beneath the weathered tan.

He said, 'I'll fetch Unis.'

Allday shook his head and gritted his teeth. '*No!* Stay with me!' He nodded heavily, and took a deep breath. 'It's goin'. I'll be all right.'

Ferguson watched the colour returning to his rugged face, the breathing becoming more even.

Allday allowed him to help him to his feet, and then said thickly, 'Not a word, mind. It comes an' goes.' He tried to grin. 'See? Bright as a bullock's bayonet!'

Ferguson shook his head, resigned. He was beaten; he should

have known. Allday and Bolitho, like master and faithful dog, someone had once said, each fearful for the other.

Together, they lifted the cask on to its trestle, and Allday said, 'I needs something stronger than ale, an' that's no error!'

Unis found them sitting by the unlit fire, her husband holding a taper for his friend's clay pipe as if they had not a care in the world. She bit her lip to contain her despair. It was all a show, for her sake. Like the new cask on its trestle. The rest she could guess.

Ferguson said, 'Must be getting back. I have to look at the books.' Allday followed him out to the yard, and watched as he swung himself up on to the seat.

He said, simply, 'Thanks, Bryan.' He stared across the fields to the glint of the river beyond the trees. 'You weren't *there*, see. Sir Richard, a full admiral, the finest ever, leading our boarders across on to that bloody renegade's deck like some wild lieutenant! You should have been there. *To me, Indoms!*' He shook his shaggy head. 'I could never leave him now.'

He raised one hand and grinned. It was one of the saddest things Ferguson had ever seen.

And one of the bravest.

Richard Bolitho sat in the corner of the carriage and stared out at the crowds and the horses, vehicles of every size jostling for position with apparent disregard for one another.

Despite the warm evening, he was wearing his boatcloak to conceal his uniform and rank. In the frenzied aftermath of Napoleon's surrender, any such reminder brought cheers and mobbing from ordinary people who had probably never displayed such emotion for any but Nelson.

A long day; a very long day. First Bethune, and then a meeting with the First Lord and his senior advisers. Napoleon had been sent into exile on the island of Elba; the giant who had raped a continent was to be marooned, forgotten. Even as the First Lord had said it, Bolitho had questioned the wisdom of the decision. It was like trying to cage a lion in an aviary, and it was too close, too close . . . .

The First Lord had spoken at length of the American war, and of Bolitho's participation with the squadron under his command. The Americans were being starved of trade due to the activity of the British squadrons, and the chain of command from Halifax to the Caribbean. Little short of a thousand American merchant ships had been captured, and, with France no longer a drain on the navy's resources, more men-of-war could now be sent to seal the last gaps in the blockade.

The First Lord had finished by saying that no war could be won by stalemate. *An example must be made*, a ready warning for the future.

Bethune had been watching Bolitho, and had tossed in some comment on the American attack on York.

The First Lord was old but he was no fool, and he had recognised in this Bethune's attempt to distract him.

'What do *you* think, Sir Richard? I know you hold advanced ideas on the war at sea, and I heard you myself say in this very building that the line of battle was, or should be, a thing of the past?'

Bolitho turned his head and saw the Thames, and the lucid glow which would promise a fine sunset.

'I'll stand by that, my lord. I also believe that a desire for revenge is no good reason for prolonging a war which neither side can hope to win.'

Even then, he had believed that some kind of attack was being planned. Now, during this slow journey from the Admiralty to Chelsea, with time to go over it again in his mind, he was certain of it. Sir Alexander Cochrane had taken over the station; a man of action in every sense, but hardly a peacemaker.

Alone with Bethune, he had asked about Valentine Keen and about his nephew. Bethune had replied cautiously, 'Rear-Admiral Keen will return to England this year. His flagship will more than likely be paid off.' He had looked up from his desk, and for an instant Bolitho had seen the midshipman again. There were only a few years between them, and beneath the charm and the confidence Bethune was much the same. Above all, he was honest. Loyal. 'I am certain that your nephew will find employment even with the fleet reduced, as it certainly will be.'

'He is probably the best frigate captain we have. To be put on the beach after what he has done and endured would be intolerable.'

It must have been at that moment that Bethune had come to his decision.

He had said, 'We are good friends, Richard, and I regret that our paths have crossed only rarely.' He had shrugged lightly. 'As is the way of our calling. I have never forgotten that I have owed everything to you, from the moment you took command of *Sparrow*. And there have been many like me, who gained everything from that contact with you.'

'And there were many who fell because of it, Graham.'

He had shaken his head, dismissing it. 'We shall see the First Lord again when he returns from his audience with the Prince Regent. Their meetings are usually brief.' He paused, and the smile was gone. 'I have to tell you that the First Lord will offer you Malta, will insist that you are the obvious choice for it. Until the peace is finally agreed amongst the Allies, the Mediterranean must serve as a reminder to friends and foes alike that no further territorial claims on land or at sea will be tolerated.' He had watched Bolitho then in silence. 'I thought you should hear it first from me.'

'That was good of you, Graham.' He had glanced around the spacious room. 'But it can be dangerous here, also, so be warned!'

He rapped the roof of the carriage, and said, 'I shall walk from here.'

The coachman in his Admiralty livery barely glanced down from the box. Perhaps he had become too used to the ways of senior officers to question any whim.

He walked beside the river. Kate's London. She had made it his London now, or this small part of it, at least.

What shall I say? What must I tell her?

The First Lord had had no doubts at all. 'Not since Collingwood held this command has there been stability and leadership. Your reputation, your sense of honour are more valuable now than in the line of battle!' He had neglected to mention that Collingwood, Nelson's second-in-command at Trafalgar, had died in the Mediterranean without ever being relieved of that command, despite his repeated requests to be allowed to come home, and despite the illness which had eventually killed him.

He walked on, disquieted by his thoughts.

It had been bad enough when he and Catherine had left Falmouth. Allday visiting the house, ostensibly to ensure that the swords were in good trim, then coming straight out with it. Not pleading, but insisting on his right to be at Bolitho's side, wherever his flag should lead. And his secretary, Yovell, a man of many faces, and the secretive Ozzard. His little crew. And now there was Avery to consider. Bethune had hinted that he had been offered a great opportunity, a chance of security and prosperity. God knew he would never find either as a lowly lieutenant.

The door was open and she was standing at the top of the steps, her hair piled above her ears, like silk in the candlelight.

She slipped his arm around her waist. 'Come into the garden, Richard. I have some wine there. I heard you were coming.' She seemed to sense his tension. 'I had a visitor.'

He turned. 'Who?'

The strain was very evident in his face.

'George Avery. He had come on a mission, with an invitation to some reception.' She caressed his hand. 'Tomorrow. After that, we can leave for Falmouth.'

He said nothing, and walked into the garden, into its deepening shadows. He heard her pour the wine, then she said quietly, 'So it is to be Malta, Richard?'

Nothing of the anger she had shown in Falmouth. This was the poised, determined woman who had dared everything for his sake, who had even shared the ordeal in an open boat off the coast of Africa.

'I have not decided, Kate . . . .'

She put her fingers lightly on his mouth. 'But you will. I know you so well, better than any other, even yourself. All those men you have led and inspired, they will expect it. For them, and the future they have been fighting for. You told me once, they are never allowed to ask, or to question why they should sacrifice so much.'

They walked together to the low wall and watched the sunset over the river.

She said, 'You are my man, Richard. I will be with you, no matter how unfair or unjust I believe this decision may be. I would die rather than lose you.' She touched his face, the cheekbone beneath the damaged eye. 'And afterwards?'

16

'*Afterwards*, Kate. That is a very beautiful word. Nothing can or will part us again.'

She took his hand and pressed it to her breast. 'Take me, Richard. Use me as you will, but always love me.'

The wine remained in the garden, untouched.

2

More Than a Duty

Captain James Tyacke sat by the small table in his room and half listened to the muffled murmur of voices from the parlour below his feet. The Cross Keys was a small but comfortable inn on the road which headed north from Plymouth to Tavistock. Few coaches paused here because of the narrowness of the track, and he had sometimes wondered how the inn managed to make a living, unless perhaps it had some connection with the smuggling trade. It suited him very well, however, away from the stares and the swiftly averted glances. The pity, the curiosity, the revulsion.

It was hard, even unnerving, to accept that he had last stayed here all of three years ago. It had been run at the time by a pleasant woman named Meg, who had spoken to him often, and had looked at him directly, without flinching. Three years ago; and when he had left the inn on that last occasion, he had known they would not meet again.

The new landlord was welcoming enough, a little ferret of a man with quick, darting movements, and he had done his best to ensure that Tyacke was not disturbed.

Three years. It was a lifetime. He had been about to take command of *Indomitable*, Sir Richard Bolitho's flagship, before they had made sail for American waters. So many miles, so many faces, some already lost from memory. And now that same *Indomitable* lay at Plymouth, paid off, an empty ship, waiting for a new future, or with no future at all.

He glanced at the big brass-bound sea chest by the bed. They had travelled a long, long way together. His whole world was contained in it.

He thought of the past weeks, spent mostly aboard his ship attending to the thousand and one details of paying off, and worse, the rough farewells and handshakes from men he had come to know, men whose confidence and loyalty he had won by his own example.

And Sir Richard Bolitho; that had been the most difficult parting of all. As admiral and flag captain they had discovered a mutual trust, and an admiration which might never be truly understood by an outsider.

And now Napoleon was beaten; the war with the old enemy was over. Perhaps he should have felt elation, or relief. But as Tyacke had watched the fleet schooner *Pickle* standing out to sea, taking Bolitho and Allday on to Falmouth, all he had been conscious of was a sense of sorrow and loss.

The port admiral was a friend of Bolitho's, and had been both cordial and helpful to his flag captain. He had no doubt thought Tyacke's request to be transferred once more to the anti-slavery patrols off the coast of West Africa, exchanging the comparative comfort of a larger ship, or some well-earned extended leave ashore for cramped quarters and the risks of fever and death, bizarre. Bolitho's written support had added a great deal of weight. But, as the admiral had explained, the transfer might not be possible for another year or more.

He remembered *Indomitable* as he had last seen her. Yards sent down, her usually immaculate decks littered with unwanted cordage and spars, her powerful cannon, which had roared defiance at the American *Retribution*, silent and disarmed. Now she was no longer needed, like the men who had served her so long and so well, men who had been pressed into the navy, for the most part. His mouth softened into a smile. But then, so had Allday been a pressed man. And the wounded, what of them? Cast ashore to try and find their places in a world which had all but forgotten them, to fend for themselves as best they could, to beg on the streets when all most people wanted now was to forget the war.

And Sir Richard Bolitho, the hero and the man. One who could inspire others when all hope seemed lost, and who could not conceal his compassion, or his grief for those who had fallen.

Again he gave the small smile. Bolitho had given him back his own hope, his pride, when he had believed them gone

19

for ever. He touched the side of his face. Scored away by fire, rendered inhuman during the great battle when Nelson had led his ships to the Nile. How the eye had survived was a miracle. *He had been so lucky*, some said. What did they know? All the years since he had been smashed down by a French broadside, when men had been killed and maimed on every side and even the captain of his ship, *Majestic*, had died in that bloody embrace, the disfigurement had haunted him. The stares, the way his young midshipmen had dropped their eyes, glanced away, anything but look at him. *The devil with half a face*, the slave-traders had called him. And now he was asking to go back to that lonely world of solitary patrols, pitting his wits against the traders, until the sighting and chase; the stinking vessels with their holds packed with chained slaves living in their filth, knowing they would be killed at the slightest provocation, their bodies pitched to the sharks. Slavers and sharks were rarely far apart.

No, they would not let Bolitho leave the navy. To many people who served in the fleet, he *was* the navy. Between them, Bolitho and his mistress had defied convention and the censure of society. Tyacke touched his face again. He remembered her climbing up *Indomitable*'s tumblehome at Falmouth, disdaining a boatswain's chair, and arriving on deck with tar on her stockings, raising the loudest cheers from the ship's company because of it. The sailor's woman who had come aboard to wish them well: men about to be carried to the other side of the world, torn from wives and families by the relentless press gangs, or felons freed by the local judges provided they were put aboard a King's ship.

And she had done it because she cared for them. She had even disdained formality that day in Falmouth, and had kissed him on the cheek in greeting. *You are so welcome here*. He could still hear the words. And then she had looked along the crowded deck at the watching crowds of seamen and marines and had said, *They will not let you down*. Nor had they.

Perhaps she had been the only one who had truly understood the torment he had suffered when he had agreed to be Bolitho's flag captain. He might be envied, feared, respected, even hated, but a captain, especially one who commanded a flagship, must be beyond self-doubt and uncertainty. Few could have guessed that those were the emotions he had felt when he had first stepped aboard to read himself in at Plymouth.

His own words then came back to him now, as if he had spoken aloud. *I would serve no other*.

He glanced around the room. He would have to leave it soon, if only to let them clean it. And suppose the appointment to the anti-slavery squadron was delayed even beyond the port admiral's estimate of a year? What then? Would it always be like this, hiding in rooms, walking out only at night, avoiding every kind of human contact?

He touched the dress coat which hung over a chair, and bore the twin gold epaulettes of a post-captain; a far, far cry from his previous command, the little brig *Larne*.

His mind explored the years since the Nile, and his slow recovery from his wounds. Fifteen years had passed since hell had burst into *Majestic*'s lower gundeck and turned it into an inferno. He had been in Haslar Hospital at Portsmouth for what little treatment could be offered, and Marion had eventually dared to come and see him. She had been young then, and pretty, and he had hoped and expected to marry her.

It had been an ordeal for her, like all the others who had ventured to Haslar in search of friends or relatives. Officers wounded in a dozen or more sea-fights, their faces so hopeful and so pitiful each time another visitor arrived. The burned, the maimed, the limbless and the blind, the living price of every victory, although few ever saw it.

After that, she had married another, an older man who had given her a pleasant house by Portsdown Hill, not far from that same hospital. There had been two children of the marriage, a boy and a girl.

Eventually her husband had died. Tyacke had received a letter from her while *Indomitable* had been at Halifax, the first news he had had of her for those fifteen years. It had been a letter written with great care, offering no excuses, no compromise, very mature, so different from the young girl he had once loved.

He had written a reply to her, and had locked it in the strongbox before the last battle with *Retribution*; she would only have received it if he had died that day. Afterwards, he had torn it into pieces and had watched them drift away beneath his ship's shot-pitted side. When he had needed her, and had sometimes found himself praying for death, she had turned away from him. He had told himself often enough that it was understandable. But she had not returned. So why had her letter disturbed him so much? The years had been another man's reward, and, like the two unknown children, were a part of something he could never share.

There was a quiet tap at the door, and after a moment it opened a few inches.

Tyacke said, 'It's all right, Jenny, I am just going out for a walk. You can see to the room.'

She gazed at him gravely. 'Not that, zur. There's a letter come for you.'

She held it out and watched him carry it to the window. She was a local girl and had six sisters, and at the inn she often saw the uniforms of army or navy, so that she did not feel so cut off from Plymouth, that bustling seaport which her sisters were always quick to compare with this place.

But she had never met anyone like this man before. He spoke only when it was necessary, although everybody knew all about him. A hero: Sir Richard Bolitho's friend and his right arm, they said. They said a lot more too, probably, when she was not within earshot.

She studied him now, his head lowered while he held the letter to the light of the window; he always turned his terrible injury away from her. He had a strong face, handsome too, and he was courteous, not like some of the gentry who called in for a glass. Her mother had warned her often enough about the dangers, about other girls who got themselves into trouble, especially with the garrison near Tavistock.

She felt herself flushing. All the same . . . .

Tyacke was unaware of the scrutiny. The note was from the port admiral. *To present himself at his earliest convenience.* Even addressed to a post-captain, that meant *immediately*.

'I'll need the carter, Jenny. I have to go to Plymouth.'

She smiled at him. 'Right away, zur!'

Tyacke picked up his coat and brushed the sleeve with his fingers. The walk would have to wait.

He stared around the room, the revelation hitting him like a fist. It was what he wanted. It was the only life he knew.

The carriage slowed, and Bolitho saw groups of idlers and

passers-by shading their eyes against the evening sun to peer in at the occupants. Some even waved their hats, although they could not possibly have recognised him, he thought.

He felt her hand on his sleeve. 'It's their way of showing their feelings.' She raised the hand to the nearest crowd and a man shouted, 'It's Sir Richard an' his lady, lads! Equality Dick!' There were cheers, and she murmured, 'You see? You have many friends there.'

The house on the river was ablaze with lights, the chandeliers burning even more brightly than this late sunshine.

How Sillitoe must hate it, Bolitho thought. Wasteful but necessary. *Necessary* was the word for it. His world.

Catherine said, 'I hear there are receptions all over London tonight to celebrate the victory.' She watched his profile, and wanted to put her arms around him, and let the crowds think what they liked.

He said restlessly, 'I wish it was young Matthew up there on the box, and we were heading down to Falmouth.' He looked at her and smiled. 'I am poor company for one so lovely, Kate.' Strangely, the realisation seemed to give him strength. She was wearing a new gown in her favourite green shot silk, high-waisted, her shoulders bared, the diamond pendant resting between her breasts. Beautiful, poised, and outwardly very calm, and yet the same woman who had given herself to him with such passion, again and again until they were exhausted, in the house on the Walk at Chelsea, around the next great sweeping bend of this river.

She said, 'At least it will not be like that terrible feast at Carlton House. I have never eaten so much in my life!' She watched his mouth lift, the way he smiled when they spoke of such things together.

She peered out at the other carriages turning in Sillitoe's drive, the crowds of footmen and grooms. Sillitoe must have gone to a great deal of expense.

There were women too, but not many wives, she decided. She never forgot that Sillitoe had helped her when there had been no one else. He had made no secret of his feelings for her after that. Like the man, it had been a statement of fact, cool and deliberate, not something open to doubt.

She glanced down at her gown. Daring perhaps, as some

would expect of her. She lifted her chin and felt the pendant shift against her skin: Bolitho's woman, for the whole world to see.

And then they were there; the door was opened, and Bolitho stepped down to assist her from the carriage.

Servants bowed and curtsied, while here and there Sillitoe's own men, hard and watchful, reminded Catherine of that last visit to Whitechapel. Some of Sillitoe's men had accompanied them then; there was always an air of mystery and danger where Sillitoe was concerned.

Bolitho handed his hat to another servant, but she retained the silk shawl, which she wore across her bare shoulders. There were no announcements, no footmen to scrutinise invitations, only waves of noisy conversation, and, from somewhere nearby, music. It was neither joyful nor martial, merely an unobtrusive background for people who quite obviously knew one another, either by sight or reputation.

'You look well, Sir Richard!' Sillitoe appeared from behind a pillar, his hooded eyes everywhere. Then he took Catherine's hand and held it to his lips. 'As always, my lady, I never find words for such beauty.'

She smiled, and saw several of the other women turning to stare. Sillitoe gestured impatiently as a footman appeared with a laden tray.

Then he said, 'Rhodes is here. I thought you should meet him, in view of the immediate future.'

Bolitho turned towards her. 'Admiral the Right Honourable Lord Rhodes is Acting Controller at the Admiralty, but he is also said to be the most likely contender for the role of First Lord.' He watched her, reading her eyes. She mistrusted the mention of senior officers she did not know, in case they meant him harm in some way.

Sillitoe said, 'I have put him in another room. I think it might be wise to see him.'

She said, 'I shall wait on the terrace, Richard.'

But Sillitoe interjected, 'This is my house and you are my guests. I see no reason to separate you.' He touched her hand lightly. 'To divide the legend?'

His small secretary was hovering close by, and Sillitoe said, 'I shall come and disturb you shortly.'

One of Sillitoe's men led the way to the library, and then

into a smaller ante-room adjoining it. There was a chair by the fireplace. Catherine recognised it. As if it had never been moved since she had sat there that day, when she had come for Sillitoe's help. When he had brushed past her, and she had felt him fighting the desire to touch her, to lay his hand on her shoulder. But he had not.

Admiral Lord James Rhodes was a tall, solidly built man who had once been handsome. His face was dominated by a strong, beaked nose, while his eyes were surprisingly small, almost incidental by comparison. He glanced quickly at Catherine, but was careful to reveal nothing. A man used to hiding his feelings, if he had any, she thought.

Bolitho said, 'May I present the Viscountess Somervell, my lord?' He felt her look at him, sensed the anxiety, in case there would be some lurking insult or rebuff. But Rhodes gave a stiff bow and said, 'I've not had the honour before, my lady.' He did not take her hand and she did not offer it.

Catherine walked to a window to watch as yet another carriage clattered across the stones. She could feel the admiral staring at her, but found no pleasure in his uncertainty.

She thought suddenly and with longing of Falmouth. To be parted again was too brutal to consider.

She leaned closer to the window and observed the new arrivals. No admiral or politician this time, only a tall lieutenant, removing his hat as he gave his hand to the woman who stepped down beside him. Even in the fading light, she could see the grey in his dark hair, saw him laugh, and the way the fair woman looked at him. So this was George Avery's lover, to whom he seemed to have lost his heart.

And yet, when he had brought Sillitoe's invitation and had warned her of the prospect of Malta, he had said nothing about staying behind when Richard was ordered to sail.

She heard Rhodes say, 'I'm giving you *Frobisher*, d'you know her?'

And Richard's reply, his mind already grappling with his new task.

'Yes, my lord. Seventy-four – Captain Jefferson, as I recall.'

Rhodes sounded relieved, she thought. 'No more, I fear. Slipped his cable two years back. Buried at sea, poor fellow.'

Bolitho said quietly, 'A French prize. She was named *Glorieux*.'

'Does that trouble you, Sir Richard? If so . . . .'

'A ship is as good as you use her.'

Rhodes grunted. 'New, too, compared with some of your recent vessels. Eight years old.'

She heard him pick up a goblet and drink noisily. Yes, he *was* relieved. She turned from the window and said, 'And when will this be required, my lord?'

He regarded her warily. 'Weeks rather than months, my lady. But you need not concern yourself with such matters. I have always found . . . .'

'Have you, my lord? I am glad to know it. Out there, people are celebrating a victory, the cost of which is still to be calculated, and *I am concerned* for this man and for myself. Is that so strange?'

Bolitho said, 'I have not yet decided.'

Rhodes looked around as though trapped. 'You were chosen because of your reputation, because of the honour you have won for your country.' He regarded Catherine grimly. 'It should be plain to see why this is of paramount importance.'

The door opened softly, and Sillitoe entered without speaking.

She said quietly, 'All I see is two islands and two men. A tyrant who has fought and murdered his way through Europe on one, and an admiral of England, a true hero, on the other. That is no comfort at all!' She touched her eyes with her glove, and when she looked again, Rhodes had departed.

Sillitoe said, 'I do regret this. Rhodes is a good controller, but he has no tact. If you decide against hoisting your flag in the Mediterranean, Richard, it will be his head on the block, not yours. And he knows it.' He glared at his secretary again, and then said, 'Join me presently. There are some people you should meet.' He gave a wry smile. 'Including my nephew's guest.'

The door closed and they were alone; only the strains of music and the muffled murmur of voices reminded them where they were.

She lowered her face. 'I am so sorry, Richard. I spoke like an angry, embittered wife. I had no right.'

He raised her chin and studied her. 'If you were my wife in the eyes of the church, I could not love you more. You had every right. You are my life.'

26

'Then let them see it.' She tossed the shawl from her shoulders and touched the pendant, and looked at him again.

'And tomorrow we shall leave London.'

Lieutenant George Avery stared around at the crowd and began to doubt the wisdom of having accepted his uncle's invitation. Important people all, well known to those who shared this unfamiliar world, politicians, senior officers of both army and navy, and a few diplomats adorned with honours he did not recognise. It was the utter transformation of his uncle's house which was the most astonishing thing. The silent austerity had been replaced by music, noise and laughter, and liveried servants pushing through the throng this way and that to satisfy the guests and refill the goblets.

He glanced down at his companion. 'Perhaps we should have made our excuses, Susanna.'

She smiled, observing him thoughtfully, like one discovering or seeking some new and unknown quality in him.

'I recognise some of the faces here. I have seen them on other occasions. I suspect that this is where all the real decisions are made, like the turn of a card.'

Avery felt vaguely jealous, without understanding why. She was used to such affairs, like the one at her own London house, where she had invited him to stay. To be her lover.

He had seen heads turn to look and compare. The beauty and the lowly lieutenant. The most junior sea officer Avery had seen so far had been a post-captain. They walked through the throng, and he saw her acknowledge one or two people. Most of the women she ignored.

When he mentioned them, she replied softly, 'Like the extra footmen, they are paid for their services!' She had gripped his arm and almost laughed at his embarrassment. 'Lord, *Mister* Avery, you still have much to learn!'

She released his arm now, and said, 'That is Lady Somervell, is it not? It must be.'

Avery saw Catherine and Bolitho by a low balustrade, and said, 'Would you care to meet them?'

But Sillitoe stepped between them, and held out his hand. 'Lady Mildmay, what a pleasure. I had been so looking forward to making your acquaintance. I hope everything is to your satisfaction? A great pity you are to be separated from my nephew so soon, but then, I shall never attempt to understand the navy!'

She looked at Avery. 'Separated? I thought. . . . I understood that you would be remaining in England until some suitable appointment could be found.'

Avery said, 'I am Sir Richard's flag lieutenant, Susanna. It is more than a duty, or an excuse. It is what I must do.'

Sillitoe shrugged. 'Believe me, I offered him an alternative, Lady Mildmay. I do, of course, admire loyalty but. . . .' He broke off as one of his footmen signalled to him. 'We will speak later.'

Avery said, 'I was going to tell you. I have been happier with you than I could have believed possible. I love you, I always have.'

'But you'd leave me, because of duty?'

She turned, startled, as Catherine said, 'I think we should meet.'

She offered her hand.

'I do know what you are thinking. I try to accept it, but I shall never do so without pain.' She glanced around the room, seeing the quick glances, the knowing smiles, recognising them. Sir Wilfred Lafargue, one of London's leading lawyers and a friend of Sillitoe's, who had helped with her unexpected inheritance from her dead husband. And a red-faced city merchant to whom she had been introduced, probably at some similar reception. Men of influence, and authority. Not the kind who fought and died in battle, at sea with Richard's ships, or those who stood shoulder to shoulder in the line. And those like Lord Rhodes, solid, reliable and unimaginative, who planned their battles behind the desks of Admiralty.

She said, 'You must ask yourself, my dear, do I love this man enough? Enough to wait?'

A man she knew to be Sillitoe's uncomplaining secretary peered up at her. 'My lady, I am asked to escort you to the terrace.' He blinked rapidly as a clock began to chime. The music had stopped, she noticed.

Bolitho said, 'I shall find your shawl. It will be cool outside.'

She smiled and touched his face. 'No matter. I want people to see us like this, as we are.'

There were lights on the terrace, but the river beyond the wall was in darkness, like black glass.

Bolitho looked over the water, his ear picking up the heavy stroke of oars. A barge of some kind, moving steadily against the current with little regard for the oarsmen.

Sillitoe turned to greet them. 'Now you will understand why I did not invite the prime minister. The Prince Regent cannot *abide* the fellow!' It seemed to amuse him.

Sillitoe glanced up at a cluster of lanterns, and took Catherine's arm.

'Here, if you please. Trust me.' She could feel the intensity, the tenacity which he did not try to conceal.

She stood quite still in the light, oblivious to the others chosen by Sillitoe to be present at this moment, feeling the cool breeze playing over her bare shoulders. She knew Richard was close by, but for just these fleeting moments, she was alone.

The oars were tossed and the barge came alongside the jetty, men leaping out to make fast the mooring lines, others to lay a scarlet carpet on the pale stones.

The Prince would pass her without a glance; he would not even remember her. He knew many women, and had an appetite to match.

She almost held her breath, and thought suddenly of Sillitoe's enigmatic words. *Trust me.* When she looked again, she saw the Prince striding towards her, exactly as she remembered him from the evening at Carlton House.

He was elegantly dressed in the very latest fashion, but even in the flickering lights it could not disguise completely the physical price he was paying for his excesses. His hair was swept forward in a style followed by many of the younger bloods, and no one could doubt his energy or the quickness of his mind.

She realised that no one was speaking, that the Prince had stopped, facing her, his eyes moving over her face and throat, and to the glittering diamond pendant shaped like an open fan. It was like being stripped naked, like an insistent caress.

He said, 'Lady Somervell! Had I known you were to be here, I would have ridden with all haste on the finest charger in the Royal Mews!' He took her hand and held it. 'Indeed, I have thought of you often. The lady who is always *too busy* to become bored, I think you said when last we met?' He

kissed her hand, taking his time. 'You are very beautiful.'
He released her hand and looked at the others. 'Ah, Lord
Rhodes. I trust you have affairs in order for me?' He did
not wait for or expect an answer. 'There you are, Sillitoe,
you rascal.' They shook hands. More like conspirators than
friends, thought Catherine.

The Prince saw Bolitho and greeted him warmly. 'My
admiral of England.' Catherine knew that was for her. What
she had said on that same occasion at Carlton House. So long
ago. Before *Indomitable*; before she had forced herself to write
and tell Richard of Zenoria's terrible death. *Tell Adam. . . .*
Like yesterday.

He continued, 'I have studied all your reports on the
American war. I agree that the sooner it is settled the better
for all concerned.' He turned and looked at Catherine. 'And
what of Malta, Sir Richard? It is important for our security.
And it is important to *me*. I must know, so what say you?' He
reached out and took Catherine's arm. 'Shall you do it?'

Catherine could sense Richard's anguish, something like
physical pain, just as she was very aware of the others standing
nearby. How would they see it, even if they understood? Arrogance, or a display of temperament, when it was neither.

Sillitoe stepped into the circle of light. 'A moment, I pray
you, sir.' He held out a piece of paper. 'This was just delivered
to me by Admiralty messenger.'

Rhodes muttered angrily, 'First I knew of it!'

Sillitoe ignored him. 'May I, sir?'

The Prince smiled, when seconds earlier he had been angered
by the interruption. 'This is *your* house, damn you.'

Sillitoe looked at Catherine but spoke to Bolitho. 'A despatch from the port admiral at Plymouth, Sir Richard. Captain
James Tyacke has withdrawn his request for transfer to the
West African squadron and has placed himself at your disposal
for his duties as flag captain.'

Catherine slipped away from the Prince's grasp, and went
to him.

'They have spoken for you, Richard. The need is theirs,
too.'

The Prince Regent pursed his lips in a little smile. 'Thank
you, Lady Catherine. Thank you. I know I have been a witness
to something, although I know not what. I am not ungrateful.'

Something might be arranged to enable you to visit Malta.'
He nodded to himself, as she had seen him do before. 'Yes,
it *shall* be done.' He seemed to relax. 'Now, there was talk of
a special claret, Sillitoe. Lead on!' But his eyes lingered on
Catherine, and her hand on Bolitho's arm. Desire certainly,
but there was also envy.

Later, much later, when they were leaving Sillitoe's house,
there were still several carriages waiting in the drive. The
Prince Regent had disappeared in his barge as quietly as he
had arrived.

Bolitho looked up at the stars, and thought, again with
disquiet, of Catherine and the Prince.

She said, 'I left my shawl behind!'

'I shall fetch it.'

He was surprised at the strength of her grip. '*No*. Let us go
to Chelsea. Be together. Lie together. It is all I want.'

Bolitho turned quickly. 'Who is that?'

It was Avery.

'Still here, George? What is it?' Although he thought he
knew. Like Tyacke. The Happy Few.

'I wondered if I could ride with you to Chelsea, Sir Richard.'

Catherine stepped between them, her shoulders pale in the
reflected lights.

'Did she leave without you, George?' She saw him nod. She
slipped her arms through theirs, linking them; she was almost
as tall as they.

'Then ride with us. And tomorrow, you will come to
Falmouth with us.'

He smiled, the sadness held at bay. 'Willingly, my lady.'

From his study window Sillitoe watched the carriage move
out on to the road. He frowned. There were still too many
overstaying their welcome. He would do something about
that.

He picked up the thin silk shawl, which she had left in the
ante-room by the library. He could smell her. Like jasmine.

Then he kissed it and folded it inside his coat and strode out
to do what he must.

3

Adam

Captain Adam Bolitho flattened the chart across his cabin table and glanced at the final calculations of the passage, although he knew them by heart. Around and above him the frigate, His Britannic Majesty's Ship *Valkyrie* of forty-two guns, held steadily on course, her reduced sails barely filling. It was early May but there was still an edge to the wind, as he had discovered during his customary morning walk on deck.

It was a time he usually liked. A ship coming to life, with the first glimpse of a horizon. Decks swabbed and holystoned, the boatswain and the carpenter comparing their lists of work for the new day. Sails to be brought down and repaired, rigging inspected and spliced wherever necessary. Water casks scoured out and prepared for refilling, and the end of stale, monotonous food, for the moment. *Valkyrie* was returning to harbour, to the main naval base at Halifax, Nova Scotia, the last real British foothold on the North American coast.

And what would they feel when they reached there? He stared around the cabin, at the lively wavelets falling astern beneath the frigate's counter, feeling again the resentment and impatience he tried so hard to conceal from his ship's company.

For *Valkyrie* was no ordinary or private ship; she was still officially the flagship of Rear-Admiral Valentine Keen, his uncle's friend. *And yours also*, a voice seemed to insist.

Somehow they had grown apart, even since the total destruction of two American frigates with the loss of only one man, a midshipman. Not so long ago, yet Adam could scarcely recall his face. Keen spent more and more time ashore concerning himself with the transport of troops. *Valkyrie* was returning from yet another such convoy. And for what purpose, he wondered. The news from England was optimistic; the war in Europe would soon be over, so that more ships could be released to fight the Americans. But for how long? The build-up of military strength here had to be for some reason.

He heard the marine sentry outside the screen door tap his musket on the deck and call, 'First Lieutenant, *sir*!'

He straightened his back as Lieutenant William Dyer stepped into the cabin.

It still came as a surprise, as if he expected John Urquhart to be presenting himself. Urquhart had gone to a command of his own, one for which he had been little envied. He had been promoted at Keen's suggestion to command the frigate *Reaper*, a ship torn apart by mutiny, inhuman discipline, and murder.

Adam had known that Urquhart could do it, and had been rewarded by the occasional news of *Reaper*'s performance and various successes. A rebirth. But Adam was missing him now.

'Ready?'

Dyer looked at a point above his captain's left shoulder. 'The master says that we shall be up to the anchorage within the hour, sir. If the wind holds steady from the nor'east, we should be in before six bells.'

A pleasant enough officer, and one who had made good use of his experience in this ship, one of the largest frigates on the station since *Indomitable*'s departure for England. But it went little beyond that.

'I shall come up directly.' He did not see the lieutenant's quick glance around the cabin, but he could imagine it. Dyer probably thought that his captain wanted for nothing. *As I once thought of mine*.

Adam had been more than successful as a frigate captain, and he was sensible enough to appreciate it, and that luck rarely came into it except to provide the opportunity to meet with an enemy, and to know his thoughts like your own. After that, it was skill, determination, and the men who depended on you. He smiled. And good gunnery.

The lieutenant saw the smile, and, encouraged, asked, 'Will we be hoisting the admiral's flag again after this, sir?'

'In truth, I do not know.' He moved restlessly to the stern windows and leaned his hands on the sill. He could feel the thud and shiver of the rudder-head, picture the ship as she would appear to any landsmen watching her careful approach.

A flagship. Only a frigate captain would understand the difference. It meant being tied to the fleet's apron strings and the whims and fancies of a flag officer. Keen was a good commander, but it was not the same. He tried to steer his mind away from his own ship, *Anemone*, which had fallen to the American commodore, Nathan Beer. Only an explosion below deck had foiled her capture and salvage, and spared her an enemy's flag. No, it was not the same.

Dyer withdrew, and Adam suspected he would soon be discussing their future with the other lieutenants. Wardroom gossip was only to be expected, but Dyer had not yet realised how quickly it could misfire.

He touched his side where the iron splinter had smashed him down, when *Anemone* had hauled down her colours and he had been unable to prevent it.

He watched the sea again, the fish leaping in *Valkyrie's* untroubled wake.

And what of Keen? Would he marry Gilia St Clair, and if so, why should he allow the prospect to torment him? Zenoria was dead, but his grief for her had not lessened. He picked up his hat and strode from the cabin. The fact was that Keen needed a wife, even if love did not enter into it.

He ran lightly up the companion ladder, and gazed at the familiar panorama which lay across the bows like a ragged barrier. Ships of every kind. Men-of-war, merchantmen, transports, captured prizes, and small, butterfly-like sails which created the movement in every living harbour.

He nodded to Ritchie, the sailing master, and saw him stand away from the compass box; he had been leaning against it. So his wounds were troubling him again. The surgeon had said that he should be discharged.

Adam frowned. Discharged? It would kill him more quickly than any American splinters.

A glance aloft at the newly trimmed sails, and the long, flapping tongue of the masthead pendant. She would make a proud sight, all sails clewed up except topsail and jib, her

company at their stations at braces and halliards, topmen
ready to take in the last of her canvas once the anchor was
dropped.

A sight which, in the past, had always warmed and excited
him. But the exhilaration eluded him now, like something
beyond his reach.

'Lee braces there! Hands wear ship!'

Bare feet thudded along the deck, and blocks squealed as
more men threw their weight on the snaking lines.

'Tops'l sheets!'

Adam folded his arms, and saw one of the young midshipmen turn to study him.

'Tops'l clew lines! Lively there! Take that man's name, Mr
M'Crea!'

'Helm a-lee!'

Adam walked to the side to watch as the big frigate came
slowly round and into the wind, the way falling off her,
her remaining sails already being dragged and fisted into
submission.

'*Let go!*'

Dyer hurried aft, his eyes everywhere as the ship came to
rest at her cable.

'Will you require the gig, sir?'

Ritchie, the master, grimaced against the pain and then
exclaimed, 'Cheering, sir!'

Adam took a telescope and trained it on two other frigates
anchored nearby. Their shrouds and rigging were filled with
shouting, waving seamen and marines.

He closed the glass with a snap. 'Yes, Mr Dyer, I shall want
the gig as soon as possible.'

Dyer stared at him. 'What does it mean, sir?'

Adam looked at the land. 'It means peace. Not here perhaps,
but peace, the hope of a lifetime.' He glanced at the staring
midshipman. 'He was not even born when the first guns in
this war were fired.'

Some of the seamen were grinning at one another, others
were shaking hands as if they had just met in some lane or
harbour street.

'I shall visit Rear-Admiral Keen. He will expect it.' He saw
the first lieutenant trying to grapple with it. 'Take charge, Mr
Dyer. I will speak with the hands later when I return.' He

35

touched his arm, and felt him jump as if he had just been nicked by a musket ball.

'They have done well. There are many who were not so fortunate.'

Later, as he climbed into the gig, he recalled his last words.

Like an epitaph.

Rear-Admiral Valentine Keen looked up from his desk and saw his flag lieutenant, the Honourable Lawford de Courcey, watching him through the door.

'Yes?'

De Courcey glanced only briefly at Keen's visitor, and said, 'It is reported, sir, that *Valkyrie* is approaching the anchorage.'

'Thank you. Let me know as soon as Captain Bolitho arrives.'

He looked around the room, which he used as his headquarters in Halifax. Charts, files, and books of signals. With de Courcey and some borrowed clerks, he had managed to stay abreast of the work as he could not have done if he had been at sea for long periods. It had made him feel that he belonged, and that what he was doing was progressive, enabling every ship and facility to give of its best. Until a few days ago, when the frigate *Wakeful* had arrived from England with news of the victory and of Napoleon's surrender. So far away, on the other side of the Atlantic, and yet the word of victory in Europe had affected him far more than the war which was being fought here against the Americans; perhaps because it had been his war for so long, with many enemies involved, but always the French.

He would have received the news earlier but *Wakeful*'s young captain had lost a couple of spars in a Western Ocean storm in his eagerness to be the first to bring the despatches. *Wakeful* had also carried a passenger.

Keen looked at him now: Captain Henry Deighton, the next acting commodore of the Halifax squadron, and soon to be directly under the command of Sir Alexander Cochrane, who had taken over the whole station.

It had all happened so quickly that Keen could not decide if he was pleased or disturbed by the unseemly haste.

There had been several letters among the despatches, including one from the First Lord, to reassure him, perhaps, that the next phase of his career was about to begin. There had been no letters from his father, a sure sign of his continuing disapproval.

And there was Gilia. He would delay no longer in asking her, and of course her father, if his proposal of marriage would be acceptable.

Deighton said, 'Captain Bolitho – what is he like, sir?'

Keen studied him. He was a senior post-captain, with several years of blockade duty and two fleet actions to his credit. Squarely built, with short, gingery hair and restless eyes. Not an easy man to serve, harder still to know, he thought.

'A good frigate captain. Successful, too.'

'Yes, I know him by reputation, of course, sir. It must have been a great asset to have Sir Richard Bolitho at his shoulder.'

Keen said nothing. Deighton had already made up his mind, or had had it made up for him.

Deighton said, 'Originally one of Sir Richard's midshipmen, I understand.'

Keen said, 'So was I. Vice-Admiral Bethune at the Admiralty was another. A good influence, it would seem.'

Deighton nodded. 'I see. I look forward to meeting him. Lost his ship, taken prisoner of war and then escaped . . . he sounds resourceful, if a trifle reckless.'

'He is my flag captain, at least until I leave here.'

It was quietly said but he saw the shot go home. Deighton had come from England; he would know better than anyone what was intended. It would mean further promotion, to vice-admiral. He still could not believe it.

He thought of Richard at home now in England, with his Catherine. He had seen and shared the legend himself. He opened the drawer very slightly and saw the miniature of the girl looking up at him. It could be his, too. *Ours*.

He half-listened to the tramp of boots outside the building, the raucous shouts of drill sergeants. This part of the place was on loan to him because of the general; it would soon revert to the army once his flag came down.

What would Adam think of the peace? He had agreed to be his flag captain, and the decision had surprised Keen. Adam was his own man, Deighton was right about that, and reckless to some degree, although Keen would never say so to someone outside the Happy Few. He could stay here and serve under the new commodore, or he could apply to be relieved, to take his chances in England while he hunted for a new command. It would not be easy; he knew that from his experience of other treaties, other respites in the long years of war.

He thought of all their faces, Inch, and Neale, and others like Tyacke who had somehow survived. The word was rarely used in the fleet, but each man was a hero. Perhaps that was what his father had implied more than once. That in war you needed heroes if you were to succeed. In peace, they were an embarrassment to those who had risked nothing.

It made him feel vaguely uneasy, as if he were letting Adam down. That was absurd. The choice was made, and by the time the next courier vessel arrived, everything might have changed yet again.

He closed the drawer, realising that de Courcey had returned.

'*Valkyrie*'s gig has been sighted, sir.'

De Courcey withdrew. The perfect aide, always there when he was needed, although Keen very clearly understood why he and Adam could not endure one another.

Deighton got to his feet. A heavy man, but he moved lightly, with an air of urgency and purpose. Commodore would be a big step for him. Sir Alexander Cochrane had gathered so many senior officers under his command that it was unlikely Deighton would rise any higher. And he would know it.

Deighton said, 'I must leave, sir. I have arrangements to complete.'

'We shall meet again this evening, Captain Deighton. I shall introduce you to Halifax society!'

Deighton stared at him, as if searching for a trap of some kind. Then he left the room.

Keen sighed, and thought, unexpectedly, of England, of Hampshire. It would be spring there. And there would be Gilia.

Suddenly, he was glad to be leaving.

Adam Bolitho opened the shutters of the two lanterns in his cabin to give it an air of welcome and seclusion. He rubbed his shin, cursing silently to himself; he had just collided with a chair in the darkness.

He touched the watch, heavy in his pocket, but did not look at it. It was about three o'clock in the morning, with *Valkyrie* riding easily at her anchor, a ship at rest, as much as she could be with some two hundred and fifty souls, seamen and marines, throughout her hull, some probably still awake after hearing of Napoleon's submission, and wondering what it might mean to them.

When he had returned from his visit to Keen's temporary headquarters he had ordered the lower deck to be cleared and the hands to muster aft. All those upturned faces: men he had come to know well, and those others who had managed to stay at arm's length from him, and all other authority. United by discipline, by the ship, and by their loyalty to one another, the strength of any man-of-war.

Later, he had explained to his officers what the immediate future might bring. With the arrival of better weather, it would almost certainly mean increased action against the Americans. That had been expected.

Dyer had been quite outraged when he had told them that there would be an acting commodore, as if the exchange of a rear-admiral's flag for a mere broad pendant was akin to a personal insult.

The day after tomorrow *Valkyrie* would sail in company with another small convoy, but her main duty would be to demonstrate to Commodore Deighton the importance and the efficiency of the squadron's scouts and offshore patrols.

Adam slumped in a chair and rubbed his shin again. He had had too much to drink, although he could scarcely remember it. And that was not like him.

He had changed into his best uniform and returned ashore for the evening reception which Keen had felt was necessary to welcome his successor. It had been a noisy, uninhibited gathering, which had shown no sign of ending even when Adam had made his excuses and walked back to the jetty, where his gig's crew had been dozing at their oars.

David St Clair and his daughter Gilia had been there, as he had known they would be, as well as local merchants and suppliers to the fleet, officers of the garrison, and several other captains. Benjamin Massey, a close friend of Keen's father, had not attended; it was said that he had returned to England. But Massey's mistress, Mrs Lovelace, had been present. She had smiled at Adam, that same direct, challenging look she had given him before. But this time her husband had accompanied her. The invitation in her eyes had been very clear.

Gilia St Clair had made a point of greeting him, and had hinted that Keen was about to propose marriage. She had watched his face while she spoke to him, remembering, perhaps, when she had asked him if he had known Keen's wife, and his unhesitating reply. *I was in love with her.* She might have told Keen while *Valkyrie* had been away, but for some strange reason he was certain that she had not.

Then she had mentioned Keen's promotion, and the possibility of his becoming port admiral at Plymouth, and the despair that was ever waiting for its chance seized him once again.

She had even mentioned the house in Plymouth. *Boscawen House.* It had been all he could do to hide his emotion.

It had been at the port admiral's house that he had met Zenoria, purely by chance. She had dropped a glove while alighting from her carriage. It had been the last time he had seen her, before she had taken her life. She had been in Plymouth to visit Boscawen House, accompanied by a London lawyer.

Had Keen, in fact, bought it as long ago as that? Did it signify nothing more to him than a suitable house for a senior officer and his wife?

Like yesterday . . . Zenoria in the admiral's house, surrounded by other officers and their wives, and yet completely alone. . . . And her glove, which he had been carrying when the American broadsides had done for his *Anemone.* That, too, was another fragment of this undying pain.

Her voice. *'Keep it for me. Think of me sometimes, will you?'*

He would never forget.

He jerked around in the chair. 'Who is that?'

It was John Whitmarsh, his servant. Another reminder. He had been the only survivor from *Anemone,* except for those men who had surrendered when they had seen their captain fall. Just a boy, who had been 'volunteered' by an uncle when his father had been drowned off the Goodwins. He could have been no more than ten or so when he had been sent to sea in *Anemone.*

'Me, zur.' He stepped carefully into the circle of light. 'I thought you would likely be staying ashore, zur.'

Adam ran his fingers through his dark hair. He must not go on like this. He would destroy himself, and those who depended on him.

'I considered it.' He gestured to his cupboard. 'A glass of cognac, if you please, John Whitmarsh.' He watched him bustling about, always so content, so eager. When Adam had offered him the position of servant the boy had treated it with open delight, as if he had been thrown a lifeline. How could he know that he, in turn, had offered the same to his captain?

And now, all the changes. What might happen next? He looked at the boy grimly. He had nobody. Father dead, and no word from his mother, although Adam had written in an attempt to discover her whereabouts, and her interest, if any, in her son. He was thirteen years old. *As I once was.*

He took the goblet and held it to the lamplight.

'Stay a while, John Whitmarsh. I have been meaning to speak with you.'

'Is something wrong, zur?'

'Have you thought about your future, in the navy, or beyond that?'

He frowned. 'I – I'm not sure, zur.'

Adam studied him for several seconds. 'I received no reply from your mother, you see. Someone must decide for you.'

The boy seemed suddenly anxious. 'I'm very happy here, zur. You've taught me so many things, how to read an' write. . . .'

'That was not all my doing, John Whitmarsh. You are a quick learner.' He looked at the goblet again. 'Would you consider being sponsored as midshipman, or transferred as a volunteer to some ship more suitable for advancement? Have you thought of that?'

The boy shook his head. 'I don't understand, zur. A midshipman . . . wear the King's coat like the young gentlemen, like Mister Lovie who was killed?' He shook his head again, determination making him suddenly vulnerable. 'I shall serve *you*, zur, an' one day perhaps I'll become your cox'n like old Mister Allday does for Sir Richard!'

Adam smiled, and was strangely moved. 'Never let Allday hear you describe him as old, my lad!' He became serious again. 'I believe you could be a midshipman, and eventually a King's officer, with some education and the right guidance.

41

And I would be prepared to sponsor you.' He saw that he was achieving nothing. 'I shall pay – even your mother cannot object to that!'

The boy stared at him, his eyes filling his face. It was all there, despair, anxiety and disbelief.

'I want to stay with you, zur. I don't want anybody else.'

Overhead feet moved back and forth, the watch changing. It must be four o'clock. But to this boy it meant nothing; all he saw was the one life he knew being taken from him.

'I shall tell you a story. There once was a young boy who lived with his mother in Penzance. They did not have much money, but they were happy together. Then his mother died, and this boy was left with nothing. Nothing but a piece of paper and the name of his uncle, whose home was in Falmouth.'

'An' be that you, zur?'

'Aye, John Whitmarsh, it was. I walked all the way to Falmouth. Not as far as India, but far enough, and there I was taken in and protected by the lady I grew to know as my Aunt Nancy. I could have stayed with her, and I would have had no fear of want again. But I waited until my uncle's ship returned to Falmouth. He was her *captain*.' He was surprised at his own voice. Pride, love for the man who was one of England's greatest admirals.

The boy nodded gravely. 'An' you became a midshipman, zur.' There was a silence, then he said, 'When I met Sir Richard that day, when he asked about you, an' what I saw when our ship went down, I *felt* it. How he felt, what you meant to him, just like me an' my father.'

'So think about it, for your own sake. And for mine. We take much from this strange life we lead. It is sometimes a comfort to put something back into it.'

The boy picked up the empty goblet but Adam shook his head, and he left it.

Then he said, 'I only ever had one real friend, zur, that was Billy, an' he was lost that day.'

Adam stood up and yawned. 'Well, now you have another, so be off and catch some rest before they pipe the hands.'

He turned to watch as the slight figure melted into the shadows, and was pleased by what he had done.

They were two days out of Halifax on passage for the Bermudas

42

once again, and *Valkyrie*, with her heavily laden charges, had barely logged five hundred miles. Long, monotonous days when some of the hands had to be chased even to their routine duties watch by watch.

In other circumstances it might have been ideal. There was a light north-easterly wind, enough to fill the sails and no more, with clear skies and sun to drive away the memories of winter cold and darkness.

At noon Adam stood by the quarterdeck rail and shaded his eyes to watch the three heavy transports lying downwind, with the outline of *Wildfire*, a smaller twenty-eight-gun frigate, almost invisible in a shimmering heat haze.

He heard the murmuring voices of the midshipmen, who were gathered with their sextants to estimate and compare their calculations from the midday sights, while Ritchie and one of his mates moved amongst them with the tired patience of schoolmasters. Lieutenant Dyer was with the boatswain by the foremast, discussing work to be done on the crosstrees, although Adam guessed that he had chosen the moment merely to keep out of his way.

This endless convoy work, soldiers and guns, stores and ammunition; it might be necessary, but it was not a life he cared for. A slow passage and limp canvas when he was more used to questions of whether to reef or not, with spray bursting over the beakhead to send the unwary flying.

He glanced at the skylight. He had scarcely seen Captain Deighton since he had come aboard. He was down there now, using the large stern cabin. Deighton was probably relishing it, thinking of the moment when it would be his stepping-stone to higher rank.

He glanced at the masthead. At least there was no broad pendant yet. *This is still my ship.*

Ritchie was writing in his log, and looked up as Adam's shadow fell across it.

The sea was empty, a glittering, blinding desert, and yet in his mind's eye he could see the land, exactly as Ritchie's spidery calculations and estimated position described it. New York lay some hundred and fifty miles to the west. Ships, movement, the enemy. But for how much longer?

'How are you feeling, Mr Ritchie?'

He saw the immediate alarm, the anxiety. Like the boy, when he had asked him about his future.

43

'Fair enough, sir.' He sighed. 'Some days is better'n others.'

Adam regarded him gravely. 'Take heed of the bad times, Mr Ritchie. Have a word with the surgeon, perhaps?'

Ritchie's worn face split into a grin. 'Of course, sir.'

George Minchin was a surgeon of the old school, one of the butchers. And yet, even sodden with rum, he had probably saved more lives in his brutal trade than others more mindful of the risks. He had been Bolitho's surgeon in the old *Hyperion* when she had fought her last fight. Drink should have sent him aloft long since, Adam thought, but he was still with them. He could understand Ritchie's reluctance to fall into his hands.

He saw Ritchie turn his head slightly. 'He's one of the walking dead if ever I saw one, sir!'

The man in question was tall, narrow-chested and bony, like a living skeleton. Except that Adam had seen him carry Captain Deighton's chest and other gear up from a boat alongside with neither a tackle nor another hand to aid him; he had muscles of steel. He was Deighton's personal servant and went by the name of Jack Norway. If that was indeed his name.

When spoken to, he would listen attentively, his gaunt head slightly on one side, his gaze never leaving the speaker. Dyer had remarked irritably, 'Never says a word, damn his eyes! More like a bodyguard than a servant, if you ask me!' He had shown no interest in mixing with those around him, and the others seemed content to keep it so.

Adam tugged out his watch and flicked open the guard. Then he turned it slightly to catch the sun's reflection on the engraved mermaid, which had immediately attracted him in the shop in Halifax. Chiming clocks, watches of every kind, and this one. His old watch had gone missing after he had been wounded in *Anemone*, or had been stolen during his imprisonment. *The little mermaid.* Like the one which was said to visit the church in Zennor, where Zenoria now lay. Or did she . . . ?

'We shall exercise the starboard battery after the hands have been fed, Mr Ritchie.' He could smell the heady aroma of rum in the warm air, another part of a ship's daily life. *Mine, too.*

He saw one of the midshipmen cleaning his sextant, then turning away as Deighton appeared on the quarterdeck.

He glanced at the men working on deck, the sailmaker's crew with their needles and palms, stitching and repairing, letting nothing go to waste. Fasken, the gunner, was bending over one of the larboard carronades, watched anxiously by Lieutenant Warren, who until recently had been a midshipman. There were probably about forty years between them.

Deighton remarked, 'Some experienced men, Captain Bolitho, but some very young ones, would you agree?'

Adam said, 'The ship has a good backbone of seasoned men, warrant officers and the like. I have been lucky. Some of the others are quite young, and I'm still short-handed despite volunteers from Halifax, but even the young ones have experience enough of battle.'

He studied Deighton's profile, the short ginger hair, the ever restless eyes.

Almost to himself, Deighton added, 'Keep them busy, drive them hard, that's the answer. But I'm sure you know that, eh?'

'This is not a ship of the line, Captain Deighton. We are often engaged in chasing enemy vessels, with a prize or two at the end of the day. We always need extra hands to crew the prizes, when and where we can find them.'

Deighton nodded slowly. 'And you have been more than successful, I hear.'

Adam gestured over the starboard side. 'There are prizes a-plenty out there for those who will run them to earth.'

Deighton took a telescope from the rack and scanned the horizon immediately ahead of the ship, pausing at each transport, and the hazy frigate beyond.

'She must be *Wildfire*. Captain Price.'

Adam half-smiled. Price, the wild-eyed Welshman. But all he said was, 'A good officer.'

'Yes, yes. We shall see.'

The afternoon watch had taken over its various stations, the men glancing at the other captain as they trooped aft, their eyes curious, perhaps hostile.

Adam wondered why. Because Deighton was a stranger? *But then, so was I.*

Deighton asked abruptly, 'And who is *that*?'

Adam saw the boy, John Whitmarsh, pausing by the boat tier to stare at the sea.

'My servant.'

Deighton smiled, for the first time. 'A damn sight prettier than mine! Where did you find him?'

45

He was surprised that Deighton could rouse such resentment in him.

'He was one of the few to survive when my ship was sunk.' He turned and looked at him directly. 'I am putting him up for advancement.'

'I see. Is he from a good family? His father, has he . . . ?'

Adam replied shortly, 'His father is dead. He has no means of support.'

'Then I don't understand.' He touched Adam's sleeve. 'Or . . . perhaps I do.'

A squad of marines had lined the quarterdeck nettings, and a sergeant was inspecting their muskets. At a signal from forward, some old pieces of boxwood were hurled outboard by the carpenter's mates.

'Marines, *ready*!'

Adam beckoned to the lieutenant of marines. 'Carry on!'

The pieces of woodwork floated past, and as the order rang out each marine fired his musket in turn. There were a few grins and some derisive cheers from idlers on the gundeck as splashes burst around the makeshift targets.

Adam reached out and took the marine officer's pistol, and tested the weight in his palm; it was heavier and clumsier than his own. He climbed up on to some bollards and took aim. The driftwood was further away now, and he heard Deighton remark, 'Not much chance there!'

'I think, Captain Deighton, that you were right the first time. You *don't* understand.'

He felt the pistol buck in his grip and saw one of the wood fragments splinter. Then he handed the pistol to the marine lieutenant, and said, 'Now, I think we all do.'

4

The Longest Day

Catherine carefully raised the window catch, and paused to glance over her shoulder at their bed. The curtain around it was partly drawn to shield his face from the first light; he was asleep, one arm flung out toward her pillow, at peace, perhaps his only refuge.

She opened the window and looked down at the garden, the rich colours of her first roses. The sun was warm on her skin even so early in the morning, the air clean, and bearing only a hint of salt from the sea.

If she had leaned out, she would have seen the blue-grey water of Falmouth Bay beyond the headland. But she did not lean out. Today, of all days, the sea was an enemy.

Her gown had fallen open and she felt the breath of that sea on her skin. There was no one to see her. The estate workers were in the fields, and she could hear the faint sound of hammers chipping on slate. She had once believed she would never get used to this place, or call it home, and now it was a part of herself.

She touched her breast as he had done, could still feel the depth of his embrace and his desire. As if he had only just withdrawn from her.

How quickly time had passed since their return from London. Riding, walking, and being alone with each other.

Now the house was so quiet, as if it was holding its breath. George Avery had visited them several times, and with Richard had gone through the canvas pouches which arrived regularly from their lordships. She had listened to them, trying to share it, to make it last. Like Richard's new flagship, *Frobisher*. They

47

discussed the ship like the professional sailors they were, as if she were human, a living creature.

Avery had stayed at the inn at Fallowfield, perhaps to allow them as much time as possible alone together, and also to ponder over his rejection by Susanna Mildmay. She knew it had saddened Richard; he had blamed himself, because Avery had put loyalty before his own personal happiness. If she was really the woman for him. . . . She watched a pair of wagtails darting amongst the flowers. *Is that not what society said about me?*

She pressed her hand to her side, feeling the ache, the heaviness, the pain which today would bring.

They had dined alone last night, although neither of them remembered the meal which had been so carefully prepared.

She had told him she wanted to ride with him all the way to Portsmouth, where *Frobisher* lay waiting to receive him. Like the other times, like the last time when she had climbed up *Indomitable*'s side. It was not to be. Richard had said that he wanted to take his leave of her in this house. *Where I always think of you.*

How could she do it? How could she let him go like this, so soon? She knew he hated the idea of her making the long journey, some one hundred and fifty miles, back from Portsmouth. Even with the roads in good condition and the coming of better weather, there was always the risk of footpads, or deserters from the army or navy who robbed or even killed if resisted. He would not be alone. He would be among friends when he saw his flag hoisted above his new flagship. Avery, Allday, Yovell, and of course Ozzard, who had given no hint of what he thought about leaving yet again. And perhaps the strongest of all, James Tyacke, who had cast aside his idea of returning to Africa. Or perhaps he had decided that there would be no escape and no solace even there.

Yes, Richard would have friends, but he needed memories also. Like last night. It had not been a last, desperate passion, an act which if missed would haunt them as something lost. It had been a *need*; she had felt it when they had come to this room, when he had turned her towards the finely carved cheval glass, and had undressed her while she had watched his hands, knowing they explored her, and yet sensing that it was happening to someone else. A stranger.

He had taken her to the bed and had said, 'Do nothing.'

He had kissed her from her throat to her thigh, from her breast to her knees and then, very slowly, back again. She could not believe that she had been able to contain her desire for him, and when she tried to pull him down to her, he had gripped her wrists and held them while he had looked down at her, wanting her, but needing it to last. Lovers, as if for the first time.

And then he had smiled at her. Even though the light had been from a single candle only, she thought it was the most beautiful thing she had ever seen.

He had entered her without hesitation, and she had cried out his name while she had arched her body to receive him.

She felt a tear fall on her breast, and wiped her skin angrily with the lace of her gown.

Not now. Not now, of all times.

She walked to the bed and pulled the curtain aside. His face was relaxed, even youthful. More like Adam than most of the other faces in those ever-watchful portraits. His hair still black across the crumpled pillow, except for the one rebellious lock above his right eye. It was almost completely white, and she knew he hated it. It concealed the savage scar which ran deeply into his hairline . . . so close to death even then.

She sat on the bed and realised he was awake, watching her. She did not resist as he released the gown from her shoulders, nor flinch when he touched what he had kissed and teased so often. She understood. It was another memory. When he was able to be alone sometimes, to be free from the demands of duty, when he might perhaps be reading the leather-bound sonnets she had given him, he would remember, and would be with her, as she was with him.

She said, 'It is a lovely day, Richard.'

He caressed her hair, which hung loosely over her bare shoulders.

He smiled, searching her face. 'You lie. It is an *awful* day!'

'I know.'

He raised himself on one elbow and looked at the clock, but said nothing.

There was no need. She thought of their walks by the sea, following a receding tide, their footmarks spread in the sand like molten silver. Holding this day at bay. They had visited his sister, and had found her strangely calm, able and willing to talk about her late husband, Lewis, 'the King of Cornwall'.

She had been very definite about one thing. 'I'll not let the estate go. The people always depended on Lewis. He'd expect it of me.' She had glanced around the huge, empty house, and had said, 'He's still here, you know.'

She realised that she had taken his hand. 'I'm sorry, Richard . . . it becomes more difficult to accept.'

They heard the discreet clatter of dishes, the soft murmur of voices beyond the door.

'Not for so long this time, Kate.'

She smiled, and wondered how it was possible. 'I shall come to Malta and torment you. Remember what Prinny said about that?'

Grace Ferguson, the housekeeper, nodded to the maid. 'Give a knock.' She smiled. 'Sounds all right.'

She thought of the barely touched meal of the previous night, the unopened champagne, which always seemed to take their fancy for some reason. But you could never be sure, especially with her ladyship. She had never forgotten when her husband had told her about that terrible day when the girl Zenoria had jumped to her death from Trystan's Leap. He had described how Lady Catherine had lifted the slight, broken body and held her like a child while she had opened her clothing to find the one mark which would identify her. Where a whip had laid open her back; the *mark of Satan*, she had called it. . . .

The maid came out and smiled. 'Good as gold, ma'am. Nothin' worries they much.'

'You mind your manners, girl!' She turned away. *That's all you know.*

Then she walked to a window and stared down at the yard. Young Matthew, as he was still called and probably always would be, was giving the carriage a wipe with his cloth. Heads would turn when they saw the Bolitho crest on the door; people would wave, but, like the maid, they would never understand.

Another Bolitho was leaving the land. She remembered her own bitterness when Bryan had returned home after the Battle of the Saintes, with one arm gone. As she had nursed him over the months and watched him slowly restored to life, she had been almost grateful. He had lost an arm, but he was still her man, and he would never have to leave her again.

Later, when she went downstairs, she saw that Sir Richard's cocked hat lay beside his sword. Ready.

She peered up at the nearest portrait, Rear-Admiral Denziel Bolitho. He had been the only other officer in the family to attain flag rank. He had been with Wolfe at Quebec, probably near to where Sir Richard and John Allday had last been, she thought. But it was not the face or the rank she noticed; it was the sword. The artist had even caught the light on it, exactly as it was falling now. The same old sword.

For some reason, she shivered.

John Allday watched the boy lead the pony and trap around the stable yard, and tried to come to terms with his feelings. All his life he had seemed to be waiting for ships, or coming back to this place from one vessel or another. In the past he had been able to face it squarely, hope for fair winds, and what Mister Herrick had always referred to as *Lady Luck*.

This time it had been hard. Unis putting on a brave face, little Kate wanting to play games with him, unaware of the pain that such partings brought. The next time he saw her she would be bigger, almost a person, and he would have missed the part in between. He grimaced. Again.

So it was another ship, but that did not trouble him. He was the admiral's coxswain, as he had always believed he would be, as he had promised Bolitho when he had been the youthful captain Allday remembered so well.

He had seen the looks on other people's faces until they had grown used to it. Admiral, England's finest, and his coxswain. But so much more. They were friends. It had even taken the flag lieutenant a while to fathom it out. And now he, too, was one of Sir Richard's little crew; he even read Unis's letters to Allday, and replied to them in a way that nobody else could do.

He saw Young Matthew, very smart in his livery, examining the baggage, ensuring it was properly stowed. From the stables Allday could hear the horses stamping their hooves, eager to go. He sighed. *Like me*. Wanting to get started now that the choice was made.

Bryan Ferguson came from the house and nodded to

Matthew. 'You can harness up now.' He joined his friend by the wall. 'Got everything you need, John?'

Allday glanced at the stout black sea-chest which was lashed beside one of the admiral's. He had made it himself; it even had secret drawers in it. He wished he had had time to show them to little Kate.

'Enough, Bryan. Leastways, we should get some good weather at this time o' year.'

Ferguson frowned, sensing the sadness and, at the same time, the overriding determination of this big man.

He said, 'You know that sea well, of course.'

Allday nodded. 'Where *Hyperion* was lost to us.'

Ferguson bit his lip. 'I shall visit Unis as often as I can. She knows we're always here and ready if she needs anything.' He ran his eye over his friend again. The landsman's idea of the true sailor, he thought, in his smart blue jacket with the buttons bearing the Bolitho crest and his nankeen breeches and silver-buckled shoes. God alone knew the people owed everything to men like him. It still did not seem possible that the fear of war and invasion were past.

He saw Allday turn as Catherine Somervell came from the house and stood for a moment in the bright sunshine. Her long, dark hair hung straight down her spine, and she wore a gown the colour of fresh cream. She shaded her eyes while she turned to speak with one of the stable-boys, her ready smile revealing nothing of her emotions.

Allday watched her and waited for her to notice him. She made a beautiful picture, he thought, and he guessed she had taken great care of her appearance. The sun glinted on the pendant Bolitho had given her, the diamond fan hung low on her breast, like pride, like defiance, like the sailor's woman she was.

When he had last visited the house he had seen them together, in her own garden by the wall. They had been holding one another, and had not seen him. Allday had left without a word. It had been too private, a moment which he could not share.

Afterwards, he had recalled the words he had used to describe Captain Adam Bolitho and the girl who had thrown herself from the cliffs. *They looked so right together*. He could have been speaking of Sir Richard and his lady.

He realised that she was looking at him and felt strangely guilty.

She came to him and took his big hands in hers.

'Take good care, John.' For the merest instant, he had seen her mouth quiver. 'And look after my man for me, will you?' She was in control again.

Then she turned and saw the horses being backed into position, Young Matthew speaking to them, careful not to catch her eye. In his quiet way, he too would know how she felt; he had driven them before when they were to be parted, just as he had driven her to the harbour when Bolitho had returned home after leaving *Indomitable* at Plymouth.

She stepped among the roses and chose one, then held it to her face. A perfect red rose, one of the earliest. There would be many more before long, when he was far away from here.

She saw him on the steps now, the house at his back, as he might remember it. He looked rested, his face showing no sign of strain or uncertainty. Her man, youthful again. No wonder people thought he and Adam were brothers, although Richard himself would dispute any such foolish notion.

He came down the steps, carrying his hat, the old sword hanging against his hip, where she had been, where her head had lain. He saw the rose, and took it from her.

'So much a part of you, Kate.' He hesitated, as if suddenly aware of the silent figures nearby. 'It is better this way.'

She touched his shirt, and felt her locket underneath.

'I shall remove it when we lie together again, dearest of men.'

Gently, he placed the rose in her gown, above her breasts.

He said, 'It is time.' He glanced around, but Allday had already climbed into the carriage, leaving them alone but sharing it, as always.

She saw him press his fingers to his eye as he faced into the sunlight, but he shook his head as he sensed her concern. 'It is nothing.' Then he held her hands tightly. 'Compared with this, nothing else signifies.'

She caressed his face and smiled at him. 'I am so proud of you, Richard. And these people too, they all love you and will miss you.' Then she said, 'Kiss me, Richard. *Here*. We are alone in every other sense.'

Then she stepped back and gave him another smile. 'Now, Richard.'

It took an age, an eternity, until at last the carriage moved through the gates. Somebody gave a cheer, and Catherine heard someone else sobbing quietly. Grace Ferguson, who had been a part of it all from the beginning.

She clutched the rose against her skin and waved with her free hand. She could scarcely see now, and yet she was determined that he would remember her like this and feel no despair and no guilt for his departure. When she looked again, the road was empty. She stared blindly at the stables and saw her big mare Tamara tossing her head over the door. She felt her resolve weakening; she would ride after him, hold him again once more.

She heard Grace Ferguson exclaim, 'My lady! My lady, you've cut yourself!'

Catherine glanced down at her breast where she had been pressing the rose; she had felt nothing. She touched the skin with her fingers and looked at the blood.

'No, Grace, it is my heart which bleeds.' Then and only then did she give in, to bury her face against the other woman's shoulder.

Ferguson waited and watched in silence. When the others had all drifted away the two women remained standing together in the sunlight. Only their shadow moved, when quite suddenly Catherine touched his wife's arm without speaking and walked slowly away towards the house, the bloodied rose still held against her breast like a talisman.

James Tyacke opened a window slightly and stared down at the busy street. Portsmouth, called by some *the heart of the British Navy*, and a place which had been so familiar to him as a young lieutenant, seemed completely different. He knew, in truth, that he was the one who had changed.

He had chosen this small boarding house on Portsmouth Point partly because he had stayed here before, and because he knew it would afford him some peace over the next few days, before he went to the dockyard to take command of *Frobisher*. He could still scarcely believe he had abandoned his decision to return to the slave coast with so little hesitation.

He watched the jostling crowds of sailors and marines, the

trusted men who were unlikely to desert, and had been allowed ashore. In peace or war, it was every captain's main concern that he might be left too short of hands to work his ship out of harbour.

He had seen for himself the mass of shipping at Spithead, the misty hump of the Isle of Wight beyond. Familiar, and yet so alien. He sighed. When would he accept it? He had no past, and his future was only today and tomorrow. It had to be enough.

The owner of the boarding house had obviously been surprised to number a post-captain among his guests, and had done everything he could to make Tyacke welcome. He was a small goblin of a man, completely bald, who wore an outdated and shabby wig, usually somewhat awry and, Tyacke thought, not properly athwartships. There was an unspoken etiquette in naval circles as to where sea officers should lodge. Senior officers stayed at the George in the High Street, where a room had already been reserved for Sir Richard Bolitho when he arrived from Cornwall. Lieutenants and the like used the Fountain further down the street, and the 'young roosters', the midshipmen of the fleet, frequented the Blue Posts, famous for its rabbit pie, if rabbit it was.

Here, too, on the Point, separated only from the respectable properties by the same rules which governed the teeming world of a ship of the line, were lodging houses, some so squalid that it was a wonder they had not been burned down; tailors, pawnbrokers and moneylenders; and narrow lanes where the ladies of the town paraded their wares, and were rarely lacking in customers. It was so often the last place a sailor would see or snatch a moment to enjoy himself, before weighing anchor and sailing perhaps to the other side of the world, often never to return.

He thought of Lieutenant George Avery; he would be arriving soon in Portsmouth if he was not already here. Another who had chosen uncertainty instead of a life ashore. For some reason, Tyacke was pleased that Avery had made the decision to join them.

And there was the ship. He had studied her details, which the Admiralty had made available to him in their weighty folder of orders and sailing instructions. A strange ship, without familiar faces, so he would start from the beginning once more. *Indomitable* had taught him that he could do it, and much more besides.

All the way to Portsmouth, he had gone through the folder. He had travelled alone. It was still difficult to accept that he was wealthy, by his own standards, as the result of slave bounty still trickling through the Admiralty channels, and prize money which he had gained under Bolitho. He touched his burned face. *His own coach.* And, had he wanted it, he could have taken a room at the George.

He closed the window and sat down. *The ship.* If he could get through the next two days, he knew he could take the next all-important step. From a commander of a schooner and a lowly brig to *Indomitable*, and now *Frobisher*, a ship of the line. And all because of one man. *I would serve no other.*

He thought of Bolitho's Catherine, and wondered how she would deal with this new appointment so soon after Bolitho's return from Halifax. He was certain that Bolitho would not bring her to Portsmouth. Crowds, cheers and mindless well-wishers. What would they know of the cost of separation?

Tyacke looked at his open chest. Another journey. This time, how might it end?

He touched his leg, where a splinter had torn into it. It had been *Indomitable*'s last battle; she would never fight again, according to the dockyard people at Plymouth.

It was like recalling someone else. He had taken a boarding-pike and driven it into the deck and had supported himself, despite the pain and the blood, until the guns had fallen silent. *Were we really like that?*

And Bolitho leading the boarding party over to the enemy's deck, that old sword dangling from his wrist, with Allday at his side.

The sounds from the street intruded again. It would be worse at night; he should have considered it. No private places to walk, to travel with his thoughts alone for company. That he did remember about the Point. Somebody had once proclaimed that it was *crowded with a class of low and abandoned beings who seem to have declared open war against every habit of decency.* Obviously not a sailor, he thought.

Then he would spend his last few days here in this room. Perhaps he might read *The Gazette*, and any newssheet that might tell him how the war with the Americans was progressing.

He looked round as the door opened an inch.

'I am sorry to intrude, Captain Tyacke, I know you insisted on privacy. We have to be careful, of course, with so many sea officers waiting for ships.'

Tyacke nodded. *Praying for them, more likely.*

The shabby wig was awry again, but his eyes were busily going around the room. Probably wondering why a post-captain, soon to assume command of a flagship, should choose such a humble place to stay.

Tyacke said patiently, 'I am all attention, Mr Tidy.'

'There is a *lady* come hence to see you, sir. Say the word, and I will make the necessary excuses. I would not like people to think . . . .'

'What is her name?'

He already knew. Had he merely been trying to avoid a decision, like tearing the letter to fragments?

'Mrs Spiers, sir.' Encouraged, he added, 'A very pleasant lady, I would say.'

'I'll come down.'

'Please use my parlour.' He paused. 'Or this room, if you prefer.'

Tyacke stood up. 'No.' How many women had been ushered into these rooms? And how often?

As he followed the small goblin figure down the creaking stairs, Tyacke was aware of something almost unknown to him. *Fear.* But of what?

She was facing the door when he entered the parlour, hands folded, the ribbons of a wide-brimmed straw hat dangling from her fingers. She must have changed over the years, had been married, borne two children, been widowed. But she was the same. Brown hair curled above her ears; the level, open gaze he had believed gone for ever, lost in that other darkness.

She spoke first. 'Don't turn away, James . . . I did that once to you. I have thought of it so many times. I wrote to you.'

'I wrote to *you*.' His mouth could not form her name. 'But you would have seen it only if I had fallen. I said . . . I said. . . .' He imagined the little man in his wig listening outside the door. But there was nothing outside, nothing beyond this room or this place. He saw her move towards him, and said, '*Don't*, Marion. Not now. Not like this. I've tried so hard . . . .'

She was very close, looking up at him; the same curved lashes. She reached up deliberately and touched his scarred face, without revulsion, without obvious emotion. Like her letter. Understanding, not asking forgiveness.

He heard himself ask, his voice that of a stranger, 'How did you know? Who told you?'

She glanced at his epaulettes. 'I read about Sir Richard Bolitho, and I knew you would be here as his captain again. The rest was easy, but you know what Portsmouth is like. A village, if you let it become one.'

'I take command the day after tomorrow. After that, who can say. . . .' He looked away and asked abruptly, 'Are you well, Marion? Provided for?'

She nodded, her eyes never leaving him. 'My husband was a good man. It was very sudden.'

He glanced around the small, untidy parlour, with its smells of tobacco and wet soot.

'And the children . . . two, you said.'

'Caroline is quite grown now.' Then she did lower her eyes. 'James is twelve. He hopes to enter the navy one day.'

Tyacke said quietly, 'They are not my children.'

She smiled. It made her look vulnerable, and suddenly defeated.

'They could be, James. If you wanted. If you wanted enough.'

He heard the landlord say loudly, 'No, Bob, I've got somebody in there.'

Tyacke turned into the light and said gently, '*Look at me*, Marion. Not at the captain, but at me, the survivor. Could you lie with me, search for a future, when we had no past?'

He had put his fingers to his face, where she had touched him. He could still feel the touch, and wanted to curse himself for his stupidity, for the hope which would betray him, if he allowed it.

He had not seen her move, but she was at the door, one hand on the catch.

'I had to come, James. I was very young . . . at that time.

Young, and transparent like gossamer. But I loved you then. I never forgot.'

She played with her hat, and shrugged. 'I'm glad I came. I had hoped we might be friends again.'

'Nothing more?'

She watched him, perhaps trying to rediscover. 'Write to me, James. I know you will be busy with your affairs, but please try to write, if you want to.'

He was reminded sharply, vividly, of Catherine and Bolitho, as if he had just seen them. What they had overcome, what it had cost them, and how they had triumphed. As he had seen that day in Falmouth, when she climbed up the ship's side to the delight of his men . . . .

. . . Of the yellow gown he had carried in his chest over the years, which Catherine had worn to cover her nakedness when *Larne* had found the open boat, when all hope of their survival had been abandoned. *Except by me . . . .*

He replied, 'I'm not much of a hand with writing, Marion.'

She smiled, for the first time.

'If you want to.'

She had put a small card in his hand. 'If you have time, James. It is not so far.'

He stared at the card, his mind, usually so cool and accurate, now like a ship taken all aback.

Where was the anger, the condemnation which had been his companions for so many years? Perhaps, like the pity, it had been something shared.

'I shall leave now.' When he did not move, she came to him again, and said, 'You are still that man, James.' She felt him hold her, carefully, as if she might break, and wanted to cry when she saw how he turned the terrible scars away as she kissed his cheek. It was a small beginning.

When Tyacke looked again, she was gone, and the landlord was in the doorway beaming at him. As if it had all been only in his mind.

'All done, sir?'

Tyacke did not answer, but climbed the stairs to his room. He propped the card on a table, and opened a bottle of cognac.

Tomorrow Avery might come, so that they could begin their preparations. Everything else would fall into place. . . .

But he knew it would not, as he should have realised when he had torn his letter into pieces.

He lay down and stared at the ceiling.

The longest day. *For all of us.*

5

The Prize

Bolitho placed his sealed letter to Catherine on the table and pictured her reading it, perhaps by her roses, or more probably in the privacy of their rooms. It had been bad enough, leaving her in Falmouth, and this letter was little comfort. Not yet; even sending it was like breaking a precious link.

He pulled out his watch and flicked open the guard: almost two o'clock in the afternoon. No turning back.

He sighed and replaced the watch in his pocket, his eyes moving around the room, its dark timbers almost black with age and the smoke from a thousand fires. He had only stayed at the famous George Inn once before, then as a young captain. It was a timeless place, which had seen more admirals and captains come and go than he could imagine.

The room looked bare now that his chests had been taken out to be sent to his new flagship, empty, ready to forget him and welcome another.

It was not difficult to see Nelson here, perhaps in this very room, on his last days ashore in England. He had left his beloved Emma at their house in Merton. What was she doing now? And what of those who had promised Nelson that she would be taken care of?

He turned away, angry with himself for making the comparison. There was none. Only the bitter rift of separation was the same.

He heard voices on the stairs; one was Avery, the other Allday. It was time.

Down the stairs, the scene was exactly as he had expected. The landlord, anxious to please, careful not to show it. There were plenty of uniforms in evidence, sea officers obviously enjoying themselves, each careful to catch his eye as he passed. Some might have served with him, most had never seen him in the flesh before. But they all knew him.

It was said that when Nelson left the George for the last time the streets had been packed with people trying to catch a glimpse of him, and show their admiration for their hero. Perhaps it had even been love.

He himself had never met 'Our Nel', although even Adam had exchanged a word or two with him when he had been carrying despatches.

He saw Avery watching him from the doorway, his eyes tawny in the reflected sunlight. Beyond him, Allday stood with his back to the inn, as if he had already rejected the land.

The street was busy, but quite ordinary. No cheering crowds or curious sightseers this time; but then, there was no war raging across the Channel.

'We'll walk to the Sally Port.' He saw Allday turn and touch his hat to him, the admiral's coxswain.

Avery observed him thoughtfully, trying to guess the mood of the man to whom he was loyal before all else.

Bolitho said, 'No bands, no parades, George.' He smiled. 'Like God, the navy is only fully appreciated when danger is at the gates!'

Avery tried to sense bitterness or regret, but there was none. He had seen the letter Bolitho had given to the landlord, and knew the truth would be in it, for her alone. For Catherine.

He said, 'The ship is short-handed, sir. I think Captain Tyacke is eager to put to sea, to learn the strengths and weaknesses amongst the people.' Even Tyacke was different, he thought. Once a hard man to know, he had become as close to a friend as was possible within their ordered lives. And he had seemed withdrawn, as if a part of him were still lingering elsewhere.

He wondered what Bolitho truly thought about the choice of flagship; he himself had only had a few days aboard *Frobisher*, and he had found little time to meet the other officers, or get the feel of the ship. In a rare moment of confidence, Tyacke had told him that *Frobisher*, if properly manned and drilled, would be a fast sailer, and had a hull so well designed that even in heavy seas she might remain a relatively dry ship.

That would prove a godsend for her seamen when required to make or reef rebellious canvas, finding what warmth and comfort they could between decks afterwards.

Avery had expected there might be some resentment at Tyacke's appointment, but he had discovered that *Frobisher*'s previous captain had been suddenly discharged as medically unfit, and sent ashore with the Admiralty's blessing. Avery had served Bolitho long enough to know that the real reason for the captain's hasty departure was probably something very different, and he had gained the impression that the ship's lieutenants, at least, were glad to see him go. Tyacke had revealed nothing of his own thoughts. He had his own methods of gaining a company's loyalty, and would tolerate nothing less than the standards he had set in *Indomitable*.

Bolitho tugged his hat down more firmly as they rounded a corner and the wind off the sea swept to greet them.

Avery had explained that Tyacke had changed the anchorage after leaving the dockyard, and the ship now lay off St Helens on the east coast of the Isle of Wight. A long, stiff pull for any barge crew, he thought, and Allday would be watching their behaviour and that of the barge with a critical eye. Like other old Jacks, he had always maintained that a ship could be judged by the appearance and handling of her boats.

He considered his own change of role. Tyacke would have attended to everything, food and stores, fresh water, and any fruit juice he could lay hands on, keeping his subordinates at arm's length until he had learned the reliability, or otherwise, of lieutenants and warrant officers, purser, gunner and boatswain. Bolitho gave a brief smile. And, of course, the midshipmen, the 'young gentlemen', for some reason he had not yet discovered always the bane of Tyacke's life.

He saw Allday on the jetty, apparently relaxed and untroubled, but Bolitho knew him so well. He would already have learned everything he could about the *Frobisher* of seventy-four guns, once the French two-decker *Glorieux*. Completed too late for Trafalgar, she had had only a brief career under the Tricolour before she was attacked and captured by two of the blockading squadron while on passage from Belle Isle to Brest. That had been four years ago. Allday would be thinking of that, too: the same year he had married Unis at Fallowfield.

Prize ships, put to work against their old masters, were

commonplace in the navy. There had been times when even ships rated as unfit through rot or disrepair had been pressed into service, like his own *Hyperion*, a ship of which they still yarned and sang in the taverns and alehouses. *How Hyperion cleared the way* . . . . Would their lordships make the same mistake of running the fleet down to the bare bones, simply because the immediate danger had been withdrawn?

He glanced at Avery, who was speaking with a waterman, noticing the stiffness with which he held and moved his shoulder when he was not conscious of it. Like Allday and his wounded chest, where a Spanish blade had hacked him down.

They were loyal; it was more than mere loyalty. But they were both sacrificing so much, perhaps a last chance, for his sake.

'Ah, here she be!' Allday scowled. 'A fresh coat of paint will be the first thing!'

Bolitho shaded his eyes to watch the barge, which had suddenly appeared around the stern of an anchored frigate. It had probably been obtained direct from the dockyard where *Frobisher* had just completed an overhaul; there would have been no time to paint it dark green, as was the custom for flag officers' barges. Again, he felt the same sense of doubt. The last captain, Charles Oliphant, might have remained as his flag captain unless he had explicitly requested James Tyacke.

He recalled Admiral Lord Rhodes's obvious eagerness for him to take *Frobisher* as flagship.

He looked at Avery again; perhaps he had noticed the flaw. Captain Oliphant was related in some capacity to Rhodes, although he could not recall where he had heard it mentioned. He frowned. But he would remember.

The barge turned in a wide arc and tossed oars, the bowman hooking on to the jetty while a seaman vaulted onto the worn stonework. Smart enough, with a lieutenant in charge, no doubt wondering what this first encounter would be like.

Avery said quietly, 'That's Pennington, second lieutenant, sir.'

Allday conceded, 'Not too bad.'

The lieutenant stepped ashore and doffed his hat.

'I am ready to take you directly to your flagship, Sir

Richard.' The eyes, Bolitho noticed, were careful not to meet his own.

'It is a long pull to St Helens, Mr Pennington.' He saw the surprise at the use of his name. 'I think they might rest easy for ten minutes.'

The lieutenant stared at the oarsmen, their raised blades dripping like wet bones.

'That will not be necessary, Sir Richard.'

Bolitho said gently, 'Have you so short a memory, sir, that you cannot remember what it was like when you first pulled an oar?'

Pennington dropped his eyes. 'I see, Sir Richard. Very well.' He turned away, and nodded to the boat's coxswain. 'Rest easy, O'Connor!'

Allday saw the ripple of surprise run through the boat. *Put that in your pipe and smoke it*, he thought.

Eventually, they were cast off and pulling strongly into the Solent. There were ships of every size and rate, and Bolitho saw sunlight flash on several telescopes as they watched him pass. It would soon be all around Spithead, he thought; the navy was a family, whether you liked it or not.

'What is the state of the ship, Mr Pennington?' Again, he was aware of an immediate caution, as if the lieutenant suspected a trap.

'All provisioned and watered, Sir Richard.'

'Short-handed?'

'Thirty trained men short, Sir Richard. Full complement of marines.'

Thirty short, out of a full company of six hundred souls, was not crippling, but the last captain should have used his time in the dockyard to recruit or poach men from other sources.

He peered over at a small brig which was scudding abeam, and preparing to set her courses. A fine-looking little ship, he thought, and he wondered if Tyacke had seen her, and was remembering his own command, *Larne*, which he had given up for *Indomitable*. *For me*.

Allday leaned forward as they passed another anchored man-of-war, and Bolitho saw the quick glance from the stroke oarsman, seeing it for himself: the admiral's coxswain who sat close to his master like a companion.

Allday said, 'There she is, Sir Richard. I'd know them Frenchie lines anywhere.'

Bolitho shaded his eyes again, aware of the blurring of his vision. The reminder. The taunt.

What Allday had said was true. The longer line of the upper hull, the planking extended beneath the beakhead to offer added strength and protection, were distinctively French. British shipbuilders had continued to end their upper gundeck with a flat bulkhead, which rendered the forepart of the ship weaker than the sides. Tyacke would have made full note of that; his own terrible injury at the Nile was the result of French fire devastating the gundeck where he was serving at the time.

Slightly broader in the beam than her English counterparts, *Frobisher* would provide a better platform for her artillery in poor sailing conditions.

He shook himself mentally. *The war was over.* It was to be Malta, not Halifax this time. He thought suddenly of Adam, and of Valentine Keen. Nothing more must happen to them, with the war in North America so nearly finished. Neither side could win, even as neither side could demonstrate a willingness to submit.

He put his hand to his eyes again as the barge swept beneath the ship's long and tapering jib boom, and did not see Avery's immediate concern. And here was the figurehead, shining in fresh paint and gilt: Sir Martin Frobisher, explorer, navigator, and one of Drake's fighting captains. He had been portrayed with jutting beard, staring blue eyes, and a black Elizabethan breastplate.

He wondered what had become of the original figurehead, so obviously unsuitable when the ship had changed names. It was not unknown for a prize to retain its old name, but the navy already had a *Glorious* on the list, and confusion might have occurred in the endless ebb and flow of signals and fleet orders.

The lieutenant called, '*Bows!*'

And there it was. The curved tumblehome, the new black and buff paint, the entry-port and the waiting rank of scarlet.

His flagship. It was a proud moment.

He touched the locket beneath his shirt, and prepared to stand as the barge surged alongside.

I am here, Kate.

He turned, momentarily off guard, convinced that he had heard her voice; he could not have been mistaken.

Don't leave me.

The Royal Marine sentry outside the screen door of the great cabin was as stiff and motionless as a man could be with the ship swaying gently at her anchor. After the bright sunlight, the shouted commands, the fifes and drums, the din of a flagship's welcome to her new lord and master, it seemed peaceful here, protected.

The ceremony had been brief, with his flag breaking at the mainmast truck, timed to the exact beat of a drum, and standing out in the Solent breeze like painted metal.

There had followed a quick presentation to the assembled ranks of lieutenants and senior warrant officers: a nod here, a nervous smile there, each man glancing surreptitiously at him before he, in turn, came under scrutiny.

Like the marine sentry, given time, he would get to know them, some better than others. It was always the hardest part to accept: the division, the barrier which rank had thrust upon him. *He was not the captain.* He could never again be as close as a captain to the people he commanded.

He nodded to the sentry, and although the man's eyes did not flicker beneath his glazed leather hat, the contact had been made.

The stern cabin was broad, spacious, and strangely welcoming. Even the strong smells of paint and fresh tar which pervaded the whole ship could not interfere with the familiarity of these things. The wine cooler with the Bolitho crest carved upon it, which Catherine had had made to replace the one lost with *Hyperion*, the high-backed chair in which he sometimes slept, his desk, his books, some old, some she had given him because of the clarity of their print. He saw Ozzard hovering by what was apparently his pantry door, and he had already seen his secretary, Yovell, observing from his own vantage point during the ceremony, when the admiral's flag had been broken out. They had worked very hard to prepare this place for him, and he had been moved by it.

Tyacke followed him into the cabin. 'All fair, Sir Richard?'

He nodded. 'You have done well, James, in so short a time.'

Tyacke glanced around. 'There's more room here than there would have been. Four eighteen-pounders were removed.'

Bolitho watched him carefully, but saw no sign of strain or discouragement. A new command, an unknown company, a way of doing things which might offend or irritate him, but Tyacke's face gave nothing away.

'Take a glass, James.' He guessed that Avery, like Allday, had purposely stayed away for this first meeting since they had shaken hands at Plymouth, where *Indomitable* had been paid off.

'I'd relish that, sir.' He made to take out his watch, and then hesitated. 'But only one glass. I've still a few ends to splice before I'm ready.'

Bolitho watched Ozzard pouring the wine, apparently indifferent to the sounds of a ship at anchor, muffled voices, the clatter of blocks and tackles as more provisions or equipment were hoisted aboard. The Caribbean, Mauritius, Halifax, and now Malta. His thoughts were unknown, the barrier here the greatest of all.

Tyacke sat, but Bolitho knew his ear was pitched to that other world.

He said, 'I've been through the books and the signals. They seem to be in order.'

Bolitho waited, knowing what was coming next.

'The punishment book lists nothing unusual.' He looked at Bolitho. 'Not like some we've seen together, sir.' He was referring to the frigate *Reaper*, but, almost superstitiously, avoided mentioning her name. 'Discipline is fair enough, but they need more gun and sail drills before I'm handing out any bouquets!'

'And what of your officers?'

Tyacke raised his glass, and paused as a boatswain's call twittered in the distance.

Then he said, 'The senior lieutenant, Kellett, seems very competent.' He looked at him directly, no longer averting the burned face, as he had in the past. 'I may be speaking out of turn, sir, but I think the first lieutenant has been carrying this ship, not just during the overhaul, but before that. I can *feel* it. Sense it.'

Bolitho sipped the wine. Perhaps it had come from the shop in St James's Street, where he had gone with her.

He would force the issue no further. It would be an intrusion, and Tyacke would tell him when he had made up his mind. When he was certain.

Tyacke said, 'The midshipmen now, they're another story. Most of them are newly joined and come from naval families. Some are young, *too* young for my taste.'

Any ship on an important commission, or Admiralty or government business, would have encouraged parents, who saw it as an opportunity only too rare in peacetime, and with the fleet being cut down. William Bligh of the ill-fated *Bounty* had had no difficulty in acquiring very young midshipmen for his command.

Tyacke said suddenly, 'But given time and a good run through Biscay, we might see the makings of something.' For a moment his blue eyes were very clear and distant, like Herrick, Bolitho thought, or perhaps more like the man Tyacke had once been. 'But I still find myself looking around expecting to see old faces, the ones who can make or break any ship.'

Who did he mean? *Indomitable, Larne*, or further back still, perhaps even before the Nile?

Bolitho said, 'I do it myself. All the time.'

He did not see the sudden, searching expression in Tyacke's eyes.

He said, 'You are satisfied, James? Being here, when perhaps you could have found a different sea to challenge?'

Tyacke seemed surprised, or relieved, that he had not asked something else. He touched his face, although Bolitho sensed that he did not even notice it.

'There is no escape, sir. There never was.' Then, firmly, 'It suits me well, sir.'

He put down the glass and got to his feet, his eyes resting briefly on the gleaming presentation sword, which Allday had already placed on its rack; *part of the show*, he once called it. Unlike the old family blade at his hip. The legend. The charisma, as his flag lieutenant Oliver Browne had described it. Another lost face. He smiled reminiscently. *Browne with an 'e'*.

Tyacke hesitated. 'I was wondering, sir . . . .'

Bolitho said, 'Ask me, James. You may always do that.'

Tyacke seemed, again, to hesitate. 'When we weigh tomorrow, will you miss England?'

Bolitho looked at him steadily. *Will I miss her*, he meant. But he did not know how to ask, without overstepping the mark.

'More than I would have believed possible, James.' He watched him leave, taking his hat from Ozzard without even seeing him. Bolitho heard Allday in the adjoining cabin, and was suddenly grateful.

It was like stumbling on to a secret, something so private that any wrong word could destroy it, and the man who carried it. The gown Tyacke had always carried in his sea chest, the one he had given Catherine to cover herself when *Larne* had plucked them from the ocean and the nearness of death. The woman . . . .

After all this time.

He stood up and walked to the stern windows, and then sat on the curved bench seat above the glistening water.

It was just as well that *Frobisher's* great anchor would show itself tomorrow.

But the voice persisted. *Don't leave me.*

Bolitho heard Allday putting his shaving gear away and speaking quietly to Ozzard in the sleeping-cabin, and walked slowly to the sloping stern windows.

Since the hands had been called, *Frobisher* had been alive with muffled sounds and occasional shouted commands. A ship preparing to sail was so familiar a sight in these waters that most people would take no notice, but in his heart he knew that this departure was different. There would be many ashore today to watch them leave. Wives, lovers, children, wondering when they would meet again. The sailor's lot. They would be pondering on the man whose flag flew from *Frobisher's* main; would he care enough for the many he commanded? Not an ordinary day for them. *Or for me.* The shave and the clean shirt were all part of it. He glanced at Ozzard's tray. He could still taste the fine coffee Catherine had bought for him; he had even eaten breakfast, slices of fat pork, fried pale brown with biscuit crumbs. He knew Ozzard disapproved of this meal, considering it fit only for a lowly lieutenant or midshipman, when the admiral he served could demand what he liked. *Neither of us will change now . . . .*

He leaned on the sill and stared at the bright water, criss-crossed by ranks of low, white crests. The wind had backed

70

overnight, perhaps to the north-east. He had had little sleep, and not because of the ship's unfamiliarity; he had overcome that sensation a long time ago. He had lain awake in his cot, half-listening to the ship's sounds, *her voices*, as his father would have described them. Creaks and mutterings, as if from the keel itself, the occasional hiss of wind and spray against the side, the responding thrum of stays and shrouds.

And once, when he had fallen asleep, he had found himself in a dream which had exploded into a nightmare. Catherine being carried away from him, her clothes torn from her, hands reaching out to touch her.

After that he had unshuttered a lantern, and had read through the last batch of instructions from the First Lord; they were lengthy, diplomatic, but meaningless. Like most senior commands, responsibility would eventually rest on the shoulders of the officer in charge.

It would be another reminder, if one were needed, of Napoleon's overwhelming power and his successes, Spain and Portugal, Italy, and onward into Egypt. Marshal Murat's crushing victory over the Egyptians at Aboukir had been the removal of the last obstacle. The gateway to India had lain open, and all Napoleon's grandiose schemes appeared to have been forged into one unstoppable force, until Nelson had taken his ships into Aboukir Bay and had destroyed the French fleet.

He glanced at some small boats passing astern, making heavy weather of it in the stiff breeze and choppy sea.

The Battle of the Nile, they called it now. Something Tyacke would never forget, or be allowed to forget. He smiled at the sharpness of memory. *Hyperion* had been there, too. Today the peace was still to be settled amongst the victors. But there would always be the predators, just outside the firelight, seeking an easy prey: the aftermath of every battle.

Allday entered the cabin, and said, 'Lively up top, Sir Richard. This will mark out the boys from the men!'

Bolitho turned to face him. He had not heard Allday leave to go on deck. A big, shambling figure, yet he could move like a fox when he wanted to. Ozzard was there too, his sharp eyes moving to the breakfast tray, the empty plate and coffee cup. And then, critically, to the coat, which he had already laid out for this occasion.

Allday saw it and smiled privately, thinking how the people

on deck would see the admiral. Not in the beautiful gold lace and gleaming buttons, but in the old, familiar sea-going coat which had even survived a battle or two. *Like us*, he thought grimly.

Ozzard patted the coat into place, almost scowling at the tarnished epaulettes.

Allday took the old sword down from its rack and turned it over in his hands. Yes, that was how they should see him. Not as the admiral, but as the man.

The ship's company would find it hard to get used to. Like the old *Indom*, when Sir Richard had made a point of speaking to the men on watch, the marines at their endless drills. He had heard him say to an officer once, 'Remember their names. In many cases, it is all that they own.'

The man.

Bolitho tugged out his watch. Tyacke would be here very soon. The shouting and the thudding bare feet were silent now. The capstan was manned, the lieutenants at their stations, on the quarterdeck, at each mast, and right forward when the anchor came home.

He thought of Avery, who had been much quieter than usual. Going over it, perhaps. Reliving what he had found, and what he had thrown away.

He saw Ozzard glide to the screen doors; his keen hearing had detected Tyacke's footsteps despite all the other noises.

Tyacke entered, his hat tucked beneath one arm. There were fine droplets of spray on his coat, and Bolitho guessed he had been up and about since before the cooks had been called.

'Ready to get under way, Sir Richard. Wind's holding fresh an' steady, nor'easterly. Once clear of St Helens, I've laid a course to weather the foreland. When we've got sea room I'll come about and steer sou'west.' He smiled briefly. 'It'll be a bit lively until then, but I shall be able to see what they can do.'

No hesitation or uncertainty, despite a different ship, people he scarcely knew, and every glass in the fleet watching him, waiting for a mistake.

'I'll come up.' The formality must wait a little longer. 'Thank you, James. I know what it cost you.'

Tyacke looked at him, perhaps remembering that other beginning. 'The cost is shared this time, sir.' As he turned to leave, he added, 'Twelve hundred miles from Spithead to Gibraltar, our first landfall.' He grinned. 'They'll have learned something of our standards by that time!'

Bolitho touched the sword at his side, and turned to Allday. 'What are *your* thoughts, old friend?'

Allday glanced up at the skylight as the boatswain's calls shrilled impatiently. Spithead Nightingales, the Jacks called them. They ruled your life.

He replied slowly, 'I'm a mite older, Sir Richard, but I *feels* the same.' He glanced at the nearest empty gunport. 'It's going to be strange, never facing an enemy broadside again.'

They went on deck, beneath the poop, and past the big double wheel where the helmsmen were already in position. Four of them: Tyacke was taking no chances.

Despite the wind, it was warmer on deck than he had expected; he felt the new pitch sticking to his shoes as he crossed to the quarterdeck rail. From here to the beakhead there were men everywhere, with more already swarming aloft to the topsail yards. Aft by the mizzen mast, the marines were waiting in squads to man the braces and halliards. The old hands claimed it was because the mizzen's sail plan was the simplest, and could mostly be handled from the deck, so that even a 'bullock' could manage it!

Bolitho saw the quick glances, the word passing along the upper deck. Avery was standing by the opposite rail, hat tugged down over the greying hair which was part of the price of his service. Tyacke was speaking with the sailing master, Tregidgo, a straight-backed man with an unsmiling, taciturn countenance. He was a Cornishman, and he had served in *Frobisher* for the four years since her capture, and under her two captains, Jefferson, whom Rhodes had casually dismissed – *slipped his cable two years back, buried at sea, poor fellow* – and Oliphant, who had left in such haste.

Tyacke faced him and touched his hat. 'Ready, Sir Richard.'

Bolitho glanced up at his flag, streaming against an almost cloudless sky.

'Carry on, Captain Tyacke.'

Calls trilled and parties of men dashed below, where they were needed on the other capstan to add their weight to the straining cable. Bolitho shaded his eyes to watch a few passing boats. There were women in one of them, whores going to greet another new arrival at Spithead. It was, unofficially, common practice to allow prostitutes on board, if only to prevent men from desertion and the aftermath of punishment.

'Anchor's hove short, sir!' That was Kellett, the first lieutenant. He was right up forward by the cathead where he could watch the lie of the cable as the heaving, straining men at the capstan bars hauled their ship to her anchor by muscle alone.

Kellett came from an admiral's family. Bolitho had seen him only once since he had come aboard, a young, serious-faced officer with deceptively mild eyes.

'Stand by on the capstan!'

'Loose the heads'ls!'

Some confusion ensued, but there were trained hands well placed to assist or knock the offender into position.

'Hands aloft, loose tops'ls!'

The men were already poised to swarm out along the tapering yards. It was no place for anyone with a bad head for heights. He smiled at himself.

Clank – clank – clank. The pawls on the capstan were slowing; he imagined the great anchor moving below the ship's shadow, a last grip upon the land.

A fifer and a fiddler broke into a tune, and across the backs of crouching seamen and those at the braces with their eyes lifted to the yards, Bolitho saw Allday watching him, as if nothing stood between them.

So that was what he had been doing.

Bolitho lifted one hand, and he saw a midshipman turn to stare at him. But he saw only Allday, with the shantyman's reedy voice rising even above the squeal of blocks to remind him. To bring it all back once more.

There was a girl in Portsmouth Town. . . . Heave, my bullies, heave!

He touched his eye. *Portsmouth Lass.* Only Allday and perhaps one other would have thought of it.

'Anchor's aweigh, sir!'

Frobisher was already swinging round, leaning above her own reflection as the anchor was hoisted up and catted home.

He beckoned to Avery. 'Walk with me, George.'

While men bustled past them and cordage slithered along the deck like snakes, they walked together, as they had before when the guns had flamed and thundered all around them.

'Is there anything I can do, Sir Richard?'

Bolitho shook his head.

How could he explain, to Avery, of all people, that he could not bear to watch the land slide away, and to be alone with his thoughts. And his sense of loss.

Instead, he looked up at his flag, high and clean above the deck.

The last command. He acknowledged it as if he had spoken aloud. Then so be it.

6

Know Your Enemy

Lieutenant George Avery felt the warmth of the noon sun across his shoulders, and walked to the quarterdeck nettings to obtain a better view of the Rock. There were vessels of every description anchored, to take on stores or to await new orders, and around and amongst them boats under sail or oars bustled in endless activity. The towering mass of Gibraltar dwarfed them all, watchful, eternal, a guardian of the gateway to the Mediterranean.

Frobisher's slow approach, the crash and echo of gun salutes, and the brisk exchange of signals were part of the tradition, and once anchored, the ship's company were soon hurrying to other duties, lowering boats and spreading awnings. As during the passage out from England, they were left little time to ponder on their first landfall.

Ten days since the Isle of Wight had vanished astern, not a fast passage by any means, but deliberately planned to exercise the whole company, sails, guns, lowering and recovering boats, until Captain Tyacke was satisfied. If satisfied he was. Hate him, curse him, it made no difference, because every one from seasoned seaman to ship's boy knew that Tyacke never spared himself, nor shied away from anything he demanded of others.

On occasion, he had ordered lieutenants and senior warrant officers to stand down, to be replaced by subordinates, or anyone Tyacke thought should discover the true responsibility of his rank or station. They had skirted Brest and the French coast and entered the Bay of Biscay, unpredictable as ever despite the shades of spring, passing close even to Lorient, where *Frobisher* had been launched.

Then the coast of Portugal, like dark blue smoke in the morning light; into bright sunshine, where, although driven hard, Avery had sensed a change in the company, had seen men pause to grin at one another. To respond.

In the wardroom he had seen it and heard it, too. But as the flag lieutenant he was never part of any company, and that suited him. Until they knew him better, other officers might imagine that he was the admiral's ear, Tyacke's too, ready to pass on their more outspoken opinions. These were divided on Tyacke's ruthless insistence upon drills. Some protested that it was pointless, as there was little likelihood now of action. Others took the view that, as flagship, it was a matter of pride.

Avery had noticed that Kellett, the deceptively mild-mannered first lieutenant, was rarely drawn into these heated discussions. Only once, he had turned suddenly on a junior lieutenant and had said, 'I fully realise that you likely speak more out of drink than conviction, Mr Wodehouse, but do so again in my presence and I'll take you aft myself!' It had been quietly said, but the wretched Wodehouse had cringed as if he had just received a torrent of obscenities.

Avery realised that one of the midshipmen was waiting to catch his eye.

'Yes, Mr Wilmot?'

'Signal from *Halcyon*, sir. *Have despatches on board.*' He pointed helpfully over the nettings. 'Yonder, sir. *Halcyon*, twenty-eight, Captain Christie.'

'Very well.' Avery smiled. 'That was quickly done. I shall inform the captain.' He saw the youth glance across at the lithe frigate. She was small, by modern standards, but still the dream of most young officers. Maybe even this midshipman, with one foot on the bottom rung.

Tyacke strode across the deck, his head turned to give some instructions to a master's mate.

He saw Avery, and said, '*Halcyon*, eh? Left Portsmouth three days after us. She'll be joining Sir Richard's command at Malta.' He glanced at the midshipman. 'Make to *Halcyon*. *Deliver despatches on board.*'

Avery watched the midshipman scurry away to his signals

party, where the flags were all ready to bend on to the halliards.

'Mr Midshipman Wilmot is a brighter one than some. Didn't wait to be told.'

But Avery had seen the midshipman drop his eyes from Tyacke's face. How could he ever come to terms with it?

Tyacke turned as the flags shot up to the yard and broke to the offshore breeze. 'We might hear some news.' He smiled wryly. 'Or it may be a recall!'

Avery said, 'Do you know Malta well, sir?'

Tyacke said, 'Look at those damned boats!' His arm shot out and he called, 'Mr Pennington? You are the officer-of-the-watch, I assume?'

The lieutenant swallowed hard. 'I *saw* the boats, sir.'

'Well, tell them to stand away. I'll not have the flagship trading with scum like that! I don't care what they're trying to sell!' He turned away. 'Drop a round shot through the first one that tries to come alongside!'

Avery sighed. Tyacke would not be drawn about the past. *We make a fine pair.*

A seaman who was intently polishing the spokes of the big double wheel glanced across at him and said, 'The admiral's comin' up, sir.'

Pleased, Avery acknowledged it. It was another beginning.

Bolitho walked over to join him. 'I have just heard about *Halcyon*.' He shaded his eyes and stared across the busy anchorage. 'Which is she?'

Avery pointed her out. He thought Bolitho looked rested and untroubled, although he knew he had been working with Yovell almost every day since they had left Spithead. Instructions, details of ships and their captains, a thousand things which Avery could only guess at.

He had seen him pacing the deck at night under the stars, or standing with his open shirt rippling in the wind when the hands were turned up to take in a reef, or to change tack on the run south. Thinking of his Catherine, perhaps. Holding on, while the leagues rolled away from *Frobisher*'s great rudder.

Perhaps he did not need sleep like other men. Or was it denied him?

'Strange to be here.' Bolitho touched his eye and massaged

it slowly. 'I was out here after the revolution, when the royalists hoped to raise a counter-action at Toulon. It was doomed from the conception, George. So much waste.'

He stared across at the opposite side: the coast of Spain, almost swallowed in heat-haze. Another memory. Algeciras He could remember someone pointing to it and saying, 'Look. Yonder lies the enemy.' But the face eluded him.

Avery wanted to speak, but after Tyacke's abruptness he was afraid to break the moment, which like all the others had become a part of his life. A part of him.

He asked, 'You will know what to expect, sir?'

Bolitho did not seem to hear. 'All that time ago, George. But later when I was here as flag captain in *Euryalus*, I can see it so clearly. The old *Navarra* being attacked by Barbary pirates. People smile when you mention them now, but they're as dangerous as they ever were. They'll not be tamed simply because we say so.'

'*Navarra*, sir? What was she?'

Bolitho looked at him. 'Just an old ship. She had no place in any line of battle. No prize court would have parted with a handful of gold for her.' He smiled, as if he was reaching out. 'Catherine was on board that ship with her husband. Where we met. Where we found and lost one another.' He paused. 'Until Antigua.'

Avery tried to imagine it, Catherine as she must have been; like *Golden Plover*, which Tyacke had described in one of these rare moments of intimacy.

Bolitho looked round as a seaman called, 'Boat's cast off from *Halcyon*, sir!' Then he said, 'I've seen so many victories and failures in this sea, but nothing could outshine that meeting.'

Tyacke appeared, and said sharply, 'If you're mistaken, Mr Pennington . . . .'

The second lieutenant stood firm. 'No, sir, the boat carries *Halcyon*'s captain!'

Tyacke glared at him. 'Then man the side, if you please.' He saw Bolitho and touched his hat. 'From England, sir. Got here ahead of us.' Then he relaxed slightly. 'Hardly surprising!'

Avery watched them. *From England*. Maybe new orders for Bolitho. And letters? It was too soon. He thought of Allday; he might want one written for him before they weighed.

The marines fell into two ranks at the entry port, and Tyacke waited to greet the visitor. Routine.

The calls trilled, the salutes were exchanged, hats raised to the quarterdeck, the flag.

Captain Christie said, 'Despatches, sir, and some personal mail.' He was a tall, serious-faced officer, probably in his late twenties, his gleaming epaulettes marking him out as a post-captain. War or no war, he had been posted, and he had his own ship.

Bolitho said, 'Come aft and take a glass.'

Avery followed them, knowing that the young captain had been unprepared for this invitation from the admiral.

They all sat down in the spacious cabin, and Ozzard appeared silently with his tray.

Christie said, 'It is an honour to be serving under your flag, Sir Richard. In these uncertain times one cannot be sure what . . . .'

He turned as Tyacke said quietly, 'Do I know you, sir?'

Christie took a goblet and almost spilled the wine. But his eyes were level enough.

'I know *you*, sir.'

Bolitho knew it was difficult for some reason, as difficult as it was important.

Christie said, '*Majestic*, sir.'

Just the name. The ship where it had happened. A ghost from the past.

Tyacke did not speak but studied Christie, trying to put the pieces together. As he had so many times, until it had almost driven him insane.

Christie said to Bolitho, 'I was a midshipman in *Majestic*, Sir Richard. My first ship, and I had barely been aboard her for more than a couple of months.' He looked around, as if searching for something. 'When Lord Nelson led us to Aboukir Bay.' He hesitated. 'To the Nile.'

Tyacke said slowly, 'I remember you.'

Christie continued, 'We were amongst the French fleet in no time at all, and were locked with the big eighty-gun liner, *Tonnant*. Broadside after broadside.' His voice was contained and unemotional, which made his description all the more vivid and terrible. 'Dead and dying lay everywhere. I was too junior to have a proper station and I was kept running

80

messages from the quarterdeck to the guns.' He stared at the misted goblet. 'Our captain was killed, people I knew were being torn to pieces, calling for help when there was none to be given. I – I almost broke that day. I was carrying a message to the lower gundeck, and I was terrified that the ship would be blown apart before I could find somewhere to hide. All the training meant nothing. I wanted to hide. To escape.' Again, he hesitated. 'And then . . . .'

Outside, Avery could hear another boat being ordered to stand away, someone laughing. But only this was real.

Christie said, 'The lieutenant in charge of the forrard division of guns called to me, Sir Richard. He put his hand on my shoulder and shook me back and forth until I was calm again.'

Avery saw Tyacke nod, his blue eyes distant, unseeing.

'He said to me, "Walk, boy. *Walk*. To these poor devils you are a King's officer, but today you are the captain's voice, so use it clearly and show them what you can do."'

Avery thought of the midshipman called Wilmot. How Christie must have been.

Christie said, 'You sent me aft. Then the French broadside found us again. But for you I would have died with all the others. I told my father about it, and he tried to write to you. I wrote to you myself, but heard nothing.' He looked directly at Bolitho. 'It is wrong of me to speak of things so personal, but they have always meant so much to me, ever since that day. It made me a man, and I hope a better one.'

He stood up and said, 'I shall return to my ship now, Sir Richard. It has been an honour.' He raised his hand as Tyacke made to follow. 'No, sir, I shall see myself over the side.' Then he smiled. Relief, gratitude, surprise, it was all there. 'In the fleet they always spoke of The Happy Few. Now I understand.'

Behind the pantry hatch Allday put down his rum, his 'wet', and considered what he had heard.

In the navy you had to expect it. Faces from the past, like old wounds, were not easily forgotten. *Always the pain.* But they were safe now. And yet, why was he so uneasy? He wanted to ask Lieutenant Avery to write a letter to Unis for him. But not about this. It was something he could not talk about through another man's pen.

Ozzard came back, frowning.

Allday tried to shrug it off. 'Did I ever tell you about the time when me an' Sir Richard was fighting them Barbary pirates, Tom?'

'Yes.' He relented slightly, and Allday thought he had felt it, too. 'But spin it again, if you like.'

'The sea's face is fair enough today.'

The two women stood side by side by the old stile at the beginning of the cliff path and looked out across Falmouth Bay. The surface of the sea was unbroken, but heaving gently in the sunlight, as if it were breathing.

Catherine glanced at her companion, Richard's youngest sister, Nancy. She was looking better than expected. In life, her husband Lewis had been too large to ignore; in death, perhaps his strength was still her support.

Catherine ran her palm over the stile, the step and beams polished by countless hands and feet. How many had paused there to rest and reflect, as she had often done? She looked along the winding cliff path, hardly used nowadays. She rarely walked there, and certainly never alone, not since Zenoria's fall from Trystan's Leap.

Nancy said gently, 'Never fear, you'll have a letter soon from him.'

'I know. He never forgets. It is like hearing his voice.' She brushed some hair from her eyes. 'Tell me, Nancy. How are your affairs progressing?'

Nancy smiled at the change of subject. This tall, beautiful woman had become dear to her, had helped her through the grief of Lewis's final days and immediately after his death. A woman known and admired, envied and hated, who, with her brother, had defied every convention to proclaim their love. The hero and his lady. Lewis, too, had always admired her, and had made no secret of it. He had always had an eye for women. She stopped her thoughts, like closing a door.

'The lawyers from London are still at the house. Lewis's affairs were in good order, despite what I may say were his occasional extravagances. They will arrange for someone to manage the estate, at least until the children become involved.' She shook her head. '*Children*. Hardly that any more!'

They turned away from the stile. Catherine could remember

him holding her beside it, the need of one for the other, after a reunion, or before another separation.

She said, 'Two weeks since he left. It will be three soon. I try to see his ship in my mind, where she is, what they may be doing.' She shrugged. 'The Mediterranean . . . where we first met. Did you know that, Nancy?'

She shook her head. 'Only that you lost one another soon afterwards. That he did tell me.' She smiled, as though remembering. 'To think what he has become, in the navy, and to this country, and he remains uncertain of himself in many ways.' She added with sudden emphasis, 'I'll be thankful when he comes home.' She touched Catherine's arm. 'And stays here.'

They turned towards the gentle slope which led down to the old grey house and its attendant cottages, so that the headland seemed to screen them from the murmur of the sea, its constant presence.

It would seem different to Nancy, daughter of a sailor, from a family of sailors, sister of Falmouth's most famous son and England's naval hero. Born and raised here with these people of the sea around her, the courageous fishermen who ventured out in all weathers to supply the tables of manor house and cottage alike. The coasters and the famous Falmouth packet ships, who sailed with the tide in peace or war. Nancy had grown up with them and their tradition.

She felt Nancy hesitate as she saw the carriage waiting in the stable yard. Perhaps their meeting and walk together had made her forget, if only for a moment. But now she would be driven back to that huge house with its folly, another of Lewis's little indulgences.

How empty it must seem now. *I count the days and weeks. But Nancy will never have even a letter to sustain her.*

Nancy said, 'You have a visitor.'

Catherine stared past the carriage, aware of her painful heartbeat. There was no other vehicle, no horse to denote some courier, or messenger from Plymouth. But she could see somebody inside the estate office, in dark clothing, his back towards her, and she heard Ferguson's sudden laugh. Perhaps he had sensed her return and was trying to reassure her. What would she do without him and without Grace? The link with Bolitho's earlier life, which she could never share.

Nancy said, 'I'll wait a moment. Just to be sure.'

Her protective caution made Catherine grip her arm. 'I am always safe, dear Nancy!'

Then, as she walked into the yard, the man with Ferguson turned and faced her. Uncertain, anxious, but, as ever, determined.

She quickened her pace. 'Rear-Admiral Herrick! I had no idea you were in Cornwall, or in England, for that matter. I am pleased to see you.' She half turned, ashamed that she had offered her right hand when Herrick's pinned-up sleeve should have reminded her. She said, 'This is Lady Roxby, Richard's sister.'

Herrick bowed stiffly. 'We met but briefly, ma'am. Some years ago.'

Nancy smiled at him. 'We *met* seldom, but through my brother you have always been a part of us.'

She allowed her coachman to help her into the carriage. 'Please call and see me again, Catherine. Soon.' She glanced briefly at Herrick. Like an unspoken question.

Catherine took Herrick into the house. Someone she should know so well, and yet he was still a stranger.

'Please be seated, and I shall fetch you something cool. Some wine, perhaps?'

He sat down carefully and looked around the room. 'Some ginger beer if you have it, my lady. Or cider.'

She regarded him steadily. 'No titles today. I am Catherine – let it be so.'

Grace Ferguson peered in at them. 'Why, 'tis Rear-Admiral Herrick! I scarce recognised you without your fine uniform!'

Catherine turned. She herself had not truly noticed. Perhaps it had been the surprise, or relief that he was not some courier bearing the news she dreaded.

Herrick said awkwardly, 'I am still of that rank, in name, in any case.' He waited for the housekeeper to leave them, and added, 'I am sent to Cornwall by their lordships.'

She watched him, his struggle to share something with her. He was not attempting to be secretive or superior, like other men she had known; he was simply unused to confiding his thoughts to any one. Perhaps only with his beloved wife Dulcie had he ever been able to do so.

His blue eyes were as clear as ever, but his hair was

84

completely grey, and there were sharp lines at the corners of his mouth which deepened, she thought with pain, when he sat, or, as now, when he leaned forward to accept the proffered glass. Richard had told her some of it, how Herrick had been captured and had had his hand savagely smashed, to destroy forever his ability to 'lift a sword for the King'. When he had been rescued, they had discovered that the wound had already succumbed to gangrene. The ship's surgeon had taken off his arm.

Most of all she remembered Bolitho's pride, his love for this stubborn, unyielding, courageous man. She sat opposite him and watched him drink the ginger beer.

She said, 'Richard is at sea.'

He nodded. 'I know, my . . . Catherine. I heard something of it. I guessed the rest.'

She waited. If she spoke now, Herrick would lose his sudden confidence. Or perhaps it was trust.

'I will never get another sea appointment. I did think I would be put out to grass, especially after the *Reaper* affair.' He looked around again. 'I have always remembered this place, and this room. I walked up from the town just now, as I did all those years ago. I was here when Richard's father was still alive, when he gave him the old sword. Over yonder, by the library door. And again, when we came back from the Indies . . . Richard's father was dead by then.'

She turned involuntarily as if she would see them, saw only Captain James Bolitho's unsmiling portrait. He, too, had lost an arm.

'I have been in Plymouth. I am appointed to the revenue service here.' He smiled briefly, and she saw him as he must once have been. 'So dress uniform is hardly appropriate for such a *popular* and respected commission.'

She thought of Nancy again; she had often mentioned the folklore of local smugglers, the 'gentlemen', as Tom the coastguard had called them. Richard had always spoken harshly of them, and of their brutal trade.

'Will it suit you, Thomas?'

She saw him flinch at the use of his name, as she had known he would.

'I needed to do something. The sea is my life. Unlike Richard, I have nothing else now.' He leaned forward and added, 'There is a lot to be done. New boats – there are four cutters building at Plymouth, and I must find men who can be trusted to perform what is sometimes a dangerous duty. The country is desperate for revenue, and free trade in the dark of night cannot be allowed to flourish unchecked.'

It was there, as Richard had described it to her. The grasp, the enthusiasm; once Herrick established a grip on something, he would never let go.

'Where are you staying, Thomas? There is plenty of room here, if you wish . . . .'

He put down his glass. 'No, I am settled at the inn. It is easier for the coach. Besides . . . .'

She nodded, careful not to smile. '*Besides*, Thomas. What a span that word must carry.'

Herrick studied her gravely. 'I shall be back and forth. If you need me, I will be easy to find.' He stood slowly, and she sensed the pain of the amputation, like so many she had seen in the streets.

'Will you not stay a while, Thomas?'

He glanced through to the library, as if to reassure himself. 'Another time, I would be honoured. Proud.' He turned away, as if unable to speak otherwise. 'When I lost Dulcie I was blind to everything, to that which I owed Richard, and above all else to you, for staying with her when she was beyond aid.' Then he faced her again, his eyes very clear. 'Blind. But not any more. You risked everything for Dulcie, and so for me. I shall not lose my way in self-pity again.'

He took her hand and kissed it with great care, and without pretence.

He took his hat from one of the servant girls and said, almost abruptly, 'You met Lord Rhodes, I believe?'

She had her hand to her breast without knowing it. She nodded. Herrick turned his hat over in his own, strong hand. Like Ferguson, he had become used to it, if ever any man could.

'A close friend of Hamett-Parker.' His mouth hardened. 'The president at my court martial.'

She followed him out into the sunlight, and he added, 'I do not trust that man. Not one inch.' Then he took her hand in his again, and smiled. 'But Richard once taught me well enough. *Know your enemy*, he said. But never reveal that knowledge!'

She watched him stride out along the track, stooped, troubled by his injury more than he would allow anyone to guess, and, out of uniform, almost shabby.

She raised her hand as he turned to look back. But at that moment, he was a giant.

James Tyacke paused outside the chart room to allow his eyes to adjust to the darkness, and then made his way beneath the poop to the quarterdeck. The ship was still strange to him, and any vessel under cover of darkness was always a threat to the unwary.

He looked up at the sky beyond the topsails, at the millions of faint stars from horizon to horizon, and the merest sliver of a moon which showed itself only occasionally on the restless water.

He saw the dark shapes of the watch on deck, the third lieutenant, Tollemache, who was officer-of-the-watch, conferring quietly with another shadow, a master's mate.

He moved to the compass box and glanced at the card: south-east-by-east, the ship moving easily but slowly under reduced canvas. According to the chart, they were some fifty miles to the south-west of the Sicilian coast. To any landsman this would seem like an ocean, an endless, open waste, but Tyacke could feel the difference, and smell it. The nearness of land, with the shores of Africa somewhere across the opposite beam. The Mediterranean was like no other sea, and always the land seemed ready to surprise or ensnare you.

Tomorrow they would sight Malta: the end of the passage. It was still too early to judge if his exercise and drills had left their mark on the ship's company. The officers remained wary of him, like Tollemache, who was standing the middle watch only a few feet away. Uneasy, perhaps, at his captain's presence, which he might interpret as a lack of trust in his ability.

Three weeks since they had weighed anchor at Spithead. Faces, names, pride and resentment. Typical enough in any company with a new captain, and an admiral's flag at the masthead.

His thoughts had repeatedly returned to *Halcyon*'s captain, Christie, the way this sea and the past kept returning. When he had taken command of *Indomitable* there had been another such recurrence, in the person of a one-legged ship's cook. The very day he had read himself in, the man, like a spectre, had brought it all back. *Majestic*, and Christie coming out with it, despite Bolitho's presence. And the cook, who as a young seaman in Tyacke's division had been smashed down by the same broadside which had left Tyacke for dead.

Would it never leave him? Sometimes, like tonight, it haunted him, so that he was unable to sleep.

He moved to the quarterdeck rail and saw the helmsman's eyes in the dim compass light as he turned to observe him.

Christie, at least, had gained something from it. *It made me a man.* Simple, genuine sincerity. *So why not me?*

He glanced around again as two seamen paused to take the slack out of some halliards before making them fast again.

Did this ship have any memories? Perhaps she was not old enough. It was difficult to imagine French voices and orders being uttered where his own men now stood.

A midshipman was writing on his slate, pencil squeaking, recording something for the log; Tyacke could see his white patches clearly in the darkness. Like Christie must have been . . . .

He walked impatiently to the empty nettings, angry with himself, with what he must regard as a weakness. It was none of those things which defied him to sleep, which put an edge to his voice when he had known he was asking, expecting, too much from people who had been allowed to *run down*, as Allday would have put it.

He had sworn to himself that it was over and done with. His anguish, his shame and his resentment had been like a defence. He had even told himself that, once out of England, it would fall back into place, into the mist of time and memory.

But it had not gone away, and his practical mind could not accept it.

He turned from the nettings and said, 'I've made a note in the log, Mr Tollemache. When the morning watch is aft, you can set the forecourse. We may sight local shipping at first light, and I shall want enough agility to avoid it.'

He felt the lieutenant staring after him as he made his way to the poop. Outside his cabin he looked aft to where the sentry stood in a pool of light, as if he had never moved. There was a faint glow beneath the screen door. Could Bolitho not sleep, either?

With his cabin door closed behind him, he unshuttered the lanterns and looked at the cot beyond the screen, and then at the cupboard where he kept his brandy, one of the bottles which Catherine Somervell had sent aboard for him, as she had before in *Indomitable*. Who else would have thought of it? Would have cared?

Eventually he sat down, his head in his hands, his ears only half-aware of the shipboard sounds, the unending chorus in any living vessel.

Then he straightened his back and pulled some writing paper from a drawer. Surprisingly he felt quite calm, unnervingly so. Like the moment of decision, before going into battle, or at the first sight of the enemy's masts and sails spanning the horizon. An awareness, simply because there was no choice, perhaps never had been.

How long he sat there, the pen gripped in his hand, he could not remember.

And then, as if driven by another force, he began to write.

Dear Marion . . . .

When Lieutenant Kellett strode aft to muster the morning watch, Tyacke was still writing.

Then, at dawn, he went on deck and examined the log. He was the captain again.

Eight bells had just chimed from the forecastle belfry when Richard Bolitho came on deck, and crossed to the weather side while *Frobisher* settled down on the final leg of her approach. His mouth was still tingling to the coffee Ozzard had prepared while Allday had been shaving him. Something which had become a routine, as much a part of the ship's own procedure.

He shaded his eyes and stared along the length of the upper deck. Malta seemed so small, so insignificant on any chart, and yet from here it reached out on either bow as if snared in the tarred shrouds and standing rigging, a sprawling mass of sandstone. They were still too far away to distinguish houses and fortifications, or the batteries which guarded the anchorage, and made Malta the most formidable obstacle to any hostile fleet or squadron which might attempt to slip through the strait between Sicily and the coast of North Africa.

This was an island fought over, occupied and reoccupied, it was said as far back as 800 BC, when the Phoenicians had arrived. Sicilians, Arabs, all had left their mark upon architecture, religion and trade.

He felt a trickle of sweat run down his spine; his fresh shirt would be like a rag within the hour, and he envied the bare-backed seamen, skins already sunburned, as they dashed up and down the ratlines in response to the shouted orders from the quarterdeck.

Some of the unemployed men stared at passing craft, brightly coloured fishing boats with bat-like sails. Most of them had an eye painted on the bow, the eye of Osiris, believed to enable the boat to see where it was going and so avoid danger. A few of the occupants waved as the black and buff seventy-four passed, but not many. Men-of-war, large and small, had become commonplace to these people throughout a war they had never truly understood.

Bolitho moved slightly into the shade of the mizzen topsail, and winced as a reflected shaft of sunlight pricked his injured eye. He saw Tyacke speaking to Tregidgo, the sailing master. They were probably satisfied with their calculations, and their arrival at the estimated time. The master was competent, Tyacke had told him, an old hand, four years in *Frobisher* and ten as a master before that. Tyacke had also said that he was not an easy man to know.

Bolitho had spoken to him only once, a fellow Cornishman, but with entirely different beginnings. Tregidgo had been the first of his family to go to sea; the others were all tin miners, Cousin Jacks, as they were called in Cornwall. He had not waited to be taken by a press gang, but had walked into Redruth and volunteered. It must have been a hard climb to his present rank, Bolitho thought.

He saw Allday moving around the boat tier, his face set in a frown of concentration. The barge had been painted green at his instruction, but it was impossible to know if Allday was pleased with it.

Lieutenant Avery joined him. 'My first visit here, sir.'

Bolitho said, 'I doubt if you'll find much time to explore.'

They looked up as more men clambered out along the topsail yards, like monkeys against the pale sky.

Bolitho had seen the date in the ship's log: the sixth of June, 1814. Adam's birthday. He thought of the war he had left behind in those disputed American waters, the risks and dangers to Adam; afraid that his despair and bitterness at Zenoria's death might make him reckless, and too eager for a fight with the enemy which had destroyed the only other thing he had loved, the frigate *Anemone*. He knew what it was like, how grief could blunt even the most experienced captain's judgement; he had suffered it himself, at a time when he believed he had nothing to live for. A death wish, someone had called it.

If only Adam were here. Another in his position would use his influence as admiral to arrange such a transfer, but it would be seen as favouritism, and Adam would decline for that very reason.

Tyacke said, 'Take in your courses, Mr Kellett, and have the marines mustered aft.'

He never seemed to raise his voice, but they were coming to know their captain, and aspire to his standards, even if they could not understand why he drove himself so hard.

Allday had come aft, but was careful to keep his distance. Thinking, perhaps, of the child who would be even more grown up when he eventually reached home again.

Bolitho bit his lip. June. His own daughter, Elizabeth, would be twelve years old this month.

I do not know her.

More shouted commands, and the way going off the ship as she moved steadily towards the land and the gleaming expanse of anchorage. The gunner was on deck speaking with Gage, the fourth lieutenant, making sure that each gun would fire exactly on time when the salutes began. A few men looked towards the quarterdeck where the admiral and his aide stood side by side, apparently beyond the reach of doubt, or any ordinary concerns.

Bolitho smiled to himself, and Avery saw the smile and found comfort in it, without knowing why.

There was a Spanish frigate anchored nearby, some of her company mustered on deck to dip her ensign in respect as the ship with the admiral's flag moved abeam.

Bolitho tried to accept it. They were enemies no longer.
He thought of Catherine's words, when they had first met.
It was as though she had just spoken them aloud.
Men are made for war, and you are no exception.
But it was not a reminder. It was a warning.

7

No Choice at All

Adam Bolitho stood by the entrance of *Valkyrie*'s great cabin
and watched in silence as Rear-Admiral Valentine Keen strode
to the stern windows, his hair almost brushing the deckhead
beams. It was impossible to know what he was thinking,
but Adam sensed that he no longer regarded this as his
flagship.

Valkyrie had anchored at Halifax in the early morning, and
with scarcely a word Captain Henry Deighton had gone ashore
to report to Keen. It had not been an easy passage, either to the
Bermudas or on the return. Deighton had questioned Adam
relentlessly about almost everything, from the various patrol
areas to recognition signals; Adam had expected that, after
their bad beginning. Deighton had hardly spoken to any of
the officers, and had confined himself to this, Keen's cabin,
for his meals and to write endless reports, for whose benefit
was still unclear.

Keen looked well, he thought, his fair hair almost white
against his tanned features. He showed no sign of strain, and
Adam suddenly realised what had changed. Here, in *Valkyrie*,
he had become a stranger.

Keen said, 'Much has happened in your absence, Adam.
I hear from Captain Deighton that you were most thorough,
by the way.'

'It was somewhat different from blockade duty, I imagine, sir.'

Keen glanced at him curiously. 'You disliked him?'

'I have served better men, sir. In *my* opinion.'

Keen nodded. 'Honesty is what I would expect from you.

As my flag captain, and as my friend.' He moved to the windows again and watched several boats pulling past the stern. 'Hard to remember all the snow and ice.' He seemed to come to a decision, visibly, like some physical effort.

'I have to tell you now that Deighton's promotion to commodore has been confirmed. I gave him his commission this morning when he came ashore.' He swung round, his eyes in shadow. 'I shall be leaving soon for England. As my flag captain, you are of course entitled to come with me.' He hesitated. 'Although with matters as they are in England I cannot make you the promise of a new command. It may take time.'

Adam tensed, his mind prepared, like waiting for the first shot in a battle. Or in a duel.

Keen said, 'Great matters are afoot. You will know soon enough, but I can assure you that *Valkyrie* will be in the thick of it. A small but experienced inshore squadron will be needed to defend some of those soldiers you have escorted of late. I should think the Bermudas might well sink under their combined weight!'

Adam said quietly, 'And Commodore Deighton, sir?'

'He will be in command of the squadron. Four frigates, including yours.'

Adam felt his jaw tighten. *Mine*. Keen had already decided. It was no choice at all. With Urquhart promoted and gone to command the redeemed *Reaper*, who of similar experience did *Valkyrie* have in her company? Dyer, the first lieutenant, was competent and reliable, when he was told exactly what to do. Two other lieutenants had been midshipmen only months ago. The sailing master was a fine seaman and navigator, but sometimes he could barely draw breath because of his wounds, although he would fall dead rather than admit it. And there was a drunken surgeon, George Minchin, who had been serving with Sir Richard Bolitho when *Hyperion* had gone down.

Keen knew him better than he realised. No captain would quit his command when his ship was on the eve of something dangerous, where skill and experience would count more than anything.

Keen said, 'Another captain could be found for *Valkyrie*. But Commodore Deighton is new amongst us. The burden of his responsibility will be great enough.'

No choice at all. 'You mentioned the army, sir?'

Keen plucked at something on his coat. 'An attack on American soil. It is all I can say.'

Adam said flatly, 'I shall stay, sir.'

He sensed that Keen had been prepared for any decision, but he could not conceal his relief.

'Your presence, your name alone, will make all the difference. And, of course, I shall be following your exploits as closely as I can.'

England. The admiral's house at Plymouth, where he had walked with Zenoria, so careful to remain in sight of the other guests. The last time he had seen her.

Keen said suddenly, 'My proposal of marriage was accepted, Adam. I wish you could have been here when it was announced.'

Adam licked his lips. 'Congratulations, sir. I would say as much to Miss St Clair, as well.'

Keen opened a drawer and closed it again. 'She is on passage to England with her father at this moment. Yes, I wish you had been here.'

Adam wondered if she had told him what he had said about Zenoria, that his absence had been planned.

He looked at Keen's open features. She had told him nothing.

The first lieutenant had appeared in the screen doorway.

'The boat is returning, sir.' He spoke to his captain, but his eyes were on the rear-admiral.

'Thank you, Mr Dyer.'

Keen glanced around the cabin, remembering perhaps the long days at sea, the boredom of routine, and the sudden fury of danger and battle. 'There is nothing of mine here.'

As the lieutenant's footsteps faded away, Keen said, 'Have the ship fully provisioned, Adam.' He hesitated. 'Be patient with him. He is an experienced officer, but he is not like us.' He tried to smile, but it evaded him. 'Not like *you.*'

They went out into the sunshine, and Keen turned once more to look at the watching seamen and marines.

He said simply, 'I shall miss you.'

Adam removed his hat, and the Royal Marine guard slapped their muskets and bayonets into a salute.

Who did he mean? Me? The ship? The assembled hands

would mean little to him; some he would already have forgotten.

Perhaps he was bidding farewell to this life, and exchanging it for higher authority, promotion too, where Adam would be the intruder.

Dyer dismissed the side party and joined him to watch Keen's boat pulling away.

'May I ask something, sir?'

Adam turned to him, surprised, even slightly shocked by the first lieutenant's nervousness.

Have I been so unapproachable? Did I forget the first responsibility of command? The most coveted gift, his uncle had called it.

He reached out and touched Dyer's arm. 'I am remaining with *Valkyrie*. Is that what you were about to ask?'

Dyer could not hide his relief, and a genuine pleasure. His was not a face which could conceal anything.

'I shall pass the word, sir!'

Adam looked towards the land, but Keen's boat had disappeared. Then he gazed up at the gently swaying masthead, where Deighton's broad pendant would soon appear. *Not like you.*

He turned sharply as a chorus of cheers broke from the forecastle, although every one was careful not to catch his eye.

Despite everything, he was glad of his decision. As if the ship had spoken for herself.

'All present, sir.' Adam waited for the other captains to be seated, and glanced around the cabin, searching for some sign or hint of its new occupant, a portrait of someone, some memento from a past ship or port of call. There was nothing. The cabin looked exactly as it had when Keen had stood here, moments before leaving it for the last time. That had been three days ago, and in the meantime, while the other vessels of the new inshore squadron had anchored nearby, Commodore Henry Deighton had spent much of his time either ashore or here in his cabin, going through the ship's books and navigational logs, and had made no attempt to meet his captains in advance of this first gathering.

Adam knew them all, Morgan Price, the wild-eyed Welshman who commanded the frigate *Wildfire*, and Isaac Lloyd, captain of *Chivalrous*, the second largest frigate in the group, who had held two commands in the West Indies and was burned as dark as any islander.

He saw Urquhart meet his eyes. His ship, *Reaper*, had been a challenge, but Keen had agreed that he was the obvious choice. There were others who had watched *Reaper*'s return to the fleet with both doubt and mistrust. A ship which had been cursed by mutiny could be seen as a threat, a dire warning to any captain who abused his authority in the name of discipline.

And there was Jacob Borradaile, commander of the fourteen-gun brig *Alfriston*. His ship had been there when *Reaper*'s mutiny had broken out, and her despairing company had turned on their captain and flogged him to death. Borradaile was probably the most unlikely figure present today, like some gaunt caricature, with sprouting, badly cut hair and deep, hollow eyes. He was no one's idea of the commander of a King's ship, but those who knew him swore by his skills and impressive knowledge of those he was fighting. James Tyacke had once described him as 'a good hand. Came up the hard way'. From Tyacke there could be no higher praise.

Commodore Deighton sat behind his table, shoulders very stiff, fingers interlocked, his restless eyes moving quickly from face to face. Adam introduced them one by one, and in response there was a quick smile, almost a grimace.

To Urquhart he said, 'And what of *Reaper*? Learned their lesson, have they?'

Urquhart replied calmly, 'I think others have, because of her, sir.'

Commodore Deighton frowned, and turned to Isaac Lloyd. 'Your ship has performed very well, I believe. I shall be looking to you.' His gaze settled on the hollow-eyed Borradaile. '*Alfriston*. I shall need you to maintain contact with the main squadron. It will be a demanding assignment.'

Borradaile watched him without expression. 'We'll be ready, sir.'

Adam saw Morgan Price glancing round. Perhaps he was expecting a glass of wine, a small thing, but usual enough at such a gathering as this. There was no wine; not even Deighton's strange-looking servant, Jack Norway, was present. A rumour, probably originating in the wardroom, had suggested that Norway had been rescued from the gallows, which might explain why he held his head at such an acute angle, and seemed barely able to speak.

Deighton was opening a long envelope and drawing out some papers. Adam could see the seals of Admiralty, and others too, which seemed to lend added importance to this meeting.

Deighton said, 'What I tell you is in the strictest confidence.' He frowned as Borradaile dragged his heels across the deck. 'A combined naval and military operation is planned, to take place while the weather is favourable, and to gain the maximum advantage. Admiral Cochrane will be in overall command, but the operation will be divided into separate sections.' He reached up and touched his ginger hair as if he were thinking of something else. Then he said deliberately, 'An attack on Washington, gentlemen.'

He had their full attention now, and Adam could see the amusement in his eyes. Pleased with his timing, with its effect.

These were experienced officers, and Adam knew that each man was regarding the challenge in a different light. Borradaile was used to prowling in American coastal waters, picking up intelligence where he could, and then making off if any enemy patrol vessel came upon him. Morgan Price was more concerned with the presence and size of American frigates; he had crossed swords with several of them already, and, like Lloyd of *Chivalrous*, he was never averse to prize money when it came his way.

Adam realised that Deighton's eyes, now quite steady, were on him.

'Captain Bolitho, what is your opinion of this honourable undertaking? You are experienced as anyone, I should have thought.'

Adam stared out at the blue-grey water beyond the stern windows. *How do I feel? Truly feel, setting aside my dislike of this man?*

He answered, 'The timing will have to be perfect, sir. Every care must be taken to avoid the leakage of information to the enemy. They would not be slow to rally against such an attack.'

'Of course, Captain.' Deighton played with the corners of his papers. 'You have no reason to love the Americans. You have had too close a contact for that.'

'I lost my ship to them, sir, and I was a prisoner of war.'

Deighton's eyes gleamed. 'Ah, but you *escaped*. I recall reading the full account.'

This was the man he could understand. 'The account of my court martial, sir?'

Price grinned wildly, and Lloyd took an interest in his cuff. Deighton nodded, unmoved.

'How did you find your captors – *the enemy*?'

'They fight for what they believe. They are like us in many ways.' He thought of his uncle. 'It is like fighting people of your own blood.'

'I shall have to take your word for that, Captain.' He smiled, but there was no warmth in it. Then he continued, 'And what are our chances of success, would you say?'

Adam saw Urquhart watching him, hating this casual interrogation in the presence of the others.

He answered, 'It can be done, sir. Others have said as much. But without ships and the necessary military strength, it has not been possible.' He paused. 'Now we have both. It would be a gesture, rather than a victory. Some might describe it as revenge for the American attack on York.'

Deighton raised a hand. 'And what do *you* say?'

Adam heard someone laugh, one of his men. One of those he had almost left behind, abandoned.

'I say *I do not care*, sir. Tomorrow we may be at peace.' He glanced around at the others, sensing that he had their understanding. 'But while we are still at war we must strike them as hard as we can. So that it will be remembered, and, with it, the many who have died for it. Too many.'

Deighton laid his hands flat on the table. 'Then we are agreed.'

His servant entered the cabin as if to a signal, with a tray of glasses.

The commodore stood up, and the others followed suit.

'I give you a sentiment, gentlemen. To the squadron.' His eyes rested on Adam again. 'And to *victory*!'

One glass each, and the servant had departed as silently as he had entered.

Deighton smiled. 'Your orders will arrive tomorrow. In the afternoon we shall weigh and take station as I direct.' The smile was fading. 'That is all, gentlemen.'

Adam was on the quarterdeck to see each captain into his gig. The last to leave was Borradaile, as he had known it would be.

Adam said quietly, 'Well, my friend? What are your feelings?'

Borradaile looked at him and made some attempt to adjust his ill-fitting uniform before going down to his waiting boat.

'I was thinking just now, sir, while I watched and listened.' His deep, hollow eyes were hidden in shadow, ageless, a man of the sea. 'So like your uncle, I was thinking. So very like that fine, caring sailor.' He almost smiled. 'But all eyes open for storms. I was thinking that too, sir.'

He shambled to the entry port, outwardly oblivious to the calls and ceremonial of his departure.

Adam found himself more moved by the simplicity and honesty of Borradaile's remarks than he had thought possible. Perhaps after Deighton's hints and suggestive asides, it had been what he most needed. He stared across the anchorage. Four frigates and a brig. At least they would be doing something again, instead of playing watchdog to helpless transports.

He saw the marines falling out and hurrying below to their messes, their barracks, as they insisted on calling them. Washington, then. But he could find no excitement in the prospect. Was that, too, gone for ever?

Whatever the outcome, the blame would lie with the man in command. The margin would be a narrow one: success or utter disaster. Then he thought of his uncle. *That fine, caring sailor.* It had made him seem closer. He smiled. And *that* was what he had needed.

Adam Bolitho stood loosely by the quarterdeck rail and stared along the full extent of his command, beyond the taut rigging and the jib sails to the empty sea ahead. It was angled now, and quite steady, as if *Valkyrie* were riding a sloping bank of dark blue, eye-searing water.

Below the larboard gangway the ritual of punishment was drawing to a close; it was something which Adam had learned to accept without flinching. Three weeks had passed since the newly formed squadron had left Halifax, and to the masthead lookouts the other frigates would still be in sight, ready to run down and investigate any suspicious vessel, or to respond to the commodore's signals.

Three weeks of drills and yet more drills, the messdecks humid in the unwavering heat, and tempers fraying. It was not unusual in any ship of *Valkyrie*'s size.

He glanced down as the boatswain's mate paused and ran his fingers through the lash, to separate each of its nine tails, then the drum rolled again and the lash came down with a crack across the naked back.

Bidmead, the master-at-arms, chanted, *'Thirty-six, sir!'*

There was something like a sigh from the ship's company, who had been piped aft to witness punishment. The victim's back was a mass of torn and bleeding flesh. But as his wrists were cut free from the upended grating he stepped clear and stood unaided, only his heaving chest revealing the pain he had suffered.

It had been a severe punishment, but Spurway was one of the ship's hard men, a troublemaker who had been flogged many times, and had boasted, and proved, that he could take it without a whimper.

Adam hated the ritual for many reasons. In a ship like this one, there were always accidents, falls, cuts and bruises as men, some inexperienced, were driven to work aloft in pitch darkness when the pipe came to shorten or make sail. For trained hands like Spurway to be excused work because of a flogging was nothing but waste. Nor would it deter others like him. But discipline was vital, and Spurway had struck a petty officer who had sworn at him for malingering.

At his back, he could sense the line of marines across the poop, a captain's final authority if all else failed.

He saw Minchin, the surgeon, peering up at him, his face as red as raw meat.

'Take him below. And don't be too soft with him.'

Minchin squinted into the sun, and grinned. 'He would have been better off in the army, sir. They'd have hanged him!' He strolled away, a man isolated from all the others.

Dyer touched his hat. 'Permission to fall out the hands, sir?'

'Yes.' Adam stared past the lieutenant's shoulder at the small courier schooner which had met with them soon after dawn to pass across a satchel of despatches for the commodore.

He watched the schooner's sails turning slowly end on in the haze, like pink shells. *Free*, he thought, her commanding officer able to move at will as he sought out his next rendezvous.

He looked at the gangway. The grating was gone, and two seamen were swilling away the remaining blood.

He said, 'Have a word with Mr Midshipman Fynmore. He hopes to sit for lieutenant soon. He should have prevented the trouble with Spurway.'

Dyer said, 'He's very young, sir.'

Adam faced him. 'He was there. He was in charge. *Tell him!*'

He turned as his servant John Whitmarsh hurried from the poop.

'What is it?' Although, in truth, he was glad of the interruption. He had been over sharp with the first lieutenant. But he, too, should have known.

Whitmarsh said, 'The commodore sends his compliments, zur. Would you join him aft.'

Adam smiled. 'Directly.' Perhaps the schooner had brought final orders for the proposed attack. So much time seemed to have passed since Deighton had announced it in his cabin that it had lost all sense of urgency.

He walked into the poop's cool shadow and saw two seamen glance at him, and as quickly look away. No one in the ship liked the man who had been punished, but a flogging was a flogging, and they would never take sides against one of their own.

He paused before entering the great cabin.

Rather like us, he thought.

Deighton was at his table, leaning on his hands while he studied an opened chart and a file of carefully written instructions.

'Ah, good – here you are.' He had raised his head, but remained in silhouette against the glistening panorama of the sea. 'Punishment carried out, eh? Just what the brutes deserve. No one respects a gentle hand, no matter how well intended.' He gestured to a chair and added, 'I thought you were against flogging, on principle.'

Adam sat down. 'I am, sir. But until some other means of punishment is suggested by their lordships or the King's regulations, I shall flog any man who tries to undermine the discipline in this or any other ship.'

'I am glad to know it, sir.' Deighton tapped the chart. 'It is all here in the admiral's despatches. The attack will take place in two weeks' time. I would like you to read the instructions as soon as possible. I have every faith in the strategy proposed, of course, but you might wish to challenge something.'

'Yes, sir.' Strange to hear someone other than his uncle or Keen referred to as 'the admiral'. It was like wearing a blindfold, not knowing the mind behind it, except by reputation. Bolitho had always known the importance, and also the folly, of such an undertaking unless it was certain of success.

'It will be a twin-pronged attack, by way of the River Potomac, and supported by another along the River Patuxent.' He opened and closed his fist, like a crab. 'Major-General Robert Ross will be in command of the land operations.' He glanced at him quickly. 'Do you know him?'

Adam said, 'He has the name of a man of action, sir.' A major-general. So it was that important.

Deighton nodded. 'Good, good. Our squadron will be placed and in position on the first day, and our main task will be to prevent any interference from the enemy while our soldiers are landed.' He waited while Adam stood and walked to the table. The charts were current, and fully corrected, something that could never be taken for granted, particularly with the Americans' insistence upon altering the names of so many towns and landmarks. He could feel Deighton watching him, perhaps searching for doubts.

He said, 'It will depend on the weather. Transferring the troops from transports to boats will take time; it always does.' He paused, expecting Deighton to interrupt. He traced the coastline with his finger. 'There are too many ships. It will take too long to prepare.'

'Are you saying it cannot be done?'

Adam bent closer to the chart; in his mind he could already see it. Soldiers tumbling into boats, many of whom had never taken part in an amphibious landing. It only needed a few small, determined vessels to work amongst them, and even with overwhelming support from the navy, any invasion would end before it began.

He straightened his back and looked at the sea. The wind was powerful but steady, with the ship still on the same tack, but he knew from experience and from what the old hands had said that it could change within the hour. Too many ships had driven aground off Chesapeake Bay to take the approaches lightly.

'It *will* be done, sir, if so ordered. I should like to discuss it with Mr Ritchie.'

Deighton stared at him. 'Ritchie? Who is he?'

'The sailing master, sir. He has great experience of these waters, and I value his judgement.'

'Oh, very well, I suppose that. . . .' He turned away. 'It is not an issue open for discussion.'

Adam waited. What did it matter? Another battle, probably planned in a comfortable room somewhere, by minds already dulled by years of war, overreached by new methods, driven by fresh ambitions which were rarely taken into account.

But it does matter. It always had, and it always must. When the drums rattled and beat to quarters and men ran to their stations, some would look aft, to see their captain, to attempt to discover in his face some hope, some hint of their chances. They never questioned what they were ordered to do. *Of course it matters.*

He said quietly, 'When we next rendezvous with *Alfriston*, I think we should speak with Commander Borradaile.'

Deighton squared his shoulders. 'If you think it useful. Coastal experience, that sort of thing?'

'We must seize and hold an advantage, sir, no matter how small.' He could see an argument forming on Deighton's face. 'As I said before, sir, the enemy are too much like us. They will fight with all they have. As we would, if the French were to sail up the Thames and attack London.'

Deighton studied him, seeking something more. But he said only, 'Signal the squadron to close on *Valkyrie*. I will pass each captain his final instructions. After that. . . .' He did not continue. Instead, he changed tack. 'I know that Rear-Admiral Keen had great faith in you. Doubtless, he had his reasons. I shall expect the same confidence and competence from you myself. Is that understood?'

'It is understood, sir.'

'Perhaps you would care to take a glass with me, Captain?'

Adam sat again. This new Deighton, the caution, the wariness, was not easy to accept.

'Thank you, sir.'

But Deighton would never allow a breach in the wall of formality, unlike Keen. *The day that Deighton calls me by my first name, I shall shake his hand.*

The strange servant entered noiselessly and prepared some goblets.

Deighton said abruptly, 'Of course, Captain, you're not married, are you?'

'No, sir.' Always a reminder, a barb.

'Not all a bed of roses, y'know.' Deighton took a glass and held it to the reflected glare. He turned to the table again, and opened a drawer. 'With all these details to examine and decide upon, it slipped my mind. There was a letter in the despatch bag for you.' He forced a smile. 'From a lady, I'll swear to it.'

Adam took it and glanced at the seal and the written instructions. It must have been passed from ship to ship before it came to the courier schooner.

Adam saw her without effort, the dark eyes and high cheekbones, and the confidence which she gave to others. *To me.*

He said, 'Catherine, Lady Somervell, sir.' He watched him, for some surprise or innuendo, that he should know her so well, well enough to receive a letter from her.

'A lady of magic, they tell me.' He raised one ginger eyebrow. 'Perhaps she will bring us luck in this great venture.'

Adam left the cabin, the taste of the wine clinging to his tongue. He did not know one vintage from another, but he did not think Keen or his elegant flag lieutenant would rate it very highly.

John Whitmarsh was in his cabin, and made to leave when he entered. He was polishing his captain's sword, the short, curved fighting blade which Adam had selected with such care after his other had been lost in *Anemone*.

'No, stay. You'll not disturb me.' He sat down beneath the skylight and slit open the letter.

My dear Adam. . . . It was dated in May, three months, a lifetime ago. How much worse it would be for her.

He could even imagine her writing it, perhaps in the library, which looked over the garden she had made her own. So many memories, countless pictures, the last being the one he carried like a penance, Catherine on the beach with Zenoria's broken body in her arms.

By the bulkhead the boy John Whitmarsh watched his captain's face, while his cloth moved up and down the keen-edged blade without a pause.

So remember, dear Adam, that you are not alone. Last week I visited Zennor again, no better place to rest. I tell you this, Adam, she is at peace now. I could feel it. The last thing she would have wanted would have been for you to lose yourself in grief. You have your life to live, and so much to offer and to discover. Do not throw it away for any cause or reason. You will find your love again. As I have.

The boy's hand stilled on the hanger as Adam unlocked his cabinet, and took out the small velvet-covered book.

Very gently, he opened it, and looked at the pressed remains of the wild rose he had picked for Zenoria. A book which Keen had casually given him, without understanding what it had meant. He held it to his cheek for several seconds, remembering, and yet very aware of the woman who had written to him, that she cared enough for him to reach out to him and give him this comfort.

The boy asked carefully, 'Is it bad, zur?'

Adam looked at him. 'No, not bad, young John.' He folded the letter, and heard her voice again. *She is at peace now.*

Catherine understood, better than anyone, that neither the love nor the peace could ever have been his; that, without her, there would only have been grief, tearing him apart.

He said quietly, 'With someone's help, I have reached an understanding.'

Catherine had returned to Zennor for his sake, to the church where he had stood with her and with Bolitho, when Keen had taken Zenoria for his wife. Perhaps she had discovered

106

that the little mermaid had gone back to the sea. And found peace. *For both of us.*

The boy watched him leave the cabin. He did not understand any of it, but that did not matter. He had been a part of it.

8

One Hand for the King

Commodore Henry Deighton prowled restlessly about his great cabin, reaching out to touch pieces of furniture and equipment, obviously without seeing them.

Adam waited beneath the cabin skylight, glad that somebody had closed it. Deighton was almost beside himself, unable to control his disbelief even in front of Adam and the hovering Lieutenant Dyer, an unwilling spectator. Anyone working on deck would otherwise have heard him.

Deighton swung round, one hand jabbing the air to emphasise each word. 'And are you telling me, Captain, that just because of some *scrap* of information which *Alfriston*'s captain. . . .' He snapped his fingers and Dyer offered helpfully, 'Borradaile, sir!'

Deighton ignored him. 'You are telling me that I should contact Rear-Admiral Cochrane's ships, and the transports, and suggest that he delay the attack! Hell's teeth, man, do you know what you're asking me to do?'

Adam felt his impatience changing to anger, but knew that any outburst now would be like a match in a powder magazine. He said, '*Alfriston* stopped a Portuguese trader, sir. One known to Commander Borradaile. In exchange for information, the trader . . . .'

Deighton shouted, '*Smuggler*, you mean!'

'Smuggler, sir. One who has proved very useful in the past.'

He waited while Deighton peered at his chart again. 'There is an American commodore named Barney. He has a flotilla of small vessels in the bay. It seems he is sheltering at the mouth of the Patuxent, perhaps because of information about us, or perhaps merely as a precaution.' His voice hardened. 'Where our ships and four thousand troops are to be conveyed and landed, *the day after tomorrow.*'

Deighton snapped, 'The admiral must be well aware of that!'

Adam glanced at Dyer and wished he was somewhere else. When *Valkyrie* was next committed to action Dyer would remember today, and the men he served.

'And there is this battery.' He did not move or indicate on the chart what Borradaile had told him. Deighton had already challenged that, too. 'Old or new, we don't know, but the Americans have been working on it these past weeks. It is not an easy approach at any time, but with a battery sited and ready, perhaps with heated shot . . . .'

Deighton sat down heavily as if the deck had given out beneath him.

'I *know* about heated shot, Captain, and I also know that a slow-moving force of vessels entering a confined passage is no match for a shore battery.'

Adam said to Dyer, 'Wait for me in my cabin.'

The lieutenant left without a word. Only then did Deighton realise he had gone.

'You are leaving me no sea room, Captain. The responsibility is mine.'

Adam thought of Dyer in his cabin. Had he guessed that he had been sent there to prevent him from describing how the new commodore had seemed snared by his own vital but damning authority?

'The whole fleet will be expecting results.' Deighton was on the move again, his hands clasped beneath his coat-tails, his head bowed under the weight of his decisions.

Adam watched him, and found no comfort in the contempt he felt. He recalled Keen's words. *Not like us. Not like you.*

Individual faces stood out in memory. His coxswain, Starr, who had been hanged by the Americans for setting charges to destroy *Anemone* when otherwise she might have been saved, to serve under the Stars and Stripes. John Allday's son, who had fallen in the battle with the USS *Unity.* And the young midshipman, Lovie, their only casualty when they had destroyed the American prize and her would-be rescuer. Wiped away, like chalk from a slate.

Washington was the impossible, the unobtainable trophy. In war, what did motives matter any more? Glory or revenge, it made little difference to the men who fought and died.

He said suddenly, 'I have a suggestion, sir.' It was like hearing someone else, a stranger: calm, impersonal.

He saw Deighton turn to stare at him, as though he were offering him a lifeline. 'Destroy the battery before the attack begins.' He watched the surprise change to disbelief, then to something like disappointment.

'No time. And besides, what chance have we?'

'Boat action, sir.' It was like a rising madness, and although he knew he should guard against it, he felt himself being carried by it.

Deighton nodded, very slowly. 'And you would lead this venture, I presume? Another laurel for the family garland? For your uncle?'

Adam said, 'That is unworthy, *sir*.'

Surprisingly, Deighton laughed. 'Well, let us assume if it were at all possible, and lead it you would – by God, where would you begin?'

He considered it, unnerved that it should seem so straightforward, something already written in orders. *You are commanded to proceed.* Like the great paintings of famous sea fights; there was never any pain or blood.

'I would transfer to *Alfriston* immediately.' He saw the caution in Deighton's eyes. 'Which would leave you with the full company of frigates.' He saw Deighton nod, although he thought he had not known that he had done so. 'I would require forty marines, and a hand-picked party of seamen.'

Deighton swallowed. '*Thirty* marines.'

Adam felt his fingers tingling. Part of the madness.

He asked quietly, 'You agree, sir?'

Deighton stared around the cabin, as if he had suddenly become a stranger there.

'I shall put your suggestion in writing.'

Their eyes met. 'And I shall sign it, sir.' That way, there could be no recriminations. 'Willingly.' He picked up his hat. 'I will attend to the transfer, and signal *Alfriston* to lie downwind in readiness.'

He left the cabin, breathing deeply. The sun had shifted, but the normal day-to-day work was going on as before. As if nothing had happened. As if he had not committed himself, and others, to disaster. Suppose he was wrong? Should he have remained silent, and so forced Deighton to make a decision?

A scarlet-coated marine stepped out smartly.

Adam looked at him: a round, sunburned face, familiar, but at a distance, observing some rule of his own making.

He said, 'Corporal Forster?'

The corporal glanced around, suddenly unsure of himself. Some other marines were watching from the starboard gangway.

'Beggin' yer pardon, sir. It's not for me to say, but I was wonderin' . . . .'

Adam said, 'Tell me.'

'Well, sir, before you asks my officer, I'd like to put me name down for the raid.'

Adam looked away. It was only a vague idea, and yet they all knew about it.

And I almost left them.

The corporal added nervously, 'I'm a fine shot, sir.'

Adam touched his sleeve and did not see the other marines nudge one another.

'That you are, Forster. Give your name to the first lieutenant.' He tried to summon a smile, some kind of reassurance. 'I'll see you a sergeant yet!'

He strode on, his mind busy with details, then paused to glance round as signal flags dashed up to the yard.

There was no time to write a letter to Catherine. Perhaps Deighton had deliberately kept hers from him.

He felt the breeze across his face and saw the sailing master watching him, as if reading his thoughts.

And if I fall, there will be no letter. Only peace.

Alfriston's chart room was small, even by a brig's standards; she had begun her life in the merchant service, and space was at a premium aboard her.

It had been a red, angry sunset, the horizon fading eventually to a hard line. But the wind was steady, and Borradaile had insisted that the weather would not 'go sour', as he had put it. Adam could feel the man close by him now, his patched

111

elbows on the chart, a large magnifying glass gripped in one bony hand.

The brig seemed to be moving beneath him, an illusion, but she felt heavier in the water with her extra seamen and thirty of *Valkyrie*'s marines packed between decks. Even at the last minute, before he had been pulled across to *Alfriston*, he had expected the commodore to change his mind, to rely on the written details of the admiral's plan, and to do nothing beyond his orders.

In the fading light he had seen faces watching him from *Valkyrie*; a few had even called out to wish him well. It had moved him more than he had expected. The first lieutenant had been almost severe.

'If you think it's too much of a risk, sir, *fall back*. We shall get you out of there, somehow.'

And Minchin, observing silently from the poop. Perhaps calculating how many would end up on his table, or in the 'wings and limbs' tub on the orlop deck.

The worst part had been the very moment of departure, glancing around his cabin so as not to leave anything vital behind. John Whitmarsh had watched him kick off his shoes and tug on the hessian boots he often wore when called to action.

'I want to come too, zur! It's my place!' He had even been wearing the dirk Adam had given him for a birthday present. It seemed likely that it was the only gift he had ever received.

Adam had heard the bark of orders, the feet on the deck and the creak of tackles, the more measured tramp of marines preparing to climb into the boats. He was well aware that it might be the last time he would stand in that cabin, in that ship, or anywhere, and yet the boy's despair had made all the rest seem insignificant.

'Not this time, John Whitmarsh. When you wear the King's coat and have someone like *old Mister Allday* at your side, you'll see the sense of it.' It had been no use.

'When we lost *Anemone*, zur, we helped each other!'

Adam had laid a hand on his shoulder. 'That we did, and we still can.'

At the door he had looked back. 'Remember all our friends who were not so lucky. Stay with the ship.'

He sighed, and felt Borradaile turn to watch him.

112

He said, 'Tell me your thoughts, my friend.'

Borradaile frowned. 'I shall land you an' your party here, sir.' He poked the chart. 'My guess is that the admiral will make an early start, to get his ships into position and to land his soldiers up here.' His bony finger jabbed the chart again, by the river called Patuxent. 'A place named Benedict, the most suitable ground for the military.' He spoke of them almost with contempt, as was often the way with sailors.

Adam said, 'The flotilla of small vessels sheltering there, they will have to be boarded and taken first.'

Borradaile grunted; it might have meant anything, and Adam could sense his impatience. Good or bad, time was against them. He could even smell the man, tar, tobacco, salt and rum.

His was a small, tight command, where there would be no secrets, their strength the dependence of one upon the other, and an utter trust in one another. He smiled in the lamplight. *Like my first command. The fourteen-gun* Firefly. *At the age of twenty-three*. How proud his uncle had been of him. He often wondered what the old veterans like Borradaile thought of the boy-captains with all their dash and arrogance. *Like me*.

Borradaile said, 'The army will have a fight on their hands, an' that's no mistake.' He chuckled. 'But then, no sense, no feeling!'

Adam stood away from the table and winced as he struck his head against a beam.

'I'll tell the others.' Their eyes met. 'If we fail, it will not be laid at your door.'

Borradaile led the way to the main messdeck where the landing party had been stowed away like so much additional cargo. In the half-light the white facings and crossbelts of the marines stood out sharply, each man gripping his weapons and various items of equipment. Their officer was Lieutenant Barlow, a competent but unimaginative man who never questioned an order and expected his men to behave in the same way. Deighton had refused to allow the captain of marines to join the landing party, and that officer would be fuming about it, no matter what their chances were.

He saw *Valkyrie*'s third lieutenant, Howard Monteith, sitting apart from the rest. He had risen from a junior lieutenant to third by way of death or promotion, and he was young, but he had the eye for detail of a much more senior officer: Adam had seen him checking his men and their weapons, have a few words with each one and getting the right responses.

There was Jago too, a gunner's mate who had been with Urquhart when they had blown up the American prize and her would-be rescuer, and a tough, reliable seaman.

Adam waited until they had all coughed and shuffled into expectant silence.

He said, 'We are a small part of much greater affairs, but one which could make the difference between success and defeat. Be mindful of that.' They would be wondering why their captain was taking charge and not some other officer. The experienced men would see it as a sign of the mission's importance; the sceptics would say that it must be without risk if the captain was sharing it with them.

He thought of Deighton, who apparently believed that such men as these had no right even to ask why they were being sent. And of his uncle, who thought it was all they did have.

He said, 'There is an enemy battery up yonder.' He saw a couple of men stare at the ship's side as if it were as near as that. 'It is not big, but, like a poacher and his piece, it is well-sited to wreak havoc amongst our people.'

He looked up, caught off-guard as canvas cracked out like gunfire; for an instant he thought the wind had defied Borradaile's predictions and was rising. Perhaps it was safer to be like Barlow, the marine lieutenant. Borradaile was making more sail. The word moved in his mind again. *Committed.*

'You will be fed now, and there will be a good measure of rum.'

He saw the grins, and thought again of his uncle, the pain in his eyes when he had said, 'Is that all they ask for what they do?'

He nodded to Monteith, and ended simply, 'Keep together, and fight bravely if you must. We shall have the sea at our backs.'

He found Borradaile waiting for him by the compass box.

'West by north, sir. Holding steady on the starboard tack.' He sounded satisfied.

Adam thought of the men he had just left, drinking their rum. *If I began now I would never be able to stop.*

114

He turned as he realised Borradaile had asked him some-thing.

'My apologies, I am leagues away at present!'

Borradaile shrugged. 'I was thinking, sir, about going ashore.' He waited, perhaps expecting a rebuff. 'After what happened to you, being a prisoner an' the like, how d'you feel about it?'

Adam looked at his gaunt shadow. 'Not fear, my friend. Perhaps it gives me an edge.' He thought suddenly of the boy Whitmarsh, and added, 'It is my place.'

After the close confines of *Alfriston*'s hull, the air across the black, heaving water felt fresh, even cold.

Adam stood in the sternsheets of the barge, his hand on the coxswain's shoulder to steady himself as he strained his eyes to see the boat ahead. Five boats in all, oars rising and falling like dark wings, with only an occasional pale splash to mark a blade cutting against the inshore current.

The next boat astern was packed with marines, and he could see the white belts and pouches without difficulty. Like the noise, looms creaking in the rowlocks, the stem thrusting toward the deeper darkness of the land. Surely someone must see or hear them?

He knew from experience that his apprehension was unfounded. The sounds of the sea and the moan of a steady breeze would muffle almost everything. Each oarsman was handpicked, some from *Valkyrie*, and others put forward by Borradaile. In the leading boat he had stationed one of his own master's mates, a veteran like himself, who was very aware of the responsibility he had been given.

No matter what happened they must keep together. If the boats lost sight of one another, the raid would become a shambles before it had begun.

He saw another faint splash, and knew that the first boat was using a lead and line simply to ensure that they were not wandering amongst the rocks he had noted on the chart. Some were as big as islets.

He felt the coxswain lean forward to gesture to the stroke oarsman. No words; they were too experienced to need more than a hint. What were they thinking? Like most sailors, probably anxious when *Alfriston*'s ghostly shape had faded into the darkness. Now, each man would be wanting to get it over and done with, to return to familiar surroundings, and their friends.

The lookout in the bows called in a hoarse whisper, 'Jolly boat's comin' about, sir!'

The coxswain snapped, '*Oars!*' Another seaman shuttered a lantern just once toward the following craft, and Adam saw the untidy disturbance of spray as the blades backed water to avoid running them down.

The jolly boat circled round until it dipped and lifted in the shallows, and Lieutenant Monteith called out as loudly as he dared, 'Ship at anchor, sir! Off the point! Brig or brigantine!'

Always the unexpected to raise the stakes, but Monteith sounded calm enough.

He could feel the coxswain's shoulder under his fingers, hard and tense. *Waiting.* They were all waiting.

Adam replied, 'Take over the others, Mr Monteith.' He glanced at the pale faces of the oarsmen, watching and listening. How many times had he seen Keen brought to the ship in this barge, or pulled ashore to meet his lady? He thrust it from his mind. *His new wife.*

The jolly boat was too small, and by the time support could be organised even the sleepiest watch might have been roused. The unknown vessel had to be taken without delay. Any sort of alarm might bring troops, even a man-of-war hurrying to head them off.

He thought of Deighton. *Another laurel for the family garland, for your uncle?* He felt a grin breaking the fierce tension in his jaw. *He could damned well think what he liked!*

He said, 'Boarding party, be ready! Cox'n, as soon as we sight the brig, or whatever she is, make for the chains where we can hook on!'

He stared around for the jolly boat, but it had already drifted clear and merged with the darkness. Monteith was left to his own devices, perhaps the first time he had carried out such a mission. *If I fall, he will be on his own.* He drew his hanger and said, 'No shooting. You know what to do!'

'Give way all!'

The barge sighed into a low trough and gathered way again.

116

Perhaps the bearing was wrong? He glanced up, but even the stars were elusive. Some of the oarsmen were beginning to breathe more heavily: it had been a long pull with an overloaded boat; they were tired. All they had left was hope, and trust.

Something moved across the faint scattering of stars, like birds on passage. He gripped his hanger until the pain steadied him, and the birds hardened into shape, into the masts and yards of the anchored vessel. She loomed out of the night, so close that it seemed impossible that no one had yet sighted them.

'Easy, lads!' It was pointless to think of the other possibility: that the bulwarks were already lined with marksmen and swivels, that their carefully guarded secret was just another myth.

The coxswain hissed, 'Oars!'

Adam groped along the boat, holding a man's arm here, another's ready hand there, until he was in the bows with the waiting boarders. Jago was one of them, and Adam guessed he had detailed the spare hands when he realised what was happening.

He watched the rigging rising above him. *'Now!'*

A grapnel flew over the bulwark and snared into place, and the gunner's mate, Jago, was up and over the vessel's side before anyone else could move. Adam found himself on a littered, unfamiliar deck, men hurrying past him, brushing him aside in their eagerness to get aboard.

There was a single cry, and Adam saw Jago drag a limp corpse down from the forecastle where the luckless seaman had been supposedly guarding the anchor cable.

Jago bent down and wiped his blade on the dead man's shirt and said between his teeth, 'Never sleep on watch! Bad for discipline!'

Incredibly, Adam heard somebody stifle a laugh.

He said, 'Rouse the others.' He walked to the vessel's deserted wheel and glanced at the masts and furled sails. Brigantine. Small, and very useful in these waters.

A few thumps and startled shouts, and then it was over. There were ten of them; the others, including the vessel's master, were ashore.

Jago said, 'They'll give no trouble, sir.'

Adam smiled. There was no point in telling Jago that the swivel guns on the brigantine's poop and foredeck were fully loaded and primed. But for the sleeping watchman, things would have been very different, and that would have left Monteith to make the biggest decision yet in his young life.

'Tie them up. Tell them what to expect if they try to raise an alarm.'

Another seaman, one of Borradaile's, as Adam did not recognise him, said, 'She's the *Redwing*, out of Baltimore, sir. Carries stores for the army.' He jerked his thumb towards the land. 'To the battery. Their last visit, they tells me.'

Adam did not ask how he obtained the information, but it was priceless. So the battery was there. And it was completed.

There was no time to spare. He beckoned to Jago. 'Could you work this vessel into open water? The truth, man – no heroics.'

Jago faced him defiantly. ''Course I can, sir! I was servin' in one such out of Dover when I first got pressed!'

Adam matched his mood and gripped his arm, hard. 'She's yours, then. When you hear the charges blow, weigh anchor and try to rejoin the supporting squadron. I shall see you get a fair share of the prize money.'

Jago was still staring after him as the barge crew climbed down to their boat. Then he spat over the side and grinned. 'If you lives after today, *Cap'n*!'

The barge felt lighter as they pulled steadily toward the darker wedge of the land, and Adam saw the gleam of Monteith's white shirt as he stood in the jolly boat to wave as they surged abeam.

A lantern shutter lifted and light blinked across the water, and in what seemed like seconds men were leaping into the shallows on either bow to control and guide the boat in the last moments before the impact of driving ashore.

The marines were wading towards the beach, their bayoneted muskets held high, their heads turning like puppets as they fanned out to protect the other boats.

Adam felt the water surge around his boots and drag at each step forward. He could almost hear Borradaile's question. *How do I feel, then, stepping once again onto a land that almost destroyed me, when even now there might be a marksman taking aim, holding his breath . . . .*

But fear? There was none. A light-headedness which was

no stranger to him, a reckless courage that matched Jago's defiance.

He waved his hanger, and saw faces turn towards him. 'Lively, lads! One hand for the King and keep one for yourselves!'

But the King was insane . . . so where was the sense of it? He knew that if he laughed now, he would be done for.

Then he thought of Bolitho, of his face when he had told him about Zenoria, and all those watching portraits which had condemned him. There had never been any choice for them, either.

Lieutenant Monteith rolled on to his side, an arm upraised as if to withstand a sudden blow, then gasped with relief as Adam dropped down beside him.

Adam pulled his small telescope from his coat. 'All quiet?'

'Yes, sir. Our people are in position and the marines have three pickets to guard each possible approach.'

He heard the anxiety in Monteith's voice. It was not unjustified. There was still enough darkness to cover them, but in less than an hour. . . . He closed his mind to it. The admiral's report had claimed that the nearest artillery post was some five miles away, but without surprise they could not hope to destroy the battery in time.

Monteith said, 'I thought I could smell fire, sir. Like burning.'

Adam glanced at him. 'It must be the new oven for heating shot.'

There was no point in deceiving the young lieutenant. If they succeeded in destroying those guns, Borradaile would be ready and waiting to pick them up. If they failed, *Alfriston* would be the battery's first victim.

Monteith said between his teeth, 'Where the *hell* is that man?'

That man was a foretopman named Brady, as nimble and sure-footed as any cat when working high above the deck in every kind of weather. But before he had agreed to join the navy rather than face deportation or worse, he had been a poacher. A man very much at home in territory like this.

Adam said, 'He'll not run, Howard.' He smiled. 'We'd know by now if he had.'

119

He felt Monteith staring at him in the darkness, surprised that he could appear so confident, or unnerved by the casual use of his first name.

A marine said in a fierce whisper, 'Here comes the little bugger now!' He must have seen Adam's epaulettes, and added, 'Brady's back, sir!'

The man in question dropped beside them. 'Five guns, sir, an' the magazine is on the side slope.' He was making slicing motions with his hands. 'Two sentries, and the rest of 'em are in a hut.'

Adam looked towards the bay, but it was still hidden in darkness. In his mind's eye he could see the battery, hacked from the hillside with the remainder of the slope rising behind it. No fear of attack from inland; the only enemy would come by sea. Five guns. A landsman would not think it much, but with heated shot they could cause a damage and destruction no landsman could begin to imagine.

'Pass the word, Brady. We will move now.' He let his words sink in. '*As planned!*' He gripped the little man's shoulder. There seemed no flesh at all, only muscle and bone. No wonder he could kick and fist freezing canvas in a screaming gale with the best of them. 'That was well done.'

He heard the marines moving carefully on the hard, sun-dried ground. They were all well concealed, but in the faintest daylight their scarlet coats would stand out like beacons.

Adam stood up. He was suddenly very thirsty, but calm enough. He searched his feelings, as if he were examining a subordinate. He had no inclination to yawn; he knew from past experience that it was a first sign of fear.

Dark shapes hurried away to the right, men used to cutting out ships in the night, so experienced that they could take out a strange vessel as if it were their own. Like Jago and the brigantine.

He heard Lieutenant Barlow draw his sword, and snap, 'Marines, *advance*!'

Adam said, 'If I fall, Howard, get them back to the boats.'

He was running now, his hanger held across his body, his heart pounding painfully, and suddenly the crudely-made wall was stretching out in front of him. Had his eyes adjusted to the darkness, or was it lighter? Nothing made sense. Only the wall. *The wall* . . . .

The crash of musket fire was deafening, the echo of the shot rebounding like a ricochet.

But the shot had come from behind; he had felt it fan past his head. One of the marines must have caught his foot on something, probably some of the building material scattered about on the slope. He raised his hanger and shouted, '*At 'em, lads!*' There was no such thing as luck now, good or bad. '*Go for the guns!*'

A marine was first on to the wall, but plummeted to the ground as someone fired up at him at what must be pointblank range. Another shot came from the other side of the clearing, but more seamen were already running across, cutlasses and boarding axes hacking at the sentry before he could reload or plead for his life.

A marine was on his knees, staring at blood on his tunic. The knowledge steadied Adam more than anything. He, too, could see the blood, and when he tore his eyes from the figures around the hut he realised that he could also see water, very still, and the colour of pewter. The bay.

He saw a marine level his bayonet and stand astride a fallen figure by one of the guns.

Adam flicked the bayonet with his hanger and said, 'Enough! Join your squad!'

But the marine could only stare from him to his victim.

'But he done for my mate Jack, sir!' The bayonet wavered, as the marine gauged the distance.

Adam repeated, '*Enough!*' He could not remember the man's name. 'You can't bring him back!'

Sergeant Whittle roared, 'Over 'ere, that man!'

The marine obeyed, hesitating only to look once more at his dead friend. Discipline was restored.

The man on the ground had been wounded, but he seemed to be attempting to grin, in spite of the pain.

'That was thoughtful of you, Captain!'

Adam looked at him. An officer, very likely the only one here. *Yet*. He called, 'Take this one, Sergeant!' To the injured officer, he said, 'You and your people are prisoners. Do not resist. I think my men are beyond the mood of reason.' Another bayonet darted between them as the American slid a hand into his coat. But the effort was too much, and the hand fell back again.

Adam knelt and reached into the coat, and drew out nothing more dangerous than a small portrait in a silver frame. He thought of Keen and the girl, Gilia.

Monteith was shouting, 'Break this door open! You, Colter, fetch the fuses.' And Lieutenant Barlow's voice restoring order and purpose, guarding their flank.

He replaced the portrait in the wounded man's coat, and said, 'A very pretty girl. Your wife?'

So much to be done. Fuses to be laid, wounded to be moved, the five guns to be spiked. But it all seemed unreal, beyond himself.

He called, 'Attend this officer, Corporal.' He realised it was Forster, the marine who had volunteered. 'Well done.'

The American gasped, 'Not yet. Maybe never. . . .' He grimaced as pain probed through him again.

Adam stood. 'Flesh wound. You'll be well enough.' The corporal leaned down with his bandages, no doubt wondering why he bothered.

The American held up his hand as Adam turned to leave him.

'Your name, sir. I would like to tell her . . . .'

Adam sheathed his hanger; there was blood on the blade, but he remembered nothing about it.

'Bolitho.'

Monteith was back again. 'I'm moving the wounded now, sir.' He glanced at Forster with his bandage. 'Theirs and ours. We lost five killed, seven wounded.'

Adam shook his arm. 'Get them to the boats.' He raised his voice. 'This officer will give his word that they will not interfere.'

Monteith listened, and wondered. He had expected to be killed, even though he had not dared to contemplate it; he had expected to fail this youthful, remote captain. But now he was shaking his arm, smiling at him. *Will I ever be so confident?*

It took an hour, and still no one raised an alarm. It seemed as if the rest of the world had ceased to exist.

Adam said, 'Go with the others, Howard. *Alfriston* will be there to collect the boats directly.' He pulled out the watch and opened the guard with its finely engraved mermaid. He imagined he could feel warmth on his cheek although he knew that the morning was still grey.

Monteith hesitated. 'Are you *certain*, sir?'

Adam walked to the parapet. The guns had been spiked, and when the magazine exploded there would be nothing left. When he glanced around, Monteith had gone. Only the dead lay where they had fallen.

At this moment more of the enemy might be marching or riding with all despatch to this place. He walked to the open trapdoor, which led down to a crude powder magazine.

He looked around at the sprawled corpses. A small price to pay for what they had done; that would be in the eventual report.

Aloud he said, 'But not small to you.'

He felt the skin on his neck tingle, an instinct he never took for granted; his pistol was in his hand and cocked before he realised it.

But it was Jago, the tough gunner's mate.

'I *ordered* you to stay with the prize!' There was an edge to his voice which warned him how close it had been.

Jago said evenly, 'The others said you was standing fast until the fuses was lit, sir.' There was no humility, and no resentment either.

'And you took it upon yourself to come looking?'

Jago almost grinned. 'No more'n what you did when you come looking for Mr Urquhart and me after we blowed up the Yankee frigate!' He peered around, and examined the dead without concern or conscience. 'Worth it, sir?'

Adam raised his arm; it felt like lead. 'Tomorrow, our soldiers will land. After that, it's only fifty miles to Washington.'

He took a slow match and held it out to Jago.

'Here. Perform the honours.' He gazed once more at the dead. 'For us all.' And, half to himself, 'And for *you*, Uncle.'

But Jago heard, and, hardened though he was, he was impressed; and for him that was something.

Then he lit the fuses.

9

Too Late for Regrets

Adam Bolitho watched the last of the boats being hoisted inboard, and then lowered on to their tier where the boatswain's party was ready to make them secure. Even the barge had survived, and had been towed with the others by Borradaile's *Alfriston*.

Lieutenant Dyer had scarcely been able to hide his excitement and pleasure. Perhaps, like the commodore, he had expected the mission to fail, and that they would all be killed or taken by the enemy.

He gripped the quarterdeck rail and suddenly realised how drained and tired he was.

Soon it would be dark. But the last sunlight was still clinging to the horizon, and touching the horns of the figurehead's helmet as if unwilling to depart.

He thought of the moment when the battery's magazine had exploded, great rocks and pieces of stonework crashing through the trees, some splashing down dangerously close to the boats as they pulled towards *Alfriston*, and was reminded of Deighton's satisfaction with the mission, tempered only by an angry disbelief that Adam should have gone personally with the landing party.

Adam had said, 'When you order men ashore to carry out a task which might normally be executed by the military, you cannot simply abandon them to it. On deck, ship against ship, that's a different matter. But in unknown and hostile territory . . . .'

Deighton had interrupted, 'And I suppose *you* could not bring yourself to abandon the chance of further glory for yourself?'

124

Eventually he had contained his sarcasm. 'I shall send a full report to the admiral, and then to their lordships. A battery destroyed, the way opened for the attacking squadron, and a useful prize to boot . . . the brigantine should fetch a good price. I hope you explained to that Borradaile fellow about the arrangements for sharing prize money?'

'I believe he is well aware of them, sir.'

Of the casualties, he had told Deighton that one of the wounded was unlikely to survive an amputation. A brave man, he had not complained once during the painful transfers from boat to brig, and then to *Valkyrie*. But when he knew he was being carried down to the surgeon, he had pleaded and sobbed like a child.

Deighton had said, 'Can't be helped.' He might have been talking about a breakage in the galley.

Adam watched the brig *Alfriston* leaning to the freshening breeze as she changed tack and headed away to the south-west. Despatches for the admiral. He tried to control his bitterness. To ensure that Deighton's own part in the attack did not pass unnoticed. . . . He himself had thought *Alfriston* should remain in company, at least until they had made contact with their own frigates again.

Deighton had scoffed at his suggestion. 'Where's your zest for battle now, Captain? My orders are to cover the squadron's flanks. *That I shall do.*'

Adam turned as one of the surgeon's loblolly boys appeared on deck, and then walked to the lee side and pitched a bloody bundle outboard. A man's leg. He thought of the dead left behind at the battery, blasted to pieces when the charges had exploded. Surely better than what he had just seen.

He ran his fingers through his hair, feeling the salt and the sand, remembering the wounded American officer with the miniature of his girl. . . . Without thinking, he touched the scar in his side where the *Unity*'s surgeon had probed for splinters. Perhaps the American would tell her one day.

He heard voices below the poop and saw the gunner's mate, Jago, with some of his messmates. He was carrying a shirt which he had just washed out after his experience ashore, and, even in the fading light, Adam could see the livid scars of the cat across his muscular back. Unjustly flogged by *Valkyrie*'s previous captain, he would carry the scars to his grave like any felon. It had been John Urquhart, then *Valkyrie*'s first lieutenant, who had protested to the captain, and had spoken up for Jago, to no avail; it was obvious that Urquhart had been damned to oblivion because of his intervention. Until Keen had given him *Reaper* to command, another ship which had been torn apart by the cruelty of a sadistic captain.

He came to a decision, and beckoned to the gunner's mate. Jago ran lightly up the quarterdeck ladder and waited. 'Sir?'

Adam saw his eyes flit over his captain's torn breeches and crumpled shirt; he himself had not found the time to change into cleaner clothes.

He said, 'I shall not forget what you did. And I wanted to ask you something.' He could almost feel Jago's guard come up, but continued, 'I lost my old cox'n.'

Jago nodded. 'We know, sir. They 'anged 'im.'

'Would you consider taking his place?'

Jago stared at him. '*Your* cox'n, sir?' He glanced up as one of the topmen yelled something to some hands working aloft.

'I'll be gettin' discharged after this, sir. I've done my share, though some might say different.' He shook his head. 'I'm a gunner's mate. That'll do for me, sir.' He looked at him in the same thoughtful manner. 'But you done kindly by me for askin'.'

Adam dismissed him and watched him rejoin his friends, and drag the damp shirt over his head, hiding the savage scars. No wonder he held Urquhart in such respect. He smiled. *If not his captain.*

Dyer murmured, 'The commodore, sir.'

Deighton strode across to the weather side and stared at the men working on the tiered boats.

'The sea and the wind are moderate, Captain. I think we shall lie-to tonight, and rejoin the squadron tomorrow.' And, sharply, to the sailing master, 'What time would *you* estimate, Mr Ritchie, all things being even?'

Ritchie regarded him with a certain wariness. 'During the dog watches we should make contact with *Wildfire*, sir.'

'Then make it so, Mr Ritchie.' He grinned. 'We have done what we set out to do, eh?'

Adam saw some of the others looking over with the same caution. This relaxed, almost jovial mood was something new to them.

He said, 'I do not think we should lie-to, sir.' He kept his voice low, but he saw Ritchie nod in agreement.

Deighton said, 'You *disagree*, Captain, is that it?'

'It is my duty to advise you, sir.'

'It is not your duty, sir, to criticize me in the presence of the ship's company!' The joviality was gone.

'The enemy will call for reinforcements, sir. It would be their first reaction.'

'And this is mine, Captain. We shall lie-to until the morning watch is mustered. Make a note of it in the log.' He gave the fierce grin again. 'Now!'

He walked away, and a few moments later a faint glow appeared at the cabin skylight.

Adam turned, and saw Lieutenant Monteith waiting for him. 'Yes?'

'The wounded man, Simpson. He died, sir.'

There was blood on his sleeve, and Adam guessed that he had stayed with the wretched Simpson until the end. He could see it as clearly as if he had been there: Monteith, and the seaman he could not recall but for his courageous silence, and the surgeon, his face as red as the blood he spilled. And he thought of Deighton's indifference. His arrogance.

Jago was right. *Leave it when you can. Walk away from it while you still have limbs, wipe it from your mind.*

Perhaps he was too tired to think. No such thing as luck, good or bad. *Was that really me?* There was always a possibility that Deighton was right; he had been an experienced and senior captain before this appointment.

He touched Monteith's arm and said, 'Dine with me tonight, Howard.' He saw the lieutenant's surprise. 'We shall drink to damnation and drown our sorrows. . . . I fear we shall be busy men tomorrow.'

Monteith said, 'I would have liked nothing better, sir. But I have the middle watch.'

He should have known. 'Then rest while you can.' He made his way down to his cabin, as the marine sentry was relieved outside the commodore's quarters.

John Whitmarsh was waiting for him, and the table had been carefully laid.

Adam shook his head. 'I find that I cannot eat. Some cognac, please.'

Then he sat down and dragged open his drawer. It was as well that Monteith had declined the invitation, he thought.

The cognac burned his throat, but it seemed to steady him. He picked up a pen and began to write. *Dear Catherine* . . . .

When Whitmarsh entered the cabin again he removed the pen from Adam's out-thrust hand, and looked at the empty sheet of notepaper. *Dear Catherine.* The captain had even done that for him, taught him to read. Like so many things. Almost shyly, he reached out and touched the bright epaulette on the shoulder; Adam, deeply asleep, did not wake.

The captain was back. It was all that mattered. Tomorrow could wait.

When the hands were piped on deck with the morning watch, their captain was already in his customary place on the weather side of the quarterdeck.

Adam watched the familiar preparations, hammocks being stowed in the nettings, petty officers checking their lists and waiting to report to their lieutenants. He had had only a few hours' sleep, but a great deal of coffee and a change into clean clothing had made all the difference. He touched his chin. And a shave. He thought of Bolitho, and the restorative power of the customary shave from his faithful Allday. Impossible to think of them being separated. But it would come . . . .

Old Mister Allday. Young Whitmarsh had better not let him hear himself so described, he thought. Whitmarsh was very quiet these days, almost withdrawn, as he went about his duties. Another separation; but it would be for the best. His aunt would be more than willing to take care of the boy while he attended a local school. You could learn a lot in a man-of-war, but if Whitmarsh was to be sponsored as a midshipman he would need preparing for the other 'young gentlemen' he would eventually meet. *As I did.* It had been his Aunt Nancy then, another stranger who had become one of his own family, who had taught him to feel at ease in a world he had never known. But that was what was troubling Whitmarsh. Leaving the ship. *Leaving me.*

He turned as Ritchie called, 'West by north, sir. Starboard tack. Wind's backed a piece overnight.' He did not need to be able to see the masthead pendant. He knew. He could feel it.

Dyer was here, too. 'Ready, sir!'

'Very well. Hands aloft, set tops'ls and forecourse.' He saw one eyebrow rise very slightly. 'We shall save the t'gallants, Mr Dyer, until we can see where we are going!' It brought a few grins from the helmsmen and the master's mate of the watch. All old hands, they knew what the captain meant. There was no sense in showing all your top canvas at first light, until you knew who else was about. He laid his hands on the quarterdeck rail, still ice-cold from the night. It would be a different story in a few hours' time.

He loved to hear a ship coming alive again; he had hardly ever given the order to lie-to, unlike some captains. Like Deighton. . . . A ship should be moving. He recalled an old sailor's advice to him once. *An equal strain on all parts, hull and spars, and she'll not let you down.*

Valkyrie leaned over to the thrust of wind, spray glinting above the beakhead as the darkness loosened its grip.

He thought about Deighton. Perhaps they were both at fault. It was not the first time he had served with a man he could scarcely tolerate. It was all too common. The cramped confines of a crowded hull made few allowances for personal dislikes.

They would receive new orders, either to continue their patrols and the stop-and-search tactics which had been so successful, or they might be returning to Halifax. All of the inshore squadron would need to be restocked with fresh water and, if possible, fruit. He turned it over in his mind. *And if I should be offered another command?* Because of Deighton, or because he needed a new beginning?

'West by north, sir. Steady as she goes!'

Dyer crossed the deck. 'Dismiss the watch below, sir?'

Adam saw a tendril of smoke from the galley funnel, earlier than usual, but sailors could eat at any time.

'Very well.' He looked for the sun. 'D'you have some good eyes aloft?'

Dyer nodded, relieved. 'I picked them myself, sir.' He hesitated, sensing the barrier which still separated them. 'Are we likely to meet with an enemy, sir?'

Adam smiled. 'Well, we know where most of our *friends* are, Mr Dyer!' Even the nearest ones would be further away by now because of the commodore's insistence on lying-to.

And it was getting lighter. He could see the pale outlines of the brigantine's sails against the heaving water, and thought of Borradaile's uncanny knack of obtaining information from any vessel he sighted . . . .

He heard a splash, and knew it was Deighton's strange servant flinging some water over the side. Perhaps he had been shaving his master.

He took a few paces across the deck, and back again. It was no use; he would have to make allowances, be ready to bend more easily, even if he never understood Deighton's sudden fits of anger and his inability to conceal it.

The figures around him were assuming identity and purpose: men flaking down lines, another splicing a damaged halliard. Two midshipmen, their white patches very clear now, were making notes on their slates, a master's mate watching with a critical eye.

Perhaps they might meet with another courier vessel. But there would be no letters, unless Catherine had written again. He wondered where his uncle was, at sea, or performing some tedious duty ashore. How they would be missing one another. How they belonged. . . . And Keen, soon to be married. He thought of her letter, her visit to Zennor, the mermaid's church. Only she would have cared enough to write of it to him.

The sort of woman who could fascinate and thrill any real man. She was never truly absent from his thoughts; once he had even dreamed about her, when she had come to him not as a friend but as a lover. He had been ashamed and disgusted with himself because of it; it had seemed a betrayal of them both. But, in the wildness of the dream, she had not rejected him.

He heard somebody mutter, 'Another early bird.'

It was Deighton, wearing a boat cloak, with his hat tugged down over his eyes. He grunted as the officers touched their hats to him.

He saw Adam and remarked, 'That coffee – like damned bilge water.'

Adam said, 'I'll have some of mine brought to you, sir. It comes from London.'

'From a lady, no doubt.' But there was no bite to his tone. 'I'd take it as a favour.' He glanced around. 'You're not under all plain sail yet.' Again, it was not a complaint. Perhaps he was making an effort.

Adam said, 'A precaution. You know, sir, first sunlight on their skyscrapers.'

Deighton said suddenly, 'Rear-Admiral Keen, you've known him for a long while?'

'Yes, sir. We've served together from time to time.'

'Lost his wife, I understand.'

Adam waited, tensed, for the next question.

But instead Deighton said, 'Getting married again, I hear. Shapely little piece, to all accounts.'

'When he's promoted, she will be an asset to him.' It was as far as he would go.

Deighton said abruptly, '*Promoted*, of course! Vice-Admiral. No stopping him now. But for the damnable blockade duty, I would have been in that fortunate position. As it is, after this . . . .'

Adam said, 'It's a question on everyone's mind.' He thought suddenly of Jago. *I've done my share.* Perhaps he was the lucky one after all.

Deighton turned to face him. 'You're young. Good reputation, successful, many would say. It will be different for you.'

It was the closest they had been, probably would ever be, and Adam was oddly moved by it.

Deighton said, 'When we rejoin the squadron I might discover more about this campaign . . . .'

'Deck there!' The masthead lookout's voice seemed unnaturally loud. 'Sail to the nor'east!'

Adam was already pulling off his coat, and tossed it to one of the midshipmen.

'I'll take a glass and go up myself. I might know better then.'

Deighton restrained him. 'An enemy?'

He knew how it would appear to the lookout. Whatever it was, it was coming out of the sun. They would not sight *Valkyrie* in the lingering darkness just yet. It was little enough.

He replied, 'Unlikely to be one of ours, sir.'

Deighton peered over the side. 'They'll not snatch our prize, damn them!'

Adam hurried to the shrouds, faces turning on every side to watch him. How could he destroy the frail confidence which Deighton was trying to build between them?

He gripped the ratlines and began to climb.

How could he explain to Deighton? *It's not the prize. It's us they're coming for!*

* * *

Adam's heels hit the deck as he completed his descent from the crosstrees by way of a backstay. It was hardly dignified for a captain, but it saved time, and he was a little surprised that he could still do it; the palms of his hands felt raw from the slide, and his clean shirt was stained with tar.

'I'd like to have a look at the chart, sir.'

Deighton's face was filled with questions, but he was experienced enough not to voice them in front of the listening watchkeepers.

It was dark in the small chart room, but he held the image as sharply in his mind as he had seen it minutes ago. The lookout had pointed unwaveringly. 'Frigate, sir. Starboard quarter!'

In the first, uncertain light he had seen the other ship for himself, a perfect pyramid of pale canvas, running before the wind with each sail hard and full. Through the telescope he had been able to see part of her hull. The lookout had good eyes indeed, but what he had not seen was a second ship, a sliver, perhaps of equal size, hull up on the shining horizon.

Deighton asked impatiently, 'What was it?'

Adam did not look up from the chart. 'One, maybe two frigates, sir. Yankees, carrying all the sail they can muster.' He tapped the chart with the dividers. 'Probably out of New York, or even Philadelphia. They hadn't sighted us just now, but it won't be long.'

Deighton stared at the chart. 'What do you think?'

'Two choices, sir. Run, and hope to meet up with the squadron or the admiral's ships.' He wished he could see Deighton's face more clearly in the shadows. Only his hand was visible, drumming on the edge of the chart table.

Deighton said, 'And the other choice?'

Adam dropped the dividers on the chart. 'Stand and fight. There'll be no surprises this time.'

Men were moving about the decks again; the initial excitement was past. But not for long; there were no secrets in any ship.

'Two frigates? We'd be outgunned.'

'The sailing master said that it would take until the dog watches to meet up with our ships. Twelve hours at best, sir.'

The hand moved again, agitated, as if separate from its owner. 'That Ritchie doesn't know everything, dammit!'

132

'He's the best sailor in the ship, sir.'

He waited, feeling no pity for the man who had insisted on letting *Alfriston* go without informing the other frigates of his intentions. To extend their patrol area and so lose signalling contact was nothing but folly. All he felt now was a sick despair.

He said, 'We have an empty ocean. By setting every sail, we might avoid a stern chase and any serious damage to masts and rigging. We would lose the prize, but we did what we came to do.'

Deighton glared at him '*You* did, that's what signifies to you!' He moved to the door, where the glare of sunlight seemed to catch him unawares.

He said thickly, 'I've never run from an enemy. Nor shall I now. What would they say of me?' He laughed, a bitter sound. 'Some would find pleasure in it, I daresay!'

Adam looked past him, at the familiar figures near the big double-wheel, the two midshipmen with their slates. Men, and boys like these, to be sacrificed because of one officer's vanity.

He heard himself ask, 'Then you'll fight, sir?' Like somebody else. A stranger's voice.

Deighton gripped his arm and as quickly released it, as if he had just realised what he was doing.

'You will fight this ship, Captain Bolitho. That is an order! *I* am going aft. I shall not be long.' He looked up at the deckhead as a muffled thud made the air shiver.

One shot. To attract the most distant vessel. *Valkyrie* had been sighted, perhaps even recognised; she was well known enough in these waters.

Deighton had gone. To do what, he wondered. To pray?

He walked out and on to the quarterdeck again, taking his coat from the midshipman who held it with barely a glance. He stared up at the masthead pendant curling and hardening in the wind; real, everyday things. All the rest had been a dream, an illusion.

He beckoned to the first lieutenant, and said, 'Two Yankees to the nor'east.' He knew others were turning to listen. 'We will continue on the same tack for the present, but you may loose the t'gallants, if only to show them we are all awake this day. Then send the remainder of the hands to breakfast.' He looked at Ritchie. 'Put it in the log. The commodore wishes it to be known. We shall fight.'

He found that Monteith was beside him. 'What is it, Howard? It is too late for regrets.'

Monteith shook his head. 'May I ask, sir? But for the order, would you have run for it?'

Do they know me so little? 'No, by Christ, I would not! Not for any man!'

Monteith nodded, and touched his hat. 'I never doubted it, sir.'

Adam saw Whitmarsh's small figure below the poop, carrying his short fighting sword, and what appeared to be his best hat; the other must have been lost somewhere between here and Chesapeake Bay. He shaded his eyes to look up at the freshly-set topgallant sails. Again, he saw the enemy ships as he had watched them through the powerful telescope. Three hours, four at the most, and then this deck would be in torment.

He raised his arm so that Whitmarsh could clip on his scabbard, then took the hat and examined it. *Make me strong today* . . . .

Valkyrie's previous captain had been a tyrant and a coward. How would he be judged?

He laid his hand on the boy's shoulder, and saw the gunner's mate, Jago, pause to watch them.

'It will be warm work today, John Whitmarsh. Take station below when we engage.'

The boy gazed up at him. 'I'll be close by, zur. If you needs me.'

It was little enough, but Adam clapped the hat with its gleaming gold lace on his unruly hair and exclaimed, 'Then so be it!' He looked over at the helmsmen and felt the grin spread across his dry mouth.

'Let us make this a day to remember!'

Adam closed his watch with a snap and said to the first lieutenant, 'That was well done, Mr Dyer. A minute off your record for clearing for action!'

After the strident rattle of drums and the seemingly uncontrolled stampede of running men, the silence seemed unreal; even the ticking of his watch was audible.

Now all was still, the crews around their guns, most of them stripped to the waist, outwardly relaxed now while they waited for the next order. *Valkyrie* was cleared for action, screens torn down, chests and cabin furniture stowed below. But the boats still lay on their tier, and no nets had been spread overhead to protect the hands from falling wreckage.

He walked aft, where the marines waited on either side, muskets resting against the packed hammock nettings, their only protection if it came to close action.

He found Deighton, alone but for his servant, right aft by the taffrail. Both the enemy ships were clearly visible now, and with a soldier's wind directly under their coat-tails were almost bows-on. The smaller of the two ships was overhauling her larger consort, with even her studding sails set to achieve her maximum speed. Twenty-eight guns. Certainly no more.

He said, 'This is what I intend, sir.' He was surprised that he could sound so formal, as if it were just another daily drill. 'The leading ship intends to close the range as quickly as possible.'

Deighton did not take his eyes off the other frigates.

'Huh, you can blow *him* out of the water!'

Adam recalled his own early days in a frigate, the ruses and tricks he had seen some captains attempt, not always successfully.

'Like a hound after a stag, sir. He intends to try and slow us down, cripple us if possible, so they can close in for a kill.' He glanced forward again; it seemed so bare without the nets spread above the gundeck.

The lieutenants would explain, and the older hands might see the sense of it. They must seem to be running away from a superior force of ships; if they dropped the boats astern and were seen to spread the nets, their intent to fight would be obvious.

He added, 'They will hold the wind-gage, but I shall use it to our advantage.'

There was a sharp bang, and seconds later he saw a ball skip across the blue water like a dolphin. The pursuing captain had used his bow-chaser to test the range; it was always a difficult shot, but it only required one good hit.

He went forward and waited for Dyer to meet him. 'I shall luff presently.' He saw Ritchie listening, taking it all in. 'Then we shall sail as close to the wind as we can. It should give us some advantage and extra elevation.' He watched his words going home. 'Double-shotted, chain-shot, too, if we have any. No full broadside.' He paused, holding Dyer's eyes. '*Gun by gun*. Do it yourself. I want that terrier dismasted before we are!'

He snatched a glass from the rack and climbed into the shrouds to search for the second vessel. He found her and settled her in the spray-dappled lens. One of their large frigates. Like Beer's *Unity* . . . .

He strode aft again, feeling the eyes upon him, knowing their thoughts.

'Sergeant Whittle. Choose your marksmen, then clear the poop. Your scarlet coats make a good aiming point!' Some of them even laughed, as if it was a huge joke.

Whittle, an impressive figure with iron-grey hair beneath his leather hat, bawled an order, and his men moved to their usual stations.

Deighton said, 'I don't see the wisdom of that, Captain. Those ships are out for a kill, you said as much yourself!'

Perhaps he felt safer with the armed marines around him. Adam almost smiled. What was *safe* today?

He flinched, although he had been expecting it, as a long orange tongue shot from the other frigate's bow, and the bang followed like an echo.

It was well aimed, but the range was still too great. Maybe a nine-pounder; he imagined he could see the brief blur as the ball reached its maximum elevation. He saw the splash, and felt the hull jerk violently as the shot found its mark below the waterline. He glanced sharply at the wheel; Ritchie had three helmsmen on it now, but she showed no sign of running free or being out of command. With the steering gone, there would be no hope at all.

He raised his hand. 'Alter course three points! Steer nor'west!'

Men were already hauling on the braces as the helm went over. The effect was immediate, the wind tilting *Valkyrie* like a toy as she came round further and further, as close to the wind as she would hold.

A whistle shrilled. 'Open the ports! *Run out!*'

Squealing like pigs, the guns were hauled up to their ports, extra men running from the opposite side to add their weight to the tackles. At this angle, it was like dragging each gun up a steep slope.

Sails cracked and thundered overhead. Ritchie called, 'Course nor'west, sir!'

Dyer was already at the starboard gangway, oblivious to the demented sails and the men slipping and falling on the spray-drenched deck. He had drawn his sword, and was standing motionless, staring at the enemy frigate as she loomed into view, as if she and not *Valkyrie* had made the violent change of tack.

'*Fire!*' Dyer ran from the side as the gun roared out and hurled itself inboard on its tackles, the crew already working with their sponges and worm to clear the barrel of any smouldering remnants which might ignite the next charge as it was rammed home. Adam had seen it happen, men driven beyond reason by the fury of battle who had neglected to sponge out a gun, and had been blown to bloody fragments when it had exploded.

There was a chorus of wild cheering which Adam could not have prevented even if he had wished to. It must have been one of the last guns to fire; they would never know.

Almost with disbelief, he saw the other frigate's foremast begin to move, in a silence which made it all the more terrible.

Slowly at first, and then like a giant tree, the entire foremast with spars, torn canvas and trailing rigging reeled forward and over the side.

He shouted, 'Stand by on the quarterdeck!' When he looked again, the mast was dragging in the sea alongside the enemy ship, snaring her, dragging her round like a great sea-anchor. From a thing of beauty and purpose to a drifting shambles; but that would not last.

The confusion amongst the flapping sails was even more violent when *Valkyrie* swung round still further, almost aback as she laboured through the eye of the wind.

Adam dragged himself to the compass. 'South-east by east, Mr Ritchie.' He saw Dyer staring at him and shouted, 'Larboard battery! *Broadside!*'

'*Fire!*' The range was about half a mile, but with a full, double-shotted broadside, they could easily have been along-side.

As the wind drove the swirling smoke away like fog, Adam raised his telescope and studied the enemy's shattered stern; the fallen mast had dragged her around to expose her full length. Only her mainmast remained standing; topmasts, spars and booms covered her decks; torn canvas and coils of severed cordage completed the picture of devastation.

Deliberately, he made himself turn, testing his emotions as he saw the second frigate, leaning over on a converging tack, her guns already run out like black teeth.

He walked to the quarterdeck rail and saw the men stand back from their guns, one gun captain lifting a fresh ball in readiness for the next shot, and the one after that. Until it was over.

He said, 'They must not board us! We're done for if they overrun the ship!'

He drew the fine, curved hanger and held it over his head. 'On the uproll, lads! Make each shot tell!'

Somebody cheered, and a petty officer silenced him with a threat.

The gun captains stood behind their breeches now, each with his trigger-line pulled taut, their crews crouched and ready with handspikes to change the elevation or training.

'*Fire!*'

The deck reeled beneath his feet, and Adam realised that the enemy had fired at the same moment. There was smoke everywhere, and he heard men screaming as splinters as large as goose quills tore amongst them. He wiped his face with his wrist and saw the enemy's sails, pockmarked with holes, but each yard properly braced, still holding her on the same tack.

The smoke was gone and he saw the upended guns now, the patterns of bright blood where men had fallen, or been crushed beneath the heated barrels.

Deighton was suddenly beside him, and seemed to be shouting, although his voice was muffled, faint.

'Disengage, Captain! That is an order, *do you hear*?'

Adam stared past him at the oncoming ship; she seemed to fill the sea, and there were men in her shrouds, waiting to board, ready to mark down the most valuable targets. As if in a dream, he noticed that Deighton had removed his bright epaulettes. Marines were clambering up the ratlines, some with two muskets slung over their shoulders. Sergeant

Whittle's best marksmen. . . . He tried to think, to clear his mind.

'I will not strike our colours, sir! You gave me an order to fight.' He knew Dyer was waiting for the order. 'Fight I will!'

Deighton winced as more iron crashed into the lower hull. 'I'll see you in hell for this!'

Adam pushed past him. 'We shall meet there, *sir*!'

He reached up to his shoulder, thinking somebody had tried to take his attention. His epaulette was gone, the cloth shredded into rag where a musket ball had torn it away.

'*Fire!*'

Men were coughing and retching as the smoke billowed inboard through the open gun ports; the enemy's sails seemed to be towering right alongside, and yet the guns still fired, and were reloaded. The dead lay where they had fallen; there were not enough spare hands either to throw them outboard, or to carry the whimpering wounded below.

Adam saw the other ship's tapering jib boom and then her bowsprit passing over the larboard bow like a giant's lance. There were shots everywhere, a rain of iron hammering the deck, ripping into the torn hammocks where several marines had already fallen.

So they would not collide. The American was carrying too much canvas.

Wildly he swung round, and shouted, '*Carronade!*' Then, 'Let her fall off, Mr Ritchie!'

A master's mate ran to throw his weight on to the wheel. Ritchie was propped against the compass box, his eyes fixed and staring as if still watching his ship's performance, even in death.

Adam waved his sword, and someone on the splintered forecastle jerked the lanyard. The carronade, the smasher as it was known, recoiled on its slide, and where seamen had been massing, ready for a chance to board, there was only a blackened heap of remains, men and fragments of men, and one officer standing, apparently untouched, his sword dangling by his side, perhaps too shocked to move.

Dyer had rallied the gun crews and had brought more men from the disengaged side. *Valkyrie* shivered to another broadside, their own or the enemy's Adam did not know.

Somebody was yelling at him. 'The commodore's bin hit, sir! They've took 'im below!'

The other frigate, her hull pockmarked with holes and with great, livid scars in her timbers, was being carried past by the press of canvas. Shots still ripped across the broadening arrowhead of water between them, but the shooting was less controlled. He saw two men fall from the shrouds as the Royal Marines in the fighting tops kept up their fire. In his heart, he knew that the engagement was over, but his reason could not accept it. One enemy crippled, and unlikely to reach safety once the other ships in the squadron came upon her. And the other – he could see her name now, in bright gold lettering across her counter, *Defender* – was unwilling to continue.

He rubbed his ear; there was cheering too, which seemed very faint, although he knew it was here, in his own ship. The guns' roar had rendered him almost deaf. He saw men peering at him and grinning, teeth white in their smoke-blackened faces.

Dyer was here, shaking his arm. 'The lookout has sighted *Reaper*, sir! The enemy must have seen her, that's why they're standing away!' He looked stunned, unable to accept that he was alive when so many had fallen.

Reaper, of all ships. So right that it should be John Urquhart, coming to the aid of his old ship, where he had been treated so badly.

'Shorten sail, Mr Dyer.' He wanted to smile, to give them something they could cling to when the final bloody bill was reckoned. 'Report damage and casualties.' He tried again. 'You did well. *Very well*.' He turned away, and did not see Dyer's expression. Pride; gratitude; affection.

He said, 'I must see the commodore. Take charge here.' He saw the man called Jago, a bare cutlass wedged through his belt.

'A victory, sir.' It seemed to have drained him. 'Or as good as.'

Adam shaded his eyes to watch the enemy frigate. *Defender*. They might still meet again. Her flag was flying as proudly as before. Defiant . . . .

He seemed to recall what Jago had said, and stared around. 'My servant! Whitmarsh! Where is he?'

Jago said, 'He's below, sir. I took 'im meself, you bein' busy at the time.'

Adam faced him. 'Tell me.' It was almost as if he had known. But how could he?

Jago answered, 'Splinter. Didn't feel nothin'.'

'And you took him below?' He looked away, at the sea. So clean, he thought. So clean. . . . 'That was bravely done. I'll not forget.'

The orlop deck was crowded with wounded men, some fearful of what might happen, others lying quietly, beyond pain.

Minchin, his familiar apron covered with blood, peered at him as a man was dragged from his table and carried into the shadows.

He said thickly, 'The commodore's dead, sir.' He gestured to a covered shape by one massive timber and Adam saw the strange servant on his knees beside the corpse, rocking back and forth, moaning like a sick animal.

Minchin wiped some blood from his knife with a rag, and cut himself a slice of apple with it. 'Quite mad, that one!'

He chewed steadily as Adam turned down a blanket and looked at the dead boy's face. There was not a mark on him; he might have been asleep. Minchin knew that the iron splinter had hit him in the spine, and must have killed him outright. He had seen many terrible things in his butcher's work, men torn apart in the name of duty, who had believed even in extremity that a miracle could save them. At least the captain's servant had been spared that. But there was nothing he could say; there never was. And there were others waiting. He could barely taste the apple because of the rum, which helped him at times like these, but down here in this hellish, lightless place, it reminded him of somewhere. Someone . . . .

He gave a great sigh. Where was the point? And the captain had done what he could. *For all of us.*

It would not help him, or anyone else, to know that Commodore Deighton had been killed by a single musket ball, but not one fired by an American weapon. It had entered the body from high up, at a steep angle. He peered at a wounded marine who was drinking some rum. It could rest.

He gestured with his knife. '*Next!*'

Adam looked at the boy's face. How he must have relived *Anemone*'s death each time the drums had beaten to quarters.

We help each other. He covered his face again with the blanket. It was all that John Whitmarsh had ever wanted.

He climbed once more up to the smoky sunlight, and almost broke when he saw his lieutenants and warrant officers waiting to make their reports, and to ask for his instructions.

One figure blocked his way. It was Jago.

'*Yes?*' He could scarcely speak.

'I was thinkin', sir. That offer of yours, cox'n, weren't it?'

Adam faced him, but barely saw him. 'You'll take it?'

Like the other time he had seized a lifeline.

Jago nodded, and held out his hand. 'I'd want to shake on it, sir.'

They shook hands in silence, men pausing in their work and perhaps forgetting their fear, merely to watch. To share it.

That evening, as predicted by Ritchie, they met with the remainder of the squadron and headed for the Bermudas, for orders. In *Valkyrie*'s wake, the stitched canvas bundles drifted down and down into eternal darkness. One of them was the commodore.

And one was a boy who wore a fine dirk strapped to his side, for the last farewell.

10

A Ship of War

His Britannic Majesty's Ship *Frobisher* lay at her anchor, unmoving above the perfect twin of her reflection in the blazing sunlight. The ensign at her stern and the admiral's flag at the mainmast truck were equally motionless, and between decks, in spite of the awnings and windsails, the air was like an open kiln.

The crash of Malta's noonday gun echoed across the water like an intrusion, but only a few gulls rose from their torpor, squawking in protest before settling down again.

In the great cabin Sir Richard Bolitho, coatless, his ruffled shirt open almost to the waist, shaded his eyes to stare at the land, the craggy battlements where, occasionally, he could see a red coat moving slowly on patrol. He pitied the soldiers in their thick uniforms as they paced up and down in the heat.

Frobisher was a well-built ship, and the sounds which reached Bolitho's quarters were muffled and remote, as if they, too, were stifled by the heat. But in many ways he envied the life and movement from which he was separated, *protected*, as his secretary Yovell had once described it. Even here, right aft, he could catch the heady smell of rum, and imagine the ship's community of some six hundred seamen and Royal Marines preparing for their midday meal.

He sighed and sat at his table again, to the litter of signals and local correspondence awaiting collection. Since their arrival here in Grand Harbour, the ship had scarcely moved. Such inactivity was bad for any fighting ship, and for one with a company far from home, with no immediate prospect of discharge or action, the strain on discipline and routine was becoming evident.

He had received two letters from Catherine; they had arrived together in a courier brig from Plymouth. It was the shortest time they had ever been parted, and yet the uncertainty of the future and the strange, lingering sense of loss he felt seemed to make it worse.

She wrote of things she knew would please him, of the house and the estate. Of the garden, *her* garden, and the roses which gave her so much pleasure.

She touched on her feelings for him, but was careful not to trouble him with her own pain of separation.

There had been one ugly note; she had mentioned it in case he should hear it from someone else. There had been a riot in Bodmin, the county town, although he found it hard to imagine in that sort of community; a local regiment had been disbanded, and the men had mounted a protest to demand work after their service to their country.

If it had happened in Falmouth, Bolitho wondered what Lewis Roxby would have done. He might well have put some of the men to work on his own large estate, and encouraged other landowners to do the same. In Bodmin, a magistrate had read the Riot Act, and called out the dragoons from Truro.

She had told him that she was going to London to see the lawyers again. She would think of him. *Dearest of men . . . always.*

He heard Ozzard's sharp voice from the pantry, and then Allday's. They were bickering about something, as usual. Without them and their concern over his welfare, he sometimes thought that the inactivity would drive him mad.

There were receptions, for him and his officers, and for visiting ships, old enemies who were now classed as allies. That would take a long, long time to accept.

He had seen little otherwise of the island itself, and although he had been offered facilities ashore with as many servants as he might need, he had remained in his flagship. As if it were a last link with the only life he knew and understood.

Malta was full of history, and as one senior officer had described it, 'the stronghold of Christianity'. When the French had been forced to withdraw because of the naval blockade, the Maltese had requested British protection, and a restoration of their rights and privileges. The island, small though it was, had once again become a stronghold. Now, with Napoleon's surrender and his incarceration on Elba, it was assumed by some that Malta would be allowed to resume its own self-government, not so different from that of the old Knights of Malta.

That same senior officer had laughed outright when Bolitho had suggested it. He had exclaimed, 'Have you ever known the flag hauled down after a victory, Sir Richard? If a place is worth dying for, it's worth holding on to, in my opinion!'

He heard the marine sentry's heels click together, and then Ozzard hurrying to the outer screen door.

It was Captain Tyacke, his scarred face very deeply tanned above the whiteness of his shirt. He was so used to the heat and the sun of Africa that he scarcely noticed it.

'Officer-of-the-Guard has just brought a message, Sir Richard.' He glanced around the cabin, made still more spacious by the removal of the eighteen-pounder guns which would otherwise have occupied even an admiral's quarters. They had been replaced by short wooden replicas, quakers as they were termed, so that, outwardly at least, the ship would appear fully armed.

Bolitho slit open the envelope. It bore a military seal on the outer flap. Another visitor . . . .

He said, 'We shall have a major-general coming aboard during the dogs, James. His name is Valancy, although it does not give a reason for this honour.'

'I shall deal with it, sir.'

Bolitho looked at him, aware of the change in him; he had seen it develop during their passage into the Mediterranean, and these dragging weeks in harbour. Perhaps he had found the challenge of the new command stimulating; he had performed miracles with some of the inexperienced hands and the junior officers. But that was only a part of it.

We are so alike in many ways. He will share it with me, when he is ready.

Tyacke said, 'Perhaps we shall be told something, sir.'

'Soon, I trust.' He stood up and walked to the quarter gallery and watched a small boat being pulled across the harbour. A boy and an old man; they did not even glance up as *Frobisher*'s big shadow passed over them.

He said quietly, 'If it does not happen, James, I shall write a suitable report to their lordships.'

Tyacke watched him, the set of his shoulders, his hair still as black as the day they had first met. And later, when Bolitho had asked him to be his flag captain. Not ordered or demanded, as most flag officers would have done, as, indeed, they were entitled to do. He had asked. And had said, *because I need you*. No wonder they spoke of the legend, the charisma, but it was both and neither of them. It was the man himself.

Tyacke said, 'If we can get to sea . . . .'

Bolitho turned towards him. 'I know. Drive her if we must, fight if we have to, but *get to sea*!'

He saw Tyacke glance down at the wine cooler, made for him after the other had been lost in *Hyperion*. Even here, Catherine was very close. He saw the disfigured side of Tyacke's face in the reflected glare from the skylight. Like melted wax, the flesh burned from the bone, the eye, miraculously unblinded, as clear and blue as the other. Even that seemed different. . . . From the moment the ship had left Spithead Tyacke had gone about his duties, explaining his standards to his lieutenants and senior warrant officers without flinching beneath the scrutiny of strangers. Landsmen and some of the younger midshipmen still could not meet his gaze without dropping their eyes; Tyacke had endured this every hour and every day since he had been smashed down at the Nile. Was it possible that he had accepted it? Or was there some other, deeper reason?

He had spoken of his feelings concerning Malta to Tyacke. The reply had been blunt, uncompromising, like the man.

'We'd be fools to let it go, sir. It may be only seventeen miles by nine, a landsman might say the same as the Isle of Wight. But it stands *here*, and who commands it holds the key to the Mediterranean. Every trading nation knows that well enough!'

Bolitho said, 'Perhaps this commission will be shorter than we thought possible.' He touched his eye as the sunlight found its mark. The cruel reminder. *Which I cannot accept.* 'Will you still go back to Africa?'

Tyacke smiled faintly. 'I would have to think on it.' He seemed to consider it. 'Yes, I would have to give it a deal of thought.' He looked at the deckhead as a call twittered, and feet padded across the tinder-dry planking. 'I must see the first lieutenant, if you will excuse me, sir.'

Bolitho watched his hand hesitate on the door, and said, 'If there is anything you wish to talk about, James, I am here.'

Tyacke paused with his hat halfway to his head. Then he smiled fully, and seemed suddenly young again.

'If you were not, sir, then neither would I be.'

Allday entered as the door closed, and glanced at the two swords on their rack.

'Might be another courier vessel soon, Sir Richard.'

So he was fretting, too. Needing to be here, but thinking of his newfound life with Unis and his daughter.

Bolitho gestured toward the cupboard. 'Have a wet, old friend. We are both all aback, it seems.'

Allday stooped beside the cupboard, and said over his shoulder, 'Get this little lot over, an' maybe we can make sail for home.'

Bolitho rubbed his eye. He must have missed something.

Allday held up a glass of rum and grinned.

'To us, Sir Richard!'

'What have you heard?'

Allday looked at the high-backed chair in green leather, which she had given Bolitho. Like the wine cooler, and the locket he always wore when they were apart from one another. *A sailor's woman*. There was no higher compliment.

He said, 'I was talkin' to the men in the guardboat just now, Sir Richard. There's a yarn goin' around about an attack on some local merchantmen. Pirates, they says.'

He felt something like a chill against his damp spine. How they had first met, all those years ago. Barbary corsairs.

He said, 'The officer-of-the-guard left no such message.'

Allday put down the empty glass, careful not to leave any wet mark, which would cause more trouble with Ozzard.

'With respect, Sir Richard, the Royals are all well an' good, in their place.' He tapped his forehead. 'But their officers don't know it all.'

Bolitho smiled. 'Off with you. And don't fret over Unis. She is in good hands.'

Allday went out, unreassured, and found Ozzard in his pantry. He sniffed suspiciously, and said, 'Been at the grog again!'

Allday ignored it. 'Sir Richard's troubled. He worries about Cap'n Tyacke, an' about me, an' about everybody but himself!'

Ozzard regarded him scornfully. 'Captain Tyacke? Don't you *know*, for God's sake?'

Allday sighed inwardly. He could kill the stooping servant with one blow, and he sometimes wondered why they had remained friends. Of a sort.

Ozzard snapped, 'It's a woman, you blockhead! It's always a bloody woman when trouble's at the door!'

Allday left the pantry, touching the little man's shoulder as he passed. If he stayed, he knew he would make matters worse.

It was like sharing a terrible secret. It was not Captain Tyacke's pain Ozzard was describing. It was his own.

Major-General Sir Ralph Valancy stepped into the stern cabin and glanced around while Ozzard took his hat. Bolitho noticed that he showed no sign of discomfort and that his uniform was perfectly pressed, his boots like black glass, although if he had been dressed in rags one would have known him to be a professional soldier. He must keep his orderly very busy, to appear so untroubled by Malta's heat and the dust.

Valancy took a chair. 'I could never have been a sailor, Sir Richard. Too confined, even for an admiral!'

Bolitho waited while Ozzard fetched wine, and wondered why this man reminded him of someone. Then it came to him. Halifax, where he had met the young captain from the King's Regiment, who had been at the siege of York, and had given a miniature of herself back to the girl, Gilia St Clair, who would soon marry Valentine Keen.

That young captain would be very like this major-general, if he lived long enough.

Valancy sipped the wine and made a sound of approval.

Bolitho said, 'It's a mite warm, but cooling anything is not easy with the ship at anchor.'

Valancy's face broke into a grin. 'Any wine tastes good to me, sir! I've ridden, marched and damned well crawled over every kind of territory, and like my men, I've had most dislikes steamed out of me!' He became serious. 'You've heard about the missing transport vessel, the *Galicia*?'

Bolitho recalled Allday's scorn for the military in general, and the marines in particular.

'I have not had an official signal as yet.'

Valancy shrugged. 'I only heard myself this morning. The *Galicia* was under charter to the army, on passage for Malta. A fisherman reported seeing her attacked by a heavily-armed vessel. He made off before he became another victim.'

'Algerine pirates?'

Valancy nodded. 'Sailing too close to the Saracen coast, as they call it. The Dey of Algiers will have had a hand in it. The whole North African coast would be part of the Turkish empire if he and the Bey of Tunis could find enough ships.'

Bolitho thought of his time as a flag captain, when he had been involved with that same coast and the notorious port of Djafou to the west of Algiers. Slavery, cruelty and torture; he had seen even his most experienced seamen sickened by what they had found. Piracy was common in these waters, and when the fleet had been fully employed against the French and maintaining a blockade, some of those same pirates had even flouted all authority to prey as far north as the Channel and the Western Approaches.

If the Mediterranean was to become stable again, this menace to trade would have to be removed. If peace and mutual trust were not restored, Britain's new allies would soon look for other means of enforcement.

Bolitho said, 'I have six frigates, and a few smaller vessels.' He glanced at the nearest quaker. 'And my flagship. Not a great force, but I have worked with far less in the past.'

'Indeed, I know, Sir Richard. You won't remember me, but I was aide to the general at Good Hope when you came to our aid.' He gave a faint smile, remembering. 'I was with the Sixty-First then. It was a fine regiment.'

It was the smile, exactly like the captain who had fought at York. The professional soldier.

'I remember.' He recalled that other general. They would not give the Cape of Good Hope back to the Dutch, either.

The soldier said, 'Yes, we'd not long heard about Trafalgar. And Nelson's death. Such a shock, although inevitable, I suppose. I often wonder what happened to his mistress after his death. Shunned by everyone, I suppose.'

Then he looked directly at Bolitho. 'That was a stupid remark. I apologise, Sir Richard.'

Bolitho said, 'It is something I think on myself, Sir Ralph.' He stood up abruptly, thinking now of Catherine, how they had first met, the deadly chebecks closing in under sail and oars, ready to fire into any larger vessel's vulnerable stern. When Catherine's Spanish husband had died. *And we lost one another* . . . .

He said, 'I shall send the only frigate I have in harbour. *Frobisher* will remain here, as she must, until more men-of-war arrive.' He could already hear Tyacke's disagreement, and his doubt.

Valancy nodded slowly, surprised, perhaps, at this sudden decision, but careful not to show it.

'The frigate's captain.' He hesitated, as he might before leading a charge. 'Will he know the instability of these people? They have countless sailors and fishermen, thrown into their rotten jails, and for no other reason than that they are Christians! Barbarians!' He became very earnest. 'And the Dey of Algiers has some six hundred guns, according to our latest intelligence . . . .'

'May I ask you something? If this matter were to be entrusted to the army, who would you send?'

Surprisingly, Valancy laughed. 'A mission like this, which might fan the flames of another war? I'd go myself! Right or wrong, it would be my responsibility.'

Bolitho smiled, and tapped his glass with a paper-knife. 'Another glass, Sir Ralph?'

When Ozzard appeared to pour the wine, Bolitho said to him, 'Ask Allday to find Captain Tyacke, and have him lay aft.' He noticed that Ozzard did not lift his eyes, nor did he show any surprise.

As he left the cabin, Bolitho said quietly to Valancy, 'I thought you would say as much.' He sipped the wine, and added, 'I shall go in *Halcyon*.' He recalled her captain's face when he had described his fear and helplessness aboard *Majestic* at the Nile, when Tyacke had given him back his courage and his pride.

Frobisher, or a larger group of ships would invite disaster . . . .

Allday entered by the other door and paused, as if uncertain. That, in itself, was unusual.

Bolitho said, 'Well?'

'Cap'n Tyacke is with the purser, Sir Richard.' He refused to look at the major-general. 'I left a message, but I thought . . . .'

Bolitho sat again. 'It is why we are here. Why I was sent.' He smiled. 'My compliments to the captain, and *ask* him to come aft.'

Allday departed, and Valancy said, 'Remarkable fellow. Although I don't see that it is possible for anyone to know what you intend.'

Bolitho touched his eye. 'Remarkable, yes. Your general said as much at Good Hope. He also said that he could use a few thousand more like him.'

The soldier got to his feet. 'I shall detain you no longer, Sir Richard.'

Bolitho shook his hand. Tonight Valancy would probably regale his staff with tales of the strange ways of the navy, and how an admiral had taken the time to reassure a common seaman.

And yet, somehow, he knew he would not.

Tyacke entered the cabin as soon as the major-general had been seen safely into his boat.

Bolitho said, 'Have *Halcyon*'s captain repair on board, James. There is something I wish to discuss with you.' He saw the immediate signs of argument. 'It is a matter of some urgency.'

'You're leaving *Frobisher*? Your flagship?'

'Presently. While I am away, I would be pleased if the guns were replaced in my quarters.'

Tyacke left the cabin without asking another question; there was no need.

The sunshine and the brightly painted boats meant nothing to him. His was still a ship of war.

Lieutenant George Avery put down his pen and passed the finished letter across his small table. 'There. I hope it does justice to your thoughts.' He watched as Allday, who had been squatting on a chest in the hutch-like cabin, made his mark carefully and deliberately at the bottom of the page. Avery had asked him once what the distinctive symbol meant, and Allday had told him that it was like the stone Cornish cross that stood outside the church in Fallowfield where he and Unis had been married.

Allday cocked his head to listen to a bosun's call, very clear and shrill in the evening stillness. 'Won't be long now,' he said.

Avery glanced around the cabin. A hutch indeed, but private when he needed to withdraw from the ship's general life and routine.

'How do you feel about it?'

Allday looked at him thoughtfully. Once he would have shown instant caution, if not mistrust.

'I've been with Sir Richard long enough to take things as they comes, but this time, I ain't so sure. Them devils ain't to be trusted an' never were. We should wait until the rest of the squadron is joined here.'

Avery thought of *Halcyon*'s young captain. A good officer, as Tyacke had confirmed, but one twenty-eight-gun frigate against well-sited batteries and, no doubt, ships ready to repel any unwanted visitors, was hardly a bargaining point.

He said, 'At least your letter will be on its way.'

Allday stood up; he had heard somebody outside the door. Avery had not written or received any letters himself, but to mention it might be pushing things too far. It was a pity, he thought. Avery was better than most of his kind. He smiled. But he was still an officer.

'I'll be ready when they calls us, sir.'

Avery got to his feet as Kellett, the first lieutenant, stepped to one side while Allday departed.

'Come in!'

They both laughed as Kellett eased his way around the screen door; the cabin was a twin of his own.

'I won't detain you.' He sat on the same chest and glanced uncuriously at the pen and paper. Avery thought he probably knew about the letters he wrote for the admiral's coxswain, but he would never remark upon it.

He knew Kellett no better than when he had joined the ship at Plymouth. Tall, about twenty-five, and obviously respected by the more seasoned hands and warrant officers; Tyacke had implied that he had carried the ship for most of the time during *Frobisher*'s lengthy overhaul. He was loyal, too; he had never complained to Tyacke about how he had been left with most of the duties, as some would, if only to ingratiate themselves with the new lord and master.

152

Kellett said, 'I would that I were coming with you. Or that *Frobisher* were carrying the flag into Algerine waters.'

Avery waited. Kellett was not here to waste his time before they transferred to *Halcyon*. He wanted to talk.

Avery said, 'You've been in this ship for three years.'

Kellett looked at him, his mild eyes very steady. 'I was appointed as second lieutenant, but my immediate superior was transferred.' He shrugged. 'I thought, ah, my future is brighter already!' But there was no humour in his voice.

Avery prompted, 'The previous first lieutenant was promoted?'

'*Transferred*. To some miserable, rat-infested bomb-vessel. I did not like him much, but he deserved better for all that.'

Avery considered it. The first lieutenant was the Honourable Granville Kellett, and the son of an admiral. His future, war or no war, should be assured. Unless . . . .

'What was the captain like? I understand that he was removed because of illness, although the surgeon claims he had no part in it.'

Kellett's smile was genuine. 'I'm surprised you got anything out of that one. He wouldn't tell you he was taking off your leg, until afterwards!' He nodded his thanks as Avery poured two glasses of cognac. 'Captain Oliphant was rarely aboard during our time in the dockyard. He was ill, but he was receiving treatment ashore.' He paused. 'But not in Haslar Hospital, as you might expect.' He swallowed some of the cognac. 'I discovered that for myself.'

'Was it sudden?'

'I thought so at first. Now, looking back, I can see that he suffered some kind of discomfort . . . pain. It affected his moods, his temper. We received the news about *Frobisher*'s appointment as Sir Richard's flagship, and I thought he was delighted about it. He would have been the flag captain, and, as Lord Rhodes' cousin, his prospects seemed excellent.' He dropped his voice. 'But I can tell you now, I thank God that Captain Tyacke is in command. I have never seen such a change in a ship, the *life* he's put into her!'

Avery smiled. 'I was in awe of him when we first met. I am closer to him now. But he still frightens me more than I'd care to admit!'

Kellett put down his empty glass. 'That was welcome, sir.'

Avery got carefully to his feet. Strange to think of French officers sitting here as they had done, discussing the prospects of battle, promotion, or perhaps love.

Kellett seemed to come to a decision. 'Captain Oliphant was very fond of women. He would get into debt because of them, if it suited. My predecessor was "transferred" because he refused to help him. I suspect I was retained merely because of my illustrious father.' He forced a smile. 'I would deny every word in court, of course!'

Avery said gravely, 'Of course.'

They both laughed, and Kellett shook his hand. 'Be careful on this mission. I would not wish to lose a friend, one so newly gained.' Then he was gone.

Avery thought about it. Rhodes had been the one who had arranged for *Frobisher* to become Sir Richard's flagship. It would have been the making of Oliphant, no matter what the future held. He heard a boat being warped alongside. It was time.

But, related or not, Rhodes would never have suggested Oliphant for flag captain if there had been even the faintest hint of scandal, especially as he valued his own prospective appointment to First Lord.

Captain Oliphant was very fond of women. Kellett's words seemed to linger in the humid air.

It was not their concern. James Tyacke's decision to join them had changed everything, and from what Kellett had said, not only for Sir Richard's little crew.

He thought he could hear Tyacke's voice through the after screen, even before he reached the great cabin. The Royal Marine sentry remained expressionless, his eyes fixed on some point at the opposite end of the ship as he rapped his musket on the deck and shouted, 'Flag lieutenant, *sir*!'

Bolitho looked up from his table and smiled at him.

'I know, George. It is almost time.' If he were glad of the interruption, he gave no sign of it.

He turned to Tyacke and said, 'You have my written orders, James. You are captain-in-charge until our return, unless despatches to the contrary direct you. The ship is in good hands. None better.' He held out his own hand, and Avery knew that although Allday, too, was present, for Bolitho, the cabin was empty but for himself and his captain.

He said, 'Trust me. This is something that must be done. If I wait for a full show of force, it might be too late. You know that.'

Tyacke sounded very calm again, but he was not resigned. 'I worked too long with slavers. I know these scum, no matter what they call themselves. It matters to *me* that we finish our work here.' He hesitated. 'And go home.'

Ozzard had insisted on joining them aboard *Halcyon*, and when he had finished supervising the lowering of the admiral's bag into the boat, he snapped, 'He can't manage his own, can he?'

Allday was still thinking about Tyacke, his mention of home, something previously unknown.

He ventured cautiously, 'About Cap'n Tyacke, an' what you said, Tom. I thought . . . .'

Ozzard peered up at him, in the first shadows of evening. '*Thought?* Leave thinking to horses, they've got bigger heads!'

Allday watched him bustle away, and was troubled by it. Tyacke's talk of home remained uppermost in his mind. *For all of us.*

As sunset touched the ancient battlements like blood, Bolitho and his companions were pulled across to the frigate *Halcyon*. There was a promising breeze, and the capstan was already manned, the sails loosened in readiness to leave.

Within the hour, it was as if she had never been.

11

A Sailor's Woman

The staircase somewhere to the rear of the main Admiralty building was narrow and, Catherine guessed, rarely used. The banister was dusty; she could feel it under her glove, and when she reached the final curve of the stairs she looked down and saw cobwebs on the hem of her gown.

The few windows were sealed despite the heavy air, and the hint of a thunderstorm which hovered over London and the river.

She had once heard Richard mention going to the Admiralty *by way of the back stairs*. This must have been what he meant.

The elderly Admiralty clerk paused to look back at her. 'I am very sorry, m'lady. Sir Graham Bethune was unavoidably detained, and asked that you meet him here.'

Here was a small ante-room, with three chairs and little else. A place of assignations, perhaps.

'Thank you. I will wait.'

She could hear the clerk's heavy breathing, almost painful. He was not used to the back stairs, obviously.

Alone again, Catherine crossed to a window, but saw only the slope of another roof. It could be anywhere. She suppressed a shiver. It was like the view from a prison.

Perhaps she should not have come. But once in London she had kept herself busy, seeing the lawyers again, and sending a note by hand to Bethune. She sighed. And tonight, another reception, as Sillitoe's guest. She would be careful. But she needed his advice, and he would know it.

Then a few more days before returning to Cornwall, to the grey house. Waiting.

She thought about the reception that evening; how different it might have been. It was yet another party in honour of the Duke of Wellington's return to England. She had heard of one held at Burlington House to which nearly two thousand guests had been invited, many wearing grotesque costumes, and with behaviour to match. The wine had been consumed in such quantity that it was doubtful many of the guests would have remembered if the Iron Duke had been there or not.

She was tired, and hoped it did not show. Now, as on other such occasions, she always felt as if she were performing, for both of them, no matter what interpretation others might choose to put upon it.

The main door opened and closed in one swift movement, so that she had only a brief glimpse of dark blue carpet and gilt chairs beyond.

Bethune seized her hands and held them to his lips.

'A thousand apologies, Lady Somervell. I only arrived back from Paris two days ago, and when your note came I could not free myself!' He did not release her hands, and studied her with a warmth and affection which she knew was genuine.

She smiled. 'How was Paris?'

He glanced toward a chair and then flicked it with his handkerchief.

'Crowded. Full of uniforms.' He looked at her again. 'Foreign.'

She sat down and turned her ankle to look for the cobweb, but it was gone. She saw his eyes follow the movement, and could understand why he was so attractive to women.

'Did Lady Bethune accompany you?'

He looked away. 'She did. She is here, at the Admiralty, now.'

It explained the back stairs, the secrecy, if there was such a thing any more.

He sat on the chair opposite her, his knees bent and apart, more like the awkward midshipman he had been than a flag officer. It made him seem more human; a friend.

He said, 'I have had little success so far, Lady Somervell.'

She raised her hand. 'Catherine.'

He smiled. 'Catherine. Sir Richard's squadron is not yet assembled at Malta, but when it is, we may expect more news.'

'And if he is allowed to come home, where then? Where next? Are they so ungrateful that they forget what they already owe him? I had hoped to join him, if only briefly, at Malta.' She looked at him until he dropped his eyes. 'It was my promise to him.'

'I remember. The situation in Malta is complicated. More so because there is trouble with the Algerines.' He tried to lighten it. 'Yet again. It is a sensitive time, not least for Sir Richard.'

'If I joined him, at my own expense and not that of the Treasury, unlike so many, it might offend the proprieties . . . marriage and religion . . . is that it?'

'Perhaps. But I have not abandoned the idea. However, there is one excellent piece of news. The frigate *Valkyrie* is to be withdrawn from the Halifax squadron. Adam will find orders waiting for him to return to England. To Plymouth.'

She shook her head, and did not see his eyes move to her hair and neck. 'I do not understand.'

'At times like these, there will be more captains than ships. It is the way of things when the guns are quiet. For how long, who can say? But there is a new frigate building and almost completed at Plymouth. I spoke with the First Lord and have written to the port admiral.'

She still could not grasp that Keen was there, a vice-admiral now. She had been invited to the wedding, which was arranged for October. She heard herself say, almost in a whisper, 'A new command, a fresh beginning.' Sharing it, seeing his face when he received his orders.

She said, 'Thank you for that, Graham. I should have known.'

He shrugged, unsure of himself, she thought. 'Neither Adam nor Richard will tolerate favouritism. So I thought *I* should do something.'

'It will do much to help both of them.' She looked down as he put his hand on hers. 'I am grateful, Graham.'

He pressed her hand very gently. 'If only, Catherine.'

She withdrew it, and faced him. 'As it is, remember? Not as it might have been. There has been damage enough already.' She gave him a folded note. 'My Chelsea address, in case you have forgotten it. If you receive any news, anything at all. . . .' She did not go on.

She tugged off one glove, and held out her hand. 'This is less dusty.'

He kissed it, lingering over it, while she watched his bowed head in silence. What might he think or say if he knew what she felt at this moment? Did he not realise that she lived on dreams and memories, homecomings and the painful farewells always so close in pursuit?

A clock chimed somewhere in the building, in that other, safe and respectable society where men in power could break the rules but still manage to shield their mistresses and keep them separate from their pious wives. But the anger would not come.

Bethune had pulled out another handkerchief. 'Please. Use this. I – I am so sorry I have upset you, Catherine.'

She shook her head and felt a tear splash against her skin. 'It is not you. Don't you understand? I miss him so much . . . each day without him, I die a little more.' She turned away and groped for the door. She had a vague impression of a figure in uniform bowing stiffly outside the room, and Bethune's curt, almost angry, 'Wait for me inside! I'll not be long!'

She did not remember reaching the bottom of the narrow staircase with him, and yet she felt the urgency, the need for Bethune to go back, where some unemployed captain was waiting to plead for a ship. As Richard had once done.

And where his wife would be waiting to hear about *that woman*.

Bethune was holding the carriage door. 'Tonight then, dear Catherine. Fear not, you have many friends.'

She looked past him at the bustling carriages and carters, the sightseers, and the red coats of soldiers off duty.

'Here, perhaps.' She glanced up at the Admiralty's arched entrance and imposing, pillared façade. 'Elsewhere, I think not.'

She climbed into the carriage and leaned back against the sun-warmed leather. She did not look round, but somehow she knew that Bethune was still gazing after her.

Hampton House, on the Thames Embankment, had been chosen as the venue for this latest of many receptions to honour the Duke of Wellington, and, indirectly, his victorious army. Although it was the London residence of Lord Castlereagh, the foreign secretary, it seemed likely that he saw less of it than anyone. Of all the statesmen and government leaders involved in negotiations with the allied powers, he had probably been the most active. The Treaties of Chaumont, followed two months later by the First Peace of Paris, which Castlereagh had settled with Metternich almost unaided, seemed no less a victory than Wellington's.

Catherine rested her hand on a footman's sleeve as she stepped down from the carriage. The air was still and heavy, with dark, brooding clouds broken only occasionally by a glimpse of early stars. There was still thunder in the air, like something physical. Perhaps, as she had thought at the Admiralty, she should not have come. She sighed, and walked slowly along a dark strip of carpet. If there was a downpour, the carpet would take the brunt of it.

The house was spacious, but seemed anonymous, unmemorable, like so many others on similar occasions. Every window glittering, every chandelier alight, strains of music, and a tide of voices audible even from here.

And now the garden, with more candles and coloured lanterns, people standing about in groups, taking advantage of any light breeze from the river. Faces turned to watch her, probably wondering who she would be with. She lifted her chin. At least Sillitoe did not care. People feared him. Needed him.

If Richard were here, he would see it differently, as no less a part of duty than firing a salute. He would make her smile at the absurdity, and the importance of appearance. Like a code, or a secret signal . . . .

'Lady Somervell?'

It was a well-dressed young man, neither servant nor guest. He bowed. 'Sir Graham Bethune has asked me to escort you to his party, my lady.' He looked at her, and must have seen the unspoken question in her eyes. 'Lord Sillitoe is delayed.'

They returned to the house. People parted to allow them to pass, young women with daring gowns and bold glances, older women in gowns which neither flattered nor suited them. Uniforms of every kind, but not many sea officers; men who tried to catch her eye, then turned to their companions as if they had succeeded.

Toiling amongst them was an army of footmen, sweating in

160

their heavy coats and wigs, and yet able to pass a glass of wine or retrieve an empty one before it was broken or trampled into the carpet.

Bethune came striding to meet her. 'Welcome, Lady Somervell!'

They both smiled, remembering the informality of that dingy ante-room.

She curtsied. 'Sir Graham, how pleasant.'

She slipped her hand through his arm and saw the eyes following them. Surprised, perhaps disappointed that there was no new scandal.

Without turning his head, Bethune murmured, 'Lord Sillitoe is with the Prince Regent. He sent word that he will not be long.'

She glanced at him. 'He trusts you, Graham.'

'I am not certain that trust means the same thing to him.'

She turned, seeing Susanna Mildmay on the arm of a major of the Royal Irish Dragoons. If Avery's lover had seen her, she did not reveal it.

Perhaps Avery had been saved from something. But he would never believe it.

Bethune said, 'The orders for Adam have been sent.' Her fingers tightened on his arm. 'We shall always need dedicated captains. It would have been a waste, otherwise.'

And the other Adam no one knew. The little mermaid . . . .
No one knows.

There was a loud bang on the floor, and a footman announced yet another prominent participant in that campaign which had ended so dramatically at Toulouse, when Napoleon had abdicated.

She said, 'You are being watched. People will talk.'

Bethune shrugged. 'They will always do that, when there is beauty like yours to envy.'

She did not have to look at him; his sincerity was obvious. 'Did you find that captain a ship?'

She spoke to calm herself, more than anything else. She had seen the group by an open window, Bethune's wife, poised and unsmiling, staring at her.

Bethune said, 'I could do nothing for him, even if I had wanted to.' He glanced at her. 'Do not concern yourself with them, Catherine. They are friends of mine.'

161

Catherine offered her hand. 'Lady Bethune, this is an unexpected pleasure.'

Bethune's wife said, 'That is a lovely gown. It shows your skin to perfection.' She gazed at the diamond pendant between her breasts. 'Yes, to perfection.' She turned away. 'More wine, I think.'

The others seemed affable enough, older officers and their wives, men employed at the Admiralty, or those who had been there when Bethune had first made his mark.

Catherine flicked open her fan to cool her face. Very dull, she thought. If only Sillitoe would arrive. He, at least, was never dull.

Bethune's wife had returned. Close to, and in spite of the expensive gown and jewellery, she was almost plain, and Catherine found herself wondering, not for the first time, how they had met, what had drawn them to one another.

'Something amuses you, Lady Somervell?'

She said, 'One hears all the time that there is a shortage of senior officers, in the navy at least. And yet, when I look around me, all I see are generals, and not a few admirals! Is that not strange?'

'Do you have any children? By your marriage, I mean to say?'

Catherine controlled her anger. *Oh yes, I know exactly what you mean.* 'No. Perhaps it is a blessing.'

Bethune's wife nodded, her lips tight. 'It could seem so. But my husband and I believe that children are the foundation of any marriage. In the navy, it is sometimes all one can cling to.'

Catherine faced her. 'And love, madam, what part does that play?'

Surprisingly, the tight lips folded into a smile. 'I should have thought you could answer that question better than I.' She raised her hand. 'Why, my dear General Lindsay, how well you are looking! You are quite recovered, I hope?'

Catherine sensed, rather than saw, the footman approach with the tray of glasses. She took one, and said, 'Wait,' and drank the contents; it was hock, and almost cool, or so it seemed. She replaced the glass on the tray and took another.

'That was most welcome. Thank you very much.'

162

If the footman had been another Allday, he might almost have winked.

Instead, he murmured, 'It sometimes 'elps, m'lady!'

Bethune was hurrying toward her.

'Catherine, what has happened?' He looked over at his wife, who was speaking to a portly officer with as much animation as if he were her greatest friend.

She answered softly, 'I should have gone when I heard about Sillitoe.'

What was the matter with her? She had dealt with far worse, endured far worse, and triumphed. But not without pain. So why could she not hide it now, treat this with the contempt it deserved? An innocent remark, then? Never . . . .

'I shall speak with her.' He looked down at her hand on his wrist, perhaps remembering how she had removed her glove for him.

'Say nothing. You have too much to lose.' She gazed at him steadily. 'I can understand why Richard cares so much for you. Please, never change!'

There was more banging on the floor, and it was with some reluctance that the din of voices died down.

But it was not a footman this time.

Catherine thought she felt Bethune tense as Admiral Lord Rhodes climbed heavily to the top of a flight of marble stairs.

'Shortly we shall dine, ladies and gentlemen!' Someone gave a loud handclap, and several of the younger women shrieked with laughter.

Rhodes did not respond. 'Just a few words, if I may.'

One of Bethune's friends murmured, 'Oh, for God's sake.'

Rhodes stared around the room, his face shining in the flickering candlelight.

'I may be biased, some claim it is a fault, but I sometimes believe that upon these occasions, and this one in particular, we tend to offer all the laurels to our military friends.' He paused while Susanna Mildmay's major gave a cheer. 'And overlook the achievements of our own service, without which no soldier would put his foot on foreign soil, nor hope to keep it there!'

This time the cheering was genuine.

Catherine glanced at Bethune again. He was unsmiling, his face grim, like a stranger's.

Rhodes was saying '. . . and, as our naval heroes cannot all be here tonight, let us remember one of our most outstanding and gallant sailors, who serves us still!'

Catherine felt her heart leap as Rhodes added, 'Sir Richard Bolitho, Admiral of the Red.' He reached out, beckoning. 'So who better? A hero's lady!'

Bethune exclaimed, 'God damn the man!'

Catherine watched as Belinda Bolitho was guided up onto the stairs. Rhodes started to clap and then others followed, some barely aware of what was happening.

Then the applause died, but the noise of conversation did not resume.

'Catherine, I had no idea!' Bethune took her hand in his. 'Believe me!'

She looked over at Bethune's wife. So poised. Smiling now, unlike those around her.

She said, 'I shall leave. Make my excuses.' It was like a nightmare, when none of the words you needed were ever there, when all you wanted to do was run.

Bethune stared around, his face cold, beyond anger. 'Sillitoe will be here soon, I am certain of it!'

She touched his arm, and looked directly into the eyes of his wife.

'Some people have short memories. I do not.' She curtsied to the others, wanting to scream at them, to spit in their faces. 'They speak of honour, when they know it not.' She turned round, her gown hissing against a pillar.

Bethune said, 'I shall accompany you to your carriage.'

His wife called, 'Graham! We are to go into the great hall!'

Bethune regarded her with contempt. 'You used my name! I had all but forgotten!'

He guided Catherine to the stairway, his hand firmly on her arm.

'I shall take you to your house.'

She felt the damp heat of the night on her face and bared shoulders, and saw, shining blackly, the Thames.

'No.' She forced a smile. 'It seems I am still vulnerable.' She did not give her hand. 'But I have a strength which others can never begin to understand.'

People moved round her and she was aided into the carriage,

while another footman ensured that her gown was clear of the door.

Like this morning . . . how could it be the same day? Bethune stood watching her, his fists bunched against his sides, then, as the horses nudged forward, he turned abruptly and strode back into the house, with something like hatred in his face.

The carriage rattled across the cobbles and Catherine stared out of the window at the passing river. So many views, so many aspects. The house she had just left; Sillitoe's on that great sweep of the river; and her own at Chelsea.

Far across the other side of this same river she saw the first lightning. Like the opening shots of a sea fight, reflected as they were in the dark water.

She gripped her fan until the pain steadied her.

She said aloud, 'God keep you safe, dearest of men.'

Perhaps he would hear her.

Catherine closed the door and went directly to her room. She heard the carriage clattering away, the driver doubtless glad to be going into shelter before the storm began in earnest.

She lighted another stand of candles near the bed; the housekeeper would ordinarily have done it, but it was her night for visiting in Shoreditch with her married sister.

She listened to another pattern of thunder, closer now but not much. Perhaps it might pass over after all. She walked to the window and watched a livid flash of lightning. How quiet the house was; Mrs Tate would be returning at six in the morning to prepare breakfast. As usual.

She pushed one curtain aside as it hung loose across the window, and with her other hand tugged the combs from her hair and tried to calm herself. But all she could see were the stares, the bewilderment, and the hostility. It had always been there, but she had managed to accept, if not ignore it. Richard must never know. He would not rest until he had dealt with the culprits, high or low.

The window shivered as another roll of thunder broke the stillness, and in the lightning she saw the first drops on the glass. Perhaps the sound of rain would make her sleep.

The air quivered again, and she reached out to raise the loose curtain. She saw the river. There would be no boats moving out there tonight.

She glanced at her reflection in the dappled glass, and felt her heart throb with sudden pain. Her thoughts were gone, scattered in a second. It was real. *It was now*.

She turned very slowly, her back to the downpour and flashes of light. The man stood by the half-open door, his face in shadow, only his eyes alive in the flickering candlelight.

He must have entered the house earlier. Had been intent on robbery, perhaps knowing that she and the housekeeper were not expected to return.

She said, 'Damn you, what are you doing here?' From the corner of her eye, she could see the commode where she kept a small carriage pistol. There was a chance. If only . . . .

The man moved suddenly into the circle of candlelight.

'Do not even think of it. I unloaded it, in any case.' He gave a slight bow. 'A precaution, you understand?'

She watched him, one fist clenched, the nails biting into her skin.

He had a level, resonant voice . . . a man of some breeding and education. As he moved closer, she saw that his shirt and breeches were well tailored. He was without shoes. She lifted her chin slightly.

'What have you stolen?'

He pushed the loosened hair from his forehead, and sounded more angry than she might have expected.

'I'm no thief, damn your eyes! It's you I came to see, *my lady*!'

She took two steps away from the window. 'I can call for help . . . .'

He moved so swiftly and lightly that she barely saw it. He was not tall, but he was very strong, as if he were gaining more strength from this violent determination.

He swung her round and pinioned her arms, his voice insistent across her shoulder. 'If you scream, it will be your last!'

'Tell me who you are – what you want . . . .'

He was muttering to himself, and she could smell gin on his breath. She tried not to show alarm, anything which might provoke him further.

'I saw you looking for the curtain cord just now.' He laughed softly, and she felt the noose dragged around her wrists. She struggled to free herself, but he pulled it tighter. Expertly. She had seen Richard's men doing it.

'There now.' He swung her round to face him. 'I have heard it said that you are something of a spitfire, but I shall have to forgo that pleasure.'

She held his gaze, seeing his eyes move over her. It was not possible, but there was something familiar about him.

She said quietly, 'Have we met?'

He laughed.

'Hardly that, my lady. You were too occupied with your *admirer* Bethune.'

She watched him, trying to give nothing away. The captain who had been asking Bethune for a favour, or for a ship.

He was staring at the diamond pendant as if suddenly mesmerised by it: he took it between his finger and thumb and lifted it slightly into the candlelight.

She said, 'Please . . . don't take it. I'll give you money . . . .'

She did not see him move or raise his arm. The blow seemed to snap her head back with such force that she thought her jaw was broken. She was conscious only of falling, down and down, and yet she was not moving.

He gripped her shoulders and shook her, his face inches away from hers.

'Don't you speak like that to me, *you whore!*' He slapped her with his free hand, again and again, and then dragged her upright and flung her on to the bed.

Her head was reeling; there was no pain, only a numbness, a sense of complete helplessness. She felt the bed beneath her, and tasted blood where he had cut her lip. She tried again, a physical striving to hold on to her wits, her understanding. *I must not lose consciousness.*

She felt the mattress yield as he sat heavily near her. She could hear the painful breathing again, and when she opened her eyes she saw him crouched on the edge of the bed, his hands thrust into his groin, moving his head from side to side, speaking to himself.

He turned, and looked at her. 'I lost my ship because of a whore. Then I saw another chance taken away, because of an act of favour.' He gripped her shoulder, the fingers bruising her skin. 'For another Bolitho! Because of another bloody whore!'

167

She cringed, waiting for another blow.

She whispered, 'It's not true. They know nothing about it.'

He was not listening. 'I was to be his flag captain. I suppose you knew that too?'

She shook her head.

What was the matter with him? Was he ill or insane? Nothing made sense.

He lurched up, and she heard him moving about the room, as if driven by something beyond his control.

Then he came back and raised her head and shoulders and wedged a cushion beneath them.

She wanted to shake her head to clear her mind, but some warning sense made her remain quite still. Perhaps he would leave. It was unlikely, but someone might call, even at this hour. She glanced at the window, the rain sheeting down it. She had been standing there, holding the curtain, and he had been here. Watching, waiting.

His shadow fell over her, and she felt him holding the pendant again.

He said, 'They take everything. They lie and deceive. They ruin you.'

'Please leave now, before it's too late.'

He began to drag the gown from her shoulders, unhurriedly and deftly.

She tried to pull away and felt the cord around her wrists tearing at the skin. In a sudden silence, she heard a clasp fall to the floor, and the more insistent tearing of silk.

She said, *'Don't! Please don't!'*

But he rolled her on her side so that she could not see him, his fingers in her hair, twisting it, making her gasp aloud with pain. She felt him kneeling, pressing against her while he tore at her clothing. He was violently aroused; she felt the warm night air across her legs, his hands on her garters, her stockings, and then hard against her skin.

She knew she must hold on, even as she knew what was happening, and that it was hopeless.

She had never been afraid of any man, except her father, but this was different.

She could feel it like a sickness in her stomach, rising up as if to choke her. Not fear; it was sheer terror. It was rape.

168

His hands were everywhere, exploring her, then dragging her round to rid her of the last of her clothing.

She screamed, and felt her head jar back again to the force of the blow.

He was holding her, his fingers insistent, probing, final.

There was a great clap of thunder, a single crack which seemed inside the very room.

She attempted to open her eyes, to move her aching body, but nothing happened. Tiny pictures flashed through her brain, like fragments in a nightmare. The shadow rising over her, the pain, and the sense of choking. Perhaps he had killed her after raping her.

A voice said, 'I have her. Cut the cord, man!'

Another hand holding hers, rough but steady, the blade barely touching her skin as the cord was pulled away.

She groped, and tried to cover her nakedness, but there was a sheet over her body, and no hands explored her thighs, her hair. A damp cloth dabbed at her mouth and cheek; somewhere, miles away, booted feet thudded on the stairs.

She opened her eyes, and realised that his arm was round her naked shoulders, holding her, while he cleaned her torn mouth. Sillitoe did not allow himself to relax even when the life returned to her eyes, and she reached up to touch the cloth.

Over his shoulder, he said, 'Deal with it. You know what to do.'

She struggled, but he held her. A man used to women, she thought, who knew how to restrain them . . . .

He said quietly, 'I know a good doctor nearby.'

She put her hands under the sheet, shaking her head. 'He did not . . . I fought him, but I couldn't . . . .'

They must have used the same stealthy manner of entry. Taking advantage of the thunder, they had come straight to this room. Otherwise. . . . She retched, and he held her until the spasm passed.

She wanted to ask so much, to discover how he had known what had happened, but all she could say was, '*Why?*'

Sillitoe took a silver flask from his pocket and unscrewed it with his teeth.

'This will burn, but it will do you good. Don't touch any of the other bottles and glasses in here, in case he used them.'

169

She choked. It was cognac, but the shock of the raw spirit on her cut mouth had the desired effect.

He said, 'His name is Charles Oliphant, former captain of what is now Sir Richard's flagship, *Frobisher*.' The hooded eyes were expressionless. 'Are you certain there was no congress?'

'Yes. . . . But for you . . . .'

He said harshly, 'He is diseased, the last stages of syphilis. He is dying from it, God damn his rotten soul!'

She thought of the spasms of apparent pain, the wildness and desperation. He had wanted revenge, but against what? She had heard of men who had been so badly infected that they had gone insane before dying. Too late to spare those they had themselves defiled.

She did not realise she had spoken aloud. 'I would have killed myself if he had done that to me.'

Sillitoe held her, recalling those last tense seconds. The lightning holding her naked body like silver, her pinioned arms, the crouching figure forcing her legs apart, oblivious to everything else. A moment later? He pursed his lips. *I would have killed him.*

She was lying against him, in shock, exhaustion, disbelief. Like a very young girl, the self she had described to him when he had gone with her to Whitechapel, after her father had died.

As his men had kicked Oliphant to the floor he had held on to that picture. Her helplessness. And he had wanted her then.

'What will become of him?'

Sillitoe considered it, without anger, and without emotion. It was not his way.

'Lord Rhodes and his clique have gained too much power by rattling other people's skeletons in public. It will be interesting to see what happens when he has a live skeleton of his own in the closet.'

She could feel his breathing; the strength of the arm around her shoulders. She was safe, even with this man whom no one trusted.

Sillitoe heard his carriage returning. Did no one in this street ever question such nocturnal comings and goings?

He looked at her hair spilling across his arm.

The one woman he could never have. The only woman he would never give up.

12

Face to Face

Richard Bolitho awoke from the dream, and for a few lingering moments was confused by the sounds and movements around him. He lay on his back in the cot and stared up into the darkness and waited for the old familiarity to return. He had once believed that he could never forget the feel of a frigate.

Instinct and experience told him that *Halcyon* was changing tack yet again; the thud of bare feet on the damp planking, the crack of unruly canvas and the squeal of blocks spoke for themselves.

He propped himself on one elbow and swallowed hard. *Halcyon*'s officers had invited him to their wardroom for a last meal before landfall. That had been strange, too. After a big cut-down two-decker like *Indomitable*, and the other ships which had flown his flag in recent years, it had all seemed so small, so intimate: Captain Robert Christie, a guest in his own ship to conform with the time-honoured custom, Avery and himself. *Halcyon*'s three lieutenants, sailing master, surgeon and captain of marines had completed the gathering. And the wardroom itself had been packed tight. One midshipman had also been invited, the youngest in the ship; he had proposed the loyal toast, but otherwise remained awed and silent throughout the meal and lively conversation.

It was hard not to make comparisons. This mixture of youthful exuberance and excitement; the way it had once been for him, when he had taken command of his first frigate, *Phalarope*. He winced and rubbed his eyes. All of thirty years ago. How was that possible? The headache would go when he went on deck. Too much wine . . . the rare chance to relax and

171

speak with just a handful of officers who were typical of all those under his command. . . . He peered over the side of the cot and saw that the door into the main cabin was unfastened, swinging this way and that while the hands on deck brought *Halcyon* back under control and laid on a new tack.

There was an early greyness from the stern windows; in no time, it would be bright and hot once again.

Captain Christie knew his ship well. They had logged six hundred miles in less than four days, in spite of contrary winds one minute and the chance of lying becalmed the next. But that was the Mediterranean, no better place for a frigate captain to work his ship and her company until they became one.

He thought of Tyacke, recalling their last words together before he had transferred to *Halcyon*. Tyacke had been opposed to the idea of his visit to Algiers from the first mention of it.

Christie, on the other hand, had confined his comments to the matters of navigation and a final landfall. He, better than most, would be aware of the possible danger to his ship if their reception was hostile, and if injury or death befell his admiral his chances of further advancement would be ruined. A thinking man, and an intelligent one.

Avery had suggested that he might go ashore and make the first contact with the Dey or his advisers. Like Tyacke, he was not convinced that his admiral was fully apprised of the risks.

Bolitho sat upright. More sleep was out of the question. He felt the ship lean over, and imagined the sea boiling around her stem while her sails filled again to the wind.

He was not here to incite another war. But the Dey had to be made to understand that that was where it would end, if the outrages committed by Barbary corsairs and Algerine pirates were allowed and encouraged to continue. In spite of all the treaties and promises, slavery remained a fact. Six years after prohibition, the trade still flourished; according to his Admiralty instructions, between fifty and sixty thousand slaves were being transported each year. And here in the Mediterranean, the Dey of Algiers condoned the seizure of luckless sailors and fishermen, mostly Sicilians and Neapolitans, simply because they were Christians. It could not be tolerated.

He smiled as he heard someone moving about in the other cabin. Allday had known or guessed he was awake.

172

He would be fetching hot water from the galley, for the morning shave which had become so much a part of their rituals and relationship.

He climbed down from the hanging cot and remembered this time to duck his head; even here down aft, *Halcyon* was smaller than *Phalarope* had been. He glanced up at the skylight. It *was* lighter. He touched the locket around his neck and tried to imagine what she was doing. If she woke missing him as he missed her. Or did she . . . .

Allday's shoes creaked on the painted deck covering.

'Fine morning, Sir Richard.' He watched his pale shape in the gloom, waiting to test his mood, like an old Jack smelling the sea changes.

'We shall anchor during the forenoon.' He saw Allday unshutter a lantern for the shave. How many times, he wondered. How many dawns like this?

Allday saw the lantern throw its light across the cabin. The watch on deck would see it. *The admiral's up and about!* Trying to fathom out a reason, when he could stay in his comfortable cot while they were lashing up and stowing their hammocks to provide some room on the crowded messdecks. The watch below had their hammocks slung so close together they were usually touching. You could hear what a man was thinking.

He grinned. They only knew the admiral. They would never know the man.

Bolitho lay back in the chair. 'What are your thoughts today, old friend?'

Allday worked busily on the blade. 'I think it's a risk. Maybe I don't believe it's worth it. Let somebody else take the weight, or get a bloody nose for a change.'

'Is that what you really think?'

No wonder the imposing major-general had not understood. How could he?

'It's what most of the Jacks will be thinking, an' that's no error!'

Bolitho heard the familiar, uneven step directly overhead. Avery was up and dressed already. There would be another argument from him. But so much better than making them seal it up and say nothing. Like the fragment of news Avery had gleaned about *Frobisher*'s previous captain, Oliphant. A man who gambled heavily and usually lost most of it; a womaniser who hardly came up to the high moral standards of his influential cousin, Rhodes. Perhaps the future First Lord had hoped and intended that Oliphant's future might be assured as flag captain? It was like a puzzle where the clues refused to fit, but sooner or later he would hear about it. Some might already be making comparisons with Hugh, his own dead brother, a gambler who had cost their father so dearly in debts and in grief.

He thought, inevitably, of Adam; but he could find small trace of Hugh in him, apart from his quickness with a sword or pistol. And what some called his recklessness. *What they said of me.*

The deck tilted, and the lantern swung giddily until the rudder took command again.

Allday stood with the razor upraised. He had seen the shaft of light pass over Bolitho's injured eye and his attempt to shield it. Like the time when Bryan Ferguson had caught him trying to lift a cask full of ale, and the agony of his old wound had knocked him witless.

Always the pain . . . .

'Done, Sir Richard.' He watched him get to his feet, his body adjusting to the deck and the lively movement. How it had always been, and they were still together. Instead of comfort, it brought him a momentary sadness.

Bolitho faced him, vaguely silhouetted now against the grey light.

'I *know*, old friend. I want that, too.'

Allday watched him return to the sleeping compartment, and then shook his head.

He could not ask Lieutenant Avery to write about that, either. He would save it and tell Unis himself. When it was all over.

'South-east by east, sir! Steady as she goes!'

Bolitho remained on the larboard side of the quarterdeck, watching the land spread away on either bow, almost colourless in a shimmering haze. The wind had dropped and had backed slightly to the north-west, and it had taken them longer to reach their destination than Christie and his sailing master had predicted.

Bolitho tried to ignore the heat across his shoulders, the stabbing reflections from the sea. A grim, inhospitable place, he thought, with deep water close inshore, so that any strange vessel would have to anchor within easy range of the guns of which Major-General Valancy had spoken.

He took a glass from the midshipman of the watch and levelled it with great care on the nearest land. Rough and broken; he could imagine the dust between his teeth, the heat rising from the ground itself.

The ship had probably been under observation since daylight: a man-of-war, unexpected, and more to the point, unaccompanied. It was a risk, but curiosity might overcome the use of direct action.

He touched the locket beneath his damp shirt. If not . . . .

He looked at the men working on deck, some pausing to peer at the land, then at the officers on the quarterdeck as if to gauge their chances. He recalled Allday's words. *What most of the Jacks will be thinking.* He was rarely wrong.

He returned the telescope to the midshipman and caught him staring at him. It would be something worthy of a letter home.

Christie joined him by the rail, his hat tugged down over his eyes to protect them from the blinding glare.

'When we reach the outer anchorage, Sir Richard, what then?'

Bolitho replied, 'We shall fire a salute to the citadel, if we can see it. Then you may anchor.'

Christie nodded doubtfully. 'The wind troubles me, sir. If it veers we shall be on a lee shore.' Unexpectedly, he chuckled. 'It might make a speedy departure difficult!'

Bolitho smiled at him, and did not see a master's mate nudge his companion by the wheel.

'The next move will be theirs.'

Christie touched his hat and moved away. 'Have the gunner lay aft.'

Another madness, some would think. To fire a salute to a lot of murdering heathen.

Avery said, 'Your flag, sir.' He glanced meaningly at the mainmast truck. 'Is it wise?'

'They must see us for what we are, George. If they fire on my flag without provocation, they will know the consequences.

I am relying,' he smiled again and touched his arm, '*depending on their curiosity!*'

He thought of Djafou, the harshness of the land, the cruelty of their enemy. Napoleon was beaten; if the allies did not stand together now, there would be another conflict. It could begin here.

The maintopsail filled and boomed and the hull tilted over very slightly. Men scampered to braces and halliards, cupping the wind while it held.

Avery said, 'Perhaps the major-general was misinformed about the guns, sir. Over six hundred, did he say?'

Bolitho turned to the midshipman. 'Give my flag lieutenant your glass.' To Avery he said, 'You will see it was no exaggeration.' He watched Avery's profile as he trained the big signals telescope; the haze had cleared a little, and he would be able to recognise the telltale stone walls of old fortifications, and newer ones along the high ground.

It would take an army to prepare such defences. *An army of slaves.*

Avery said, 'A lot of shipping, sir. One of them must be the vessel they seized, *Galicia.*'

Bolitho turned away. Avery missed nothing, but rarely seemed to write anything down. It was a great pity about the fair Susanna, like his uncle's offer of security and a prosperous future. He had given up both. *For me. For us.*

Ozzard appeared on the gangway and, after a quick, incurious glance at the land, threw something over the side. He was giving up nothing. This was all he had.

Bolitho saw *Halcyon*'s gunner speaking to his selected gun captains. One of them glanced aft, and his expression was as clear as if a voice had shouted it.

A proper salute? For them bastards!

But whoever was watching their slow approach would be waiting for it, the one gesture of peaceful intent when *Halcyon*'s guns would be empty. When she would be at the mercy of those hidden batteries.

'Hand me the glass.' He was surprised by a sudden edge in his voice. 'Mr Simpson, is it not?' He saw the midshipman's alarm give way to astonishment that he should know his name. 'I shall require your shoulder also!'

It was the worst part. Tricks born out of experience.

Deceit. . . . If he was wrong, this youth could be dead within the hour, and yet he was grinning at one of his companions, the midshipman who had called the loyal toast in the wardroom.

He eased the draw of the glass very slowly and saw the outline of the citadel harden into something solid, like a mist clearing away. As marked and described on the chart, and the information on the chart was about all they knew of this place.

And there it was. A tiny patch of scarlet floating above it as if detached. The flag. He measured the distance with his eye. Half an hour, perhaps less if this breeze continued to favour them.

Christie was there again. 'The salute, Sir Richard?'

Bolitho kept his eye on the land. 'Seventeen guns, if you please.'

Christie said nothing. He did not need to. Seventeen guns: an admiral's salute. He would probably be wishing it was a full broadside instead.

Avery watched him, and thought of Catherine; she must have seen him like this when they had been together in the open boat after shipwreck. Jenour had been his flag lieutenant then, and afterwards, Bolitho had given him a command of his own, when all Jenour had really wanted was to remain with his admiral.

Am I so like poor Jenour? I watch his moods, I share his excitement, and often his pain in the aftermath of victory. And now, we are sailing towards an unknown force, a power of evil. He half-smiled. How his father, the clergyman, would have described it.

And yet I feel no fear, nor would I be anywhere else.

He saw Allday standing by the companion way, his arms folded while he looked along the deck, recognising each move, understanding every sheet and halliard, the *bones* of a ship as he had once described them. Briefly their eyes met, and Allday gave a slight nod. Like that very first time, when Avery had known that he was accepted by others of Bolitho's 'little crew'.

He saw Bolitho return the big telescope and say something to the midshipman. He wondered what it had been. Words which had suddenly made the lively midshipman become so serious. So proud.

Bolitho turned and looked at him, his hand touching the hilt of the old sword.

'Soon now, George.'

Someone yelped with alarm as a single shot crashed out from the land, the sound lingering long afterwards. Every glass was raised, but nobody moved, as if the whole ship were under a spell.

Then there was a yell. 'They'm dippin' their flag, sir!'

Bolitho gripped the old sword and stared at the land. His eye was painful, and he could not see the distant citadel. But in his mind it was very clear, like an image in a telescope.

Dipping their flag, not to him, but to His Majesty King George the Third. Perhaps they did not know that His Majesty was shut away, insane. Maybe it no longer counted for anything. He wanted to dab his eye, but knew Avery would see and become anxious.

He said, 'Begin the salute, if you please.'

Halcyon's gunner took charge himself, striding to each crew in turn. As the first shot banged out and the gun recoiled inboard on its tackles, he was already moving on to the next, repeating the couplet slowly and deliberately to time each shot.

If I wasn't a gunner I wouldn't be here. 'Number two gun, *fire!*'

Between shots, Bolitho said, 'Now is the time for eyes and ears, George.' To Christie he called, 'There is a guard boat yonder, Captain! Anchor when it suits you.'

Then he looked at the men who were running to their stations for shortening sail, and murmured, 'Well done.'

Allday heard and understood that, too. He was speaking to the ship.

Captain Christie lowered his telescope and said, 'They're sending a boat, sir.'

Bolitho walked across the quarterdeck, feeling the impact of the heat as *Halcyon* swung listlessly to her anchor. Close inshore now, he could see the old fortifications. You could lose an army trying to work around the town from inland, and a fleet would fare little better against the many guns facing the bay.

Allday was watching the approaching boat with obvious

suspicion. It was double-banked, with two men to every oar, more like a galley than a longboat.

'Man the side!'

Avery murmured, 'It is not difficult to imagine what the marines are thinking about, sir.'

Christie said, 'There's an officer of some kind, sir.' He took another quick glance with his telescope and exclaimed, 'A white man, by God!'

Bolitho watched the oncoming galley, graceful, yet somehow sinister.

He said, 'If things go wrong, Captain Christie, you will cut your cable and put to sea. Fight your way out if you must, *but do it!*' He saw the immediate opposition in Christie's face. 'That is an order. You must get word to Malta.'

He moved nearer to the side and saw the oars backing smartly, holding the galley and then turning it towards the frigate's side. No barge crew could do it better.

The boatswain's mates moistened their calls on their tongues and glanced expectantly at the entry port.

'*Pipe!*'

The squeal of calls died away just as suddenly, and Bolitho stepped forward to meet their visitor.

A white man certainly, perhaps with a mixture of other blood. His uniform was remarkably plain, its only decoration being a pair of tarnished epaulettes.

He doffed his cocked hat and gave a slight bow to the assembled officers.

'Your visit is without invitation, but nevertheless I am commanded to offer you welcome.'

He spoke flawless English, with an inflection Bolitho had heard before.

He said, 'I am . . . .'

The man bowed again, and smiled faintly. 'I know of you, sir. *Bo-lye-tho*, His Majesty's admiral of fame and reputation.'

'And whom have I the honour of addressing, sir?'

'I am Captain Martinez, adviser,' again the small smile, 'and friend to Mehmet Pasha, the Governor and Commander-in-Chief in Algiers.'

'Would you care to come to my quarters, Captain Martinez?'

Martinez held up his hat to shade his eyes from the sun.

His hair was sleek, and as dark as Bolitho's own, his skin tanned to the colour of leather; there were deep crows' feet around the eyes. He could have been any age from forty to sixty.

He glanced at the guns, their crews standing by with sponges and worms to clean out the barrels after the salute.

'That will not be possible. I have orders to escort you to the citadel myself.' He made an elegant gesture. 'You will find the craft quite comfortable.' His dark eyes flitted around the upper deck. 'An improvement, I would think?'

Captain Christie said sharply, 'I must *protest*, Sir Richard. Once you were in the citadel, we would be powerless to assist you!'

Bolitho shook his head. 'I am ready, Captain Martinez. My aide will accompany me.'

Martinez frowned as Allday joined Avery by the entry port. 'And who is this?'

Bolitho said simply, 'He is always with me. I trust that will suffice?'

'Yes.'

Bolitho touched his hat to the side party: Christie and his lieutenants, so many faces staring at him, anxious and without understanding. Men he did not even know.

Martinez ushered them to the stern of the galley. It was ornate, with gilded carvings, and long shades to provide privacy for the passengers.

Bolitho heard him giving orders to the boat's crew: a different voice again, fluent and without hesitation.

Avery whispered, 'Martinez is no Turk, sir. Spanish, more likely.' He frowned. 'But there's something else . . . .'

Bolitho nodded. 'It is my belief that he learned his English in America, a long time ago.'

Avery looked relieved. 'I agree, sir.'

Allday loosened the cutlass at his side. 'I'd not trust one of 'em!'

Bolitho raised one of the blinds and was surprised to see *Halcyon* lying half a cable away, so fast were the oars rising and dipping.

He recalled Christie's concern, and hoped he would remember to keep his men working as normally as possible. A thousand pairs of eyes were probably watching the ship at this very moment. The first sign of preparation for action would destroy everything. He touched the locket again.

It was suddenly cool and almost dark, and he realised that the galley had entered something like a cave, a seaward entrance to the citadel here, where there were no tides. It made the place almost impregnable.

They were alongside a stone-flagged jetty, and he saw more uniforms, soldiers this time, observing them in silence, fingering their weapons as if unsure.

Most of the muskets were French, but there were a few British ones among them. Demand probably outpaced supply, hence the seizure of the chartered *Galicia*, which had been carrying powder and shot, and perhaps an unlawful cargo of weapons. It was common enough; army quartermasters were like pursers, not averse to some private profit if it was offered without risk to themselves.

He considered Martinez, his role here, and where he had originated. A survivor of the American Revolution, perhaps? Or a mercenary who had changed sides once too often.

He was striding ahead of them now, full of energy and purpose. Bolitho found he could almost smile. A man you would not turn your back on.

He heard Allday breathing heavily on the steps; Martinez probably reminded him of the day when a Spanish sword had cut him down. He was paying for it now.

'Easy, old friend. We can rest a while . . . .'

Allday turned towards him, his brow furrowed with pain.

'I'll keep with you, Cap. . . .' He shook himself, angry because he had almost called him *Cap'n*, as in those other, reckless days.

Doors opened to receive them and Bolitho saw rich rugs hanging from the walls. There was incense too, and the smell of sandalwood.

Martinez paused and held up his hands. 'We must proceed alone, Admiral Bolitho.' He glanced disdainfully at Allday. 'He can rest here.' He moved his dark eyes to Avery. 'There will be refreshment. Companionship, if you wish.' He smiled again. 'It is permitted.'

Bolitho snapped, 'Women? But I thought the Dey was opposed to such behaviour.'

The glance was almost pitying. '*Captives*, Admiral Bolitho.'

Bolitho's eyes moved quickly to an open, unguarded window. Avery did not even blink. He understood.

Instead he said, 'We shall be here, Sir Richard.'

Bolitho said, 'I never doubted it.'

More doors closed behind him and he saw Mehmet Pasha seated at the opposite end of the room. Another surprise; he had expected him to be rotund and soft, someone used to the spoils and rewards of his rank.

But the man he saw was neat and slight, with bright, intelligent eyes and a cruel mouth. The face of a warrior, or a tyrant.

Martinez said, 'Mehmet Pasha speaks no English.' It seemed to amuse him. 'So you will have to trust me.'

Bolitho gave a stiff bow, and said, 'I am here to represent His Britannic Majesty, Excellency. On behalf of our two nations, and the peace we presently enjoy.'

He half-listened to Martinez's guttural translation and was reassured by it. Mehmet Pasha was not listening. He had understood every word he had said.

Bolitho continued, 'The vessel *Galicia* and her cargo were seized by one of your ships. I ask that you release *Galicia*'s master, so that I may arrange a solution.' He looked at the other man calmly. 'And the release of her company.'

Martinez touched his arm and beckoned him to a window. 'Some of them are there, Admiral. They resisted, they were punished.' He watched him curiously. 'Perhaps you would have done the same?'

The corpses lay where they had been thrown, like so much rubbish. As a warning to others, or with total indifference. The pools of dried blood were still apparent by the rotting remains. They had suffered terribly before they had died.

Martinez returned to his position facing his master.

Bolitho had seen more than the decaying corpses; he had caught sight of some of the guns pointing out across the bay. Perhaps Martinez had intended him to see them. Like a threat.

Mehmet Pasha was speaking, his tone unhurried, and without any sort of emotion. Martinez explained, 'The vessel was carrying an unlawful cargo. It was using waters governed only by the Dey, that also was *unlawful*. You are received here as a guest.' His eyes moved between them. 'But you

182

have no authority, no power in these waters. He has spoken.'

'I shall send his words to His Majesty, Captain Martinez. Of his response, I am not privileged to speak.'

Martinez looked less confident, and said quickly, 'Mehmet Pasha commands here, Admiral Bolitho!'

Bolitho watched the other man. Outwardly calm, even contemptuous, but something, an instinct perhaps, gave another impression. He was waiting to hear Bolitho's answer, and not through his 'interpreter'.

'Please tell him,' he pointed suddenly to the window, the blinding edge of the horizon, 'that I command *out there*!'

In the sudden silence he could hear the echo of his own words, a sentence of death if Mehmet Pasha recognised his bluff.

The other man rose slowly from his chair, his face thoughtful. At any moment he would call for the guards. He would have proved nothing.

Martinez said huskily, 'There will be some refreshment, Admiral, for you and your . . . friends.' He bowed as the slight figure walked unhurriedly to another door. Then he murmured, 'You may take the *Galicia* when you depart from here, but her cargo remains.' He glanced at the closed doors. 'You are a very fortunate man, permit me to say!'

Bolitho saw Avery being ushered into the room, the astonishment and relief in his tawny eyes.

'For a moment, Sir Richard . . . .'

Bolitho forced a smile. 'For a *moment*, George. But it was not to be.'

Martinez persisted, 'Your little ship would stand no chance, but you knew that?'

Bolitho shrugged. 'There would be other ships, as many as might be needed, as well you know. The rightful release of *Galicia* is not an understanding, but it may be the beginning of one.'

Martinez said, 'One of my officers will attend your return to the ship, Admiral Bolitho.'

Bolitho understood. He needed to know what his master's reactions truly were, and Bolitho could accept that he had a kind of courage to serve here, for whatever reason. He thought of the rotting remains by the wall. Martinez would need no warning to remind himself of the constant danger he was in.

Avery fell into step beside him, eager to leave, and perhaps unable to accept that they would be allowed to do so.

'I did as you bid me.' He revealed the end of a small telescope inside his coat. 'A good view of the main anchorage from up there.' He glanced round at Bolitho and said, 'There are two frigates at anchor. Fifth-rates, I'd say, no flags but well guarded. Did you *know*, sir?'

'I'm not certain, George.' He shaded his eyes to watch the same galley gliding towards the jetty. Mehmet Pasha wanted them away from here quickly, hence the release of *Galicia*. But two frigates? From where, and to what purpose?

He thought of the erect figure in the ornate chair. The bluff had not been one-sided after all.

Avery saw the galley come to rest, and a bearded officer in a flowing robe stepped ashore to receive them. He could scarcely conceal his relief.

'And we could have stayed a while longer for "refreshment"!'

Allday glared, and just as suddenly grinned at him.

'A ship's biscuit full o' weevils would do me after this damnable place, an' that's no error!'

Bolitho climbed down into the galley and waited for the bright sunshine to greet them again. With luck, they might be clear of Algiers by dusk. Christie would need no encouragement after this.

He touched the locket, and knew Avery was watching him. Later, he might admit it to himself. It had been a very close thing. How close, only Martinez had known at the time.

'*Boat ahoy?*' Sunlight flashed on fixed bayonets along *Halcyon*'s gangway.

Allday cupped his hands. '*Flag!*'

Bolitho stared at the land, and then up at the frigate's side and rigging.

He was back. He smiled at a memory. Lady Luck had been with him.

13

So Private and So Strong

Captain James Tyacke sat in Bolitho's high-backed chair and watched as his admiral strode from the adjoining cabin, Ozzard trotting behind him trying to adjust the clean shirt, without success.

Tyacke felt vaguely uneasy, uncomfortable seated while Bolitho stood. He paced the cabin, describing what he had discovered at Algiers, pausing from time to time to make sure that his round-shouldered secretary was keeping pace, and that he was not thinking and speaking too quickly for the pen.

It was more than that; Tyacke had felt it within an hour of *Halcyon*'s return to the Grand Harbour. An almost boyish eagerness to put his thoughts into motion, to be doing something again. But Tyacke knew him well enough now to see beyond it. There was a brittleness, a need, perhaps, to convince himself as well as those in the far-off Admiralty.

Bolitho's return had been something else Tyacke would remember: order and discipline momentarily forgotten as *Frobisher*'s hands had swarmed into the shrouds and rigging to cheer *Halcyon*'s boat, as it pulled alongside and hooked on to the chains with a flourish.

Tyacke had seen the effect for himself on Bolitho's features when he had climbed aboard, the wild cheering, from men he scarcely knew, echoed by those from *Halcyon* and the other ships which had joined the squadron during the admiral's absence.

Tyacke shifted in the chair. He had shared it, and his anxiety and relief had been forgotten in that very personal moment.

'The Dey knows he has a strong position, James. All those

guns – it would take a fleet, and even then the cost might outweigh the gains.' He paused, and waited for Ozzard to tug his neckcloth into place. 'And had I requested permission to anchor beforehand it would have been refused, or ignored like those of my predecessors.'

Tyacke nodded. It was pointless to remind him of the risk, and the possible consequences. Bolitho might have spoken the words himself. *That was then. This is now.*

Instead he said, 'The two frigates are another matter. If they are to fly the Dey's colours we might take precautions, but if they are corsairs,' he frowned, '*pirates*, it would put a great strain upon our ships.' He glanced at an open gunport. 'We now have seven frigates, including *Halcyon*, under your flag. There are brigs and schooners too, but no match for fifth-rates.' He looked over at the flag lieutenant, who was leaning comfortably across the stern bench. 'If you are sure of it?'

Avery said, 'I am certain, sir.'

Tyacke touched his disfigured face. 'It is said that Spain intended to dispose of some of her men-of-war. It is possible. But this Captain Martinez . . . I know nothing of him, as a slaver or in any other role.'

Bolitho walked to the sloping stern windows. The sun was high overhead, the buildings along the shore sandy yellow in a dusty glare. The weather would change soon, and it would take weeks more for a decision to be made. He felt the old restlessness churning within him. *Everything took so long . . . .*

He turned his back on the others to study a passing dhow, but his mind was still upon the letter which had arrived with the courier brig. *Time.* Catherine would be thinking of it also. The ever-present barrier. But it was not even that; it was the tone of her letter, different in some way. Or was it his own fatigue after the fast passage from Algiers? He knew it was not.

Tyacke said, 'The frigates are there for a reason. At anchor they are useless, no threat to anybody.' He was thinking aloud. Did he suspect something? *That I am being torn apart?*

Suppose Catherine had given up the fight. She was beautiful; she was rich in her own right. She did not need to endure the separations and the anxieties being thrust upon her. Someone else, then? He thought of her last words in that letter.

Whatever you do, wherever you are, remember that I love you and only you, nothing could change that.

He would read it again, slowly, when he was alone. But first . . . .

He said, 'Something from your anti-slavery days, James? Make *them* come out to us?'

Tyacke smiled, but not with his eyes. '*Frobisher*, sir.' He glanced around the cabin, less spacious with the eighteen-pounders returned to their ports. 'They will know she is your flagship. After your visit they might be expecting more to join us. They will not want to risk losing the two frigates.' He shrugged. 'And if their presence is proved innocent, we have lost nothing.'

Bolitho walked away from the windows and the glare, pausing to rest one hand on Tyacke's shoulder. 'Another bluff!'

Tyacke glanced at the hand on his shoulder, strong and tanned, an extension to this man's brain and experience. He was not easily moved, and was careful not to show it now.

'It might succeed.' He looked at Avery. 'At least it will get this ship's company working again!'

They laughed, the tension gone.

Bolitho thought of the big room overlooking the battery, and the scattered remnants of the corpses. *I command out there!* He said, 'There are a few of the *Galicia*'s original company, who were allowed to leave with our prize crew. Captain Christie had them separated. Perhaps they could be questioned, now that their safety is assured.' He recalled Christie's own description, the terror, the disbelief and hysteria amongst the few sailors who had been spared the brutality and eventual death meted out to *Galicia*'s master, and others who had 'resisted'.

Avery glanced at the others, sensing the bond, the quiet understanding. He had seen Bolitho take the letter from the despatch bag, and the expression in the grey eyes as he had read through it. It must be like a hand reaching out, a security which few could understand. He thought of Susanna. Still no letter, but then, he had not hoped for one. He gave a rueful smile. Even that was a lie.

Bolitho said, 'I shall send orders to the squadron, so that each captain is left in no doubt of the kind of enemy we are facing.'

Tyacke watched him. *So that you will carry the blame if we are proved wrong.*

He was glad about Christie. *Majestic* had done precious little for anyone else.

The sentry bawled, 'First lieutenant, *sir!*'

Bolitho looked at his secretary. 'You are frowning.'

Yovell smiled gently, behind his small, gold-rimmed spectacles.

'I was asking myself, Sir Richard, why do the marines always shout so loudly?'

Lieutenant Kellett stood in the doorway, his hat beneath his arm. 'Officer-of-the-guard, sir.' He spoke to Tyacke, but his deceptively mild eyes were on Bolitho.

Tyacke took an envelope from him, and then said, 'Major-General Valancy requests the pleasure of your company at his headquarters for dinner.' He looked up from the page in time to see the disappointment and frustration which, in those few seconds, Bolitho had been unable to hide.

Bolitho said only, 'Make the necessary arrangements, James. It may be important.'

Yovell gathered up his papers. It was time to go.

He said, 'I will have these copied at once, Sir Richard. I have a clerk and one of the young gentlemen to assist me.'

Avery said, 'I shall accompany you, Sir Richard.' He saw the unspoken protest, and added, 'The *army*, Sir Richard. They will expect it.'

He left, and Tyacke said, 'You could refuse, sir.'

Bolitho smiled, rather bitterly, he thought. 'People think we are inspired by duty. In truth, we are its slaves!'

Later, with the barge alongside, the crew in their best chequered shirts and tarred hats and Allday poised massively in the sternsheets, the marines and boatswain's mates were ready and waiting. *Frobisher*'s captain and senior lieutenant saw the admiral over the side.

Allday waited for Bolitho to settle himself beside Avery, and then gave the order to cast off.

He saw it in the eyes of the bargemen as they laid back on their looms. Their admiral, who wanted for nothing.

Allday scowled at the bow oarsman as he stowed his boathook.

How could they ever know? At moments like these, *nothing* was all he had.

The day after Bolitho's return to Malta, *Frobisher* weighed anchor and put to sea. At first light two of the frigates, *Huntress* and *Condor*, had also departed with orders to take station outside Algiers, where their presence would be seen and understood.

Bolitho had been on deck to watch them leave, his heart and mind responding to the sight of the two sleek frigates spreading their sails, and leaning obediently to an early breeze. He had wanted more than anything to have an opportunity to know all of his captains, but he was again reminded that time was the enemy. The ships in his new squadron were mostly known to him by name or reputation, even the small brig *Black Swan*, which was to be the flagship's only companion.

After *Frobisher* had cleared the harbour Bolitho went to his quarters, surprised that he felt no trace of fatigue from the previous evening, despite the heavy meal and entertainment by the army. Avery had fallen asleep at the table, but he had not been alone; their hosts seemed to expect it, and made no comment.

He had returned to the ship to find Captain Christie waiting for him in Tyacke's cabin.

A small thing, a fragment of information, but it was all they had. Of the handful of men who had been released with the *Galicia*, one had been the boatswain, a Greek who, because of his captors, had feared for his life more than the others. He had described to Christie how they had been attacked and boarded, as if *Galicia*'s presence had been known to the Algerines. Every man had been robbed and the vessel looted, and two of the seamen had been killed for no apparent reason. The master's son had been aboard; the attackers had known that, too. Unable to obtain information from the wretched master, they had beaten his son, and then nailed him to a crudely fashioned cross, where he had died. There had been other pirate vessels nearby, which had altered course to the east once the attack had been completed. The boatswain had been certain he had heard someone mention Bona. On the chart it was shown as a small port, little more than a segment of a bay, some hundred and fifty miles from Algiers. *Halcyon* had sailed past it only days ago, and Christie was probably cursing his misfortune that he had not known it was being used as a base by Algerine pirates.

Tregidgo, the sailing master, had confined himself to saying that Bona was known to be used by fishermen for shelter, and sometimes for trade. It would be a likely choice for ships waiting to pounce on some unwary merchantman.

A show of force, then. Afterwards, they would meet up with the two frigates outside Algiers. It would be interesting to know what Captain Martinez would have to tell his master about that.

He sat down and thought once more of Catherine's letter. He had read it very carefully when he had returned from his visit to the garrison. With the lantern unshuttered, and the ship silent but for the secret noises in any living hull, he had sensed again the reserve, the unspoken, as if she wanted to protect him from something, like the riots of which she had written earlier.

The roses are at their best just now. I would that they might last for ever.

The summer would soon be over in Cornwall. In his mind, he could see her on the old path, *their* path. Watching the empty horizon. Waiting. Hoping . . . .

Ozzard hurried to the door and opened it, although Bolitho had heard nothing.

It was Tyacke, outwardly relaxed, glad to be at sea again, even if it proved a worthless exercise.

His blue eyes moved quickly to the untouched coffee, and back again to his admiral.

'*Black Swan* is taking up her station ahead of us, sir.'

Bolitho nodded. The brig might remind Tyacke of his old command, but her commander was not of his world. A forceful, determined young officer, he might go far, if fate was kind to him. When the fleet was reduced in strength and numbers, he would be only one of many trying to prosper in the career of his choosing.

Tyacke had commented bluntly, 'A big mouth to match his head, that one!'

Bolitho said, 'When you hear of slavery even here, does it bring the past back to you, James?'

Tyacke squinted against the sudden glare as *Frobisher* altered course very slightly.

'It was different then.' He did not explain. 'But where there's gold you'll find slavers. In the end they'll not be so quick to run – they'll stand and fight. Turks, Arabs, they are always the hardest to control.' He saw Ozzard by the pantry. 'Would you fetch a chart for me? The master knows which one.'

Ozzard almost frowned, but hurried away after glancing at Bolitho.

When the door closed, Tyacke said, 'I am sorry about the trick, sir. I wanted to talk. A ship can be a small market-place where privacy is concerned.'

Bolitho waited. This was the moment.

Tyacke said, 'Years ago, there was a girl in my life. That was before. . . .' He hesitated. 'The Nile. Then I lost her. I never thought I'd ever see her again. Or want to, for that matter.' He looked at his hands and added simply, 'So I lost her.'

Bolitho wanted to tell him that he understood, but if Tyacke lost the will to speak now, it would not return.

'She wrote to me, and I wrote to her, but never posted it.'

Bolitho said nothing. It was the letter he had put in the strongbox before *Indomitable*'s battle, with another of his own addressed to Catherine. *But we both survived that day.*

Tyacke turned to look at the door, expecting Ozzard or someone else to be there.

'Then, in Portsmouth, just before we commissioned, she came to see me.' He spread his hands, as if he still could not understand or believe it. 'I knew we would meet one day.' He looked now at Bolitho, very directly. 'As you must have known, sir.'

Bolitho said, 'I hoped.'

'I had another letter when the courier came. I should have penned a reply, but with you away, and the future uncertain, I thought I would wait.'

'You still care for her, and for what happened. Do you care enough, James?'

'That's it, sir. I don't know. I have no right. . . . I've lived so much apart from ordinary, decent people for so long that I'm not sure any more.'

He thought of the gown Tyacke had carried in his chest, for

191

the girl who had rejected him. The same gown he had given to Catherine.

'Did you ever tell her about the gown, James? The way you told Catherine?'

Tyacke shook his head. 'There are two children to consider, sir.'

Bolitho saw the door edge open. 'Ah, Ozzard. Some cool wine, if you can lay hands on it!'

Ozzard said, 'The master didn't know about a chart, sir.' It sounded like an accusation. Then he hurried away: always alone.

Bolitho said gently, 'When you write, James, tell her. About the gown. Tell her.'

Tyacke touched his scarred face. 'I never see this. I'm always looking out, watching others.'

Ozzard reappeared, without any change of expression. 'This is cool, Sir Richard.'

Bolitho said, 'Let me.' He held the bottle; in the unmoving air it felt almost cold. Ozzard must have stowed it in the bilges somewhere. It was clear Rhenish wine, from that shop in St James's, in her London. Perhaps she had even held this bottle, before it was packed and sent to Portsmouth.

Tyacke watched, his uncertainty, his inability to speak like this before, momentarily forgotten. Unimportant.

He could never have what this man had and shared with his lovely Catherine, who had kissed him on board *Indomitable* that day in Falmouth, to the delight of the assembled ship's company.

He could see it in Bolitho's grey eyes, the way he shaded the damaged eye to study some detail of the label. So private, and yet so strong that he felt like an intruder.

But aloud he said, 'I shall try, sir. When I write.' He stared at the deckhead, and sensed Ozzard placing a glass within reach. 'Then I shall exercise the gun crews, and blow away these Maltese cobwebs!'

Bolitho raised his glass. 'Let Mr Kellett do it, James. He admires you greatly, you know.'

Unexpectedly, Tyacke laughed, the tension draining away. Bolitho regarded him for several seconds; his wine remained untouched.

'I think we shall fight.' He brushed the rebellious lock of

hair from his forehead, and Tyacke saw the livid scar. 'In fact, I am certain of it.' He smiled, the man he must have been when he had first met Catherine.

'I am glad you told me . . . shared it with me, James. Now we are truly of one company.'

Vice-Admiral Sir Graham Bethune got to his feet, startled by the interruption as the doors of his room were thrown open and Sillitoe, followed nervously by a protesting clerk, strode towards him.

Bethune exclaimed, 'My lord, I had no idea. . . .' He tried again, angry with himself that he was so easily disturbed by this man, powerful or not. 'You were not expected!'

Sillitoe stared around and into the adjoining room, and waited for the clerk to withdraw.

He said, 'I am here to see Rhodes. I trust that will present no obstacles?'

Bethune gestured to a chair. 'I shall see what I can do, my lord. At any other time . . . .'

Sillitoe sat down, outwardly calm, unmoved. '*At any other time* I would prefer not to visit this place. However, I shall use the opportunity to mention a matter to you first.'

Bethune watched him across his desk, dressed all in grey, elegant, assured, with droplets of rain on his coat. He must have walked here from some nearby building. For exercise, or to prepare himself for a meeting with Admiral Lord Rhodes, although Bethune had heard no mention of it; his clerk would have told him.

Lean and sleek; a man who rode, walked and fenced to keep his mind and body sharp. Bethune had heard he used a very respectable house not so far from the Admiralty. Was he like that with women, also, habit rather than need?

Sillitoe said, 'I have just had news of the attack on Washington last month, the burning and destruction of government buildings and stores, and the sinking of American ships there.'

Bethune felt suddenly wary, uneasy. The Admiralty had only received the information this morning, on the telegraph from Portsmouth. The first person to be informed had been the Prince Regent; Sillitoe must have been with him at the time.

'I was relieved to know that the attack had been successful.

Surprised, too.' He ignored Bethune's resentment, and continued, 'I understand that Captain Adam Bolitho is to be given a new command.'

Bethune swallowed. Sillitoe's change of tack was like the man, swift and unpredictable. 'He should have received his orders, and be returning to England as we speak, my lord. *Valkyrie* was severely damaged. She will be withdrawn from service.'

Sillitoe studied him coolly, his hooded eyes revealing nothing. 'The squadron commodore was killed? Unfortunate, although it would seem, in my experience, that officers chosen of necessity for this or that command are not always the right ones for the task.' He raised his hand. 'There is another matter. One which I would prefer to remain between us only.' He watched Bethune's growing discomfort, but felt no triumph; if anything, he sensed anger and contempt.

He said, 'Lady Somervell. You were there at the reception for the Duke of Wellington. You attended Lady Somervell when I was detained by His Royal Highness.' He leaned forward as if to emphasise his words. 'As I requested of you!'

'She left before your arrival, my lord.'

Sillitoe leaned back, his head resting on the chair.

'Sir Graham, do not take me for a fool. I know all of that. She left because she was angered by remarks made by Lord Rhodes, his arrogance in introducing Lady Bolitho as an honoured guest. It was an insult.'

'The last thing I wanted was for her to be humiliated!'

Sillitoe regarded him coldly. 'She was not. She was angry. Had I been there, I would have spoken out rather forcefully.'

Bethune looked away. 'I know. I was in no position to prevent it.'

Sillitoe smiled. 'Had you known about it beforehand, I would not be sitting here now.' His eyes flashed. 'And neither, sir, would you!'

Bethune said, 'I wrote to Lady Somervell, to explain. But she had gone down to Falmouth. I shall endeavour to . . . .'

Sillitoe said quietly, 'I thought perhaps you had mislaid her London address?' He watched, waiting for some sign, some hint. But there was none. Bethune might deceive his wife, but he doubted even that. He held out his hand and opened it slowly.

'This piece of paper has her address written upon it.' He saw Bethune's eyes widen; there was a certain anxiety as well. He felt his anger returning. 'It was found on a man I now know to be Charles Oliphant, at one time a captain in command of the seventy-four *Frobisher*.'

Bethune stared at it. 'She gave it to me. In case I had any news of Sir Richard. I must have mislaid it when . . . .'

'When Oliphant came crawling to you to beg for a command before the truth became known.'

'I do not understand.' Bethune leaned forward. 'Please tell me, if anything has happened to disturb Lady Somervell, I must know!'

Sillitoe waited, counting the seconds. 'Oliphant was waiting for her in Chelsea. The house was empty; she was alone.' He paused. 'Mainly because she was allowed to proceed there without an escort.' He saw the shots slam home. 'She was attacked, but I had received word about Oliphant. People tell me things. I got to the house in time to prevent . . . .'

'To . . . prevent what, for God's sake?'

Sillitoe said harshly, 'Oliphant, the officer chosen to be Sir Richard's flag captain, is not only a gambler and a thief, he is one so rotten with disease that he wanted only revenge, in the last and only way he knew.'

'Tell me, sir – is she safe?'

Sillitoe felt his muscles slackening. Had Bethune given a single hint of involvement, he would not have trusted himself.

'She is safe. With no thanks to those who might have protected her.'

Bethune persisted, 'And Oliphant?'

'He is in care.' His mouth hardened. 'And under guard. It seems likely he will either die or be driven to the bounds of madness before much longer. If not, he will face a court martial, where the severest penalty will be demanded.' He dabbed his mouth with his handkerchief. 'And deserved!'

Bethune thought of the night when it had happened. Weeks ago; he should have suspected something. But his wife had been against his becoming further involved. *I should have known . . . .*

Sillitoe added, 'I have a few small suggestions to make to Lord Rhodes. I am confident that they will be easy to act upon.'

Bethune looked at the clock. 'I fear Lord Rhodes has a prior engagement, my lord. As I explained . . . .'

Sillitoe said, 'Announce me.'

Bethune repeated wretchedly, 'A prior engagement . . . .'

Sillitoe gave a faint smile. 'I know. With the new inspector-general.' He laid the envelope on his desk. 'Here are my credentials, Sir Graham.'

Bethune stared from him to the buff-coloured envelope with its royal seal.

'I shall attend to it immediately!'

Sillitoe walked to a window and stared down at the wet streets, the bowed heads and shoulders of people hurrying for shelter. He should feel something beyond the contempt and impatience they afforded him. But all he could think about was the woman, naked and bound in that small, quiet house in Chelsea. Holding her, protecting her. Wanting her.

The doors opened again; Rhodes had come himself.

'I must *congratulate* you – I had no idea!' He darted a quick glance at Bethune, and another officer who had followed him. He smiled. 'I think our meeting should be recorded, Sillitoe. Everything out in the open, eh?'

Sillitoe did not return the smile. 'As you wish. There are several items. To begin with, the desertion from duty by your cousin, Captain Oliphant, and the failure to provide medical evidence when you agreed to discharge him. Court-martial offences, you will not dispute. Gambling debts, frequenting premises used by prostitutes and becoming diseased to such an extent that he is all but out of his mind. And an attempted rape.' He balanced lightly on one foot. 'Need I continue, Lord Rhodes?'

Rhodes stared around, barely able to speak. 'I shall not need you, gentlemen.' When the door closed again he exclaimed thickly, 'I did not *know* about the extent of his illness, I swear it! I wanted only the best chance for him to improve his circumstances.'

'Yes. Under Sir Richard Bolitho, the man you tried to humiliate through another.'

'What must I do?'

Sillitoe glanced at the painting of a sea fight, Bethune's old ship. Men fighting and dying. He suppressed his mounting fury. *For arrogant fools like this.*

196

'Continue as before, my lord, what else might you expect? Your cousin will not disturb you. You have my word on it.' He reached down and took his hat from a chair. 'I am the new inspector-general, not judge and jury.'

Rhodes made a final attempt. 'When I am offered the post of First Lord . . . .'

Sillitoe waited for the doors to open for him.

'Be assured, Rhodes.' He gave a cold smile. 'You will not.'

He walked out of the building, and was suddenly glad of the wet pavings and the cool, damp air on his face. He could walk for a while, and think. He recalled Bethune's wife on the night of the reception when he had arrived late, to find Catherine gone; it was the closest he had ever seen her to elation. A conniving woman, who would use her husband when he believed it was the other way about.

He nodded to himself, and was unaware of the scrutiny of passers-by. That was it. It would be better for Bethune, for all concerned perhaps, if he was sent to a new appointment. Somewhere a long, long way from England.

Grace Ferguson watched as a housemaid placed a vase of freshly cut roses by the window and gave them her approval.

'Saw you cutting them yourself, m'lady. Did my heart good.'

Catherine smiled. 'I hate it when they are finished.' She glanced at the window, to the grey-blue line of the horizon beyond the headland. 'I shall try to make them last, in case . . . .'

Grace busied herself tidying some books which did not require it. She had mentioned her thoughts to her husband several times, but Bryan had insisted that her ladyship was well enough, missing Sir Richard, but otherwise the same.

Grace was not so sure, but Bryan was like that. All men were. Lady Catherine was a lovely woman. But she was a human being, for all that. Of course she missed her lover, as she herself had fretted over Bryan all those years ago when he had been snatched up by the hated press gang, along with John Allday. *And now look at us . . . .*

She thought of Catherine's eventual return from London, the strain and tension in her face. One night Grace had arranged a bath for her, and had seen the bruises on her arm, the healed cut on her neck. She had said nothing, not even to Bryan.

Catherine said, 'Lady Roxby will be coming this afternoon, Grace.'

Lady Roxby she might be to the outside world, but as Richard's sister she could never be anything but Nancy to Catherine. With only the servants for company, she still lived in the big house, with a steward taking care of the estate. Lewis Roxby's presence was still very tangible whenever Catherine had visited, and she thought that Nancy, in her way, was less lonely than herself.

Grace Ferguson faced her, having made up her mind. 'You'm not eating right, m'lady. You'll fade away if you don't eat! When Lady Roxby comes I shall bring some of those little cakes you like, I made them myself.'

'I don't mean to worry you, Grace – we've all had enough of that in the past few years. All I want is to have him here, with me, with us. He's done so much – can't they see that?'

She seemed suddenly troubled by the watching portraits. 'I want to be strong, to be patient, like all the others must have been.'

Grace said, 'You'll be strong, m'lady. I knows it.'

Later, when the Roxby carriage rolled on to the cobbles, Catherine saw that there were two visitors. Nancy was accompanied by a young woman with fair hair. She was neatly but plainly dressed, a servant, or perhaps a companion. She heard Grace Ferguson greeting them and then went to the door, hoping her anxiety and lack of sleep would not be as apparent to Nancy as it obviously was to her housekeeper.

Nancy embraced her, and said, 'This is Melwyn. Her mother is a dressmaker and seamstress over in St Austell. I've known her family for years, since I was a child.'

Catherine looked at the girl, for that was all that she was. Serious, almost grave features, but when she smiled she had an elfin prettiness which would soon draw some young man's attention.

'Melwyn has been staying at the house with me for the past few days. She works hard, and is pleasant company. A fine seamstress too, like her mother.' She smiled, and Catherine saw Richard's warmth in it. 'As you have lost your Sophie, I thought you might consider taking her into your service.'

Catherine said, 'Melwyn. What a pretty name.'

Nancy said, 'It means "honey-fair" in the old Cornish tongue.'

Catherine asked quietly, 'Do you want to leave home, Melwyn?'

The girl seemed to consider it. 'I – I think so, m'lady. I need the work.' She looked at one of the portraits, her eyes distant. 'My father went for a soldier, to the West Indies. He died there. I do still think about him.' She turned again. 'Do 'ee know the West Indies, m'lady?'

Nancy said with unusual severity, 'Don't ask so many questions, my girl.'

But Catherine said gently, 'Yes, I know them. Where I found my love again, after losing him.' She felt the girl's shoulder tremble slightly beneath her hand. *As I once was.*

'They do say that you travelled all over the world, m'lady.'

Catherine patted her shoulder and smiled at her. 'That story grows in the telling!'

Nancy watched, quietly satisfied. Melwyn was not like most of the local girls who served the big houses and estates. She was a dainty worker; her fingers could skim over a piece of silk or linen as if enchanted, and she was sometimes withdrawn, and a bit of a dreamer. Like her remarks about her dead father: a sergeant in the Eighty-Seventh Foot, true enough. But a foul-mouthed braggart until the army had recruited him, probably while he was drunk. Perhaps it was safer to be a dreamer.

Catherine said, 'If you want it, Melwyn, I would be happy to employ you.'

The girl smiled, beautifully. 'Oh my dear life! Wait till they hear about *this*.'

Catherine looked away. Her voice was reminiscent of Zenoria, although she was completely different in every other way.

The door opened slightly; Grace, she thought, to tempt her with her little cakes.

But it was Bryan. She kept her hand on the girl's shoulder, feeling the sudden chill in her body in spite of the room's heavy warmth.

'What is it?'

'A letter, m'lady. I told the post boy to wait, in case. . . .'

He looked round, relieved as his wife entered and took the letter from his hand.

Nancy spoke, saying that she would remain, but Catherine did not hear her. She picked up a knife and slit the envelope; her hand was quite steady, and yet she felt as if her whole body was shaking. The girl made to move away but Catherine said, 'No. Stay with me.' She dashed her hand across her face, angry with the sudden tears. The writing was blurred, unfamiliar. She persisted, turning it to the light, hardly daring to draw breath.

Then she said, 'Bryan, have you heard of a ship named the *Saladin*?'

Bryan watched her, seeing the strength and determination, and something more.

'Aye, m'lady. She's a big Indiaman, fine-looking vessel. Put into Falmouth once – John Allday an' me went down to see her.'

'The *Saladin* sails from Plymouth next week.' They were all waiting, listening, but she was speaking to him. To Richard. 'She sails for Naples, but will stop at Malta. . . . Will you come with me, Melwyn?'

Nancy exclaimed, 'Malta? How is it possible?' She was near tears, and also proud that she was still a part of it, of them.

'It has been arranged. By a friend.' She stared around the room, seeing it come to life again. The loneliness, which she had been forced to share with the memory of that night when she had known raw terror, would now be gone.

A friend. She could almost sense Sillitoe's amusement.

14

The Edge of Darkness

Lieutenant George Avery spread the chart across the cabin table and watched as his admiral examined some notes, before leaning over it in the fading light.

In the afternoon the wind had backed again, and had risen unexpectedly. Tyacke had discussed it with Bolitho and they had decided to reef *Frobisher*'s bulging topsails. Men had fought their way out along the treacherous yards, the wind hot across their bodies as if it were from the desert itself.

Now, looking at the well-used chart with its bearings and the hourly calculations of their progress from Malta, Avery saw that the nearest land was about eighty miles away. The little brig *Black Swan* had taken up her station for the night, and Avery had last seen her through a telescope, tossing about under minimum canvas like a gull in distress. A lively command at the best of times, and Avery had wondered what her youthful captain thought of his present position, under the very eyes of the flagship.

He knew that Bolitho was troubled by the lack of contact and knowledge of his various captains. He had heard him speaking to Tyacke about Norton Sackville of the *Black Swan*. Only recently promoted from lieutenant and highly recommended by his previous flag officer, he was in his early twenties, and eager for a chance to distinguish himself. Tyacke had replied to a question, 'Sackville is clever enough, to all accounts.' He had tapped his forehead. 'But a little lacking in wisdom.'

The ship felt quieter now under reefed topsails, but she yawed occasionally to broken water; so different from the days of calm seas and limp canvas.

Bolitho was aware of Avery's scrutiny, and thought he was probably questioning why it was necessary to divide the squadron on the strength of an idea, a rumour.

Perhaps I am driving myself for the wrong reasons?

He felt the deck shiver, the heavy rudder taking the brunt of sea and wind.

Two days and ten hours to reach this position: the port of Bona was lying to the south of them. To tack any nearer overnight would be inviting disaster; a lee shore would offer no hope if they misjudged the final approach.

He had been thinking, too, of *Black Swan*, and had tried to put himself in her captain's place. Sackville's lookouts would be the vital link, would make the first landfall, and Sackville himself might have to decide on a course of action.

He half-listened to the sounds around and above him, the creak of straining rigging and the rebellious crack of loose canvas. Voices too; the thud of hard, bare feet overhead. Allday was on deck, Ozzard was in his pantry. The ship carried them all.

He glanced across the table and winced as the lantern's light swung across his eyes. Surely it was no worse? Or was it another attempt to delude himself?

He remarked, 'I have asked the surgeon to come aft, George.'

So calmly said. Like a man chatting to his second before a duel.

Avery secured the chart, and did not look up. 'He seems a steady enough fellow, Sir Richard. Not like some we've seen.'

They were both thinking of Minchin and his bloody apron.

Avery ventured, 'Does it trouble you much, sir?'

Months ago he would have turned on anyone, no matter how close, who might have suggested a weakness. He would have regretted it instantly, but even that eluded him now.

Almost distantly, he said, 'You have not been what Allday would term a North Sea sailor, George. It has been like that. A mist on the sea's face when the light is too strong, but gone soon afterwards. At other times, I can see things so clearly I find myself searching for reasons, solutions.' He shrugged. 'But I cannot *accept* it. Not now, not yet.'

He heard the bell chime out, the responding pound of feet

as the watch on deck was relieved. He had observed it, and done it so many times that he could see it, as if he were up there with them. Only the ship was different.

Avery was troubled by his mood. Resisting, but already resigned . . . .

He said suddenly, 'After this is over, sir – '

Bolitho looked at him and smiled suddenly, the doubts and the strain falling away.

'Then what shall we do, George? What shall we become?' He paused, as if he had heard something.

'You have been a good and loyal friend to us, George. Neither of us will forget.'

He did not need to explain *us*, and Avery was moved by his intensity.

The sentry tapped his musket and called, 'Surgeon, *sir!*'

He said, 'I shall be in my cabin, sir.' Their eyes met. 'You will not be disturbed.' He opened the door for the surgeon and passed him without a glance. Like strangers, even though they shared the same wardroom.

Paul Lefroy, *Frobisher*'s surgeon, was round, even cherubic, more like a country parson than a man used to the grim sights of the orlop deck. He was completely bald but for a narrow garland of grey hair, and his skull was the colour of polished mahogany.

He waited until Bolitho was seated in his high-backed chair and then began the examination, his fingers probing around the injured eye like instruments rather than skin and bone.

Lefroy said, 'I had occasion to meet a young colleague who once served under you. You sponsored him, I believe, to the College of Surgeons in London.'

Bolitho stared at the light until his vision blurred. 'Philip Beauclerk. Yes, he was in *Indomitable* with me. A fine and promising surgeon.' But all he could remember was Beauclerk's eyes, the palest he had ever seen.

Lefroy wiped his hands on a cloth. 'We spoke of you, Sir Richard, as doctors will.' He beamed, the parson again. '*Must*, if we are to improve the lot of our people. He spoke, too, of the great man, Sir Piers Blachford.'

Another memory. Blachford and the rum-sodden Minchin, working as one while *Hyperion* gave up the fight and was starting to sink under them.

Bolitho said, quietly, 'He thinks nothing more can be done.'

Lefroy nodded slowly, his round figure tilted, untroubled by the angle of the deck.

'For someone in a position of retirement, free of the demands, to say nothing of the risks which beset every sailor, this damage might be contained for years.' He gazed around the cabin, the heavy guns straining at their breeching ropes while the ship heeled over. 'This is no such position, Sir Richard, and I think you know it well.'

Ozzard had appeared and murmured, 'Captain Tyacke is here, Sir Richard.' He shot a wary glance at the surgeon.

'Tell the captain I am ready.'

Lefroy was closing his battered bag. 'I am sorry, Sir Richard. You could attend another surgeon, much better qualified, were you not at sea.'

As he reached the door he paused and said, 'The drops you are using are excellent in their way, but. . . .' He bowed himself out, his baldness shining in the swinging lanterns.

His last word lingered like an echo in the air. As if someone had just slammed a great door. Like something final.

Tyacke strode in, his head bent to avoid the curving deckhead beams. He had seen the surgeon, but they had not spoken.

He did not ask Bolitho about it. He had seen enough of pain to read it now in the grey eyes watching him.

He recalled the words. *Now we are truly of one company.*

He said, 'Now, concerning tomorrow, Sir Richard . . . .'

Bolitho leaned over the chart. *The lifeline.* The rest could wait.

Allday stood quite still, his razor reflecting the lantern light. Bolitho was leaning forward in the chair, his head on one side as if he had heard some new sound. But there was nothing, only a few muffled noises, and a sense of heavy stillness.

'The wind?'

Allday nodded. 'Aye, it's left us. Like the last time, an' the times afore that.'

He was talking to give himself time; he had no need to remind Bolitho of the moods and the madness of the weather. He knew them all, as he could feel the ship around him, her strength and her weakness. It was his life.

It was none of those things now. Bolitho had suddenly

gripped the arms of the chair and dragged himself upright, his mind wholly intent upon the ship, and the wind which had deserted them.

Allday glanced at the razor; he had been moving it downwards for the first stroke of the morning shave. He had barely a second to twist it away from Bolitho's face before its well-stropped edge laid open his cheek to the bone. Bolitho had not seen it.

Allday tried to relax the relentless grip of dread in his stomach. *He had not been able to see it.*

Bolitho was looking keenly into his face, his eyes clear in the light from the lantern.

'What is it, old friend? The pain?'

Allday waited for him to lie back again, unable to look at him.

'It comes an' goes, Sir Richard.'

He began to shave him with great care. *A close thing.*

There were voices now, loud and angry. Bolitho recognised Tyacke's, the other was Pennington, the second lieutenant. Then there was silence again, the ship holding her breath, creaking and clattering as she began to drift, her sails flat against the stays.

Tyacke hesitated by the door. 'I am sorry to disturb you, Sir Richard.'

Allday was mopping the shaved skin, relieved at the captain's interruption.

'The wind, James – is that it? We were warned we might expect it.'

Tyacke moved into the light. His shirt was torn, and streaked with tar.

He said, 'No, sir. We've lost *Black Swan*.' He was unable to contain his anger. 'I should have known! I ought to have picked the morning watch lookouts myself.'

Bolitho said, 'You command, James. You cannot carry every man's burden all of the time.'

Tyacke stared down at him. '*Black Swan* knows full well that she must be in company with the Flag at first light. A lookout with half an eye should have seen that she had gone from her station – at the first hint of dawn it should have been clear enough.' He waved curtly toward the stern windows, now grey-blue in the strengthening light. '*Gone!* And the fool only just reported it!'

Bolitho stood up, and felt the listless movement of the deck. Tyacke must have gone aloft himself to be certain, and vented his anger on Pennington when he had found the horizon empty, just as he was now blaming himself for another's carelessness.

He said, 'The wind will return, perhaps sooner than we think. Closer inshore, there could still be enough for the brig.'

He knew what Tyacke believed. That *Black Swan*'s eager commander had used the darkness to tack nearer to the land, to be the first to discover any shipping there and still return in time to resume his position for making and receiving signals. The dying wind had changed that dramatically. *Black Swan* was now without support, and *Frobisher* would be unable to see her, even if she required help.

The sentry's voice broke into their thoughts.

'First lieutenant, *sir*!'

Kellett stepped into the cabin, his face composed, probably prepared for this by the humiliated Pennington.

'Sir?'

Tyacke spoke instead to his admiral. 'I thought we should put down the boats and take the ship in tow, keep her head round, and cut the drift as much as possible.'

Bolitho said, 'I agree. God knows I've done it often enough myself.'

He saw Kellett relax slightly as Tyacke said, 'Detail the boats' crews yourself, Mr Kellett. Two-hour spells at the oars, more than enough when the sun finds them. Put the spare hands aloft to dampen the sails. I don't want to lose a cupful of wind.' As Kellett turned away, he added, 'It was not your fault. Sometimes we all expect too much.'

Kellett's mild eyes widened very slightly. 'I shall inform the second lieutenant, sir.'

Bolitho waved Ozzard aside and loosened his shirt. 'Not yet.'

He heard the trill of calls and the boatswain's harsh voice as he urged more men to the boat-hoisting tackles. Sam Gilpin was a boatswain of the old school, quick with an oath or one of his fists, but he rarely took a man aft for punishment if either of the options would suffice.

'Visibility?'

Tyacke dragged his mind back to the present. 'Heavy mist

inshore, sir. We are no more than ten miles out, but we're useless like this.' He glared around, as if the cabin were restricting him like a cage. 'I just hope young Sackville keeps his lust for glory on the leash!' Then he seemed to relent. 'That was unfair. I scarce know the fellow.'

Avery had arrived, stifling a huge yawn as he listened to what was being said, and to the urgent noises overhead.

He glanced quickly at Allday. 'Trouble?'

Allday shrugged. 'The wind's gone, so has *Black Swan*.' He wondered if he should tell him what had nearly happened with the razor, and decided against it.

Tyacke left the cabin and was heard calling out instructions to his lieutenants, and there was a responding creak of tackles as the first boats were hoisted up and over the gangways, ready to be lowered alongside. Avery imagined them all, all the faces he was coming to know, and the qualities behind them. Tregidgo the sailing master, the true professional, waiting with his mates by the unmoving helm, ready for the first hint of steerage way. Sam Gilpin the boatswain, whose voice was never silent for long: another old Jack, every finger a marlinspike, as he had heard Allday describe him. Kellett, always outwardly calm and unruffled; he would make a good captain if he ever got the chance. And all the midshipmen; *Frobisher* carried nine of them, with the usual contrast between the first voyage squeakers, aged about twelve, to the more serious-minded ones who fretted on the threshold of that first, unimaginable step, to the rank of lieutenant. A step so vast, from cramped berth to wardroom, that it was almost impossible to imagine, except for those with influence or favour.

A ship's company, then, no better or worse than most; but this was a flagship, and the man whose flag flew from the main truck was a legend. That made the true difference.

He heard men calling from the upper yards and could see them, too, in his mind, hauling up bucket after bucket of sea water to pour over each limp sail. The salt would harden the canvas, so that when the wind found them again they would not lose even what Tyacke had called a cupful. He had seen the marine sentry grinning to himself at that, enjoying what he heard. He was not involved.

Ozzard had brought coffee, resigned, Avery thought, to his admiral's refusal to allow him to fetch his dress coat and hat.

Avery sipped the coffee. It was strong, and very good. One would never know Ozzard in a thousand years, but he could spirit food and drink out of thin air like a wizard.

He glanced at the discarded dress coat. Perhaps Bolitho needed, or wanted, to remain the ordinary man for a moment longer. He smiled privately. He could never be ordinary, no matter what he tried . . . .

Bolitho was waiting for Ozzard to refill his cup, unconsciously touching the locket against his skin, beneath the open shirt. Avery saw it, and was moved by what he saw. So far apart, and yet so close. It made him think of Susanna. It was hopeless, and yet he knew that if she merely crooked her finger, he would be her willing slave.

Bolitho said, 'I shall go on deck. A walk, George, before we begin to earn our keep?'

Ozzard almost ran for the admiral's coat, but let it fall again as Bolitho strode past him to the screen door.

He muttered quietly, 'What's the use?'

Allday looked over at the old sword on its rack. 'Use, matey? Only God knows that, an' he won't tell it to any poor Jack!'

He thought Ozzard unusually troubled. 'But how does he know, John? How *can* he know?'

Allday touched the sword. It was so unlike Ozzard to ask an opinion, let alone call him by name, that he was uneasy.

'I've never known him to be wrong.' He forced a grin. ''Cept in his choice of servants, that is!'

Ozzard snapped something and hurried away, pausing only to look back yet again at the discarded coat.

On the broad quarterdeck the air was almost unmoving; the seamen's bodies shone with sweat, and the salt water dripping from the limp sails pattered over them like tropical rain.

Bolitho walked back and forth, his feet avoiding the various ringbolts and gun tackles without conscious effort. How many times? How many places? Lieutenants touched their hats when they realised it was their admiral amongst them, and a nervous midshipman almost turned the half-hour glass a fraction too soon, until a scowl from a master's mate checked him.

Bolitho took a telescope from the signals midshipman, and, as he trained it along the ship and beyond the bows, he said casually, 'It will soon be time for your examination for lieutenant, Mr Singleton. I trust you are well acquainted with the signals procedure of our new allies?'

He did not see the youth's pleasure at being noticed and spoken to, and barely heard his stammered reply.

The boats were standing ahead of the ship, the tow lines rising at regular intervals to the pull of the oars. They were the launch and two cutters; any more would have caused unnecessary confusion. He saw a lieutenant in the leading boat, midshipmen in the others. Some might use a starter on their oarsmen to get better results, but he guessed that Tyacke's influence had made itself felt even in that.

And there was the shore. Africa, solid and hostile; no landsmen would recognise it on the chart.

'I can see the headland, Mr Tregidgo. A fair landfall, despite all else, eh?'

He heard the master's calm agreement. A far cry from being a Cousin Jack, but Cornwall was still clear in his voice. A fragment of home. He moved the glass slowly, careful to avoid the reflections from the sea. The haze or mist still shrouded the division between land and water; you could hide a fleet in it. *Frobisher* had probably been sighted, and her becalmed impotence noted with satisfaction. If, indeed, there was anybody to care.

He felt a nerve jump as a raucous squawk shattered the silence and expanded into a drawn-out crowing.

It was the ship's cockerel, penned in its coop. He heard Kellett saying something to Tyacke, and when he turned Bolitho saw the first lieutenant staring at the sea with obvious bewilderment. Tregidgo was actually grinning. He looked over at Bolitho and called, 'Old Jonas is never wrong, zur! Always crows when 'e 'ears a wind comin'!'

They all looked up as a voice shouted, 'Deck there! Gunfire to the south'rd!'

Bolitho strode to the nettings and stared at the empty sea. Like polished glass. No wind, then: Jonas had been mistaken.

Then he heard it. Sharp and irregular, with an occasional echo of a larger gun.

Avery was saying, 'I don't see how they can manoeuvre and fight without wind!'

Bolitho handed the telescope to the signals midshipman. He

recognised the sound of *Black Swan*'s small guns; the other was something much heavier, able to lie off and make every shot tell.

He said, 'Chebecks, George. Magnificent sailers – properly handled, they can outrun anything but a fast frigate.' He knew the others had fallen silent, and were pressing closer to hear his words. 'And when there is little wind they can use their sweeps to work around an enemy until they have discovered a blind spot.' A loud bang echoed across the water again. 'Like that.'

Kellett exclaimed, 'And here comes the wind, by God!'

It crossed the sea, ruffling it like silk, and then, as it found the ship, Bolitho felt the sails come alive again, heard the attendant clatter of blocks and rigging, and men calling to one another as the helm gave a shiver and then had to be restrained.

Tyacke said sharply, 'Recall the boats, Mr Kellett!' He saw Bolitho, and paused. 'Sir?'

'Recover the crews, James. We can tow the boats. It might give us time.'

He did not explain, but Avery saw in Tyacke's eyes that he understood, and was sharing each move with Bolitho, each thought, as if they were one.

Bolitho said, 'Take your glass, Mr Singleton, and go aloft.' He restrained the midshipman, gripping his shoulder. He felt the wind pressing his damp shirt against his skin. 'Tell me what you *see*, Mr Singleton, not what I might wish to hear.' He squeezed the young shoulder. 'You are my eyes today.'

Frobisher had reached her boats, and men were already swarming up the tumblehome to help warp them aft, to be secured astern.

Bolitho said, 'When you are ready, Captain Tyacke.' It was abrupt, and strangely formal. 'You may beat to quarters and clear for action. Have the gunner open the arms chests. I want each man ready!'

Tyacke touched his hat, equally formal. 'Aye, aye, sir!'

Bolitho felt the deck tilt very slightly, and heard the topsails and topgallants bang noisily until they were filled like breastplates.

'Sou'east by east, sir! Full an' bye!'

The master looked at Bolitho, the question unspoken.

Bolitho said, 'Hold her as she is. As close as we dare. There may be no time to wear ship!'

The rest was lost in the staccato rattle of drums and the immediate rush of feet as seamen and marines stampeded to their stations, to clear the ship from bow to stern. To make her a floating battery, a fortress under sail.

'Ozzard's here, sir.'

Bolitho held out his arms and slipped into the heavy coat with its epaulettes and bright stars. How she had laughed when he had forgotten to tell her of the promotion. *My admiral of England* . . . .

He tugged on his hat, hoping it would shade the damaged eye.

'You may go below, Ozzard.'

Ozzard pouted stubbornly. 'Because of those pirates?' He sounded outraged that he should hide from such rabble.

Bolitho glanced up as the midshipman yelled, 'Six vessels on starboard bow, sir!' A slight hesitation, perhaps remembering his admiral's words. '*Black Swan* is all but dismasted!'

Tyacke swore softly. 'Stood no chance!' Thinking of his own *Larne*, how it might have been.

Bolitho snatched another glass. The mist had almost gone and the chebecks were clearly silhouetted against the dull land mass beyond. The same raked hulls he remembered, but more powerful now, with a square-rigged mainmast to give them additional power and speed; he could see the banks of oars churning at the water, the din and confusion quite silent in the lens. They were on a lee shore, and would need their long sweeps to regain sea room. One was still firing her heavy cannon, and Bolitho watched, his heart cold as more wreckage exploded from the helpless brig.

He said, 'Chain shot, Captain Tyacke.' He saw him nod, could sense his anguish as he urged his ship through the water.

'Get the royals on her, Mr Kellett! Put more hands aloft!'

Tyacke must have been right about *Black Swan*'s young commander. Using the darkness to break free for a moment from the flagship's apron strings, to see and act for himself. It was common enough. *I did it myself in* Sparrow, *a lifetime ago*. He lowered the glass as more smoke and sparks burst from the embattled brig. Sackville was paying for it now. But here and there a gun still fired, and splashes fell amongst the chebecks, when before they had been unable to bear.

He felt the sudden fury rising inside him. Captain Martinez must have been well aware of these Algerine pirates and what they were doing. Like the two frigates they had seen from the citadel; they knew. But, for him, it was like being in the dark.

Tyacke said, 'I can open fire in half an hour, sir. Extreme range, but any longer and I think we'll lose them.'

'Very well, James. If we cannot take *Black Swan* in tow, we'll lift off her people in our boats.' He glanced aft, and saw them still towing astern.

Kellett shouted, 'Two of the chebecks are coming for us, sir,' incredulous that such frail-looking craft would dare to challenge a powerful two-decker.

There was a dull report, and then a loud slap as a ball punched a brown-rimmed hole in the foretopsail.

Bolitho said quietly, 'They can still bite, Mr Kellett.'

'Stand by to alter course to larboard!' Tyacke sounded very calm, totally absorbed. 'Alter course three points. That should do it.' He looked at Kellett. 'Pass the word to the starboard battery, and see that the lower gundeck understands what we are about!'

The helmsmen leaned back on their spokes and watched the driver flapping slightly, spilling wind while *Frobisher* answered the rudder.

'East-south-east, sir! Steady she goes!'

The two chebecks changed bearing as *Frobisher* edged around, every gun on the starboard side run out and ready. To most of *Frobisher*'s men, it would seem sheer madness to challenge a ship of seventy-four guns, and some of the crews were leaning through the open ports to jeer.

But the chebecks were moving faster now, and were using their square and lateen rigged sails to stand closer into the wind than any other vessel.

Tyacke had realised the danger; perhaps he had faced it before, when dealing with Arab slavers. If they could work around *Frobisher* and attack her from astern, any lucky shot could leave her rudderless.

He shouted, 'Full elevation, Mr Kellett! We can't wait any longer!'

His eyes found Bolitho across the crouching crews. He could have spoken it aloud. *We dare not.*

As if to give an edge to his words, another ball slammed into the lower hull. Through the telescope Bolitho saw several robed figures leaping up and down on the nearest chebeck's ramlike beakhead in what appeared to be a wild dance, beyond fear and beyond doubt. There was silence on the gundeck now, and only a handspike moving here and there to adjust the elevation or the training of each weapon.

'*As you bear!*' The pause seemed endless, each gun captain bent behind his port, trigger-line taut, his crew waiting to sponge and reload with the chain shot, hated almost as much by those who used it as by those who were its target.

The two chebecks were almost bows-on, and another flash of gunfire came from one of them, the ball smashing through the hammocks in the nettings and hurling two seamen to the deck, their blood like tar on the pale planking.

'*Fire!*'

Even the sound of the broadside was different, and as each gun threw itself inboard on its tackles it was possible to hear the chain shot, moaning and screaming like the fury of a hurricane. Bolitho imagined he could see its passage over the water, the sea's face torn into sharp fins as the whirling shot blasted above it.

The nearest chebeck seemed to stagger, as if it had struck a reef. The brightly-coloured sails were ripped away in the wind, spars, bulwarks, and men were smashed down in one bloody tangle. But a few figures still leapt about by the big cannon, and even when the chebeck began to heel over they were still there, waving their weapons and screaming defiance at their destroyer.

Tyacke lowered his glass. 'The others are coming about, sir! They intend to attack from the opposite side!' He gestured to Kellett. 'Larboard battery, run out. Those bastards are closely bunched. We'll give them a tune to dance to!'

But Bolitho was watching the first chebeck; somehow it had survived the broadside, and if anything had increased speed, even as her consort was torn apart.

Avery cleared his throat. 'Straight for us, sir! It's madness!'

Bolitho touched the old sword at his hip; he had not recalled Allday clipping it into place.

'They don't think so, George.'

'*Fire!*' The hull shook violently as the two larboard gundecks fired almost simultaneously. The range was down to half a mile. Not what British sailors had become used to, with an enemy hard alongside, and ships pounding one another into submission until one of the flags was cut down.

A single chebeck had survived the devastating broadside, and, like the first, showed no intention of retreating, or pausing to rescue the survivors who floundered amongst the flotsam and the drifting carnage.

'Marines, *stand to*!'

Tyacke turned toward Bolitho, his scarred face strangely calm. 'No time to reload, sir.' He drew his sword, and then raised his voice, so that men who were snatching up cutlasses and boarding axes faltered and stared at him. 'They intend to board us, lads! If one man, *just one man*, can get below, it will bring disaster!' He saw the uncertainty, and the doubt, especially on the more seasoned faces. 'This will be their last fight. Let it not be yours.' He looked at the dark blood where the two wounded seamen had been dragged away. 'So stand together!'

The marines were already crouching at the nettings, muskets trained, bayonets like ice in the sunlight. A seaman stood in the shrouds and took aim with his musket. Then he fell, his mouth wide in a final cry as he hit the water.

Frobisher's seamen abandoned their guns and clambered up to repel boarders.

Bolitho saw it all with an immense detachment, as if he were someone else, an onlooker, untouched by the sudden bang of muskets, and a deep baying chorus as the first chebeck surged alongside, sweeps splintering in the impact, men falling and yelling as the marines fired down amongst them at a few yards' range. They had no chance, but, as that onlooker, Bolitho felt no surprise when figures swarmed up and over the gangway, hacking with their curved swords, some still firing muskets and pistols while they clung to the chains and then the shrouds, driven onward by something even the stabbing bayonets could not repulse.

Avery drew his sword, and Allday moved closer to Bolitho, his cutlass resting on his shoulder, his eyes on the surging, swaying mass. But the squads of scarlet-coated marines were gaining the upper hand, their boots stamping in unison as, with bayonets parrying and pointing, they formed a barrier between the Algerines and the quarterdeck.

One marine slipped on the bloody deck and lost his balance. As though it were a scene in a nightmare, Bolitho saw a bearded giant whose robes were already soaked in blood swing his blade like a scythe, and heard the cries of outrage and horror as the marine's head rolled down amongst the litter of dead and wounded.

Lieutenant Pennington, a deep cut on his forehead, lunged at the giant but had his sword torn from his hand, and would have shared the marine's hideous death but for the diversion his admiral provided.

The giant, feet apart, raised his sword and held it in both hands, his eyes fixed on Bolitho, as if nothing and no one else existed. He must have been wounded several times; there was blood pouring unheeded down his thigh. His teeth were bared, in hatred or agony it was impossible to tell, but to Bolitho he appeared to be grinning, his teeth like fangs against his black beard.

Allday rasped, '*Leave it*, Sir Richard!' and bounded forward, but the great sword swung again. Sparks flew from the steel as the two blades clanged together, and Allday reeled across one of the guns.

Voices came from far away. '*Kill that bastard, Sergeant Bazely!*'

The crack of the musket was deafening, and Bolitho felt the sting of powder in his eyes as the marine fired, even as the sword rose again above his attacker's head.

When he looked again, the bearded giant had fallen among the others, a bayonet putting an end to his last, incredible strength. Weapons were being thrown down, but not many of the Algerines had survived, or perhaps they had been given no chance to surrender.

Tyacke was beside him, his hat gone, his sword still gripped in his hand. There was blood on its blade. He did not speak immediately, allowing the fury and the madness of the fight to release him.

'We lost a dozen men, Sir Richard, maybe a couple more. They're taking the wounded below . . . we'll know about them soon enough, I daresay.'

Bolitho stared up at the sails: unmoving again. Becalmed, with the remaining chebecks drifting alongside, crewed only by the dead.

Tyacke was still speaking. 'I've sent the boats for *Black Swan*'s people. We're safe enough here.' Then, with sudden venom, 'I'll be glad to see the last of this hellish place!'

Avery had joined them, and was gazing at the dead pirate as if he expected to see that inhuman strength rise up again.

He said, 'It was you he came for, Sir Richard.'

'I doubt that, George.' He turned suddenly. 'Sergeant Bazely saved me just now. He must have been the only one left with a loaded musket!' He touched his sword, without knowing why. 'Where is he? I would like to thank him.'

Bazely exclaimed, 'I'm *here*, Sir Richard. With you.' He was grinning. 'Where a good Royal Marine belongs!'

Bolitho turned once more, and then covered his undamaged eye with his hand. There was no image, sharp or misty. There was nothing, only darkness.

15

The Next Horizon

Catherine Somervell gripped a vibrating stay and felt her cloak lift around her legs in the gusty wind. She had become used to ships and had always respected the sea, even before she had learned so much about its moods and hidden cruelties from the man she loved.

Grace and Bryan Ferguson had been openly despairing about her decision to take passage to Malta, and even Nancy, with the sea in her blood, had been concerned.

Catherine had travelled in all kinds of vessel, from humble merchantman to the ill-fated *Golden Plover*. None could compare with the East India Company's lordly and powerful *Saladin*. Even in the unreliable waters of the Bay of Biscay, *Saladin*, as large and imposing as any naval three-decker, had made the voyage more of an adventure than a discomfort.

She pulled the cloak tighter around her; it was the faded boatcloak of Richard's which she used for her cliff walks, doubly welcome now, like an old friend.

It was strange that she had hardly seen or spoken with Sillitoe since they had departed from Plymouth five days ago. There were a dozen other passengers, mostly merchants and their wives, privileged to be in this ship which was sailing to Naples to restore the severed links between Britain and the Neapolitan government after the escape of Naples from French rule, and the bloody recriminations which had followed it.

Strange, too, that Sillitoe should hold the same important role as her late husband, Viscount Somervell, although his appointment had been by the King when he had been in the early stages of madness. Whatever else the Prince Regent might appear to the public, he was genuinely determined to recoup the losses in trade brought about by the years of war with France.

She heard some sailors laughing together as they ran to deal with some rebellious cordage. Richard had told her a great deal about 'John Company' and its ships. Carrying trade to the ends of the earth, and when their flag was hoisted, it rarely came down. Well-manned and armed to full capacity, the company's ships were a match for any pirate or privateer, and had won several battles with enemy men-of-war. Richard had spoken of them with a kind of wistfulness, if not envy.

'Their men are well-paid and cared for, and carry a protection against impressment. They are true seamen, not held against their will. Perhaps when all this is over, Adam will be in a position to see those conditions in his navy. Think of that . . . .'

Sillitoe had touched only briefly upon his actual business in Naples, except to confirm that he was going to sign a new treaty and an agreement on trade. Nelson was still remembered there for his part in crushing the rebels and their French protectors, although Sillitoe had referred to the Neapolitans as 'fiddlers, poets, whores and scoundrels'. He had smiled at her surprise, and had added gently, 'Nelson's appraisal, not mine.'

She watched the gulls cutting back and forth across the ship's high stern and thought of the open boat, and their survival. *Tonight those gulls will sleep in Africa.* And the day after tomorrow, *Saladin* would anchor at Gibraltar. There might even be news of Richard and his ships.

One evening she and Sillitoe had supped alone, the other passengers apparently too sickened by Biscay. Even her new companion and maid, Melwyn, had crept quietly into her cot.

While they had sat listening to the sea against the hull and the muffled voices of men on deck, Sillitoe had said, 'I fear you cannot remain in Malta for long. When this ship returns from Naples, you must leave with her.' He had given that fleeting, wry smile again. 'With me. Nobody may question my arrangements; you have no such protection. In Malta's *society*, there would be talk of scandal. It could harm Sir Richard.' He had looked at her very directly. 'I can always offer that defence against envy and hypocrisy, things you know

218

only too well. I can sometimes turn such hostility aside, and use it to advantage.'

Not once had he mentioned Oliphant and his attempt to rape her.

She had spoken to only a few of the other passengers, but had enjoyed her daily conversations with the captain, a bluff and very experienced officer who had once served in the navy as a lieutenant. He seemed much older than the captains she had met through Richard: boys who became men in the aftermath of battle.

And there was a master's mate, whom she had seen watching her when she had been walking on the poop. Not unlike Allday, a true man of the sea; like so many sailors he had been almost too shy to speak to her.

He had served with Richard in a frigate named *Tempest*, and it had been like sharing a fragment of his past. Richard had told her of the ship and her cruise in the Great South Sea, when he had almost died of fever, and Valentine Keen's first love, a Tahitian girl, had fallen to the same fate.

The man had fumbled with his belt and had said, 'We'm all that pleased to 'ave you aboard with us, m'lady. There's many o' th' lads who've served with Sir Richard Bolitho or knows all about him.' Then he had grinned, the shyness suddenly gone. 'We'll ne'er see *his* like again!'

She could almost hear Allday say, *An' that's no error.*

She could think of nothing but seeing him again; the reality of leaving so soon afterwards must not spoil it. She had agreed; they were Sillitoe's terms for this privileged passage. She had learned from one of the officers that *Saladin* would not have been calling at Malta but for Sillitoe's instruction. Powerful indeed. . . . Almost hesitantly, she thrust her arm outside the cloak and studied her wrist in the hard light. The marks were still there, like the memory of the cord tightening around her arms.

If he knew, or sensed in some way . . . .

We have no secrets. It was easy enough to say.

And she remembered Sillitoe's last words at their undisturbed supper, while the sea and the wind had boomed around them, but she had felt no fear.

He had said quietly, 'I am a willing party to this, and you must be sensible of my feelings for you. But I am curious to know what drives you . . . what carries you in the face of everything? Sir Richard is as safe as any flag officer can be. He has a good ship, to all accounts, and a reliable squadron. Not what he has been used to. So I have to ask myself, why?'

She had answered simply, without pausing to consider it.

'Because he needs me.'

Richard Bolitho stepped into *Frobisher*'s sick-bay and hesitated, unprepared for the brightness of its interior, the white-painted bulkhead and partitions, and the shelves of bottles and jars which rattled occasionally in time with the ship's motion. A world completely apart from the rest of the ship; Lefroy's domain. It was said that he even slept down here, rather than use one of the wardroom cabins, which, built as they were only of screens, could be torn down whenever the ship cleared for action. They were only temporary; here on the orlop deck, below the waterline, a place which had never seen the light of day since *Frobisher* had been built at Lorient, there was an air of permanence. On deck, in that other world, which he understood, Bolitho knew the hour was close to noon, the sky almost empty of cloud. In the sick-bay, time had no measure.

Lefroy was regarding him thoughtfully, more like a country parson than ever in the curious white smock he favoured when working among the wounded.

He said, 'Another has died, Sir Richard.' He sighed. 'Two amputations. A strong man, but. . . .' He shrugged, almost apologetically. 'Miracles are hard to come by.'

'Yes. Captain Tyacke told me. Fifteen killed in all. Too many.'

Lefroy heard the bitterness, and wondered at it. But he said, 'His name was Quintin.'

'I know. He was a Manxman. I spoke with him one night when it was his trick at the wheel.' He repeated, 'Too many.'

He glanced at the spiralling lanterns, and said, 'It's no better.'

Lefroy gestured to a chair. 'It was most unfortunate that the musket was discharged so close to your face. It could only aggravate the original injury.'

Bolitho sat and leaned back in the chair. 'I would be dead but for that Royal Marine's aim, my friend!'

220

Lefroy was wiping his hands, but thinking of the hours which had followed the fanatical attack on the flagship. He had only served under one admiral before, and could not have imagined him visiting the orlop as Bolitho had done, to talk with the wounded, or to take a hand in a strong clasp, and watch the life ebb from a man's face.

'I shall try this patch again.' The steely fingers adjusted a patch and placed it firmly over Bolitho's uninjured eye. The fingers again. Probing, stinging, another kind of ointment. He felt the heat of a lamp, so close that he could smell the wick. His eyelid was held, the eye wide open, while Lefroy said, 'Look right. Look left. Up. Down.'

He tried not to clench his fists, to contain the rising fear. What he had known from the beginning, when he had been unable to see the sergeant who had been right beside him. What he had been unable to accept.

Lefroy said, 'Anything?' He bit his lip as Bolitho shook his head.

'Nothing. Not a glimmer.'

Lefroy replaced the lantern. He had held it very close, so there could be no deception.

He untied the patch and turned away from the chair.

Bolitho looked around him. Everything the same as before; everything completely different.

He said quietly, 'As you said, miracles are hard to come by.'

Lefroy said, 'Yes,' and watched Bolitho stand again, the casual way he adjusted his coat, then touched his hip as if he expected to find his sword still there. A remarkable man, one who had been wounded several times in the service of his King and country, although he somehow doubted if the admiral would regard it in that light.

'I shall prepare something for it, Sir Richard. It should afford you no discomfort.'

Bolitho glanced at his reflection in a hanging mirror. How could it be? The same face, the same eyes, the same lock of hair which hid the deep scar there.

He thought of Catherine, that night in Antigua when he had found her again. When he had stumbled in a shaft of light. Now he would not stumble; there was nothing to deceive him.

'When we return to Malta, Sir Richard. . . .' He was caught

221

off guard as Bolitho answered, 'Tomorrow morning, early, if Mr Tregidgo can be believed.'

'I was going to suggest that you might visit a local doctor. I am no expert in this field.'

Bolitho touched his arm and reached for the door. 'See to the wounded. I shall be all right.'

On the quarterdeck once more, he stood for a few minutes staring at the dark blue water, the spray leaping over the beakhead with a movement like flying fish.

Tyacke had been waiting for him, but Bolitho knew he would never admit it.

'All well, sir?'

Bolitho smiled at him, warmed by his concern. A man who had suffered so much, and had never been allowed to forget it; who had almost broken when the woman he had loved had turned away. *And all I think about is what Catherine will see when she looks at me again.*

He said, 'I shall walk with you a while, James.' He paused. 'But for Sergeant Bazely, I would not be doing that!'

Avery had been looking at the signals log with Singleton, the midshipman in charge. Bolitho had been down on the orlop for only a short while, although it had felt like hours.

He heard Bolitho say, 'There may be some letters for us when we anchor – that would sweeten the pill, eh?'

He heard them laugh, saw some seamen look up to watch them pass.

Midshipman Singleton said, 'My ambition is to be like that, sir.'

Avery turned sharply, surprised by the seriousness and the sincerity of this youth who had seen men die screaming on this same deck.

He said, 'Keep to your studies, my lad. One day you might remember what you just told me. I hope you do.' He stared unseeingly at the open log. 'For all our sakes!'

Singleton was still gazing at the two pacing figures, remembering how the admiral had gone to speak to each of the survivors from the brig *Black Swan*. It had been impossible to save the brig, and she had been set alight to prevent her capture and repair by the Algerines.

He would remember that most of all. *Black Swan*'s young commander, wounded, but too stricken to accept attention while he had watched the dirty column of smoke against the blue sky. The end of his ship. He had heard the lieutenants saying it would finish his career too, at a court-martial table.

Bolitho had joined him by the nettings and had gripped his uninjured arm, held it until the other officer had turned towards him.

Singleton could still hear it. *The worst lies behind you now. Think only of the next horizon.*

He turned to Avery, but the tall lieutenant with the tawny eyes and the grey streaks in his hair was gone.

The first lieutenant called wearily, 'When you are through with your dreams, Mr Singleton, I would be *obliged* if you would bring me your log!'

Singleton stammered, 'Aye, *aye*, sir!'

Order and routine. But for him, things would never be quite the same again.

Daniel Yovell, Bolitho's round-shouldered secretary, dripped the red, official wax on to yet another envelope before sealing it. Then he shifted slightly in his chair, and peered through the salt-dappled stern windows, where the sun was touching the bright sails of some local craft as *Frobisher* made her final approach. He heard Allday moving restlessly in the sleeping cabin, still brooding over the short, savage fight on the upper deck when one twist of the Algerine's great blade had rendered him helpless to defend his admiral. His friend.

Yovell's frown softened slightly. People mocked him behind his back. *Old Yovell and his Bible.* But it had helped him in more ways in the past than people would ever know. Allday had no such release.

He was here now, looking at the pile of letters and despatches which had kept Bolitho, and Yovell's pen, busy for much of the time since the encounter with the chebecks.

Allday asked, 'What d'you think will happen?'

Yovell adjusted his small gold-rimmed spectacles. 'It depends. On what orders are waiting for us in Malta. On what the patrols may or may not have discovered about the two frigates at Algiers. I sometimes wonder if anyone ever takes heed of all this intelligence.' He made another attempt, for he was a kindly man. 'Try to forget what happened that day. You did your best. The pirate, from what I've heard, was a giant, and a savage, probably filled with some devil's potion as well as an unholy lust to kill.' He added gently, 'We get no younger, John. We sometimes forget that.'

Allday punched one fist into another. 'I should have stopped the bastard! Not left it to some bloody bullock!'

Yovell half-listened to the stamp of bare feet, and the sudden squeal of blocks as the ship began to change tack again.

He said, 'Sir Richard seems well enough. I think he always knew his eye would eventually fail him. It could have been worse. Much worse.' He folded his hands on Bolitho's desk. 'I prayed. I hope I was heard.'

Allday turned on him, but was moved to silence by the simple assurance.

He growled, 'Well, I think we should stop now. Haul down the flag an' let some other up-an'-comin' Nelson take the strain!'

Yovell smiled at that. 'Within a month you'd be burrowing round, looking for some job to keep you occupied. I would lay odds on it, and you know I am not a gambling man.'

Allday sat heavily on the bench seat, and glared at the nearest eighteen-pounder.

'I don't never want to become like most of the old Jacks you see. You knows 'em well enough, swingin' the lamp and sayin' how great an' fine it was to be raked by some bloody mounseer, an' to lose a spar like poor Bryan Ferguson.' He shook his shaggy head. 'Never! What we done, we done *together*. That's how I wants to remember it!'

The door opened and Avery entered the cabin. He, too, glanced at the pile of waiting letters and despatches, and shook his head.

'I don't know what drives him so!' He waved Allday back to his seat and remarked, 'There might be some fleet mail for us.' He peered through an open gunport. 'I just saw a sight, a big Indiaman, making all plain sail with the skill and swagger of a first-rate! Young Singleton told me she was *Saladin*, on passage to Naples. On the King's business for a change, by the sound of it.'

Allday looked at him. 'I knows her, sir. We was just talking about Bryan Ferguson, back home. Him an' me went down to see her once when she dropped her hook at Falmouth.'

Avery said something vague in acknowledgement. Like

Singleton, this seasoned, unflinching sailor could still surprise him. *Back home. . . .* Not many landsmen would ever understand what that meant to men like Allday, worn out by war and unready for peace. *And what of me?*

He could hear Ozzard rattling glasses in his pantry, preparing for the ship's first visitors after they had anchored. He smiled faintly. *Dropped her hook . . . .*

Yovell was saying, 'In a few weeks it will be Christmas again. And we don't even know if the war with the Yankees is over.'

Avery, still gazing out idly, saw another local sailing craft pass *Frobisher*'s quarter. Eyes everywhere. The news of their destruction of the Algerine pirates would have preceded them, too. He thought of *Black Swan*'s commander, Norton Sackville. Even in the crowded wardroom, he remained alone. Avery knew what such isolation was like, while he had been waiting for the unwarranted court martial, and had seen former friends cross the road to avoid contact with him.

Ozzard appeared and said stiffly, 'Sir Richard's not here, then? Must be still on deck for entering harbour.'

Allday stood up abruptly. 'I'll take his sword.' It was suddenly important, and he knew Avery was watching him with his steady cat's eyes.

Avery said, 'It'll be a while yet. Another hour, the master informs me.'

Allday took down the sword, nonetheless. Remembering all those other times, the excitement, the madness, the survival. *Always the pain.*

It was still damp on deck, and the air was surprisingly cool, reminding him of what Yovell had said. It was November now, but hard to compare with England's bare trees and angry, autumnal coastline.

The watch on deck were at their stations, and Allday noticed the extra lookouts aloft for the final approach. He thought of Captain Tyacke blaming himself for losing the *Black Swan*; you could never be too careful with so many mindless natives controlling all these hundreds of small vessels. *Not a true seaman amongst them.*

He found Bolitho with Tyacke by the quarterdeck rail, shading his eyes while he watched the land opening out to greet them. There was an anchored sloop-of-war close by, her

225

yards and rigging full of cheering seamen as their flagship passed slowly abeam.

Allday gave a satisfied grin. *As it should be.*

Bolitho saw him, and the sword. 'That was thoughtful, old friend. . . . I was looking at the harbour, preparing myself for what we might expect.'

Allday fastened the sword into place. The belt needed adjusting; Sir Richard was losing weight. He frowned. One of Unis's pork pies, now, that would be more like it.

Kellett called, 'Signal that fool to stand away!' He sounded sharper than usual, on edge.

A master's mate said, 'Guard boat, sir!'

Bolitho walked to the side and saw the smart pinnace with a midshipman and a captain of marines in the sternsheets coming about to lead them in; the marine stood to raise his hat in salute. He had always enjoyed the moment of entering harbour, no matter where it might be, but his heart refused to rise to it. He thought suddenly of Keen; he would be married by now, and a port admiral in his own right. He wondered who else would have been at the wedding. Bethune, perhaps even Thomas Herrick. He bit his lip. No, not Thomas. He had never healed the rift between himself and Keen.

She would be good for Val. Strong enough to stand up to his overbearing father, woman enough to help him forget.

'Guard boat is comin' alongside, sir!' The master's mate sounded shocked at such a breach of procedure.

Kellett shouted, 'They have a message for the admiral! Lively there, Mr Armytage! Your people are all like old women this morning!'

'Stand by for entering harbour! Hands aloft, Mr Gilpin!'

Bolitho raised his arm to the guard boat as the oars backed water, and swung the stem towards the sand-coloured fortifications once again.

Tyacke said, 'Carry on, Mr Kellett.'

Armytage arrived on the quarterdeck, still flushing from Kellett's rebuke and the grins from various seamen. It was his first commission as a lieutenant.

He saw Avery and hurried across, a small package, wrapped in oilcloth, in his hand.

Bolitho said, 'Here, Mr Armytage!'

He felt the others watching him, as if unable to move

while the ship and her tall shadow carried them forward, some invisible force in command.

'Thank you, Mr Armytage.' He unfolded the oilcloth carefully, his head turned very slightly to correct the imbalance of his vision. Then the paper; for a moment he held it in his hands. A carefully pressed rose, velvet-red, as he had seen them so many times. Again he read the card, the writing he knew so well. *I am here. We are together.*

Avery's voice broke in anxiously. 'Is something amiss, Sir Richard? Can I . . . .'

Bolitho could not look at him, remembering yesterday's verdict from Lefroy. He answered quietly, 'A miracle, George. They do happen after all.'

They stood side by side on a small balcony which looked down over a cobbled courtyard and an arched entrance from the street. There was a fountain in the centre of the courtyard, but, like the cobbles, uncared for, and full of weeds browned by the Maltese sun. There were servants, unobtrusive and unseen, their presence marked by fresh fruit and wine in the room behind them.

Even the island's sounds were distant and muffled, someone singing, or perhaps chanting in a strange, quavering voice, and the regular clang of a chapel bell.

She turned slightly inside his arm, which had never left her waist since they had stepped on to the balcony. She felt his fingers tighten, as if he still could not believe it, as if he was afraid to release her, and like a dream it would all be lost.

She said, 'I wanted to go to the jetty and watch you come ashore. To meet you and hold you. I wanted it so much. Instead . . . .'

They both glanced down as an old dog turned over, panting in the sunshine before dragging itself into the retreating shadows.

He tightened his hold around her waist, thinking of the haste with which he had cut short his immediate duties to come ashore, to this quiet street, to her.

She had told him about Sillitoe, how he had arranged this passage, how even this house belonged to one of his friends or associates, someone who owed him favours. He had felt no resentment or jealousy. It was as if he had known.

As he had slipped out of his heavy coat she had told him the rest of the story, or most of it. How Sillitoe had come with his men to her aid, and had saved her.

Then Bolitho had held her for the first time, pressing her face to his, stroking her hair, his words muffled until he had lifted her chin in his fingers and had said without emotion, 'I would have killed him. I *will* kill him.'

She had kissed him, and had whispered, 'Sillitoe is a law unto himself. He will deal with it.'

'He is in love with you, Kate.' She had flinched at the familiar use of the name. 'Who would not be?'

'I am in love with you.'

He thought of the piles of despatches which had been brought by the last courier from England. Once so important; he had barely scanned them, and had left Tyacke to sift through them.

She turned again in his arms and looked directly into his face.

'I would have done anything to be here with you. When the ship sailed into the harbour and your *Frobisher* was not at anchor, I thought I would die.' She moved against him. 'And then you came. My admiral of England.' She struggled with the words. 'Will you be able to stay? *Saladin* is returning in a matter of days. If only . . . .'

He kissed her face and her throat, and felt the pain draining away like sand. 'It is more than I dared to hope for.'

She led him into the room and closed the shutters.

'They know you are here?'

He nodded, and she said softly, 'Then they will know what we are doing.' He reached out for her, but she twisted away from him. 'Pour some wine. I must do things.' She smiled, and pushed some hair from her face. 'Oh, Richard, I love thee so!' Then, like the dream, she was gone.

Bolitho thought of Avery and Allday, who had accompanied him ashore. Each unwilling to abandon him in a strange port, and yet both so determined not to display their anxieties.

And she was here. It was not another dream, wherein she was torn away from him. He felt again the anger and shock as he recalled her careful description of the attack, and what

Oliphant had intended. It was as if Oliphant represented all those nightmare figures, the rivals and lovers which were always a part of his fears.

And she had shown a courage which he could only imagine; it was not even something he could compare with the shipwreck, or their first embattled meeting aboard the *Navarra*.

She called through the door, 'What of tomorrow?'

'I must meet the garrison commander, and receive some officials.'

'Afterwards?'

He felt the sudden excitement. 'I shall be meeting a very beautiful girl.'

She came into the room very quietly, her feet bare, her body clothed from neck to ankles in a fine, white gown.

She put her arms around his neck and held him tightly.

'A girl? If only I still were.' She gasped as he cupped her shoulders and ran his hands down her spine.

She said softly, 'And I missed your birthday. It was all done in such a hurry. Perhaps I shall buy something here in Malta . . . .'

She stood quite still, her arms at her sides as he found the gold cord and pulled it towards him. The gown was so thin that, in falling, it scarcely made a sound, and she watched him, her lips suddenly moist and parted in the filtered sunlight, as he held her against him before lifting her, and carrying her to the bed.

Her fingers were like claws in the sheets as he kissed her nakedness, her mouth and her throat, each breast, with a lingering pressure which made her cry out as if in pain as her nipples hardened in his lips. Once she had dreaded that this reunion would only bring back the disgust and the terror of that night. But it was as if she had no memory, and no control at all; she felt her body writhing as he came to her and she drew him down, touching and caressing, taking him into her, as if it was for the first time.

He kissed her, deeply, and tasted what might have been tears. But their need of one another drove all reserve, all memory, into the shadows. She arched her back so that he could lift her, to join them even more closely; they were one.

She turned her head from side to side, her hair spreading across the disordered sheets, her face damp as if from fever.

'I can't wait, Richard . . . I can't wait . . . it's been so long . . . .'

The rest was lost as they fell, entwined like broken statuary, and there was nothing, only the sound of their urgent breathing.

When, eventually, they stood again at the shuttered doors the shadows were deeper, and the old dog had disappeared. Together they drank the wine, neither noticing that the glasses were hot from the sun.

She put her arm around his shoulder, and did not look away when he turned his head to see her more fully.

'I know, dearest of men. I *know*.'

He felt her move against him, and the need of her again.

She tossed the mood aside. 'I am out of practice! Come, my love . . . I shall do better this time!'

Faint stars were in the sky when they finally fell asleep, in one another's arms.

There was a smell of jasmine in the room. The miracle was complete.

Lifeline

Captain Adam Bolitho walked slowly to the quarterdeck rail and, for only a few seconds, laid his hand upon it. Like the rest of the ship, it was cold and damp, and he felt a shiver run down his spine like some ghostly reminder. He was very aware of the crowded maindeck, the upturned faces, still anonymous and unknown to him, the swaying lines of scarlet-coated marines, the blue and white groups of officers and those of warrant rank. Soon to be a ship's company. *His* ship's company. People, individuals, the good and the bad, but on this bitter December day they were strangers. And Captain Adam Bolitho was quite alone.

On the lively passage back from Halifax to England, he had still imagined that he would be replaced at the last moment. That his one hope would be gone.

It was not a dream. It was not a reward. It was now, today. What his uncle had sometimes described as *the most coveted gift* was his by right. His Britannic Majesty's Ship *Unrivalled*, a fifth-rate of forty-six guns, was in almost every sense ready to join the fleet and perform whatever task might be ordered. So fresh from the builders' hands that in places below decks the paint was not yet dry, but up here, even to the inexperienced eye, she was a thing of beauty. She moved restlessly on the current, her holds and stores yet to be filled, like her magazines and shot-lockers, to give the graceful hull stability and purpose.

It was an important day for all of them. The fruitless, bitter war with the United States was all but over. *Unrivalled* was not only the first ship of her name on the Navy List, but also the first to be commissioned under the promise of peace.

Adam glanced at the taut shrouds and blacked-down stays, the new cordage touched with frost like entwined, frozen webs, and he saw the breath of one seaman hanging over him like smoke.

It was misty, too, and the houses and fortifications of Plymouth were still blurred, like a glass out of focus.

He felt the ship move again, and pictured the Tamar River which he had seen when he had first arrived. Beyond it was Cornwall, his home, his roots. He had heard that Catherine had gone to Malta to visit his uncle, and it had seemed pointless to challenge the rutted, treacherous roads merely to visit an empty house. Even more so to venture further, perhaps to Zennor.

He pushed the thought away, and drew the scroll from inside his damp coat. This was all that mattered, all that counted now. There was *nothing else*, and he must never forget that.

He looked steadily at the assembled company for the first time. The seamen were uniformly dressed in new clothing from the purser's slop chest, chequered shirts and white trousers. A new beginning.

Unlike any other ship in which he had served, Adam knew that *Unrivalled* carried not a single pressed man. The ship was undermanned, and some of her company he knew were felons from the assizes and local courts who had been given a choice: the King's service or deportation. Or worse. There were seasoned hands too, a tattoo or some skilled piece of tackle to mark them out from the rest. With ships and men being paid off with unseemly haste, why did some choose to remain in this harsh world of discipline and duty? Perhaps because, despite whatever they had sacrificed or endured, it was all they trusted.

Most of them would have heard other captains read themselves in at some time in their service, but as always it was a moment of significance for every one. The captain, any captain, was their lord and master for as long as the commission dictated.

Adam had known good captains, the best. He had also known the tyrants and the petty-minded, who could make any man's life a misery, or just as easily take his life from him.

He unrolled the scroll, and saw men leaning towards him

to hear more clearly. There were visitors as well, including two vice-admirals, and a small group of burly men in rougher clothing. They had been surprised to be invited, and proud, too; they had built this ship, had created her, and had given her life.

The commission was addressed to Adam Bolitho Esq, in large, round copperplate writing; it could have been Yovell's, he thought.

'*Willing and requiring you forthwith to go on board and take upon you charge and command of captain in her accordingly.*'

It was like listening to someone else, so that he was able both to speak and take note of individual faces: Vice-Admiral Valentine Keen, now the port admiral at Plymouth, and, with him, Vice-Admiral Sir Graham Bethune, who had come from the Admiralty in London for the occasion.

He recalled the moment when he had been pulled around the ship, and she had been warped to her first mooring. The figurehead had intrigued him: a beautiful woman, her nude body arched back beneath the beakhead, her hands clasped behind her head and beneath her long hair, her breasts out-thrust, her eyes looking straight ahead, challenging and defiant. It had been made by a well-known local carver named Ben Littlehales, and was said to be the best work he had ever done. Adam had heard some of the riggers saying that Littlehales always used living models, but none of them knew who she was, and the old carver would never tell. He had died on the day *Unrivalled* had first quit the slipway.

Adam saw Bethune and Keen exchange glances as he drew near to the end of the commission. Strange to realise that both of them, like himself, had been midshipmen under Sir Richard Bolitho's command.

If only he were here today . . . .

'. . . *hereof, not you nor any of you may fail as you will answer to the contrary at your peril.*' He pulled his hat from beneath his arm and raised it slowly, saw their eyes following it. So many strangers. Even the gunner's mate, Jago, who had accepted the invitation to become his coxswain, looked like a different man in his new jacket and trousers. Jago was probably more bemused than anyone at the turn of events.

He thought suddenly of the boy, John Whitmarsh, who had

died in that brief, bloody fight. He would have been here, should have been here. . . . and *Anemone*, the ship he had loved more than any other. Could this ship, and this new beginning, replace either of them?

He called, 'God Save the King!'

The cheering was loud, unexpectedly so, and he had to fight to contain his emotion.

He thought again of the figurehead; the old carver had chiselled an inscription at the foot of his creation. *Second to None.*

. . . . He would have to entertain his guests in the great cabin. It seemed so large and so bare, devoid of every comfort, and occupied at the moment only by some of the frigate's armament.

Valentine Keen stood back as the builders and senior carpenters crowded round *Unrivalled*'s first captain. Adam had done well today. Keen had sensed the thoughts possessing him, the memories, on this bleak morning.

So very like his uncle; changed in some inexplicable way from the flag captain he had left in Halifax. The confidence and resolve remained, but there was a new maturity in Adam. And it suited him.

And what of me? It was still all so new, and a little overwhelming at times. Keen had a full staff, two captains, six lieutenants and a veritable army of clerks and servants.

Gilia had surprised him with her grasp of this new life, her ability to win hearts, and to be equally firm when she thought it was necessary. With each passing day the old shipboard life seemed to fade further into the distance; perhaps eventually, he thought, he would be like Bethune, with only a painting or two of a ship or a battle to remind him of the life he had known, for which he had bitterly fought his father, and now had, voluntarily, given up.

Boscawen House, his new home, was an imposing place with fine views over the Sound; sometimes, when he was alone, he had tried to imagine Zenoria there. *The admiral's lady.* . . . He stared at the land. Like the image in his mind, it was misty, and eluded him.

Graham Bethune felt the damp, cold air on his face, and was glad he had come for this day. By using what influence he possessed, he had made certain that *Unrivalled* would go

234

to no other captain. It was for Richard Bolitho; it was what he would want more than anything.

He recalled Catherine's pride and anger at the reception when Rhodes had presented Bolitho's wife. And later, when he himself had faced Sillitoe's fury and unrestrained contempt, he had known that this commission was for her sake also.

She was said to be in Malta with Bolitho; if anyone could manage it, she would. He thought of his wife's hostility, her shock and astonishment when he had turned on her and said coldly, 'Honour? What would you or your family know of that?' She had scarcely spoken to him since.

He sighed. But neither had she spoken out against 'that woman'.

He walked over to Adam Bolitho and thrust out his hand.

'I am so glad for you. It is a day one never forgets.' He saw the shadow in the dark eyes, and added kindly, 'There will always be thoughts.'

Adam bent his head. He had once said as much to John Whitmarsh.

'She's a fine ship, Sir Graham.'

Bethune said, 'I envy you. You cannot know how much.'

Adam joined the others and walked aft to his quarters, where a party of Royal Marines had been detailed to act as messmen. When they had all departed the ship would close in on him, and make her own demands.

He paused, the first laughter and the clink of glasses washing over him, unheeded. There was so much to do before they would be ready to put to sea, to teach, to learn, and to lead.

He pulled out the heavy watch and held it in the grey light. In his mind he could still see the shop in Halifax, the ticking, chiming clocks, the proprietor's interest when he had chosen this odd, old-fashioned watch with the mermaid engraved on its guard.

Aloud, he said, '*Unrivalled*. Second to none.' He thought of his uncle, and smiled. 'So be it!'

Paul Sillitoe sat at his broad desk and stared moodily through the windows, across the swirling curve of the river to the leafless trees on the opposite bank. Everything was dripping from an overnight rain; it seemed that it would never stop.

The new year of 1815 was only two days old; he should

be filled with ideas and proposals to put before the Prince Regent at their next meeting. Today, if His Royal Highness was sufficiently recovered from yet another celebration.

The unwanted and costly war with the United States was over, ended by the Treaty of Ghent, which had been signed on Christmas Eve. There would still be battles between ships or even armies until the news was officially confirmed and carried; he had known several such incidents, partly due to the difficulties of communication across sea and wilderness, but also, he suspected, because the officers in command were not prepared to ignore any prospect of action.

He knew that his valet was hovering behind him with his coat. He pushed some papers aside, angry at his inability to summon any enthusiasm for the day's work, let alone a sense of urgency.

His valet said, 'The carriage will be here at the half hour, m'lord.'

Sillitoe said curtly, 'Don't fuss, Guthrie. I shall be ready!'

He stared at the river again, remembering the night when he had burst into her house in Chelsea. It was rarely out of his thoughts, like a curse or a fever from which there was no escape.

He had been surprised at his own behaviour on board the Indiaman *Saladin*, that he had been able to see her and greet her as if they were total strangers. *Which we are.* Sometimes he had confined himself to his quarters in order not to meet her, in case she should think he had forced the encounter. But when they had met, and supped alone, there had been a new awareness, something he had never known.

He had not greeted her when she had rejoined the ship on the return from Naples, but had found her on deck, hours after *Saladin* had worked out of Grand Harbour and had suddenly been totally becalmed, the island still in sight, like copper in the sunset.

She had repeated, 'I am all right, I am all right,' and for a moment longer Sillitoe had believed she had heard him approaching, and had wanted to be left alone.

Then she had turned towards him, and he had realised that she had not known he was there.

'I am sorry. I shall take my leave.'

She had shaken her head. 'No. Please stay. It is hard

236

enough to leave him. To be tortured like this is cruel beyond measure!'

He had heard himself say, 'When I reach London, I will do what I can.' Even that had astonished him, to offer to seek on her behalf a favour which, if granted, would deprive him of any chance he might have believed he had.

He smiled grimly. Nevertheless, Vice-Admiral Sir Graham Bethune would be leaving for the Mediterranean in a matter of days, to take charge of a squadron of frigates which could be used against pirate or corsair. A sea-going appointment; there would be no accommodation for Lady Bethune.

He had seen the orders himself. They would release Sir Richard Bolitho from duty, and he could return to England. To Catherine.

He had also been kept informed of Captain Adam Bolitho's affairs. Why anyone should want to throw his life away on the sea was quite beyond him. Ships, to him, meant only trade, communication, and a means of travel. And even that . . . .

He glanced round angrily, but it was Marlow, his secretary, this time.

'Yes, what is it?'

'Some letters, my lord.' Marlow's cautious eyes took in the unread news sheets on the floor beside the desk, the coffee and the glass of madeira untouched. They were inauspicious signs, and, with Sillitoe, almost unknown.

Sillitoe shook his head dismissively.

'I'll attend to them later. Make my excuses, Marlow. I shall go now to the Prince Regent.'

'I have all the necessary papers, my lord.' He broke off. Sillitoe had not even heard him.

'After that, I shall be engaged.' Their eyes met. 'Understood?'

Marlow did understand. He was going to that house, so discreet, so private. Where a man of influence could lose himself completely in the arms of a woman, without fear of scandal or condemnation. He had become used to Sillitoe's difficult ways and scathing comments, but it troubled him to see him so disturbed, like some ordinary being.

To his knowledge, Sillitoe had not visited the brothel since the incident in Chelsea.

Sillitoe allowed his valet to help him into his coat, and stared around the room as if he had mislaid something.

Then he said, 'There is one letter, Marlow, for Lady Somervell in Falmouth. Please send it post-haste. She will want to know.'

He could already see it in his mind, the tears and the joy with which she would receive the news that her lover had been ordered home. He could deceive himself no longer. He heard the carriage on the cobbles and strode from the room.

Like a duel, when you have fired and your opponent is still standing. He had lost.

His Britannic Majesty's schooner *Tireless*, messenger, courier and bearer of news, good or bad, lived up to her name. Rarely in port for longer than required for storing and watering, she would be off again with all haste to her next rendezvous.

She was a smart, lively little vessel, a young man's command. On this February morning the lookout had reported sighting the flagship *Frobisher*, and, taking full advantage of a soldier's wind under her coat-tails, she had set more sail to run down on the slow-moving two-decker. Lieutenant Harry Penrose, the schooner's captain, was well aware of the significance of his despatches, and very concerned that he should make a perfect approach to the flag of one so famous; it was a name with which he had been acquainted even before he had entered the navy.

Penrose would have been astonished had he known that the admiral had been watching *Tireless* since first light with equal anxiety.

In *Frobisher*'s great cabin, the man in question listened to the bark of orders and the tramp of hardened, bare feet, as the flagship altered course slightly to meet the schooner and afford her some protection, although the sea was little more than a gentle swell. He clenched his fists. Weeks of it, of lack of news, of uncertainty, and of this sense of no purpose. There had been some activity when Barbary corsairs had attacked other small and defenceless vessels, but they had fled before any of Bolitho's thinly-stretched squadron could find and destroy them. And until more ships were released from the Channel Fleet and the Downs squadrons, it seemed unlikely that matters would improve.

Tireless might bring something. He tried not to hope for it. Perhaps a letter from Catherine. . . . So many times, he had recalled every detail of their reunion, the ache of parting after the big Indiaman *Saladin* had returned from Naples, in what must have been record time. He had thought of it again when Tyacke had come to report the sighting of *Tireless*, remembering with anguish how the Indiaman's pyramid of canvas, gold in the sunset, had remained becalmed outside the harbour as if to taunt him. He had watched the ship until darkness had hidden her. And he had known, even before her letter from England, that she had done the same. She had written to him about Adam, and the confirmation of his new command. Of the dazed reaction to the combined attack on Washington, and the burning of government buildings in retaliation for the American attack on York. As Tyacke had once said, *and for what?* He had watched Tyacke while he had trained a glass on the approaching schooner. Remembering his own first command, perhaps, or the powers of fate which had brought them so close together, as his friend and flag captain? And Avery. He would remember his own service in the schooner *Jolie*, which had ended in disaster and court martial. The tawny eyes gave little away; he might even have been thinking of the letter for which he waited. The letter that never came.

The strain of weeks at sea without activity was telling on *Frobisher*'s people. Ships and men being paid off: a sailor's dream rather than a safe reality, but it gave rise to flarings of temper and outbreaks of violence, even in a well-disciplined company. He could hear Gilpin the boatswain, bawling out to some of his working party. A grating was to be rigged immediately after the despatches had been passed across, and *Frobisher*'s own mail sent into *Tireless* in exchange. It was anyone's guess when those letters would reach their destinations.

He knew Tyacke hated the ritual of punishment, as much as he did himself. But he, more than most, knew the dangers of sailing alone when the ringing phrases of the Articles of War were not always enough. The Royal Marines of the afterguard, and the lash, were the only known alternative.

Yovell stood by the other door, his spectacles on his forehead.

'Everything has been signed and sealed, Sir Richard. I've had the satchel sent on deck.' Unruffled, unchanged, and yet the one man he might have expected to remain a misfit. Amused, gentle, devout: they were not qualities common in a man-of-war.

Allday was there, too. Pretending to examine the two swords on their rack, but obviously fretting more than ever about the possibility of a letter from that other, quiet world of the Helford River. Avery would read it to him as usual, if it arrived; theirs was an odd and a warm relationship, upon which neither of them ever remarked. Avery would be thinking of the fair Susanna. In vain . . . .

And Sillitoe, the one man he had never expected to become involved on his behalf. He could hear Catherine's voice in the darkness, remember her warm breath on his shoulder, while she had spoken of that night in Chelsea, distancing herself from it, more like an impartial witness than one who had been face to face with terror. He had wanted to feel doubt, suspicion, even hatred. But Sillitoe remained as before, remote, even in the desire he so obviously felt for Catherine.

And all the while I remain here in the Mediterranean, waiting. Probably with no less intolerance than the seaman who would be flogged at six bells of the forenoon watch.

Avery entered by the screen door and removed his hat.

'*Tireless* is shortening sail, Sir Richard.' He glanced briefly at Allday. 'She has signalled that her captain is coming aboard.' He added, 'Penrose, Lieutenant.' And then, more lightly, 'I would have thought he'd be here and gone, in case his admiral finds him some errand!'

Bolitho laughed. Avery had not forgotten.

'Very well. Bring him aft, and I'll speak with him myself.'

It took another hour for the ships to draw close enough for a boat to be put down and pulled over to the flagship, where young Lieutenant Harry Penrose was received with no less respect than if he were a post-captain.

Two seamen carried the satchels of mail and the despatches, and when Allday finally returned to the great cabin Bolitho knew that he had been lucky. Just a nod. That was all it took.

Lieutenant Penrose had a small bag of letters for Bolitho.

'From the courier-brig when I was last at the Rock, Sir Richard.' He became almost confidential. 'Her captain made me promise that I would deliver them personally.'

Bolitho took the letters; there seemed to be four of them. The link, the lifeline. He would make them last.

Penrose was saying, 'I fell in with the frigate *Halcyon*, Sir Richard. Captain Christie was making for Malta, but sent word to you in case I found you beforehand.'

He raised his eyes from the letters.

'What "word"?'

'The two frigates reported in Algiers have put to sea.' Penrose looked suddenly troubled, as if it were his fault.

Avery watched Bolitho as he slit open the first, crumpled letter, saw the way he turned his head as if to read it better, the damaged eye now obviously useless. By his appearance, one would never guess, and to share the knowledge was both moving and terrible.

He recalled the moment when Catherine had left Malta. He thought it had been Tyacke's idea; they had sent *Frobisher*'s barge for her, each oar pulled by a captain or one of the squadron's officers, with the admiral's own coxswain at the tiller.

As people saw them, and remembered them; as they spoke of them in the alehouses and the coaching inns from Falmouth to London. *The admiral and his lady.*

Bolitho looked up at him. 'I thought we might learn something of their intentions, but we were unlucky. They could be anywhere, under any flag. It would take a fleet to break into Algiers, not merely this squadron, and even then . . . .'

Avery said, 'Even then, nobody would thank you for beginning another conflict, though it would seem inevitable, whichever aspect presents itself.'

Penrose coughed politely. 'I must take my leave, Sir Richard. The wind favours me, and . . . .'

Bolitho held out his hand. 'My best wishes to your company, Mr Penrose. When next we meet, I shall expect to see epaulettes on your shoulder.'

The door closed as Avery led the schooner's captain away.

Yovell remarked, 'That was kindly said, Sir Richard. That young man will remember this day.'

He heard the trill of calls, and imagined the schooner's gig pulling away from the flagship's side. *Tireless* would soon be gone. Meeting and departure. Their world.

Then the calls shrilled a different tune.

'All hands! All hands lay aft to witness punishment!' The immediate response of hurrying feet, the boots of the Royal Marines as they took up their stations across the poop.

Allday passed him without a word to close the cabin skylight, so that the sound of the punishment would be muffled.

It was a strange fact about Allday, Yovell thought. He loathed officers who abused their authority, but showed no sympathy for any man who raised his hand against it.

Bolitho said, 'I shall dictate orders for the squadron. Some will already know, but if the two frigates intend to reinforce the Barbary corsairs against allied commerce, it is essential that each captain recognises them as the enemy.'

He looked at her letters. She must have written every day. So that he could live her life with her, and share it, week by week, season by season. He clenched his fingers again as the drums beat out their staccato roll. Then the lash, a loud crack across the naked flesh, followed by the shout from M'Clune, the master-at-arms. '*One!*'

Then the drums again, and the sharp crack of the cat. One of the ship's hard men, Tyacke had said, who had threatened a petty officer.

'*Two!*'

Yovell looked at his interlaced fingers below the table. It only took one rotten apple, Allday had often proclaimed.

'*Three!*'

Yovell glanced up again, and then stared as Bolitho got abruptly to his feet, a canvas envelope still gripped in one hand.

He said, with great anxiety, 'What is it, Sir Richard?' conscious only of the expression on Bolitho's tanned face. Surprise, disbelief, but above all, a release which he had rarely seen before.

Bolitho seemed to hear him for the first time.

He answered quietly, and yet even the urgent drums could not quench it, 'From the Admiralty.' He turned, and looked for Allday. 'We are to pay off, old friend. *We're going home.*'

Allday let out his breath, very slowly.

'Well, that's it an' all about it!'

The waiting was over.

17

'Until Hell Freezes'

Yet another forenoon watch was ending, working parties preparing to gather up their tools and equipment, eyes alert for any over-zealous petty officer. The sailmaker and his crew had squatted cross-legged in any shade they could find, needles and palms moving busily like backstreet tailors. The carpenter and his men had continued their endless search for material in need of repair. At times like this, the upper deck was aptly known as the market-place.

Aft, below the poop, some of *Frobisher*'s midshipmen waited with their sextants to shoot the noon sun, some frowning with concentration, and very aware of their captain's tall figure by the quarterdeck rail.

In his mind, Tyacke was seeing the ship's slow progress, east by south, and some one hundred miles to the east of the Sardinian island. It was a sailor's vision, and that of a navigator, but to any layman the sea would appear an empty, glittering desert, as it had been for days. For weeks. They had met only one of their frigates, and had been in contact with another courier vessel; otherwise, they had seen nothing. He saw the first lieutenant making his way aft, pausing to speak with one of the bosun's mates. Like the other officers, Kellett was showing signs of strain. *Frobisher* had been shorthanded even before her fight with the chebecks, shorthanded long before she had commissioned at Portsmouth, and that, he thought, was due largely to her last captain's indifference.

The thought of Portsmouth brought another stab of anger. More men had been excused from duties because of sickness: poisoned meat, the surgeon had insisted.

Tyacke had an innate distrust of all victualling yards, and an immense dislike and suspicion of the common run of ships' pursers. Between them, yard and purser could dispense food already rotten in the casks without any captain's knowledge, until it was too late. A lot of money changed hands this way, and Tyacke had often heard it said that half of any naval port was owned by dishonest pursers and suppliers.

The casks in question had been put aboard at Portsmouth a year ago. How old they really were would remain a mystery; the date markings burned into every such barrel had been carefully defaced, and men were laid off as a result. Tyacke tightened his jaw. It would not end there.

He glanced at the poop, and imagined the admiral going through his despatches yet again. Was all this a waste of time? Who could say? But, as the captain, Tyacke had to consider the demands of his company, the growing shortages of fresh fruit and even of drinking water. An armed marine sentry by the water cask on deck was evidence of that.

He was staring at one of the midshipmen without realising it, and saw the sextant quiver in his hands. This, perhaps, was not what he had expected when he had donned the King's coat.

He turned away and gave his attention to the topsails, filled but only just; the weather was part of the general malaise. It was the usual north-westerly wind, but without life, sultry, more like the sirocco of this region at a later time of the year.

He considered the orders Bolitho had given him to study. When *Frobisher* eventually ended her mission and returned to Malta, Bolitho's successor would be there to relieve him; he had very probably already arrived. Vice-Admiral Sir Graham Bethune. Tyacke had sensed Bolitho's surprise at the choice; he knew the officer, and they had served together. The navy was a family . . . .

The thought uppermost in his mind returned; it had come, increasingly, to haunt him. *Frobisher* would be returning to England; Sir Richard would be allowed to lower his flag, to pass the burden to someone else. For a change.

He had heard Kellett and the others discussing it, when they thought he was out of earshot.

Going home. He had to come to terms with it; it was a concept totally unknown to him in all his years of service. *Going home.* He knew what it meant to Bolitho, even to

Allday. But to him, England had become something alien, a place only of more scrutiny, more revulsion, more pain. Until that last letter from the woman he had once intended to marry. Interesting, warm, mature, truthful. . . . He had tried to dismiss it, to laugh at himself, to accept that there was nothing for him.

In his heart, he knew that Bolitho had guessed some of it, but had said little. That was their strength.

It had all come to a head when Kellett had blurted it out, a day after they had parted with the schooner. The whole wardroom had been alive with speculation and concern for the future. What would happen to *Frobisher*? To them?

Tyacke had already asked himself that. Would she end up an empty hulk, in ordinary in some crowded dockyard, or allowed to sink still further to the status of a storeship or a floating prison? It had happened to other ships; Bolitho's *Hyperion* and even Nelson's *Victory* had been dragged from ignominy to serve again when the country was in danger of invasion and defeat. To find glory when others had been prepared to let them rot.

Kellett had asked him in his usual quiet fashion, 'When we return to the fleet, sir, may I ask, what shall *you* do?'

It had been then, without any hint or warning, that Tyacke had found his way, his purpose.

'I shall remain with the ship.'

Running away was not the answer. It never had been. He belonged.

And Marion would be there to help him. For all kinds of reasons, reasons he would have previously denied, or laughed at, they needed each other.

He thought of Bolitho and his Catherine.. Love was the strongest bond.

He heard a step on the deck beside him, but it was not the first lieutenant; it was Avery, squinting at the sea and tugging at his shirt while he stared around from horizon to horizon.

Tyacke said, 'I have to see Sir Richard.' He hesitated over his choice of words. 'It is my duty to advise him.'

'I know.' Avery watched the vivid blue eyes, Tyacke coming to a decision. He said, 'Sir Richard knows this cannot continue much longer. As soon as we return to Malta, it will be out of his hands. But you know him well enough – he cannot let it

246

rest. It seems there is some flaw in it, in the pattern, which refuses to fit.'

'I know. He spoke of the Spaniard, Captain Martinez, the one you met in Algiers.'

Avery nodded, and felt more sweat run down his spine. He often thought of that fine house in London, and of the lovely Susanna; even those, he would exchange at this moment for a bath in pure, clean water.

'There was a brief mention of him in the last despatches from Admiralty. Someone took the time and trouble to look into Sir Richard's report, a lowly clerk most likely!'

Tyacke watched some seamen loitering by an open hatch; they could smell the rum being issued. With little fresh water, and all the beer long gone, rum might be all the spark that was needed.

'A renegade, and an agent for the French when they were preparing to drag Spain into the war. Not that they needed much encouragement!' He heard Kellett clear his throat, and added impatiently, 'Is that all the information we have?'

Avery said, 'It troubles Sir Richard.'

Tyacke turned to Kellett. 'This afternoon, Mr Kellett – is that what you were about to ask?'

Kellett gave one of his rare smiles. 'Aye, sir.'

'Lower gundeck. Both batteries. See if you can knock a minute or two off their time.'

He turned back to Avery, his voice very calm. 'If Sir Richard requires it, I shall wait until hell freezes.' He paused. 'But it may take more than extra gun drills to keep the people mindful of their duties, if we delay much longer, eh?'

The cabin skylight was open, and Bolitho heard Avery laugh. Tyacke was a patient man, and he knew his trade better than any he had met.

He returned to the chart, and pictured *Frobisher* sailing sedately above her own reflection in this Tyrrhenian Sea. So wrong for a ship of her size and quality; this was a place more used to beak-prowed galleys with banked oars, and bearded warriors in plumed helmets. A place of the gods, of the myths of Greece and Rome.

He smiled at the notion, and opened his notes once again; he held his hand over his blind eye, out of habit, and was surprised that he could accept it. Catherine's letter had given him the strength; their lordships of Admiralty had done the rest.

It was strange about Bethune; he had seemed so suited to the ways and powers of London. Perhaps he had offended someone, which was easy enough at the Admiralty. Even Lord Rhodes' name seemed to have been dropped from despatches and orders. Was Sillitoe's hand in that, too?

He dragged his mind back to that meeting with Mehmet Pasha and his Spanish adviser, Martinez. They had known all about the two frigates moored there; nothing could move without the governor's permission, and his complicity. Martinez had been a successful and daring agent for the French revolutionary government. For Napoleon.

Tyacke needed to provide for his ship, and Bethune was probably waiting in Malta to assume command of the Mediterranean squadron.

I must go home. He did not realise he had spoken aloud to the empty cabin and its dancing, dazzling reflections.

There was no proof that Martinez was any more than he proclaimed. His roles had become less important and possibly more dangerous over the years, and in his own country he would never be trusted again. He thought of his brother, Hugh. A traitor was always remembered for his treachery.

If only he had more ships, especially frigates. This venture was a needle in a haystack; or was it merely vanity, a belief that no one else could see the hidden dangers?

He could smell the rum, and imagined the seamen and marines throughout the flagship, isolated now, and idle, no longer participating in the great events of other times and places.

As he leaned over the table he felt the locket, filmed with sweat, adhering to his skin. It would be spring when they reached England again. So much time lost, so much to rediscover.

He heard Tyacke's shoes outside the door, and, quite suddenly, made up his mind.

Tyacke entered and removed his hat; with his face in shadow, it was barely possible to see the full extent of the terrible scars.

'Join me in a glass, James.' Ozzard had appeared, as if by magic. 'I think I have pursued my instincts too far this time.'

They both watched the wine filling the glasses for a moment, then he said, 'We may run down upon *Huntress* before sunset. I would wish to speak with her captain.'

Tyacke nodded. 'It is possible, Sir Richard.'

Bolitho raised his glass. 'Either way, we shall return to Malta.' He smiled. 'In all truth, James, I wish you the happiness you deserve in your new life!'

Their glasses clinked, and the watchful Ozzard saw some wine splash across the admiral's white breeches. Like blood, he thought. But the admiral had not seen it.

Tyacke was on his feet again. 'I shall pass the word, Sir Richard. It may lessen the toils of gun drill!'

Ozzard went into his pantry and found Allday there, carving yet another model ship.

Ozzard could usually conceal his feelings, but on this occasion he was glad that his friend was so engrossed.

Now, even Captain Tyacke had somebody waiting for him.

He thought of the street in Wapping, and heard her dying screams. There was nothing left.

Lieutenant Harry Penrose gripped the companion ladder, and leaned back to stare at the sky while his schooner, *Tireless*, scythed through a ridge of broken water. It never failed to excite him, like riding something alive, which, of course, she was.

The rectangle of sky was duller than usual, with large patches of cloud moving like an untidy flock of sheep. Against it he could see the towering fin of the schooner's mainsail; that, too, seemed darker. Perhaps it would rain. They were not short of water, but just to hear rain running through the scuppers and wetting the sun-dried planking would make a welcome change.

He continued on his way, and heard the squeak of a fiddle from one of the tiny messdecks. She was a small ship, and a happy ship, a command for the young. Penrose was twenty-two years old and knew he was lucky to have *Tireless*, and would be sad to leave her when the time came; just as he knew he would not shirk his duty when it called him elsewhere. It was his life, all he had ever wanted, and had dreamed about as a child. His father and grandfather had been sea officers before him. He smiled. Like Bolitho. He had thought many times since of that unexpected meeting, when he had delivered despatches to the flagship. What had he anticipated? That the hero, the navy's own legend, might prove to be only another imposing figure in gold lace?

He had written to his mother about it, embroidering the story a little, but the truth was still fixed firmly in his mind. *The next time we meet, I shall expect to see epaulettes on your shoulders.* The sort of man you could talk to. The kind of leader you would follow to the cannon's mouth.

He felt the wind on his face, damp, clinging, but still enough to fill the schooner's sails.

Tireless's only other officer, Lieutenant Jack Tyler, waved vaguely toward the bows.

'Masthead just reported a sail to the sou'east, sir.'

Penrose glanced at the sea creaming back from the raked stem.

'I heard the hail. Who is the lookout?'

'Thomas.'

'Good enough for me, Jack.'

They worked watch and watch, with a master's mate standing in when it was convenient. You got to know the ability and strength of every man aboard, and any weakness too.

Tyler said, 'He thinks it's a frigate, but the light's so bad, we may have to wait until tomorrow.'

Penrose rubbed his chin. 'First light? Another day lost. She must be *Huntress*, our last rendezvous.' He thought of the solitary bag in his cabin and added wryly, 'Important, no doubt. Officers' tailoring bills, tearful letters for the mothers' boys, all vital stuff!'

They laughed, more like brothers than captain and first lieutenant.

They both looked up as the masthead pendant cracked out like a coachman's whip, and Penrose said, 'I think we might do it before dark, Jack. When she sights us she's bound to claw up as quickly as she can. They must be sick of being the last of the patrols, a guardship of nothing!'

He made up his mind. 'All hands, Jack! Let's get the tops'ls on her!' He could not contain his excitement. 'Let's show those *old men* how she can shift herself!'

Only one pipe was necessary; the fiddle fell silent, and the schooner's narrow deck was soon filled with bustling figures.

Tireless did not have a wheel like most vessels, but still mounted a long tiller-bar fixed directly to the rudder head. The helmsmen gripped it between them, glancing at the mainsail and masthead pendant, with only an occasional scrutiny of the compass. For a moment longer all was confusion, or so it might appear to the ignorant landsman, and then, heeling to the thrust of canvas and rudder, *Tireless* settled on her new course, spray bursting over her jib and spurting through the sealed gunports, where her sole armament of four four-pounders tugged at their breechings.

'Sou'east, steady she goes, sir!' Even the senior helmsman was grinning, his sunburned face wet with spray, as if it had indeed started to pour.

The lookout called again, 'Frigate, sir! Larboard bow! *Huntress* right 'nough!'

Penrose nodded. Thomas would know; he had eyes like a heron. And they had met with *Huntress* more than a few times on her endless patrols. Penrose thought of her captain. Older than most frigate men, with experience in other ships, and probably in merchantmen too, he was friendly enough, but one who stood no nonsense. Penrose had noticed that he never received anything but official letters with the despatches.

He lifted a telescope and waited for the image to settle in the lens, and at the same time accustomed his legs to the schooner's lively plunges. The habit and the motion had become part of himself.

Even in the dull light he could see the familiar outline, the shining black and buff hull, the chequered line of closed gunports. A fifth-rate, not new, but a fine command. He smiled to himself. For a younger man, of course.

He saw her ensign curling from the peak, so clean and white against the dull backdrop. Ant-like figures in her tops, some watching, hoping for a letter to bring back the precious memories, a face, a touch.

Tyler said, 'The bugger's not changing tack! Making us do all the work!'

Penrose grinned. The light was holding. They would pass the bag across and be away before dark, back to Malta. And after that? Not that it truly mattered . . . .

Tyler was speaking to the master's mate. 'We'll overreach

251

him at this pace, Ned.' He looked at Penrose. 'We shall have to come about, sir!'

'I know. Take in the mains'l!' He moved the glass again as a tiny patch of colour appeared at the frigate's yard.

'She's made her number, sir!'

Tyler was yelling to his men, and the air was alive with banging canvas and the squeal of blocks.

Penrose did not move. He could not.

He shouted, '*Belay that order!*' He did not recognise his own voice, hard and desperate.

He ran up the slippery planking and stared at the compass. 'Let her fall off, steer due south! She can take it!'

He seized the lieutenant's arm and saw him staring at him like a stranger.

'Why should he make his number to *us*, for God's sake?'

'Look, sir!' The seaman was almost incoherent. 'Christ Almighty!'

The telescope in Penrose's wet fingers felt like ice. He had just seen it. A moment later when they would have been wallowing round on to a new tack, they would have been close enough to hear it: the sound of trucks, even as the line of ports opened along the frigate's side to reveal the guns, and the men who had been crouching there, prepared to fire them.

The great sails filled again, and the taut rigging rattled and hummed in protest. But nothing carried away.

Penrose watched the other ship, his mind as cold as the glass in his hands; everything was clear. *Huntress* had been taken, and within minutes it would have been too late. Someone had tried to warn them, in the only way a seaman would know and recognise.

He felt a muscle jerk in his throat as smoke billowed from the frigate's side to blow instantly inboard again, so that the long tongues of fire looked solid, like furnace bars.

He heard voices crying out as iron crashed across the schooner's deck, and a length of the larboard bulwark was shivered to fragments. Men had fallen, how badly injured Penrose could not tell. But the masts were still standing, and the sails as hard as steel. Only a topsail had been punctured by a shot fired too soon, the wind tearing the canvas to ribbons like a giant ripping paper.

He levelled the glass again, shutting his mind to the pitiful cries, and to the fear which would follow if he allowed it.

The *Huntress* was changing tack; no wonder she had left it so late. Even in the spray and fading light, he could see the battering she had taken on her opposite side. They had not surrendered without a fight, although that was little enough, for what they had given in exchange.

He swung round and saw the master's mate tying the lieutenant's wrist with his neckerchief.

He strode to his friend, and steadied him. 'Hold on, Jack.' He did not blink as another ragged broadside exploded somewhere. As if it were happening in a dream, and to somebody else.

'We must find the flagship, Jack. The admiral must be told.'

Tyler tried to speak but the pain made him gasp.

Penrose persisted, '*Huntress* was the last patrol. The guard-ship.'

Tyler tried again, and managed to say one word. '*Elba.*'

It was enough.

Bolitho leaned back in his chair, his shirt clinging damply to the warm leather. Beyond the stern windows there was only darkness, whilst here in the cabin the shaded light from a solitary lantern threw shadows across the paintwork and the chequered deck covering, like strange dancers keeping time with *Frobisher*'s uneven movements.

How could a ship so large be so silent? There was only an occasional sound of feet overhead, or cordage being man-handled to trim a yard, or take the slack out of a sail.

He knew that he should sleep, just as he knew that he would be unable to do so. He covered his blind eye and looked at the unfinished letter which lay open on top of his chart.

Writing to Catherine always gave him a sense of conversing, of sharing the days and nights with her. *Frobisher* might be on passage for England before this particular letter was concluded.

He stood up and moved about the cabin, his hand brushing against one of the tethered guns. Even the metal felt warm, as if it had been fired only hours earlier.

They had not met with *Huntress*, and in his heart he knew

Tyacke had been humouring him with the belief that they would make a final contact before Bolitho handed over his command.

At first light they would come about and head for Malta. But until then . . . .

Allday was taking great care not to intrude upon his thoughts, but he was unable to conceal his relief that they were finally going home.

How would Allday settle down, what would he do? Proprietor of a small country inn, seeing the same faces every day, in a world where men discussed crops, livestock and the weather with equal authority. Not the sea. . . . But he would have Unis and little Kate. He would have to begin learning all over again. A different life. *Like me.*

He thought of going on deck, but knew that his presence would worry the watchkeepers. On the same tack and under reduced canvas, it would be hard enough for some of them to stay awake without their admiral pacing up and down. Tyacke would be in his cabin, planning, preparing for his ship's immediate future, and his own. Tyacke was probably the one person who had never expected hope to hold out its hand to him; the one man who so richly deserved it.

And what of Avery; would he remain in the navy or reconsider his uncle's offer? It was hard to imagine any one of his little crew in any life but this.

In fact Avery was on deck, clinging to the empty hammock nettings, and listening to the ship shuddering and groaning above and around him. Alan Tollemache, the third lieutenant, had the watch, but he had retreated to the poop after two attempts to open a conversation.

It was not that Avery disliked him, even though he tended to brag about himself and his family; it was simply that he wanted to be alone, to have only his thoughts and memories for company. It was difficult enough for any flag lieutenant to fit completely into wardroom life with its rules and traditions, and where every thought and idea was shared. It had to be that way; the lieutenants were a group apart, *us* and *them*. It was natural enough, but Avery had never been able to be anything but himself, and solitary.

He had been thinking deeply about the future, and what he might do when Bolitho's flag came down. Promotion, and perhaps a small command of his own? He could sense a hundred arguments before he could even consider it. He served Sir Richard; to be appointed aide to some other flag officer was out of the question. His powerful uncle, Baron Sillitoe of Chiswick, then? He admired Sillitoe for having offered him a future, one of substance and prosperity, partly because he sensed what it had cost him to bend so far. He smiled, and tasted the raw salt on his lips. The prospect would certainly attract the beautiful Susanna. But even poor luffs had pride, and pride pulled in both directions.

With a sigh, he walked aft, tossing a casual wave to the dark group of figures around the compass box, and pausing as the poop's black outline loomed over him to glance again at the sky. No moon, and only an occasional star. It was a fine night after all, even during the hated middle watch. He was about to feel his way to the companion ladder when something caused him to hesitate, and to turn, as if someone had called his name.

But there was nothing. It was an intrusion into thoughts which had been quiet, meditative, and for some reason he was troubled by it.

When he climbed into his swaying cot the disquiet remained with him, and sleep was denied him.

As in all men-of-war, shorthanded or not, *Frobisher*'s company were turned-to when there was barely enough light to mark sea from sky. It was always a time of bustle and purpose, and on this day there was not a man jack aboard who did not know that the ship, which was their home, their way of life, their reason for being, would soon be turning her jib boom towards the west, and eventually to England.

Kellett, the first lieutenant, was in charge of the morning watch, as the decks were washed down and the water casks filled with some of their last supply. The lazy breeze was heavy with greasy smells from the galley funnel.

Kellett saw the signals midshipman watching him, and said, 'Aloft with you, Mr Singleton, and see if you can be the first to sight the wretched *Huntress*! And cling to the thought while you climb: after this, *you* may be the one giving orders to some snotty midshipman, if your wits serve you well in your examination!'

The midshipman ran to the shrouds and began the long climb up the ratlines.

Someone whispered, 'Cap'n, sir.'

Tyacke strode to the compass and glanced at the topsails, then his eyes found Singleton clawing his way past the maintop.

'He'll see nothing, I daresay.'

Kellett was watching the working parties being dismissed, and thought of the tasks he had detailed for the day.

Tyacke was saying, 'If the wind holds steady, we should make a fair passage.'

Kellett listened with some curiosity. The captain rarely made idle observations, any more than he ever showed uncertainty in the presence of his officers. He had been in awe of Tyacke when he had suddenly accepted this command, and resentful also. Now he could not imagine *Frobisher* without him.

Tyacke was observing Singleton's progress, remembering how Bolitho had once confided in him, and told him how the fear of heights had disturbed him as a 'young gentleman'. He had heard Kellett's remarks to the youth concerning promotion, and, reluctantly, he had concluded that Singleton might make a good officer, provided he had a captain to drive him.

Oblivious to all of them, the midshipman had reached the crosstrees, where a tanned and scarred seaman was already on duty. Singleton had seen him fumbling with a packet when he had appeared beside him, and guessed that the man had been chewing tobacco, a punishable offence while on watch.

Singleton unslung his telescope, pleased that he was not out of breath. He would not report the offender, and he knew that the seaman, an old hand, would remember him for it. He trained the glass with great care, recalling the admiral's words to him. *My eyes.*

There was an horizon at last, very thin and hard, like polished silver.

It would be strange to leave this ship, he thought, to take that once unimaginable step from midshipman's berth to wardroom. To be able to speak openly with fellow lieutenants, who, up until now, had seemed bent on making every midshipman's life a perfect misery.

The old seaman was studying him, the seriousness on his young features. With one or two of the others, he would have remained silent, but the signals midshipman had always seemed fair enough.

He said calmly, 'There's a ship out yonder, Mr Singleton.'

Singleton lowered the heavy glass and stared at him. 'If I can't see it with this, then I. . . .' He grinned, and raised it again. 'Where away?'

'Larboard bow, very fine.'

Singleton tried again. Nothing. He knew about some of the older lookouts; it was a second sense, someone had told him.

He held his breath and waited for *Frobisher* to lift again. *And there it was.* How could he not have seen it?

He screwed his eye closer and saw the image strengthen. Catching the light from somewhere. A sail, touched with yellow gold, standing up from the hard horizon; like a feather, he thought.

He looked at his companion. 'I see her.' He smiled. 'My thanks.'

On the quarterdeck, every face was raised as Singleton's voice echoed down from the mainmast.

'Deck there! Sail, fine on the larboard bow!'

Tyacke exclaimed, 'Well, I'll be damned!'

Kellett said, 'Shall I inform the admiral, sir?'

Tyacke looked at him. 'When we know a bit more.' As Kellett hurried away, he added, 'He won't need telling.'

It was another hour before the masthead could recognise the newcomer. Tyacke watched Bolitho's face keenly as he told him.

'*Tireless*, James? Not *Huntress* after all?' He smiled, but the mood seemed to elude him. 'Well, she may have news for us, although from that direction I doubt it.'

When admiral and flag lieutenant joined the others on the quarterdeck, Tyacke noticed that Bolitho was dressed in a clean shirt and breeches. He looked rested and alert now, even though there had been a light burning in his cabin throughout the night watches.

Avery said, 'May *Tireless* not have seen *Huntress*, Sir Richard?'

Bolitho did not answer, trying to gauge the depth of his feelings. He could feel nothing but a sense of inevitability, of destiny. As if his reluctance to return to Malta had been

257

justified. He saw Allday watching him; even Yovell was here on this bright morning.

Singleton yelled down, '*Tireless* has hoisted a signal, sir!'

Lieutenant Pennington murmured, 'We are all agog, sir.' Nobody laughed.

Singleton must have been very aware of the signal and its importance, even though he would not understand it. But his voice did not break or quiver.

'From *Tireless. Enemy in Sight!*'

Bolitho looked at Tyacke, ignoring or detached from the babble of disbelief and astonishment which separated them.

'So now we know, James. The trap is sprung. All else was delusion.'

He turned away, one hand on his shirt, and Tyacke thought he murmured, 'Don't leave me.'

Then he smiled, as if he had heard her voice.

18

Final Embrace

Bolitho pressed his face against the thick glass of the quarter-gallery, and watched the little schooner's distorted shape as she clawed her way across the wind.

When he turned he saw the stains of salt water on the deck covering, where *Tireless*'s captain had stood after a hasty pull to the flagship.

So young, so earnest, perhaps not able to grasp the magnitude of these events. He had almost pleaded, 'I can stay in company, Sir Richard. We're no match for close action, but surely we could do something?'

Bolitho had said, 'You have done enough. The signal, for instance.'

Penrose had forced a smile. 'I heard it said that you used the same ruse to deceive a more powerful enemy, so that he should believe you had sighted friendly ships.'

How could Penrose have known? It was beyond trickery now.

Bolitho had said, 'They will not run. They dare not. There is too much at stake.' He had taken his hand. 'Go to Malta with all haste. Tell the senior officer. I shall rely on it.'

Tyacke was standing by the table now, Avery by the fine wine cooler, his hand touching it as if to reassure himself. Beyond the screen there was utter silence except for the muffled sounds of sea and rigging. A ship holding her breath.

Tyacke said, 'Shall I remain on this course, Sir Richard?'

Bolitho walked to the table and lifted a corner of the chart. His unfinished letter still lay there; it had been hidden by the chart. Lieutenant Penrose could have picked it up, put it inside his spray-dappled coat before returning to his little command. And, sooner or later, she would have read it . . . .

He recalled what Tyacke had asked him; he had not questioned or even doubted him. So much trust. It was like a betrayal, and he was suddenly angry.

'Those *fools* in London, what do they know or even care, until all at once it is too late! All they can think about is grand receptions, peerages and self-congratulation! Men have died because of their arrogance and complacency! And will go on dying!'

Avery had stepped away from the cooler, his eyes very bright in the filtered sunshine. He had never seen Bolitho reveal his anger before, even though, many times, he had guessed it was there.

Bolitho said, '*Huntress* was taken, a vital link in the chain of an overstretched squadron! What did their lordships expect? Perhaps that the tyrant would remain passive, indifferent? This is not merely a man, but a colossus, one who has cowed and conquered every force that stood against him, from Egypt to the snows of Russia, from the Indian Ocean to the Spanish Main. What in hell's name did they expect?'

He calmed himself with an effort. 'There are hundreds, perhaps thousands of men who owed their power and influence to Napoleon. Without him to direct them, they are nothing.' He thought of Penrose again, and his signal. 'Oh, they will come, and we shall be ready for them.' He plucked his shirt from his body. 'But the trap is sprung. The *maybes* and the *if onlys* have no place here.'

He looked at Tyacke, his eyes very clear. 'You thought, perhaps, that nobody but a fool would challenge a ship of the line?'

Tyacke glanced at the chart, and saw the letter beneath it.

'*Frobisher* will dish them up, Sir Richard, you have my word on it!'

Yovell had appeared silently, and ventured, 'Then it will be war, Sir Richard?'

Bolitho said, 'We shall soon know.'

They all looked at the open skylight as the lookout's voice pealed, 'Deck there! Sail to the nor'east!'

Bolitho turned to Avery. 'Take a glass, George. I need your experience today.'

Avery snatched up his hat. 'Could it be *Huntress*, Sir Richard?'

Another voice reached down to the great cabin. It was Midshipman Singleton this time.

'Deck there! Another sail to the nor'east!'

Bolitho pushed the lock of hair from his forehead. 'I think not, George.' Then he smiled, and Avery was very conscious of the warmth in it. 'And fetch down Mr Singleton, or he'll have no lungs left!'

The door closed and Tyacke waited, blue eyes watching every movement, every changing mood, like reflections on the sea's face.

Bolitho nodded slowly. 'Yes, James, the two we saw in Algiers. Privateers, renegades, pirates, who can say? They will fight. They cannot afford to fail.'

Tyacke glanced around the cabin, imagining it stripped of all things personal, precious to this unbreakable man. A place of war.

'I would like to speak with the people, Sir Richard.'

Bolitho touched his arm as he walked to the opposite side. 'Good. It is their right.'

Tyacke understood. *What you would do in my place.* What so many would not.

Their eyes met, and Bolitho said quietly, 'Ten minutes, then? It will be enough, I think.'

Tyacke closed the door behind him, and Yovell, too, prepared to leave.

Bolitho said, 'Wait a moment, Daniel. Bring me a pen. Then you may put this letter in the strongbox.'

Yovell went to the desk where he kept his pens. Pipes shrilled, and he was surprised that he was unafraid.

'All hands! Clear the lower deck and lay aft!'

He looked toward the tall figure by the table, remembering. *It is their right.* Then he pulled open a drawer, his mind clear. He would fetch his Bible; it had never failed to comfort him. He placed a fresh pen on the table and saw Bolitho press the letter between his hands. His profile was composed, as if he was able to detach himself and his mind from the din of running feet, and the voices calling to one another. Voices offering hope and reassurance, and he was moved by them.

And then there was utter silence again; he thought of

the flag lieutenant up in the crosstrees with his telescope, probably looking down at the ship and the assembled seamen and marines, so rarely seen all together at one time.

Bolitho did not look up as Yovell padded quietly from the cabin. He read the first part of the letter very slowly, and hoped she would hear his voice when she read it. How could he be so sure that she would even receive it, or that they would be victorious today?

The pen hesitated above the letter, and then he smiled. There was nothing to add.

He wrote, *I love thee, Kate, my rose.* Then he kissed it, and sealed it with great care.

He was aware of the Royal Marine sentry outside the door, shuffling his feet and probably trying to hear what the captain was saying on deck.

The adjoining door opened and Allday entered, pausing only to close the skylight. His own way of holding the things he hated at bay. He said offhandedly, 'Young Mr Singleton says there are two frigates, Sir Richard.' He glanced at the eighteen-pounder gun near him. 'They'll not do much, no matter what they thinks, an' that's no error!'

Bolitho smiled at him, and hoped that there was no sadness in his heart.

But we know differently, my dear friend. We have done it ourselves. Can you not remember?

Instead he said, 'We've a fine day for it, old friend.' He saw Allday's eyes move to the swords on their rack. 'So let's be about it!'

Ozzard was here also, Bolitho's coat over his narrow shoulder. 'This one, Sir Richard?'

'Yes.'

It would be a hard fight, no matter what Allday thought about it. *Frobisher*'s company would need to see him. To know they were not alone, and that someone cared for them.

Then the drums began to rattle, urgent and insistent.

'Hands to quarters! Clear for action!'

He slipped his arms into the sleeves and took his hat from Ozzard. The one she had persuaded him to buy in that other, timeless shop in St James's.

My admiral of England.

He held out his arms and waited for Allday to fasten the

262

old sword into position. Ozzard would take the glittering presentation blade with him when he went down to the orlop, when the guns began their deadly symphony.

Allday opened the door for him and the marine sentry slammed his heels together, waiting to be released from this duty so that he could be with his comrades.

Allday closed the door from habit, even though the ship would soon be cleared from bow to stern, screens and cabins torn down, personal possessions stowed away until they were recovered by their owners, or sold to their mates if fate turned against them.

He found time to notice that Bolitho did not look back.

Captain James Tyacke stood by the quarterdeck rail, his arms folded while he surveyed the ship, *his* ship, in this moment of instinct and experience when nothing could be overlooked. He could feel the first lieutenant watching him, perhaps seeking approval, or preparing for some sharp criticism. But he was a good officer, and he had done well. The chain slings had been rigged to the yards, and nets spread to protect men on the maindeck from falling debris. There were boarding nets also. They could not estimate the strength or the determination of the enemy. If fanatics from a chebeck could hack their way aboard, this was no time to take chances.

He looked along each line of guns, the eighteen-pounders which made up half of *Frobisher*'s artillery. Until action was joined, each remained a separate unit, the gun captains sorting over the rows of black balls in the shot garlands. A good gun captain could select a perfectly moulded shot just by turning it in his hands.

A glance aloft, to the small scarlet clusters in each fighting top: marine marksmen and others who could aim and fire the deadly swivel guns. Known by the Royals as daisy cutters, they could scythe anything more than an inch high to the ground, or to the deck. Most sailors hated the swivels; they were unpredictable, and could be equally dangerous to friend and foe alike.

The decks had been well sanded. It was said to prevent men from slipping in the heat of action, although everyone knew the real reason for it.

'Well done, Mr Kellett.' Tyacke took a telescope from the rack and raised it to his eye. Without looking, he knew that Kellett was smiling his deceptively gentle smile, satisfied.

He felt his jaw tighten as the first pyramid of sails appeared to rise out of the shark-blue water like a phantom. He moved the glass again. The second frigate had luffed, and was drawing away from her consort. Almost to himself, he said, 'They hope to divide our fire.'

He lowered the glass slightly and glanced up at *Frobisher*'s spread of canvas, topsails and forecourse, flying and outer jib, with the big driver angled across the poop, the White Ensign streaming out from the peak. He knew that Tregidgo, the sailing master, was watching him. He ignored him. They all had their vital roles to play, but he was the captain. He must decide.

The wind was as before, from the north-west, not strong, but steady. Enough to change tack when required. She would handle even better when the order was given to slip the boats from their tow-lines astern; the main deck looked strangely clean and bare without them. Always a bad moment for sailors, when they saw their means of survival cast adrift. But the risk of flying splinters was far greater.

The sky was clearing, so different from the dawn. Long banks of pale clouds, but the sun already stronger and higher. He grimaced. A perfect setting.

He turned to face Kellett. 'I want to make this quite clear. When we get to grips with those fellows, I want every available man at his station. Provided he can walk, I need him *today*, and I'll not stand for carrying passengers! The lower gundeck is the key to any fight with faster vessels. Inform Mr Gage and Mr Armytage that I expect them to maintain rapid fire no matter what may be happening up here. Is that understood?'

Kellett nodded. He had heard about Tyacke's experience at the Nile, when he had been on the lower gundeck with the big thirty-two pounders. Guns which, if properly laid and trained, could pierce nearly three feet of solid oak. Or so it was claimed.

Kellett had only served on a lower gundeck once, as a very junior lieutenant. The noise and the inferno of fire and smoke had been enough to drive some men to panic. It was a place and a time where only discipline and rigid training could overcome fear and madness. How it must have been for Tyacke . . . .

He remarked, 'They wear no colours, sir.' It was something to say, to ease the tension.

Tyacke raised his glass again. 'They soon will. And by God they'll lose them, too!'

He concentrated on the leading frigate. There was a fine display of gilded carving around her beakhead. He smiled, unconsciously. She was Spanish, or had been once. He wondered what had happened to *Huntress*; perhaps they had put her down after the failure to lure *Tireless* beneath her broadside. He thought of his own depleted company. He must keep the enemy at a distance, cripple at least one of them.

How easy it was to regard strange ships as enemies; he had been doing it for most of his life. He thought suddenly of Bolitho. He was in the chart room, probably keeping out of the way, when every fibre in his body was tugging at him to take command, as a captain again. But there was neither fleet nor squadron this time, and some of the waiting seamen would be thinking as much. Their fate lay in the hands of three captains, and the man whose flag whipped out from the mainmast truck.

Tyacke heard Midshipman Singleton instructing his signals party by the halliards. The boy seemed different in some way, not yet mature, but indefinably different.

Tyacke moved to the compass box and gazed at the group there, the backbone of any company committed to action. The master and his mates, three midshipmen to carry messages, four helmsmen at the tall double wheel, and beyond them, the rest of the afterguard, the marines and nine-pounder crews. Protected by nothing more than tightly-packed hammocks in the nettings, they would be the first target for any sharpshooter.

He said, 'Converging tack, Mr Tregidgo.' He saw him nod; Tregidgo was not one to waste words. 'We will engage from either side.' He looked at their faces, stiff, empty. It was too late for anything else. *I have decided.*

He walked to the rail and gripped it. Warm, but nothing more. He smiled tightly. That would soon change. He looked along his command yet again, sobered by the thought that she might not be his for much longer. At the Nile, his own captain had fallen, and so many others on that bloody day. Could Kellett fight the ship if that happened? He shook himself angrily. It was not that. He had faced and accepted death many times. It was the navy's way, perhaps the only way. To make men confront and accept what was, in truth, unacceptable.

It was Marion. The new belief, the hope that a hand had reached out for him. Something he had sometimes dreamed about, but too often dreaded. He thought of Portsmouth, gazing at the nearest gun's crew. When all this had begun, when she had come to find him. With such quiet warmth, and such pride.

He thought of Bolitho's unfinished letter, hidden by the chart in the great cabin. Marion could never have realised what strength he had found in her.

He heard Allday's voice from the poop, and turned in readiness. He saw Bolitho, apparently quite calm, and Allday walking with him. As a friend, an equal. He smiled. No wonder it was so hard for people to understand, let alone share.

He touched his hat. 'I would like to alter course, Sir Richard. Those two beauties will try to harry us, to use haste to avoid being dismasted.' He waited while Bolitho took the big signals telescope from Midshipman Singleton, saw the way he held his head at an angle to obtain the best image. It was not possible to believe that he was blind in one eye.

'They'm running up their colours, sir!'

Tyacke levelled his glass on the leading frigate. Had he really clung to a last doubt, a hope? He could see the Tricolour standing out to the wind. More than a gesture; it meant that this was war again, even if the rest of the world was ignorant of it. Napoleon had escaped from what had been, at best, a token captivity. He recalled Bolitho's rare anger, his despair for the men he had led, who, in his eyes, had been betrayed by complacency. Tyacke glanced at him now, and saw the bitterness on his features as he returned the glass to Singleton.

Then he looked directly at his flag captain. 'So it is war once more, James.' There was a cold edge to his voice. 'So much for the Bourbon Restoration.' He looked around at the silent gun crews and the waiting seamen, and the marines, faces shadowed beneath their leather hats. Very quietly, he said, 'Too much blood, too many good men.'

Then he smiled, his teeth very white in his tanned face, and only those close enough could see the pain and the anger which lay there.

'So cast the boats adrift, Captain Tyacke, and let us give these scum a lesson, teach them that now, as before, *we are here*, and ready!'

Somebody gave a wild cheer, and it was carried along the deck to the forecastle and the men crouching at the carronades, although they could not have heard a single word.

It was infectious. A madness, and yet so much more.

Tyacke touched his hat with equal formality. 'I am yours to command, Sir Richard.'

Allday watched the cluster of boats drift haphazardly away from the counter. There was no cheering now, nor would there be until the flag came down. Theirs or ours, the rules never changed.

He touched his chest as the pain moved through him like a warning. Then he grinned. One more time. And they were still together.

Bolitho stood beside Tyacke and watched the oncoming ships. The range was closing, and, at a guess, stood at about three miles. An hour and a half had passed since *Frobisher* had cleared for action; it felt like an eternity.

The two frigates were almost in line ahead, their sails overlapping, as if they were joined. It was the usual illusion; they were perhaps a mile apart, and pointing directly towards *Frobisher*'s larboard bow. The wind had not varied by a degree; it was still north-westerly, light but steady enough. The frigates were close-hauled on the starboard tack, probably as near to the wind as they could manage.

'Shall I run out, Sir Richard?'

Bolitho glanced at him, at his burned profile, and the steady blue eye.

'I think they intend to tackle us separately. They'd never risk a fight broadside-to-broadside, not against our armament. If I were in command, I would change tack at the last possible moment. The leader could then lie athwart our hawse and be able to rake us as he passes, and we'd not be able to bring a single gun to bear.'

Tyacke nodded slowly, seeing it. 'If we try to follow him round, which we can do with the wind in our favour, the other one will go for our stern, and pour a broadside through us while we are engaged. I think we should run out now, and try to cripple one of them with our heavy battery.' He looked at Bolitho. 'What do *you* suggest? You're a frigate captain, and always will be. I'd welcome your experience!'

Bolitho smiled. 'That was bravely said. It is just a feeling.' He could not keep the excitement out of his voice. 'Those two captains are desperate, to engage us, to cripple us, above all to provoke close action. The wind is in our favour, but they can match our strength with their agility. I think that the *unexpected* will win the day. We can come about into the wind, be taken aback in all probability, but we can give each a broadside before either captain can stand away. What say you, James?'

Tyacke was staring at the two oncoming frigates, as if they were being drawn towards *Frobisher* by an invisible force, like a line on a chart.

'I'll pass the word.'

He looked down as Bolitho touched his sleeve. 'When we turn, run out the upper guns, James. Keep the lower gundeck sealed. It will give them something to ponder over.'

Tyacke smiled. 'It might just work, by God! Trick for trick!'

Bolitho saw Avery watching him, brushing threads of cordage from his breeches after his hasty descent to the deck.

'I'll send *him*, if I may, James. Captains and admirals should sometimes keep their distance.'

He saw Tyacke's smile open into a grin. Because of the unlikely plan of action, or because he had not been too proud to ask for advice? But he was already calling to Kellett and the other lieutenants to outline what he required of them.

Avery listened to Bolitho without comment, his expression thoughtful, curious.

Bolitho repeated, 'No double-shotting, no grape. I want every shot to find its target. Tell the lieutenant on the lower gundeck to keep firing, no matter what!' His grey eyes moved towards the waiting gun crews. 'Otherwise it will be bloody work up here.'

Avery looked at the other ships. Was it only his imagination, or were they much closer?

'And Napoleon, Sir Richard? Where will he be, at this moment?'

Bolitho heard the crash of a solitary gun, but could see no

telltale fall of shot. A signal, one ship to the other? A misfire, perhaps?

He answered, 'He could be anywhere.' He added quietly, 'He may have gone to his home in Corsica, but a few miles from Elba. Can you imagine a more reckless place to imprison such a man? But my guess is France, where his real strength lies, where people will rise up and follow him yet again.'

'You admire him, don't you, Sir Richard?'

'*Admire*? That is too strong a word. He is the enemy.' Then he gripped his arm, the mood changing again. 'But if I were a Frenchman, I would be there to welcome him.'

He watched Avery move away, and said, 'Take young Singleton, for the experience.' He shaded his eye to look at the masthead. 'I shall need no signals today.'

Avery hesitated, and saw some of the seamen running to the braces and halliards, Tyacke consulting the sailing master and his mates by the compass. In a moment the ship would alter course to larboard, into the wind, into the enemy. He looked at the distant pyramids of sails. Half an hour, at the most. He beckoned to the midshipman and together they hurried to the companion ladder.

After the brightness of the upper deck, the lower hull seemed like a musty vault.

When they reached the lower gundeck, Avery had to stand for several seconds to accustom his eyes to the gloom, and the sudden sense of danger. A little, feeble light filtered through the tiny observation ports on either bow, and from lanterns protected behind thick glass. The guns were manned and loaded, and he could see the eyes of some of the seamen glinting as they turned to watch him. Was that why Bolitho had told him to take Singleton with him? Because he was known to these men, young or not, and because as flag lieutenant he himself would be, and would remain, a stranger?

Objects were taking shape on either side, the great black humps of the breeches, the powerful thirty-two pounders, fourteen on either side. Tiny pin-pricks of light, like malevolent eyes, flickered in each match tub, slow matches in readiness if the more modern flintlock should fail or misfire.

He was joined by the two lieutenants in charge, 'Holly' Gage and Walter Armytage. He met them often enough in the wardroom, but it went no further than that.

He could feel the intensity of their concentration as he explained what was intended.

Gage said doubtfully, 'Might work.'

His friend laughed, and some of his men leaned over to listen. 'I shall tell our people we need a miracle today!'

Avery touched his arm. 'If the order comes, you'll know they're trying to board us.' He gestured toward the guns. 'Seal the ports and clear the deck. We'll need every man jack to repel an attack in strength!'

As they moved to the ladder again, he saw the side of the hull, dull red in the feeble light. If the enemy's iron burst into this crowded deck, at least the paint would conceal the blood.

Singleton said, '*Will* it work, sir?' He sounded very serious, but not afraid.

Avery thought of all those other times, and replied, 'If anyone can do it, *he* can.'

The light seemed blinding on the upper deck. Avery saw Tyacke turn towards the admiral, one arm half-raised as he said, 'Now, sir?'

Bolitho nodded, and gripped his sword against his hip.

'Stand by on the quarterdeck!'

'*Ready ho!*'

Tyacke barely raised his voice. 'Put the helm down!'

As the wheel was hauled over and the ship began to turn to larboard, men were already running like demons to let go the headsail sheets, spilling out the wind so as not to hamper the ship's head from swinging.

Instead of the peace and the menace of their approach, everything was noise and orderly confusion, the sails banging and flapping wildly as the ship continued to turn.

Bolitho walked to the opposite side and watched the enemy. Perhaps they had been expecting *Frobisher* to stand downwind to give battle to the leader, exposing her stern to the other frigate. Now it appeared as if they and not *Frobisher* were turning, separating, one on either bow.

He glanced aloft, at the writhing sails pressed against masts and yards. The ship was aback, unable to pay off on either tack, but the frigates were in a worse plight, sailing so close to the wind that they had no choice but to alter course. *Frobisher* was almost hove-to, and might even have lost steerage way, but it made no difference now.

He shouted, 'At 'em, lads!'

The port lids were hauled up, and to the shrill of a whistle the main deck eighteen-pounders trundled their black muzzles out into the sunlight.

'As you bear! *Fire!*' That was Lieutenant Pennington, his face scarred from the fight with the Algerines. The leading frigate seemed to turn away, her foremast and rigging reeling over in the carefully-aimed broadside, gun by gun, each shot controlled by Pennington and another lieutenant. Up forward, the breathless crews were already sponging out and ramming home new charges, oblivious to the banging canvas and the yells of topmen high above them.

'As you bear!' Tyacke's sword blinked in the sun as he brought it down. '*Fire!*'

The second frigate had recovered and was already setting more sails, to continue with her original attack or to escape further setbacks, Bolitho could not tell. She was standing across the starboard bow, changing tack, close enough to her damaged consort to be able to see the destruction and the upended guns.

Bolitho looked at Avery. '*Now!*'

Avery, with Singleton at his heels, ran for the companion ladder, tugging a whistle from his shirt as he stumbled and almost fell down the last steps.

Smoky daylight scythed through the gundeck as the port lids opened as one, and the crews threw themselves on the tackles to haul their massive charges towards the enemy. Each 'Long Nine', as these guns were nicknamed, weighed three tons, and the naked backs of the seamen were soon shining with sweat.

Lieutenant Gage was pressed up to his small spy-hole, then he turned, his face wild. 'On the uproll, lads!'

Avery heard Singleton shout, 'Cover your ears, sir!' Then the world seemed to explode, smoke billowing through the deck, where men were already serving their guns and others waited with handspikes and rammers to compete with their messmates. The same men who served these guns slept and ate beside them; the guns were the first things they saw upon waking every day, and, too often, in dying, the last.

Each gun captain held up his fist, and Armytage yelled, 'Ready, sir!'

271

'Fire!'

Again the guns crashed inboard on their tackles, but suddenly another whistle shrilled, and the same crews were struggling to secure them and close the ports to prevent the enemy boarders from attacking them in their midst. In their home.

Armytage was shouting, 'Arm yourselves!' As he ran past Avery, he called, 'We're going to foul the first bugger, George! We've done for the other one!' He was grinning, mad with excitement, but all Avery could think was that it was the first time he had called him by name.

On deck, Bolitho watched the second frigate with something like disbelief. An enemy, driven by hatred and revenge, but a thing of beauty, two broadsides from those thirty-two-pounders had reduced her to a mastless wreck. He turned and stared at the mainmast of the frigate which had taken their first, carefully aimed broadside, when *Frobisher* had caught the enemy completely by surprise. A collision was inevitable; *Frobisher* had not regained the wind, and the other ship was out of command. Seamen and marines were already running to the point of impact, bayonets and cutlasses shining through the seemingly immovable pall of pale smoke.

There were cheers, too, as more men came pouring from the lower gundeck, either already armed or snatching up weapons from the chests prepared earlier by the gunner.

Bolitho saw Captain Wise of the Royal Marines striding, not deigning to run after his men as they crouched by the hammock nettings and searched for targets.

Shots cracked and whined overhead or smacked through the heavy canvas, and here and there a man fell, or was dragged away by his companions. But their blood was up; no boarder would survive this day.

He saw Avery and Singleton hurrying toward the quarterdeck; the midshipman was almost knocked over by a charging, wild-eyed marine.

Tyacke waved his sword. 'Board 'em, lads! Cut that bloody flag down!'

Bolitho strained his eyes through the smoke, and saw men already on the frigate's forecastle. There was resistance, but the harsh blast of a swivel gun scattered the defiant ones like torn rags.

Singleton's voice cracked for the first time. 'They've struck, sir! They're done for!' He was almost weeping with excitement.

Bolitho turned to Allday. So it was war again. But even war would not keep him from her.

A seaman running with a boarding pike slipped on blood and would have fallen, but for Bolitho's grip on his arm.

He lifted his eyes in disbelief, and managed to stammer, '*Thankee*, Sir Richard! I be all right now!'

Allday was about to say something, he did not know what, when he felt the pain again, so intense that he could barely move. But it was not the old wound this time. He saw Bolitho turn and stare at him, as if he would speak, but seemed unable to find the words.

He heard Avery shout, '*Hold him!*' Then he saw Bolitho fall. It was like being given new life, new strength; he leaped forward and caught him around the shoulders, holding him, lowering him carefully, everything else without meaning or purpose.

Men were cheering, some firing their muskets. It meant nothing.

From the starboard gangway Tyacke saw him fall, but knew he must not leave his men while they boarded the enemy, following his orders. Midshipman Singleton, who had become a man this day, also saw him fall, and was on his knees beside him with Allday and Avery.

Bolitho turned his face away from the sunlight which lanced down between the shrouds and the limp sails. His eye was stinging in the smoke, and he wanted to rub it. But when he attempted to move, there was no response, no sensation, only numbness.

Shadows moved across the sun, and he could hear faint cheers, as if they came from another time, another victory.

They were all here, then. *Waiting*. A sudden anxiety ran through him.

Where was Herrick? Herrick should be here . . . .

Someone reached around him and dabbed his face with a wet cloth. He recognised the sleeve; it was Lefroy, the bald surgeon.

He heard Allday's painful breathing, and needed to tell him, to reassure him. Everything would be the same.

273

But when he tried to reach out for him, he realised for the first time that his hand was tightly gripped between Allday's. Then he saw him, watching him, his hair shaggy against the smoke and the sun.

Allday murmured, 'Mr Herrick's not here, Cap'n. But don't you fret now.'

It was wrong that he should be so distressed. One who had done so much. He tried again, and said, 'Easy, old friend, be easy now.' He felt Allday nod. 'No grief, we always knew . . . .'

Lefroy stood slowly, and said, 'He's gone, I'm afraid.'

Tyacke was here now, his sword still in his hand. He stood in silence, unable to accept it, and yet knowing that all the others were looking to him. To the captain.

Then something made him reach down and grip the sobbing midshipman's shoulder. Like that time at the Nile.

He said, 'Haul down his flag, Mr Singleton.' And then, gazing unseeingly at Allday's bowed head, 'Help him, will you? There's none better for the task.'

He saw Kellett and the others watching, the fight forgotten, the victory now pointless, empty.

He turned, as Avery stood and said quietly, 'Goodbye, dearest of men.'

As if she had spoken through him.

It was over.

Epilogue

The carriage wheeled into the stable yard and came to a halt with practised ease, and a stable boy ran to take the horses' heads. To pacify them, perhaps, after so short a journey from the harbour.

Adam Bolitho opened the door without hesitation. This was the only way he knew, to go through with it.

He climbed down and stood on the worn cobbles and stared at the old grey house with a certain defiance.

Young Matthew had remained on the carriage, his face grim and downcast, almost a stranger, like the stable boy.

It had been Bryan Ferguson's idea to send the carriage, as soon as he had received word that the frigate *Unrivalled* had anchored in Carrick Roads.

Adam glanced around now, at the carpets of daffodils and bluebells amongst the trees, seeing none of it.

This was the place where he had come for help, for sanctuary, when his mother had died. Then, from midshipman to post-captain, a life full of excitement, elation and pain; and he owed it all to one man, his uncle. And now he, too, was dead. It was still stark and unreal, and yet, in some strange way, he had sensed it.

When *Unrivalled* had entered Plymouth after her first weeks under his command, he had known it then. The port admiral, Vice-Admiral Valentine Keen, had put off in his barge to meet him personally. To tell him. *We Happy Few.*

Napoleon had escaped from Elba, and a few days later had landed near Cannes, to be greeted not with hostility or fear but like a conquering hero, especially by his marshals and Old Guard, who had never lost their faith in him.

He had walked the streets of Plymouth, grappling with it, fighting it. His uncle had fallen on the very day that Napoleon had stepped ashore.

Even through his grief, he had sensed the mood in that seaport which had seen so much. Anger, frustration, a sense of betrayal. He understood their bitterness; there was hardly a village in England which had not lost someone in a war against the old enemy. And in seaports like Plymouth and in garrison towns, there were too many cripples in evidence to allow them to forget.

In Falmouth, it had been much worse. Falmouth was no city but lived off the sea, and the ships of every size and flag which came and went on the tides. *Bad news rides a fast horse*, Ferguson had said. Enemies were nothing new to these people; like the sea, the dangers were always there. But this was different, close, personal. Falmouth had lost her most beloved son. The flag above the church of King Charles the Martyr was at half-mast, and idlers had dropped their eyes when he had climbed from his gig, as if they were unable to face him. During the short journey from the town square, past familiar fields where he had seen men and women working together in the warm spring sunlight, some had looked up as the coach with its familiar crest rattled past, as if they still believed, dared to hope, then, as quickly, they had looked away.

The pleasure of his new command seemed unimportant; there was no one with whom to share it now. Even the names and faces of his ship's company were blurred, a part of something else, irrelevant.

He himself had remained composed, withdrawn; he had seen too many men die in battle to be unprepared, or to reveal the distress which was now tearing him apart.

He saw Ferguson climb down from the carriage, using his solitary arm as if he had never known anything different. He was a good man, a reliable one, and a friend. Ferguson understood him well enough to ensure that he was spared the agony of being greeted by the people who worked here and on the estate, especially his wife Grace, who would have been unable to contain her tears.

How quiet it seemed, the windows in shadow, watching.

Ferguson said, 'We got the news two days back. A cutter

came into port. I told Lady Catherine myself. She left for London immediately.'

Adam turned and looked back at the stables, at the big mare Tamara, tossing her head up and down.

Ferguson saw his glance, and said, 'Lady Catherine will come back. She'd not leave Tamara.' He hesitated, his hand twisting at his belt. 'John Allday. D'you happen to know . . . .'

'Safe.' Bethune had sent a full report to Keen, probably quite a different kind from that which he would write for the Admiralty. But until the others came home, they would not know the full story.

Keen had tried to explain to him, and Adam had guessed much of it. *Frobisher* had returned to Malta to land her dead and wounded, although there had been few of either. Bethune, Tyacke, Avery; someone close to Sir Richard must have suggested a sea burial. To avoid the splendid ritual which had attended Nelson's death, the ostentatious displays of grief and mourning from people who had hated England's hero in life. To spare Catherine the agony of seeing the same mockery made of her lover's sacrifice.

They had buried him at sea. Adam had seen it as vividly as if he had been there. Wrapped in his flag, an admiral of England, at a place marked on a chart of which few would know. Surely no better resting-place, by his old ship *Hyperion*, and so many of her company whom he had never forgotten.

He found that he was on the stone steps, and knew Ferguson had stopped by the tall, double doors to allow him the time and the solitude for this reunion.

It was all exactly as he remembered it, the grave portraits, the great hearth where he had lain with Zenoria, some fresh flowers on a table, the door to the library partly open, as if somebody might appear there; he could even imagine the smell of jasmine.

He clenched his fists as he saw the sword, lying on a table in a patch of sunshine. Bethune must have sent it with his courier, perhaps not knowing what he should do with it. And Keen had sent a cutter to Falmouth with his own letter of condolence to Catherine. It was strange that he had not mentioned it in Plymouth.

He picked up the old sword very slowly, and saw the sheet of paper which had been folded beneath it.

It was Catherine's writing. What it must have cost her to sit here in anguish, and yet be able to think of him.

Dearest Adam,
  The sword outwore its scabbard. Wear it with pride, as he always wanted. God bless you.

Ferguson stepped quietly into the room and watched, holding his breath, as Adam Bolitho unfastened his own sword and clipped the old blade in its place.

In this room, and in this light, it was not Adam but Richard standing there, all those years ago, and he was deeply moved by it.

When he looked again, Adam was smiling, and holding out both hands to him.

It needed no words.

The last Bolitho had come home.

Second to None

Especially for you, Kim,
With all my love.

CONTENTS

The wave cry, the wind cry, the vast waters
Of the petrel and the porpoise. In my end is my beginning.

T. S. ELIOT

The midshipman stood beneath the cabin skylight, his body accepting the heavy motion of the ship around him. After the cramped quarters of the midshipmen's berth of the frigate in which he had taken passage from Plymouth, this powerful man-of-war seemed like a rock, and the great stern cabin a palace by comparison.

It was the anticipation which had sustained him when everything else seemed lost. Hope, despair, even fear had been ready companions until this moment.

The shipboard sounds were muffled, distant, voices far off and without meaning or purpose. Someone had warned him that joining a ship already in commission was always hard; there would be no friends or familiar faces to ease the jolts and scrapes. And this was to be his first ship.

It was still impossible to accept that he was here. He moved his head slightly and watched the cabin's other occupant, who was sitting behind a desk, the document the midshipman had carried so carefully inside his coat to avoid spray from the boat's oars turned towards the light of the sloping stern windows, and their glittering panorama of sea and sky.

The captain. The one man upon whom he had placed so much hope; a man he had never met before. His whole body was as taut as a signal halliard, his mouth like dust. It might be nothing. A cruel disappointment, the end of everything.

He realised with a start that the captain was looking at him, had asked him something. His age?

'Fourteen, sir.' It did not even sound like his own voice. He

1

saw the captain's eyes for the first time, more grey than blue, not unlike the sea beyond the spray-dappled windows.

There were other voices, nearer now. There was no more time.

Almost desperately he thrust his hand into his coat again, and held out the letter which he had guarded and nursed all the way from Falmouth.

'This is for you, sir. I was told to give it to no one else.'

He watched the captain slit open the envelope, his expression suddenly guarded. What was he thinking? He wished he had torn it up without even reading it himself.

He saw the captain's sun-browned hand tighten suddenly on the letter, so that it shivered in the reflected light. Anger, disapproval, emotion? He no longer knew what to expect. He thought of his mother, only minutes before she had died, thrusting a crumpled paper into his hands. How long ago? Weeks, months? It was like yesterday. An address in Falmouth, some twenty miles from Penzance where they had lived. He had walked all the way, his mother's note his only strength, his guide.

He heard the captain fold the letter and put it in his pocket. Again, the searching look, but there was no hostility. If anything, there was sadness.

'Your father, boy. What do you know of him?'

The midshipman faltered, off guard, but when he answered he sensed the change. 'He was a King's officer, sir. He was killed by a runaway horse in America.' He could see his mother in those final moments, holding out her arms to embrace him and then to push him away, before either of them broke down. He continued in the same quiet tone, 'My mother often described him to me. When she was dying she told me to make my way to Falmouth and seek your family, sir. I – I know my mother never married him, sir. I have always known, but . . .'

He broke off, unable to continue but very aware that the captain was on his feet, one hand on his arm, his face suddenly close, the face of the man, perhaps as few others ever saw him.

Captain Richard Bolitho said gently, 'As you must know, your father was my brother.'

It was becoming blurred. The tap at the door. Someone with a message for the captain.

2

Adam Bolitho awoke, his body tensed like a spring as he felt the uncertain grip on his arm. It came to him with the stark clarity of a pistol shot. The ship's motion was more unsteady, the sea noises intruding while his practised ear assessed each in turn.

In the dim glow of a shaded lantern he could see the swaying figure beside his cot, the white patches of a midshipman. He groaned and tried to thrust the dream from his mind.

He swung his legs to the deck, his feet searching for his hessian boots in this still unfamiliar cabin.

'What is it, Mr Fielding?' He had even managed to remember the young midshipman's name. He almost smiled. Fielding was fourteen. The same age as the midshipman in the dream which refused to leave him.

'Mr Wynter's respects, sir, but the wind is freshening and he thought . . .'

Adam Bolitho touched his arm and groped for his faded sea-going coat.

'He did right to call me. I'd rather lose an hour's sleep than lose my ship. I shall come up directly!' The boy fled.

He stood up and adjusted to the motion of His Britannic Majesty's frigate *Unrivalled. My ship*. What his beloved uncle had described as 'the most coveted gift'.

And it should have been his greatest prize. A ship so new that the paint had been scarcely dry when he had read himself in, a frigate of the finest design, fast and powerful. He glanced at the dark stern windows, as if he were still in the old *Hyperion*'s great cabin, his life suddenly changed. And by one man.

He touched his pockets without even noticing it, ensuring that he had all he needed. He would go on deck, where the officer-of-the-watch would be anxiously waiting to gauge his mood, more nervous at the prospect of disturbing his captain than at the threat of the wind.

He knew it was mostly his own fault; he had remained apart and aloof from his officers since taking command. It must not, could not continue.

He turned away from the stern windows. The rest was just a dream. His uncle was dead, and only the ship was reality. And he, Captain Adam Bolitho, was quite alone.

3

1

A Hero Remembered

Lieutenant Leigh Galbraith strode aft along the frigate's maindeck and into the shadows of the poop. He was careful not to hurry, or to show any unusual concern which might create rumour amongst the groups of seamen and marines working at their various forenoon tasks.

Galbraith was tall and powerfully built, and had learned the hard way to accustom himself to low deckhead beams in one of His Britannic Majesty's ships of war. He was *Unrivalled*'s first lieutenant, the one officer who was expected to maintain order and discipline as well as oversee the training of a new ship's company. To assure his captain that she was in all respects an efficient unit of the fleet, even to assume command at any time should some disaster befall him.

The first lieutenant was twenty-nine years old, and had been in the navy since the tender age of twelve like many of his contemporaries. It was all he had known, all he had ever wanted, and when he had been promoted to acting commander and given a ship of his own he had thought himself the luckiest man alive. A senior officer had assured him that as soon as convenient he would take the next step, make the impossible leap to full captain, something which had once seemed like a dream.

He paused by an open gunport and leaned on one of the frigate's thirty eighteen-pounders, and stared at the harbour and the other anchored ships. Carrick Roads, Falmouth, glittering in the May sunshine. He tried to contain the returning bitterness, the anger. He might have had a command like this fine ship. *Could. Might.* He felt the gun's barrel warm under his fingers, as if it had been fired. Like all those other times. At Camperdown with Duncan, and at Copenhagen following Nelson's flag. He had been commended for his coolness under fire, his ability to contain a dangerous situation when his ship was locked in battle with an enemy. His last captain had put his name forward for a command. That had been the brig *Vixen*, one of the fleet's workhorses, expected with limited resources to perform the deeds of a frigate.

Just before he had been appointed to *Unrivalled* he had seen his old command lying like a neglected wreck, awaiting disposal or worse. The war with France was over, Napoleon had abdicated and been sent into exile on Elba. The impossible had happened, and with the conflict in North America being brought thankfully to a close by Britain and the United States alike, the prospect of peace was hard to accept. Galbraith was no different; he had never known anything but war. With ships being paid off, and men discharged with unseemly haste with neither prospects nor experience of anything but the sea, he was lucky to have this appointment. More than he deserved, some said behind his back.

He had been pulled around the ship an hour earlier in the jolly boat, to study the trim as she lay motionless above her own reflection. She had been in commission for five months, and with her rigging and shrouds blacked-down, each sail neatly furled to its yard, she was a perfect picture of the shipbuilder's art. Even her figurehead, the naked body of a beautiful woman arched beneath the beakhead, hands clasped behind her head, breasts thrust out in a daring challenge, was breathtaking. *Unrivalled* was the first to carry that name on the Navy List, the first of the bigger frigates which had been hastily laid down to meet the American threat, which had cost them dearly in a war neither side could win. A war which was already becoming a part of history.

Galbraith plucked his uniform coat away from his chest and tried to push the resentment aside. He *was* lucky. The navy was all he knew, all he wanted. He must remember that at all times.

He heard the Royal Marine sentry's heels click together as he approached the screen door to the aftermost cabins.

'First lieutenant, *sir*!'

Galbraith gave him a nod, but the sentry's eyes did not waver beneath the brim of his leather hat.

A servant opened the door and stood aside as Galbraith entered the captain's quarters. Any man would be proud, honoured to have her. When Galbraith had stood watching with the assembled ship's company and guests as the ship's new captain, her *first* captain, had unrolled his commission to read himself in and so assume command, he had tried to banish all envy and accept the man he was to serve.

After five months, all the training and the drills, the struggle to recruit more landmen to fill the gaps once the pressed hands had been discharged, he realised that Captain Adam Bolitho was still a stranger. In a ship of the line it might be expected, especially with a new company, but in frigates and smaller vessels like his *Vixen* it was rare.

He watched him warily. Slim, hair so dark it could have been black, and when he turned away from the stern windows and the reflected green of the land, the same restlessness Galbraith had noticed at their first meeting. Like most sea officers, he knew a lot about the Bolitho family, Sir Richard in particular. The whole country did, or seemed to, and had been stunned by the news of his death in the Mediterranean. Killed by a marksman in the enemy's rigging, the very day Napoleon had stepped ashore in France after escaping from Elba. The day peace had become another memory.

Of this man, Sir Richard Bolitho's nephew, he had heard only titbits, although nothing remained secret for long in the fleet. The best frigate captain, some said; brave to a point of recklessness, others described him. He had been given his first command, a brig like Galbraith's, at the age of twenty-three; and later lost his frigate *Anemone* fighting a vastly superior American force. Taken prisoner, he had escaped, to become flag captain to the man who was now Flag Officer, Plymouth.

Adam was looking at him now, his dark eyes revealing strain, although he was making an effort to smile. A youthful, alert face, one which would be very attractive to women, Galbraith decided. And if some of the gossip was to be believed, that was also true.

6

Galbraith said, 'The gig is lowered, sir. The crew will be piped at four bells, unless . . .'

Adam Bolitho moved to the table and touched the sword which was lying there. Old in design, straight-bladed, and lighter than the new regulation blades. It was part of the legend, the Bolitho sword, worn by so many of the family. Worn by Richard Bolitho when he had been marked down by the enemy.

Galbraith glanced around the cabin, the eighteen-pounders intruding even here. When cleared for action from bow to stern *Unrivalled* could present a formidable broadside. He bit his lip. Even if they were so badly undermanned. There were cases of wine waiting to be unpacked and stowed; he had seen them swayed aboard earlier, and knew they had come from the Bolitho house here in Falmouth, which would be the captain's property now. Somehow it did not seem to fit this youthful man with the bright epaulettes. He noticed, too, that the cases were marked with a London address, in St James's Street.

Galbraith clenched his fist. He had been there once. When he had visited London, when his world had started to collapse.

Adam forced his mind into the present. 'Thank you, Mr Galbraith. That will suit well.' He waited, saw the questions forming in the first lieutenant's eyes. A good man, he thought, firm but not impatient with the new hands, and wary of the old Jacks who might seek favours from an unknown officer.

He could feel the ship moving very gently beneath his feet. Eager to move, to be free of the land. *And what of me, her captain?*

He had seen Galbraith looking at the wine; it was from Catherine. Despite all that had happened, her despair and sense of loss, she had remembered. Or had she been thinking of one who had gone?

'Is there something else?' He had not meant to sound impatient, but he seemed unable to control his tone. Galbraith had not apparently noticed. Or had he simply become accustomed to the moods of his new lord and master?

Galbraith said, 'If it is not an imposition, sir, I was wondering . . .' He hesitated as Adam's eyes settled coldly on him. Like someone watching the fall of shot, he thought.

Then Adam said, 'I am sorry. Please tell me.'

7

'I should like to pay my respects, sir. For the ship.' He did not flinch as a voice on deck yelled obscenely at a passing bumboat to stand away. 'And for myself.'

Adam dragged out the watch from his pocket and knew Galbraith had noticed it. It was heavy and old, and he could recall exactly the moment when he had seen it in the shop in Halifax. The ticking, chiming clocks all around him, and yet it had seemed a place of peace. Escape, so many times. At the change of duties on deck, reefing or making sail, altering course, or entering harbour after a successful landfall . . . The old watch which had once belonged to another 'seafaring officer'. One thing had made it different, the little mermaid engraved on the case.

He said, 'If you think we can both be spared from the ship?' It was not what he had meant to say. It was the mermaid which had distracted him, the girl's face, so clear, as in the shop. *Zenoria.*

Then he said, 'I would take it kindly, Mr Galbraith.' He looked at him steadily and thought he could see a momentary warmth, something he had tried not to encourage. 'Impress on the others, extra vigilance. We are under orders. I don't want any deserters now. We'd not have enough to work ship, let alone fight.'

'I shall deal with it, sir.' Galbraith moved towards the door. It was not much, but it was the closest they had yet been.

Adam Bolitho waited for the door to close, then walked to an open quarter window and stared down at the water rippling beneath the counter.

A beautiful ship. Working with the local squadron, he had felt the power of her. The fastest he had known. Soon the anonymous faces would become people, individuals, the strength and the weakness of any ship. *But not too close. Not again.* As if someone had whispered a warning.

He sighed and looked at the cases of wine. How would Catherine manage, what would she do without the man who had become her life?

He heard three bells chime faintly from the forecastle.

It was going to be hard, even harder than he had imagined. People watching him, as they had watched his beloved uncle, with love, hatred, admiration and envy, none of them ever far away.

He knew Galbraith's background, and what had smashed his chance of promotion to the coveted post rank. It could happen to anybody. *To me.* He thought of Zenoria again, and of what he had done, but he felt no shame, only a deep sense of loss.

He was about to walk beneath the open skylight when he heard Galbraith's voice.

'When the Pendennis battery fires one gun, you will dip the flag and ensign, Mr Massie, and all hands will face aft and uncover.'

Adam waited. It was like an intrusion, but he felt unable to move. Massie was the second lieutenant, a serious young man who held the appointment because his father was a vice-admiral. He was, as yet, an unknown quantity.

Massie said, 'I wonder if Sir Richard's lady will be there.'

He heard their feet move away. An innocent remark? And who did he mean? Catherine, or Belinda, Lady Bolitho?

And there would be spite to bring out the worst. Shortly after *Unrivalled* had commissioned, the news of Emma Hamilton's death had been released. Nelson's lover and inspiration and the nation's darling, but she had been allowed to die alone in Calais, in poverty, abandoned by so-called friends and those who had been entrusted with her care.

The ship moved slightly to her cable and he saw his reflection in the thick glass.

Brokenly he said, 'I'll never forget, Uncle!'

But the ship moved again, and he was alone.

Bryan Ferguson, the Bolitho estate's one-armed steward, stared at the two ledgers on his table. Both had remained unopened. It was late evening but through the window he could still see tall trees silhouetted against the sky, as if the day was reluctant to end. He stood up and walked to the cupboard, pausing as the creeper outside the window rustled slightly. A wind, freshening from the south-east at last, as some of the fishermen had said it would. After all that stillness. Ferguson opened the cupboard and took out a stone bottle and one glass. *After all that sadness.*

There was another glass in there, too, kept especially for

the times when John Allday came over on some pretext or other from the little inn at Fallowfield on the Helford River. The Old Hyperion: even the name had a deeper significance this day.

It might be a while yet before John Allday came here. The *Frobisher*, Sir Richard Bolitho's flagship, was coming home to be paid off. Or maybe not, now that Napoleon was in France on the rampage again. And it was only last year that the town had gone wild at the news: the allied armies were in Paris, Bonaparte was finished. Exile in Elba had not been enough; he had heard Lady Catherine say that it was like putting an eagle in an aviary. Others were of the opinion that Boney should have been hanged after all the misery and murder he had caused.

But Allday would not remain on board the ship where Sir Richard had fallen. Only when he was back, perhaps sitting here with a wet between those big hands, would they know the real story. Unis, his wife, who ran the Old Hyperion, often received letters from him, but Allday himself could not write, so his words came through George Avery, Bolitho's flag lieutenant. Theirs was a rare and strange relationship within the rigid bounds of the navy, and Allday had once remarked that it seemed wrong that while the flag lieutenant read and wrote his letters for him, he never received any himself. And from the moment when the dreadful news had broken in Falmouth, Ferguson had known that Allday would never entrust that moment to anyone, or share it, or commit it to paper. He would tell them himself, in person. If he could.

He coughed; he had swallowed a measure of rum without noticing that he had poured it. He sat down again and stared at the unopened ledgers. Above his head he could hear his wife Grace moving about. Unable to rest, unable even to deal with her usual duties as housekeeper, a position of which she was very proud. As he was.

He gripped the glass tightly with the one hand which was now able to do so much. Once he had believed he would be useless, just another piece of human flotsam left behind in this seemingly endless war. But Grace had nursed him through all of it. Now he found himself recalling the moment mostly at times like these, in the shadows, when it was easier to picture the towering pyramids of sails, the lines of French ships, the deafening crash and roar of broadsides as the two fleets had joined in a bloody embrace. It had seemed to take all day for them to draw together, and all the while the sailors, especially the new ones, pressed men like himself, had been forced to watch the enemy's topsails rising like banners until they had filled the horizon. One officer had later described the awesome sight as resembling the armoured knights at Agincourt.

And all the while, aboard the frigate *Phalarope*, so puny she had seemed against that great line of battle, he had seen their young captain, Richard Bolitho, urging and encouraging, and once, before Ferguson himself had been smashed down, he had seen him kneel to hold the hand of a dying sailor. He had never forgotten his face on that terrible day, never would forget it.

And now he was the steward of this estate, its farm and its cottages, and all the characters who made it a good place to work. Many of them were former sailors, men who had served with Bolitho in so many ships and in every part of the world where the flag had been hoisted. He had seen many of them at the church today, for Sir Richard Bolitho was one of them, and Falmouth's most famous son. Son of a sailor, from generations of sea officers, and this house below Pendennis Castle was a part of their history.

Across the yard he could see lights now in some of the rooms, and imagined the line of portraits, including the painting of Sir Richard as the young captain he had known. His wife Cheney had commissioned it while Bolitho had been away with the fleet. Bolitho had never seen his wife again; she had been killed with their unborn child when her carriage had shed a wheel and overturned. Ferguson himself had carried her, seeking help when it was already too late. He smiled sadly, reminiscently. *And with only one arm.*

The Church of King Charles the Martyr, where the lives and deaths of other Bolithos were commemorated, had been filled to capacity, servants from the house, farm workers, strangers and friends pressed close together to pray and to remember.

He allowed his mind to dwell on the family pew near the pulpit. Richard Bolitho's younger sister Nancy, who had not yet come to terms with her own husband's death. Roxby, 'the

11

King of Cornwall', would not be an easy man to lay aside. Next to her Catherine, Lady Somervell, tall and very erect, all in black, her face covered by a veil, and only the diamond pendant shaped like an opened fan which Bolitho had given her moving on her breast to betray her emotion.

And, beside her, Adam Bolitho, his eyes upon the altar, his chin lifted. Defiant. Determined. And, like the moment when he had come to the house after his uncle's death, and had read Catherine's note and clipped on the old family sword, so like the young, vanished sea officer who had grown up here in Falmouth.

There had been another officer with him, a lieutenant, but Ferguson had noticed only Adam Bolitho and the beautiful woman beside him.

It had reminded him painfully of the day in that same church when a memorial service had been conducted following the news that Sir Richard and his mistress had been lost in the wreck of the *Golden Plover* off the African coast. Many of the same people had been there, as well as Bolitho's wife. Ferguson could remember her look of utter disbelief when one of Adam's officers had burst in with the revelation that Bolitho and his companions were alive, and had been rescued against all odds. And when Lady Catherine's part had become known, how she had given hope and faith to the survivors in that open boat, she had been taken to their hearts. It had seemed to sweep aside the scandal, and the outrage which had been previously voiced at their liaison.

Together or alone, Ferguson could see them clearly. Catherine, her dark hair streaming unchecked in the wind while she walked on the cliff path, or paused by the stile where he had seen them once, as if to watch some approaching ship. Perhaps hoping . . .

Now there was no hope, and her man, her lover and the nation's hero, was buried at sea. Near his old *Hyperion*, where so many had died, men Ferguson had never forgotten. The same ship Adam had joined as a fourteen year old midshipman. Nancy, Lady Roxby, would be remembering that too, Adam in a captain's uniform, but to her still the boy who had walked from Penzance when his mother had died. The name 'Bolitho' written on a scrap of paper was all he had had. And now he was the last Bolitho.

There were to be other, grander ceremonies in the near future, in Plymouth, and then at Westminster Abbey, and he wondered if Lady Catherine would go to London and risk the prying eyes and the jealous tongues which had dogged her relationship with the nation's hero.

He heard a step in the yard and guessed it was Young Matthew, the senior coachman, making his rounds, visiting the horses, his dog Bosun puffing slowly behind him. Old now, the dog was partly deaf and had failing eyesight, but no stranger would ever pass him without his croaking bark.

Matthew had been in church also. Still called 'young', but a married man now, he was another part of the family, *the little crew* as Sir Richard had called them.

Buried at sea. Perhaps it was better. No aftermath, no false display of grief. Or would there be?

He thought of the tablet on the wall of the church beneath the marble bust of Captain Julius Bolitho, who had fallen in battle in 1664.

> The spirits of their fathers
> Shall start from every wave;
> For the deck it was their field of fame,
> And ocean was their grave.

It said it all, especially to those assembled in the old church in this place of seafarers, the navy and the coastguard, fishermen and sailors from the packets and traders which sailed on every tide throughout the year. The sea was their life. It was also the enemy.

He had sensed it when the church had resounded at the last to *The Sailors' Hymn*.

He had heard the bang of a solitary gun, like the one which had preceded the service, and seen Adam turn once to look at his first lieutenant. People had parted to allow the family to leave. Lady Catherine had reached out to touch Ferguson's sleeve as she had passed; he had seen the veil clinging to her face.

He went to the window again. The lights were still burning.

He would send one of the girls to deal with it, if Grace was too stricken to do it.

He thought of the shipwreck again. Adam had come to the house when Vice-Admiral Keen's young wife had been there; Keen, too, had been aboard the *Golden Plover*.

Zenoria, from the village of Zennor. He knew Allday had suspected something between them, and he himself had wondered what had happened that night. Then the girl lost her only child, her son by Keen, in an accident, and had thrown herself off the cliff at the notorious Trystan's Leap. He had been with Catherine Somervell when they had brought the small, broken body ashore.

Adam Bolitho had certainly changed in some way. Matured? He considered it. No, it went far deeper than that.

Something Allday had said stood out in his mind, like the epitaph.

They looked so right together.

Captain Adam Bolitho sat in one of the high-backed chairs by the open hearth and half-listened to the occasional moan of the wind. It was freshening, south-easterly; they would have to keep their wits about them tomorrow when *Unrivalled* weighed anchor.

He shifted slightly in the chair, which with its twin was amongst the oldest furniture in the house. It was turned away from the dark windows, away from the sea.

He stared at the goblet of brandy on the table beside him, catching the candlelight which brought life to this room, the grave portraits, the paintings of unknown ships and forgotten battles.

How many Bolithos had sat here like this, he wondered, not knowing what the next horizon might bring, or if they would ever return?

His uncle must have thought it on that last day when he had left this house to join his flagship. Leaving Catherine outside where there was only darkness now, except for Ferguson's cottage. His lights would remain until the old house was asleep.

He had been surprised by Lieutenant Galbraith's request to join him at the church; he had never met Richard Bolitho as far as Adam knew. But even in *Unrivalled* he had felt it. Something lost. Something shared.

He wondered if Catherine was able to sleep. He had pleaded with her to stay, but she had insisted on accompanying Nancy back to her house on the adjoining estate.

He stood, and looked at the stairway where she had said farewell. Without the veil she had looked strained and tired. And beautiful.

'It would be a bad beginning – for you, Adam. If we stayed here together there would be food for rumour. I would spare you that!' She had spoken so forcefully that he had felt her pain, the anguish which she had tried to contain in the church and afterwards.

She had looked around this same room. Remembering. 'You have your new ship, Adam, so this must be your new beginning. I shall watch over matters here in Falmouth. It is yours now. *Yours by right.*' Again, she had spoken as if to emphasise what she herself had already foreseen.

He walked abruptly to the big family Bible, on the table where it had always lain. He had gone through it several times; it contained the history of a seafaring family, a roll of honour.

He opened it at the page with great care, imagining the faces watching him, the portraits at his back and lining the stairway. A separate entry in the familiar, sweeping handwriting he had come to know, to love, in letters from his uncle, and in various log books and despatches when he had served him as a junior officer.

Perhaps this was what troubled Catherine, the subject of his rights and his inheritance. The date was that upon which his surname of Pascoe had been changed to Bolitho. His uncle had written, *To the memory of my brother Hugh, Adam's father, once lieutenant in His Britannic Majesty's Navy, who died on 7th May 1795.*

The Call of Duty was the Path to Glory.

His father, who had brought disgrace to this family, and who had left his son illegitimate.

He closed the Bible and picked up a candlestick. The stair creaked as he passed the portrait of Captain James Bolitho, who had lost an arm in India. *My grandfather.* Bryan Ferguson had shown him how, if you stood in the right place and the daylight favoured you, you could see where the artist had overpainted the arm with a pinned-up, empty sleeve after his return home.

The stair had protested that night when Zenoria had come down to find him weeping, unable to come to terms with the news that his uncle, Catherine, and Valentine Keen had been reported lost in the *Golden Plover*. And the madness which had followed; the love which he could not share. It was all contained, so much passion, so much grief, in this old house below Pendennis Castle.

He pushed open the door and hesitated as if someone was watching. As if she might still be here.

He strode across the room and opened the heavy curtains. There was a moon now, he could see the streaks of cloud passing swiftly across it like tattered banners.

He turned and looked at the room, the bed, the candlelight playing over the two portraits, one of his uncle as a young captain, in the outdated coat with its white lapels which his wife Cheney had liked so much, and one of Cheney on the same wall, restored by Catherine after Belinda had thrown it aside.

He held the candles closer to the third portrait, which Catherine had given to Richard after the *Golden Plover* disaster. Of herself, in the seamen's clothing with which she had covered her body in the boat she had shared with the despairing survivors. 'The other Catherine', she had called it. The woman few had ever seen, he thought, apart from the man she had loved more than life itself. She must have paused here before leaving with Nancy; there was a smell of jasmine, like her skin when she had kissed him, had held him tightly as if unable or unwilling to break away.

He had taken her hand to his lips but she had shaken her head, and had looked into his face, as if afraid to lose something. He could still feel it like a physical force.

'No, dear Adam. Just hold me.' She had lifted her chin. 'Kiss me.'

He touched the bed, trying to keep the image at bay. *Kiss me.* Were they both so alone now that they needed reassurance? Was that the true reason for Catherine's departure on this terrible day?

He closed the door behind them and walked down the stairs. Some of the candles had gone, or had burned so low as to be useless, but those by the hearth had been replaced. One of the servant girls must have done it. He smiled. No secrets in this old house.

He swallowed some brandy and ran his fingers along the carvings above the fireplace. The family motto, *For My Country's Freedom*, worn smooth by many hands. Men leaving home. Men inspired by great deeds. Men in doubt, or afraid.

He sat down again.

The house, the reputation he must follow, the people who relied on him, it would all take time to accept or even understand.

And tomorrow he would be the captain again, all he had ever wanted.

He looked at the darkening stairs and imagined Bolitho coming down to face some new challenge, to accept a responsibility which might and did finally destroy him.

I would give everything I have just to hear your voice and take your hand again, Uncle.

But only the wind answered him.

The two riders had dismounted and stood partly sheltered by fallen rock, holding their horses' heads, staring out at the whitecapped waters of Falmouth Bay.

'Reckon she'll come, Tom?'

The senior coastguard tugged his hat more securely over his forehead. 'Mister Ferguson seemed to think so. Wanted us to keep an eye open, just in case.'

The other man wanted to talk. ''Course, you *knows* her ladyship, Tom.'

'We've had a few words once or twice.' He would have smiled, but his heart was too heavy. His young companion meant well enough, and with a few years of service along these shores he might amount to something. Know Lady Catherine Somervell? How could he describe her? Even if he had wanted to?

He watched the great span of uneasy water, the serried ranks of short waves broken as if by some giant's comb, while the wind tested its strength.

It was noon, or soon would be. When they had ridden up from town along the cliff path he had seen the small groups of people. It was uncanny, like some part of a Cornish myth, and there were plenty of those to choose from. A town, a port which lived off the sea, and had lost far too many of its sons to have no respect for the dangers.

Describe her? Like the time he had tried to prevent her from seeing the slight, battered corpse of the girl who had committed suicide from Trystan's Leap. He had watched her hold the girl in her arms, unfasten her torn and soaking clothes to seek a scar, some identifying mark, when all features had been destroyed by the fall and the sea. On that little crescent of beach in the dropping tide after they had dragged her through the surf. It was something he would never forget, nor wanted to.

At length he said, 'A beautiful lady.' He recalled what one of Ferguson's friends had said of her. 'A sailor's woman.'

He had been in the church with all the others, had seen her then, so upright, so proud. *Describe her?*

'Never too busy or too important to pass the time o' day. Made you feel like you *was* somebody. Not like a few I could mention!'

His companion looked at him and thought he understood.

Then he said, 'You was right, Tom. She's comin' now.'

Tom removed his hat and watched the solitary figure approaching.

'Say nothing. Not today.'

She was wearing the faded old boat cloak she often used for these clifftop walks, and her hair was unfastened and blowing freely in the wind. She turned and faced the sea at the place where she often paused on her walks; the best view of all, the locals said.

The young coastguard said uneasily, 'You don't think she . . .'

Tom turned his head, his eye trained to every movement and mood of the sea and these approaches.

'*No.*' He saw the fine edge of the ship as she tacked around Pendennis Point and its brooding castle, close-hauled and hard over, clawing into the wind before standing towards St Anthony Head. She carried more canvas than might be expected, but he

18

knew what the captain intended, to weather the headland and those frothing reefs before coming about to head into open waters for more sea-room, with the wind as an ally.

A tight manoeuvre, well executed if *Unrivalled* was as short-handed as was rumoured. Some might call it reckless. Tom recalled the dark, restless young captain in the church and all those other times. He had seen him grow from midshipman to this moment in his life, which must be the greatest challenge of all.

He saw the woman unfasten her shabby boat cloak and stand unmoving in the blustery wind. Not in black, but in a dark green robe. Tom had seen her waiting on this same path for the first sign of another ship. So that he would see her, sense her welcome.

He watched the frigate heeling over and imagined the squeal of blocks and the bang of wild canvas as the yards were hauled round. He had seen it all so many times before. He was a simple man who did his duty, peace or war.

What ship did *she* see, he wondered. What moment was she sharing?

Catherine walked past the two horses but did not speak.
Don't leave me!

2

No Longer A Stranger

Adam Bolitho rested one hand on the quarterdeck rail and watched the misty horizon tilt as if to dislodge the entire ship. For most of the forenoon they had been engaged in sail drill, an exercise made even more uncomfortable than usual by the blustery wind. It was directly from the north, and strong enough to force *Unrivalled* to lean until the sea spattered against the sealed gunports and drenched the men working aloft and on deck like a tropical storm.

Three days since the rugged Cornish coastline had vanished astern, and each one had been put to good use.

The hands were sliding down to the deck now, the landsmen and others less confident holding tightly to the ratlines when the ship heeled over to leeward, so that the sea appeared to be directly beneath them. There was a smell of rum even in the wind, and he had already noticed a thin trail of greasy smoke from the galley funnel.

He saw the first lieutenant waiting by the starboard ladder, his face giving nothing away.

'That was better, Mr Galbraith.' He thought he saw Galbraith's eyes drop to the pocket where he carried the old timepiece and wondered what it must be like to take orders as a lieutenant again, instead of being in command. 'Dismiss the watch below.' He heard the seamen running from their stations, glad to be spared further discomfort, and to curse their captain over a tot of rum.

He knew the sailing master was watching him from his usual position, near his helmsmen whenever the ship was altering course or changing tack.

20

Adam walked to the weather side and wiped spray from his face, his body angled to the deck as the sails filled out like breastplates again. The sea was lively with cruising white horses, although it was calmer than when they had been in Biscay. There was too much spray to make out the lie of the land, but it was there, a long, purple hump, as if a bank of cloud had dropped from the sky. Cape St Vincent. And despite all the drills, the alterations of course to test the topmen and new hands alike, this was the exact landfall. He had seen the sailing master's calculations and his daily estimates of distance covered.

His name was Joshua Cristie, and he had a face so weathered and creased that he looked like the Old Man of the Sea, although Adam knew he was in his forties. He had served in almost every size and class of vessel from schooner to second-rate, and had been a sailing master for some ten years. If the senior warrant officers were the backbone of any man-of-war, the sailing master must surely be her rudder. *Unrivalled* was lucky to have him.

Adam joined him and said, 'Gibraltar tomorrow, eh?'

Cristie regarded him impassively. 'I see no problems, sir.' He had a clipped, matter-of-fact manner, and did not waste words.

Adam realised that Galbraith had come aft again, this time with one of the ship's five midshipmen. He tested his memory. Sandell, that was his name.

Galbraith was saying, 'I was observing you, Mr Sandell. *Twice*, I've warned you before. Discipline is one thing, force another!'

The midshipman retorted, 'He was doing it on purpose, sir. Hanging back so that my party was delayed.'

It was unusual for Galbraith to reveal such anger, especially with some of the watchkeepers close enough to hear. He seemed to calm himself with an effort.

'I know you must control the men in your charge. If you are to become a King's officer that is all a part of it. Inspire them, persuade them if you like, but *do not abuse them*. I'll not remind you again!'

The midshipman touched his hat and retreated. Adam caught only a glimpse of his profile. Galbraith had made an enemy there, as was the way of first lieutenants everywhere.

Galbraith walked up the sloping deck and said, 'Young ruffian! Too ready with his starter by far. I know his part of the drill was held up by the man in question, I saw it myself. But with sixty hands short, and some of those aboard little better than bumpkins, it needs more care.'

It was like mist clearing from a telescope. Adam suddenly remembered hearing that a midshipman had been put ashore to await a court martial after a sailor had been accidentally killed at sea. The matter had never come to court martial and the midshipman had been sent to another vessel. He had been an admiral's son. It had been about the time when Galbraith had seen his promised promotion cancelled. Nobody could prove there was a connection; few would even care. Except Galbraith. And he was here, second-in-command of one of the navy's most powerful frigates. Would he remain content, or would he be too afraid for what was left of his career to show the spirit which had once earned him a command of his own?

'Any orders, sir?'

Adam glanced at the nearest eighteen-pounders. Another difference. *Unrivalled*'s armament consisted mainly of such guns, and they made up the bulk of her topweight. The designers had insisted that these eighteen-pounders, usually nine feet in length, be cast a foot shorter in an effort to reduce some of the weight.

A frigate was only as good as her firepower and her agility, and he had taken careful note of the sea creaming almost as high as the ports on the lee side. In a fierce ship-to-ship action, a captain could no longer rely on supremacy merely by taking and holding the wind-gage.

He said, 'We shall exercise the larboard battery this afternoon, Mr Galbraith. I want our people to know their guns like their own minds. As you remarked, we are short-handed, and if required to engage on both sides at once we shall be busy indeed.' He saw the slight frown. 'I know we may not be called to fight. The war might be over already for all we know.' He touched his arm and felt him flinch at the contact. 'But *if* we fight, I intend this ship to be the victor!'

Galbraith touched his hat and walked away, no doubt to face the questions and displeasures of the wardroom.

Adam walked to the dripping hammock nettings and stead-ied himself as the deck lurched to another strong gust. The land was almost gone from view. Cape St Vincent, the scene of one of the war's greatest engagements, where Nelson had scorned the rigidity of Fighting Instructions and attacked the Spanish flagship *Santissima Trinidad* of one hundred and thirty guns, the largest warship in the world. So like his uncle, he thought. Sir Richard Bolitho had never allowed the conventional rules of battle to preclude initiative and personal daring. It seemed wrong that the admirals so admired and so loved by those they had led had never met face to face.

He ran a sodden handkerchief over skin streaming now with spray. Identical to the handkerchief he had given Catherine in the church, knowing she had used it to dry her eyes behind the veil. Galbraith had seen that too . . .

He shook himself angrily and walked to the rail. A few of the hands were splicing and repairing; as in any frigate, the miles of cordage needed constant attention. Some of them raised their eyes and immediately looked away. Men who could make or break any ship. He smiled grimly. *Any captain.* Some of them were from the assize courts, debtors and thieves, tyrants and cowards. The alternatives were transportation or the rope. He watched spray bursting through the beakhead, making the beautiful figurehead shine like a nymph rising from the sea itself.

Unrivalled would draw them together, as a team, as one company.

And when they reached Gibraltar, what orders would he find waiting? To return to England, or be redirected to some other squadron in a different ocean? If nothing had changed he would continue on to Malta, to join the new squadron under the flag of Vice-Admiral Sir Graham Bethune. He was dismayed by the return of the pain. Bethune had been sent to relieve Sir Richard Bolitho, but Fate had decided otherwise. But for that, it might have been Bethune who had died, and Richard Bolitho would have been reunited with his Catherine. *Kate.*

Like himself, Bethune had been one of Bolitho's midship-men, in his first command, the little *Sparrow.* As Valentine Keen had been a midshipman when Sir Richard had been captain of a frigate. So many missing faces. *We Happy Few.* Now there were hardly any.

He saw two of the 'young gentlemen' dodging along the slippery maindeck, calling to one another above the bang of canvas and the sluice of water, apparently without a care in the world.

Here there were only five of them. He would make an effort to get to know each one. Galbraith's sharp comment about inspiration and leadership cut both ways; it always had. In larger ships, which carried broods of midshipmen, there was always the risk of bullying and petty tyranny. He had discovered it soon enough for himself, like so many things which had taught him to defend himself and stand up for those less able to do so.

Today, his reputation with both blade and pistol would end any trouble before it could begin. But it had not been easy. How slow he had been to understand, to come to terms with it. The regular lessons with a local teacher, and later, when he had learned to handle a sword, the intricacies of defence and attack. Slow? Or had he merely decided that he did not want to know how it was all paid for? Until he heard his teacher in the next room, in bed with his mother. And the others.

It was different now. They could think what they liked, but they dared not slander her name in his presence.

But the memory remained, like an unhealed wound.

He saw the midshipman of the watch, Fielding, writing something on his slate, his lip pouting with concentration. The same midshipman who had called him one morning when he had been powerless to break that same dream.

He thought of Catherine again, that last desperate kiss before she had left the house. *To protect my reputation.* There was no defence against dreams. Just as, in those same dreams, she had never resisted him.

He heard a slight cough behind him. That was Usher, the captain's clerk, who had once been the purser's assistant, a small, nervous man who seemed totally out of place in a ship of war. O'Beirne, the ruddy-faced surgeon, had confided that the man was dying, 'a day at a time', as he had put it. His lungs were diseased, only too common in the confines of a ship. He thought of Yovell, the clerk who had become

24

his uncle's secretary. A scholar who was never without his Bible. He would have been there when . . . He turned away and closed his mind to it.

'Yes, Usher?'

'I've done copies of the lists, sir. Three of each.' He always found it necessary to explain every detail of his work.

'Very well. I shall sign them after I have eaten.'

'Deck there! Sail on the larboard quarter!'

Everyone looked up. The voice of the masthead lookout had been heard only rarely on this passage.

The master tugged down his hat and said, 'Shall I send another man aloft, sir?'

Adam glanced at him. Cristie was a professional; he would not be here otherwise. It was not an idle comment. And here was Wynter, the third lieutenant and officer-of-the-watch, hurrying from the chart room, but with biscuit crumbs on his coat to betray his other activities. Young, efficient and keen, when required he could put on such a blank expression that it was impossible to know what he was thinking, which was unusual for a junior lieutenant. But his father was a member of Parliament, so perhaps that might explain it.

Adam said, 'Your glass, Mr Fielding. I shall go up directly.' He thought he saw Cristie's deepset eyes sharpen. 'I shall not shorten sail. Yet.' He wedged his hat inside the companion way and felt his hair wet against his forehead. 'A trader seeking the company of a frigate?' He shook his head as if someone had answered. 'I think not. I know a few King's officers who would not be slow to press a few prime hands, no matter what the Admiralty directs us to do!'

Cristie gave a rare grin. He would know. Even sailors with the genuine Protection, the document which should have defended them against the demands of a hungry fleet, had been pressed. It would take months for someone to find out and do something about it.

Cristie said, 'If she holds up to wind'rd we'll never be able to reach her.'

Adam looked up at the towering masts. *Why?* Was it a demonstration of something? Bravado, perhaps?

He slung the big telescope over his shoulder and strode forward to the main chains before gazing up again at the swaying crosstrees, where the lookout would be perched like a sea bird, uncaring, or indifferent to the other world far beneath his dangling legs.

The others watched until Lieutenant Wynter exclaimed, 'What ails him, Mr Cristie? How can he know anything more than the rest of us?'

'The Cap'n don't miss much, Mr Wynter.' He gestured to the biscuit crumbs. 'Your little pleasures, for instance!'

A seaman murmured, 'First lieutenant's comin' up, sir!'

'Damn!' Wynter stared at the captain's slim figure, leaning back and outwards above the creaming water surging from the finely raked stem. Wynter was twenty-two years old and could remember the congratulations and the envy alike when he had been appointed to *Unrivalled*. The first of her class, the kind of frigate which had been denied them when they had needed them most in the war against the new American navy. With the fleet being cut down and officers as well as seamen being discharged or put on half-pay without any visible prospects, he had been fortunate. Like Galbraith, the senior, who seemed old for his rank when compared with most lieutenants; he must have seen this appointment as a last chance rather than a new beginning.

A new ship, and commanded by one already proclaimed a brave and resourceful officer. The name alone was enough, part of the legend, and now of the mourning for the admiral who had inspired and shocked the nation.

Wynter had been serving in an elderly third-rate when his appointment had been posted. He still had no idea why he had been selected. His father, a rising member of Parliament and one well known for his outspoken criticism of naval and military affairs, was certainly not behind it. Even when he had first gone to sea as a midshipman, his father had offered little encouragement.

'A good regiment would have been preferable. I could have bought you a comfortable living where you would have served with gentlemen, not uncouth ruffians! Don't come to me for pity when you lose an arm or a leg through some captain's hunger for glory!'

And Wynter had never been in a sea fight, mainly because the old seventy-four had been too slow to chase an enemy, and was often left far behind the rest of the squadron. She would doubtless be hulked, like so many of the other worn-out ships which had stood between England and her natural enemies for so many years. He saw Bellairs, the senior midshipman, in charge of *Unrivalled*'s signals and with any luck the next in line for lieutenant's examination, talking to the sailing master, ready to muster his men if something unusual happened. Even *he* had seen action, several times if he was to be believed, when he had served with the Channel Fleet in a small thirty-two gun frigate.

Wynter stared up at the captain again. He was almost there now, apparently untroubled by the height, and the unnerving shake and quiver of the masts under their great weight of spars and cordage.

He knew something of Captain Adam Bolitho's past. A command at twenty-three, and a list of successes against the Americans and the French, with prize money to show for it. Nobody spoke of the other matter, the disgrace to his family when his father had changed sides to command a privateer against his own country during the American War of Independence. But everybody knew about it. How must he feel? He turned away as a shaft of watery sunlight lanced into his eyes. *How would I feel?*

He heard Cristie telling the first lieutenant about the masthead's sighting. He did not hear any reply or comment, but Galbraith was like that. Easy to talk to in the wardroom, on matters relating to shipboard duties or the watch bill. Ready to give advice about the suitability of certain men for the various parts of ship. On a personal level, or when asked to offer an opinion about the course of the war or the reliability of the higher command, he would close up like a clam. Unlike some of the others. Captain Louis Bosanquet, the officer in charge of the ship's Royal Marines, was the complete opposite. Like a steel blade to his men, he was outspoken about almost everything in the mess, especially when he had had too much to drink. His second-in-command, Lieutenant John Luxmore, on the other hand, went by the book, and seemed to live only for the drilling and betterment of his 'bullocks'. O'Beirne, the surgeon from Galway, who knew more jokes than anyone Wynter had ever met, and Tregillis the purser were easy enough to share a mess with, no better or worse than men in any other ship of this size. The exception was Vivian Massie, the swarthy second lieutenant, who had seen plenty of action and did not bother to hide a driving ambition. Beyond that he could be withdrawn, almost secretive, as if any personal revelation might be considered weakness. Good in a battle, but a bad enemy, Wynter had decided.

He stiffened as Galbraith joined him by the rail.

Captain Bolitho had almost reached the crosstrees. But even he could make a mistake. If he slipped and fell, if he missed hitting a spar or the ship herself, the fall would knock him senseless. It would take far too long to heave to and lower a boat. He glanced at Galbraith's strong profile. Then *he* would be in command. Perhaps only temporarily, but it would offer him the recognition he needed and must crave. It happened in battle, just as it had struck down the captain's uncle. *Dead men's shoes.* Nobody mentioned it, but it was on most people's minds when it came to promotion.

Wynter shaded his eyes and peered up again through the maze of rigging and flapping canvas.

Why should the captain do it? Did he trust no one? He had heard Bosanquet remark once that he knew the captain no better than when he had stepped aboard. Galbraith had been present, and had answered, 'I could say the same about you, sir!' That had ended it. That time.

A figure moved from the gundeck and paused, gazing at the sea. It was Jago, the captain's coxswain, the only man aboard who had actually served with Adam Bolitho before. He had a lean, darkly tanned face and hair tied in a neat, old-fashioned queue, like the gunner's mate he had been. A man with a past, he had been flogged in another ship, wrongly it was said, by a sadistic captain, and there was still a certain anger about him, a contained defiance. Wynter had seen him stripped and sluicing his body at the washdeck pump; the scars had been familiar enough, but Jago carried them differently, almost with pride. Bloody arrogance, Massie had called it.

Whatever the truth of it, he would know their captain better than any of them. He had been with him when they had stormed a battery during an attack by the combined forces on the dockyards and principal buildings in Washington. Some claimed that raid was revenge for the American invasion of Canada and the attack on York; others said it was a final show of strength in a war no one could win.

Luke Jago knew the officers on the quarterdeck were watching him and could make a fair bet as to their thoughts. He, too, was surprised to find himself here, in his new station, when all he had wanted was to quit the navy, with only bitterness in his soul.

He could recall exactly when Captain Bolitho had asked him to be his coxswain; could remember his refusal. Bolitho was one of only a few officers Jago had ever liked or trusted, but his mind had been made up. Determined. Until that last battle, the deck raked by the enemy's fire, men crying out and falling from aloft. When the commodore had pitched on to his side, already beyond aid. He knew the rumours like all the rest of them, that the commodore had been shot by somebody aboard their own ship, but he had heard no more about it. He gave a quick grin. He couldn't even remember the bloody man's name any more.

Unlike the boy John Whitmarsh, the captain's servant, who had survived when *Anemone* had gone down. He remembered him well enough. The smile faded. The Yankees had hanged Bolitho's old coxswain for ensuring that *Anemone* would not live to become their prize.

Captain Bolitho had taken a liking to the boy; maybe he had seen something of himself in him. He had wanted to sponsor him with his own money, so he could finish his education and wear the King's coat some day. Jago could remember the boy showing him the dirk the captain had given him, probably the only gift he had ever received. Without a tremor in his voice, he had told Jago that he wanted to stay with his captain. It was all he wanted, he said.

He had watched Adam Bolitho's face when he had told him Whitmarsh had been killed. A ball had shattered against one of the guns, and the iron splinter had ended his young life instantly; he had died without a trace of pain or terror.

And the exact moment when he had made up his mind, or had it made up for him. He was still uncertain, unwilling to believe it was not his decision alone. They had shaken hands on it with the smoke still hanging in the air, when the enemy frigate had broken off the action. 'A victory, sir,' he had heard himself say. 'Or as good as.' He had thought himself mad then. Until they had buried their dead, including the boy John Whitmarsh, with the beautiful dirk still strapped to his side.

One hundred and sixty feet above their heads and oblivious to their thoughts, Adam Bolitho eased himself into position and looked down at the ship, which seemed to pivot from side to side as if his perch in the crosstrees was motionless. He had never tired of the sight since he had made his first dash aloft as a midshipman in his uncle's old *Hyperion*. Even when he had been mastheaded for some prank or indiscretion, he had always managed to marvel at what he saw. The ship, far beneath his shoes, the little blue and white shapes of the officers and master's mates, the clusters of seamen and scarlet-coated marines. *His ship*, all one hundred and fifty feet of her, over a thousand tons of weapons, masts and spars, and the men to serve and fight her.

His uncle had confided that he had always hated heights, had feared going aloft when his ship had made or reefed sails. Another lesson Adam had learned, that fear could be contained if it seemed more dangerous to reveal it.

He glanced at his companion. A leathery face and a pair of the keenest eyes he had seen, like polished glass.

He hesitated. 'Sullivan, isn't it?'

The seaman showed his uneven teeth. 'Thass me, sir.' He smiled slightly as Adam unslung the telescope.

'Where away?' It was strange: despite his attempt to stay at arm's length, the ship was closing in. A face he could barely recall. A typical Jack, some would say. Hard, rough, and, in their way, simple men.

'Same bearin', sir.'

He steadied the glass, raising it very carefully as breaking crests leaped into view, magnified into small tidal waves in the powerful lens.

He felt the spar quiver and shake against his body, mast upon mast, down to the ship's keelson. He could remember the genuine pleasure and pride of the men who had built her when he had insisted they come aboard for her commissioning.

And there she was, rising and dipping, her canvas dark against the scudding clouds.

The lookout said, 'Square-rigged at the fore, sir.'

Adam nodded and waited for the glass to steady again. A brigantine, handling well in the offshore wind, almost bows-on. When he lowered the glass she seemed to drop away to a mere sliver of colour and movement. It never failed to surprise him that men like Sullivan, who would scorn a telescope, or trade it for a new knife or fresh clothing, or drink if it was offered, could still see and recognise another vessel when a landsman might not even notice it.

'Local, d' you think?'

Sullivan watched him with sudden interest. 'Spaniard, I'd say, sir. I seen 'em afore, as far to the south'rd as Good Hope. Handy little craft.' He added doubtfully, 'Rightly 'andled, er course, sir!'

Adam took another look. The master was right. They would never catch her with the wind against them. And why should they care? Lose more time and distance when tomorrow they should lie in the shadow of the Rock?

It was like yesterday. He had been returning to Plymouth and it had been reported that a boat had been heading out to meet them. Not merely a boat: an admiral's barge, the flag officer himself coming to tell him, to be the first to prepare him for the news of his uncle's death. Vice-Admiral Valentine Keen. His uncle's friend. He felt the same stab of guilt; he would never lose it. Zenoria's husband. After her death he had married again. But like that moment alone in the silence of the house, he had thought only of Zenoria. What he had done.

Keen had told him what he knew, the circumstances of Bolitho's death and of his burial at sea. Nothing was definite, except that his flagship had engaged two frigates, manned by renegades and traitors who, with others, had aided Napoleon's escape from Elba; he had marched on Paris almost before the allies had recovered from the shock.

Bethune would know more of the details by now, where the frigates had taken refuge prior to their unexpected meeting with *Frobisher*, who was involved, how it had been planned. He found he was gripping the telescope so tightly that his knuckles were almost white. Spain was an ally now. And yet a Spaniard had been involved.

He repeated quietly, 'Spaniard, you say?'

The man regarded him thoughtfully. Sir Richard Bolitho's nephew. A fire-eater, they said. A fighter. Sullivan had been at sea on and off for most of his forty years, and had served several captains, but could not recall ever speaking to one. And this one had even known his name.

'I'd wager a wet on it, sir.'

A wet. What John Allday would say. Where was he now? How would he go on? The old dog without his master.

Adam smiled. 'A wager it is then. A wet you shall have!' He seized a stay and began to slide towards the deck, heedless of the tar on his white breeches. Instinct? Or the need to prove something? When he reached the deck the others were waiting for him.

'Sir?' Galbraith, poised and guarded.

'Spanish brigantine. He's a damned good lookout.'

Galbraith relaxed slowly. 'Sullivan? The best, sir.'

Adam did not hear him. 'That vessel is following us.' He looked at him directly. It was there. Doubt. Caution. Uncertainty. 'I shall not forget that craft, Mr Galbraith.'

Wynter leaned forward and said eagerly, 'An enemy, sir?'

'An assassin, I believe, Mr Wynter.'

He swung away; Jago was holding his hat for him. 'See that the wardroom mess provides a double tot for Sullivan when he is relieved.'

They watched him walk to the companion way, as if, like the two midshipmen he had seen earlier, he did not have a care in the world.

Midshipman Fielding stood examining the telescope which the captain had just returned to him. He would put it in the next letter to his parents, when he got round to it. How the captain had spoken to him. No longer a stranger . . . He smiled, pleased at the aptness of the phrase. That was it.

He recalled the time he had gone to waken the captain when Lieutenant Wynter had been concerned about the wind. He had dared to touch his arm. It had been hot, as if the captain had had a fever. And he had called out something. A woman's name.

He would leave that out of the letter. It was private.

But he wondered who the woman was.

It was like sharing something. He thought of the captain's easy confidence when he had slithered down to the

32

deck like one of the topmen. Perhaps the others had not noticed it.

He smiled again, pleased with himself. *No longer a stranger.*

Vice-Admiral Sir Graham Bethune walked to the quarter window of the great cabin and observed the activity of countless small craft in the shadow of the Rock. He had visited Gibraltar many times throughout his career, never thinking that one day his own flagship would be lying here, with himself at the peak of his profession. Although a frigate captain earlier in the war, he had been surprised and not a little dismayed to discover how his post at the Admiralty had softened him.

He glanced at the dress coat with its heavy gold-laced epaulettes which hung on one of the chairs, the measure of the success which had brought him to this. He was one of the youngest flag officers on the Navy List. He had always told himself that he would not change, that he was no different from that young, untried captain in his first serious encounter with the enemy, with only his own skills and determination to sustain him.

Or from the midshipman. He stared at the shadowed side of the Rock. Aboard the little sloop-of-war *Sparrow*, Richard Bolitho's first command.

He still could not come to terms with it. He could remember the signal being brought to his spacious rooms at the Admiralty, the writing blurring as he had read and understood that the impossible had happened: Napoleon had surrendered. Abdicated. It had ended. A release for so many, but for him like a great door being slammed shut.

He stared around the cabin, the rippling reflections of water on the low deckhead. It had seemed so small, so cramped after his life in London. He *had* changed.

He could hear the movement of the men on the upper deck, the creak of tackles as stores sent across from one of the supply vessels from England were hoisted inboard.

His thoughts returned to Catherine Somervell, from whom they were never far away. That night at the reception at Castlereagh's home, when Admiral Lord Rhodes had stunned the guests by calling Bolitho's wife to join him and share the applause for her absent husband. When Bethune had begged to be allowed to escort Catherine to her Chelsea house, she had refused. She had been composed enough to consider him; there was enough scandal. Later he had heard of the attack at her home, a disgusting attempt to rape her by a Captain Oliphant, apparently a cousin of Rhodes. After that, things had moved quickly. Rhodes had not become First Lord as he had hoped and expected, and his cousin had not been heard of since.

He looked at the heavy coat again. *And I was ordered here.* In command of a small group of frigates entrusted with patrol and search operations, too late to relieve Sir Richard Bolitho at Malta, nor even in England when the news of his death had broken. No wonder he had changed. He had once imagined himself comfortably, if not happily, married to a woman who suited his role and shared his ambitions. Now even their life together had been soured by those events, and he suspected his wife had been a willing partner in Rhodes' attempt to humiliate and insult Catherine at that reception for Wellington.

He crossed to the opposite quarter and shaded his eyes against the glare to gaze at the mainland. Spain. It was hard not to think of it as the enemy; in Algeciras there had always been eyes watching for the arrival of a new sail, with riders ready to gallop to the next post where the message could be relayed. *Another ship from England. Where bound? For what purpose?*

And there were many who still believed Spain harboured enemies who had already taken advantage of Napoleon's downfall to settle old scores in these waters, to resume piracy and the running of slaves to a ready market in America and the Indies, despite the laws so piously passed to forbid it. The new allies. Would it last? Could they ever forget?

A cutter pulled strongly past the counter and the crew tossed oars in salute, a midshipman in charge rising to remove his hat within the shadow of the flagship. His Britannic Majesty's Ship *Montrose* of forty-two guns was little different from any other frigate to the casual observer, but Bethune knew that his blue command flag at the fore made her unique.

He heard voices beyond the screen door. His flag captain, Victor Forbes, was a brisk, no-nonsense man who was very aware that this was no longer a private ship, and that flag had made all the difference to him in particular; he had even had to vacate these quarters for his admiral. Bethune had seen the seamen and marines glancing at him when he took his regular walks up and down the quarterdeck. A far cry from the Thames Embankment or the London parks, but it was better than nothing. He touched his stomach. He would not let himself go to seed like some of the flag officers he knew. In case . . . *In case what?*

Tomorrow *Montrose* would weigh and return to Malta, unless new orders came to direct otherwise. It was becoming ever more difficult to keep a part of his mind in the world of the Admiralty, to assess or disregard the next possible strategy, which had once been so clear to him. Even to know the true deployment of the allied armies, or whether Napoleon was indeed fighting a rearguard action.

Today he might receive fresh information. That was the irony of it. The ship which had been sighted just an hour ago was *Unrivalled*. He had felt a certain involuntary shock when he had seen his flag lieutenant's report in the log, *Unrivalled (46). Captain Bolitho.* Not like a step forward; rather, looking back. The names, the faces . . .

And now Adam Bolitho was here. In a new ship. *At least I was able to send word of that before he was struck down.*

He clenched his fists. He had heard one of the seamen saying to his mate when they had been splicing below the quarterdeck:

'I tell 'ee, Ted. We'll ne'er see his like again, an' that's God's truth!'

The sailor's simple tribute, shared by so many. And yet, like so many, that unknown sailor had never laid eyes on Richard Bolitho.

The door opened and he saw Captain Forbes looking around the cabin, probably to ensure his admiral had not changed it out of all recognition.

'What is it, Victor?'

The reflected sunlight was too strong for him to see the captain's expression, but he sensed it was one of uncertainty, if not actual disapproval.

We are about the same age, and yet he behaves like my superior officer. He tried to smile, but it would not come.

Captain Forbes said, '*Unrivalled* has anchored, sir.' Then, as an afterthought, 'She's big. We could have done with a few more like her when . . .'

He did not go on. There was no need.

'Yes. A fine ship. I envy her captain.'

That did surprise Forbes, and this time he was unable to conceal it. His vice-admiral, who was both liked and respected, and would no doubt rise to some even more exalted post when the Admiralty directed, lacked for nothing. He could use favour or dislike as he chose, and no one would question him. To profess envy was unthinkable.

'I shall make the signal, sir.'

'Very well. *Captain repair on board*.' How many times he had seen it break out at the yard, for himself and for others. And now for Adam Bolitho. Every new meeting like this one would be an additional strain. *For us both*.

Forbes was still here, hand on the screen door.

'I was thinking, sir. Perhaps we might entertain *Unrivalled*'s captain. I'm sure the wardroom would be honoured.' He hesitated under Bethune's stare. 'You know the way of it, sir. Word from home.' He added warily, 'You would be our guest too, of course, sir.'

'I am certain Captain Bolitho would be delighted.' He looked away. 'I would also be pleased. None of us should ever forget how or why we are here.'

He heard Forbes marching across the quarterdeck, calling for the midshipman of the watch. Bethune had not even seen him leave the cabin.

Unrivalled was joining his squadron. This was the best way. He thought of Bolitho again. *No show of favouritism*.

But they would have a glass together first, while he read his despatches from that other world. He smiled again, and it was very sad. *No looking back*.

Adam Bolitho sat in one of the cabin chairs and crossed his legs, as if the action would force him to relax. He had been greeted very correctly when he had climbed up *Montrose*'s tumblehome, amid the twitter of boatswain's calls, the slap and crack of muskets being brought to the present under a cloud of pipeclay. All due respects to a captain, and he wondered why it surprised him. He had been so received aboard many ships large and small, and in all conditions. When it had been hard to prevent his hat from being blown away, or with a boat cloak tangling around his legs. He had never forgotten a story his uncle had told him about a captain who had tripped over his own sword and pitched back into his barge, to the delight of the assembled midshipmen.

Perhaps, like the vice-admiral sitting opposite him, turning over the pages of his despatches with practised speed, he too had changed. On his way across to the flagship he had glanced astern at his own command. Above her reflection, sails neatly furled, all boats in the water to seal their seams, she would make any would-be captain jealous. *And she is mine.* But as of this moment she would be a part of a squadron, and, like her, he would have to *belong.* He watched Bethune's bowed head, the lock of hair falling over his brow. More like a lieutenant than a Vice-Admiral of the Blue.

It had been an awkward meeting, which even the din of the reception could not hide or cover. Friends? They were hardly that. But they had always been a part of something. Of someone.

He had mentioned the brigantine and his suspicions to Bethune. It would be in his report, but he felt he should use it to dispel the lingering stiffness between them. Instead of dismissing it, the vice-admiral had seemed very interested.

'It is the kind of secret war we are fighting out here, Adam. Algerine pirates, slavers – we are sitting on a powder keg.'

Bethune looked up suddenly. 'It seems the lords of the Admiralty are as much in the dark as we are!'

Adam said, 'You would know better than most, sir.' They both laughed, the tension all but gone.

He liked what he saw. Bethune had an open, intelligent face, a mouth which had not forgotten how to smile. He knew from Catherine's letters that she had trusted him. He could understand why.

Bethune said, 'I almost forgot. When we reach Malta I should have more information to act upon.' He was making up his mind. 'There is a Lieutenant George Avery at my headquarters there. You will know him?'

'Sir Richard's flag lieutenant, sir.' He felt his muscles tense, but made another attempt. 'They were very close, I believe. I thought he had returned to England in *Frobisher*.'

'I did not force him to stay, but his knowledge is very valuable to me – to us. He was with Sir Richard when he dealt with the Algerines. And with a certain Spanish connection.' He smiled slightly. 'I see that interests you?' He turned as muffled thuds came from the direction of the wardroom. Adam knew of the invitation, and that *Montrose*'s captain would be there also. As a guest, as was the custom, although Adam had never known any captain refused entry to a wardroom in his own ship.

Bethune said, 'In any case, I did not have to press Lieutenant Avery. It seems he has nothing for which to return.'

I have a ship. George Avery has nothing.

'I look forward to meeting him again. My uncle,' he hesitated, 'and Lady Somervell spoke highly of him. As a friend.'

Bethune picked up his untouched glass of wine.

'I give you a sentiment, Adam. "To absent friends."' He drank deeply and grimaced. 'God, what foul stuff!'

They both knew it was to hold at bay something far deeper, but when Captain Forbes and his first lieutenant arrived to escort them to the wardroom, they sensed nothing unusual.

Adam saw Forbes' eyes rest briefly on the old Bolitho sword, which lay beside Bethune's.

Why had he not seen it for himself? How could he have doubted it? It was still there, like a hand reaching out.

The lifeline.

3

A Matter of Pride

Sir Wilfred Lafargue waited while Spicer, his clerk, gathered up a bulky file of documents, and then folded his hands on the empty desk.

'I foresee several problems, perhaps serious ones, arising in the near future. But insurmountable? I think not.'

Normally, such a comment would leave a client hopeful, if not entirely satisfied. But Lafargue, as a lawyer and the senior partner of this prestigious firm which bore his name, was conscious only of its lack of substance.

He knew it was because of his visitor, standing now by the far window in this vast office. It was Lafargue's favourite view of the City of London, and the dome of St Paul's, a constant reminder of its power and influence.

Lafargue was always in command; from the moment the tall doors were opened to admit a client, potential or familiar, his routine never varied. There was a chair directly opposite this imposing desk, forcing the client to face the full light of the windows, more like a victim than one who would eventually be charged a fee which might make him blanch and reconsider before returning. Except that they always did return.

But this one was different. He had known Sillitoe for a good many years; Baron Sillitoe of Chiswick, as he now was. The Prince Regent's Inspector-General, and a man of formidable connections long before that. Feared, hated, but never ignored. Those who did regretted it dearly.

Sillitoe was a man of moods, and this again unsettled Lafargue; it broke the pattern of things and was disconcerting.

Restless, unable to remain still for more than a few minutes, he seemed disturbed by something which had not yet been revealed.

Lafargue, as usual, was expensively dressed, his coat and breeches cut by one of London's leading tailors, but the clothing could not completely disguise the signs of good living which made him appear older than his fifty-eight years. Sillitoe on the other hand had never changed; he was lean, hard, as if anything superfluous or wasteful had long since been honed away. A good horseman, he was said to exercise regularly, his secretary panting beside him while he outlined one or another of his schemes. He was also a swordsman of repute. For Lafargue it made the comparison even more difficult to accept. Sillitoe was the same age as himself.

Sillitoe was motionless, watching something below, perhaps the carriages wending their way towards Fleet Street, perhaps merely waiting for something. Lafargue saw that the doors were once more closed; Spicer had departed. As senior clerk he was invaluable, and although he appeared to be very dull he never missed the slightest nuance or inflection. Even here, at Lincoln's Inn, which Lafargue considered the very centre of English law, there were some things which should and must remain private. This conversation was one of them.

He said, 'I have studied all the deeds available. Sir Richard's nephew Adam Bolitho, once known as Pascoe, is deemed the legal heir to the Bolitho estate and adjoining properties as listed . . .' He stopped, frowning, as Sillitoe said, 'Get on with it, man.' He had not raised his voice.

Lafargue swallowed hard. 'However, Sir Richard's widow and dependant, the daughter, will have some rights in the matter. They are supported by the trust instituted by Sir Richard. It may well be that Lady Bolitho will want to install herself at Falmouth where she did, in fact, enjoy a conjugal residency at one time.'

Sillitoe rubbed his forehead. What was the point? Why had he come? Lafargue was a celebrated lawyer. *Otherwise neither of us would be here.* He controlled his impatience. Lafargue would act when the time came. If it did . . .

He looked across at the other buildings, the small green expanses of parks and quiet squares, and saw St Paul's. Where the nation, or a select few, would gather to pay homage to a hero. Some with genuine grief, others there only to be seen and admired. Sillitoe had never understood why any sane man would volunteer to spend his life at sea. To him, a ship was only a necessary form of transport. Like being caged, unable to move or act for himself. But he had accepted that others had different views, his nephew George Avery among them.

When they had last met he had offered him a position, one both important and, in time, lucrative. Sillitoe never threw money to the winds without proof of ability, and his nephew was a mere lieutenant, who had been passed over for promotion after being taken prisoner by the French; he had been freed only to face a court martial for losing his ship.

Any other man would have jumped at the opportunity, or at least shown some gratitude. Instead, Avery had returned to his appointment as Sir Richard Bolitho's flag lieutenant, and must have been with him when he had been killed.

He said flatly, 'And what of Viscountess Somervell?' He did not turn from the window, although he heard the intake of breath. Another lawyer's ploy.

'In the eyes of the law, she has no rights. Had they been at liberty to marry . . .'

'And the people? What will they say? The woman who inspired their hero, who displayed courage when most would fall back in despair? What of her part?'

He knew Lafargue would think he was referring to Catherine's bravery and strength in the open boat after the shipwreck; he was intended to. But Sillitoe was seeing something very different, something which had preyed on his mind and had never released him since he and his men had burst into the house by the river. Bruised and bleeding, stripped naked and with her wrists tied cruelly behind her back, she had fought her attacker. Sillitoe had held her against his body and covered her with a sheet or curtain, he could not remember what it had been or the exact order of things. His men beating her attacker, dragging him down the stairs, and then those moments alone with her, her head against his shoulder, her hair beautiful in disarray.

A nightmare. And he had wanted her. Then and there.

'The people? Who listens to the *people*?' Lafargue was regaining his self-control. His old arrogance.

41

Sillitoe turned his back on the city, his face in shadow.

'In France they listened. Eventually!'

Lafargue watched him, sensing the bitterness, the anger. And something else. He recalled Catherine Somervell coming here to consult him, at Sillitoe's suggestion, on a matter of purchasing the lease of a building where Bolitho's estranged wife lived, at her husband's expense. Belinda Bolitho had been horrified to discover that her home was owned by the woman she most hated. A woman scorned.

Lafargue's eyes sharpened professionally. No, there was far more to it than that. He watched Sillitoe, dressed all in grey as was his habit, move swiftly to the opposite side of the room. He had the ear of the Prince Regent, and when the King, drifting in madness, eventually died, who could say to what heights he might not rise?

Lady Somervell . . . he had thought of her as Catherine just now, which showed that he was unusually overwrought . . . was the key. Lafargue remembered her entering this room. She had walked straight towards him, her eyes never leaving his. To call her beautiful was an understatement. But a symbol could be soiled, and envy and spite were well known to Lafargue in the world of law.

They had praised Nelson to the skies, and those who had cried out the loudest had been the biggest hypocrites. A dead hero was safe, and could be remembered without anxiety or inconvenience.

Edward Berry, Nelson's favourite flag captain, had once quoted, *God and the navy we adore, when danger threatens but not before.*

Napoleon was said to be in retreat; it might soon be over. Not like the last time. Truly over . . .

How soon after that would those same people turn on the woman who had defied society and protocol for the man she loved?

He ventured, 'If Lady Somervell were to remarry . . . Her husband was killed in a duel, I understand.'

Sillitoe sat down abruptly. Everyone knew about Somervell, a gambler and a waster who had used much of Catherine's money to extricate himself from debt. A man who had plotted with Bolitho's wife to have his mistress imprisoned and transported as a common thief. One of Bolitho's officers had called him out and had mortally wounded him. He had paid for it with his own life.

I would have killed him myself.

How much did Lafargue really know?

He would know, for instance, that the post of Inspector-General had once been Viscount Somervell's. Another bitter twist.

'I think it unlikely.' He tugged out his watch. 'I must leave now.'

Lafargue asked, too casually, 'And how goes the war?'

Sillitoe glanced around the room. 'I shall see the Prince Regent this afternoon. He is more concerned with the army than the fleet at this moment. As well he might be.'

Lafargue stood. He felt unusually drained and could not explain it. He said, 'I have received an invitation to the memorial service at St Paul's. The cathedral will be crowded to the full, I have no doubt.'

It was a question. Sillitoe said, 'I shall be there.'

'And Lady Somervell?'

Sillitoe saw the double doors open silently. Perhaps there was a hidden bell, some sort of secret signal.

'She has been invited.' Their eyes met. 'Privately.'

It told Lafargue nothing. He took his hat from the clerk, and sighed. It told him everything.

Unis Allday walked slowly around the small parlour, making certain that everything was as it should be. She knew she had already done it several times, but she could not help it. Beyond the open door she could hear voices, the only two customers at the Old Hyperion inn. Auctioneers from the sound of them, on their way to Falmouth for tomorrow's market.

Everything looked neat. There was a smell of freshly baked bread, and new casks of ale on their trestles, each with its own clean towel. She paused, and with her hands on her hips stared at her reflection in the looking-glass. She did not smile, but examined every feature as she would a new girl applying for work in the kitchen.

She shivered, staring at herself. As he would see her. His friend Bryan Ferguson had brought the news. The man-of-war

Frobisher which had taken her man away from her last year was at Plymouth. John Allday was back, and coming home. She looked around the parlour again. Coming home. She allowed her mind to explore it. Never to leave her.

She could hear her brother, also named John, chopping wood for the kitchen. She had told him not to, with only one leg, but he was doing it for her. Allowing her this time to be alone.

She walked through the outer parlour. The auctioneers were still there but one was counting out money, and their horses were already at the door. She walked past them into the afternoon sunshine. Almost June, the summer of 1815. Where had it all gone, and so quickly?

She gazed down the empty road, the hedgerows rippling slightly under the breeze off Falmouth Bay, campion and fox-glove splashing colour against the many shades of green. She turned and looked at the inn. She could not have done it without her brother. He had lost his leg in the line while serving with the Thirty-First regiment of foot, the Old Huntingtonshires. If it had been her, she thought, she would have given up. Now, freshly painted, the inn sign with the ship which had become so important in their lives was moving restlessly, as if the old *Hyperion* was remembering also.

Unis was well acquainted with the ways of the sea, its demands and its cruelties. Her first husband had been a master's mate in that same old ship and had died aboard her, like so many others. John Allday had burst into her life not far from here, when she had been attacked by two footpads while on her way to this very inn.

Big, shambling, but there was no man like him. As he had dealt with her attackers she had realised that he was in pain; he was suffering from an old wound, which she knew now had been a sword-thrust to the chest. She had seen the scar many times. She wiped her eyes. *He was coming home.* Bryan Ferguson had said it would be today or tomorrow. She knew it was today. How could she? But she knew.

The two auctioneers were leaving, heaving themselves into their saddles, well filled with rabbit pie and the vegetables she grew behind the inn. They waved to her, and cantered away.

She was small, pretty and neat, but customers did not take liberties with her. Not more than once.

44

She smiled. Anyway, she was a foreigner, from over the border in Devon, the fishing port of Brixham where she had been born and had lived until her man had been reported killed. *Discharged dead*, the navy termed it.

She pushed some hair from her eyes and looked at the hillside, which was alive with young lambs either grazing or frolicking in the pale sunshine. Foreigner maybe, but she would be in no other place.

Bryan Ferguson had warned her, or had tried to; her brother had also done his best. It would be difficult, most of all for John Allday. She thought of that last visit, when Bryan had brought the news that Sir Richard Bolitho was ordered to sea again. Even Unis had been angry; he had been back in England no time at all. The house below Pendennis was empty now, except for the Fergusons and the servants.

She recalled the young Captain Bolitho at the church. So erect, brave in his dress uniform, with the old sword at his hip which had been pointed out to her. All that was left of the man they were remembering.

And Lady Catherine. She had come here to the inn whenever she had wanted a friend, and Unis ventured to call herself that, when Sir Richard was away at sea. She had been in the parlour that night Squire Roxby had died, and had gone from here to comfort his widow. A family, but it was more than that. In the room where John had finally found himself able to tell her about his son John Bankart, who had died in battle, how he had carried him himself, and had put him over the side for his burial.

She glanced at the narrow stairway. And together they had had Kate. That would be different this time, too. She nodded firmly. *From now on.* She had seen the hurt on the strong, weathered features when he had returned from sea, and his own child had run from him to Unis's brother.

Little Kate was upstairs now in the beautiful cot John had made for her. Like the toys, and the perfect ship models; his big, clumsy-looking hands could perform miracles.

Her brother had said, 'When I got back from the war, a pin missing and all, I was grateful. I was thankful to be spared, crippled or not. When things were bad I remembered, or tried to, all those lines of men. Friends I'd known, lying out in the field, bleeding to death, calling out with nobody to hear. Waiting to die, quickly, to be spared the crows and the scum who rob the likes of poor soldiers after a battle. What I hated most was pity, well meant or otherwise. All I had left was my pride.' He had looked at the old tattoo on his arm and had managed to smile. 'Even in the old bloody regiment!'

Unis knew what John's standing as the admiral's coxswain had meant to him. How he had belonged. That was what he had said, right here, just before he had left. Not merely the personal coxswain of England's most famous sailor, but his friend. And he had been there. Bryan Ferguson had told them about it after Adam Bolitho's return, and he had heard it from the admiral at Plymouth. John had been at Richard Bolitho's side when he had been shot down.

Horses' hooves and the rattle of wheels startled her from her thoughts, but the sounds went on, and were lost around the curve of the road.

She stared at the hand pressed under her heart. Was it fear? John was safe. He would never go back to sea. She knew he and Bryan Ferguson had discussed it, talked about the point at which a man was reckoned too old to fight for King and country. It was like a red rag to a bull for John Allday.

She thought of his letters; how she had waited for them, yearned for them. And had often wondered about the officer who had written them on John's behalf. George Avery was a good man, and had stayed at the Old Hyperion. She had often thought of him reading her letters aloud to John, a little like having letters from home for himself, although John had told her he never received any.

How long would it take? What would he do? He had often said he would never become just another old Jack, yarning and 'swinging the lamp'.

But it would be hard, perhaps for all of them. Bryan Ferguson had told her that he and her John had been pressed together here in Cornwall, and taken to a King's ship in Falmouth. Bolitho's ship. What had grown from that unlikely meeting was stronger than any rock.

Here on the edge of the little village of Fallowfield, it was not like Brixham or Falmouth. Farm workers and passing tradesmen were more common than men of the sea. But there would still be talk. Everyone knew the Bolitho family. And Catherine was in London, they said. There would be more ceremonies there; how could she endure it? There was gossip enough in any town or village. How much worse it must be in the city.

She heard her brother descending the stairs, the regular thump of his wooden leg. His spar, John Allday called it.

'Little Kate's fast asleep.' He limped towards her. 'Still thinking on it, Unis love? We'll make it right for him, see?'

'Thank you for that, John. I don't know what I'd have done –' She looked into his face and froze, unable to move. She whispered, 'Oh, dear God, make my man happy again!'

The sound of Bryan Ferguson's pony and trap seemed louder than it had ever been.

She tugged at her skirt and pushed some hair from her face again.

'I can't! I can't!'

Nobody moved, nobody spoke. He was suddenly just there, filling the entrance, his hat in one hand, his hair shaggy against the sunlight.

She tried to speak, but instead he held out his arms, as though unable to come forward. Her brother remembered it for a long time afterwards. John Allday, who had rescued and won his only sister, was in the room, as if he had never been away.

He was wearing the fine blue coat with the gilt buttons bearing the Bolitho crest, which had been made especially for him, and nankeen breeches and buckled shoes. The landsman's ideal of the English sailor, the Heart of Oak. So easily said by those who had not shared the horrors of close action at sea or on land.

John Allday held her close against him, but gently, as he would a child or some small animal, and touched her hair, her ears, her cheek, afraid he might hurt her in some way, unable to let go of her.

He thought he heard a door close, very quietly. They were alone. Even his best friend Bryan was silent, out there with his fat little pony named Poppy.

'You're a picture, Unis.' He tilted her chin with the same care. 'I've thought about this moment for a long time.'

She asked, 'The officer, Mister Avery?'

47

Allday shook his head. 'Stayed with the ship. Thought he was needed.' He held her away from him, his big hands cupping her shoulders, his eyes moving over her, as if he was only now realising what had happened.

She stood quite still, feeling the strength, the warmth of his hard hands. So strong and yet so unsure, so wistful.

'You're here. That's all I care about. I've missed you so much, even when I tried to be with you over the miles . . .' She broke off. She was not reaching him even now.

Suddenly he took her hand in his, and led her like a young girl to the nook where his model, his first gift to her, was carefully mounted.

'I was there, y' see. All the while. Comin' home, we was. We'd got the orders. I never seen such a change in the man.' He looked at her with something like anguish. 'Comin' home. What we both wanted.'

They sat down on a scrubbed wooden bench, side by side, like strangers. But he held her hand, and spoke so quietly that she had to put her head against his arm to hear him.

'He often asked about you an' little Kate.' The sound of the child's name seemed to unsteady him. 'Is she safe? An' well?'

She nodded, afraid of breaking the spell. 'You'll see.'

He smiled, something faraway. Perhaps another memory.

He said, 'He knew, y' see. When we went up on deck. He knew. I felt it.'

She heard her brother by the door, and thought she saw Bryan Ferguson's shadow motionless in a shaft of light. Sharing it. As they had every right.

She found she was gripping his hand more tightly, and said, 'I want you as my man again, John Allday. I'll give you the love you need. I'll help you!'

But when he turned his face to hers there was no pain, no despair.

He said, 'I was with him to the end, love. Just like we always was, from the first broadside at the Saintes.'

He seemed to realise that they were no longer alone. 'I held him.' He nodded slowly. Seeing it. Confronting it. 'He said, *easy, old friend.* Just to me, like he always did. *No grief. We always knew.*' He looked at her and smiled, perhaps truly

48

aware of her for the first time. 'Then he died, an' I was still holdin' him.'

She stood up and put her arms around him, sharing his loss, feeling such love for this one man.

She murmured, 'Let it go, John. Later we shall lie together. It's all that matters now.'

Allday held her for several minutes.

Then he said, 'Get the others, eh?'

She shook him gently, embracing him, her heart too full for words.

A life was gone. Hers was complete.

Brush . . . brush . . . brush . . .

Catherine, Lady Somervell, sat facing the tilted oval mirror, her hand rising and falling without conscious thought, her long hair spilling over one shoulder. In the candlelight it looked almost black, like silk, but she did not notice.

The hour was late and beyond the windows the evening had darkened, the Thames revealed only by the light of an occasional lantern, a wherryman, or some sailor on his way to one of the riverside taverns.

But here in the Walk, there were very few people, and the air was heavy, as if with storm. She saw the candles beside the mirror shiver and stared at the reflection of the bed behind her. There were far too many candles in the room; they were probably the cause of the stuffiness. But there were always too many, had been since that night of raw terror. *In this room. On that bed.* She had overcome it. But it had never left her.

She continued to brush her hair, pausing only at the sound of a fast-moving carriage. But it did not slow or stop.

She thought of the housekeeper, Mrs Tate, who was somewhere downstairs. Even she had changed her way of life since that night, when she had been visiting her sister in Shoreditch as had been her habit. Now she never left the house unattended, and watched over her with a tenderness Catherine had never suspected. And she had never once mentioned it. Her own thoughts had been too full, too chaotic in those first weeks after the attack. Even then it had been like witnessing the horrific violation of someone else, not herself. A stranger.

Except on nights like these. Warm, even clammy, the thin

gown clinging to her body like another skin, despite the bath she had taken before coming upstairs.

She hesitated, and then pulled open a drawer deliberately and took out the fan. Richard had given it to her after his ship had called at Madeira. So long ago.

She looked at the diamond pendant which hung low on her breast. It, too, was shaped like a fan. So that she would not forget, he had said. The pendant the intruder had turned over in his fingers while she had been helpless, her wrists pinioned behind her. She looked involuntarily at the nearest window. He had used the cord. He had struck her, so that she had almost lost her senses, when she had called him a thief. Outraged, like a madman. And then he had begun to torment her, to strip her there, on that bed.

She touched her breast and felt her heart beating against her hand. But not like then, or all those other times, when the memory had returned.

And afterwards . . . The word seemed quite separate from her other thoughts. Sillitoe and his men had burst into the room, and he had held her, protected her while her attacker had been dragged away. It had been like a sudden calm after a terrible storm.

She thought of Malta, her brief visit in an Indiaman, which had been on government business and bound for Naples. Sillitoe had arranged for her to be landed at Malta, even though she knew he would once have done anything to keep her from Richard, and he had made no attempt to gain any advantage either on the passage out or on the journey back to England. If anything, he had been withdrawn, perhaps at last understanding what it had cost her to leave the man she loved behind in Malta.

Forever.

She had seen him only twice since Richard's death. He had offered his condolences, and assured her of his readiness to help in any way he could. As with the lawyer, Lafargue, he had understood immediately her concern for Adam. He had been correct in every way, and had made it his business to begin enquiries of his own.

Catherine thought she understood men, had learned much out of necessity.

But after Richard, how could she survive? Where would be the point?

She recalled the exact moment when they had been reunited, at English Harbour over ten years ago. She had been married to Somervell, the King's Inspector-General.

Dazed and yet on guard because of the unexpectedness of the meeting, and the danger she had known it would offer. Telling him he needed love, *as the desert craves for rain.*

Or was I speaking of myself? My own desires?

And now he is dead.

And tomorrow, another challenge. All those staring eyes. Not those of the men who had stood with him and had faced death a hundred times, or the women who had loved and welcomed them when they had returned home. Without limbs. Without sight. Without hope.

No. They would be the faces and the eyes she had seen that evening at the celebration of Wellington's victory. Rhodes, who had been championed as the new First Lord of the Admiralty. Richard's wife, bowing to applause she would never earn or deserve. And the unsmiling wife of Graham Bethune. Unsmiling until the moment of insult, as if she had been a part of it. All enemies.

She had turned her back on them. Had come here, half blind with anger and humiliation. She stood up quickly and stared at the bed. *And he was waiting for me.*

Tomorrow, then. The bells would toll, the drums echo through the empty streets. They would be remembering her Richard, her dearest of men, but they would be looking at her. *At me.*

And what would they see? The woman who had inspired a hero? The woman who had endured a shipwreck, and fought the danger and misery so that they might all hope to live, when most of them had already accepted a lingering death. The woman who had loved him. *Loved him.*

Or would they see only a whore?

She faced the mirror again and unfastened her gown, so that it fell and was held until she released it and stood naked, the hair warm against her spine.

As the desert craves for rain.

She sat again and recovered the brush. She heard a step on

the stairs, quick and light. It would be Melwyn, her maid and companion. Cornish, from St Austell, a fair girl with an elusive, elfin prettiness. She was fifteen.

She stared unwaveringly at the mirror. Fifteen. *As I was when I was with child. When my world began to change.* Richard had known of that; Sillitoe also knew.

She heard a tap at the door and pulled the gown up to her shoulders. Melwyn entered the room and closed the door.

'You've not eaten, m' lady.' She stood her ground, quietly determined. 'Tesn't right. Cook thought . . .'

She stood quite still as Catherine twisted round to look at her. Then she said simply, 'You'm so beautiful, m' lady. You must take more care. Tomorrow d' be so important, and I can't be with you. No room for servants . . .'

Catherine clasped her round the shoulders and pressed her face into the fair hair. Richard's sister had told her that Melwyn meant *honey-fair* in the old Cornish tongue.

'You're no mere servant, Melwyn.' She embraced her again. 'Tomorrow, then.'

The girl said, 'Sir Richard will expect it.'

Catherine nodded very slowly. She had nearly given in, broken down, unable to go through with it. She lifted her chin, felt the anger giving way to pride.

She said, 'He will, indeed,' and smiled at a memory the girl would never know or understand. 'So let's be about it, then!'

4

New Beginning

Captain Adam Bolitho ran lightly up the companion ladder and paused as the bright sunshine momentarily dazzled him. He glanced around the quarterdeck, fitting names to faces, noting what each man was doing.

Lieutenant Vivian Massie had the afternoon watch, and seemed surprised by his appearance on deck. Midshipman Bellairs was working with his signals party, observing each man to see if he was quick to recognise every flag, folded in its locker or not. It was hard enough with other ships in company, but alone, with no chance to regularly send and receive signals, there was always a danger that mistakes born out of boredom would be made.

Four bells had just chimed from the forecastle. He looked up at the masthead pendant, whipping out half-heartedly in a wind which barely filled the sails. He walked to the compass box. East-by-south. He could feel the eyes of the helmsmen on him, while a master's mate made a business of examining a midshipman's slate. All as usual. And yet . . .

'I heard a hail from the masthead, Mr Massie?'

'Aye, sir.' He gestured vaguely towards the starboard bow. 'Driftwood.'

Adam frowned and looked at the master's log book. Eight hundred miles since leaving Gibraltar, in just under five days. The ship was a good sailer despite these unreliable winds, conditions which might be expected in the Mediterranean.

No sight of land. They could be alone on some vast, uncharted ocean. The sun was hot but not oppressively so, and he had seen a few burns and blisters amongst the sea-men.

'Who is the lookout?'

He did not turn, but guessed Massie was surprised by what seemed so trivial a question.

He did not recognise the name.

'Send Sullivan,' he said.

The master's mate said, 'He's off watch below, sir.'

Adam stared at the chart. Unlike those in the chart room, it was stained and well used; there was even a dark ring of something where a watchkeeper had carelessly left a mug.

'Send him.' He traced the coastline with his fingers. Fifty miles or so to the south lay Algiers. Dangerous, hostile, and little known except by those unfortunate enough to fall into the hands of Algerine pirates.

He saw the seaman Sullivan hurrying to the main shrouds, his bare feet hooking over the hard ratlines. His soles were like leather, unlike some of the landsmen, who could scarcely hobble after a few hours working aloft, although even they were improving. He heard Partridge, the ship's barrel-chested boatswain, call out something, and saw Sullivan's brown face split into a grin.

He knew that Cristie, the master, had arrived on deck. That was not unusual. He checked his log at least twice in every watch. His entire world was the wind and the currents, the tides and the soundings; he could probably discover the exact condition of the seabed merely by arming the lead with tallow and smelling the fragment hauled up from the bottom. Without his breed of mariner a ship was blind, could fall a victim to any reef or sandbar. Charts were never enough. To men like Cristie, they never would be, either.

Adam shaded his eyes and peered up at the mainmast again.

'Deck, there!'

Adam waited, picturing Sullivan's bright, clear eyes, like those of a much younger man peering through a mask.

'Wreckage off the starboard bow!'

He heard Massie say irritably, 'Could have been there for months!'

Nobody answered, and he sensed that they were all looking at their captain.

He turned to the sailing master. 'What do *you* think, Mr Cristie?'

Cristie shrugged. 'Aye. In this sea it could have been drifting hereabouts for quite a while.'

He was no doubt thinking, *why*? To investigate some useless wreckage would mean changing tack, and in this uncertain wind it might take half a day to resume their course.

The master's mate said, 'Here's Sullivan, sir.'

Sullivan walked from the shrouds, gazing around the quarter-deck as if he had never seen it before.

'Well, Sullivan? A fool's errand this time?'

Surprisingly, the man did not respond. He said, 'Somethin's wrong, sir.' He looked directly at his captain for the first time. Then he nodded, more certain, knowing that the captain would not dismiss his beliefs, his sailor's instinct.

He seemed to make up his mind. 'Gulls, sir, circlin' over the wreckage.'

Adam heard the midshipman of the watch suppress a snigger, and the master's mate's angry rebuke.

A shadow fell across the compass box. It was Galbraith, the first lieutenant.

'Trouble, sir? I heard what he said.'

Gulls on the water meant pickings. Circling low above it meant they were afraid to go nearer. He thought of the boy John Whitmarsh, who had been found alive after *Anemone* had gone down.

'Call all hands, Mr Galbraith. We shall heave to and lower the gig.' He heard the brief, almost curt orders being translated into trilling calls and the responding rush of feet. *What's the bloody captain want this time?*

He raised his voice slightly. 'Mr Bellairs, take charge of the gig.' He turned to watch the hands rushing to halliards and braces. 'Good experience for your examination!' He saw the midshipman touch his hat and smile. *Was it so easy?*

He saw Jago by the nettings and beckoned him across. 'Go with him. A weather eye.'

Jago shrugged. 'Aye, sir.'

Galbraith watched the sails thundering in disorder as *Unrivalled* lurched unsteadily into the wind.

55

He said, 'I would have gone, sir. Mr Bellairs is not very experienced.'

Adam looked at him. 'And he never will be, if he is protected from such duties.'

Galbraith hurried to the rail as the gig was swayed up and over the gangway.

Did he take it as a slight because one so junior had been sent? Or as a lack of trust, because of what had happened in his past?

Adam turned aside, angry that such things could still touch him.

'Gig's away, sir!'

The boat was pulling strongly from the side, oars rising and cutting into the water as one. A good boat's crew. He could see Jago hunched by the tiller, remembered shaking hands with him on that littered deck after the American had broken off the action. And John Whitmarsh lay dead on the orlop.

'Glass, Mr Cousens!' He reached out and took the telescope, not noticing that the name had come to him without effort.

The gig loomed into view, up and down so that sometimes she appeared to be foundering. No wonder the frigate was rolling so badly. He thought of Cristie's comment. *In this sea.*

He saw the oars rise and stay motionless, a man standing in the bows with a boathook. Jago was on his feet too, but steadying the tiller-bar as if he was calming the boat and the movement. The hard man, and a true sailor, who hated officers and detested the navy. But he was still here. *With me.*

Bellairs was trying to keep his footing, and was staring astern at *Unrivalled.* He held up his arms and crossed them.

Massie grunted, 'He's found something.'

Cristie barely spared him a glance. 'Somebody, more like.'

Adam lowered the glass. They were pulling a body from the sea, the bowman fending off the surrounding wreckage with his boathook. Midshipman Bellairs, who would sit for lieutenant when the admiral so ordered, was hanging over the gunwale vomiting, with Jago holding his belt, setting the oars in motion again as if all else was secondary.

'Fetch the surgeon.'

'Done, sir.'

'Extra hands on the tackles, Mr Partridge!' The boatswain was not grinning now.

He thought again of Whitmarsh, the twelve year old who had been 'volunteered' by a so-called uncle. He had told him how he had drifted from the sinking frigate, holding his friend's hand, unaware that the other boy had been dead for some while.

He turned to speak to Sullivan but he had gone. He handed the telescope to the midshipman of the watch; he did not need to look again to know the gulls were swooping down once more, their screams lost in distance. The spirits of dead sailors, the old Jacks called them. Scavengers fitted them better, he thought. He heard O'Beirne giving instructions to two of his loblolly boys. A good surgeon, or another butcher? You might never know until it was too late.

Adam walked to the side, two marines springing out of his way to allow him to pass. The gig was almost here, and he noticed that Bellairs was on his feet again.

Why should it matter? We all had to learn. But it did matter.

A block squeaked, and he knew Partridge's mates were lowering a canvas cradle to hoist the survivor inboard. It would probably finish him, if he was not dead already.

Other men were running now to guide the cradle over the gangway, clear of the boat-tier.

Adam said, 'Secure the gig and get the ship under way, if you please. Take over, Mr Galbraith.' He did not see the sudden light in Galbraith's eyes, but he knew it was there. He was being given the ship. *Trusted.*

The surgeon was on his knees, sleeves rolled up, his red face squinting with concentration. Large and heavy though he was, he had the small hands and wrists of a very much younger person.

'I cannot move him far, sir.'

To the sickbay, the orlop. There was no time.

'Carry him aft, to my quarters. More room for you.'

He leaned over and looked at the man they had pulled from the sea. From death.

One bare arm showed a faint tattoo. The other was like raw meat, a bone protruding through the blackened flesh. He was so badly burned it was a marvel he had lived this long. A fire, then. Every sailor's most dreaded enemy.

Someone held out a knife. ''E were carryin' this, sir! English, right enough.'

O'Beirne was cutting away the scorched rags from the body. He murmured, 'Very bad, sir. I'm afraid . . .' He gripped the man's uninjured wrist as his mouth moved, as if even that were agonising.

Perhaps it was the sound of the ship coming about, her sails refilling, slapping and banging as the great yards were braced hard round, or the sense of men around him again. A sailor's world. His mouth opened very slightly.

''Ere, matey.' A tarred hand with a mug of water pushed through the crouching onlookers, but O'Beirne shook his head and put a finger to his lips.

'Not yct, lad.'

Jago was here, on his knees opposite the surgeon, lowering his dark head until it seemed to be touching the man's blistered face.

He murmured, 'He's *here*, mate. Right here with us.' He looked up at Adam. 'Askin' for the Captain. You, sir . . .' He broke off and lowered his face again. 'Ship's name, sir.' He held the man's bare shoulder. 'Try again, mate!'

Then he said harshly, 'No good, sir. He's goin'.'

Adam knelt and took the man's hand. Even that was badly burned, but he would not feel it now.

As his shadow fell across the man's face he saw the eyes open. For the first time, as if only they lived. What did he see, he wondered. Someone in a grubby shirt, unfastened, and without the coat and the gold lace of authority. Hardly a captain . . .

He said quietly, 'I command here. You are safe now.'

It was a lie; he could feel his life draining away like sand in an hourglass, and even the unwavering eyes knew it.

He was using all his strength. The eyes moved suddenly to the shrouds and running rigging overhead.

Who was he? What did he remember? What was his ship? It was no use. He heard Bellairs say, 'There were four others, sir. All burned. Tied together. He must have been the last one left alive . . .' He could not continue.

Adam felt the man's hand tighten very slightly in his. He watched his mouth, saw it forming a word, a name.

O'Beirne said, '*Fortune*, sir.'

Someone else said, 'Probably a trader. They was English anyway, poor devils!'

But the hand was moving again. Agitated. Desperate.

Adam leaned closer, until his face was only inches from the dying man's. He could smell his agony, his despair, but he did not release his hand.

'Tell me, *what is it*?'

Then, with great care, he lowered the hand to the deck. The sand had run out. It was as if only one thing had kept him alive, long enough. For what? Revenge?

He rose and stood for a few moments looking down at the dead man. An unknown sailor. Then he looked around at their intent faces. Troubled, curious, some openly distressed. It was perhaps the closest he had been to them since he had taken command.

He said, 'Not "fortune". He got it out, though.' The man's eyes were still open, as if he were alive, and listening. 'It was *La Fortune*. A Frenchman who sank his ship.'

Jago said, 'Shall I have him put over, sir?'

He was still on his knees, and glanced at Adam's hand as it rested briefly on his shoulder.

'No. We shall bury him during the last dog watch. It is the least we can do.'

He saw Bellairs, deathly pale despite his sunburn, and said, 'That was well done, Mr Bellairs. I shall enter it in your report. It will do you no harm.'

Bellairs tried to smile but his mouth would not move.

'That man, sir –'

But the deck was empty, and the sailmaker's crew would soon be stitching up the nameless sailor for his last journey on earth.

'I intend to find out. And when I do, I shall see that he does not leave us unavenged!'

The sun stood high in a clear sky, so that the reflected glare from the anchorage was almost a physical presence. *Unrivalled*, with all sails clewed up except topsails and jib, seemed to be gliding towards the sprawled panorama of battlements and sand-coloured buildings, her stem hardly causing a ripple.

Adam Bolitho raised a telescope and examined the other vessels anchored nearby. *Montrose*, the forty-two gun frigate which Sir Graham Bethune had chosen for his flagship, was surrounded by boats and lighters. She had left Gibraltar two days ahead of *Unrivalled*, but from the activity of storing and watering ship it seemed she had arrived in Malta only today, more evidence of their own fast passage despite the contrary winds.

Adam was still not sure what he thought of Bethune's decision to sail separately. In company they might have exercised together, anything to break the day-to-day routine.

He did not know the vice-admiral very well, although what he had seen of him he had liked, and had trusted. He had been a frigate captain himself, and a successful one, and in Adam's book that rated very high. Against that, he had spent several years employed ashore, latterly at the Admiralty. *Something I could never do.* It might make an officer over cautious, more aware of the risks and the perils of responsibility in a sea command. He had even heard Forbes, *Montrose*'s captain, question the need for such caution. It was unlike the man to criticise his admiral, but they had all had too much to drink.

He moved the glass further and saw three other frigates anchored in line, flags barely moving, windsails rigged to provide a suggestion of air in the crowded quarters between decks.

Not a large force, something else which would weigh heavily on Bethune's mind. With Napoleon at large on the French mainland again, no one could predict the direction the conflict might take. The French might drive north to the Channel ports, and seize ships and men to attack and delay vital supplies for Wellington's armies. And what of the old enemies? There would still be some who were prepared and eager to renew their allegiance to the arrogant Corsican.

'Guardboat, sir!'

Adam shifted the glass, and beyond the motionless launch saw other buildings which appeared to merge with the wall of the nearest battery.

Catherine had been here. For a few days, before she had been forced to take passage back to England.

The last time, the last place she had seen his uncle. He tried to turn aside from the thought. The last time they had been lovers.

Cristie called, 'Ready, sir!'

Adam walked to the rail and stared along the length of his command. The anchor swaying slightly to the small movement, ready to let go, men at halliards and braces, petty officers staring aft to the quarterdeck. To their captain. He saw Galbraith on the opposite side, a speaking trumpet in his hands, but his eyes were on Wynter, the third lieutenant, who was up forward with the anchor party. Galbraith had intended to take charge himself, and Adam had been surprised by this discovery, more so because he had not noticed it earlier. A strong, capable officer, but he could not or would not delegate, as in the matter of Bellairs and the wreckage, the pathetic corpses, the screaming gulls.

He said, 'Carry on, Mr Galbraith!'

'Lee braces, there! Hands wear ship!'

'Tops'l sheets! Tops'l clew lines!'

Galbraith's voice pursued the seamen as they hauled and stamped in unison on the sun-dried planking, waiting to belay each snaking line of cordage.

'Helm a'lee!'

Adam stood very still, watching the land pass slowly across the bowsprit and the proud figurehead.

'Let go!' Galbraith nodded curtly and the great anchor hit the water, flinging spray over the bustling seamen.

The Jack broke from the bows almost immediately, and he saw Midshipman Bellairs turn to smile at one of his signals party. But he had not forgotten the man they had plucked from the sea, only to surrender him again. Adam had seen the boy when they had cleared lower deck for the ceremony. Even the wind had dropped.

It had been strangely moving for new hands and old Jacks alike. Most of them had seen men they knew, and had shared their meagre resources with in one messdeck or another, pitched outboard like so much rubbish after a battle. But for some reason the burial of this unknown sailor had been different.

He had known Galbraith was watching him as he had

read from the worn and salt-stained prayer book. He smiled. His aunt Nancy had given it to him before he had joined *Hyperion.*

Take good care of it, Adam. It will take good care of you.

It was the only thing he still possessed from that day, a lifetime ago.

He looked up now at the monkey-like figures of seamen securing sails, and freeing the boat tackles. How long this time? What orders? His mind refused to submit. *And what of a ship named* La Fortune*?*

The dying man might have been mistaken, his reeling mind betraying him, clinging perhaps to a memory which, like him, was now dead.

But suppose? There had been many French ships at sea when Napoleon had abdicated. The two frigates which had engaged *Frobisher* on the day of his uncle's death had not come from nowhere.

'Orders, sir?'

'Post sentries, Mr Galbraith. I don't want any unlawful visitors. And have a boat prepared for the purser – he'll need to go ashore to look for fruit.'

Even a man-of-war invited attention when she lay at anchor. With gunports left open to afford some relief to men off watch, there was easy access for dealers and women, too, given half a chance. He smiled again, privately. *Especially a man-of-war.*

A boatswain's mate called, 'Guardboat coming alongside, sir!'

Galbraith seemed to come abruptly out of his habitual reserve.

'Letters from home, maybe, sir? We might learn what's happening!'

Adam glanced at him, this Galbraith who was still unknown to him.

'Passenger on board, sir!' He thought Bellairs sounded disappointed. 'A lieutenant, sir!'

Adam walked to the entry port, and saw the officer in question shaking hands with the Royal Marine lieutenant who was in charge of the boat. A tall man, dark hair streaked with grey. Adam clenched his fist without realising it. It had to come. But not now, not like this. He was unprepared. Vulnerable.

Perhaps Bethune had been trying to warn him at Gibraltar.

Galbraith said uncertainly, 'I do not recognise him, sir.'

'Why should you?' He touched his arm, aware of the sharp sarcasm. 'Forgive me. My rank does not afford me a licence to insult you.' He stared at the entry port. 'He is – was – my uncle's flag lieutenant. And friend.'

Then he walked to meet his visitor, and all he could feel was envy.

Lieutenant George Avery seated himself in a high-backed chair and watched as the cabin servant placed two goblets of wine on a table. The chair felt hard, unused, like the ship herself.

Strange how it became with ships, he thought. In a King's ship you always expected to see a familiar face, catch a name you had once known. The navy was a family, some said; you were always a part of it.

He had been introduced to the senior lieutenant, a powerfully built man with an honest face and a firm handshake. But he was a stranger.

He studied the captain. He had been prepared for this meeting, although he guessed Adam Bolitho had been disconcerted by it.

But it was not that. He observed him now, in profile as he wrote briefly on a pad for a small, sickly-looking man who must be a clerk.

They had met several times, and Avery had always remembered his quick, observant approach to his work and the people he met, in retrospect always youthful, always restless. *Like a young colt*, Richard Bolitho had once said.

The resemblance was there, to the portraits in the house in Falmouth. And, above all, to the man he had served, and had loved.

We are about the same age, but whereas he has his career and his future ahead like a beacon, I have nothing. Adam Bolitho and his uncle had been kept apart far more than they had been together, and yet, in his mind, Avery had always thought of one as being in the mould of the other. It was not so. Adam had changed in some way, matured as was inevitable for any man of his rank and responsibility. But it went far deeper. He was guarded, withdrawn. Perhaps still unable or unwilling to accept that the cloak, the guardian presence, was gone, that there was not even a shadow.

Adam was looking at him now, holding out the goblet.

'You will like this.'

But he was not telling him; he was asking him to share something.

Avery held up the goblet, and thought of the wines she had sent aboard for Richard Bolitho.

'I am told that you saw Lady Somervell when you were in England, sir? Before you sailed.'

'Aye. She was concerned that I would not care enough to order some wine for myself!' Then he did smile, and, only briefly, he was the young, headstrong officer Avery had first met.

Avery said, 'She never forgets,' and the smile faded. Like sunlight dying even as you watched, he thought.

'We were at Falmouth . . . I pray to God she is able to come to terms with this terrible loss.' He changed tack swiftly, in the manner Avery remembered. 'And what of you? Shall you remain here in Malta?'

Avery put down the goblet. It was empty, and he could taste the wine on his lips, but he did not recall drinking it.

'I am able to elaborate on the information already to hand, sir.' He hesitated. 'Sir Richard had cause to meet Mehmet Pasha, the man who commands and governs in Algiers. I was with him, and was privileged to share the intelligence we gained there. If I may be of help?'

He moved his shoulder and Adam saw him wince: the old wound which had brought him down and had cost him his ship. *We have so much in common.* He had seen his own flag cut down in surrender when, like Avery, he had been too badly wounded to resist. And he also had been a prisoner of war, before making his escape. A court martial had cleared and had praised him. The verdict could just as easily have destroyed him.

He said, 'I would be grateful. Sir Graham Bethune has very little on which to proceed.'

Above and around them the anchored frigate was alive with shipboard sounds, and once during their conversation he got up and closed the cabin skylight against them. As if, for these moments, he wanted to share it with nobody else.

Avery spoke evenly and without any obvious emotion, but Adam understood what it was costing, and what it meant to him. At last, here was someone who had been there. Had seen what had happened.

Avery said simply, 'I saw him fall.' The tawny eyes were distant. He almost smiled. 'Allday was with me.'

Adam nodded, but dared not speak or interrupt. For Avery's sake, but mostly for his own.

Avery was looking at the sloping stern windows, and the anchored ships beyond.

'He was the bravest and the most compassionate man I ever served, ever knew. When I was pulled out to your ship just now, I almost asked to be taken ashore. But I had to come. Not out of duty or respect – they are mere words. Not even because it was your right to be told. Above all, I thought I would feel resentment, because you are here and he is not. I now know that I did the right thing. He spoke of you often, even on the day he fell. He was proud of you, of what you had become. *More like a son*, he said.'

Adam said, quietly, 'Did he suffer?'

Avery shook his head.

'I think not. He spoke to Allday. I could not hear what he said, and I had not the heart to question him afterwards.'

Afterwards.

Avery's eyes moved to the table, and the envelope which was addressed to Vice-Admiral Bethune.

'I shall take it to him when I leave, sir.'

Duty, so often used as an escape from tragedy. Adam had learned it the hard way, better than most.

He said, 'You could return later. We might sup together. Nobody else.' He felt like a hypocrite, but was glad when Avery declined. 'Tomorrow, then. There will be a conference, I believe?'

Avery glanced down, and almost unconsciously plucked a solitary gold thread from his coat. Where he had once worn a twist of gold lace to distinguish him as an admiral's aide, his flag lieutenant.

Bethune would already have one of his own, as Valentine Keen had had at Halifax. There could be resentment.

Avery said, 'If you so requested, I should be pleased . . .' He smiled again, faintly, as though his mind were somewhere else. 'Honoured to accompany you. I can still stand a fair watch, and I have nothing to go home for as yet.'

Adam recalled that Avery was the nephew of Sillitoe, that man of power whose name was rarely out of the newssheets. Another nephew. Another coincidence.

He held out his hand. 'I'm glad you came. I'll not forget.'

Avery took a small package from his pocket and unwrapped it with great care.

The locket. He had seen his uncle wearing it whenever he had been on deck with his shirt unfastened. *As I do.* He took it and held it to the sunlight, the perfect likeness, Catherine's bare shoulders and high cheekbones. He was about to turn it over to examine the inscription when he saw the broken clasp and severed chain. As clean a cut as if done by a knife. His fingers closed tightly upon it. No knife. The marksman's shot must have done it.

Avery was watching him.

'I have been unable to find a local craftsman with skill enough to repair it. I would have sent it to her . . . Now, I think it better that you should be the one, sir.'

They faced one another, and Adam understood. In his way Avery had been in love with her also. Now that she needed help, there was no one.

'Thank you for saying that. Perhaps I shall be able to return it myself.'

Avery picked up his hat, knowing he would do nothing of the kind. Suddenly he was pleased at what he had done. He looked at Adam, and for a fleeting moment he saw the other face. He smiled. *Like a good flag lieutenant.*

Galbraith was at the entry port when they came on deck, and saw them shake hands, as if each was reluctant to break the contact. He noticed, too, that the visitor paused and glanced almost involuntarily at the mainmast truck, as if he still expected to see a flag there.

In his cabin once more, Adam took out the locket and read

the inscription, and her voice seemed to speak to him as it did whenever he received a letter from her.

May Fate always guide you.
May love always protect you.

She must have remembered those words when she had watched *Unrivalled* standing out into Falmouth Bay. As she would always look for the ship which would never come.

He turned as Galbraith appeared by the open screen door.

'Concerning tomorrow, sir?'

It was the only way. Perhaps Galbraith understood, and in time might share it.

'Take a glass with me first, eh?'

He slipped the locket into his pocket, out of sight. But the voice still persisted.

'There is something we must discuss, before I meet the vice-admiral tomorrow. You see, I have a plan . . .'

It was a new beginning for all of them.

5

A Contest

Lieutenant Leigh Galbraith strode across the quarterdeck and reported, 'The watch is aft, sir!' Like his unerring steps over and past ringbolts and other obstacles, it was part of an unchanging routine at sea. He even touched his hat to the shadowy shape of Lieutenant Massie, whom he was about to relieve.

It was still quite dark, but when his eyes eventually became accustomed he would see the approach of dawn in the fading stars, the hardening of the horizon. Massie stifled a yawn.

'West-by-south, sir.' He stared up at the pale outlines of the sails, filling only occasionally with the wind across the starboard quarter.

Galbraith glanced at the helmsmen, eyes flickering in the shaded light from the compass. Other shapes were moving into position: the morning watch, when the ship would come alive again.

Galbraith looked at the tiny glow from the cabin skylight. Was the captain awake, or was it a ploy to keep the watch on its toes?

He thought of Captain Bolitho's return from his meeting with the vice-admiral. Galbraith had no idea what had been said, but the captain had come back on board barely able to conceal his anger.

Galbraith tried to dismiss it. At first light they would sight and resume contact with another frigate, *Matchless* of forty-two guns. She had been in the Mediterranean for three years attached to one squadron or another, and would therefore be very familiar with shipping movements and the lurking danger of pirates. Corsairs.

Matchless was commanded by a senior post-captain named Emlyn Bouverie, a man who came from a proud naval family, and was thought likely for promotion to flag rank in the near future. Galbraith did not know him, but those who did apparently heartily disliked him. Not a tyrant or martinet like some he had known, but a perfectionist, who was quick to reprimand or punish anyone who fell below his own high standards.

He said, 'You are relieved, sir.' He lifted the canvas hood from the master's chart table and peered at the log with the aid of a tiny lantern. They would sight land before noon, according to Cristie. He had never known him to be wrong.

He steadied the light with care. The coast of North Africa: to most sailors a place of mystery and strange superstitions, and best avoided.

He studied Cristie's fine handwriting. *6th June, 1815.* What would this day bring?

Captain Bolitho had called his officers and those of senior warrant rank together in his cabin. Galbraith straightened his back and glanced at the skylight again. Remembering it.

The captain had described the mission. A visit to Algiers, to investigate. Their intentions were peaceful, but guns' crews would exercise twice a day all the same. It was said that Algiers was protected by some six hundred guns. It would not be much of a contest if the worst happened.

The captain had looked at their faces and had said, 'There was a French frigate named *La Fortune* in the Western Mediterranean before Napoleon's surrender. Others too, and it is known that the Dey of Algiers and the Bey of Tunis have offered sanctuary to such men-of-war in exchange for their services. The prisons are still filled with Christians, people snatched from passing vessels, and held on no more serious charge than their religious beliefs. Torture, slavery, and open acts of aggression against merchantmen sailing under our protection – the list is endless. With our "allies" . . .' he had made no effort to conceal his contempt '. . . we had a chance to put paid to this piracy once and for all. Now with Napoleon at the head of his armies again, the Dey in particular may use our predicament to gain even more control of these waters, and beyond.'

Somebody, Galbraith had thought Captain Bosanquet of the Royal Marines, had asked about the sailor they had rescued and later buried at sea.

Captain Bolitho had answered shortly, 'Probably one of many.' And again something like bitterness had crept into his voice. 'Which is why Captain Bouverie intends to make a peaceful approach. Vice-Admiral Bethune's squadron is hard pressed as it is. He sees no alternative.'

Bouverie was the senior captain, as he reminded them often enough by hoisting signals at every opportunity. Galbraith half-smiled. He would make a good admiral one day.

The master's mate of the watch said softly, 'Cabin light's out, sir.'

'Thank you, Mr Woodthorpe. I am glad *you* are awake!' He saw the man's teeth in the dimness.

How would it be this time? He thought of the moment when they had shared wine together; it had shown him another side of Adam Bolitho. He had even touched on his early days at sea as a midshipman, and had spoken of his uncle, his first captain. Opening out, demonstrating a warmth which Galbraith had not suspected.

After his visit to the flagship, he had shut that same door. At first Galbraith thought that he had expected some priority, a preference because of his famous surname, and had resented Bouverie's slower, more cautious approach. But Adam Bolitho was a post-captain of some fame, and had not come by it easily. He would be used to Bouveries in the navy's tight world.

It was deeper than that. Driving him, like some unstoppable force. Something personal.

Like the brigantine, which might or might not be following *Unrivalled*. Twice on this passage they had sighted an unknown sail. The lookouts had not been certain; even the impressive Sullivan could not swear to it. But Captain Bolitho had no such doubts. When he had signalled Bouverie for permission to break company and give chase, the request had been denied with a curt *negative*.

Galbraith had heard him exclaim, 'This is a ship of war! I'm no grocery captain, damn his eyes!'

Galbraith recognised the light step now, and heard his passing comment to the master's mate. Then he saw the open shirt, rippling in the soft wind, and remembered the savage scar he had seen above his ribs when he had found him shaving in his cabin. He was lucky to be alive.

Bolitho had seen his eyes, and said, 'They made a good job of it!' And had grinned, and only for a second or so Galbraith had seen the youth override the experience and the memories.

A good job. Galbraith had heard the surgeon mention that when Adam Bolitho had been captured, more dead than alive, he had been operated on by the American ship's surgeon, who had in fact been French.

'Good morning, Mr Galbraith. Everything is as it was, I see?' He was looking up at the topsails. 'I could make her *fly* if I got the word!'

Pride? It was stronger than that. It was more like love.

He moved to the compass box and nodded to the helmsmen, and their eyes followed him further still, to the canvas-covered table.

'We shall exercise the main battery during the forenoon, Mr Galbraith.'

Galbraith smiled. That would go round the ship like a fast fuse. But it had to be said that the gun crews were improving.

'And call the hands a quarter-hour earlier. I expect a smart ship today. And I want our people properly fed, not making do with muck!'

Another side. Captain Bolitho had already disrated the cook for wasting food and careless preparation. Many captains would not have cared.

He was holding the same little lamp, but did not seem to be looking at the chart, and Galbraith heard him say quietly, 'June sixth. I had all but forgot!'

'May I share it, sir?'

For a moment he thought he had gone too far. But Adam merely looked at him, his face hidden in shadow.

'I was thinking of some wild roses, and a lady.' He turned away, as if afraid of what he might disclose. 'On my birthday.' Then, abruptly, 'The wind! By God, *the wind!*'

71

It was as though the ship had sensed his change of mood. Blocks and halliards rattled, and above their heads the main topsail boomed like a drum.

Adam said, 'Belay my last order! Call all hands directly!' He gripped Galbraith's arm as if to emphasise the importance of what he was saying. 'We shall sight land today! Don't you see, if we *are* being followed it's their last chance to outreach us!'

Galbraith knew it was pointless to question his sudden excitement. At first light they should be changing tack to take station on *Matchless* again. There was not a shred of evidence that the occasional sightings of a far-off sail were significant, or connected in any way. But the impetuous grip on his arm seemed to cast all doubt to the rising wind.

He swung round. 'Pipe all hands, Mr Woodthorpe! And send for the master, fast as you can!'

He turned back to the indistinct outline. 'Captain Bouverie may not approve, sir.'

Adam Bolitho said quietly, 'But Captain Bouverie is not yet in sight, is he?'

Men rushed out of the shadows, some still dazed by sleep, staring around at the flapping canvas and straining rigging until order and discipline took command.

The master, feet bare, stumped across the sloping deck, muttering, 'Is there no peace?' Then he saw the captain. 'New course, sir?'

'We will wear ship, Mr Cristie! As close to the wind as she'll come!'

Calls shrilled and men scrambled aloft, the perils of working in darkness no longer a threat now to most of them.

Blocks squealed, and someone stumbled over a snaking line, which was slithering across the damp planking as if it were truly alive.

But she was answering, from the instant that the big double-wheel was hauled over.

Galbraith gripped a backstay and felt the deck tilting still further. In the darkness everything was wilder, louder, as if the ship were responding to her captain's recklessness. He dashed spray from his face and saw pale stars spiralling around the masthead pendant. It was all but dawn. He looked towards the captain. Suppose the sea was empty? And there was no other vessel? He thought of Bouverie, what might happen, and knew, without understanding why, that this was a contest.

Unrivalled completed her turn, water rushing down the lee scuppers as the sails refilled on the opposite tack, the jib cracking loudly, as close to the wind as she could hold.

Cristie shouted, 'Steady as she goes, sir! East-by-south!'

Afterwards, Galbraith thought it was the only time he had ever heard the master either impressed or surprised.

'Make fast! *Belay!*'

Men ran to obey each command; to any landsman it would appear a single, confused tangle of canvas and straining cordage.

Adam Bolitho gripped the rail and said, 'Now she *flies*! Feel her!'

Galbraith turned, but shook his head and did not speak. The captain was quite alone with his ship.

'Hands aloft, Mr Lomax! Get the t'gallants on her and put more men on the maincourse! They're like a pack of old women today!'

Lieutenant George Avery stood beneath the mizzen mast, where the marines of the afterguard had been mustered for nearly an hour. He had heard a few whispered curses when the galley fire had been doused before some of the watchkeepers had managed to snatch a quick meal.

He felt out of place aboard *Matchless*, alien. Everything worked smoothly enough, as might be expected in a frigate which had been in commission for over three years. But he had sensed a lack of the companionship he himself had come to recognise and accept. Every move, each change of tack or direction, seemed to flow from one man. No chain of command as Avery knew it, but a single man.

He could see him now, feet apart, hand on his hip, a square figure in the strengthening daylight. He considered the word; it described Captain Emlyn Bouverie exactly. Even when the ship heeled to a change of tack, Bouverie remained like a rock. His hands were square too, strong and hard, like the man.

Bouverie said, 'Attend the lookouts, Mr Foster, you should know my orders by now!' His voice always carried without

73

any apparent effort, and Avery had never seen him deign to use a speaking trumpet, even in the one patch of wind they had encountered after leaving Malta.

He heard a lieutenant yelling out names, and thought he knew why. Soon now *Unrivalled* would be sighted, provided Adam Bolitho had kept on station as instructed. He recalled the meeting aboard the flagship. Bouverie had vetoed the suggestion that Avery should sail with *Unrivalled* instead of 'the senior officer's ship', and Bethune had concurred. Looking back, Avery still wondered if it was because he had truly agreed, or if he had simply needed to demonstrate that no favouritism would be shown Sir Richard Bolitho's nephew.

He gazed aloft as the topgallant sails broke free from their yards and filled to the wind, the topmen spread out on either side, all aware of their captain's standards.

Pride, jealousy? It was difficult to have one without the other. *Matchless* had been in these waters for more than three years, and despite her coppered hull was heavy with weed and marine growths. *Unrivalled* had been forced to shorten sail several times during the day to remain on station, while at night they must be almost hove to. He could imagine Adam Bolitho's frustration and impatience. *And yet I hardly know him.* That was the strangest part. Like handing over the locket. *When I wanted it for myself.*

He realised that Bouverie had joined him by the mizzen. He could move swiftly when it suited him.

'Bored, Mr Avery? This may seem a mite tame after your last appointment!'

Avery said, 'I feel like a passenger, sir.'

'Well spoken! But I cannot disrupt the running of my command with a wrong note, eh?'

He laughed. In fact, Bouverie laughed frequently, but it rarely reached his eyes.

'All secure, sir!' Somebody scuttled past; nobody walked in *Matchless*.

Bouverie nodded. 'I've read the notes and observations on your last visit to Algiers. Could be useful.' He broke off and shouted, 'Take that man's name, Mr Munro! I'll have no damned laggards this day!'

That man. After three years in commission, a captain should have known the name of every soul aboard.

Again, the ambush of memory. How Richard Bolitho had impressed upon his officers the importance of remembering men's names. *It is often all they can call their own.*

He turned, startled, as Bouverie said, 'You must miss the admiral,' as if he had been reading his thoughts.

'I do indeed, sir.'

'I never met him. Although I too was at Copenhagen, in *Amazon*, Captain Riou. My first stint as a lieutenant. A real blooding, I can tell you!' He laughed again, but nobody turned from his duties to watch or listen. Not in *Matchless*.

Bouverie's arm jerked out once more. 'Another pull on the weather forebrace and belay! *Far too slow!*'

He changed, just as suddenly. 'Did you have much to do with Lady Somervell? Turn a man's heart to water with a glance, I'm told. A true beauty – caused more than a few ripples in her time!'

'A woman of courage also, sir.'

Bouverie was studying him in the gloom. Avery could feel it, like the stare of a prosecuting officer at a court martial. As he could feel his own rising resentment.

Bouverie swayed back on his heels. 'If you say so. I'd have thought –' He broke off and almost lost his balance. 'What the *hell* was that?'

Someone shouted, 'Gunfire, sir!'

Bouverie swallowed hard. 'Clod!' He strode to the opposite side. 'Mr Lomax! *Where away?*'

Avery licked his lips, tasting the brine. A single shot. It could only mean one thing, a signal to heave to. He stared at the horizon until his eyes throbbed. Every morning since leaving Malta it had been like this. As soon as *Unrivalled* was sighted Bouverie would make a signal, as if he was always trying to catch them out. Without looking he knew that the first signal of the day was already bent on, ready to soar up to the yard, when most ships would have been content to remain in close company. He shivered, from more than the rising wind, recalling Adam Bolitho's impatience at the meeting when doubts had been voiced about the brigantine. Only some ridiculous obsession, something to command attention, to impress. *Not any more.*

He heard the first lieutenant say, '*Unrivalled* must be off her station, sir!'

'I know that, God damn it! We are to alter course when . . .' He turned towards Avery. 'Well, what do you think? Or do "passengers" have no opinions?'

Avery felt very calm.

'I believe *Unrivalled* has found something useful, sir.'

'Oh, *very* diplomatic, sir! And what of Captain Adam Bolitho? Does he truly believe he is above obeying orders, and beyond the discipline that binds the rest of us?'

An inner voice warned him, *take care.* Another insisted, *you have nothing more to lose.*

He said, 'I was with Sir Richard Bolitho at Algiers, sir. Things have changed since then. If we attempt to enter without permission . . .' He glanced round, seeing the first touch of gold spill over the horizon. The moment he had always loved. But that, too, was past. 'This ship will be destroyed. Your ship, sir, will be blasted apart before you can come about. I have seen the anchorage, and the citadel, and some of the fanatics who control those guns.'

'I have faced worse!'

Avery relaxed. He had always been able to recognise bluster.

'Then you will know the consequences, sir.'

Bouverie stared at him. 'God damn you for your impertinence!' Then, surprisingly, he grinned. 'But bravely said, for all that!' He looked at the clearing sky as a voice yelled, 'Sail on the starboard quarter!' The merest pause. '*Two* sail, sir!'

Bouverie nodded slowly. 'A prize, then.'

The first lieutenant climbed down from the shrouds with a telescope.

'She's a brigantine, sir.'

Avery looked at his hands. They were quite still, and warm in the first frail sunlight. They felt as if they were shaking.

Bouverie was saying, 'No, not that signal, Mr Adams.' He took a glass from the signals midshipman and steadied it with care. He was studying *Unrivalled*'s topsails, like pink shells in the clear light, although the sun had not yet revealed itself.

76

'When she is on station again, make *Captain repair on board.*'

Avery turned away. How many times would Adam Bolitho read that signal with different eyes from other men? When his uncle had called him to his flagship to tell him of the death of Zenoria Keen. *We Happy Few* . . . It had been their secret.

Bouverie said, 'Breakfast, I think. Then we shall hear what our gallant Captain Bolitho has to say.' The good humour seemed even more volatile than his usual mood. 'I hope it pleases me!'

But, out of habit or memory, Avery was watching the signals party bending on the flags.

Bouverie sat squarely in a broad leather chair, hands gripping the arms as if to restrain himself.

He said, 'Now, Captain Bolitho. In your own words, of course. Share your discoveries with me, eh?' He glanced towards his table where Avery was sitting with a leather satchel and some charts, while beside him the ship's clerk was poised with his quill at the ready. 'For both our sakes, I think some record of this conversation should be kept. Sir Graham Bethune will expect it.'

Adam Bolitho walked to the stern windows and stared at his own ship, her sheer lines and shining hull distorted in the weathered glass. Hard to believe that it had all happened so quickly, and yet it was exactly as he had imagined when he had ordered *Unrivalled*'s change of course. They had all thought him mad. They were probably right.

He could recall the calm, professional eye of old Stranace, the ship's gunner, when he had explained what he required. Stranace was more used to the deadly quiet of the magazine and powder store, but like most of his breed he had never forgotten his trade, or how to lay and train an eighteen-pounder.

It must have taken the brigantine's people completely by surprise. Day in, day out, following the two frigates, knowing almost to the minute when they would reduce sail for the night, then to see one of the quarry suddenly looming out of the last, lingering darkness with every sail set, on a converging tack with no room for manoeuvre and no time to run . . .

One shot, the first *Unrivalled* had fired in anger.

Adam had watched the splash, the succession of jagged fins of spray as the ball had skipped across the water no more than a boat's length from her bows. He had touched the gunner's shoulder; it had felt like iron itself. No words were needed. It was a perfect shot, and the brigantine, now seen to be named *Rosario*, had hove to, her sails in confusion in the wind which had changed everything.

He heard the quill scratching across the paper and realised he had been describing it. He looked again and saw the brigantine's outline, more like a blurred shadow than reality. *Unrivalled* had put down two boats, and they had done well, he thought, with the lively sea, and their movements hampered by their weapons. Jago had been with him. Amused, but deadly when one of *Rosario*'s crew had raised a pistol as the boarders had flung their grapnels and swarmed aboard. He had not even seen Jago move, his blade rising and falling with the speed of light. Then the scream, and the severed hand like a glove on the deck.

Lieutenant Wynter had been in the second boat, and with his own party had put the crew under guard. After Jago's example there was no further resistance.

Rosario was Portuguese but had been chartered repeatedly, at one time by the English squadron at Gibraltar. The master, a dirty, unshaven little man, seemed to speak no English, although he produced some charts to prove his lawful occasions. The charts, like *Rosario*, were almost too filthy to examine. As Cristie later remarked, 'By guess an' by God, that's how these heathen navigate!'

A sense of failure then; he had sensed it in the restlessness of the boarding party, the apparent confidence of *Rosario*'s master. Until Wynter, perhaps the least experienced officer in the ship, had commented on the brigantine's armament, six swivel guns mounted aft and near the hold. And the smell . . .

Adam had ordered the hatches to be broached. Only one cargo had a stench like that, and they found the chains and the manacles where slaves could be packed out of sight, to exist, if they could, in terror and their own filth until they were shipped to a suitable market. There had been blood on one set of irons, and Adam guessed that the wretched prisoner had been pitched overboard.

He had seen Wynter's eyes widening with shocked surprise when he had said coldly, 'A slaver then. Worthless to me. Fetch a halter and run this bugger up to the main yard, as an example to others!'

Wynter's expression had changed to admiring comprehension when the vessel's master had thrown himself at Adam's feet, pleading and sobbing in rough but completely adequate English.

'I thought he might remember!'

Confident and less gentle, they had continued their search. There was a safe, and the gibbering master was even able to produce a key.

Adam turned now as Avery opened the satchel.

'*Rosario* had no papers as such. That alone makes her a prize.' He smiled faintly. 'For the moment.'

Avery laid out the contents of the satchel. A bill of lading, Spanish. A delivery of oil to some garrison, Portuguese. A log book, crudely marked with dates and what could be estimated positions. Some shadowed *Unrivalled*.

Bouverie said abruptly, 'Many such men are paid to spy and inform their masters of ship movements, theirs and ours.' He gave the characteristic nod. 'But I'll give you this, Bolitho. You did not imagine it!'

Adam felt the sudden surge of excitement. *The first time since* . . . He said, 'And there is a letter. I do not speak French, but I recognise it well enough.'

Avery was holding it. 'For the captain of the frigate *La Fortune*.' He gave a grave smile. 'I learned my French the hard way. As their prisoner.'

Bouverie rubbed his chin. 'So she is in Algiers. Under a great battery, you say.'

Adam said, 'The bait in the trap, sir. They will not expect us to ignore it.'

It was as if some invisible bonds had been cut. Bouverie almost sprang out of the chair.

'Out of the question! Even if we hold *Rosamund* –'

Avery heard himself correcting gently, '*Rosario*, sir,' and cursed himself. Always the good flag lieutenant . . .

Adam persisted, 'No, sir, we use her. To spring the trap. They know we are trailing our cloaks, and they will be expecting the brigantine. I am sure she is a regular visitor there.'

He was aware of the tawny eyes on him, Avery watching but not seeing him. As if he were somewhere else . . . He was suddenly deeply moved. *With my uncle.*

'*Rosario* appears to be an agile vessel, sir. It would seem only fair if we were to "chase" her into Algiers?'

Bouverie swallowed. 'A cutting-out expedition? I'm not at all certain –' Then he nodded again, vigorously. 'It might work, it's daring enough. Foolhardy, some will say.'

Adam returned to the stern windows. One of the *Rosario*'s crew had told him that they had often carried female slaves, some very young girls. The master had delighted in abusing them.

He thought of Zenoria, her back laid open by a whip. Keen had rescued her, and she had married him. Not out of love. Out of gratitude.

The mark of Satan, she had called it.

He heard himself say, 'Time is short, sir. We cannot delay.'

'The authority for such an act, which might provoke another outbreak of war . . .'

'Is yours, sir.'

Why should it matter? Bouverie would not be the first or the last officer to await a decision from a higher authority. But it did matter. It had to.

He said, 'I can take *Rosario*. I am short-handed, but we could share the burden between us. Then so would the laurels be equally divided.'

He saw the shot go home. Like one of old Stranace's.

'We'll do it. I'll send you some good hands within the hour.' Bouverie was thinking fast, like a flood-gate bursting open. 'Will you take the *Rosario*'s master with you, in case . . . ?'

Adam picked up his hat and saw blood on his sleeve. Jago's cutlass.

'I shall take him. Later, I shall see him hang.' He looked at Avery. 'By the authority vested in *me*!'

Adam Bolitho lowered his telescope and moved into the shadow of the brigantine's foresail. There would be hundreds of eyes watching from the shore. One mistake would be enough to betray them.

Bang.

He saw a waterspout burst from the sea. Close. But was it near enough to deceive their audience?

He had seen *Matchless* leaning over as she had changed tack for her final approach, and he had seen the citadel, all and more than Avery had described. It looked as if it had been there for centuries, since time began. Avery had told him about a secret, cave-like entrance to which they had been taken in a large galley. You could lose an army trying to storm such a place. Or a fleet.

He glanced at the *Rosario*'s master. Once aboard and in command of his own vessel again, he seemed to have grown in stature, as if all the pathetic pleading and whimpering for his life had been forgotten. Slumped by the bulwark, Jago sat with both legs outthrust, his eyes never leaving the man's face.

Nothing was certain. The master had intended to hoist some sort of recognition signal as they had tacked closer to the protective headland. Adam had said, 'No. They will know *Rosario*. They will not expect a signal when she is being chased by an enemy!'

Somebody had even laughed.

He turned to look at the swivel guns, all loaded and primed. And the hatch covers. He could imagine the extra seamen and marines crammed in the holds, listening to the occasional bang of *Matchless*'s bow-chaser, sweating it out. Captain Bosanquet was down there with them, apparently more concerned with the state of his uniform in the filthy hold than the prospect of being dead within the next hour.

He stepped into the shadow again and held his breath, and carefully raised his glass and trained it on the citadel, and the main wall which Avery had remembered so clearly. A movement. He watched, hardly daring to blink. Guns, an entire line of them, thrusting their muzzles through the embrasures, the menace undiminished by distance. He could almost hear their iron trucks squeaking over the worn stone.

He felt the hull shiver. Whatever else he was, *Rosario*'s master knew these waters well. They were in the shallows now, heading for the anchorage. Avery was right. He felt almost light-headed. *Right.* The great guns would not depress enough to endanger the brigantine. Like the batteries he had seen at Halifax, carefully sited on the mainland and on a small island in the harbour, so that no enemy ship could slip past them undetected.

But here there was no island.

He saw the first gun fire and recoil, smoke writhing above the old walls like a ragged spectre. Then, one by one, the others followed. The sound seemed to be all around them, like an unending echo. Probably bronzed guns. They were just as deadly to a wooden hull.

He thought of *Unrivalled* outside, somewhere around the headland and still out of sight. Galbraith and Cristie, and all the others who despite his own attempts to remain detached were no longer strangers to him.

Could he never accept it? Like the moment when Galbraith had picked men for the *Rosario*'s raiding party. It had been difficult for him; almost everybody, even the green hands, had volunteered. Madness, then. What would Galbraith be thinking now? Feeling pride at having been left in command? Or seeing a chance of permanent promotion if things went badly wrong?

A seaman called, 'One o' them galleys headin' this way, sir! Starboard bow!'

Matchless was firing again, a broadside this time; it was impossible to tell where the shots were falling. There were more local vessels in evidence. Lateen sails and elderly schooners, with dhows etched against the water like bats.

He felt his mouth go dry as splashes burst around *Matchless*'s bows. Close. Too damned close. He bit his lip and scrambled to the opposite side.

When he lifted his head again, it was all he could do to stop himself from shouting aloud.

Directly across the larboard bow, and framed against the citadel's high walls, was the frigate. He tried to take it in, to hold it in his mind, like all those other times. The range and the bearing, the point of embrace. To see the frigate lying at her anchor, brailed-up sails filling and emptying in the offshore wind the only suggestion of movement, was unnerving. Unreal.

He cleared his throat. 'Ready about! Warn all hands, Mr Wynter!'

He groped for the short, curved fighting sword and loosened it. He could hear Jago's voice in his thoughts. 'Take the old one, sir. *The* sword!'

And his own reply. Like somebody else. 'When I've earned it!'

The *Rosario*'s ragged seamen were hauling on halliards and braces, their bare feet gripping the deck like claws, without feeling.

It only needed one of them to shout, to signal. He found his fingers clenched on the hilt of the hanger. They must not be taken. There would be no quarter. No pity.

He moved around the mast and watched the helmsman putting down the wheel, one of *Unrivalled*'s topmen at his side, a dirk in his fist.

'*Matchless* 'as gone about, sir!' The man breathed out noisily. 'They're best off out o' this little lot!'

Adam stared at the frigate. Old but well maintained, her name, *La Fortune*, in faded gilt lettering across her counter. Thirty guns at a guess. A giant to the local craft on which she preyed in the name of France. There were faces along her gangway and poop, but no muzzles were run out. Adam felt his body trembling. Why should they be? Those great guns had seen off the impudent intruder. He could hear some of them cheering, laughing. Not too many of them, however; the rest were probably ashore, evidence of their security here.

Rosario's master jumped away from the helmsman and cupped his hands, staring wild-eyed as the frigate's masts towered over them. The dirk drove into his side and he fell without even a murmur.

Even at the end he must have realised that nothing Adam could do would match the horror his new masters would have unleashed on those who betrayed them.

It was already too late. With the helm hard over and the distance falling away, *Rosario*'s bowsprit mounted the frigate's quarter like a tusk and splintered into fragments, cordage and flapping canvas shielding Wynter's boarding party as they swarmed up and over the side.

Adam drew his hanger and waved it.

'*At 'em, lads!*' Hatches were bursting open and men ran, half blinded by the sunlight, carried forward by their companions, reason already forgotten.

Adam grasped a dangling line and dragged himself over the frigate's rail, slipping and almost falling between the two hulls.

An unknown voice rasped, 'Don't leave us *now*, sir!' And laughed, a terrible sound. Matched only by the scarlet-coated marines, somehow holding formation, bayonets like ice in the sun's glare, Captain Bosanquet shouting, 'Together, Marines! *Together!*'

Adam noticed that his face was the colour of his fine tunic.

A horn or trumpet had added its mournful call to the din of shouting, the clash of steel, the screams of men being hacked down.

The boarding party needed no urging. Beyond the smoke and the scattering sailing craft was open water. *The sea.* All they had. All that mattered.

Adam stopped in his tracks as a young lieutenant blocked his way. He was probably the only officer left aboard.

'*Surrender!*' It had never left him. Not at moments like this. 'Surrender, damn your eyes!'

The lieutenant lowered his sword but drew a pistol from inside his coat. He was actually grinning, grinning while he took aim, already beyond reach.

Jago lunged forward but halted beside Adam as the French officer coughed and staggered against the gangway. There was a boarding axe embedded in his back.

Adam stared up at the masthead pendant. The wind was still with them.

'Hands aloft! Loose tops'ls!'

How could they hope to do it? To cut out a ship from a protected harbour?

'Cut the cable!' He wiped his mouth and tasted blood on his hand, but could recall no contest. Men were surrendering, others were being thrown over the side, dead or alive it did not matter.

La Fortune was free of the ground, her hull already moving as the first topsails and a jib steadied her against the thrust of wind, the demands of her rudder.

Guns were firing, but *La Fortune* moved on, untouched by the battery which could not be brought to bear.

He saw the *Rosario* drifting away, an oared galley already attempting to grapple her.

Wynter was shouting, 'She's answering, sir!' Not so blank and self-contained now, but wild-eyed, dangerous. His father the member of Parliament would scarcely have recognised him.

Jago said, 'Lost three men, sir. Another'll go afore long.'

He winced as iron hammered against the hull, grape or canister from *Rosario*'s swivels, and licked his parched lips. A Froggie ship. There would be wine on board. He turned to mention it to the captain.

Adam was watching a Royal Marine hoist a White Ensign to the frigate's gaff. Without surprise that they had done it. That they had survived.

But he said, 'For you, Uncle! For you!'

6

None Braver

Adam Bolitho closed his small log book and leaned his elbows on the cabin table. For a moment he watched the dying light, the shadows moving evenly across the checkered deck as *Unrivalled* tilted to a steady wind across the quarter. A fine sunset, the thick glass and the cabin skylight the colour of bronze.

He massaged his eyes and tried to thrust aside the lingering disappointment, and accept what he had perceived as unfairness. Not to himself, but to the ship.

They had done what many would have considered foolhardy, and, having cut out a valuable prize from under the noses of the Dey's defenders, they had joined the other ships outside the port in an atmosphere of triumph and excitement.

Now *Unrivalled* sailed alone. At any other time Adam would have welcomed this, the independence beloved of frigate captains.

But he had sensed the resentment when Captain Bouverie had decided to return to Malta with the captured *La Fortune*, and, as senior officer, to reap the praise and the lion's share of any reward which might be forthcoming. From what Adam had managed to glean from the French frigate's log, it seemed that her captain had been employed along the North African coast, snatching up or destroying local shipping with little or no opposition. The circumstances of war must have changed his role to that of a mercenary, under French colours now that Napoleon was back in Europe, but living off whichever ally found his services most useful when there was no other choice.

Adam had known nothing but war all his life, and even while he had been at sea he had been well aware of the constant threat of invasion. He thought of *La Fortune*'s captain and others like him. *How would I feel, if England was overrun by a ruthless enemy? Would I continue to fight? And for what?*

He felt the rudder shudder beneath the counter. The glass was steady, but Cristie insisted that the wind which had given them *Rosario* and their one chance to cut out the frigate was the forerunner of stronger gusts. It was not unknown in the Mediterranean, even in June.

Two of the cutting-out party who had died of their wounds had been from *Unrivalled*, and they had been buried immediately. But it was another source of grievance, and then open protest, now that the prize had disappeared with *Matchless*. There had been an outbreak of violence in one of the messes, and a petty officer had been threatened when he had intervened. So there would be two men for punishment tomorrow.

Adam disliked the grim ritual of flogging. It too often broke a man who might have made something of himself had he been properly guided. He recalled Galbraith's words to the midshipman. *Inspired.* The hard man would only become harder and more unruly. But until there was an alternative . . .

He frowned as the cabin servant entered and walked down the tilting deck towards him. One of the ship's boys, his name was Napier, and he had been trained originally to serve the officers in the wardroom. He took his duties very seriously and wore an habitual expression of set determination.

Galbraith had made the choice himself, no doubt wondering why a post-captain did not have a servant of his own.

Click . . . click . . . click. Napier wore ill-fitting shoes for this new employment, probably bought from one of the traders who hung around the King's ships, and the sound grated on Adam's nerves.

'Napier!' He saw the youth stiffen, and changed his mind. 'No matter. Fetch me some of that wine.' He curbed his impatience, knowing he himself was at fault. *What is the matter with me?* The boy he was going to sponsor for midshipman, the boy he had been trying to fashion in his own image, if he was honest enough to admit it, was dead.

Napier hurried away, pleased to be doing something. *Click*

. . . click . . . click. He thought of the state of the French frigate's stores. *La Fortune* had been down to her last resources when she had been seized, her powder and shot, salted meat, and even the cheese the Frenchmen took as a part of life almost finished.

He recalled Jago's remarks about wine, and smiled. There had indeed been plenty of that, under lock and key until Bosanquet of the Royal Marines had shattered it with a well-aimed pistol shot.

Napier brought the bottle and a glass and placed them with great care beside the log book.

Adam could feel the eyes on him as he poured a glass. *The Captain.* Who lived in this fine cabin and was oblivious to the cramped conditions and brutal humour of the messdecks. Who wanted for nothing.

The wine was cool, and he imagined Catherine selecting it for him. Who else would care about such things? He would eke it out. Like the memory: hold on to it.

The glass almost broke in his fingers as he exclaimed, *'Hell's teeth,* boy!' He saw Napier cringe, and said urgently, 'No! Not you!' Like calming a frightened animal; he was ashamed that it was always so easy. For the Captain.

He said evenly, 'Tell the sentry to fetch the first lieutenant, will you?'

Napier twisted his hands together, staring at the glass.

'Did I do somethin' wrong, sir?'

Adam shook his head.

'A bad lookout is the one who sees only what he expects to see, or what others have told him to expect.' He raised his voice. *'Sentry!'* When the marine thrust his head around the screen door he said, 'My compliments to the first lieutenant, and would you ask him to come aft.' He looked back at the boy. 'Today, I am that bad lookout!'

Napier said slowly, 'I see, sir.'

Adam smiled. 'I think not, but fetch another bottle, will you?'

It was probably only a flaw in his memory. Something to cover his anger at Bouverie's arrogant but justified action over the prize.

And what of *La Fortune?* Were there still people who did not know or believe that ships had souls? She was not a new vessel, and must have seen action often enough against the flag which the marine had hoisted at her peak. Now she would probably be sold, most likely to the Dutch government. Another old enemy. Several prizes had already been disposed of in that manner, and yet, as the vice-admiral himself had pointed out, the fleet was as short of frigates as ever.

Galbraith entered the cabin, his eyes taking in the wine, and the anxious servant.

'Sir?'

'Be seated. Some wine?'

He saw the first lieutenant relax slightly.

'The Frenchman we took – she was short of everything, especially powder and shot.'

Galbraith took time to pick up and examine the glass. 'We were saying as much earlier, sir.'

So they had been discussing it in the wardroom, and most of all, he had no doubt, the prize money which might eventually be shared out.

'And yet there was a letter, which Lieutenant Avery translated.' Remembering his bitterness. 'To *La Fortune*'s captain. Supposedly from a lady.' He noted the immediate interest, and then the doubt. 'I can see you think as I did.' He grinned ruefully. 'Eventually!'

Galbraith said, 'It seems strange that anyone would be able to send a letter to a ship whose whereabouts were largely unknown.'

Adam nodded, his skin ice-cold in spite of the cabin's warmth.

'To promise the delivery of the one thing they did not need. Wine!'

Galbraith stared past him. 'Daniel . . . I mean, Mr Wynter made a note of the dates in *Rosario*'s log, sir.'

'Did he indeed? We may have cause to thank him for his dedication.'

He was on his feet, his shadow angled across the white-painted timbers, as if the hull was leaning hard over.

'My orders are to remain on this station and to await instructions. That I must do. But we shall be *seen* to be here. There are those who might believe that *Matchless* has gone to obtain assistance, and that time is now more precious than ever.'

Galbraith watched him, seeing the changing emotions, could almost feel him thinking aloud.

He ventured, 'They are expecting supplies, above all powder and shot. If there are other ships sheltering in Algiers . . .'

Adam paused and touched his shoulder. 'And they still have *La Fortune*'s captain to help matters along, remember?'

'And we are alone, sir.'

Adam nodded slowly, seeing the chart in his mind. 'The Corsican tyrant once said, "Wherever wood can swim, there I am sure to find this flag of England."' The mood left him as quickly. 'The truest words he ever spoke.' He realised for the first time that the servant, Napier, had been in the cabin the whole time, and was already refilling the glasses. With the wine from St James's Street in London. He said, 'We have no choice.'

He walked to the stern windows, but there was only a fine line to separate sky from sea. Almost dark. *My birthday.*

He thought of her, whom he had loved and had lost, and when he looked at the old sword hanging from its rack, reflecting the lantern light, he thought of another who had helped him and was rarely out of his thoughts. Neither had been his to lose in the first place.

He said suddenly, 'How did it feel today, having a command of your own again?'

Galbraith did not appear to hesitate.

'Like me, sir, I think the ship felt uneasy without her captain.'

Their eyes met, and held. The barrier was down.

There was nothing else. For either of them.

The carriage with its perfectly matched greys wheeled sharply into the drive and halted at the foot of the steps. Sillitoe jumped down with barely a glance at his coachman.

'Change the horses, man! Quick as you can!'

He knew he was allowing his agitation to show itself, but he was powerless against it. He left the carriage door open, the watery sunlight playing on its crest. Baron Sillitoe of Chiswick.

A servant was sweeping the steps but removed the broom and averted his eyes as Sillitoe ran past him and threw open the double doors before anyone could be there to greet him.

He was late. Too late. And all because he had been delayed by the Prime Minister: some errand for the Prince Regent. It could have waited. *Should* have waited.

He saw his minute secretary, Marlow, coming towards him from the library. A man who knew all his master's moods but had remained loyal to him, perhaps because of rather than in spite of them, Marlow recognised his displeasure now, and that there was no point in attempting to appease him.

'She is not here, m' lord.'

Sillitoe stared up and around the bare, elegant staircase. There were few paintings, although the portrait of his father, the slaver, was a notable exception, and fewer objets d'art. Spartan, some called it. It suited him.

'Lady Somervell was to wait here for me! I told you exactly what I intended –' He stopped abruptly; he was wasting more time. 'Tell me.'

He felt empty, shocked that it had been so simple to deceive him. It had to be the case. No one else would dare, dare even to consider it.

Marlow said, 'Lady Somervell *was* here, m' lord.' He glanced at the open library door, seeing her in his mind. All in black but so beautiful, so contained. 'I tried to make her comfortable, but as time passed she became . . . troubled.'

Sillitoe waited, controlling his impatience, and surprised by Marlow's concern. He had never thought of his small, mild-mannered secretary as anything but an efficient and trustworthy extension of his own machinations.

Another door opened soundlessly and Guthrie, his valet, stood watching him, his battered features wary. More like a prizefighter than a servant, as were most of the men entrusted with Sillitoe's affairs.

'She wanted a carriage, m' lord. I told her there would be great crowds. Difficulties. But she insisted, and I knew you would expect me to act in your absence. I hope I did right, m' lord?'

Sillitoe walked past him and stared at the river, the boats, the moored barges. Passengers and crews alike always pointed to this mansion on the bank of the Thames. Known to so many, truly known by none of them.

'You did right, Marlow.' He heard horses stamping on flagstones, his coachman speaking to each by name.

He considered his anger as he would a physical opponent, along the length of a keen blade or beyond the muzzle of a duelling pistol.

He was the Prince Regent's Inspector-General, and his friend and confidential adviser. On most matters. On expenditure, the manipulations of both army and naval staffs, even on the subject of women. And when the King finally died, still imprisoned in his all-consuming madness, he could expect an even greater authority. *Above all, the Prince Regent was his friend.*

He attempted to look at it coldly, logically, as was his way with all obstacles. The Prince, 'Prinny', knew better than most the dangers of envy and spite. He was quick to see it among those closest to him, and would do what he could to preserve what he called 'a visible stability'. Perhaps he had already tried to warn him what might become of that stability, if his inspector-general were to lose his wits to a woman who had openly scorned and defied that same society for the man she loved.

And I did not realise. He could even accept that. But to believe that the future King had betrayed him, had given him a mission merely to keep him away and safe from slander and ridicule, was beyond belief. Even as he knew it was true. It was the only explanation.

Marlow coughed quietly. 'The horses have been changed, m' lord. Shall I tell William to stand down now?'

Sillitoe regarded him calmly. So Marlow knew too, or guessed.

He thought of Catherine, in this house or around the river's sweeping bend in Chelsea. Of the night he had burst in with Guthrie and the others and had saved her. *Saved her.* It was stark in his mind, like blood under the guillotine during the Terror.

He thought of Bethune's stupid, conniving wife, and Rhodes, who had expected to be created First Lord of the Admiralty. Of Richard Bolitho's wife; of so many who would be there today. Not to honour a dead hero, but to see Catherine shamed. Destroyed.

Now he could only wonder why he had hesitated.

He said curtly, 'I am ready.' He brushed past his valet without seeing the cloak which was to conceal his identity. 'That fellow from the *Times*, the one who wrote so well of Nelson . . .' He snapped his fingers. 'Laurence, yes?'

Marlow nodded, off guard only for a moment.

'I remember him, m' lord.'

'Find him. Today. I don't care how, or what it costs. I believe I am owed a favour or two.'

Marlow walked to the entrance and watched Sillitoe climb into the carriage. He could see the mud spattered on the side, evidence of a hard drive. No wonder the horses had been changed.

The carriage was already wheeling round, heading for the fine gates on which the Prince Regent himself had once commented.

He shook his head, recalling without effort the grand display of Nelson's procession and funeral. A vast armada of boats which had escorted the coffin by barge, from Greenwich to Whitehall, and from the Admiralty to St Paul's. A procession so long that it reached its destination before the rear had started to move.

Today there would be no body, no procession, but, like the man, it would be long remembered.

And only this morning he had heard that the end of the war was imminent. No longer merely a hope, a prayer. Could one final battle destroy so monstrous, so immortal an influence? He smiled to himself, sadly. Strange that on a day like this it seemed almost secondary.

Sillitoe pressed himself into a corner of the carriage and listened to the changing sound of the iron-shod wheels as the horses entered yet another narrow street. Grey stone buildings, blank windows, the offices of bankers and lawyers, of wealthy merchants whose trade reached across the world. The hub, as Sir Wilfred Lafargue liked to call it. The coachman, William, knew this part of London, and had managed to avoid the main roads, most of which had been filled with aimless crowds, so different from its usual bustle and purpose. For this was Sunday, and around St Paul's it would be even worse. He felt for his watch but decided against it. Half an hour at the most. But for the delay with the Prime Minister, he would have had ample time in hand, no matter what.

He leaned forward and tapped the roof with his sword.

'What is it now? Why are we slowing down, man?'

William hung over the side of his perch.

'Street's blocked, m' lord!' He sounded apprehensive; he had already had a taste of Sillitoe's temper on the drive to Chiswick House.

Sillitoe jerked a strap and lowered the window. So narrow here. Like a cavern. The smell of horses and soot . . .

He could see a mass of people, and what appeared to be a carriage. There were soldiers, too, and one, a helmeted officer, was already trotting towards them. Young, but lacking neither intelligence nor experience, his eyes moved swiftly to take in Sillitoe's clothing and the bright sash of the order across his chest, and then the coat of arms on the door.

'The way is blocked, sir!'

William glared down at him.

'"My lord"!'

The officer exclaimed, 'I beg your pardon, my lord, I did not know . . .'

Sillitoe snapped, 'Must get through to St Paul's. I do not have to explain why, I trust.' He could feel the anger rising again; this was only the calm before the storm. He studied the officer coldly. 'Fourteenth Light Dragoons. I know your agent, at Gray's Inn, I believe?'

He saw the shot go home.

'A vehicle has lost a wheel, my lord. It could not have happened in a worse place. I have already had to turn back one carriage – a lady –'

'A lady?' It was Catherine. It had to be. He glanced at the shining helmets and restless horses, and said sharply, 'I suggest you dismount those pretty warriors and remove the obstruction.'

'I – I am not certain. My orders –'

Sillitoe leaned back. 'If you value your commission, Lieutenant.'

It took only minutes for the dragoons to drag the vehicle to one side, and for William to drive the length of the street.

Deliberate? An accident? Or was it what Richard Bolitho had always called Fate?

He thought of her. On foot, hemmed in by gaping, curious faces. He looked out again and saw St Paul's. Close to, it dominated everything, so that the silence was all the more impressive.

'Stop now!'

He knew William was against it, and was probably wishing the massive Guthrie was here with him, but he climbed down to calm the horses before they became troubled by the slow-moving crowds, and the unnatural silence.

What might they have done? Would they have dared to turn her back at the cathedral's imposing entrance, on some paltry excuse, perhaps because there was no record of her invitation? Catherine, of all people. On this damnable day.

He quickened his pace, used to staring eyes and peering faces, beyond their reach, or so he believed now.

A hand plucked at his coat. 'Would you buy some flowers to honour his memory, sir?'

Sillitoe thrust him aside with a curt, 'Out of my way!'

Then he stopped, as if he had no control of his limbs. It explained the silence, the complete stillness, the like of which this place had never witnessed.

Catherine, too, stood quite still, and erect, surrounded by people and yet utterly detached from them..

Across the cathedral steps was an uneven rank of men. Sailors, or they had been before they had been cut down in battle. Men without arms, or hobbling on wooden stumps. Men with burned and scarred faces, victims of a hundred different battles and as many ships, but today joined as one. Sillitoe tried to reason with it, coldly, as was his habit. They were probably from the naval hospital at Greenwich and must have come upriver for this occasion, as if they had been drawn to it by the same power which had stopped him in his tracks. All wore scraps of uniform, some displayed tattoos on their arms; one, in a sea officer's uniform, was wearing his sword.

Sillitoe wanted to go to her. Not to speak, but only to be beside her. But he did not move.

Catherine was aware of the silence; she had even seen the mounted dragoons ordered to remove the wrecked vehicle. But it was all somewhere else. Not here. Not now.

She stood, unmoving, watching the man in the officer's uniform as he stepped slowly forward from the watching barrier of crippled sailors. The ones with wooden spars. Half-timbered Jacks, as Allday called them. She trembled. But he always said it without contempt, and without pity, for they were himself.

The officer was closer now, and she realised that his uniform was that of a lieutenant. Clean and well-pressed, but the careful stitching and repairs were evident. He had one hand on another man's shoulder, and when she saw his eyes she knew that he was blind, although they were clear and bright. And motionless.

His companion murmured something, and he removed his cocked hat with a flourish. His grey hair and threadbare uniform did not belong to this moment; he was the young lieutenant again. And these were his men.

He held out his hand and for an instant she saw him falter, until she reached out to him and took it in hers.

'You are welcome here.' Very gently, he kissed her hand. Still no one spoke or moved. As if this vignette were caught in time, like these ragged, proud reminders who had come to honour her.

Then he said, 'We all knew Sir Richard. Some of us served with or under him. He would have wished you to be so met today.'

She heard a step beside her and knew it was Sillitoe.

She murmured, 'I thought . . . I thought . . .'

He slipped his hand beneath her elbow and said, 'I know what you thought. What you were intended to think.'

Without looking above or beyond the watching figures, he knew that the great doors had opened.

He said, 'Thank you, gentlemen. No admiral's lady could ever have a braver guard of honour!'

There were smiles now, and one man reached out to touch Catherine's gown, muttering something, beaming at her while tears streamed down his cheeks. She removed her black veil, and stared up the steps.

'I do not have the words, Lieutenant. But later . . .' But there was no grey-haired officer, or perhaps her eyes were too blurred to see. A ghost, then. Like those who lay with Richard.

'Take me in, please.'

She did not hear the stir of surprise that ran through that towering place like a sudden wind through dry leaves, nor see the admiration, or outrage, or the angry disappointment, as Sillitoe guided her to his pew, which otherwise would have been empty.

She gripped her left hand in her right, feeling the ring her lover had placed there on Zenoria Keen's wedding day.

In the eyes of God, we are married.

She could not look ahead, and dared not think of what was past, that which she could never regain.

It was a proud day, for Richard, and for all those who had loved him.

And, only for this moment, they would be together.

It was just before dawn that the full force of the wind made itself known. Joshua Cristie, *Unrivalled*'s taciturn sailing master, found no comfort in the fact that his predictions had proved right, for this was the enemy. Others might fear the cannon's roar and the surgeon's knife, but Cristie was a sailor to his fingertips, like most of his forebears, and saw the weather's moods as his foes. As he gripped a stanchion to steady himself on the lurching deck he watched the sky, burning like molten copper, with long, dark clouds scudding beneath it as if they were already ashes.

They had shortened sail during the middle watch; he had heard the captain giving orders as he had hurried to the chart room to collect his precious instruments.

The captain seemed well able to make his immediate demands understood. On the face of it, *Unrivalled* was a smart and disciplined ship. *On the face of it.* But Cristie knew that it was only on the surface. Until men were truly tested to the limit, they would not know. She was still a new ship, and like any other was only as strong as the men who served her, and the chain of command which directed them as surely as any rudder. *Unless.*

The captain was here now, his old seagoing coat flapping in the wind, the dark hair pressed against his face by the flying spray. Even that looked like droplets of copper in the strange light.

'Let her fall off a point, Mr Cristie! Steer south-west-by-south!'

More men ran across to halliards and braces, some only half-dressed after the urgent call for all hands.

Cristie shouted, 'Still backing a piece, sir! She'll not hold this close to the wind for much longer!'

The captain seemed to hang on to his words, then swung round to face him. Cristie tested the moment, as he would a sounding or a compass bearing.

'We could come about and run with it, sir.' He hesitated, his mind grappling with the crack and thunder of canvas, the drone of straining rigging. 'Or we could lie-to under close-reefed main tops'l!'

Galbraith was yelling for more hands, and a few anonymous figures were in the mizzen top, cutting away broken cordage.

Cristie heard the captain say, '*No*. We'll hold as close as we can.' He was staring up at the swaying yards, the sickening motion making each plunge seem as if the ship were out of control.

But there were two more men on the big double-wheel, and as a solid curtain of spray burst over them and the quartermasters, they looked like survivors clinging to a capsizing wreck.

Adam Bolitho watched a party of seamen securing the hammock nettings. It was not vital. Seamen had slept in sodden hammocks before, and they would again. But it gave them a sense of purpose, kept them occupied when, even now, fear might be striding amongst them.

Unrivalled was leaning hard over, her lee bulwark almost awash, water spurting past the forward carronades and knocking men off their feet like skittles.

He held his breath, counting seconds as the bows dipped yet again, the hull quivering as it smashed into solid water, as if she had driven ashore.

He cupped his hands. 'Fore t'gan's'l's carried away!' He

saw Galbraith staring at him. *'Leave it!* Not worth risking lives!'

He watched the sail destroy itself, being ripped apart as if by giant, invisible hands until there were only shreds.

Men were clambering across the boat-tier now, urged on by the boatswain's powerful bellow. If a boat came adrift it would run amok on the deck, maiming and killing if not secured.

He heard Partridge shout, 'Make a bloody seaman of ye yet, damned if I don't!'

Old Stranace would be down there too. Dragging himself from gun to gun, checking each breeching rope, making sure that *his* equipment was not being lost or damaged.

Adam shivered, and felt the icy water exploring his spine and buttocks. But it was not that. It was a wildness, an elation he had not felt since he had lost *Anemone*.

The ship's backbone, the professionals. They never broke.

Midshipman Fielding was knocked sideways by a block swinging from a severed halliard. A seaman caught his arm and pulled him to his feet. Adam recognised the man as one of those due to be flogged. *Today* . . . He even saw the man grin. Like Jago. Amused. Contemptuous.

He seemed to hear John Allday's voice, when they had served together. His summing up of a ship's ability or otherwise.

Aft the most honour, mebbe, but forrard the better men!

He could see the horizon now, blurred with spray, writhing in the fierce light. Men's faces, bodies soaked and bruised, some with nails torn out by the tormented canvas they had fisted and kicked into submission, their world confined to a dizzily swaying yard, their strength that of the men up there with them.

But was it worth it? To risk so much, everything, on a frail belief?

A boatswain's mate ran past him, one arm outthrust, his mouth a soundless hole as the wind's fury increased to an insane scream. Adam thought he had seen something fall, probably from the main topsail yard, hardly making a splash as it hit the sea and was swamped by the water surging back from the stem.

Not even a cry. The fall had probably killed him. But

suppose he lived long enough to break surface and see his ship already fading into the storm?

It happened often enough, something which landsmen never considered when they saw a King's ship passing proudly at a safe distance.

Midshipman Bellairs wiped his face with his sleeve and gasped, 'It can't go on!'

Cristie heard him, and exclaimed harshly, 'Later on you'll remember this, my lad! When you're striding your own deck and making poor Jack's life a bloody misery! Leastways I hope you'll remember, for all our sakes!'

He watched the captain, his body angled to the quarterdeck, his voice carrying above the wild chorus of wind and sea.

'It's what *you* want to be, right?' He liked Bellairs; he would make a good officer, given the chance. He glanced at the captain again. *And the example.* Cristie had seen the best and the worst of them in his day. His own family had grown up in Tynemouth, in the next street to Collingwood, Nelson's friend and second-in-command at Trafalgar.

He heard Lieutenant Massie say, 'I'll not answer for the jib if we try to come about!'

Cristie nudged the midshipman and repeated, '*Remember it*, see!'

He moved away as the captain strode towards him.

'What say you, Mr Cristie? Do you think me mad to drive her so?'

Cristie did not know if Bellairs was listening, nor did he care. It was nothing he could mark on his chart, or record in the log. And nobody else would understand. The captain, the one who drove himself and everybody else, who had not hesitated to lead his own men on a cutting-out raid which had seemed an almost certain disaster, had *asked* him. Not told him, as was every captain's right.

He heard himself say, 'There's your answer, sir!' He watched his face as he looked at the widening bank of blue sky as it spread from horizon to horizon. The wind had lessened, so that the rattle of broken rigging and the flapping tails of torn canvas intruded for the first time. Soon the sun would show above the retreating cloud, and steam would rise from these wet, treacherous decks.

Men were pausing to draw breath, to peer around for messmates or for a special friend, as they might after action. Two of the younger midshipmen were actually grinning at one another and shaking hands with a kind of jubilant triumph.

Adam saw all and none of it. He was staring up, at the first lookout to risk the perilous climb aloft.

'Deck there! Sail on th' weather bow!'

He turned to Cristie and said quietly, 'And *there*, my friend, lies the enemy.'

7

A Bad Ship

Lieutenant Galbraith pivoted round on his heels and stared up to the quarterdeck rail, eyes slitted against the first hard sunshine.

'Ship cleared for action, sir!'

Adam did not take out his watch; he had no need to. From the moment the small marine drummer boys had begun the staccato rattle of beating to quarters, he had watched the ship come alive again, the savage wind almost forgotten. Only fragments of canvas and snapped cordage, flapping 'Irish pennants', as the old hands called them, gave any hint of the storm which had passed as quickly as it had found them.

Seven o'clock in the morning: six bells had just chimed from the forecastle. It was all routine, normal, and yet so different.

Adam had stood by the rail, feeling the ship preparing for whatever challenge she might meet within the next few hours. Screens torn down, hutchlike cabins folded away and stowed in the holds with furniture and all unnecessary personal belongings. A bad moment, when some might pause to reflect that their owners might not need them after this day was past.

It had taken ten minutes to clear the ship from bow to stern. Even his cabin, the largest he had ever occupied and a place which still lacked personality, was open, so that gun crews and powder monkeys could move unhindered if the shot began to fly.

The galley fire had been doused at the beginning of the storm, and there had been no time to relight it. Men fought better on a full belly, especially when they had already been contesting wind and sea for most of the night.

He stared along the maindeck, at the gun crews standing by their charges, the long eighteen-pounders which made up the bulk of *Unrivalled*'s artillery. Most of them were stripped to the waist, new hands and landsmen following the example of the seasoned men who had seen and done it all before. Any clothing was precious to a working sailor, and costly to replace out of his meagre pay. Fabric also attracted gangrene, and hampered treatment should a man be wounded.

Adam thought he could smell the rum even from the quarterdeck. The purser had been quietly outraged by the extra issue he had ordered, a double tot for every man, as if the cost would be extracted from his own pocket.

But it had bridged the gap, and would do no harm at all.

Six seamen to each gun, including its captain, but hauling the heavy cannon up a tilting deck if the ship was to leeward of an enemy would require many more. An experienced crew should be able to fire a shot every ninety seconds, at the outset of battle in any case, although Adam had known some gun captains prepared and ready to fire three shots every two minutes. It had been so in *Hyperion*, an exceptional ship; a legend, like her captain.

He smiled, but did not see Galbraith's quick answering grin.

The ship was moving steadily and, apparently, unhurriedly, with courses and staysails clewed up or furled. It seemed to open up the sea on either beam, and Adam had seen several of the unemployed seamen clambering up to seek out the enemy. To watch and prepare themselves as best they could. He considered it. *The enemy.* There were two of them, one large, a cut-down man-of-war by her appearance, the other smaller, a brig.

It was still so peaceful. So full of quiet menace.

Who were they? What had prompted their mission to Algiers?

He saw Lieutenant Massie by the foremast, ready to direct the opening shots, his own little group of midshipmen, messengers and petty officers waiting to pass his orders, and to close their eyes and ears to all else around them.

He turned away from the rail and saw the Royal Marines stationed across the deck, scarlet ranks moving evenly to the ship's motion. Cristie, and Lieutenant Wynter, Midshipman Bellairs and his signals party, the helmsmen and master's mates. A centre. The ship's brain. He glanced at the tightly packed hammock nettings, slight protection for such a prize target.

He raised his eyes and saw more marines in the fighting tops. He had always thought of it when facing an action at sea. The marksmen, one of whom he knew had been a poacher before enlisting, not out of patriotism but rather to avoid prison or deportation. They were all first-class shots.

He looked at the horizon again, the tiny patches of sails against the hard blue line. He would think even more of it now, since Avery had described those final moments, so quietly, so intimately. He bit his lip, controlling it. All these men, good and bad, would be looking to him. *Aft, the most honour.* He touched the old sword at his hip, remembering the note she had left with it. *For me.* He had seen Jago's searching glance when he had come on deck. The old sword, the bright epaulettes. What had he thought? Arrogance, or vanity?

Jago was climbing the quarterdeck ladder now, his dark eyes barely moving, but missing nothing. A man he might never know, but one he did not want to lose.

Jago joined him by the rail and stood with his arms folded, as if to show his contempt for some of those watching. Like Lieutenant Massie, or the sulky midshipman named Sandell. San*dell*, as he insisted on being called.

Jago said, 'The first ship, sir. Old Creagh thinks he knows her.'

So casually spoken. *Testing me?*

The face formed in his mind. Creagh was one of the boatswain's mates, and would have been carrying out a flogging if *Unrivalled* had turned back instead of forcing her passage into the teeth of the storm. A lot of people might be thinking that, and cursing their captain for his stubborn refusal to give way.

'One of Mr Partridge's mates.' He did not see Jago's quiet smile, although he sensed it.

'He swears she's the *Tetrarch*. Served in her some years back.'

Adam nodded. Like a family. Like the men who served them, there were bad ships too.

Tetrarch was a fourth-rate, one of a rare breed now virtually erased from the Navy List. Classed as ships of the line, they had been rendered obsolete by the mounting savagery and improved gunnery of this everlasting war. The fourth-rate was neither one thing nor the other, not fast enough to serve as a frigate, and, mounting less than sixty guns, no match for the battering she must withstand in the line of battle. Ship to ship. Gun to gun.

Tetrarch had been caught off Ushant some three years ago. Attacked and captured by two French frigates, she had not been heard of since.

Now she was back. And she was here.

Jago said, 'Cut down, she is.' He rubbed his chin, a rasping sound like an armourer's iron. 'But still, she could give a fair account of herself. And with that other little bugger in company.'

Adam tried to put himself in the enemy's position, assessing the distant vessels as if he were looking down on them. Like impersonal markers on an admiral's chart. The brig would be sacrificed first. She had to be, if the bigger ship was indeed loaded with supplies and powder for others still sheltering in Algiers, enjoying what Bethune had called the Dey's one-sided neutrality. After losing *La Fortune* to such a calculated trick, they would be doubly eager to even the score.

On a converging tack, both close-hauled, but the enemy would have the wind's advantage. And there was not enough time to replace the fore topgallant sail.

Galbraith had joined him, his face full of questions.

Adam asked, 'How long, d' you think?'

Galbraith looked up at the masthead pendant, flapping and drooping. How could the wind change so completely?

He answered, 'An hour. No more.' He hesitated. 'She has the wind-gage, sir.'

'It's the little terrier which concerns me. We shortened sail in time last night. But our lady will be hard put to lift her skirts in a hurry!' He studied the set of each sail, the yards braced round. The wind would decide it. 'I want to hit them before they can do too much damage.'

The men at the quarterdeck nine-pounders glanced at one another. *Too much damage.* Not just timber and cordage, but flesh and blood.

Adam walked to the compass box and back again. 'Our best shots must be all about today, Mr Galbraith.' He smiled suddenly. 'A guinea for the man who marks down the captain. Theirs, not ours!'

Some of those same men actually laughed aloud. Captain Bouverie would not approve of such slack behaviour aboard *Matchless.*

He turned aside. 'Be watchful of powder. The decks will soon be bone dry. One spark . . .' He did not need to continue.

He took a glass and held it to his eye; it was already warm against his skin.

Three ships, drawing together as if by invisible warps. Soon to be close, real, deadly.

I must not fail. Must not.

But his voice sounded flat and without emotion, betraying nothing of his thoughts.

'Load in ten minutes, Mr Galbraith. But do not run out. Let the people take their time. Gunnery is god today!'

If I fall. He had his hand on his pocket and could feel the locket there, carefully wrapped. *Who would care?*

He thought suddenly of the old house, empty now, except for the portraits. Waiting.

They would care.

It was time.

Galbraith glanced quickly at his captain and then leaned over the quarterdeck rail.

The final scrutiny. There was always the chance of a flaw in the rigid pattern of battle.

Decks sanded, particularly around each gun, to prevent men from slipping in the madness of action on blown spray or blood. Nets had been spread above the deck to protect the gun crews and sail-handling parties from falling debris, and impede any enemy reckless enough to try and board them.

The gunner and his mates had already gone to the magazine to prepare and issue charges to the powder monkeys, most of whom were mere boys. With no experience to plague them, they were less concerned than some of the older hands, who would look for reassurance at familiar faces around them, every man very aware of the two pyramids of sail, so much nearer now, although seemingly motionless on the glistening water.

Galbraith shouted, *'All guns load!'*

Each eighteen-pounder was an island, its crew oblivious to the rest. Just as during the constant drills when they had roundly cursed every officer from the captain downwards, they were testing the training tackles, casting off the heavy breeching ropes, freeing the guns for loading. That too was a routine, a ritual, the bulky charge taken by the assistant loader from the breathless powder monkey, to be eased into the waiting muzzle and tamped home by the loader. No mistakes. Two sharp knocks to bed it in, and a wad tamped in to secure it.

Experienced gun captains had already selected their shots from the garlands, holding each ball, weighing it, feeling it, making sure it was a perfect shape, for the opening roar of battle.

It had all been done deliberately and without haste, and Galbraith knew why the captain had ordered them to take their time, for this first attempt at least. Now there was a stillness, each crew grouped around its gun, every captain staring aft at the blue and white figures of discipline and authority. As familiar as the guns which were their reason for being, in the company of which they greeted every dawn, and which were constant reminders of a ship's hard comradeship.

And yet despite the toughness of such men, Galbraith knew the other side of the coin. Like the seaman who had been lost overboard, without even a cry. Later there would be a sale of his few possessions, before the mast, as they called it, and messmates and others who had barely known him would dip into their purses and pay exorbitant prices so that money could be sent to a wife or mother somewhere in that other world.

He turned and looked at his captain, speaking quietly with the master, gesturing occasionally as if to emphasise something. He gazed at the oncoming vessels. The moment of embrace. There would be more possessions to bargain for if today turned sour on them.

He blinked as a shaft of sunlight glanced down between the braced yards. The smaller vessel had tacked, widening the distance from her consort. The terrier, the captain had called her. Ready to dart in and snap at *Unrivalled*'s vulnerable stern and quarter. One shot could do it: a vital spar, or worse, damage to the rudder and steering gear would end the fight before *Unrivalled* had bared her teeth. He looked at the captain again. *He would know.* His first command had been a brig. He had been twenty-three, someone had said. He would know . . .

The enemy had the advantage of the wind, and yet Captain Adam Bolitho showed no sign of anxiety.

'We will load both broadsides and engage first at full range, gun by gun. Tell the second lieutenant to sight each one himself. We will then luff, and if the wind is kind to us we can rake the enemy with the other full broadside.'

Galbraith dragged his mind back to the present. Extra hands at the foremast ready to set the big forecourse, until now brailed up like the others. With the fore topgallant sail missing, they would need every cupful of wind when they came about. And even then . . .

Adam called, *'Open the ports!'*

He imagined the port lids lifting along either beam, could see the water creaming past the lee side. *Unrivalled* was leaning over, and she would lean still further when they set the forecourse. He had guessed what Galbraith was thinking. If the wind deserted them now, the enemy ships could divide and outmanoeuvre him. He touched his pocket again. If not, the long eighteen-pounders on the weather side, at full elevation, would outrange the others. He smiled. So easily said . . .

Cristie had told him something about the *Tetrarch* which he had not known. She had been in a state of near mutiny when she had been attacked by the French frigates. Another bad captain, he thought, like *Reaper*, in which the company had mutinied against their captain's inhuman treatment and had joined together to flog him to death. *Reaper* was back with the fleet now, commanded by a good officer, a friend of Adam's, but he doubted that she would ever entirely cleanse herself of the stigma.

And *Tetrarch* might be the same. Her armament had been

reduced in order to allow for more hold space, but she could give a good account of herself.

He looked up at the black, vibrating shrouds, the soft underbelly of the main topsail, seeing it in his mind even now. *Anemone* torn apart by the American's heavy artillery. Men falling and dying. *Because of me.*

He squared his shoulders, and felt his shirt drag against the ragged scar where the iron splinter had cut him down.

It was enough.

He said, 'Run out!'

Every spare man, even the Royal Marines were on the tackles, hauling the guns up the tilting deck to thrust their black muzzles through the ports. The enemy was faceless, unknown. But it would be madness to show *Unrivalled*'s shortage of hands from the outset. After that . . .

There were a few hoarse cheers as the crouching gun crews saw the enemy angled across each port, and he heard Lieutenant Massie's sharp response.

'Keep silent, you deadheads! Stand to your guns! I'll have none of it!'

Adam walked to the rail and watched the nearest vessel, the brig. Like his old *Firefly*. Well handled, leaning over while she changed tack. Probably steering south-east. He thought of Cristie. *By guess and by God.* He measured the range, surprised still that he could do it without hesitation. The *Tetrarch* had taken in her fore and main courses and was preparing to await her chance, poised across the starboard bow as if nothing could prevent a collision.

There was a dull bang, and seconds later a hole appeared in the main topsail. A sighting shot. He clenched his fists. *Not yet, not yet.* Another shot came from somewhere, sharper, one of the brig's bow-chasers probably. He saw the feathers of spray dart from wave to wave, like flying fish. Still short.

'Forecourse, Mr Galbraith!' He strode to the opposite side. 'Lay for the mainmast, Mr Massie! On the uproll!'

The enemy might be expecting a ragged broadside, and be waiting for a chance to close the range before *Unrivalled* could reload.

Adam heard Massie yell, 'Ready! *Fire!*'

He kept his eyes fixed on the other ship. Massie was

managing on his own, pausing at each breech, one hand on the gun captain's shoulder, the trigger-line taut, ready, the target framed in the open port like a painting come to life.

'*Fire!*'

Gun by gun, the full length of *Unrivalled*'s spray-dashed hull, each one hurling itself inboard on its tackles to be seized, sponged out and reloaded, the men racing one another to run out again, whilst on the opposite side the crews waited their turn, with only the empty sea to distract them from the regular crash of gunfire.

Someone gave a wild cheer.

'Thar goes 'er main topmast! B' Jesus, look at 'er, mates!'

But the other ship was firing now, iron hammering into *Unrivalled*'s lower hull, a stray ball slamming through a port and breaking into splinters.

Adam tore his eyes from the spouting orange tongues of fire, feeling the blows beneath his feet like wounds to his own body. Men were down, one rolling across the deck, kicking and coughing blood, another crouched against a gun, fingers interlaced across his stomach, his final scream dying as he was dragged aside and the gun run up to its port again.

Galbraith yelled, 'He's standing off, sir!' He flinched as a powder monkey spun round, his leg severed by another haphazard shot. Adam saw another run and snatch up the fallen charge, eyes terrified, and averted from someone who had probably been his friend.

He turned. 'Wouldn't you? If you were full to the gills with powder and shot?' He shut them from his mind. 'Stand by on the quarterdeck!' There was smoke everywhere, choking, stinging, blinding.

He could no longer see the other ship; the forecourse was filled to the wind, blotting out the enemy's intentions.

'Put the helm down!' He dashed his wrist across his eyes and thought he saw the ship's head already answering the helm, swinging bowsprit and flapping jib across the wind.

'Helm's a' lee, sir!'

Adam heard someone cry out and knew a ball had missed him by inches.

Come on! Come on! If *Unrivalled* was caught aback across

the eye of the wind she would be helpless, doomed. He felt the deck planking jump again and knew the ship had been hit.

'Off tacks and sheets!' He walked level with the quarterdeck rail, his hand brushing against the smooth woodwork. Without seeing, he knew the forward sails were writhing in confusion, spilling the wind, allowing the bows to swing still further, unhampered.

'Fores'l haul! Haul, lads!'

One man slipped on blood and another dragged him to his feet. Neither spoke, nor looked at one another.

She was answering. Adam gripped the rail, and felt her standing into the opposite tack, sails filling and booming, the yards being hauled round until to an onlooker they would appear almost fore-and-aft.

'Hold her! Steer east-by-south!' Adam glanced swiftly at Cristie. Only a second, but it was enough to see a wild satisfaction. The pride might come later.

'Starboard battery!' Massie was there now, his sword in the air, his face a mask of concentration as he watched the brig swinging away, caught and unprepared for *Unrivalled*'s change of tack.

'Fire!'

It must have been like an avalanche, an avalanche of iron. When the whirling smoke, swept aside by the wind, laid bare the other vessel it was hard to recognise her, almost mastless, her shattered stumps and rigging dragging outboard like weed. She was a wreck.

Adam took a telescope from Midshipman Fielding, and felt the youth's hand shaking. *Or is it mine?*

'Again, Mr Cristie! Man the braces and stand by to wear ship!' He tried to calm himself and steady the glass.

The terrier was dead. The real target could never outpace them.

'All loaded, sir!'

He watched the other ship. Saw the scars left by *Unrivalled*'s first controlled broadside, the holes punched in her darkly tanned canvas.

Galbraith called, 'Ready, sir!' He sounded hoarse.

'Bring her about and lay her on the starboard tack.' He

111

glanced up at the forecourse, at scorched holes which had not been there earlier. *Earlier? On my birthday.*

Galbraith's voice again. 'We could call on him to strike, sir.'

'*No.* I know what that feels like. We will open fire when we are in position.' The smile would not come. 'The wind will not help him now.' He saw Midshipman Bellairs watching him fixedly, and said, 'Signal the brig to lie-to. We will board her presently.'

Bellairs beckoned to his signals party. 'A prize, sir?' Like Galbraith he sounded parched, as if he could scarcely speak.

'No. A trophy, Mr Bellairs.' He looked at Galbraith. 'Bring her about and take in the t'gallants. We shall commence firing.' He measured the distance again. 'A mile, would you say? Close enough. Then we will see.'

He watched the sudden activity on deck, the shadows swinging across the flapping sails while the frigate continued to turn, the grim faces of the nearest gun crews.

It was neither a contest nor a game, and they must know it.

He saw Massie pointing with his sword and passing his orders, the words lost in the din of canvas and tackles.

Unless that flag came down, it would be murder.

Using the wind across his quarter to best advantage, *Tetrarch*'s captain had decided to wear ship, not to close the range but to outmanoeuvre and avoid *Unrivalled*'s challenge.

Adam observed it in silence, able to ignore the bark of commands, the sudden protesting bang of canvas as his ship came as close to the wind as she could manage.

He raised his telescope again and trained it on the other vessel as she began to come about; he could even discern her figurehead, scarred and rendered almost shapeless by time and weather, but once a proud Roman governor with a garland of laurel around his head. Her captain might try to elude his adversary until nightfall. But there was little chance of that. It would only prolong the inevitable. He stared at the other ship's outline, shortening, the masts overlapping while she continued to turn.

He could sense Galbraith and some of the others watching him, all probably full of their own ideas and solutions.

If they came too close and the other ship caught fire, her lethal cargo could destroy all of them. Adam had done it himself. Jago had been there then, also.

He said sharply, 'Stand by to starboard as before, Mr Massie! Gun by gun!'

He wiped his eye and looked again. The enemy was bows-on, and in the powerful lens it looked as if her bowsprit would parry with *Unrivalled*'s jib boom.

'As you bear!'

He saw the *Tetrarch*'s canvas billow and fill, the bright Tricolour showing itself briefly beyond the braced driver. What did the flag mean to those men, he wondered? A symbol of something which might already have been defeated.

He thought of *Frobisher*, the cruel twist of fate which had brought her and her admiral to an unplanned rendezvous with two such ships as this one.

'Fire!' He watched the first shots tearing through the enemy's forecourse and topsails, and felt although he could not hear the sickening crash of falling spars and rigging.

Like *Anemone* . . .

But she continued to turn, exposing her broadside and the bright flashes from her most forward guns. Some hit *Unrivalled*'s hull, others hurled waterspouts over the side, where gun crews were working like fiends to sponge out and reload.

He heard Lieutenant Luxmore of the Royal Marines yelling a name as one of his marksmen in the maintop fired his Brown Bess at the enemy without waiting for the order. At this range, it was like throwing a pike at a church steeple. *The madness.* No one could completely contain it.

There was a wild cheer as with tired dignity *Tetrarch*'s fore topmast appeared to stagger, held upright only by the rigging. Adam watched, unable to blink, as the mast seemed to gain control, tearing shrouds and running rigging alike as if the stout cordage were made of mere twine, the sails adding to the confusion and destruction until the entire mast with upper spars and reeling foretop spilled down into the smoke.

Only a part of his mind recorded the shouts from the gun captains, yelling like men possessed as each eighteen-pounder slammed against its open port. Ready to fire.

He moved the glass very slightly. There was a thin plume of smoke from the maindeck of the other ship. Any fire was dangerous, in a fight or otherwise, but with holds full of gunpowder it was certain death. He glanced at *Unrivalled*'s upper yards and the whipping masthead pendant.

'Fall off a point!'

He saw Massie staring aft towards him, his sword already half raised.

There was no room for doubt, less for compassion. *Because that captain could be me.*

Tetrarch was still turning, her bows dragging at the mass of fallen spars and cordage. There were men too, struggling in the water, calling for help which would never come.

The next slow broadside would finish her. At almost full range, high-angled to the rise of the deck, it would smash through the remaining masts and canvas before *Tetrarch*'s main battery could be brought to bear.

'As you bear!' It was not even his own voice. He thought he saw the sun lance from Massie's upraised blade, and somehow knew that the gun crews on the larboard side had left their stations to watch, their own danger forgotten.

He stiffened and steadied the glass again. This time, he knew it was his own hand shaking.

'Belay that order!'

There was too much smoke, but certain things stood out as clearly as if the enemy had been alongside.

The forward guns were unmanned, and there were figures running across the ship's poop and halfdeck, apparently out of control. For an instant he imagined that the fire had taken control, and the ship's company were making a frantic attempt to escape the imminent explosion.

And then he saw it. The French flag, the only patch of colour on that broken ship, was falling, seemingly quite slowly, until somebody hacked the halliards apart so that it drifted across the water like a dying sea bird.

Cristie grunted, 'Sensible man, I'd say!'

Someone else said harshly, 'A lucky one too, God damn his eyes!'

Tetrarch was falling downwind, her maincourse and mizzen already being brailed up, as if to confirm her submission.

Adam raised the glass again. There were small groups of men standing around the decks; others, dead or wounded it was impossible to tell, lay unheeded by the abandoned guns.

Midshipman Bellairs called, 'White flag, sir!' Even he seemed unable to grasp what was happening, even less that he was a part of it.

'Heave to, if you please!' Adam lowered the glass. He had seen someone on that other deck watching him. With despair, hate; he needed no reminding. 'Take the quarter-boat, Mr Galbraith, and pick your boarding party. If you find it safe for us to come alongside, then signal me. At any sign of treachery, you know what to do.'

Their eyes held. *Know what to do. Unrivalled* would fire that final broadside. Any boarding party would be butchered.

Galbraith said steadily, 'I shall be ready, sir!'

'A close thing.'

'We would have run them down, sir. The way you handled her . . .'

Adam touched his sleeve. 'Not that, Leigh. I wanted them dead.'

Galbraith turned away, beckoning urgently to one of his petty officers. Even when the quarter-boat had been warped alongside and men were clambering down the frigate's tumble-home, he was still reliving it.

The Captain had called him by his first name, like an old and trusted friend. But more, he remembered and was disturbed by the look of pain on the dark features. Anguish, as if he had almost betrayed something. Or someone.

'Bear off forrard! Give way all!'

They were dipping and rising over the choppy water, the boat's stem already clattering through drifting flotsam and lolling corpses. Galbraith shaded his eyes to look up at the other vessel, huge now as they pulled past her bows, seeing the damage which *Unrivalled*'s guns had inflicted.

'Marines, take the poop! Creagh, put your party below!' He saw the boatswain's mate nod, his weatherbeaten face unusually grim. He was the man who had first recognised *Tetrarch*, and perhaps remembered the blackest moment in her life, when she had been surrendered to the enemy.

Sergeant Everett of the marines called, 'Watch yer back, sir! I'd not trust a one of 'em!'

Galbraith thought of the captain again. *It might have been us.* Then he lurched to his feet, one hand on the shoulder of an oarsman in this overcrowded boat, his mind empty of everything but the grapnel thudding into the scarred timbers and the hull grating alongside.

'With me, lads!'

Within a second he might be dead, or floating out there with the other corpses.

And then he was up and over the first gunport lid, tearing his leg on something jagged but feeling nothing.

There were more people on deck than he had expected. For the most part ragged and outwardly undisciplined, the sweepings of a dozen countries, renegades and deserters, and yet . . . He stared around, taking in the discarded weapons, the sprawled shapes of men killed by *Unrivalled*'s slow and accurate fire. It would need more than greed or some obscure cause to weld this rabble into one company, to stand and fight a King's ship which for all they knew might have been expecting support from other men-of-war.

He thought of the hand on his sleeve, and pointed with his hanger.

'Where is your captain?' He could not recall having drawn the blade as he had scrambled aboard.

A man stepped or was pushed towards him. An officer of sorts, his uniform coat without facings or rank.

He said huskily, 'He is dying.' He spread his hands. '*We* pulled down the flag. It was necessary!'

One of Creagh's seamen shouted, 'Fire's out!' He glared at the silent figures below the poop as if he would have cut each one down himself. 'Lantern, sir! Knocked over!'

The ship was safe. Galbraith said, 'Run up our flag.' He glanced at *Unrivalled*, moving so slowly, the guns like black teeth along her side. Then he looked up at the squad of Royal Marines with their bayoneted muskets. They had even managed to depress a swivel gun towards the listless men who were now their prisoners. A blast of canister shot would deter any last-minute resistance.

Sergeant Everett called, 'Captain's up here, sir!'

Galbraith sheathed his hanger. It would be useless in any case if some hothead tried to retake the ship. The groups of men parted to allow him through, and he saw defeat in their strained features. The will to fight was gone, if it had ever been there. Apathy, despair, fear, the face of surrender and all it represented.

Tetrarch's captain was not what he had expected. Propped between one of his officers and a pale-faced youth, he was at a guess about Galbraith's age. He had fair hair, tied in an old-style queue, and there was blood on his waistcoat, which the officer was attempting to staunch.

Galbraith said, 'M'sieur, I must tell you . . .'

The eyes opened and stared up at him, a clear hazel. The breathing was sharp and painful.

'No formalities, Lieutenant. I speak English.' He coughed, and blood ran over the other man's fingers. 'I suppose I *am* English. So strange, that it should come to this.'

Galbraith stared around. 'Surgeon?'

'None. So many shortages.'

'I will take you to my ship. Can you manage that?'

What did it matter? A renegade Englishman; there was a slight accent, possibly American. Perhaps one of the original privateers. And yet he did not seem old enough. He stood up; he was wasting time.

'Rig a bosun's chair. You, Corporal Sykes, attend this officer's wound.' He saw the doubt in the marine's eyes. 'It is important!'

Creagh shouted, ''Nother boat shovin' off, sir!'

Galbraith nodded. Captain Bolitho had seen or guessed what was happening. A prize crew, then. And there was still the dismasted brig to deal with. He needed to act quickly, to organise his boarding party, to have the prisoners searched for concealed weapons.

But something made him ask, 'What is your name, Captain?'

He lay back against the others, his eyes quite calm despite the pain.

'Lovatt.' He attempted to smile. 'Roddie – Lovatt.'

'Bosun's chair rigged, sir!'

Galbraith said, 'We have a good surgeon. What is the nature of your wound?'

He could hear the other boat hooking on, voices shouting to one another, thankful that reinforcements had arrived. All danger forgotten, perhaps until the night watches, when there would be thoughts for all men.

Lovatt did not conceal his contempt as he said bitterly, 'A pistol ball. From one of my gallant sailors yonder. When I refused to haul down the flag.'

Galbraith put his hand on the shoulder of the boy, who had not left the wounded man.

'Go with the others!'

His mind was full. An English captain who was probably an American; a ship which had been handed to the enemy after a mutiny; and a French flag.

The boy tried to free himself and Lovatt said quietly, 'Please, Lieutenant. Paul is my son.'

Two seamen carried him to the hastily rigged boatswain's chair. Once, Lovatt cried out, the sound torn from him, and reached for his son's hand. His eyes moved to the newly hoisted flag at the peak, the White Ensign, so fresh, so clean above the pain and the smell of death.

He whispered, '*Your* flag now, Lieutenant.'

Galbraith signalled to the waiting boat's crew and saw Midshipman Bellairs peering up at him. He would learn another lesson today.

Lovatt was muttering, 'Flags, Lieutenant . . . We are all mercenaries in war.'

Galbraith saw blood on the deck and realised it was his own, from the leg he had cut when climbing aboard.

The chair was being hoisted and then swayed out over the gangway.

He said, 'Go with him, boy. Lively now!'

Creagh joined him by the side as the chair was lowered into the boat, where Bellairs was waiting to receive it.

'Found this, sir.' He held out a sword. 'Th' cap'n's, they says.'

Galbraith took it and felt the drying blood adhering to his fingers. A sword. All that was left of a man. Something to be handed on. He thought of the old Bolitho blade, which today his captain had worn. *Or forgotten.*

He studied the hilt. One of the early patterns, with a five-ball

118

design, which had been so resented by sea officers when it had been introduced as the first regulation sword. Most officers had preferred their own choice of blade.

Deliberately, he half-drew it from its leather scabbard and read the engraving. He could even picture the establishment, in the Strand in London, the same sword-cutlers from whom he had obtained the hanger at his hip.

He stared across at his own ship, and at the boat rising and dipping in the swell on its errand of mercy.

Better he had been killed, he thought. A King's officer who had become a traitor: if he lived through this, he might soon wish otherwise.

He sighed. Wounded to be dealt with, dead to be put over. And a meal of sorts. After that . . . He felt his dried lips crack into a smile.

He was alive, and they had won the day. It was enough. It had to be.

8

No Escape

Denis O'Beirne, *Unrivalled*'s surgeon, climbed wearily up the quarterdeck ladder and paused to recover his breath. The sea was calmer, the sun very low on the horizon.

The ship's company was still hard at work. There were men high in the yards, splicing a few remaining breakages, and on the maindeck the sailmaker and his crew were sitting cross-legged like so many tailors, their palms and needles moving in unison, ensuring that not a scrap of canvas would be wasted. Apart from the unusual disorder, it was hard to believe that the ship had exchanged fire on this same day, that men had died. Not many, but enough in a small, self-contained company.

O'Beirne had served in the navy for twelve years, mostly in larger vessels, ships of the line, always teeming with humanity, overcrowded and, to a man of his temperament, oppressive. Blockade duty in all weathers, men forced aloft in a screaming gale, only to be recalled to set more sail if the weather changed in their favour. Bad food, crude conditions; he had often wondered how the sailors endured it.

A frigate was something else. Lively, independent if her captain was ambitious and able to free himself from the fleet's apron strings, and imbued with a sense of companionship which was entirely different. He had observed it with his usual interest, seen it deepen in the few months since *Unrivalled* had commissioned on that bitterly cold day at Plymouth, and the ship's first captain had read himself in.

As surgeon he was privileged to share the wardroom with

the officers, and during that period he had learned more about his companions than they probably knew. He had always been a good listener, a man who enjoyed sharing the lives of others without becoming a part of them.

A surgeon was classed as a warrant officer, his status somewhere between sailing master and purser. A craftsman rather than a gentleman. Or as one old sawbones had commented, neither profitable, comfortable, nor respectable.

In recent years the Sick and Hurt Office had worked diligently to improve the naval surgeon's lot, and to bring them into line with army medical officers. Either way, O'Beirne could not imagine himself doing anything else.

He was entitled to one of the hutch-like cabins allotted to the lieutenants, but preferred his own company in the sickbay below the waterline. His world. Those who visited him voluntarily came in awe; others who were carried to him, like those he had left on the orlop deck, or had seen being put over the side in a hasty burial, had no choice.

He glanced around the quarterdeck. Here, in this place of authority and purpose, the roles were reversed.

Unrivalled was rolling steeply despite the sea's calmer face, lying to as she had for the entire day, with the battered *Tetrarch* under her lee, the air alive with hammers and squealing blocks as the boarding party had used every trick and skill known to seamen to erect a jury-rig, enough for *Tetrarch* to get under way again, and be escorted to Malta.

The little brig had capsized and vanished even before many of her wounded could be ferried to safety. He had heard few regrets from anyone, and even the loss of potential prize money had seemed insignificant.

Two ships, and the sun already low above its reflection. He saw the captain staring up at their new fore topgallant sail, while Cristie, the master, pointed out something where the topmen were still working.

O'Beirne thought of his latest charge, *Tetrarch*'s captain. He had borne up well, considering the angle of the pistol shot and a great loss of blood. The ball had been fired point-blank, and his waistcoat had been singed and stained with powder smoke. Only one thing had saved his life: he had been wearing one of the outdated crossbelts which some

121

officers had still been using when O'Beirne had first gone to sea. It had a heavy buckle, like a small horseshoe. The ball had been deflected by it, and had broken in half.

They had stripped him naked and the loblolly boys had held him spreadeagled on the makeshift table, already ingrained with the blood of those who had gone before him.

O'Beirne could shut his ears and concentrate on the work in hand, but his mind was still able to record the inert shapes which lay in the shadows, or propped against the frigate's curved timbers. There had been no time to separate or distinguish the living from the dead. He had become accustomed to it, but still liked to believe he had not become hardened by it. He remembered the powder monkey who had lost a leg: it had been a challenge not to watch his face, his eyes so filled with terror as the knife had made its first incision. He had died on the table before the saw could complete the necessary surgery.

O'Beirne had seen his surgeon's mate scribble in a dog-eared log book. The powder monkey had been ten years old.

O'Beirne came from a large family, seven boys and three girls. Three brothers had entered the Church, two had donned the King's coat in a local regiment of foot, another had gone to sea in a packet ship. His sisters had married honest farmers and were raising families of their own. The brother who had gone to sea was no more; neither were the two who had 'gone for a soldier'.

He smiled to himself. There was something to be said for the Church after all.

He realised that the captain was looking at him. He seemed clear-eyed and attentive while he listened to what Cristie had to say, and yet O'Beirne knew he had been on deck or close to it since dawn.

Adam walked away from the rail and stared down at the sailmaker's crew.

'What is it?'

'The captain, sir.' He hesitated as the dark eyes met his. 'Captain Lovatt.'

'The prisoner, you mean. Is he dead?'

O'Beirne shook his head. 'I've done what I could, sir.

There is some internal bleeding, but the wound may heal, given time.'

He had not considered the man a prisoner, or anything but a wounded survivor. He had fainted several times, but had managed to smile when he had finally come to his senses. O'Beirne had prevented him from moving his arms, telling him it might aggravate the inner wound, but they all did it, usually after they had been rendered incapable of thought or protest by liberal helpings of rum. Just to make certain their arms were still there, and not pitched into the limbs and wings tub like so much condemned meat.

He saw a muscle tighten in the captain's jaw. Not impatience, but strain. Something he was determined to conceal.

He said, 'He asked about you, sir, while I was dressing the wound. I told him, of course. It helps to keep their minds busy.'

'If that is all . . .' He turned away, and then back abruptly. 'I am sorry. You are probably more tired than all the rest of us!'

O'Beirne observed him thoughtfully. It was there again, a kind of youthful uncertainty, so at odds with his role as captain, of this ship and all their destinies.

He knew Lieutenant Wynter and a master's mate were trying to catch the captain's eye; the list of questions and demands seemed endless.

He said, 'He knew your name, sir.'

Adam looked at him sharply.

'Because of my uncle, no doubt.'

'Because of your father, sir.'

Adam returned to the rail and pressed both palms upon it, feeling the ship's life pulsating through the warm woodwork. Shivering, every stay and shroud, halliard and brace, extensions of himself. Like hearing his first sailing master in *Hyperion*, so many years ago. *An equal strain on all parts and you can't do better.*

And now it was back. Was there no escape? No answers to all those unspoken questions?

Midshipman Bellairs called, 'Signal from *Tetrarch*, sir! *Ready to proceed*!'

He stared across the water, purple now with shadow, and saw

the other ship angled across the dying sunlight, pale patches of new canvas marking the extent of Galbraith's efforts.

'Thank you, Mr Bellairs. Acknowledge.' He looked at the portly surgeon without seeing him. 'Make to Mr Galbraith, *With fair winds. Good luck*.' Then, aware of the lengthening shadows, 'Roundly does it!'

O'Beirne was surprised, that this youthful man should take the time to send a personal message when he had so many urgent matters demanding his attention, and more so that he himself could be moved by it.

Adam was very conscious of the scrutiny, and moved away from it to the rail again and stood watching the greasy smoke rising from the galley funnel. The working parties were fewer, and some of the old hands were loitering, looking on as *Tetrarch* tested her jury-rig for the first time.

Men had died this day, and others lay in fear of living. But there was a smell of pitch and tar in the air, spunyarn and paint, *Unrivalled* shaking off the barbs of war, and her first sea fight.

'I shall get the ship under way.' He saw the surgeon turn, and knew he thought his visit had been in vain. 'After that, I shall come below and see the prisoner, if that is what you desire.'

Calls shrilled and men ran once more to halliards and braces: the sailors' way, exhausted one minute, all energy the next.

O'Beirne lowered himself carefully down the steep ladder, his mind lingering on the captain's last remark.

Half aloud, he said, 'What *you* need, more like, if I'm any judge.'

But it was lost in the hiss and boom of canvas as *Unrivalled* once again responded to those who served her.

They faced one another, the moment intensified by the stillness of O'Beirné's sickbay below the waterline. Adam Bolitho seated himself in the surgeon's big leather chair, which seemed to dominate this private place like a throne.

He looked at the other man, who was propped in a kind of trestle, one of O'Beirne's own inventions. It helped to ease the breathing, and lessened the risk of the lung filling with blood.

Two captains. He could not think of them as victor and vanquished. *We are only two men.*

124

Lovatt was not what he had expected. A strong but sensitive face, with hair as fair as Valentine Keen's. The hands, too, were well shaped, one clenching and unclenching against the throbbing pain of his wound, the other resting as if untroubled against the curved timbers of the hull.

Lovatt spoke first.

'A fine ship, Captain. You must be proud to have her.' He gazed at the nearest frame. 'Grown, not cut by saw. Natural strength, rare enough in these hard times.'

Adam nodded. It was indeed rare, with most of the oak forests hacked down over the years to supply the demands of the fleet.

He thought of Galbraith's hastily written message, and said, 'What did you hope to achieve?'

Lovatt almost shrugged. 'I obey orders. Like you, Captain. Like all of us.' The fist opened and closed again as if he had no control over it. 'You will know that I was expecting to be met, to be escorted the remainder of the passage to Algiers.'

Adam said quietly, '*La Fortune* was taken. She is a prize, like *Tetrarch*.' Half his mind was still with the scene he had left on deck. A lively breeze, a steadier motion with the wind almost across the taffrail. A soldier's wind, the old hands called it. It would help Galbraith's jury-rig, and it allowed *Unrivalled* to hold up to windward in case they required assistance.

He glanced around O'Beirne's domain, at the piles of well-thumbed books, the cupboards, and racks of bottles and jars clinking occasionally with the vibration of the rudder-head.

The smell here was different too. Potions and powders, rum and pain. Adam hated the world of medicine and what it could do to a man, even the bravest, under knife and saw. The price of victory. He looked at his companion again. And defeat.

'You asked to see me?' He curbed his impatience. His was the need.

Lovatt regarded him with calm eyes.

'My father fought alongside yours in the struggle for independence. They knew one another, although I did not know about you, the son.'

Adam wanted to leave, but something compelled him to remain. 'But you were a King's officer.'

'When I am handed over to the right authority I shall be

125

condemned as one. No matter – my son is all I have now. He will forget.'

Adam heard boots scrape outside the door. A marine sentry. O'Beirne was taking no chances. *On either of us.*

Lovatt was saying, 'I left America and returned to England, to Canterbury, where I was born. I had an uncle who sponsored my entry as midshipman. The rest is past history.'

'Tell me about *Tetrarch*.'

'I was third lieutenant in her . . . a long time ago. She was a fourth-rate then, but past her best. There was bad feeling 'twixt the captain and the senior lieutenant, and the people suffered because of it. When I spoke up on their behalf I discovered I had stepped into a trap. Because of my father, an Englishman *on the wrong side*, I was left in no doubt as to how my future would be destroyed. Even the second lieutenant, whom I had thought a friend, saw me as a threat to his own advancement.' He gave a sad smile. 'Not unknown to you perhaps, sir?'

Midshipman Fielding peered around the door. 'Mr Wynter's respects, sir, and he wishes to take in another reef.' His eyes were fixed on Lovatt.

'I shall come up.' Adam turned back, and saw something like desperation in the hazel eyes.

'There was no mutiny. They simply refused to stand to their guns. I agreed to remain aboard until their case had been put to the French.' The eyes were distant now. 'Most of them were exchanged, I believe. I was branded a traitor. But an American privateer came into Brest . . . Until then I had been a trusted prisoner of the French navy. On parole, *on my honour*.' It seemed to amuse him. 'And I had met a girl there. Paul is our son.'

Adam stood, his hair brushing the deckhead. 'And now you are a prisoner again. Did you think your mention of my father could buy you privilege? If so, then you do not know me.' It was time to go. *Now.*

Lovatt sank back against the trestle. 'I knew your name, what it has come to mean to sailors of all flags. My wife is dead. There is only Paul. I was planning to obtain passage to England. Instead, I was given command of *Tetrarch*.' He shook his head. 'That damned, wretched ship. I should have forced you to fire on us. Finished it!'

The deck moved slightly. They would all be up there waiting for him. The chain of command.

Adam stopped, his hand on the door. 'Canterbury? You have people there still?'

Lovatt nodded. The effort of conversation was taking its toll. 'Good friends. They will care for Paul.' He looked away, and Adam saw the despair in his clenched fist. 'But he will come to hate me, I think.'

'He is still your son.'

Again the faint smile. 'Be content, Captain. *You* have your ship.'

O'Beirne filled the doorway, his eyes everywhere.

Adam said, 'I have finished here.' He regarded Lovatt coldly. *The enemy*, no matter which flag he served or for what reason.

But he said, 'I shall do what I can.'

O'Beirne opened a cupboard and took out a bottle of brandy, which he had been saving for some special occasion although he had not known what. He recalled the even, Cornish voice as the captain had spoken a simple prayer before the corpses were put over the side. Most of the dead were unknown. Protestant, Catholic, pagan or Jew, it made no difference to them now.

He found two glasses and held them up to the light of the gently spiralling lantern to see if they were clean, and noticed the dried blood, like paint, on his cuff.

Lovatt cleared his throat, and said, 'I believe he meant it.'

O'Beirne pushed a glass towards him. 'Here – kill or cure. Then you must rest.'

He lingered over the glass. Some special occasion . . . He saw the brandy tilting with the rhythm of the sea, and imagined Captain Bolitho with his men, watching the stars, holding station on this man's ship.

He said, 'Of course he meant it.' But Lovatt had fallen into an exhausted sleep.

From somewhere aft he heard the sound of a fiddle, probably in the junior warrant officers' mess. Badly played, and out of tune.

To Denis O'Beirne, ship's surgeon, it was the most beautiful sound he had heard for a long time.

*   *   *

Vice-Admiral Sir Graham Bethune walked across the tiled floor and stood by one of the tall windows, careful to remain in the shadows, but feeling the heat of the noon sun like something physical. He shaded his eyes to stare at the anchored ships, his ships, knowing what made each distinct from the others, just as he now knew the faces and characters of each of his captains, from his bluff flag captain Forbes in *Montrose*, out there now with her awnings and windsails shimmering in the harsh glare, to the young but experienced Christie in the smaller twenty-eight gun *Halcyon*. It was something he could now accept, as he had come to accept the responsibility of his rank, one of the youngest flag officers on the Navy List.

The sense of loss was still there, as strong as ever, and if anything he felt even more impatient, conscious of a certain disappointment which was new to him.

Whenever he was at sea in *Montrose* he felt this same restlessness. He had confided to Sir Richard Bolitho more than once his discomfort at commanding, but not being in command, of his own flagship. Each change of watch or unexpected trill of a bosun's call, any sound or movement would find him alert, ready to go on deck and deal with every kind of incident. To leave it to others, to wait for the respectful knock on the screen door, had been almost unbearable.

Bethune had grasped at the chance of a seagoing appointment, having imagined that the corridors of the Admiralty were not for him.

He had been wrong, but it was hard to come to terms with it.

He watched the small boats pulling around the captured French frigate, *La Fortune*. A prize indeed. It had been a risk, and he had seen Adam Bolitho's face clearly in his mind as he had read the report. But a risk skilfully undertaken. If their lordships required any further proof that the Dey of Algiers was intent on even more dangerous escapades, this was it.

He recalled Bouverie's description of the cutting-out expedition. It was wrong to take sides, and Bethune had always despised senior officers who did so, but Bouverie had given the impression that the capture of the frigate had been entirely his own idea.

He turned his back on the grand harbour and its crumbling

backdrop of ancient fortifications, and waited for his eyes to become accustomed to the dimness of this room which was a part of his official headquarters. Once owned by a wealthy merchant, it was almost palatial. There was even a fountain in the small courtyard, and a balcony. In this house was the room where Catherine Somervell had made her final visit to her beloved Richard.

Bethune had ordered that it be kept locked, and could guess what his staff thought about it. He had visited the room only once. So still, so quiet, and yet when he had thrown open the shutters the din and turmoil of Malta seemed to swamp the place. It was uncanny.

There was a bell on a table. He had only to ring it and a servant would appear. Wine, perhaps? Or something stronger? He almost smiled. That was not like him, either; he had seen the results of over-indulgence only too often at the Admiralty.

He walked to another window. When he thought of his wife in England, and of their two young children, he could feel only guilt. Because he had been glad to leave, or because he had not trusted his own feelings for Richard Bolitho's mistress? It seemed absurd out here. He turned as someone tapped on the door.

Or was it?

It was his flag lieutenant, Charles Onslow. Young, eager, attentive. And dull, so dull. He was a distant cousin, and the appointment had been a favour to his wife.

Onslow stood just inside the door, his hat beneath his arm, his youthful features set in a half-smile.

'I am sorry to interrupt you, Sir Graham.' He usually prefaced any remark to Bethune with an apology, not like the Onslow he had heard barking at his subordinates. Favour or not, he would be rid of him.

'I welcome it!' Bethune stared at the heavy dress coat which was hanging carelessly on the back of a chair. So many officers envied him, and looked to him in hope of their own advancement.

I do not belong here.

'What is it?'

'A report from the lookout, Sir Graham. *Unrivalled* has been

129

sighted. She will enter harbour in late afternoon if the wind prevails.'

Bethune dragged his thoughts into the present. *Unrivalled* had quit her station. Adam must have had good reason. If not . . .

Onslow added helpfully, 'She has a ship in company. A prize.'

Another from Algiers, perhaps, although it seemed unlikely. He was reminded of Richard Bolitho's insistence that, unpopular though it might be with some senior officers, the bare bones of the written Fighting Instructions were no substitute for a captain's initiative.

Always provided that the end justified the methods.

'You may signal *Unrivalled* when she enters harbour, *Captain repair here when convenient.*'

Onslow frowned; perhaps he thought it too leisurely. Slack.

He was turning in the doorway. 'I all but forgot, Sir Graham.' He dropped his eyes. 'A lieutenant named Avery desires an audience with you.'

Bethune plucked his shirt from his ribs. 'How long has he been waiting?'

'The secretary brought word an hour back. I was dealing with signals at the time. It was an unusual request, I thought.'

He was enjoying it. He, more than any, would know that Avery had been flag lieutenant to Sir Richard Bolitho. He would also know that Avery had volunteered to remain at Malta to offer his assistance and the experience he had gained when he had visited the lion's den, Algiers.

'Ask him to come up. I shall apologise to him myself.'

It was almost worth it to see the rebuke go home like the sounding-shot before a broadside.

He made to pick up his heavy coat but decided against it.

He heard Avery in the corridor; he had come to recognise the uneven, dragging step.

Avery paused and gazed almost uncertainly around the room, like so many sea officers out of place on dry land. He would have to get used to it, Bethune thought.

He offered his hand, smiling.

'I regret the delay. It was unnecessary.' He gestured to

the envelope on the table. 'Your orders. You are free to leave Malta, and take passage in the next available vessel. Go home. You have done more than enough here.' He saw the tawny eyes come finally into focus, as if Avery's mind had been elsewhere.

'Thank you, Sir Graham. I was ready to leave.' The eyes searched him. 'I came to see you because . . .' He hesitated.

Bethune tensed, anticipating it. Avery would know this place. The room. Where there was now only silence.

Avery said, almost abruptly, 'I heard that *Unrivalled* has been sighted. With a prize.'

Bethune did not question how he knew, although he himself had only just been told. It was something beyond explanation: the way of sailors, he had heard an old admiral call it.

He said, 'Forgive me. I spoke of home. It was thoughtless.'

Avery regarded him without emotion, vaguely surprised that he should remember, let alone care. He had no home. He had lived at Falmouth. As Allday had put it often enough, 'like one of the family'. Now there was no family.

He shrugged. 'I might be needed here. I have a presentiment about this prize, something Captain Bolitho and I discussed. He is a shrewd man – his uncle would be proud of him.'

Bethune said gently, 'And of you, I think.' He swung round as another tap came from the door. *'Come!'*

It was Onslow again, his eyes moving quickly from the envelope on the table to his admiral's dishevelled appearance, coatless in the presence of a junior officer. He avoided looking at Avery completely.

'I beg your pardon, Sir Graham. Another report from the lookout. The schooner *Gertrude* has been sighted.'

Bethune spread his hands. 'We are busy, it seems!' Then he turned on his flag lieutenant, his mind suddenly clear. *'Gertrude*? She is not due for several days, surely, wind or no wind. Send a messenger to the lookout immediately.'

Onslow added unhappily, 'And Captain Bouverie of *Matchless* is here, Sir Graham.'

Avery said, 'I shall leave, sir.'

Bethune held out his hand.

'Sup with me tonight. Here.' He knew Avery disliked Bouverie, mainly, he suspected, because he had brought him

131

back to Malta with the French frigate, when Avery would have preferred Adam's company. The same bond which held them all together. He allowed himself to explore the thought. *And Catherine, who has touched us all.*

Avery smiled. 'I would relish that, sir.' And meant it.

Bethune watched him leave, and heard the uneven step retreating. There were many things to deal with: *Unrivalled's* unexpected return, and the early arrival of the courier schooner *Gertrude*. Despatches. Letters from England, orders for the ships and men under his command. It could all wait. He would ask Adam to join them, and, out of courtesy, his flag captain as well. Show no favouritism . . .

There would be others here tonight. He looked across at the empty balcony and the sealed shutters. Invisible, perhaps, but they would be very close.

He realised that Onslow was still there.

'I will see Captain Bouverie now. After that, I shall discuss the wine for this evening.' He pulled on the heavy coat with its bright epaulettes and silver stars. It seemed to make a difference to everyone else around him, but he was the same man underneath.

Poor Onslow; it was not entirely his fault. He caught him at the half-open door.

'You are invited too, of course.'

For once, Onslow was unable to control his pleasure. Bethune hoped he would not regret the impulse.

He thought of Avery, wanting to leave this place, but afraid of the life he might find waiting for him.

He smiled to himself and faced the door, ready to perform.

Catherine had visited him once at the Admiralty, privately, if not actually in secret. She had removed her glove so that he could kiss her hand. The knowledge hit him like a fist. Adam, George Avery, and one of the youngest flag officers on the Navy List . . . they were all in love with her.

The night was warm, but a soft breeze from the sea had driven away the day's clinging humidity.

Three officers stood side by side at an open window, watching the lights, boats bobbing like fireflies on the dark water. There were a few pale stars, and from the narrow streets they could hear singing and cheering. Earlier there had been a raucous ringing of bells, until some drunken sailors had been chased out of the church.

Captain Forbes had made his excuses and had remained in his ship, the captured *Tetrarch* needing his full attention. She looked larger in harbour against the sloops and brigs, and her valuable cargo of powder, shot and supplies, to say nothing of the vessel herself, would fetch a substantial reward in the prize court.

But even that seemed secondary, especially in this cool room with its banks of flickering candles.

It had been a boisterous meal, interspersed with countless toasts and good wishes for absent friends. Lieutenant Onslow had been fast asleep for most of it, and even the servants had been surprised by the amount of wine he had swallowed before sliding on to the floor.

The little schooner *Gertrude* had carried overwhelming news: the British and allied armies under the Duke of Wellington had met and fought Napoleon at a place called Waterloo. When *Gertrude* had weighed anchor to carry her despatches around the fleet there had been little more information than that, except that there had been horrific casualties in a battle fought in mud and thunderstorms, and victory had more than once hung in the balance. But it had been reported that the French army was in retreat. To Paris perhaps, although even as they waited there might still be a reverse in fortune.

But out there in the harbour aboard ships of every size and type men were cheering, men who had known nothing but war and sacrifice. Bethune remembered that day in London when the news of Napoleon's defeat had been brought to the Admiralty; he himself had been the one to interrupt the First Lord's conference and announce it. Fourteen months ago, almost to the day. And since then, the chain of events which had freed the tyrant from Elba, and had set his feet once more on the march for Paris . . .

He glanced at Adam's profile, knowing that he was remembering also. When England's hero, their beloved friend, had fallen to the enemy's marksman.

Tomorrow he must draft new orders to his captains and commanders, for no matter how the war was waged ashore the requirements for this squadron, like the whole fleet, were unchanged. To show the flag, to protect, to fight, and if need be, to intimidate, and maintain mastery of the sea which had been won with so much blood.

Adam felt the scrutiny but kept his eyes on the dark harbour, and the place where he knew *Unrivalled* was lying. Thinking of them all . . . Galbraith, quietly proud one moment, openly emotional the next. The imposing surgeon, O'Beirne, forgetting himself and capering in a little jig to the shantyman's fiddle. And the others, faces he had come to know. Faces he had once attempted to hold at a distance.

And the prisoner, Roddie Lovatt, delirious, but reaching out for his son, speaking in both English and French with equal intensity. Adam had seen the boy, and had recalled Lovatt's words to him. If there had been any name for the expression on the face of one so young, it could only be hatred.

A servant had brought yet another tray of filled glasses, one of which he placed carefully with the rest where Onslow still lay snoring loudly.

Bethune called, 'To our special friends! They will live forever!'

Adam felt the locket in his pocket, and shared the moment. And the guilt.

The three glasses clinked together and a voice said, 'To Catherine!'

Across the darkened courtyard Bethune thought he heard her laugh.

9

Luckier Than Most

Unis Allday paused and brushed a stray hair from her eyes and listened to some of the customers in the 'long room', as her brother called it, laughing and banging their tankards on the scrubbed tables. The Old Hyperion had been busy today, busier than she could remember for some months.

She scraped the slices of apple into a dish and stared out of the kitchen window. Flowers everywhere, bees tapping against the glass, the sun warm across her bare arms. The news of the great battle 'over there' had been brought to Falmouth by courier brig and had gone through the port and surrounding villages like wildfire, eventually reaching this little inn which nestled on the Helford River at Fallowfield.

It was not a rumour this time, it was far beyond that. The people who worked on the farms and estates in the area could only speak of victory, and no longer *when* or *if*. Men could go about their affairs without fear of being called to the Colours or snatched up by the hated press gangs. The war had levied a heavy toll; there were still very few young men to be seen in the lanes or around the harbours, unless they held the precious Protection. Even then, they could never be certain how some zealous lieutenant, desperate for recruits and fearful of what his captain might say if he returned to his ship empty-handed, might interpret his duty if the chance offered itself. And there were cripples a-plenty to remind anyone who might believe that the war had kept its distance from Cornwall.

She thought of her brother John, who had lost a leg when he had been serving with the Thirty-First regiment of foot.

She could not have managed without him, when she had taken this inn and had made it prosper. Then her other John, Allday, had come into her life, and they had been wed here in Fallowfield.

Her brother had said very little since the news of the French collapse had been shouted around the villages, and had seemed to distance himself from the customers. Perhaps he despised the lively banter and the steady sale of cider and ale which kept it close company, remembering now more than ever what the war had cost him, and all those who had stood shoulder to shoulder with him on the right of the line.

Maybe he would get over it, she thought. He was a kindly man, and had been so good with little Kate when she had been born, with John away at sea. She inspected a pot on its hook without seeing it, and then turned to look at the model of the *Hyperion* which John Allday had made for her. The old ship which had changed and directed the lives of so many, hers among them. Her first husband had served in *Hyperion* as a master's mate and had been killed in battle. John Allday had been pressed in Falmouth and put aboard a frigate commanded by Captain Richard Bolitho; *Hyperion* had later become their ship. She would always think of them together, although she knew little of men-of-war, except those which came and left on the tide. It had seemed only right that this inn should now bear *Hyperion*'s name.

John Allday was not very good at hiding things from her, neither his love for her and their child, nor his grief.

People who did not understand always wanted to know, were always asking him, despite her warnings, about Sir Richard Bolitho. What he was like, truly like as a man. And always asking about his death.

Allday had tried, and was still trying, to fill every day, as if that was the only way he could come to terms with it. As his best friend Bryan Ferguson had confided, 'Like the old dog losing his master. No point any more.'

And Unis knew that the old wound was troubling him, although if she had asked him he would have denied it. Ferguson had said that he should have quit the sea long ago, even as he had known, better than anyone, that John

136

Allday would never leave the side of his admiral, his friend, while they were both still needed.

Unis saw the pain in his face more frequently now, as he made himself useful about the inn, especially when he was lifting barrels of ale on to their trestles. She would get some of the other men to do it in future, if she could manage it without Allday finding out.

She knew that he went occasionally across to Falmouth, and this was something she could not share, nor attempt to. The ships, the sailors, and the memories. Missing being a part of it, not wanting to become just another old Jack, 'swinging the lamp', as he put it.

Unis often thought of the ones who had become close to her. George Avery, who had stayed here several times, and who wrote her husband's letters at sea for him, and read hers to him. John had told her that Avery never received any letters himself, and it had saddened her in some way.

And Catherine, who had called here when she had needed *to be with friends*. Unis had never forgotten that, nor would she.

Nothing was the same, even at the big grey house below Pendennis Castle. Ferguson had said little about it, but she knew he was deeply concerned. Lawyers had been to the house from London, pursuing the matter of a settlement, he had said. The estate had been left to Captain Adam Bolitho; it had been signed and sealed. But there were complications. Sir Richard's widow and his daughter Elizabeth had to be considered. No matter what Sir Richard had wanted, nor what Catherine had meant to him.

Where would she go now? What would she do? Bryan Ferguson would not be drawn on the possibilities. He was worried about his own future; he and his wife had lived and worked at the estate for many years. How could lawyers from London know anything about such things as trust and loyalty?

She thought, too, of the memorial service at Falmouth. She had heard of the grander services at Plymouth and in the City of London, but she doubted they could match the united bond of pride and love, as well as sorrow, that day in the crowded church.

Her brother walked into the kitchen, his wooden leg thumping heavily on the flagstones.

He reached for his long clay pipe. 'Just spoke with Bob, the farrier's son.' He took a taper from the mantel and held it to the flames, careful not to look at her. 'There's a frigate in Carrick Roads. Came in this morning.' He saw her fingers bunch into her apron, and added, 'Don't fret, lass, none of her people will come this far out.'

She looked at the old clock. 'He'll be down there, then. Watching.'

He studied the smoke from his pipe, almost motionless in the warm air. Like that day when he had been struck down. All in a line, like toy soldiers. The smoke had lingered there too. For days. While men had called out, and had eventually died.

'He's got you, and young Kate. He's lucky. Luckier than most.'

She put her arms round him. 'And we've got *you*, thank God!'

Someone banged his tankard on a table and she dabbed her face with her apron.

'There now, no rest for the wicked!'

Her brother watched her bustle out of the kitchen, and heard her call out to somebody by name.

Hold fast there, John. He did not know if he had spoken aloud, or to whom he had been speaking, himself, or the sailor home from the sea.

He heard a gust of laughter and was suddenly proud of his neat little sister, and even perhaps ashamed that he had given way to his bitter memories. It had not always been so. He squared his shoulders and tapped out his pipe in the palm of his hand, carefully, so as not to break it. Then he strode in to the adjoining room and picked up an empty tankard. Like the old Thirty-First. *Stand together, and face your front.*

He was back.

Catherine Somervell gripped a tasselled handle and leaned forward as the carriage with its matching greys turned into the imposing gateway. The sky over the Thames was clear, but after several days of thunderstorms and heavy rain nothing seemed certain.

She was alone, and had left her companion Melwyn to pay the men who were repairing the front door of her Chelsea

138

house. Sillitoe had sent his carriage to collect her, and she had seen several people in the Walk turn to watch, some to smile and wave.

It was still hard to accept. To come to terms with. To understand.

Some had left flowers for her; one had even placed an expensive arrangement of roses on her doorstep with the simple message, *For the Admiral's Lady. With admiration and love.*

And by contrast, last night, probably during the thunderstorm, someone had scratched the word *whore* on the same door. Melwyn had been outraged, the affront sitting strangely on one so young. Because she felt a part of it.

She watched the horses' ears twitching as the carriage rolled to a halt. She could see the Thames again. The same river, but a world apart.

As speculation about the war had hardened into fact, she had wondered how the news would affect Adam. She had written to him, but she knew from bitter experience that letters took their time reaching the King's ships.

Once, when she had been passing the Admiralty, she had realised how complete her isolation from Richard's world had become. She knew no one in those busy corridors, or even 'by way of the back stairs', as he had called it. Bethune was in the Mediterranean, in Richard's old command, and Valentine Keen was in Plymouth. She thought of Graham Bethune's concern for her, and his furious estrangement from his wife. He was an attractive man, and good company. It was probably for the best that he was so far away.

A boy in a leather apron had opened the door and was lowering the step. He, at least, should be spared the suffering and the separation of war.

She climbed down and looked up at the coachman.

'Thank you, William. That was most comfortable.' She sensed his surprise, that she had remembered his name, or because she had spoken at all. She saw his eyes move to her breast and the diamond pendant there, and just as swiftly move away. Like the men painting the front door. She had seen their expressions. Their curiosity.

Then she thought of the blind lieutenant and the crippled

sailors at the cathedral. It made the others seem lower than the dust.

A servant opened the doors for her, a man she did not know. He gave a quick bow.

'If you will wait in the library, m' lady. Lord Sillitoe will join you presently.'

She walked into the room and saw the chair where she had sat, waiting for Sillitoe on the day of the memorial service. Only two weeks ago. A lifetime.

And now she was here again. Sillitoe had taken it upon himself to deal with the legal complications; she had seen another carriage in the drive, and somehow knew it was that of the City lawyer, Sir Wilfred Lafargue. Sillitoe seemed to know everyone of consequence, friend or enemy. Like the private article someone had shown her in the *Times* newssheet, a very personal appraisal, a dedication to the one man she had loved.

Sir Richard practised total war, and inspired others to seek a total victory. To the Navy, his will remain an abiding influence. We shall never forget him, nor the woman he loved to the end.

Her name had not been mentioned. There was no need.

Sillitoe had said nothing about it. There had been no need for that, either.

The door opened and he strode into the room, his quick, keen glance taking in the dark green gown, the wide-brimmed straw hat with its matching ribbon. Perhaps surprised to see her out of mourning; the hooded eyes gave little away, but she recognised approval in them.

He kissed her hand, and half-turned as horses clattered across the drive.

'Lafargue can make even a single word into an overture.' He waited for her to sit and arrange her gown. 'But I think the way has become clear.'

She felt the eyes upon her, the power of the man. An intensity which so many had found cause to fear.

She had only once seen him off guard, that day at the cathedral, when he had pushed through the silent crowd to be at her side. As if he believed he had failed her in some way, something which he was unable to conceal.

And other times. When he had arranged passage for her to Malta . . . *For that last time.* She clenched her fist around her parasol. She must not think of it. She had often found him watching her, like this moment, in this great, silent house overlooking the Thames. Perhaps remembering yet again the night he had burst into her room, and had held her, shielded her, as his men had dragged away the madman who had attempted to rape her.

He had made no secret of his feelings for her. Once, in this house, he had even mentioned marriage. But after that terrible night, how did he really regard her?

She thought of the lightning over the river last night, probably while the unknown pervert had been scratching his poison on the door. It had all come back to her. Melwyn had felt it too, and had climbed into bed with her, holding her hand, a child again, until the storm had abated.

Sillitoe said, 'Lady Bolitho will have the right to visit Falmouth. A lawyer acceptable to Lafargue,' he almost smiled, 'and, of course, to me, will be present. Certain items . . .' He broke off, suddenly tired of evasion. 'It would not be advisable for you to be present. Captain Bolitho is the accepted heir, but in his absence we may have to make allowances.'

She said quietly, 'I had no intention of returning to Falmouth.' She raised her chin and regarded him steadily. 'There would be some who would say that the mare was hasty to change saddles!'

Sillitoe nodded. 'Bravely spoken.'

'Time will pass. I shall become a stranger there.'

'Adam will ask you to visit or take up residence, whichever you choose. When he eventually returns.'

She was on her feet without knowing that she had left the chair. She looked down at the river: people working on barges, a man walking his dog. Ordinary things. She bit her lip. Beyond her reach.

She said, 'I think that might be dangerous.'

She did not explain. She did not need to.

And she spoke the truth. What would she do there? Watch the ships, listen to the sailors, torture herself with memories they had shared with no one?

Sillitoe waited, watched her turn, framed against the sun-dappled window, her throat and shoulders as brown as any country lass working in the fields, the pendant glittering between her breasts. The one woman he truly wanted; he had never considered it as a need before. And the only one he could never have.

He said abruptly, 'I have to leave London. Tomorrow or the next day.' He saw her hand close into a fist again. What was troubling her? 'To Deptford. I was going to suggest that you stay here. You would be well taken care of, and I would feel safer.'

She looked at the river once more. 'That would do your reputation injury, surely?'

'It is of no consequence.' He was standing beside her, like that day at St Paul's. 'After this *duty* I shall be spending more time in the pursuit of my own affairs, unless . . .'

She turned towards him, unnerved by the realisation that this was the true reason for asking her here. 'Unless?'

'The Prince Regent seems to feel that my work as Inspector-General has run its course.' He shrugged. 'He is probably right.'

She could feel the beat of her heart, like a hammer, and said again, 'Unless what?'

'I think you know, Catherine.'

'Because of me. What they will say. How it would look. They would pillory you, just as they tried to destroy Richard.' She repeated, 'Because of me.'

'And do you think I care what people say about me? What they have always been careful to conceal to my face? Power is like a fine blade – you must always use it with care, and for the right purpose!'

A bell was ringing somewhere, another visitor. But she could not move.

It had been wrong, stupid, to allow herself to become dependent on this hard, remote man. And yet she had known it was there. As at St Paul's, when he had risked the stares and the condemnation.

She said softly, 'You should have married someone suitable.'

He smiled. 'I did. Or I thought she suited. But she went with another. Greener pastures, I believe it is called.'

He said it without anger or emotion, as though it were something forgotten. Or was that, too, another form of defence?

142

There were voices now, probably the secretary Marlow or one of his burly servants.

He put his hand on her arm and held it, and she watched, detached, as if she were watching someone else.

She said, 'Would you have me as your mistress, my lord?'

She lifted her eyes and looked at him. Angry, wanting to hurt this unreachable man.

He took her other arm and turned her towards him, holding her only inches away.

'As I said before, Catherine. As my wife. I can give you the security you need and deserve. I loved you at a distance, and sometimes I fought against it. So now it is said.'

She did not resist as he pulled her against him, did not even flinch when he touched her hair and her skin. A voice was screaming, *what is the matter with you*? But all she could see was the damaged door. *Whore.*

She whispered, 'No. Please don't.'

He held her away and studied her face, feature by feature.

'Come with me on this last duty, Catherine. Then I will know.' He tried to smile. 'And so will the Prince Regent!'

Again it came to her. When she had met Richard at Antigua, so long ago, it seemed, she had told him that he needed love, *as the desert craves for rain.* She had been describing herself.

She thought of all the rare, precious times they had spent together. As one. And the endless waiting in between. And the finality.

Don't leave me.

But there was no reply.

John Allday rested against the iron railings at the top of the jetty, so well-worn throughout the years that they were quite smooth, and stared across the crowded anchorage. One of the local carriers had given him a ride into Falmouth; he would doubtless be calling at the inn later on for some free ale.

Allday was glad he had come. It was something he could not explain to Unis, to anybody. It was probably bad for him, holding on to the past. Was it that . . . ?

She was a frigate of some thirty-eight guns, although he had noticed that some of her ports were empty, as if her main armament had been cut down for some reason. She was named

143

Kestrel, and even without a glass he had seen her figurehead, the spread wings and curved beak. As if it were alive. He did not know the ship, and that troubled him. Before long, there would be many more ships coming and leaving which were strangers to him, in name and reputation. No reminders.

He studied the frigate with a critical eye. A fine-looking vessel, freshly painted, and her furled or brailed-up canvas all new from the sailmakers. There were few local craft around her, so she was not in Falmouth to take on stores. He had heard someone say that *Kestrel* was already armed and provisioned, in readiness for a long voyage. Not Biscay or the Mediterranean this time; somewhere far away, perhaps. There were scarlet uniforms at the gangways and forecastle; her captain was taking no chances on last-minute desertions. A change of heart caused by the news of more advances across the Channel, the end finally in sight.

But the navy would still be needed. And there would always be deserters.

He heard some old sailors discussing the ship, their voices loud, as if they wanted to be noticed. In a moment they would try to draw him into it.

He moved a few paces along the jetty, and looked down at the water lapping over the stone stairs which had seen so many thousands arrive and depart. It was as if his life had begun here, when he had been taken aboard Bolitho's frigate *Phalarope*. With Bryan Ferguson, and some others who had not been quick enough to avoid a landing party. An unlikely way to begin something so strong. It was not as if he had been a green recruit; he had served in the fleet before. He frowned and glanced down at his good blue coat with the buttons which Bolitho had had made for him. The Bolitho crest, for an admiral's coxswain. He sighed. *And friend.*

Unis was doing all she could to make his life comfortable. She gave him encouragement, and she gave him love. And there was little Kate. He recalled how pleased Lady Catherine had been when she had heard their decision to name her Kate. The same name Sir Richard used for her.

And now she was gone from the old grey house. It seemed so empty without her; even his best friend Bryan had said as much. He went there when he could, if only to share a wet with him, or to yarn about old times.

There was talk that Sir Richard's widow might return. No one seemed to know anything for certain. Lawyers and snotty clerks, what did they understand about this place and its people? Even the smell of it. Paint and tar, fishing nets hung to dry in the June sunshine, and the sounds. Winches and hammers, local dealers haggling with some of the fishing skippers who had come into the harbour earlier than usual. And always the sea.

He touched his chest, but the pain hesitated, like a warning at the door. Fallowfield was quiet, and usually peaceful. He knew that Unis got worried when sailors came so far out to the Old Hyperion. He had seen her watching, caring.

'Oars!'

The order rang out sharply, but a little too shrill for the occasion. Allday turned as a jolly-boat thrust around the jetty, the bowman scrambling to his feet to seize a boathook. There was a smart-looking midshipman by the tiller, his hat tilted against the sunlight.

'Up!'

The oars rose as one, like white bones, while the midshipman brought the hull against the wooden piles with barely a shudder.

Allday nodded. Rakishly done. So far. You never knew with the young gentlemen, ready to listen and learn one minute, tyrants the next.

One of the old sailors on the jetty cackled, 'Look at *'im*! Proper little 'ero, eh, lads?'

Allday frowned. The speaker would not be saying that if he was back in the *perfect* navy he was usually describing in one of the local taverns.

The midshipman was clattering up the stone steps, a shining new dirk pressed against his side. Allday made to move aside, but the boy, and he was little more than that, blocked his way.

'Mister Allday, sir?' He was gazing at him anxiously, while the boat's crew looked on with interest.

Very new and very young. Calling him 'mister' and 'sir'. He would have to learn quickly, otherwise . . . It hit him like the pain in his chest. His was a different world now. He did not belong any more.

'That's me.' The midshipman reminded him of someone . . . A face formed in his mind. Midshipman Neale of the *Phalarope*, who had eventually become captain of a frigate himself. Neale had died after being taken prisoner of war. With Richard Bolitho. He felt it again. *And me.*

The midshipman breathed out with relief. 'My captain saw you, sir.' It was as if he were afraid to turn towards the anchored ship, in case he was being watched.

'He sends his respects, sir.'

Allday shook his head, and corrected roughly, 'Compliments!'

The midshipman was equally firm. '*Respects*, sir. And would you come aboard, if you have the time?'

Allday touched his arm. 'Lead on.' It was worth it just to see the idlers on the jetty staring down at them. The loud-mouthed one could put that in his pipe and smoke it!

He threw his leg over the gunwale and said, 'So long as I'm not being pressed!'

Some of the oarsmen grinned. *Because they think I'm too bloody old.*

'Bear off forrard! Out oars! Give way together!'

Then the midshipman turned to stare at him, and said, 'Never fear, sir, they'll be up to your standard soon!' And he was proud of it.

Allday looked around, avoiding the eyes as the seamen lay back on their looms, unable to accept it. The midshipman knew who he was. *Knew him.*

Eventually he managed to ask, 'And who is your captain?'

The boy looked surprised, and almost misjudged the tug of the tiller-bar.

'Why, Captain Tyacke, sir! Sir Richard Bolitho's flag captain!'

Allday looked up at the fierce kestrel with its spread wings, at a seaman using a marlin spike but pausing in the middle of a splice to peer down at him. Captain James Tyacke. A face from yesterday. Or half a face, with that terrible disfigurement, his legacy from the Nile.

And the midshipman stood and removed his hat as the boat hooked on to the main chains, and Allday climbed up the 'stairs' to the entry port. His mind was too crowded to record that he did it with ease and without pain.

It was like one of those things you think about, in a dream or a part-remembered story from someone else. A lieutenant greeted him, older than most for his rank, so probably from the lower deck. *Come up the hard way.* He had heard Tyacke speak of others like that. From him, with his qualities of seamanship and professional skill, there was no higher praise.

Beneath the quarterdeck, his mind trying to take in everything. Neat stands of pikes, and smartly flaked lines. The smell of fresh paint and new cordage. Just months since he had seen Bolitho fall, had caught and held him to the last. Tyacke had been there, too, but because of the close action he had been prevented from leaving his men. He nodded to himself, as if someone had spoken. *Yesterday.*

A Royal Marine sentry drew his boots together as the lieutenant tapped on the screen door. She could have been any ship . . . He almost expected Ozzard to open the door.

But it was Captain Tyacke. He shook his hand, waved aside all formality and guided him into the great cabin. Through the broad, sloping stern windows Allday was aware of Carrick Roads, stationary masts and moving patches of sails. But, in truth, he saw none of it.

Tyacke seated him by a table, and said, 'I called at Falmouth in the hope that I might see Lady Somervell. But when I sent word to the house I was told that she is in London.' He looked at the skylight, and made no attempt, as he had used to do, to turn aside to hide the hideous scars.

Allday said, 'She would have wanted to see you, sir.'

Tyacke held up his hand. 'No rank here. I shall write to her. I am under orders for the West African station. But when I saw you through the glass just now, I had to speak with you. Chance, like happiness, does not come so easily.'

Allday said, awkwardly, 'But we thought . . .' He tried again. 'My wife Unis was certain that you were to be married, if and when *Frobisher* was paid off. I thought you might spend some time ashore.' He tried to grin. 'You've earned it more 'n most!'

Tyacke glanced at the adjoining sleeping cabin, glad that his big sea chest had at last been taken below. His companion for so many years. Thousands and thousands of miles logged, icy gales and blistering heat. Guns and death. The chest had been standing near the door of Marion's house, waiting for men to come and take it to his new command. This ship.

He said, 'I always thought I'd like to return to Africa. Their lordships were good to me, and granted my request.' He looked up at the skylight again; maybe he could see the mainmast truck from there. No admiral's flag any more. A private ship. His own.

Allday heard someone bringing glasses. He thought of Unis, how lucky he was to have her.

Tyacke was speaking again, with no discernible emotion in his voice.

'It would not have worked, you see. The two children . . .' He touched his scarred face, reliving it. 'I can understand how they felt about it.'

Allday watched him sadly. *No, you don't.*

Tyacke gestured to the unknown servant.

'Nelson's blood, am I right?'

Allday saw the servant give him a quick glance, and was glad he had put on his best coat today. As if he had known.

'It will do me good to get away from all of it. There's nothing for me here. Not any more.' Tyacke took a full goblet. 'It's something we shared, were a part of. Nothing can alter that.' He swallowed some of his drink, his blue eyes very clear.

Then he said, after a silence, 'He gave me back my *pride*, my hope, when I had thought them gone forever. I'll never forget him, and what he gave to me.' He smiled briefly. 'It's all we can do now. Remember.'

He poured another generous measure of the rum and thought of Marion, her face when he had left the neat house, the children hiding in another room. Another man's home, another man's children.

Then he stared around the cabin and knew it was what he wanted. It was the only life he knew, or could expect.

Back to the anti-slavery patrols where he had been serving when he had first met Richard Bolitho. The trade was more extensive and more lucrative than ever despite all the treaties and promises; the slavers would have the pick of the ships as soon as this war was finally ended. Like the ones which had been there that day. When he had seen him fall, and this big, shambling man with the goblet almost lost in one of his hands had held him with a tenderness which few could imagine. Unless they had shared it. Been there. *With us.*

He smiled suddenly. And he never had told Marion about the yellow gown which he had always carried in that old sea chest.

Later in the afternoon they went on deck. There was a hint of mist below Pendennis Castle, but the glass was steady and the wind was fair. *Kestrel* would clear harbour before most good people were awake and about their business.

Allday stood by the entry port, feeling the ship stir slightly beneath his fine shoes. He was surprised that he could accept it, without pain and without pity. He would never lose it, any more than the tall captain with the burned and melted face would forget.

The jolly-boat was already coming alongside, and the same midshipman was at the tiller. For some reason Allday was glad of it.

They faced one another and shook hands, each somehow knowing they would not meet again. As was the way with most sailors.

Tyacke waved to the boat, and asked, 'Where to now, old friend?'

Allday smiled. 'Goin' home, Cap'n.'

Then he walked to the entry port, and paused and touched his forehead to the quarterdeck, and to the great ensign curling lazily from aft. For John Allday, admiral's coxswain, it would never end.

He climbed down into the boat and grinned at the young midshipman. The worst part was behind him.

The midshipman eased over the tiller-bar and said shyly, 'Will you, sir?'

Allday nodded, and waited for the bowman to cast off.

'Bear off forrard! Out oars! Give way *together!*'

It would never end.

10

Captain To Captain

Luke Jago made his way unhurriedly aft, his lean body angled easily to the deck. *Unrivalled* was heading west again, steering close-hauled on the starboard tack under topsails and topgallants, the wind light but enough to hold her steady.

Here on the ship's messdeck the air was heady with rum, and the smell of the midday meal. Unlike a ship of the line, there were no guns on this deck. Each mess was allotted a scrubbed table and bench seats, with hooks overhead where the hammocks would be slung when the ship piped down for the night. In larger vessels the guns were a constant reminder to seamen and marines alike, when they swung themselves into their hammocks, and when they were piped on deck for any emergency. Their reason for being.

Jago glanced at the tables as he passed. Some of the men looked at him and nodded, others avoided his eye. It suited him well enough. He recalled that the captain had said he could use the little store which adjoined the cabin pantry for his meals, but he had declined. He had been surprised by Captain Bolitho's offer, and that he should even care about it.

He half-listened to the loud murmur of voices and the clatter of plates. The forenoon watchkeepers were already tucking into their boiled meat, and what looked like oatmeal. The new cook was far better than his predecessor; at least he was not so mean with his beef and pork. And there was bread, too. The captain had sent a working party to one of the garrisons in Malta: the army always seemed to live well when it was not in the field. And there was butter, while it lasted. When the purser had supervised the issue to all the messes, you would have thought he was parting with his own skin. But they were always like that.

To these men, experienced or raw recruits, such small items, taken for granted by those ashore, were luxuries. When they were exhausted it would be back to iron-hard ship's biscuits, with slush skimmed off the galley coppers to make them edible. He grinned inwardly. A sailor's lot.

He saw the glint of metal and scarlet coats, marine sentries, and, crowded together while the food was ladled out, the prisoners from the ill-fated *Tetrarch*. Jago had seen them eating so voraciously when they had been brought aboard that it seemed they had not been properly fed for years. Now some were even working with the various parts of ship, under supervision of sorts. But Jago thought that no matter what lay ahead for these men, they were somehow glad to be back in the world which had once been their own.

The admiral at Malta, Bethune, had wanted to get rid of them as quickly as possible, the British ones at any rate. Someone else would have to decide their fate. Would anybody bother to investigate the circumstances, he wondered? Mutineers, deserters, or men who had been misled? The end of a rope was the usual solution.

He thought of the captain again. He had given orders that these men were to receive the same rations as the ship's company. Troublemakers would be punished. *Instantly*. He could see Bolitho's face as he had said it. Jago knew that most captains would have kept these men on deck in all weathers, and in irons. As an example. As a warning. And it was cheaper, too.

He paused by one of the tables and studied a finely carved model of a seventy-four. *Unrivalled* had been in commission for only six months, and during that time he had watched this superb carving take on meaning and life.

The seaman raised his head. It was Sullivan, the keen-eyed lookout.

'Almost done, 'Swain.'

Jago rested one hand on his shoulder. He knew the history of the model: she was the *Spartiate*, a two-decker which had been in Nelson's Weather Division at Trafalgar. Sullivan kept to himself, but was a popular man by any standard. Trafalgar: even the word gave him a sort of presence. He had been there, in the greatest naval battle of all time, had cheered with all the others when they had broken through the French line, only to be stunned by the signal that Lord Nelson, 'Our Nel', had fallen.

When Jago had watched the captain he had found himself wondering if he ever compared the death of his uncle, Sir Richard Bolitho, a man who had been as well liked and respected as Nelson, but had been killed in what might have been an accidental engagement. In the end, it was the same for both of them.

He looked over Sullivan's head at the next mess, where the ship's boys were quartered. Signed on by parents who wanted to be rid of them, and others like Napier, who had been appointed the captain's servant, living in the hope of outside sponsorship, and the eventual chance of a commission. He remembered the captain's face when he had told him that the boy John Whitmarsh had been killed. He had intended to sponsor the boy as midshipman, and all the while Whitmarsh had wanted only to remain with him.

There was another boy at the mess table, the one called Paul, son of the *Tetrarch*'s renegade captain. Had he continued the fight and faced one of *Unrivalled*'s broadsides with his holds filled to the deckhead beams with powder . . . at least it would have been a quick death, Jago thought.

Sullivan did not look up, but said, 'What'll they do with 'im?'

Jago shrugged. 'Put him ashore, maybe.' He frowned, angry without knowing why. 'War is no game for children!'

Sullivan chuckled. 'Since when?'

Jago glanced around the partly filled messdeck, the swaying rays of sunlight probing down through the gratings and an open hatchway.

This was his world, where he belonged, where he could catch the *feel* of the ship, something which would be denied him if he accepted the captain's offer.

His eyes fell on the burly seaman named Campbell, who had been sentenced to a flogging for threatening a petty officer. There had been two men brought aft for punishment, but the other had been killed during the opening shots of the engagement, and the captain had ordered that Campbell's punishment should be stood over. He was sitting there now, his face blotchy with sweat from too much rum. Wets from others, for favours done, or perhaps the need to keep on the good side of this seemingly unbreakable troublemaker.

One of the hard men, Campbell had received a checkered shirt at the gangway several times. Jago knew what it was like to be flogged; although the punishment had been carried out unjustly, and despite the intervention of an officer on his behalf, he would carry the scars to the grave. No wonder men deserted. He had nearly run himself, twice, in other ships, and for reasons he could scarcely remember.

What had held him back? He grimaced. Certainly not loyalty or devotion to duty.

Again he recalled the day he had shaken hands with Captain Bolitho after they had driven off the big Yankee. A bargain, something done on the spur of the moment while the blood was still pounding with the wildness of battle. It was something new to him, which he did not understand. And that, too, troubled him.

Campbell looked at him. 'This is an unexpected honour, eh, lads? To 'ave the Cap'n's cox'n amongst the likes of us!'

Jago relaxed. Men like Campbell he could handle.

'Far enough, Campbell. I'll take no lip from you. You've been lucky, so make the best of it.'

Campbell seemed disappointed. 'I never meant nuthin'!'

'*One foot*, just put one foot wrong and I shall drag you aft myself!'

Somebody asked, 'Why are we goin' to Gib again, 'Swain?'

Jago shrugged. 'Despatches, to land *Tetrarch*'s people –'

Campbell said harshly, 'Run 'em up to the mainyard, that's what I'd do!' He pointed at the boy in the other mess. '*'Is* bloody father for a start!'

Jago smiled. 'That's more like it, Campbell. A ten year old boy. A fair match, I'd say!'

Sullivan said softly, 'Officer on the deck, 'Swain!'

Someone else murmured, 'Bloody piglet, more like!'

It was Midshipman Sandell, striding importantly past the messes, chin in the air and not bothering to remove his hat,

153

a courtesy observed by most officers. Jago ducked beneath one of the massive deckhead beams and realised that the midshipman was still able to walk upright, even wearing the hat. Sandell was carrying a gleaming, and, Jago guessed, very expensive sextant, probably a parting gift from his parents. Earlier he had seen the midshipmen assembled on the quarter-deck taking their noon sights, watched critically by Cristie, the master, as they had tried to estimate the ship's position for their logs.

Cristie missed very little, and Jago had heard him give Sandell the rough edge of his tongue more than once, to the obvious glee of the others.

Jago faced him calmly. It made upstarts like him dangerous.

'Oh, you're here, are you?' Sandell peered around, as if he had never set foot on the lower deck before. 'I want the boy, Lovatt. He is to lay aft, *now*.'

'I'll fetch him, Mr Sandell.'

'How many times do I have to tell people?' He was almost beside himself. 'San*dell*! That's easy enough, surely?'

Jago murmured, 'Sorry, sir.' It had been worth it just to see the shot go home. As he had intended it would.

He beckoned to the boy, and asked, 'The captain wants him, sir?'

Sandell stared at him, as if astonished that anyone should dare to question him. But, angry or not, some inner warning seemed to prevent another outburst. Jago's demeanour, and the fine blue jacket with gilt buttons, appeared to make him hesitate.

He said loftily, 'The captain, yes.' He snapped his fingers. 'Move yourself, boy!'

Jago watched them leave. Sandell would never change. He had shown no sign of fear during the fight, but that meant little; his kind were usually more afraid of revealing their fear to others than of fear itself. He winked at Sullivan. But if Sandell wanted to climb the ladder of promotion, he would be wise not to turn his back.

Unrivalled's wardroom, which was built into the poop structure on the gundeck, seemed spacious after other frigates George Avery had known. Unlike the lower deck, the ship's officers shared the cabin and dining space with six eighteen-pounders, three on either side.

The midday meal had been cleared away, and Avery sat by an open gunport watching some gulls diving and screaming alongside, probably because the cook had pitched some scraps outboard.

Two days out of Malta, on passage for Gibraltar, as if everything else was unreal. The dinner with Vice-Admiral Bethune and Adam Bolitho, then the excitement at being a part of something which he had begun with Sir Richard, had all been dashed by the arrival of another courier vessel. *Unrivalled* would take Bethune's despatches to the Rock and pass them on to the first available ship bound for England. Whatever Bethune really thought about it, he had made himself very clear. His latest orders were to contain the activities of the Dey's corsairs, but to do nothing to aggravate the situation until more ships were put under his flag.

Adam had been quietly resentful, although *Unrivalled* was the obvious choice: she was faster and better armed than any other frigate here or anywhere else in the fleet. There had been reports of several smaller vessels being attacked, taken or destroyed by the corsairs, and communications between the various squadrons and bases had never been so important. There was still no definite news of a total victory over Napoleon's army. Waterloo had broken his hold over the line, and it seemed as if all French forces were in full retreat. Even Marshal Ney's formidable cavalry had been defeated by the red-coated squares of infantry.

And he, Lieutenant George Avery, had received orders which countermanded all others. He was to return to England and present himself to their lordships, perhaps to add his report to all those which must have gone before. He laid his hand on the gun, warm, as if it had been recently fired. Perhaps he was too close. It was not another report they wanted. It was a post-mortem.

He looked around at his companions. It was a friendly enough wardroom, and he was after all a stranger, a temporary member of their small community.

And it was always in the air. It was only natural, and he

knew he was being unreasonable to expect otherwise. *I was there. When he fell.*

Galbraith, the first lieutenant, understood, and confined his questions to the subject of Avery's visit to the Dey's stronghold, and if there was any real risk that the attacks on shipping and the seizure of Christians would spark off a bigger confrontation. The war with France would soon be over; it probably already was. Galbraith would be thinking of his own future, thankful that he was at least in a stronger position than many, in a new and powerful frigate, with a captain whose name was known because of his famous uncle as well as his own past successes.

Massie, the second lieutenant, remained scornful, if not openly critical of Bethune's change of direction.

'When Boney surrenders this time, their lordships will cut the fleet to the bare bones! We'll have less chance than ever to topple these would-be tyrants!' To recover from such a costly war every nation, former friends and enemies alike, would be seeking fresh trade routes, and would still need the ships and men to protect them.

He saw Noel Tregillis, the purser, poring over one of his ledgers. He rarely stopped work even in here.

Captain Bosanquet of the Royal Marines was asleep in his chair, an empty goblet still clasped in his fingers, and his second-in-command Lieutenant Luxmore had gone to share a drink with his sergeant.

The portly surgeon, O'Beirne, had made his excuses and had gone aft to the great cabin, leaving his food untouched. The prisoner, Lovatt, was unwell; the wound was not healing to O'Beirne's satisfaction.

He had said sharply, 'He should have been put ashore in Malta. All this is quite unnecessary.' The severity of the comment was uncharacteristic of this generally quiet, affable man, who Avery knew took his work very seriously.

Even O'Beirne had touched on the subject, on their first night at sea. He had known Lefroy, *Frobisher*'s bald surgeon. It was to be expected: the fraternity of fleet surgeons was even more close-knit than the family of sea officers.

But once more it had all come back. The surgeon rising from his knees, from the bloodstained deck where Allday had held his admiral with such terrible anguish, and saying, 'He's gone, I'm afraid.' In so few words.

Through a skylight he heard someone laugh. It was young Bellairs, sharing the afternoon watch with Lieutenant Wynter. What must it be like to be seventeen again, with the examination for lieutenant anticipated with every despatch satchel? A boy to a man, midshipman to officer, and Bellairs would deserve it. Avery thought of Adam, and how he had changed, confidence and maturing tempering him like the old sword he now wore. He smiled. A man of war. Perhaps . . .

And me? A passed-over luff with memories but no prospects.

He thought of Sillitoe, his energy, his manipulations, and of the last time they had met and parted. He had never believed that he could have felt something like pity for him.

Feet scraped outside the screen door, and Galbraith looked up from an old and much handled newssheet.

'What is it, Parker? D' you want me?'

The boatswain's mate nodded towards Avery and said, 'The cap'n's compliments, zur, an' 'e'd like you to step aft, directly.'

Galbraith stood up. 'The prisoner?'

The boatswain's mate gazed curiously around the wardroom. Just another part of the same ship. But so different.

He said, 'Dyin', I thinks, zur.'

The purser glanced up from his ledger, his face trained to give nothing away. *One less mouth to feed.*

Galbraith reached out and took the empty goblet from Bosanquet's limp hand. He said, 'If you need me . . .'

Avery picked up his hat. 'Thank you. I know.'

He walked into the deeper shadows of the poop and saw the Royal Marine sentry standing outside the screen door of the great cabin. The seat of command, which he himself would never know. Also the loneliest place in any King's ship.

The sentry straightened his back and tapped his musket smartly on the deck.

'Flag lieutenant, *sir*!'

Avery glanced at him. A homely, unknown face.

'Not any more, I'm afraid.'

157

The marine's eyes did not even flicker beneath his leather hat.

'You always will be to us, sir!'

Afterwards, he thought it was like a hand reaching out to him.

So let's be about it.

Adam Bolitho put a finger to his lips as Avery began to speak.

He said quietly, 'Come aft,' and led the way to the sloping stern windows. With the sun directly overhead, the panorama of blue water and cloudless sky was like some vast painting.

'Thank you for coming so quickly.' He turned his head as he heard Lovatt's rambling voice again. More like a conversation than one man. Questions and answers, and, just once, a tired laugh. And coughing. 'He's dying. O'Beirne's done all he can. I've been with him, too.'

Avery watched the dark profile, the strain around the eyes and mouth. He could feel the energy too, refusing to submit. When he had entered the cabin, his mind still clinging to the sentry's words, he had taken in the coat tossed carelessly on to a chair, one of Cristie's charts weighed down on a table by the bench seat, some brass dividers, the master's notebook. An untouched cup of coffee and an empty glass beside it. The captain was driving himself again; perhaps in truth he did resent the change of orders. Avery knew well enough that there were few bonds as strong as the one he had enjoyed with Richard Bolitho anywhere in the navy. Rank and responsibility did not allow it.

Or did he blame himself in some way? What captain would tolerate a prisoner, even a wounded one, in his own quarters?

Adam said, 'He's delirious for much of the time. Young Napier's in there with the surgeon – he's a good lad.' He added with some bitterness, 'Lovatt believes he's his son!'

Avery had seen Lovatt's son on the way here, waiting with one of the midshipmen as escort. He could guess the rest.

When Adam turned, he was calm again.

'I asked you to come here because I think you can help me.'

Why had he sent for him, and not the first lieutenant?

Adam said, 'In your original report to Sir Graham Bethune, you made mention of a Captain Martinez, whom you described as adviser to Mehmet Pasha, the governor and commander-in-chief in Algiers. Spanish . . .'

He broke off as Lovatt shouted, 'Helm *a-lee*, man! Are you blind, damn you!' It was followed by a bout of coughing, and Avery heard O'Beirne's resonant voice for the first time.

Adam continued, 'A renegade, you said?'

Avery forced himself to think, aware of the controlled urgency in the captain's tone.

'Yes, sir. He changed sides several times, but is useful to the Dey. He has or had connections in Spain when we met him. But the Dey is a hard man to serve, and Martinez will be very aware of it.'

Adam said, 'Lovatt spoke of him this morning. He said that the powder and shot, and other supplies not listed, were provided by Spanish sources, the whole of *Tetrarch*'s cargo to be exact.'

Avery tried to shut his ears to the pitiful muttering and retching from the sleeping compartment. This was important, it had to be, and yet it made no sense.

Adam said, 'He also told me that a second supply ship was to follow *Tetrarch*.' He gestured impatiently to the chart. 'Tomorrow we shall be north of Bona. The hornets' nest, eh?' He almost smiled. 'You will doubtless remember it well?'

Avery was silent for a moment, seeing it in his mind, as he had done in the past.

'It would make sense, sir. Our patrols, such as they are, would be less likely to sight them, and even then . . .'

Adam touched his sleeve. 'And *even then*, supporting ships would be required, and the admiral would have to be informed, and consulted – it is an old and familiar story!'

So he was bitter about Bethune's change of heart. Avery said, 'News travels fast in these waters, sir. *Tetrarch*'s capture, and your cutting out of *La Fortune*, will put an edge on things.'

The louvred door opened slightly, and O'Beirne peered into the cabin.

'If you still wish it, sir, I think this might be the time.'

159

Adam acknowledged it. He meant, *the only time*.

'So be it.' He looked briefly at his coat, hesitated and then slipped his arms into the sleeves. Then, to Avery, he said softly, 'Captain to captain, remember?'

To Avery the scene was nightmarish. Lovatt was propped up in the surgeon's makeshift trestle, one hand gripping it as if it was moving, his arm around the waist of the boy called Napier. O'Beirne was wedged into a corner, fingers interlaced on his knees, as if he had to force them to stay still.

'Aha, Captain! No urgent matters to keep you occupied?'

Lovatt's voice was stronger again, but that was all. His face seemed sunken, and his hazel eyes very bright, like somebody else looking out from a feverish mask.

Avery saw his hand tighten around the boy's body, and noticed that Napier had removed the noisy shoes, and his feet were bare on the checkered deck covering.

'Young Paul here is a comfort!' He contained another cough, and Napier dabbed his forehead with a damp cloth, gently and without hesitation, as if he had been trained for it.

But he was nothing like Lovatt's son in appearance, being taller and about four years older. Was Lovatt really deceived? Or perhaps it was a need, a desperate need.

Adam rested his hands on the trestle. 'You spoke earlier of the other supply ship, Captain Lovatt?'

Lovatt twisted his head from side to side, as if he could hear something. Or someone.

'Mercenaries! War makes us all hunger for something!' He was quiet again as the cloth moved gently over his brow. 'I could not offer my men a reason for dying, you see? It was a gesture. A final conceit!'

He seemed to see Avery for the first time.

'*Who is this?* A spy? A witness?'

O'Beirne moved as if to restrain him but Adam shook his head.

'This is George Avery. He is a friend.'

'Good.' Lovatt closed his eyes and O'Beirne gestured quickly to another basin. It contained a folded dressing, soaked in blood.

Avery watched a thin tendril drip from Lovatt's mouth, like red silk against his ashen skin. The boy dabbed it away,

160

frowning with concentration as Avery had seen him do when he had poured the captain's wine.

'Thanks, Paul. I – I'm so *sorry* . . .'

Avery had seen many men suffer, and had endured great pain himself. And yet still he thought, with immense bitterness, why did death have to be so ugly, so without dignity?

Pain, suffering, humiliation. A man who had once hoped and loved, and lost.

'Where lies the land, Captain?' Stronger again.

Adam said quietly, 'We are nor'-east of Bona. Ship's head, west-by-south.'

The eyes found and settled on his face. 'You *will* see to his safety, Captain?'

'I will do what I can.' He hesitated. *Where was the point?* 'You have my word on it, Captain Lovatt.'

Lovatt let his head fall back and stared at the white deckhead. Adam saw the boy Napier show fear for the first time, and guessed that he thought Lovatt had died.

He must not leave it now. Could not.

'There were two other frigates in harbour.' He repeated the question, and saw the hazel eyes focus again.

'Two. Did I tell you that?' He looked at Napier and tried to smile. 'So like your mother, you know? *So . . . like . . . her.*'

Adam leaned over the trestle, hating it, the despair, the pain, the surrender. The very stench of death.

He asked sharply, *'Will they sail?'*

He could feel O'Beirne's disapproval, his unspoken objections. Avery was very still, a witness; it was impossible to guess what he was thinking.

Something thudded on the deck overhead, and there were sounds of tackle being hauled through the blocks. Normal, everyday shipboard noises. And there were men up there too. *Who depend on me.*

I must not care what others think.

He persisted, *'Will they sail?'*

'Yes.' Lovatt seemed to nod. 'So run while you can, Captain.' His voice was failing, but he tried once more. *'But promise me . . .'* He gave one small cry and more blood choked the words in his throat. This time it did not stop.

O'Beirne dragged the dead man's arm from Napier's waist

161

and pushed him away, knowing that any show of sentiment would make a lasting impression.

Adam laid his hand on the boy's shoulder.

'That was well done. I am proud of you.'

Napier was still staring at Lovatt's contorted, bloodied face. Although he seemed quite calm, his body was shaking uncontrollably.

Adam said, 'Send for the first lieutenant.'

He kept his hand on Napier's shoulder. *For his sake or for mine?*

O'Beirne said, 'I shall have my people clean up in here, sir.' He studied the captain, as if he was discovering something he had previously missed. 'He should be buried soon, I think.'

'Tell the sailmaker. Did he have any possessions?' *Did.* Already in the past. Not a man any more. A thing.

As if reading his thoughts, O'Beirne said bluntly, 'It were better he had been killed outright!'

Galbraith was already in the great cabin, grim-faced, reassuring.

Adam said, 'We shall bury him at dusk.'

Avery listened intently, afraid something had eluded him. Some seamen were here now, accustomed to death, and to concealing their feelings in its presence.

Galbraith said, 'He had nothing but the sword, sir.'

Adam looked at him, his eyes distant. *But promise me . . .* What had he been going to say? He turned and saw the dead man's son standing just inside the door, his eyes wide and unblinking. He stared at the trestle bed, and may have seen Lovatt's face before one of the seamen covered it with a piece of canvas. The same boy who had refused to come to his father's side when he was dying, even at the last . . . His anger faded as quickly as it had flared. The boy was quite alone. *As I once was. As I am now.* He had nothing left.

He turned away, aware that Avery was watching him. There was so much to do. Lovatt had called it a final conceit. Was that all it meant?

The boy said, 'I would like the sword, *capitaine*.' His voice was very controlled, and clear, so that even his mother's French inflection was noticeable.

162

Adam said to Napier, 'Take him forrard and report to my cox'n. He will tell you what to do.'

Then, to the boy, he said, 'We will speak of the sword later.'

He walked to the stern windows and stared at the sky, feeling the ship around him. *Second to none.*

Galbraith was back. 'Orders, sir?' Once again, the lifeline. To normality. To their world.

'Sail drill, Mr Galbraith. See if the topmen can improve their timing.'

Galbraith smiled.

'And tomorrow I thought we might exercise the eighteen-pounders, sir.'

Adam looked back at the sleeping compartment. It was bare but for his own cot, which he had been unable to use. There was only Lovatt's sword leaning against the hanging wardrobe. Final.

He recalled Galbraith's remark.

'I think not, Leigh.' He saw Avery clench his fist. So he already knew. 'I fear that tomorrow it will be in earnest.'

11

The Last Farewell

Galbraith stifled a yawn and walked up to the weather side of the quarterdeck. Another morning watch, when a ship came alive again and found her personality. A time for every competent first lieutenant to delegate work, and to discover any flaws in the pattern of things before his captain drew his attention to them.

He felt a growing warmth on his cheek, and the ship sway to a sudden gust of wind. He saw the helmsmen glance from the flapping driver to the masthead pendant, licking out now across the larboard bow, easing the spokes with care to allow for it.

It would be hot today, whatever the wind decided. The decks had been washed down at first light, and were now almost dry, and some of the boatswain's crew were filling the boats with water to prevent the seams opening when the sun rose to its zenith. His eye moved on. Hammocks neatly stowed, lines flaked down ready for instant use, without the danger of tangling and causing an infuriating delay.

A brief glance aloft told him that more men were out on the yards, searching for breaks and frayed ends, another daily task.

He saw the cabin servant, Napier, making his way aft, a covered dish balanced in one hand, and recalled the burial, Lovatt's body sliding over the side after the captain had spoken a few words. A seaman, one of Lovatt's, tugged off his tarred hat: respect or guilt, it was hard to tell. Napier had been there also, standing in the dying light beside Lovatt's son. As the body had been tipped on a grating Napier had put his arm around the other boy's shoulder.

Galbraith saw another gust crossing the heaving water, ruffling it like a cat's fur. The large ensign was standing out from the peak, and beyond the naked figurehead the hazy horizon tilted to a steeper angle. *In for a blow* . . . He smiled. As the master had predicted. The wind had shifted, veered overnight, north-easterly across the starboard quarter.

He walked to the opposite side again and looked at the compass, the helmsman's eyes noting every move. Due west. Gibraltar in three days, less if the wind increased. He watched a seaman on the gundeck splicing a rope's end, his face stiff with concentration. Another, who had been applying grease to a gun truck, reached out and took it from him. The strong, tarred fingers moved like marlin spikes, there was a quick exchange of grins, and the job was done. One of the prisoners, helping a new hand still mystified by the intricacies of splicing and rope work. *If only they were not so undermanned.* He paced impatiently up the tilting deck. There was still half the morning watch to run, and a hundred things he needed to supervise.

The lookouts had sighted a few distant sails, doubtless fishermen. It was as well they were not hostile. What would happen if they could get no more men at Gibraltar? He looked towards the cabin skylight, imagining Captain Adam Bolitho down there, alone with his thoughts. No matter what orders the vice-admiral had given him, or any other flag officer for that matter, he had nothing with which to rebuke himself. So short a time in commission, and together they had welded a mixed collection of hands into one company, had cut out a frigate and had taken a supply ship. It could have gone against them if *Tetrarch* had fought to the finish; they might both have been destroyed. And yet, despite all this, Galbraith still found his captain impossible to know. Sometimes almost bursting with spirit and enthusiasm, and then suddenly remote, as if he were afraid to draw too close to any one person. He thought of Lovatt, and the captain's determination to extract all available intelligence, even though the man was dying. What *was* Lovatt after all? A traitor, most would say; an idealist at best. Yet there had been compassion in the captain's voice when he had buried that unhappy man.

He heard a step on the companion ladder and saw Lieutenant Avery staring at the sea and the sky.

'No breakfast, then?'

Avery grimaced and joined him by the compass. 'Too much wine last night. It was stupid of me.' He peered aft. 'The captain about yet?'

Galbraith studied him. Avery sounded depressed, and he guessed it had nothing to do with the wine.

'Once or twice. Sometimes I think he never sleeps.' Then, 'Walk with me. Blow away the cobwebs, eh?'

They fell into step together. They were both tall men, and like most sea officers who cared to take regular exercise they were able to walk without difficulty among watchkeepers and working parties alike, their feet avoiding ringbolts and gun tackles without conscious effort, when any one of those obstacles would have sent a landsman sprawling.

Galbraith said, 'You've known Captain Bolitho for a long time, I gather.'

Avery glanced covertly at him. '*Of* him. We have not met very often.'

Galbraith paused as a halliard snaked past his thigh. 'I should think he'd be a hellish fine target for women, but he's not married.'

Avery thought of the girl who had killed herself. He sensed that Galbraith was not merely seeking gossip to pass it on elsewhere. He wanted to know his captain, perhaps to understand him. *But not from me.*

Galbraith continued to walk, aware of Avery's unwillingness to discuss it, and changed the subject.

'When all this is over, what do you intend for yourself?'

Avery winced at the pain in his head. 'On the beach. There will be too many officers in better positions than mine for me to compete any more.' *Like you.*

Galbraith said, 'You have a very famous uncle, I hear. If I were in your shoes –'

Avery halted abruptly and faced him. 'I hope you never are, my friend!' He thought of the locket the admiral had been wearing when he had been shot down, which he had given to Adam. What would become of Catherine?

Midshipman Fielding said, 'The captain's on his way, sir.' He had been trying very hard not to look as if he had been eavesdropping.

Galbraith touched Avery's arm. 'I did not mean to pry, George. but I need to understand this man. For all our sakes.'

Avery smiled, for the first time. 'One day, when he is down there in his cabin, the *man* without the bright epaulettes, ask him. Just ask him. His uncle taught me that, and so much more.'

Adam Bolitho walked from the companion way and nodded to the master's mate of the watch.

'A promising start to the day, Mr Woodthorpe.' He looked up at the braced yards, the canvas full-bellied now, cracking occasionally in the breeze. Seeing the ship as Galbraith had this morning, but viewing it so differently.

'We shall set the maincourse directly, Mr Galbraith.' He shaded his eyes to look at the compass as it flashed in reflected sunlight. 'Then bring her up a point. She can take it. Steer west-by-north.' He gestured at the midshipman. 'And, Mr Fielding, after you have brushed the crumbs off your coat, you will note the change in the log and inform Mr Cristie!'

One of the helmsmen glanced at his mate and grinned. So little, Adam thought, and yet it was infectious. He walked to the rail and pressed his hands on it. Hot, bone-dry already. He looked at the boats on their tier, the trapped water slopping over the bottom boards as *Unrivalled* dipped her stem into a trough, and spray pitched over the bowsprit.

A wind. Please God, a wind.

He saw some seamen splicing, and one he did not recognise showing another how to twist and fashion the strands into shape. The man must have sensed it and stared up at the quarterdeck. Where might his loyalty lie? Perhaps like Jago, it was *just another officer*.

He said suddenly, 'You have a key to the strongbox, Mr Galbraith?' He turned his back to watch a solitary bird, motionless above the mizzen truck. 'Use it as you will. Any letters, documents and the like.'

Galbraith seemed uncertain, and shook his head.

'None, sir.'

Adam saw the master's head and shoulders hesitate in the companion hatch. Cristie's eyes were already on the masthead pendant.

Adam joined Avery by the nettings, sensing his isolation from the others. Knowing the reason for it.

'Think, George, it will be full summer when you walk ashore in England.'

Avery did not respond. He had thought of little else since his change of orders. He gazed at the working parties on deck, the sure-footed topmen moving like monkeys in the shrouds; even the greasy smell from the galley funnel was like a part of himself.

And the letters he had written for Allday, and the replies he had read from his wife. *Belonging.*

He tried to think of London, of the Admiralty, where there would be polite interest or indifference to what he had to say. And he did not care. That was almost the worst part.

Had he really lain in bed in that gracious house, with the tantalising Susanna Mildmay? Beautiful Susanna . . . beautiful and faithless.

Adam said, 'Is there something I can do?'

Avery studied him, memories stirring and fading like ghosts. 'When I reach England . . .'

They stared up as the lookout's voice turned every head.

'Deck there! Sail, fine on the starboard bow!'

Galbraith shouted, 'Mr Bellairs, aloft with you! Take your glass, man!'

Avery smiled, and reached out as if to take Adam's hand. 'I shall think of you.' The rest was lost in the sudden rush of feet and another cry from the masthead.

He said softly, 'No matter.'

The moment was past.

Midshipman Bellairs' voice carried easily above the sounds of sea and flapping canvas.

'Deck there! Square-rigger, sir!'

Adam folded his arms and looked along the length of his command. The forenoon watch had not been piped, but the deck and gangways seemed to be crowded with men. And yet there was hardly a sound. Some stared ahead to the darker line of the horizon, others inboard at the ship, at one another.

Cristie muttered, 'No fisherman this time, then.'

Adam waited, feeling the uncertainty. The doubt.

He said, 'Frigate.'

Galbraith was peering up at the mainmast crosstrees, as if willing Bellairs to confirm or deny it.

'Beat to quarters, sir?' Even his voice seemed hushed.

'Not yet.' Adam held out his hand, remembering Avery's despair. 'There'll be another out there somewhere.' He watched the low banks of cloud. 'They will have had plenty of time to prepare. We've had the sun behind us since first light – a blind man could see us.'

Galbraith moved closer, excluding all the others.

'We still have time, too, sir.'

Adam looked at him.

'To run?'

'We shall be hard put to stand and fight.'

Adam touched his arm, and felt it tense as if he had been expecting a blow.

'That was well said, Leigh. I respect you for it.'

He could see the two ships in his mind, as if they were within range instead of miles distant, visible only to the masthead lookout and Bellairs. He would learn something today. If he lived through it.

'How many extra hands do we have aboard?'

'Fifty-five, and two injured. I'll clap the whole lot in irons if you think –'

What had Lovatt called it? *A gesture. But too late.*

He said suddenly, 'Clear lower deck, and have all hands lay aft.' He attempted to smile, but his mouth refused. 'Though it would seem they are already here!'

He walked to the compass once more, hearing the sound of his shoes on the deck, like that day at his court martial at Portsmouth. So impossibly long ago. He heard the trill of calls below decks, and a few idlers running to join the mass of figures already on deck.

Galbraith said, 'Lower deck cleared, sir.'

Adam touched the compass box, remembering the brief moments of clarity before Lovatt had died.

I could not offer them a reason for dying.

He could have been speaking at this very moment.

Adam turned and strode to the quarterdeck rail and looked out across the sea of upturned faces. The others he had already seen, the afterguard, and the swarthy Lieutenant Massie who was responsible for the gunnery of this ship. And young Wynter, whose father was a member of Parliament. And the two scarlet-coated marine officers, standing a little apart from the others; the midshipmen and the master's mates; men and faces which had become so familiar within six months.

'You will know by now that two ships are standing to the west'rd of us.'

There were some quick, uncertain glances, and he sensed the sudden understanding as Bellairs' clear voice called, 'Second ship, starboard bow! Square-rigged, sir!'

'They are not there by accident. It is their intention to engage, seize, or destroy *Unrivalled*.'

He saw some of them looking at the black eighteen-pounders, perhaps already considering the hazards – the older men would call it folly – of engaging two frigates at once. Heeling to the wind, it would require brute force to haul the guns back to their ports on the weather side once they had been fired.

'The war with Napoleon has likely been over for some time. We shall be told eventually. *I hope.*'

He saw old Stranace, the gunner, offer a dour grin. It was little enough, but it was all he had.

Adam pointed at the empty sea.

'These ships will respect no treaty, no pieces of paper applauded by old men in government. They are already outlaws!' He let his arm drop and recalled Lovatt's words. *We are all mercenaries in war.*

He laid both hands on the rail and said deliberately, 'I need trained men today.' He saw some of *Unrivalled*'s people looking at those who had been thrust amongst them. None had forgotten the days, so recently passed, when men had been seized and dragged aboard King's ships by the hated press gangs with no less severity.

'I can promise you nothing, but I can offer the chance of a new beginning. If we lose the day, our fate at the hands of the enemy will be prolonged and terrible. If we win, there is the possibility of freedom.' He thought of Avery, and said, 'Of England. You have my word upon it.' What he had said to Lovatt . . .

Galbraith pointed. 'That man! Speak up!'

It was a seaman who would not have seemed out of place in any ship, any port.

'An' if we refuse, Cap'n? If we stands by our rights?'

There was a growl of agreement.

'Rights?' Adam patted a quarterdeck nine-pounder by his knee. 'Speak to me of those rights when these are silent, eh?'

He nodded to Galbraith. He had made a mistake; the gesture had misfired. Galbraith joined him by the rail.

'Show of hands!'

The silence was physical. Crushing. Far worse than if they had jeered at his inability to reach them.

Then he heard Partridge, the massive boatswain, bawling out as if it were a part of normal routine.

'Right, then, you lot over 'ere. Lively, lads! Creagh, take their names, if you still knows 'ow to write!'

And somebody laughed. *Laughed.*

Adam turned towards them again. The crowd was breaking into groups, pushed and sorted into small parties, the blues and whites of warrant officers moving amongst them, taking control. He tried to remember; how many had Galbraith mentioned? Over fifty: not an army, but it might make the difference. Men who had been cheated, lied to and ill-treated for most of their lives, when loyalty to one another carried far more weight than flag or country, they had decided.

Galbraith was beside him again.

'I would never have believed it, sir.' He hesitated. 'Would you tell me? How did you do it?'

Adam saw the one man who had challenged him. Their eyes met across the bustling figures and frantic petty officers, and then the man gave a shrug. Resignation, or was it trust after all?

He murmured, 'Perhaps I offered them a reason for living.'

He felt spray dash across his cheek. The wind was still rising. The *chance*.

But all he heard was Lovatt's mocking laugh.

He turned on his heel and said, 'Now you may beat to quarters, and clear for action, Mr Galbraith.' He saw the boy Napier watching from beside the capstan, and called, 'Fetch my coat, will you. My sword, too.' But Jago was already there, the old sword held casually, almost indifferently.

'Here, sir.'

Adam held out his arms and felt him clip the sword into place. Was this, too, a final conceit?

Jago stood back. 'Scum they may be, sir, but fight they will. Like me, they don't know nothing else!'

At that moment the drums began their staccato roll to beat to quarters.

Adam stared at the sea until his eyes misted over. He felt no fear. If anything, it was pride.

Adam Bolitho brushed a lock of loose hair from his eyes and used his sleeve as a shield against the glare from a lively sea, broken now by the strengthening wind.

One bell chimed from forward, and he saw Midshipman Fielding apparently jerk out of his thoughts and turn the half-hour glass before someone rebuked him.

So little time since the first hint of danger; two hours, or less. It was hard to remember, but it would all be noted in the log. He licked his dry lips. For posterity.

Even the ship had changed in that time. Cleared for action, *Unrivalled* was stripped, like the gun crews who had discarded their shirts but retained their neckerchiefs to tie over their ears against the roar of battle, of her main and mizzen courses and staysails, so that the deck felt open and vulnerable. Under topsails and topgallants, with the big forecourse loosely brailed, she was making a fair speed through the water, spray constantly breaking over the beakhead and forecastle. Nets had been rigged to protect the gun deck from falling wreckage. Adam faced each possibility like a challenge, the margin between winning and losing. And lastly the boats. He did not move from his place on the weather side of the quarterdeck but could see the boat-tier, each hull already bailed and steaming in the hot sunshine.

It was always a bad moment when the boats were lowered and cast adrift on a sea-anchor, to await collection by the victors. Even seasoned sailors never accepted or became accustomed to it. The boats were their last hope of survival. Adam had seen some of them watching Partridge's crew rigging the tackles in readiness for hoisting and then swinging each boat outboard. Abandoned . . .

But Adam had seen hideous casualties caused by splinters ripped from tiered boats, like flying razors when they cut into human flesh. It was the last task.

He took a telescope from its rack and trained it across the nettings. It was no longer a suspicion, or a flaw on the dawn horizon, but brutal reality. The enemy.

Two ships. Frigates, their hazy silhouettes overlapping as if joined, a common illusion. They were probably some five miles away; he could see each sail, braced so hard round that they were almost fore-and-aft. Another trick perhaps, but each captain was hard put to hold his ship up into the wind, as close-hauled as any professional officer could manage.

Who were they? What did they hope for today, apart from victory? Perhaps it was better not to know your enemy, to see his face. You might recognise yourself in him.

He gazed across the deck. They were all present, the Royal Marines at the barrier of packed hammocks, extra hands on the big double-wheel, Lieutenant Wynter with the afterguard, his midshipman, Homey, close by. Cristie and his senior master's mate, and Avery, arms folded, hat tilted over his eyes, observing. As he must have done so many times with . . .

Adam swung away. 'Very well, Mr Galbraith, cast off the boats!'

He saw faces turn away from the guns to watch. This was the worst moment. Especially for newcomers.

Galbraith returned to the quarterdeck and waited for the gap left in the nets to be sealed. He did not look astern at the drifting cluster of boats.

'If I might make a suggestion, sir.'

Adam said, 'I know. My coat, it troubles you.'

'You have me all aback, sir. But any marksman will be looking for the chance to mark down the captain. You know that well enough!'

Adam smiled, touched by the concern. Genuine, like the man.

'The enemy will know *Unrivalled* has a captain, Leigh. I want our people to know it, too!'

He raised the glass again. The frigate astern of her consort had hoisted a signal of some kind. Two flags, nothing more. A private signal, perhaps? It could also be a ruse, to make

173

him believe it was the senior ship. He recalled Francis Inch, his first lieutenant in *Hyperion*, telling the midshipmen that in ship-to-ship actions beyond the control of the ponderous line of battle a good captain often survived by trickery as much as agility.

He considered it. Two frigates, neither as powerful as *Unrivalled*, but, used aggressively and with determination, they were formidable.

He said, almost to himself, 'They will try to divide our strength. Tell Mr Massie to point each gun himself, no matter which side we engage first. The opening shots will decide.' He paused, and repeated, '*Must* decide.'

He walked from one side of the deck to the other, hearing Galbraith calling to Massie. If *Unrivalled* altered course away from those ships, they would gain the advantage from the wind. He imagined the two frigates, like counters on an admiral's chart. From line ahead to line abeam, they would have no choice, nor would they want one.

He heard the spray pattering over the lee side, and thought, *no, Captain Lovatt, not running away.*

When Galbraith returned he found his captain by the compass, his shirt and coat opened to the hot wind. There was no sign of the strain he had glimpsed earlier. He found himself thinking of the woman again, the one Avery so pointedly had not discussed. What had happened, he wondered. What would she feel if she could see him now on this bright, deadly forenoon?

Adam said, 'Pass the word to load. Single-shotted to starboard, double-shotted to larboard, but do not run out. At the turn of the glass, we shall alter course and steer south-west.' He almost smiled. 'What the enemy intended, I believe. A lively chase with the wind under their coattails without too much risk to themselves, and if all else fails they will hope to run us ashore on the African coast. What say you?'

Galbraith stared up at the rippling masthead pendant. 'It would make sense, sir.' He sounded doubtful, surprised.

Adam said, 'We will luff at the right moment and rake the nearest one. Tell Massie, each ball must make its mark.'

'I did tell him, sir.'

But Adam was not listening; he was seeing it. 'We must get

174

to grips, it's our only way out. So get all spare hands off the upper deck. We are short-handed, remember? And they will know it!'

Galbraith saw him turn away and gesture urgently to the cabin servant, Napier.

'You! Over here!'

Napier hurried across, past grim-faced seamen and marines, a cutlass thrust through his belt, his shoes clicking on the sun-dried planking and bringing some unexpected grins from the crew of a nine-pounder. One called, 'Look, boyos! We've nowt to fear now! We're all in good hands!'

Adam said gently, 'Your place is below. You know what to do.'

Napier faced him anxiously, with something like desperation. 'My place is here, sir, with you.'

There was no laughter now, and Cristie looked away, perhaps remembering somebody.

Adam said, 'Do as I ask. I shall know where you are. I mean it.'

Jago heard it, too, feeling the handshake again, the strange sense of sharing what he could not contain or understand.

Galbraith watched the boy return to the companion way, head high, the cutlass almost dragging along the deck.

Adam raised the glass once more, and remembered that Midshipman Bellairs was still at the masthead.

'Carry on, Mr Galbraith. Bring her about. Let's see her fly today!' His hand was raised and Galbraith waited, remembering every phase, and each mood, like pictures in a child's most treasured book.

And saw his captain suddenly give a broad grin, teeth very white against his tanned skin.

'And be of good heart, my friend. We shall win this day!'

Cristie's voice was harsh, his Tyneside accent even more pronounced as he shouted, 'Steady as she goes, sir! Sou'-west-by-south!'

Another bang echoed across the choppy water, the second gun to be fired. Adam clenched his knuckles against his thighs, counting seconds and then feeling the ball smash

175

into *Unrivalled*'s lower hull. He did not need the glass; he had seen the smoke from the nearest pursuer before it was shredded in the wind. The second shot, and both had come from the frigate on *Unrivalled*'s starboard quarter. Not because the other, on almost exactly the opposite quarter, could not bear but, he suspected, because the ship which had fired was the senior, and probably mounted heavier bow-chasers.

The ship which had made that brief signal. No trick, then; she was the main danger. *Unrivalled*'s stern was vulnerable to any shot, no matter how badly aimed. The rudder, the steering tackles . . . He shut his mind to it.

'*Stand by to come about, Mr Galbraith!*' He strode to the rail again, and shaded his eyes. Two shots; it was enough. He dared not risk it any further. Disabled, *Unrivalled* would be destroyed piecemeal.

As he turned he saw the staring eyes of those at the gun tackles along the starboard side, muzzles pointing at the empty sea. The breechings were cast off, the guns were loaded, and men with sponges, worms and rammers were already poised for the next order, their bodies shining with sweat, as if they had been drenched by a tropical rain.

'*Stand by on the quarterdeck!*'

Massie would be ready with his gun captains. All those drills . . . it was now or not at all.

'*Put the helm down!*'

Feet skidded on wet gratings as the three helmsmen hauled over the spokes. With her topsails filled to the wind *Unrivalled* began to respond immediately, her head swinging even as more men freed the headsail sheets, spilling out the wind, to allow the bows to thrust unimpeded into and across the eye. Sails flapped and banged in confusion, and as the deck tilted hard over the nearest enemy ship appeared to be charging towards the concealed broadside.

It must have taken the other captain completely by surprise. From a steady, unhampered chase to this: *Unrivalled* pivoting round, revealing her full broadside, and none of his own guns yet able to bear.

'Open the ports! *Run out!*'

All order had gone. Men yelled and cursed with each heave

on the tackles until every port was filled, and there was no longer an empty sea for a target.

Massie strode past the empty boat-tier. *'Fire!'* A slap on a man's tense shoulder. 'As you bear, *fire!'*

As each trigger line was jerked an eighteen-pounder thundered inboard to be seized and sponged out, charge and ball tamped home.

Adam shouted, 'Hold her now! Steer north-west!'

There were more yells, and he imagined that he heard the splintering crack of a falling spar, although it was unlikely above the din of canvas and straining rigging, and the last echoes of a full broadside.

The other frigate was falling downwind, her bowsprit and jib boom shot away, the tangle of severed cordage and wildly flapping sails dragging her round.

Adam cupped his hands. 'On the uproll! *Fire!'*

It was a ragged broadside, some of the guns had not yet run out, but he saw the iron smash home, and bulwarks and planking, broken rigging and men being flung like flotsam in a high wind.

It might have been us.

Galbraith was shouting, 'The other one's coming for us, sir!'

The second frigate seemed so near, towering above the larboard quarter, stark in the hard sunlight. He could even see the patches on her forecourse, and the pointing sword of a once-proud figurehead.

He winced as more iron smashed into the hull, feeling the deck lurch beneath his feet, and hearing the heavy crash of a ball ripping into the poop. The enemy's jib boom was already overreaching the larboard quarter.

He dashed the smoke from his eyes and saw a man fall on the opposite side, his scream lost in the report of a solitary gun.

He waved to Cristie. *'Now!'*

The wheel was moving again, but one of the helmsmen was sprawled in blood. *Unrivalled* turned only a point, so that it appeared as if the other ship must ride up and over her poop. The jib boom was above the nettings now, men were firing, and through the swirling smoke Adam saw vague figures swarming out on the other frigate's beakhead and bowsprit, cutlasses glinting dully in the haze of gunfire.

Going to board us. It was like another voice.

'Clear lower deck, Mr Galbraith!' Suppose it failed? He thrust the thought away and dragged out his sword, conscious of Avery beside him, and Jago striding just ahead, a short-bladed weapon in his fist.

Adam raised the sword. 'To me, *Unrivalled*!'

She was a well-armed ship. He could remember the admiration, the envy. Apart from her two batteries of eighteen-pounders, she also mounted eight thirty-two pound carronades, two of which were almost directly below his feet.

It happened within seconds, and yet each moment remained separate, stamped forever in his memory.

Midshipman Homey slipping and falling to his knees, then being hit in the skull by a heavy ball even as he struggled to his feet. Flesh, blood and fragments of bone splashed across Adam's breeches. The carronades roared out together, crashing inboard on their slides and hurling their massive balls, packed with grape and jagged metal, directly into the enemy forecastle.

Avery turned and stared at him, shook his sword, shouted something. But the stare did not waver, and he fell face down, and the packed mass of boarders surged across his body and on to the other ship's deck.

It was useless to hesitate. There were too many who depended . . . But for only a second Adam halted, looking for the man who had been his uncle's friend.

Jago was dragging at his arm.

'Come *on*, sir! We've got the bastards on the run!'

A dream, a nightmare; scenes of desperate brutality, all mercy forgotten. Men falling and dying. Others dropping between the two hulls, the only escape. A face loomed out of the yelling, hacking mob: it was Campbell, the hard man, waving a flag and screaming, 'The flag! They've struck!'

Now there were different faces, and he realised that, like Avery, he had fallen and was lying on the deck. He felt for the sword, and saw Midshipman Bellairs holding it; it must have been knocked out of his hand.

And then the pain reached him, a searing agony, which

punched the breath from his lungs. He groped for his thigh, his groin; it was everywhere. A hand was gripping his wrist and he saw it was O'Beirne, and understood that he was on *Unrivalled*'s gun deck; he must have lost consciousness, and he felt something akin to panic.

He said, 'The orlop! You belong with the wounded, *not here*, man!'

O'Beirne nodded grimly, his face sliding out of focus like melting wax. Then it was Jago's turn. He had torn down the front of Adam's breeches and was holding something in the hazy sunlight. No blood. No gaping wound. It was the watch, which he always carried in the pocket above his groin. A shot had smashed it almost in two pieces.

He was losing control again. The shop in Halifax. The chiming chorus of clocks. The little mermaid . . .

Jago was saying, 'Christ, you were lucky, sir!' He wanted to lessen it, in his usual way. But the levity would not come. Then he said, *'Just hold on.'*

Men were cheering, hugging one another, the marines were rounding up prisoners . . . so much to do, the prizes to be secured, the wounded to be tended. He gasped as someone tried to lift him. And Avery. Avery . . . *I shall have to tell Catherine. A letter. And the locket.*

Somehow he was on his feet, staring up at the flag as if to reassure himself. But all he could think of was the little mermaid. Perhaps it was her way; the last farewell.

Then he fainted.

12

Aftermath

Like an unhurried but purposeful beetle, *Unrivalled*'s gig pulled steadily around and among the many vessels which lay at anchor in Gibraltar's shadow.

It was a time of pride, and of triumph, climaxing when they had entered the bay with one prize in tow and the other in the hands of a prize crew. To the men of the fleet, hardened by so many years of setbacks and pain, it had been something to share, to celebrate. Ships had manned their yards to cheer, boats from the shore had formed an unofficial procession until the anchors had splashed down, and order and discipline was resumed.

And the war was over. Finally over. That was the hardest thing to confront. Napoleon, once believed invincible, had surrendered, and had placed himself under the authority of Captain Frederick Maitland of the old *Bellerophon* in Basque Roads, to be conveyed to Plymouth.

The officer of the guard who had boarded *Unrivalled* within minutes of her dropping anchor had exclaimed, 'When you fought and took the two frigates, *we* were at peace!'

Adam had heard himself answer shortly, 'It made no difference.'

He thought of the men who had fallen in that brief, savage action. Of the letters he had written. To the parents of Midshipman Thomas Homey, who had been killed even as the second frigate had surged into their quarter. Fourteen years old. A life not even begun.

And to Catherine, a long and difficult letter. Seeing

Avery's shocked and unwavering gaze, like an unanswered question.

Midshipman Bellairs was sitting behind him, beside Jago at the tiller.

'Flagship, sir!'

Adam nodded. He had taken a calculated risk, and had won. It was pointless to consider the alternatives. *Unrivalled* might have been caught in stays, taken aback as she tried to swing through the wind. The two frigates would have used the confusion to cross her stern and rake her, each broadside ripping through the hull. A slaughterhouse.

He stared at the big two-decker which lay directly across their approach, His Britannic Majesty's Ship *Prince Rupert* of eighty guns, a rear-admiral's flag rising and drooping at her mizzen truck.

He made to touch his thigh and saw the stroke oar's eyes on him, and controlled the impulse. He had examined his body in the looking-glass in his cabin, and found a great, livid bruise, showing the force of the impact. A stray shot perhaps, fired at random as his men had hacked their way on board the enemy. Even now, four days after the engagement, the pain was almost constant, and caught him unaware, like a reminder.

The surgeon, rarely at a loss for words, had been strangely taciturn. Perhaps when he had fallen unconscious again he had said something, revealed the despair which had tormented him for so long.

O'Beirne had said only, 'You are in luck, Captain. Another inch, and I fear the ladies would have been in dire distress!'

He looked up now and saw the flagship towering above them, the gig's bowman already standing with his boathook, and prepared himself for the physical effort of boarding. Seeing his eyes on the ship's massive tumblehome, the 'stairs' up to the gilded entry port, Jago said quietly, 'Steady she goes, sir!'

Adam glanced at him, remembering his face when he had torn open his breeches to deal with the wound. Poor Homey's blood and brains had made it look worse than it was.

He seized the handrope, gritting his teeth as he took the first step.

An unknown voice sang out, 'Cap'n comin' aboard! Stand by . . . *pipe*!'

Adam climbed, step by step, each movement bringing a shaft of pain to his thigh.

The calls shrilled, and as his head rose above the sill he saw the scarlet-coated guard, the seemingly vast area of the flagship's impeccable deck.

The guard presented arms, and a duplicate of Captain Bosanquet brought down his blade with a flourish.

The flag captain strode to greet him. Adam held his breath. Pym, that was his name. The pain was receding, playing with him.

'Welcome aboard, Captain Bolitho! Your recent exploits had us all drained with envy!' He looked at him more closely. 'You were wounded, I hear?'

Adam smiled. It seemed so long since he had done that. 'Damaged, sir, nothing lasting!'

They walked together into the poop's shadow, so huge after *Unrivalled*. He allowed his mind to stray. *Or* Anemone . . .

The flag captain paused. 'Rear-Admiral Marlow is still studying your report. I have had your despatches transferred to a courier – she will leave this afternoon. If there is anything else I can do to assist you while you are here, you have only to ask.' He hesitated. 'Rear-Admiral Marlow is newly appointed. He still likes to deal with things at first hand.'

It was as good as any warning. Captain to flag rank; he had seen it before. *Trust nobody*.

Rear-Admiral Elliot Marlow stood with his back to the high stern windows, hands beneath his coattails, as if he had been in the same position for some time. A sharp, intelligent face, younger than Adam had expected.

'Good to meet you at last, Bolitho. Take a chair. Some wine, I think.' He did not move or offer his hand.

Adam sat. He knew he was strained and tired, and unreasonable, but even the chair seemed carefully placed. Staged, so that Marlow's outline remained in silhouette against the reflected sunlight.

Two servants were moving soundlessly around the other side of the cabin, each careful not to look at the visitor.

Marlow said, 'Read your report. You were lucky to get the

182

better of two enemies at once, eh? Even if, the perfectionists may insist, you were at war with neither.' He smiled. 'But then, I doubt that the Dey of Algiers will wish to associate himself with people who have failed him.' He glanced at his flag captain, and added, 'As to your request respecting the son of that damned renegade, I suppose I can have no objection. It is hardly important . . .'

Pym interrupted smoothly, 'And Captain Bolitho has offered to pay all the costs for the boy's passage, sir.'

'Quite so.' He gestured at the nearest servant. 'A glass, eh?'

Adam was glad of a chance to regain his bearings.

He said, 'With regard to the prizes, sir.'

Marlow subjected his glass to a pitiless scrutiny. 'The prizes, yes. Of course, their role may also have changed in view of the French position. I have heard it said that frigate captains sometimes see prize money as the price of glory. A view I find difficult to comprehend.'

Adam realised that his glass was empty, and said bluntly, 'The Dey of Algiers had three frigates at his disposal, sir. With the re-opening of trade routes, those ships could have been a constant threat. That threat was removed, and at some cost. I think it fair enough.'

Captain Pym adroitly changed the subject.

'How long will your repair take, d' you think?'

Adam looked at him and smiled thinly.

'We did much of it after the fight.' He considered it, seeing the dangling cordage, the limping wounded, the canvas bundles going over the side. 'A week.'

Marlow waved one hand. 'Give him all the help you can . . .' He pointed at the table. 'That despatch from the Admiralty, where is it?'

Adam relaxed very slowly. The real reason for his visit. Not to congratulate or to crucify him. That was Bethune's domain. Marlow had not even mentioned his use of the prisoners to fill the gaps in *Unrivalled*'s company.

Marlow put his glass down with great care and took some papers from his flag captain.

'You are instructed to take passengers when you return to Malta. Sir Lewis Bazeley and his party, of some importance, I gather. It is all explained in the orders.'

Captain Pym said hastily, 'Because of the danger from corsairs and other renegades, a man-of-war is the only safe option.' He gave a tight smile. 'As your own recent fight against odds has proved. I am sure that Vice-Admiral Bethune would have chosen your ship, had he been consulted.'

Adam found he could return the smile. He could understand why Pym was a flag captain.

'Anything else?' Marlow stared at him. 'Now is the time to ask.'

'I have a midshipman named Bellairs, sir. He is due for examination shortly, but in the meantime I would like to rate him acting-lieutenant, and pay him accordingly. He has done extremely well during this commission.'

He had not seen Marlow all aback before, and neither, he suspected, had Pym.

'Bellairs? Has he family? Connections?'

'He is my senior midshipman, sir. That is all that concerns me.'

Marlow seemed vaguely disappointed.

'You deal with it.' He turned away, dismissing him. 'And, er – good fortune, Captain Bolitho.'

The door closed behind them.

Pym grinned widely. 'That was damned refreshing! Leave it with me!'

He was still grinning when the calls trilled again, and Adam lowered himself into the waiting gig.

'Bear off forrard! Give way all!'

Bellairs stood to watch a passing trader, ready to warn them away if they came too near.

Adam said, 'By the way, Mr Bellairs, you will be moving shortly.'

Bellairs forgot his poise in the captain's gig, and said, '*Move*, sir? But I hoped to . . .'

Adam watched Jago's face over the midshipman's shoulder. 'To the wardroom.'

It was only a small thing, after all. But it made it seem very worthwhile.

Catherine, Lady Somervell, moved slightly in her seat and tilted her wide-brimmed straw hat to shade her eyes from the sun. With the windows all but closed it was hot, and her gown was damp against her skin.

The City of London had never featured largely in her life, and yet in the past few months she had come here several times. It was always busy, always teeming. The carriage could have been open, but she was constantly aware of the need for discretion, and had noticed that the coachman never seemed to use the same route; today, as on those other visits, the vehicle was unmarked, never the one Sillitoe had been using on the day of the service at St Paul's. She had seen the cathedral this morning, dominating its surroundings as it had on that day, which she would never forget nor wanted to relinquish.

She looked at the passing scene; the carriage was moving slowly in the congestion of the road. Grey-faced offices, one of which she had visited with Sillitoe when he had kept an appointment with some shipping agent; she had been politely entertained in another room.

There were stalls here, flowers and fruit, someone elsewhere making a speech, another drawing a crowd with a performing monkey.

Now they were returning to Sillitoe's house in Chiswick. Never once had he forced his presence on her, but he was always ready to help her, to escort her, or if necessary to give his opinion on her decisions for the immediate future.

She glanced at him now, on the seat opposite, frowning slightly as he leafed through yet another sheaf of papers. His mind was ever agile, ever restless. Like their last visit to Sir Wilfred Lafargue at Lincoln's Inn. He was a lawyer of repute, but when he and Sillitoe were together they were more like conspirators than legal adviser and client.

She thought of the letter she had received from Captain James Tyacke, a concise, unemotional account of why marriage to the woman he had once loved had proved impossible. It had saddened her, but she had understood his reasons, and the sensitivity he would never reveal. A man who had been utterly withdrawn, almost shy, when he had been forced to leave the only world he understood; she was proud to call him her friend, as he had been Richard's. Perhaps for him the sea was the only solution, but it was not, and never could be, an escape.

185

She realised that Sillitoe was looking at her, as he often did, when he believed she did not know.

'I have to go to Spain.' Calmly said, as was his habit, but not the same. This was a mood she had not seen or sensed before.

'You said that it was possible.'

He smiled. 'And I asked you if you would come with me.'

'And I told you that there has been enough damage done already because of me. And you know that is true.'

She averted her eyes to look at a passing vehicle, but saw only her reflection in the dusty glass.

Sillitoe's sphere of influence encompassed both politics and trade, although he was no longer Inspector-General. The Prince Regent, who was notorious for his infidelities, had feared whatever stain a liaison between his adviser and confidante and the admiral's whore might cast on his reputation as the future monarch. She felt the old, familiar bitterness. The men in power with their mistresses and their homosexual lovers were forgiven if their affairs were kept separate from rank and authority, and were not conducted where they might offend the royal eye.

She had rarely seen Sillitoe reveal anger. A week ago, a cruel cartoon had appeared in the *Globe*. It had depicted her standing nude and looking at ships below in a harbour. The caption had been, *Who will be next?*

She had seen his anger then. There had been apologies. Someone had been dismissed. But it was there all the same. Hate, envy, malice.

Perhaps even the Prince's courtiers had had a hand in it.

She recalled Lafargue's advice on Belinda, Lady Bolitho. *Never underrate the wrath of an unloved woman.*

Sillitoe said, 'You need security, Catherine. And protection. I can offer you both. My feelings remain unchanged.' He glanced round, frowning as a gap appeared in the buildings and the river was revealed. Masts and loose, flapping sails. Arriving and departing; sailors from every corner of the world. She wondered briefly if the coachman, who seemed to know London like the back of his own hand, had been ordered to avoid ships and sailors also.

She looked at him again. His face was tense, his mind obviously exploring something which troubled him.

He said, 'You could stay at my house. You would not be molested by anything or anybody, my staff would see to that.' As he had said when someone had carved the word *whore* on the door of her Chelsea house.

He said abruptly, 'There is always danger. I see it often enough.'

'And what would people say?'

He did not answer her directly, but the hooded eyes seemed calmer.

'If you come to Spain, you may be yourself again. I go first to Vigo, where I must see some people, and then on to Madrid.' He laid the papers aside and leaned forward. 'You like Spain, you speak the language. It would be a great help to me.' He reached out and took her hand. 'I should be a very proud man.'

She gently withdrew the hand, and said, 'You are a difficult man to refuse. But I must confront whatever future remains for me.'

She heard the coachman making his usual clucking sounds to the horses, a habit she had noticed whenever they were approaching the Chiswick house. The journey had passed, and now she must do something, say something; he had done so much to help, to support her in the aftermath of Richard's death.

There was another vehicle in the drive. So he had known she would refuse; the carriage was waiting to take her to Chelsea, a lonely place now without her companion Melwyn, whom she had sent back to St Austell temporarily to help her mother with work for a forthcoming county wedding.

They would surely notice the change in the girl. She had become confident, almost worldly. *As I once was at that age.*

She was aware now of Sillitoe's expression; ever alert, he seemed suddenly apprehensive, before he regained his habitual self-assurance. She followed his eyes and felt the chill on her spine. The carriage door bore the fouled anchors of Admiralty, and there was a sea officer standing beside it, speaking with Sillitoe's secretary.

So many times. Messages, orders, letters from Richard. But always the dread.

'What is it?'

He waited for a servant to run up and open the door for her. Afterwards, she thought it had been to give himself time.

He said, 'I shall not keep you. The Admiralty still needs me, it would appear.' But his eyes spoke differently.

Marlow accompanied her into the house and guided her to the library, where she had always waited for Sillitoe.

'Is something wrong?'

The secretary murmured, 'I fear so, m' lady,' and withdrew, closing the tall doors.

She heard voices, the sound of hooves; the visitor had departed without partaking of hospitality. Sillitoe drank little, but always remembered those to whom the gesture was welcome.

He came into the library and stood looking at her without speaking, then, without turning his head, he called, 'Some cognac.'

Then he crossed the room and took her hand, gently, without emotion.

'The Admiralty has just received news on the telegraph from Portsmouth. There has been a fight between one of our frigates and two pirates.'

Without being told, she knew it was *Unrivalled*, and that there was something more.

Sillitoe said, 'Lieutenant George Avery, my nephew and Sir Richard's aide, was killed.' He remained silent for a moment, then said, 'Captain Adam Bolitho was injured, but not badly so.'

She stared past him, at the trees, the misty sky. The river. The war was over. Napoleon was a prisoner, and probably even now being conveyed to some other place of internment. And yet, although it was over, it was not yet over; the war was here, in this quiet library.

Sillitoe said, 'George Avery was your friend also.' And then, with sudden bitterness, 'I never found the time to know him.' He gazed at the window. 'I see him now, leaving to rejoin Sir Richard when I wanted him to stay with me. I do believe that he felt sorry for me.' He waved his hand, and the gesture seemed uncharacteristically loose and vague. 'All this – and his loyalty came first.'

The door opened and Guthrie placed a tray and the cognac on a table, glancing at Catherine. She shook her head, and the door closed again.

Sillitoe took the glass, and sat in one of the uncomfortable chairs.

'He was coming home, damn it. It was what we both needed. What we both *fought*!'

She looked around, feeling the silence, as if the great house were holding its breath.

Adam was safe. There would be a letter from him as soon as it was possible. In the meantime, he was at sea, in the one element he knew and trusted. Like James Tyacke.

She walked past the chair, her mind suddenly quite clear, with that familiar sensation of detachment.

She put her hand on his shoulder and waited for him to turn his head, to look at the hand, and then at her.

As she had been, defenceless.

She said softly, 'My Spanish is not so perfect, Paul.' She saw the light returning to his eyes, and did not flinch as he took both her hands and kissed them. 'Perhaps . . . we can both find ourselves again.'

He stood, and then held her fully against his body, for the first time.

He said nothing. There were no words.

Eventually there was a gentle tap on the door, and Marlow's voice. Unreal.

'Is there anything I can do, m' lord?'

She answered for him. 'Tell William to put away the carriage, please. It will not be required again today.'

It was done.

Bryan Ferguson hurried into the kitchen and all but slammed the door behind him.

He looked at his friend, seated in the chair he always occupied when he visited them, the familiar stone bottle on the table.

'Sorry to have left you so long, old friend. I'm bad company today.' He shook his head as Allday pushed the bottle towards

189

him. 'I think not, John. Her ladyship might think badly of the "servants" having a wet!'

Allday watched him thoughtfully.

'She changed much?'

Ferguson walked to the window and stared at the stable yard, giving himself time to consider it. The smart carriage was as before, and Young Matthew was talking to the coachman. He smiled sadly. *Young* Matthew, the Bolitho household's senior coachman. Filling out now, and a little stooped. But he had always been called 'young', even after his father had died.

He said, 'Yes. More than I thought.' It stuck in his throat. Like a betrayal.

Allday said it for him. 'High an' mighty, is she? Thought so, when I last seen her.'

Ferguson said, 'She walks from room to room with that damned lawyer, making notes, asking questions, treating my Grace like she's a kitchen maid! Can't understand it!'

Allday sipped the rum. It, at least, was good. 'I can remember when Lady Bolitho was no more'n a paid companion to the wife of some bloody-minded old judge! She may have *looked* like Sir Richard's wife, but it went no deeper. That's it an' all about it!'

Ferguson only partly heard. 'As if she owns the place!'

Allday said, 'Young Cap'n Adam's away, Bryan, an' there's only the lawyers to fight over it. It's nothin' to them.'

Ferguson touched his empty sleeve, as he often did when he was upset, although he was not aware of it.

'She asked about the sword.' He could not stop himself now. 'When I told her that Lady Catherine had given it to Captain Adam, like Sir Richard had intended, all she said was, *she had no right*!' He looked at his oldest friend. 'Who had any better right, eh? God damn them, I wish she was back in the house where she belongs!'

Allday waited. It was worse than he thought, worse than Unis had warned him it might be. 'She done the right thing to stay away while this is goin' on, an' you knows it. How would it look, that's what a lot of people would say. A sailor's woman, but she got pride too, an' that's no error! Look what happened to Lady Hamilton. All the promises and the smiles came to naught. Our Lady Catherine's not like any of 'em.

I know, I seen her in that damned boat after the wreck, an' other times, the two o' them laughin' and walkin' together, just like you have. We'll not see the likes o' them again, you mark me well!'

Ferguson felt the empty sleeve again. 'Seemed to think I was getting past my duties here. That's how it sounded to me anyway. God damn it, John, I don't *know* anything else!'

'It's all written down. Your position here is safe. Sir Richard took care o' that, like he did for everyone else.' He looked away suddenly. '''Cept for himself, God rest him.'

Ferguson sat at the table. Sir Richard had always called Allday his oak, and suddenly he understood, and was grateful for it.

He said in a calmer voice, 'An' then she went into the big room, *their* room.' He gestured towards the house. 'She told the lawyer that Sir Richard's picture should be down with all the others of the family. The ones of Cheney and Catherine she said could be removed as far as she was concerned.'

Allday asked, 'She stayin' overnight?'

'No. Plymouth. With Vice-Admiral Keen.'

Allday nodded sagely, his head shaggy in the reflected sunshine. He enjoyed his visits here. One of the family, he had always described it, until good fortune had offered him Unis, and the little inn in Fallowfield.

'I hopes that one'll be on the lookout for squalls!'

A stable boy thrust his head around the door, but hesitated when he saw Allday, who had become something of a legend around Falmouth since Sir Richard Bolitho's last battle.

Ferguson said, 'What is it, Seth?'

'They'm comin' now, Mister Ferguson!'

Ferguson stood up and took a deep breath.

'I won't be long.'

Allday said, 'We done a lot worse together, Bryan, remember?'

Ferguson opened the door, and smiled for the first time.

'That was then, old friend.'

He walked across the yard, so familiar underfoot that he would have known every cobble in the dark.

He considered Allday's question. *Has she changed much?* He saw her now, on the broad steps leading up to the entrance, elegant in a dark red gown, a hat which he guessed was fashionable in London shading her face. In her late forties, with the same autumn-coloured hair, like the young wife she had replaced when Cheney Bolitho had been killed in a carriage accident. It was hard to believe that he himself, with only one arm, had carried her, seeking help, when she and her unborn child were already dead.

It was one of fate's cruellest ironies that Richard Bolitho and his 'oak' had found Belinda in almost exactly the same circumstances after an accident on the road.

Her face was unsmiling, the mouth tighter than he remembered it. He tried not to think of Allday's pungent summing-up. *High and mighty.*

She was speaking to the lawyer, a watchful, bird-like man, while Grace waited to one side, her bunch of keys in her hand.

Ferguson saw her expression, and felt his own anger rising again. Grace, the finest housekeeper anyone could wish for, and a wife who had nursed him through pain and depression after losing his arm at the Saintes, hovering like a nobody.

'There you are, Ferguson. I shall be leaving now. But I expect to return on Monday, weather permitting.' She walked across the yard, and paused. 'And I should like to see a little more discipline among the servants.'

Her eyes were amused, contemptuous. Ferguson said, 'They are all trained and trustworthy, m' lady. Local people.'

She laughed softly. 'Not foreigners like me, you mean? I think that quaint.'

He could smell her, too. Heady, not what he might have expected. He thought of the delicate scent of jasmine in his estate office.

She said, 'Are all the horses accounted for among the other livestock?'

Ferguson saw her eyes move to the nearest stall, where the big mare Tamara was tossing her head in the warm sunlight.

He said, 'That one was a gift from Sir Richard.'

She tapped his arm very gently. 'I am aware of it. She will need exercise, then.'

Ferguson was suddenly aware of the hurt, like that which he had seen in Grace's eyes.

'No, m' lady, she was ridden regularly, until . . .'

She smiled again; she had perfect teeth. 'That has an amusing ring, don't you think?' She glanced towards the carriage, as though impatient. 'I might take her for a ride myself on Monday.' She was looking at the house again, the windows where the room faced the sea. 'You have a suitable saddle, I trust?'

Ferguson felt that she knew, that she was enjoying it, mocking him.

'I can get one if you intend . . .'

She nodded slowly. '*She* used a saddle like a man, I believe? How apt!'

She turned away abruptly and was assisted into the carriage. They watched it until it was out on the narrow road, and then walked together to their cottage.

Ferguson said, 'I'll take John back to Fallowfield presently.'

Grace took his arm and turned him towards her. She had seen his face when they had been in the room with the three portraits, and the admiral's bed. Lady Bolitho had got rid of Cheney's portrait before; it had been Catherine who had found and restored it. Bryan was a good man in every way, but he would never understand women, especially the Belindas of this world. Catherine would always be an enemy to Belinda, but Cheney's love she could never usurp.

Allday made to rise from his chair as they entered, but Grace waved him down.

'Bad?' was all he said.

Ferguson answered sharply, 'We shall have no say in things, that's certain.'

Grace put down another glass. 'Here, my love. You deserve it.' She looked from them to the empty hearth, the old cat curled up in one corner. Home. It was everything; it was all they had.

She remembered how Bryan had described those moments of Adam's first visit here after his uncle's death, when he had picked up the old sword and read the letter Catherine had left for him.

Like rolling back the years, he had said, like seeing the young Captain Bolitho again. Surely nothing could destroy all that.

193

She said with soft determination, 'I must lock up,' and looked at them both, saddened rather than angered by one woman's petty spite. 'God will have His say. I shall have a word with Him.'

It was Tom, the coastguard, who found her body. A year or so ago, he would have done so earlier. He had been riding loosely in the saddle, his chin tucked into his neckcloth, his mind only half aware. Like his horse, he was so familiar with every track and footpath along this wild coastline that he had always taken it for granted. Behind him, his young companion was careful not to disturb him or annoy him with unnecessary questions and observations; he was a good fellow, inexperienced though he was, and should make a competent coastguard. He had been thinking, *and he is replacing me next week.* It had been hard to accept, even though he had known to the day when his service was to be ended, and he had already been offered employment with the mail at Truro. But after all he had seen and done on these lonely and often dangerous patrols, it would be something unknown, and perhaps lacking in a certain savour.

He had heard all about the comings and goings at the old grey house, the Bolitho home for generations. Lawyers and clerks, officials, all Londoners and strangers to him. What did they know of the man and the memory? Tom had been there at the harbour when news of the admiral's death had arrived. He had been at the old church for the memorial service, when the flags had been dipped to half-mast, and young Captain Adam Bolitho had taken his place with Lady Somervell. He had thought of the times he had met her along this same coast, walking or riding, or just watching for a ship. *His* ship, which would never come any more.

And at first he had thought that it *was* her, that patch of colour, a piece of clothing moving occasionally in the breeze off Falmouth Bay. It was one of her favourite places.

Like that other time when she had joined him in the cove below Trystan's Leap and had cradled the small, broken body of the girl named Zenoria. All those times.

He had found himself dropping from the saddle, running the last few yards down the slope where the old broken wall stood half-buried in gorse and wild roses.

And then he had seen her horse, Tamara, another familiar sight on his lonely patrols above the sea.

But it had not been Catherine Somervell. He had thrust his hand into her clothing, cupping her breast, aware of her eyes watching him through the veil over her hat. But the heart, like the eyes, had been still.

He should have known; the angle of the head told him some of it, the riding crop on its lanyard around the gloved, clenched hand and the bloody weals on the mare's flank told the rest.

Tamara would have known. Would have pulled back, even if beaten, from jumping the old wall. She would have known . . .

'What is it, Tom?'

He had forgotten his companion. He stared up at the dark outline of the old house, just visible above the hillside.

'Fetch help. I'll stay here.' He glanced at the side-saddle, which had slipped when the woman had been thrown.

'It's got a lot to answer for.' He had been describing the house. But his companion was already riding hard down the slope, and there was no sound but the wind off the bay.

13

Envy

Eight days after her arrival at Gibraltar, *Unrivalled* was to all intents once more ready for sea. Pym, the rear-admiral's flag captain, had been true to his word, and had supplied as much as he could to speed repairs and replace standing and running rigging which was beyond recovery.

But it went far deeper than that. Adam Bolitho had seen and felt it from the first day. There was a new stubbornness in the men, and a kind of resentment that anyone should think *Unrivalled*'s own ship's company could not manage without outside help or interference.

Some of the wounded who had been transferred ashore to more comfortable surroundings had returned on board, eager to help, unwilling to be separated from the faces and voices they knew.

Adam had imagined that he would be able to weigh and sail unimpeded by the passenger Rear-Admiral Marlow had described. The written orders had explained little, merely emphasising the need for haste and, above all, safety. As Pym had said, 'No more battles, Bolitho!'

Curiously, it had been the third lieutenant, Daniel Wynter, who had been able to supply more information. Sir Lewis Bazeley was well known in the political circles frequented by Wynter's father. A hard-headed businessman who had been largely responsible for designing and building defences along England's south coast from Plymouth to the Nore when a French invasion had seemed a very real possibility, he had been knighted for his efforts, and it was suggested that his next appointment was Malta, where the fortifications had altered little since the first cannon had been mounted. If there had been any lingering doubts about Malta's future, they had been dispersed. A fortress in the Mediterranean's narrows, who commanded it held the key to Gibraltar and the Levant.

But Adam's hopes were dashed by the arrival at the Rock of the *Cumberland*, a stately Indiaman; he had been with Galbraith the previous morning when she had dropped anchor. Like most of John Company's ships she was impressively armed, and, he had no doubt, equally well manned. The H.E.I.C. paid generously, and offered other financial benefits to officers and seamen alike. Adam's thoughts on that score were shared by most sea officers: if as much money and care had been lavished on the King's navy, the war might have ended in half the time.

There was to be no ceremony, he had been told; the great man would transfer to the more spartan comforts of the frigate and be on his way.

The sooner the better, Adam thought.

He had visited the flagship this morning, and Pym had congratulated him on the appearance of his ship, and the speed with which the scars of battle had been hidden, if not removed. Tar, paint and polish could work wonders, and Adam was proud of the men who had done it.

The severe bruising to his groin had been given little opportunity to improve, and inevitably the pain returned when he most needed all his energy and patience.

The greater, and far more pleasant, surprise had been at the twenty or so seamen who had volunteered to sign on, after his promise to do what he could for anyone who would fight for *Unrivalled*. Galbraith had not shared the surprise, and said only that he thought the whole lot should have put their names down without question. Ten of those same men had been killed or wounded in the fight.

Adam wondered what Lovatt would have made of it.

As he had written in his report to the Admiralty, *'I gave them my word. Without them, my ship would have been lost.'* It might blow a few cobwebs away from that place. He also wondered what Bethune might have done, given the same choice. A man between two separate roles. The one he had known as a young captain. The one he was living now.

Unrivalled's gig was turning in a wide arc as she returned from the flagship. Adam leaned forward, his eyes slitted against the glare, studying the line and the trim of his command. He had been pulled around the ship every day, making certain that the additional stores, even the movement of powder and shot from one part of the hull to another, would in no way impede her agility under all conditions. He smiled to himself. Even in action again.

He thought of the noisy celebration to welcome Bellairs to the wardroom. He had made the right decision; Bellairs had all the marks of a fine officer. He recalled the rear-admiral's interest. *Has he family? Connections?* But there were many senior officers who thought exactly like Marlow when it came to promotion; he could recall one post-captain who had been quite frank about his reluctance to promote any man from the lower deck to commissioned rank. 'All you do,' he had insisted, 'is lose a good man, and create a bad officer!'

Midshipman Fielding had the tiller, and Adam guessed it had been Galbraith's decision. Homey, the midshipman who had been killed, had been his best friend. A good choice for two reasons.

Fielding said, 'Boats alongside, sir!'

Sir Lewis Bazeley and his party had arrived in his absence. No ceremony, Marlow had said.

Adam said, 'Pull right round the ship, Mr Fielding. I am not yet done.'

Jago was watching Fielding's performance on the tiller, but his thoughts were elsewhere, on the day when the dead Lovatt's son had been sent for. Told to collect his gear and report to the quarterdeck. Just a boy, with a long journey before him, to caring people in Kent. Jago had heard the captain dictating a letter to his clerk. And all paid for out of Adam Bolitho's pocket. There had been a sea fight and men had died. It happened, and would continue to happen as long as ships sailed the seven seas and men were mad enough to serve them. Lovatt had died, but so had the flag lieutenant who had served the captain's uncle. And young Homey, who had not been a bad little nipper for a 'young gentleman'. He thought

198

of the other one, Sandell. San-*dell*. Nobody would have shed a tear for that little ratbag.

He looked over at the captain now. Remembering his face when he had torn open his breeches, the dead midshipman's blood and bone clinging to his fingers. Then the surprise when he had found the smashed watch, pieces of broken glass like bloody thorns. Why surprise? *That I should care?*

He felt the captain touch his arm. 'Bring her round now.' They both looked up as the jib boom swung overhead like a lance, the beautiful figurehead too proud to offer them a glance, her eyes already on another horizon.

He heard him say, 'Fine sight, eh?'

But all Jago could think of was the small figure of Lovatt's son, his father's sword tucked under one arm, pausing only to hold the hand of the cabin servant Napier, who had cared for him.

Jago had felt anger then. Not even a word or a look for the one man who had tried to help his father. And him.

He stared over towards the two prizes. They had done it, together . . .

Adam was watching the Indiaman, already making sail, her yards alive with men, and imagined what Catherine must have felt, leaving Malta for the last time in such a vessel.

Midshipman Fielding cleared his throat noisily. *'Bows!'*

The side party was already in position. *The captain was coming aboard.* Adam tested his leg and felt the pain again. The decks of that same Indiaman were probably lined with rich passengers, observing the little ceremony about to take place aboard just another of His Majesty's ships.

'Toss your oars . . . *up!*'

Jago winced, and saw the bowman thrust out to soften the impact alongside. But he would learn. He saw the captain reach for the first handhold, felt his muscles tighten in sympathy as if sharing his uncertainty.

Then the captain turned and looked down at him, and Jago saw the grin he remembered from that day when they had blown up the battery, before the attack on Washington.

Adam said, 'Equal strain on all parts, eh?'

Jago saw the young midshipman standing in the boat, hat in

hand but grinning up at his captain, all else, for the moment, forgotten.

Jago nodded slowly. 'You'll do me, *sir*!' Then he laughed out loud, because he found that he meant it.

Sir Lewis Bazeley was tall, but gave an immediate impression of strength rather than height. Broad-shouldered, and with a mane of thick grey hair which, although cut in the modern style, still singled him out from anyone else.

Adam strode from the entry port and extended his hand.

'I am sorry that I was not aboard to greet you, Sir Lewis.'

The handshake too was strong: a man not afraid of hard work, or of showing an example to others.

Bazeley smiled and waved vaguely towards the open sea.

'I knew this was not one of John Company's ships, Captain. I'll expect no special favours. A quick passage, and I can see for myself she's a fine sailer, and I'll ask no more of any man.' The smile broadened. 'I am sure that the women will endure it for three days.'

Adam glanced at Galbraith. 'Women? I was not told –' He saw the quick, answering nod; Galbraith had dealt with it.

Bazeley was already thinking of something else. 'I promised to pay a private visit to the lieutenant-governor, Captain. If you can provide a boat for me?'

Adam said, 'Mr Galbraith, call away the gig again,' and lowered his voice as Bazeley moved away to speak with one of his own men. 'What the hell is going on?'

'I took the women aft, sir, as you would have wished. And I've already told Mr Partridge to make sure all working parties are decently dressed, and to mark their language.'

Adam stared aft. 'How many?'

Galbraith turned as Bazeley called out something, and said, 'Only two, sir.' He hesitated. 'I will happily vacate my cabin, sir.'

'No. The chart room will suffice. I doubt I shall get much sleep, fast passage or not.'

He saw Bazeley waiting for him, feet tapping restlessly. He seemed full of energy, as if he could barely contain it. He appeared to be in his late forties, although possibly older; it was difficult to tell. Even his style of dress was unusual, more like a uniform than the clothing of a successful man of business. Or *trade*, as Rear-Admiral Marlow would no doubt describe it.

He recalled the discreet wording of his orders. *To offer every facility.* Bethune would know what to do; he was used to it.

He said, 'Perhaps you would care to sup with me and my officers, Sir Lewis. Once we are clear of the approaches.'

It would be a far cry from the Indiaman's table, he thought, and expected Bazeley to make his excuses. But he said immediately, 'A pleasure. Look forward to it.' He saw the gig being warped alongside and beckoned to one of his party.

He paused in the entry port. 'I shall not miss the ship, Captain.'

Adam touched his hat, and said to Galbraith, 'Is everyone accounted for?'

'The purser's due back on board shortly, sir. The surgeon is at the garrison – there are still two of our people there.'

Adam saw Napier hovering by the quarterdeck ladder. 'Call me when you're ready.' And grimaced as another pain lanced through him. 'I'll not be much of a host tonight!'

He made his way aft, where seamen were stowing away chests and some cases of wine which obviously belonged to Bazeley's group. Something else for Partridge to keep his eye on.

The marine sentry straightened his back as Adam passed, then leaned towards the slatted screen with sudden interest.

Adam thrust open the door, and stared at the litter of bags and boxes which appeared to cover the deck of the main cabin. A woman was sitting on one of the boxes, frowning with apparent pain while another, younger woman was kneeling at her feet, trying to drag off one of her shoes.

Adam said, 'I – I am sorry, I did not realise . . .'

The younger woman twisted round and looked up at him. Woman; she was no more than a girl, with long hair, and a wide-brimmed straw hat which was hanging down over her back. In her efforts to drag off the offending shoe some of the hair had fallen across her eyes, and one shoulder was bare and luminous in the reflected sunlight.

Adam saw all this, and that her eyes were blue, and also that she was angry. He made another attempt. 'We were not forewarned of your arrival, otherwise you would have been offered more assistance.' He gestured wordlessly at the disordered cabin. 'Your father said nothing to me about all this!'

She seemed to relax slightly, and sat on the deck looking up at him.

'Sir Lewis is my husband, Lieutenant. That you *should* have been told.'

Adam could feel the other woman watching him, and, he thought, enjoying his discomfort.

'I am Captain Adam Bolitho, ma'am.'

She stood lightly and pushed the hair from her forehead, all in one movement.

'There now, *Captain*. We all make mistakes, it would seem!' She looked around the cabin. 'Yours, I believe.' It seemed to amuse her. 'We are honoured.'

The other woman had managed to remove her shoe, and was staring glumly at her swollen foot. Lady Bazeley said gravely, 'This is Hilda. She takes care of everything.'

She laughed, and the other woman's face responded as if she had never learned to resist the sound.

The girl moved just as swiftly to the stern windows and looked at the panorama of masts and colourful lateen sails, then she faced him again, her body outlined against the blue water. 'And this is a man-of-war.' She sat on the bench seat, the hair falling across her bare shoulder. 'And you are her captain.'

Adam wondered at his own silence, his inability to answer, to be himself. She was laughing at him, teasing him, and probably very aware of the effect it had on him and anyone else she cared to confront.

She pointed at the adjoining sleeping cabin. 'I see you are not married, Captain.'

He said coolly, 'You have a keen eye, ma'am.'

'And that surprises you? Perhaps you take a dim view of a woman's place in the scheme of things!' She laughed again, and did not wait for a reply. 'You have been in a battle, I understand, and you have been injured?'

'Many were less fortunate.'

She nodded slowly. 'I am sorry for it. I have not experienced war at close quarters, but I have seen what it has done to people. Those close to me.' She tossed her head, the mood passing as quickly. 'Now you really must excuse me, Captain. I must prepare myself.' She walked past him, and he could feel the impact of her presence as if they had touched. She was lovely, and she would know it, and that alone must act as a warning, before he made a complete fool of himself. Bazeley was not the sort of man who would forgive even a casual offence.

'If you will excuse me also, m' lady, *I* must prepare the ship for leaving harbour.'

She regarded him steadily, her eyes much darker in this confined space. Violet.

He glanced at the sleeping cabin, where his cot had already been folded away. Where he had dreamed, and remembered. He turned away from it. Where Lovatt had coughed out his life . . .

'My servant will assist you. He is a good lad. If you require anything else, my officers will do their best to make your stay aboard as comfortable as possible.'

'In the *Cumberland*, the captain said I was to ask *him*. Are the King's ships so different?'

She was playing with him again. Was she so young that she did not understand what she could do, was doing? Or did she not care?

He answered, 'Then ask me, m' lady, and I will try to oblige you.'

She watched him, one hand resting on the empty sword rack, her eyes thoughtful.

'A duty, then?'

He smiled and heard the sentry move away from the door. *To offer every facility.*

'I hope it may also be a pleasure, m' lady.'

He turned to the door and the pain hit him again like a bullet.

A reminder; if so, it was just in time. He walked quickly to the companion ladder, his mind clearing as the pain retreated.

Galbraith was waiting for him, with one of his lists already in his hands.

He said, 'I've spread Sir Lewis's people as evenly as

203

possible amongst the warrant officers. Two will be in the wardroom.'

Rank and status. Always separated, no matter how small the ship. He heard her voice again, mocking him. *Are the King's ships so different?*

Galbraith said, 'Lady Bazeley is a very striking woman, sir. I shall endeavour to make certain that she is not offended by some careless word or deed.'

He was so serious that Adam wanted to laugh, and did, at the sheer absurdity of it.

'And that includes the captain, I take it?'

Acting Lieutenant Bellairs heard him laugh, and saw the surprise and bewilderment on Galbraith's face.

He thought of the lovely woman in the cabin; she had smiled at him.

And he was a part of it.

Adam Bolitho tried to ease the discomfort in his legs on the makeshift mattress and stared at the spiralling lantern above the chart table. It was an effort to think clearly, to determine each sound and movement. Here, in the chart room, it even felt different. Like another ship.

He rubbed his eyes, and knew he would get no more sleep. He had already been on deck when *Unrivalled* had shortened sail for the night, and had sensed the growing strength of the wind, holding the ship over; the darkness had been filled with flying spray.

It had done something to clear his head. But not much.

He heard the muffled sounds of blocks, the stamp of bare feet somewhere overhead; even that seemed strangely distorted.

It was useless. He swung his legs over the side of the mattress and felt the ship rising, rising, before ploughing down again. He could see it in his mind, as clearly as if he were up there with Massie. He licked his dry lips. The middle watch. How much wine had they had?

The three lieutenants, and O'Beirne the surgeon, sitting around the table in his cabin. Lady Bazeley's servant Hilda had supervised the flow of dishes and wines, assisted by young Napier. Bazeley himself had been in good form, recounting his various trips, visits to other countries, and, in passing, his building of fortifications and harbour facilities under government contract. Most of the wine had been his, and he had insisted that they should try whatever they fancied.

Adam had been very conscious of the young woman opposite him, her eyes giving little away while she listened to each officer in turn. He had been conscious, also, of the lack of personal comforts in the great cabin; no wonder she had guessed he was unmarried. The women had probably laughed about it when they had been left alone together.

He felt for a beaker of water but it was empty. And there would be more incidents like the one which had so unreasonably disturbed him. Bazeley had left the table to select a particular bottle of wine, and had paused by one of the cabin lanterns to show them his own name, engraved on the medallion around its neck.

'A Château Lafite, 1806. Now this will appeal to you, Captain.'

The ship had been close-hauled, the deck rising and shuddering to the pressure of sea and rudder. Adam had seen Bazeley put his other hand on his wife's shoulder as if to steady himself as he had stressed the significance of that particular chateau or vintage, Adam could remember neither. He had been watching the hand gripping her naked shoulder, the strong fingers moving occasionally like a small, private intimacy.

And all the while she had been looking at him across the table; her eyes had never left his. Not once did she glance up at the man by her chair, nor had she responded to his touch. Perhaps it meant nothing, although he had heard that they had been married for only six months.

He had tasted the claret; it meant nothing to him. It might as easily have been cider.

He had seen her hand move only once, to readjust the gown across her shoulder. And even then she had looked at him.

He saw the old sword hanging beside his boat cloak, swaying with the heavy motion. Was he so stupid that he could not recognise the danger? A single wrong move, and he would lose everything. He reached out and touched the damp timbers. The ship *was* everything.

He stood slowly, waiting for the pain, but it did not come. He spread his hands on the chart table and stared at Cristie's scribbled notes and the soft cloth he used to polish the ship's chronometer, something he entrusted to no one but himself. A man who had grown up in the same streets as Collingwood; what would he think of his captain if he knew his weakness? Like a false bearing or sounding on a chart. Not to be trusted.

There was a tap on the door: someone needing to examine the chart, to make some new calculation. *If in doubt, call the Captain.* That, too, seemed to mock him.

But it was the boy Napier, his shirt soaked with spray, carrying his shoes in one hand.

'What is it?' Adam seized his wet arm. 'Where have you been?'

Napier said quietly, 'I – I thought I should call you, sir.' He swallowed, perhaps already regretting that he was here. 'The lady –'

'Lady Bazeley? What's happened?' His mind was suddenly quite clear. 'Easy, now. Tell me – take your time.'

The boy stared at him in the swaying light. 'I heard somethin', sir. I was in the pantry, like you told me.' He stared out into the poop's inner darkness. 'She were out there, sir. I tried to help, but she wouldn't move. She was sick, sir.'

Adam snatched his boat cloak and said, 'Show me.'

Once outside the chart room the sound of sea and banging canvas was almost deafening. The deck was streaming with water, shipped each time *Unrivalled* ploughed into the heavy swell.

'Here, sir!' His voice was full of relief, that he had told his captain, that she was still where he had left her.

She was below the quarterdeck ladder on the leeward side of the upper deck; seamen on watch could have passed without seeing her. She could have fallen against one of the tethered eighteen-pounders, broken a rib or her skull. It happened even to experienced sailors.

Adam crouched under the ladder and gathered her into a sitting position. She felt very light in his arms, her hair hiding her face, her feet pale in the darkness. She was wet to the skin and her body was like ice.

'Cloak, *here*!' He held her again, feeling her shivering, with cold or nausea, it could be either.

He dragged the cloak round her shoulders, wrapping it with great care as more spray rattled against the ladder and drenched his shirt. He felt her body contract in another spasm and saw Napier with a sand bucket under the ladder.

'Easy, easy!' He did not realise he had spoken aloud. 'I'll bring some help.'

She seemed to understand then what he had said. Who he was. She tried to turn, to struggle round, one hand pushing the hair from her face. As he restrained her he felt the coldness of her skin. She was naked under the dripping gown.

She gasped, 'No.' But when he pulled away she shook her head and said, 'No! Don't go.'

He said, 'Get someone, fast!' But Napier had already disappeared.

Slowly and carefully, he began to drag the girl from beneath the ladder. At any second now someone would come, perhaps call Massie, who was in charge of the watch. And then Bazeley.

She lolled against him and he felt her grip his hand, pulling it against her, across her. She would remember none of it. The rest did not matter.

He felt someone kneel beside him, caught the rich tang of rum. It was Jago, the boy Napier hovering behind him like a nervous ghost.

Jago said between his teeth, 'Trouble, sir?' He did not wait for or seem to expect a reply. 'All women is trouble!'

They guided and half-carried her into the poop again, the sounds becoming muffled, insignificant.

The wardroom door was closed, and there was no sentry at the cabin screen. Jago muttered, 'Just to be on the safe side, sir.'

They found the woman Hilda in a state of anxiety and disbelief.

Adam said, 'Dry her, and get her body warm again. D' you know what to do?'

She took the girl in her arms and led her to the couch which had been prepared in the sleeping cabin. There was no sign of Bazeley, nor were his clothes anywhere to be seen.

She said, 'Too much wine. I tried to warn her.' She combed the wet hair from the girl's face with her fingers. 'You should go now. I can manage.' She called after them, 'Thank you, Captain!'

Outside, it was as if nothing had happened. The sentry had reappeared at the screen, but stood aside as they passed. A ship's boy was climbing the companion ladder, carrying a tarpaulin coat for one of the watchkeepers.

Adam stared at the deckhead, measuring the sounds of rigging and canvas. They would have to take in a reef if the wind did not cease.

'In for a squall.' He had spoken aloud, unconsciously.

Jago thought of the girl sprawled on the couch, the gown plastered to her body, hiding nothing.

Half to himself, he murmured, 'It'll be a bloody hurricane if this little lot gets out!'

Adam reached the chart room and paused. 'Thank you.' But Jago was already melting into the darkness.

He closed the door and stared at the chart, and then down at his shirt and breeches, dark with spray and probably vomit, still feeling the fingers, cold on his wrist where she had pressed his hand against her. She would not remember. And if she did, her shame and disgust would soon change to affront and worse.

He heard footsteps clattering on a ladder: the midshipman of the watch coming to tell his captain that the wind was rising, or it had veered, or it was lessening. *And I shall deal with it.*

He sat on the mattress and waited. But this time the footsteps scurried past.

He lay back and stared at the lantern. And just as they had left the great cabin he had heard the woman Hilda speaking quietly, firmly.

Lifeline or death wish, it no longer seemed to matter.

Her name was Rozanne.

Tomorrow, today, it would be all through the ship. And yet, he knew it would not.

A dream then, soon over, and best forgotten.

When Galbraith came aft to relieve the middle watch, he found his captain fast asleep.

The echoes of the gun salute rolled across the crowded harbour like dying thunder, the smoke barely moving while *Unrivalled* crept to her allotted anchorage preceded by the guardboat, and let go.

Adam Bolitho tugged at his shirt beneath the heavy dress coat and watched the pale buildings of Malta's shoreline shimmering in haze like a mirage. How different from the brusque and fickle winds on their passage from the Rock, and the exhilaration of changing tack in time to outwit every trick.

And then, almost becalmed, they had crawled the last miles to this anchorage, with courses and topsails all but flat against the rigging.

The guardboat was pulling for the shore now, to warn Bethune of his visitors, he thought. Bethune was welcome to this part of it.

He walked to the opposite side of the quarterdeck and saw a few traders already idling nearby, holding up their wares, probably the very same oddments they had offered *Unrivalled* on her first visit here.

Chests and baggage were already being hauled on deck, and cargo nets were laid out in readiness to lower them into the boats. Partridge and his men were swarming around the boat-tier, doubtless speculating on their chances of getting ashore, being free from routine and discipline, perhaps to lose themselves in some of the island's more dubious attractions.

He saw the cabin skylight open and remain so. Lady Bazeley would soon be leaving. He could see it now as it was, in its true perspective, as he might assess the evidence of some offender brought before him for sentence. He had scarcely seen her since that first night. She had been on deck once or twice, but always with the woman Hilda, and once the surgeon, for company.

She had remained for the most part in the great cabin, and had had all her meals sent there. Napier confided that very little had been eaten.

Their eyes had met only once, when he had been standing by the foremast discussing some final repairs with Blane, the carpenter. She had seemed about to raise her hand to him, but had used it instead to adjust the brim of her hat.

Bazeley had spoken to him hardly at all, and then only on matters relating to their progress, the ship's time of arrival, and aspects of her routine. He had made no mention at all of his wife's behaviour, or her illness. Galbraith had solved one mystery. Bazeley had been drinking with some of his companions in the warrant officers' mess when she had left the cabin in her night attire, apparently the worse for drink.

Whenever Bazeley did mention her it was as though he were speaking of a possession. Like the hand on her shoulder that night at the table, it was deliberate. He could not imagine Bazeley doing anything on a whim.

He moved into a patch of shade, angry at himself. Like some moonstruck midshipman . . . It was unlikely that they would ever meet again, and it was just as well. He had been mad even to think about it. And it was dangerous.

Bellairs called, 'They're about to leave, I think, sir.'

Adam watched her stepping through the companion hatch; she even did that gracefully, in spite of her gown. For a moment she stood alone by the untended wheel, looking around, at the men working on deck and up in the yards, and then towards the land, veiled in its dusty heat. And then, finally, at him.

Adam crossed the deck and removed his hat. 'I hope you are feeling well, m' lady?'

He saw her eyes flash. Then she said, 'Better. Much better. Thank you, Captain.'

He relaxed a little. Either she did not remember, or she wanted only to forget.

She said, 'So this is Malta. A place worth fighting and dying for, I'm told.' There was no contempt or sarcasm; if anything, it was resignation.

'Shall you be here long, m' lady?' A voice seemed to warn him. *Stop now.*

'Who can tell?' She looked at him directly, her eyes changing again. Like the sea, he thought. 'And you, Captain? Some other port, perhaps? Some new adventure?' She tossed her head, impatient with the game. 'Some adoring woman?'

Galbraith called, 'Sir Lewis insists that our boats will not be required, sir.'

Adam stared at the shore, and saw several boats pulling smartly towards them. Bazeley was obviously a man of influence. Even Vice-Admiral Bethune was apparently eager to make his acquaintance.

Galbraith strode away to rearrange his preparations for the passengers' departure, and Adam said, almost to himself, 'I have learned that gratitude in a woman can be harmful. To *her*, m' lady.' He saw the sudden uncertainty on her face. 'I had hoped to escort you ashore.' He smiled. 'Another time, maybe.'

Bazeley was here now, calling over his shoulder to one man, beckoning impatiently to another.

He said, 'We take our leave, Captain. Perhaps one day –' And swung round again. 'Be careful with that, you clumsy oaf!'

It was then that she thrust out her hand, and said softly, 'Thank you, Captain Bolitho. You will know what for. It is something we will share with no one.'

He kissed her hand, feeling her eyes on him, and imagining that her fingers closed very slightly around his own.

A bosun's chair was already rigged, and she allowed herself to be settled in it, her gown protected from grease and tar by a canvas apron.

'Hoist away, *'andsomely*!'

Every unemployed hand turned to watch as she was hoisted and then guyed out with great care to be lowered into a waiting boat. Bethune had even sent his flag lieutenant to assist.

Bazeley glanced around, patting his pockets as if to be sure he had left nothing personal below.

Adam thought of the mattresses and bedding strewn across the sleeping cabin. Where they had lain together. Where Bazeley had taken and used her like a plaything.

Bazeley said, 'Good sailing, Captain.' He glanced briefly at his wife in the boat alongside. 'I was told you were reckless.' He held up one hand. 'You get results, that's all important in my view!' Then he laughed, and Adam saw her look up, shading her eyes. 'But you know caution when you see it, eh? And that's no bad thing, either!'

Adam watched the boat bearing off, and said, 'I shall be going ashore in one hour, Mr Galbraith.' He sensed the unspoken question, and added flatly, 'To see the admiral. Perhaps we may be given something useful to do!'

Galbraith watched him walk to the companion way before picking up the duty midshipman's telescope.

Sunlight on her cream-coloured gown, a scarlet ribbon on

her wide-brimmed hat which matched the other one in her hair. All compressed into one small, silent picture. There could be nothing between them. How could there be? But today, she had dressed with obvious care, and he had seen her expression when the captain had pressed his lips to her hand.

Wynter had told him what he knew of Sir Lewis Bazeley. A man who had forced himself to the top, offering and no doubt receiving favours on the way. People less accustomed to deception might describe them as bribes, but one thing was certain: he would be a ruthless man to cross. Galbraith had lost his own command because of another's malignant influence and dislike. *Unrivalled* was his only chance of obtaining another.

He smiled grimly. And yet, all he could feel for Adam Bolitho was envy.

Below in the great cabin, Adam looked around; the place was suddenly spacious and bare again, the quarter gallery open as if to clear away the last vestige of their presence here. The bedding had vanished, his own cot was in its place. No wonder she had played with him, when all the time . . .

He saw his boat cloak hanging from the deckhead, where it was never kept. He took it down and folded the collar. The entire garment had been sponged and cleaned, the stains from that night gone completely. He felt inside the deep pocket, although he did not know why.

It was a small, sealed paper. He carried it to the quarter gallery and opened it.

There was no note. But there was a lock of her hair, tied with a piece of scarlet ribbon.

14

Destiny

Vice-Admiral Sir Graham Bethune pushed some of the unopened despatches to one side and got up from the ornate desk.

'Deal with these, Grimes. My head is too full for much more at present.'

He felt the clerk's eyes following him to the window, which looked across the small, sun-drenched courtyard.

The day had started badly with the guardboat's officer reporting that *Unrivalled*'s arrival meant more than simply the delivery of despatches or letters – there were visitors to accommodate and entertain. Bethune felt the same resentment returning as he heard a woman's voice, and saw the gleam of colour from the opposite balcony. His flag lieutenant had insisted that that particular room was the obvious choice for guests who had come with the full blessing of the government and the lords of the Admiralty. He could hear Bazeley's voice too, loud, demanding, authoritative. Full of himself.

He sighed, and walked back to the desk. There was a letter from his wife as well, asking about the possibility of joining him in Malta, or of his coming back to London. She made it sound like the only civilised place to live.

He glanced at Adam Bolitho's report. Two more prizes. Surely their lordships would offer him extra ships now. There was proof enough that the activities of the Dey of Algiers and his equally unpredictable ally in Tunis required swifter, sharper measures. He almost smiled. It would also make an impressive spearhead for his return to another post in London.

Bethune enjoyed the company of women, and they his, but

213

he had always been discreet. The prospect of his wife joining him in Malta made him realise just how far they had grown apart since her attempts to humiliate Catherine, perhaps even long before that. Of course, he thought bitterly, there were always the children . . .

He looked at the other window, thinking of Lieutenant Avery standing beside him, sharing it, remembering it. And now he was dead. The Happy Few were only ghosts, only memories.

Bazeley's young wife would turn a few heads here when her presence became known. She had probably married the great man for his fortune, which, allegedly, was considerable, but if any of the young bloods from the local garrison got the wrong ideas, they had better watch out. He wondered how Adam had managed to resist her very obvious charm on the passage here from Gibraltar. He was reckless. But he was not a fool.

The flag lieutenant was back. 'Captain Bouverie is here, Sir Graham.'

Bethune nodded. It was even harder to recall Onslow as he had been on that last night together, lying on his back, snoring and drunk. But almost human.

'Very well.'

Onslow smiled, as always apologetic. 'And Captain Bolitho is due shortly. His boat was reported a few minutes ago.'

Bethune turned away and looked across the courtyard.

'I will see them.' He added abruptly, 'Separately.'

Onslow understood, or thought he did. He would do it by seniority.

Bethune was well aware of the peculiar rivalry between Adam Bolitho and Emlyn Bouverie of the frigate *Matchless*. They scarcely knew one another, and yet it had leaped into being. He thought of the successes his small squadron had achieved, despite, or perhaps even because of this personal conflict. It might even be used to greater advantage if he could enlarge his chain of command here. He smiled again. He could never go back to being a mere captain, and he wondered why he had not noticed the change in himself before.

Adam Bolitho stood aside to allow two heavily laden donkeys to push their way through the narrow street. When he glanced up at the strip of blue sky overhead, it seemed the buildings were almost touching.

He had deliberately taken a longer route from the jetty where he had landed from the gig, perhaps for the exercise, maybe to think; his mind was only vaguely aware of the babble of voices around him. So many tongues, so many different nationalities crammed together in apparent harmony. Plenty of uniforms, too. The Union Flag was obviously here to stay.

There were stairs across this part of the street, and he felt the stabbing pain, when earlier he had all but forgotten it.

He paused to give himself time and heard the gentle tap of a hammer. Here the open-fronted shops were as varied as the passers-by. A man selling grain, another asleep beside a pile of gaudy carpets. He ducked beneath a canopy and saw a man sitting cross-legged at a low table. The sound was that of his hammer against a miniature anvil.

He looked up as Adam's shadow fell across shallow baskets full of metal, probably Spanish silver like the chain on Catherine's locket, and asked in faultless English, 'Something for a lady, Captain? I have much to offer.'

Adam shook his head.

'I may return later . . .' He hesitated, and bent to examine a perfect replica of a sword. 'What is this?'

The silversmith shrugged. 'Not old, Captain. Made for a French officer who was here,' he gave a polite smile, 'before you came. But never collected. The war, you understand.'

Adam picked up the sword, so small, but heavy for its size. A brooch, or a clasp of some kind. He smiled; he was being ridiculous, and he knew it.

The silversmith watched him calmly. 'There is an inscription, very small. It must have been important. It says *Destiny*, Captain.' He paused. 'I have other pieces also.'

Adam turned it over in the palm of his hand. 'You speak very good English.'

Again the shrug. 'I learned in Bristol, many years ago!' He laughed, and several people who had paused to observe the transaction joined in.

Adam heard none of them. '*Destiny*.' Like the horizon which never got any nearer.

Somewhere a bell began to chime, and he clapped his hand

to his empty watch pocket. He was late. Outwardly at least, Bethune was tolerant enough, but he was still a vice-admiral.

He said, 'I would like to have it.'

The silversmith watched him take out his purse, and when he was satisfied held up one hand.

'That is *enough*, Captain.' He smiled as Adam held it to the light. 'If the lady declines it, sir, I will buy it back from you, at a consideration, of course.'

Adam returned to the sunlight a little dazed, amazed at his own foolish innocence.

He touched his hat to a Royal Marine sentry and walked into the courtyard.

An unknown French officer, and a silversmith from Bristol.

Then he saw her on the balcony, in the same gown she had been wearing when she had left *Unrivalled*. She was looking down at him, but she did not smile or wave to him.

He felt it again, like a challenge. Destiny. The horizon.

And he knew it was already too late for caution.

Adam was surprised by the warmth of Bethune's welcome, as if he were genuinely pleased, relieved even, to see him.

'Sit here.' He gestured to a chair far from the reflected glare. 'I saw you come through the gates just now – limping, I thought. I read the full report.' He glanced at the dour-faced clerk at the other table. 'Most of it, in any case. I am glad it was nothing worse.'

'The shot struck my watch. Which is why I was late, sir.'

He saw Bethune look meaningly at his flag lieutenant. So they had noticed.

'You are here and you are safe, that's the main thing. I am so damned short of vessels I am beginning to think that nobody cares in the Admiralty.' He laughed, and Adam saw the young officer again.

Bethune said, 'We shall take wine in a moment. I would ask you to stay for a meal, but I have matters which require prompt action.' The easy smile again. 'But you've heard all that before, eh? We all have!'

Adam realised for the first time that Bethune was adrift here in Malta. Perhaps high command was even lonelier than the life of a captain.

'No matter, sir. I have to return to my ship. But thank you.'

Bethune walked to the window, one hand tapping against the flaking shutter.

'Captain Bouverie of *Matchless* was here.'

'I saw him briefly, sir.'

'Not a happy man, I fear. His ship badly requires an overhaul. She has been the longest out here, as far as I am aware.'

Adam thought of something he had heard Jago say. *Like a man who's found a penny but lost a guinea.* It fitted Bouverie well.

And Adam did not need to be told. If *Matchless* was sent to a dockyard in England she might be paid off, laid up, her company disbanded.

It could happen to me. To us.

He saw Bethune step back from the shutter, and knew he had been watching the balcony. Watching *her.* The revelation surprised him, and he began to see him in quite a different light, recalling that Catherine had spoken of him favourably in her letters. Rank had its privileges, and its drawbacks too, apparently.

Bethune said, 'We have received information from what is judged to be a reliable source.' He waited for Adam to join him at the other table where Onslow had arranged a chart, weighed down with carved ivory figurines. 'These islands to the south-west of Malta. Owned by nobody, claimed by many.' He tapped the chart. 'Almost midway 'twixt here and the coast of Tunis. They are useless for trade or habitation except for a few fishermen, and not many of those, with the corsairs so active in these waters.'

He stood aside as Adam bent over the chart.

'I know them, sir, but at a distance. Dangerous shoals, not even safe for an anchorage. But small craft,' he looked up and saw Bethune nod, '*they* would find the islands useful.' There was a sudden silence, broken only by the scratching of the clerk's pen. Even the sounds of the street did not penetrate to this room.

'Some of the islands have high points of ground.' He touched the chart as if to confirm it. 'When this one was last corrected, it stated that two of them could be three hundred feet or more above sea level.'

Bethune rubbed his chin thoughtfully. 'I believe the corsairs are sheltering their chebecks among these islands. The high ground rules out any kind of normal approach. A blind lookout would see our t'gallants before we got within five leagues of the place!'

'And the information is good, sir?'

Bethune glanced towards the window again, but seemed to change his mind.

'Two traders have been attacked in the past week, another is missing. A Sicilian vessel saw the chebecks – her master has given us some useful information over the years. Us *and* the French, of course!'

Adam said quietly, 'My uncle always had the greatest respect for the chebecks, sir. His flagship *Frobisher* was attacked by some of them. Lieutenant Avery told me about it.'

They both looked at the empty chair, and Bethune said, 'He saw what many of us missed.'

Adam walked a few paces. 'A landing party. At night. Volunteers.'

'Royal Marines?'

'I think not, sir. They are fine fighters, but they are foot soldiers at heart. This would require stealth, men used to working aloft in all weathers, sure-footed, eager.'

A door opened and he heard the clink of glasses. No wonder Bouverie had looked so depressed and so angry. His ship was too slow. By the time *Matchless* was restored to her proper trim it might be too late. For him.

Bethune said, 'I can offer *Halcyon* in support. I cannot spare my flagship, and the rest of the squadron is deployed elsewhere.' He banged the table with his fist. 'God, I could find work for ten more frigates!'

Adam knew the other frigate, half *Unrivalled*'s size, twenty-eight guns, with a youthful and zealous captain named Christie. The family again . . . Christie had been a midshipman under James Tyacke at the Nile. They had both been scarred, in different ways, on that terrible day.

Adam could feel Bethune watching him, perhaps seeing

himself already there, confronted by an operation which at the best of times could spell disaster. But if the corsairs were using the islands they could not have chosen a more effective lair. A thorn in the side; no. Far deeper than any thorn.

Hazardous or not, Captain Bouverie would perceive it as an act of favouritism. *As I would.* He felt the piece of silver inside his shirt, and wanted to laugh at the absurdity of it.

He recalled a captain who had once said to him after a bitter hand-to-hand engagement, 'You might have been killed, you young idiot! Did you ever pause to consider that?'

He straightened his back and took a goblet from the hovering servant.

'I think it can be done, sir.'

'I hoped you might say that.' Bethune could scarcely conceal his relief. 'But no unnecessary risks.'

Adam smiled tightly. Bethune had never lost his ship, witnessed her agony, and that of her people who had trusted in him.

Perhaps it made it easier for him.

Onslow ventured, 'The reception, Sir Graham?'

Bethune frowned at him. 'It would be better if you weighed at first light. I will have your orders prepared immediately, Christie's too.' He looked at the pile of documents awaiting his signature, and said abruptly, 'Sir Lewis and Lady Bazeley, were they any trouble?'

'We had a fast enough passage, sir.'

Bethune looked at him and smiled. It was not what he had asked.

'There is a reception for them this evening. Short notice, but they are used to that in Malta. *I* am not.'

He walked with him to the door, while Onslow made a display of folding the charts, probably in readiness for the next visitor.

Bethune said, 'Captain Forbes will give you all the help he can. He has served in these waters for many years.' Then, at a complete tangent, 'I am truly sorry that you cannot join us this evening. Everything must appear normal.' He paused, as if he had gone too far. 'A king once said, if you tell your best friend a secret, it is no longer a secret!'

The mood did not last, and he said almost brusquely, 'I will

219

see you when you sign for your orders. No matter what I am doing, I want to be told.'

Adam descended the marble stairs, his mind already on the details of his mission. Total responsibility. He had heard it from his uncle several times. *If you succeed, others will get the reward; if you fail, yours is the total responsibility.*

He saw the flag captain's stocky figure by the entrance. Ready to play his role.

Unrivalled had arrived that morning; tomorrow she would weigh and proceed to sea once more. And suddenly he knew he was not sorry to leave.

Leigh Galbraith stood by the hammock nettings and studied the boats alongside. One of them was *Halcyon*'s gig, her crew very smart in checkered shirts and tarred hats. He smiled. *A ship shall be judged by her boats.*

The other frigate's captain had been down in the great cabin for more than an hour. Each seeing his own ship's part in what lay ahead, the selection of men, and who would lead them.

A landing party. A raid, to flush out the corsairs so that the frigates could get amongst them before they could make good their escape.

He heard Lieutenant Massie, who had the watch, speaking sharply to a boatswain's mate, a man not known for his quick response to anything beyond routine. Massie had little patience with anyone who could not keep up. He was a good gunnery officer, one of the best Galbraith had known, but he was not a man for whom it was possible to feel any affection.

Massie joined him now, breathing hard. 'A bloody block of wood, that man!' Galbraith glanced at the open skylight. *Soon now.* He heard Bolitho laugh. A small thing, but reassuring.

The captain had said to him while they had been waiting for Christie to arrive from *Halcyon*, 'I want you to take charge of the landing party. I've a few suggestions which we can discuss later, but mostly it will be your initiative, and your decision when you get there.' His dark eyes had been intense. 'Not a battle, Leigh. I need you as my senior lieutenant, not as a dead hero. But you are the obvious choice.' He had smiled. 'The *right* choice.'

Massie said, 'One man to be flogged, so why all the fuss?'

220

A seaman had been found in his mess, off duty and drunk. It seemed they had only just dropped anchor, and now they were leaving again . . . *There will be danger.* Aboard ship it was different. Faces and voices to sustain you, the strength of the timbers surrounding you.

Galbraith said, 'A flogging helps no one at a time like this.'

'They'd laugh in your face without firm, strong discipline, and you know it!' Massie sounded triumphant when Galbraith did not respond. 'They offer us scum to be made into seamen. Well, so be it!'

Galbraith stared at the other ships, their reflections less sharp now in a freshening breeze.

Massie seemed to read his thoughts, and said angrily, 'I expect half of Malta knows what we are about! When we reach those damned islands the birds will have flown, and good riddance, I say!'

Is that what I was hoping? Galbraith thought suddenly of the gathering in the captain's cabin when they had entertained Sir Lewis Bazeley and his young wife at supper. The wine, like the endless procession of tempting and distracting adventures with which Bazeley had dominated the conversation, disappearing bottle by bottle. Like most sea officers, Galbraith had little experience of fine wines. You took what was available, in a far different world from that described by Sir Lewis. But once or twice he had received the impression that Bazeley had not always known the luxury of good food and wine, or beautiful women. He was a hard man in more ways than Galbraith had yet fathomed.

Massie waved an arm towards the shore. 'And a reception, no less! We should be there, after all we've achieved since we joined this damned squadron!'

Galbraith remembered most of all how the young woman had looked at the captain whenever he had answered one of Bazeley's many questions. As if she were learning something. About him, perhaps . . .

He answered wearily, 'Next time, maybe.'

Midshipman Cousens said, 'The captain's coming up, sir.'

Galbraith nodded, glad that the conversation had been interrupted, and that Massie would be quiet for a while.

'Man the side!'

The two captains stood together by the rail and waited for the gig to grapple alongside.

Christie turned and smiled at Galbraith. 'My second lieutenant will be supporting you on this venture. Tom Colpoys – he's an experienced officer, so you'll have no complaint on that score!'

So easily said. As if neither of these young captains had a care or a doubt in the world.

The muskets slapped to the present, a sword sliced through the dusty air, the calls squealed, and moments later Christie's gig pulled smartly out from *Unrivalled*'s shadow.

Adam Bolitho swung on his heel. 'A man for punishment, I understand?'

Galbraith watched his face as Massie reeled off the offences.

'Willis, you say?' Adam paced to the rail and back again. 'Foretopman, starboard watch, correct?'

Massie seemed surprised. 'Aye, sir.'

'First offence?'

Massie was out of his depth. 'Of this kind, sir.'

Adam pointed towards the shimmering rooftops and battlements.

'Over yonder, a good many will be too drunk to stand tonight, Mr Massie. Officers, no less, so think on that too! They shall not be flogged and neither shall Willis. Give him a warning, this time.' He looked keenly at the lieutenant, as if searching for something. 'And a warning for the one who brought him aft in the first place. Responsibility pulls in two directions. I'll not have it used for working off old scores.'

Massie strode away, and Galbraith said, 'I should have dealt with it, sir.' Massie had probably never been spoken to in that manner in his life. Few captains would have cared, in any case.

Adam said, 'I shall be going ashore directly.' And smiled, at something Galbraith did not understand. 'To sign for my destiny.' He looked along his command, and Galbraith wondered how he saw her. Only a captain could answer, and Bolitho would share that with nobody. Unless . . . 'When I return offshore, you will join me in a glass.' The rare, infectious smile again. '*Not* claret, I think.'

222

Then the mood was gone, just as quickly, and he said, 'The man Willis. His wife has died.' He paused, the memory stirring. 'In Penzance.'

'I did not know, sir.'

'Why should you? But Massie is his lieutenant. *He* should have known, and cared enough to prevent this unnecessary affront.'

Bellairs was hurrying towards them, but he waited for the captain to leave before he produced a list of items he had been told to muster for the proposed landing party.

Galbraith put his hand on the young man's shoulder. 'Later, but not now, my lad.' He shook the shoulder gently. 'I wish you had been here just now. You'd have learned something which would have had your promotion board agog with admiration.' He thought of the captain's expression, the dignity and the fire in the quiet voice. 'About the true qualities which make a King's officer. I certainly did, believe me!'

He knew Bellairs was still gazing after him when he walked away to call the gig's crew. And he was glad he had shared it with him.

Adam chose the same leisurely approach to Bethune's house without truly knowing why. The narrow street was in deeper shadow now, and most of the stalls had been closed or abandoned for the night. He looked towards the low-canopied shop where he had spoken with the silversmith, but that, too, was deserted. As if he had imagined it.

He had left the gig at the jetty alone and had sensed Jago's disapproval; he had even ventured to suggest that he should keep him company. *The whole place is probably full of cutthroats an' thieves.* But he had remained with the boat's crew when Adam had told him that there would not be a man left, hand-picked or not, when he returned.

Like that handshake; Jago had still come only halfway towards sharing his innermost thoughts.

But the old sword at his hip had been loosened in its scabbard all the same.

There had been a couple of small boys begging, and a savage-looking guard dog, but otherwise his walk was undisturbed.

The air was cooler as evening lengthened the shadows, but not much. He thought without pleasure of the reception at Bethune's headquarters, and imagined the press of sweating bodies, and the wine. *Unrivalled* would put to sea in the morning. He had to keep a clear head, to deal with any remaining problems before the two frigates were committed.

He turned the corner and saw the pale gates looming out of the dusk. Every window seemed to be ablaze with light. He could smell cooking, and felt his stomach contract. He had eaten nothing since breakfast; Jago probably knew about that, too.

He touched his hat to a sentry and strode into the courtyard, aware of vague shapes, murmured instructions, and the continuous clatter of dishes and glassware.

He recalled Bethune's casual question about the passage from Gibraltar. Did he see his unwanted visitor as a burden, or a possible stepping-stone to some new appointment? He was welcome to it. His was a world Adam had never known, and had repeatedly told himself he would never willingly share.

There was music, hesitant at first, violins, seemingly at odds with one another and then suddenly sweeping through the courtyard in a single chord.

He stopped and listened as the music faded away, and somebody called out for attention. *Short notice.* Bethune had not approved of that, either.

'Why, Captain Bolitho, is it not? Standing alone and so thoughtful. You are *very* early!'

He turned and saw her in a curved entrance he had not noticed on his previous visit. In the deepening shadows her gown looked blue, perhaps chosen to match her eyes. Her dark hair was piled above her ears, Hilda's work, he thought, and she was wearing earrings, shining like droplets of fire in the last sunlight.

He removed his hat and bowed.

'My lady, I am a visitor, not a guest. I shall be on my way as soon as I have met with Sir Graham or his aide.'

'Ah, I see. More duty, then?' She laughed and flicked open a small fan which had been dangling on a cord at her wrist. 'I had thought we might see more of you.'

He joined her in the paved entrance and caught her perfume,

her warmth. The same woman, and yet so different from the one he had held and restrained in her moment of nausea and despair.

'It seems you are well cared for, m' lady.' He looked past her as the music began again. 'I hope the reception is a great success.'

She took his arm, suddenly and deliberately, turning him towards the music, towards her, until they were only inches apart.

'I do not care a fig for the reception, *Captain*! I have seen so many, too many . . . I am concerned that you choose to blame me because of such . . .' She seemed angry that she could not find the word to express her displeasure.

'Necessities, m' lady?'

'No, never that!' She calmed herself; he could feel her fingers gripping his arm, like the night Napier had brought him to her.

She said, 'Walk with me. There is a view of the harbour on the other side.' Her fingers tightened as if to drive away his resistance. 'Nobody will see us. Nobody will care.'

'I do not think you understand . . .'

She shook his arm again. 'Oh, but I do, Captain! I am well aware of the rules, the *etiquette* of King's officers. No talk of women in the mess. But a knowing nod and a quick wink betrays such chivalry!' She laughed, and the sound echoed in the curved archway. 'Listen! D' you hear that?'

They came out on to a paved parapet, beyond which Adam saw the sea, sunset already bronze on the water, the riding lights and small moving craft making patterns all their own.

The hidden orchestra was playing now, and the other sounds of preparation seemed to pause as if servants and orderlies had stopped to listen.

She said almost in a whisper, 'It's beautiful,' and turned to look at him. 'Don't you agree?'

He put his hand on hers and felt her tense. A woman one moment, a child the next. Or was he deluding himself yet again?

'As you have observed, my lady, I am somewhat aback when it comes to the finer points of etiquette.'

She did not respond, but said a moment later, as if she had

225

not heard him, 'A waltz. D' you know that some people still claim it is too risqué, too bold, for public performance?'

He smiled. She was teasing him.

'I am thankful I am spared such hazards!'

She turned towards him again, and removed his hand from hers as if she was about to walk away. Then she took his hands once more, and stood looking at him, her head slightly on one side, deciding perhaps if she had already gone too far.

'Listen. Hear it now? Let it take charge of you.'

She placed his right hand on her waist, pressing it there, like the night when she had refused to release him.

'Now hold me, guide with your left hand, so.'

Adam tightened his grip and felt her move against him. Even in the uncertain light he could see the bare shoulders, the darker shadow between her breasts. His heart was pounding to match the madness, the pain of his longing. And madness it was. At any moment somebody would discover them; rumour could run faster than any wind. And jealousy could match and overwhelm any sense or caution.

But she was moving, taking him closer, and his feet were following hers as if they had always been waiting for this moment.

She said, 'You lead,' and leaned back on his arm, her eyes wide. 'Then I shall *yield*.'

And laughed again. The music had stopped, like the slamming of a single door.

How long they stood in the same position was impossible to know. She did not move, even when he pressed harder against her thighs, until he could feel the heat of her body, her shocked awareness of what was happening.

Then, carefully, firmly, he held her away, gripping the naked shoulders until she was able to look at him again.

He said, 'Now you know, *my lady*, this is no game for tricksters. Bones mend, but not hearts. You would do well to remember that!'

She dragged her hand away and raised it as if to strike him, but shook her head when he seized her wrist. 'It was not a game or a trick, not to me. I cannot explain . . .' She stared at him, her eyes shining with tears, and he felt her come against him again, without protest or amusement. He wanted

226

to push her away, no matter what it might do to each or both of them.

Think what you are doing, of the consequences. Are you beyond reason because of a loss you could never have prevented, a happiness which was never yours to explore?

But there was no solution. Only the realisation that he wanted this woman, this girl, another man's wife.

He heard himself say, 'I must leave you. Now. I have to see the admiral.'

She nodded very slowly, as if the action was painful.

'I understand.' He felt her face against his chest, her mouth damp through his shirt. 'You may despise me now, Captain Bolitho.'

He kissed her shoulder, felt her body tighten, shock, disbelief, it no longer mattered.

There were voices now, and laughter, someone announcing an arrival. She was fading into the shadows, moving away, but with one arm held out.

He followed her through the same low archway, and she said, 'No, no – it was wrong of me!' She shook herself as if to free her body of something. 'Go now, please go!'

He held her, kissing her shoulder again, lingeringly, and with a deep sensuality. There were more voices, closer. Someone looking for him, or for her.

He pressed the small silver sword into her hand and closed her fingers around it, then he walked through the archway and into the courtyard once more, his mind and body fighting every step, almost daring to hope she might run after him and prevent him from leaving. But all he heard was the sound of metal on stone. She had flung the little clasp away from her.

He saw Lieutenant Onslow peering out from the opposite doorway and felt something like relief.

'Captain Bolitho, sir! Sir Graham sends his compliments, but he is unable to receive you this evening. He is with Sir Lewis Bazeley, and before the guests arrived he thought –'

Adam touched his sleeve. 'No matter. I will sign for my orders and leave.'

Onslow said lamely, 'He wishes you every success, sir.'

Adam did not glance up at the balcony. She was there, and

she would know that he knew it. Anything more would be insanity.

He followed the flag lieutenant into another room. While Onslow was taking out the written orders, Adam held out his hand and examined it. It should be shaking, but it was quite steady. He picked up the pen, and thought of Jago down there with the gig's crew.

There were far more dangerous forces abroad this evening than cutthroats and thieves. Perhaps Jago had realised that also.

I wanted her. And she will know it.

He could hear her voice still. *Then I shall yield.*

Perhaps they would never meet again. She would know the perils of any liaison. Even as a game.

The gig's crew sat to attention when he appeared, and the bowman steadied the gunwale for him to step aboard. Jago took the tiller.

'Cast off!'

Captain Bolitho had said nothing. But he could smell perfume, the same she had been using when they had carried her, almost insensible, below.

'Bear off forrard! Out oars!'

Jago smiled to himself. *Get back to sea. Good thing all round.*

'Give way all!'

Adam saw the riding light of his ship drawing nearer and sighed.

Destiny.

15

Close Action

Lieutenant Leigh Galbraith got down on his knees in the cutter's sternsheets and ducked his head under the canvas canopy to peer at the compass. When he opened the lantern's small shutter it seemed as bright as a rocket, just as the normal sounds around him were deafening.

He closed the shutter and regained his seat beside the helmsman. By contrast it was even darker than ever now, and he could imagine the man enjoying his lieutenant's uncertainty. He was Rist, one of *Unrivalled*'s senior master's mates, and the most experienced. The stars, which paved the sky from horizon to horizon, were already paler, but Rist navigated with the assurance of one who lived by them.

Galbraith watched the regular rise and fall of oars, not too fast, not enough to sap a man's strength when he might need it most. Even they sounded particularly loud. He tried to dismiss it from his thoughts and concentrate. The cutter's rowlocks were clogged with grease, the oar looms muffled with sackcloth; nothing had been left to chance.

He imagined their progress as a sea bird might have seen them, had there been any at this hour. Three cutters, each astern of the other, followed by a smaller boat which had been hoisted aboard *Unrivalled* under cover of darkness. Was it only two nights ago? It felt like a week since they had made that early morning departure from Malta.

It had been a quiet night when they had hoisted the other boat aboard, in spite of a steady breeze through the rigging and furled sails, quiet enough to hear the music carried across the harbour from the big white building used by Vice-Admiral Bethune and his staff.

Galbraith had seen the captain by the quarterdeck rail, his hands resting on it as he watched the boat being manhandled into a position away from the others. His head had been turned towards the music, as if his thoughts were elsewhere.

Rist said quietly, 'Not long now, sir.'

Galbraith failed to find comfort in his confidence. A point off-course and the boats might pass the poorly described and charted islet; and he was in command. When daylight came in a mere two hours' time it would lay them bare, all secrecy would be gone, and the chebecks, if they were there, would make their escape.

There were thirty-five all told in the landing party, not an army, but any larger force would increase the risk and the danger of discovery. Captain Bolitho had decided to include some marines after all, only ten, and each man, as well as their own Sergeant Everett, was an expert shot. When Galbraith had carried out a final inspection of the party before they had disembarked he had noticed that even without their uniforms they managed to look smart and disciplined. The others could have been pirates, but all were trained and experienced hands. Even the foul-mouthed hard man, Campbell, was here in the boat. In a fight he would ask no quarter, nor offer any.

Halcyon's second lieutenant, Tom Colpoys, was in the boat furthest astern. It would be his decision either to fight or to run if his leader encountered trouble.

Colpoys was a tough, surprisingly quiet-spoken man, old for his rank, and indeed the oldest man in the landing party. Galbraith had been immediately aware of the respect he was shown by his own sailors, and of a calm assurance which could not have come easily to him. From the lower deck, he had probably served all kinds of officer before rising to that same rank.

It was good to know that he was second-in-command of what his young captain had called this 'venture'.

Galbraith had taken part in several such raids throughout his varied service, but never in this sea. Here there was no running tide to cover your approach, no boom of surf to warn or guide your final decision to land.

He thought of the Algerine chebecks he had seen and had heard described by the old Jacks. They were laughed at by those who had never encountered them, as relics from a dead past, from the pharaohs to the rise of the slave trade. But those who had experience of them treated them with respect. Even their rig had improved over the years, so that they could outsail most of the smaller traders on which they preyed. Their long sweeps gave them a manoeuvrability which compensated for their lack of armament. A man-of-war, with a fully trained and disciplined company, but becalmed, could become a victim in minutes. A chebeck could pull around the ship's stern and fire point-blank with her one heavy cannon through the unprotected poop. And then the Algerines would board their victim, without either fear or mercy. It was said that the dead were the lucky ones, compared with the horrors which inevitably followed.

He saw Williams, one of *Unrivalled*'s gunner's mates, bending over the heavy bag he had brought with him. Another professional, he had been entrusted with fuses, powder, and the combining of both into a floating inferno. Galbraith had seen him clambering over the small boat they had hoisted aboard, supervising the placing and lashing of each deadly parcel. If anything could dislodge the chebecks, this miniature fireship would do it. If they were driven from shelter and forced into deeper water, even they would be no match for *Unrivalled*'s speed and armament.

'*Now*, sir!' Rist eased the tiller-bar without waiting for an order. Galbraith saw the man in the bows waving his arm above his head, and then pointing firmly across the starboard bow. Nothing was said, nobody turned to watch, and so break the steady stroke of oars.

Galbraith wanted to wipe his face with his hand. 'Ease the stroke – allow the others to see what we are about!'

He was surprised at the calmness of his own voice. At any moment a shot might shatter the stillness, another boat forge out from the invisible islet. Only the handful of marines had loaded muskets. Anything else would be madness. He himself had been in the middle of a raid when someone had tripped and fallen, exploding his musket and rousing the enemy.

It was no consolation now. He touched the hanger at his side and wondered if he would have time to load his pistol if the worst happened. And then he saw it. Not a shape, not an outline, but like a presence which must have been visible for a long time, and yet hidden, betrayed only by the missing stars which formed its backcloth.

He gripped Rist's shoulder. 'We'll go in! *Beach her!*' Afterwards he wondered how he had managed to grin. 'If there *is* a poxy beach!'

Then he was scrambling through the boat, steadying himself on a shoulder here, an oarsman's arm there. Men he knew, or thought he did, who would trust him, because there was no other choice.

'Boat your oars. Roundly, there!'

Galbraith heaved himself over and almost fell as the water surged around his thighs and boots, dragging at him, while the cutter plunged on towards the paler patch of land.

More men were over the side now, and one gasped aloud as he stumbled on hard sand or shingle. The boat grated noisily aground, men rocking and guiding the suddenly clumsy hull until it eventually came to rest.

Galbraith wiped spray from his mouth and eyes. Figures were hurrying away, like the spokes of a wheel, and he had to shake himself to recall the next details. But all he could think was that *they* had remembered what to do. Exactly as it had been outlined to them on the frigate's familiar deck. Yesterday . . . it was impossible.

Someone said hoarsely, 'Next boat comin' in, sir!'

Galbraith pointed. 'Tell Mr Rist! Then go and help them to beach!'

And suddenly the small hump of beach was full of figures, men seizing their weapons, others making the boats secure, and the gunner's mate, Williams, floundering almost chest-deep in water while he controlled the last boat in the procession.

Lieutenant Colpoys sounded satisfied. 'They'll lie easy enough here, sir.' He was peering up at the ridge of high ground. 'The buggers would be down on us by now if they'd heard anything!'

'I'm going up to get my bearings, Tom.' Galbraith touched his arm. 'Call me Leigh, if you like. Not *sir*, in this god-forsaken place!'

He began to climb, Rist close on his heels, breathing

heavily, more used to *Unrivalled*'s quarterdeck than this kind of exercise.

Galbraith paused and dropped on one knee. He could see the extent of the ridge now, jutting up from nowhere. *Like a cocked hat*, one survey had described it. Darker now, because the stars had almost gone, and sharper in depth and outline as his eyes became accustomed to their barren surroundings.

Then he stood, as if someone had called to him. And there it was, the crude anchorage, with another, larger island beginning to be visible in the far distance. He swore under his breath. *The one they should have landed on.* Despite everything, he had misjudged it.

He felt Rist beside him, watching, listening, wary.

Then he said, 'Fires down yonder, sir!'

Galbraith stared until his eyes watered. Fires on the shore. For warmth, or for cooking? It did not matter. At a guess, they were exactly where his boats would have grated ashore. The rest did not bear thinking about.

Rist summed it up. 'We was lucky, sir.'

Galbraith asked curtly, 'First light?'

'Half an hour, sir. No cloud about.' He nodded to confirm it. 'No longer.'

Galbraith turned his back on the flickering points of fire. It might be long enough. If it failed . . .

He quickened his pace, hearing Adam Bolitho's voice. *Mostly, it will be up to you.*

And that was now.

He was not even breathless when he reached the beach. He had heard it said often enough that the British seaman could adapt to anything, given a little time, and it was true, he thought. Men stood in small groups, some quietly loading muskets, others checking the deadly array of weapons, cutlasses, dirks or boarding axes, the latter always a favourite in a hand-to-hand fight. Colpoys strode to meet him, and listened intently as Galbraith told him what he had seen, and the only possible location for an anchorage. Chebecks drew little water; they could lie close inshore without risk to their graceful hulls.

Colpoys held up his hand and said flatly, 'Wind's backed, si . . .' And grinned awkwardly. 'It will help our ships.' He glanced at the one boat still afloat. 'But it rules out sailing *that* directly amongst the Algerines. One mast and a scrap of sail – they'll see it coming, cut their cables if necessary. No chance!'

Galbraith saw Rist nod, angry with himself for not noticing the slight change of wind.

He said, 'But they're *there*, Tom, I know it. Fires, too.' He pictured the other island, high ground like this. A lookout would be posted as a matter of course at first light, to warn of the approach of danger or a possible victim. It was so simple that he wanted to damn the eyes of everyone who had considered this plan at the beginning. Bethune perhaps, spurred on by some sharp reminder from the Admiralty? Whatever it was, it was too late now.

Colpoys said, 'Not your fault, Leigh. Wrong time, wrong place, that's all.'

Williams, the gunner's mate, leaned towards them, his Welsh accent very pronounced.

'I've trimmed the fuses, sir. It'll go up like a beacon, see?' If anything, he sounded dismayed that his fireship was not going to be used.

Colpoys said, 'The wind. That's all there is to it.'

Galbraith said, 'Unless . . .' *Stop now. Finish it. Pull out while you can.*

He looked around at their faces, vague shapes in the lingering darkness. They had no choice at all.

'Unless we *pull* all the way. We could still do it. I doubt if they'll have much of a watch on deck, as we would!'

Somebody chuckled. Another said, 'Heathen, th' lot of 'em!'

Galbraith licked his lips. His guts felt clenched, as if anticipating the split second before the fatal impact of ball or blade.

'Three volunteers. I shall go myself.'

Colpoys did not question it or argue; he was already thinking ahead, reaching out to separate and to choose as shadowy figures pushed around him.

Two of *Halcyon*'s seamen, and Campbell, as somehow Galbraith had known it would be.

Williams exclaimed, '*I* must be there, sir!'

Galbraith stared at the sky. Lighter still. And they might be seen before . . . He closed his mind, like slamming a hatch.

'Very well. Into the boat!' He paused and gripped Colpoys' arm. 'Take care of them, Tom. Tell my captain about it.'

He threw his coat into the boat and climbed down beside the carefully packed charges. A few voices pursued him but he could not hear them. Colpoys was wading with the others, pushing the boat away from the beach.

Four oars, and a hard, hard pull. He doubted if any of them could swim; few sailors could. For them, the sea was always the real enemy.

He lay back on the loom, his muscles cracking in protest. Williams took the tiller, a slowmatch by his foot shining like a solitary, evil eye.

Campbell said, 'Nice an' steady, lads! We don't want to tire the officer, do we?'

Galbraith pulled steadily; he could not recall when he had last handled an oar. As a midshipman? Was he ever that?

Tell my captain about it. What had he meant? Because there was no one else who would care?

He thought of the girl he had hoped to marry, but he had been about to take up his first command, so the wedding had been postponed.

He closed his eyes and pressed his feet hard into the stretchers, sweat running down his back like ice water.

But she had not waited, and had married another. Why had he thought of her now?

And all for this. A moment's madness, then oblivion. Like George Avery, matter-of-fact about some things, sensitive, even shy, about others. And the traitor Lovatt who had died in the captain's cabin; perhaps he had had some purpose, even to the end . . .

Williams called softly, 'Half a cable!'

Galbraith gasped, *'Oars!'*

The blades still, dripping into the dark water alongside. When he twisted round on the thwart, he saw what he thought at first was a single large vessel, but when he dashed the sweat from his eyes he realised there were two, chebecks, overlapping one another, masts and furled sails stark against the clear sky, rakish hulls still hidden in shadow.

He said, 'We shall grapple the first one, and light the fuses.' He saw Williams nod, apparently untroubled now that he was here to do it. 'Then we'll swim for the land. Together.' He paused, and Williams said gently, 'Can't swim, sir. Never thought to learn.'

One of the others murmured, 'Me neither.'

Galbraith repeated, '*Together*. Take the bottom boards, we shall manage.' He looked at Campbell, and saw the evil, answering grin.

'I'd walk on water just to 'elp an officer, *sir!*'

The long bowsprit and ramlike beakhead swept over them, as if the chebeck and not the boat was moving.

It was a miracle nobody had seen or challenged them.

Galbraith lurched to his feet and balanced the grapnel on his hand. Up and over. *Now.*

Even as the grapnel jagged into the vessel's beakhead the stillness was broken by a wild shout. More like a fiend than something human. Galbraith staggered and ducked as a musket exploded directly above him, the sickening crack of the shot slamming into flesh and bone so close that it must have passed within inches.

Someone was gasping, 'Oh, dear God, help me! Oh, dear God, help me!' Over and over, until Campbell silenced him with a blow to the chin.

The fuse was alight, sparking along the boat, alive, deadly.

'Over, lads!' The water knocked the breath out of him but he could still think. No more shots. There was still time before the chebeck's crew discovered what was happening.

And then he was swimming strongly, Williams and the other man floundering and kicking between them. The wounded seaman had vanished.

Two shots echoed across the water, and then Galbraith heard a chorus of yells and screams. They must have realised that the bobbing boat under their bows was not merely a visitor.

It was madness, and he wanted to laugh even as he spat out water, trying to guess how far they had come, and if the Algerines had managed to stop the fuses. Then he gasped as his foot grated painfully between two sharp stones, and he realised that he had lost or kicked off his boots. He staggered into the shallows, one hand groping for his hanger, the other still clinging to the choking gunner's mate.

Campbell was already on his feet, pulling the other seaman on to firm ground.

Galbraith wanted to tell them something, but saw Campbell's eyes light up like the fires he had seen on the beach.

'Get down!' But it came out as a croak. Then the whole world exploded.

Adam Bolitho rested his hands on the quarterdeck rail and listened to the regular creak of rigging, the clatter of a block. Otherwise it seemed unnaturally quiet, the ship forging into the deeper darkness, as if she was not under control.

He shivered; the rail was like ice. But it was not that and he knew it. He could see *Unrivalled* in his mind's eye, ghosting along under topsails and forecourse; to set more canvas would deny them even a faint chance of surprise. He stared up at the main-topmast and thought he could see the masthead pendant licking out towards the lee bow. It would be plain for everyone to see when daylight finally parted sea from sky. To set the topgallants, the 'skyscrapers', would be a gift to any lookout.

He felt the twinge of doubt again. There might be nothing.

They had cleared for action as soon as they had cast off the boats. There had been no excitement, no cheering. It had been like watching men going to their deaths, pulling away into the darkness. *Not just a captain's decision. But mine.*

He walked to the compass box again, the faces of the helmsmen turning towards him like masks in the binnacle light.

One said, 'Sou'-west-by-south, sir. Full an' bye.'

'Very well.' He saw Cristie with a master's mate. Their charts had been taken below; their part was done. The master was probably thinking of his senior mate, Rist, who had gone with Galbraith and the others. Too valuable a man to lose. To throw away.

Suppose Galbraith had misjudged his approach. It was easy enough. It would give the enemy time to cut and run for it, if they were there . . . The slight shift of wind had been noted. Galbraith might have ignored it.

He saw Lieutenant Massie's dark shadow on the opposite

side of the deck, standing in Galbraith's place, but with his heart most likely with his gun crews. The eighteen-pounders were already loaded, double-shotted and with grape. It was inaccurate but devastating, and there would be little time to reload. *If they were there.*

He wondered briefly if Massie was still brooding over the reprimand he had been given. Resenting it, or taking it personally. What did one man matter in any case?

It was an argument Adam had heard many times. He could recall his uncle's insistence that there had to be an alternative, beginning with the conditions under which men were forced to serve in times of war. Strange that Sir Lewis Bazeley had made the same point during that meal in the cabin. To impress the officers, or had he really cared? He had drawn comparisons with the Honourable East India Company's ships, where men were not ruled by the Articles of War, or subject to the moods and temper of a captain.

Adam had heard himself responding, very aware of the girl's eyes, and her hand lying still on the table. The same hand which had later gripped his wrist like steel, refusing to release him.

'So what is the alternative for the captain of a King's ship, Sir Lewis? Restrict their freedom to come and go, when they have none? Deny them their privileges, when they are afforded none? Cut their pay, when it is so meagre after the purser's deductions that were it gone they would scarcely miss it?'

Bazeley had smiled without warmth. 'So you favour the lash?'

Adam had seen her hand clench suddenly, as if she had been sharing it in some way.

He had answered, 'The lash only brutalises the victim, and the man who administers it. But mostly, I think, the man who orders it to be carried out.'

He came out of his thoughts abruptly and stared at the masthead. Colour. Not much, but it was there, the red and white of the long pendant, and even as he watched he saw the first touch of sunlight run down the topgallant mast like paint.

He took a telescope brusquely from Midshipman Cousens and strode to the shrouds, extending the glass as he moved. He rested it on the tightly packed hammocks and stared across

238

the bow. Land, fragments. As if they had been scattered by the gods.

He said, 'Are the leadsmen ready, Mr Bellairs?'

'Aye, sir.'

Cristie said, 'Closer inshore there's some seven fathoms, sir.' He did not add, *or so the notes state*. He knew his captain needed no reminding. Seven fathoms. *Unrivalled* drew three.

Adam looked up at the gently bulging main topsail. He could see most of it, the head in contrast with the foot, which was still in deep shadow. Not long now.

He steadied the glass once more and trained it slowly across the craggy humps of land. He could see the higher ground also, and that one small islet had a solitary pinnacle at its end, like something man-made.

'Bring her up a point. Steer sou'-west.' There was an edge to his voice but he could not help it. 'Rouse the lookouts, Mr Wynter – they must be asleep up there!'

Suppose Galbraith had been taken by surprise and overwhelmed? Thirty-five men. He had not forgotten what Avery had told him about the barbarity of the Algerines towards their captives.

He rested his forehead against the hammock nettings. So cool. Soon it would be a furnace here.

'Sou'-west, sir! Steady she goes!'

A quick glance at the topsails again. Steady enough. Braced close to the wind, such as it was.

He thought of *Halcyon*, in position by now on the other side of this miserable group of tiny islands. The trap was set. He touched his empty watch pocket and felt the pain again.

Somebody moved past him and he saw that it was Napier, his feet bare, as if to avoid being noticed.

Adam said, 'We are cleared for action, Napier. You know your station. Go to it.'

He swung round and stared up again. Very soon now, and the whole ship would be in broad daylight. Or so it would feel.

He realised that the boy was still there. 'Well?'

'I – I'm not afraid, sir. The others think I'm not to be trusted on deck!'

Adam stared at him, surprised that the simplicity could move him, even distract him at this moment.

'I understand. Stand with me, then.' He thought he saw Jago grin. 'Madness is catching, it seems!'

'Deck there! Somethin' flashin' from the middle high ground!'

Adam licked his lips. The voice was Sullivan's. Something flashing: it could only be one thing, early sunshine reflecting from a glass. A lookout. *They were there.*

Then came the explosion, which seemed to linger in a slow climax before rolling across the sea and sighing against the ship. *Unrivalled* seemed to quiver in its path.

'One craft under way, sir. 'Nother on fire!' Sullivan was barely able to contain his excitement, which was rare for him.

On the upper deck the gun crews were staring into the retreating shadows or aft at the quarterdeck, trying to guess what was happening. A great pall of smoke had begun to rise, staining the clear, clean sky like something grotesque, obscene. There were more explosions, puny after the first, and smoke spreading still further as if to confirm the success of Galbraith's attack.

But sails were moving, suddenly very bright and sharp in the new sunlight, and Adam had to force himself to see it as it really was. A vessel destroyed: impossible to guess how many had died to achieve that. But the explosion was on a different bearing, so that the alleged anchorage must also be wrongly charted.

Galbraith would stand no chance of getting away. Another chebeck, perhaps two, were using the change of wind which had delayed his attack. They would escape. He steadied the glass again, ignoring everything but the tall triangles of sails, a flurry of foam as the chebeck used her long sweeps to work around the blazing wreck, which was burned almost to the waterline.

Between and beyond was the gleam of water: the line of escape. And *Halcyon* would not be there to prevent it. He swallowed as a second set of sails moved from the smoke, like the fins of a marauding shark. They still had time for revenge. Galbraith's boats would stand no chance, and even if his men broke and scattered ashore they would hunt them down and slaughter them. Revenge . . . *I should have known that, only too well.*

240

'We will come about, Mr Cristie! Steer nor'-east!'

They were staring at him, and he heard the reluctance in Cristie's response.

'The channel, sir? We don't even know if . . .' It was the closest he had ever come to open disagreement.

Adam swung on him, his dark eyes blazing. '*Men*, Mr Cristie! Remember? I'll roast in hell before I leave Galbraith to die in their hands!'

He strode to the opposite side, ignoring the sudden bustle of seamen and marines as they ran to braces and halliards, as if they had been shaken from a trance.

The leadsmen were in position in the chains, one on either bow, their lines already loosely coiled, ready to heave.

Adam bit his lip. Like a blind man with his stick. There was not a minute more to measure the danger. There was no alternative.

He said, 'Carry on! Put the helm down!' He saw Massie staring at him over the confusion of men already lying back on the braces, his face wild, that of a stranger.

Cristie stood near his helmsmen, one hand almost touching the spokes as the big double-wheel began to turn, and *Unrivalled*'s figurehead gazed at what appeared to be an unbroken line of sun-scorched rocks.

Adam gripped the old sword and forced it against his hip, to steady himself. To remember.

His voice sounded quite level, as if someone else had spoken.

'Then get the hands aloft and shake out the t'gallants!'

He touched his face as the sun reached down between the flapping canvas, and did not see Bellairs pause to watch him.

Then he held out one hand, like someone quieting a nervous horse.

'Steady now! *Steady!*'

Trust.

Adam remained by the nettings and watched the shadows of *Unrivalled*'s topgallants and topsails glide over a long strip of sand and rock, as if some phantom ship were in close company. Some of the gun crews and unemployed seamen were peering into the water, the more experienced to study the patches of weed, black in the weak sunlight, which seemed to line the side of the channel through the islands. They were bedded in rock, any one of which could turn the ship into a wreck.

As if to drive home their danger, the leadsman's voice echoed aft from the chains. 'By the mark ten!'

Adam watched the man hauling in his lead, his bare arm moving deftly, perhaps too engrossed to consider the peril beneath the keel.

Cristie said, 'Narrows a bit here, sir.' It was the first time he had spoken since they had laid the ship on the new tack, and his way of reminding his captain that after this there would be less room to come about, even if that was still possible.

'Wreckage ahead, sir!' That was Midshipman Cousens, very calm, and aware of his new responsibilities now that Bellairs was promoted. Almost.

Adam leaned over to stare at the charred timbers as they parted across *Unrivalled*'s stem. Galbraith's people must have got right alongside the vessel to cause such complete devastation. Perhaps they had all been killed. Somehow he knew Galbraith had done it himself; he would never delegate, particularly when lives were at risk. *And because I would expect it of him.* It was like a taunt.

He could smell it, too. The boat must have exploded like a giant grenade; the fire had done the rest. There were corpses as well, pieces of men, lolling wearily in the frigate's small wash.

'Deep *six*!'

If he went to the side he knew he would be able to see the ship's great shadow on the seabed. He did not move. Men were watching him, seeing their own fate in him. Lieutenant Wynter was by the foremast, staring at another, larger island which appeared to be reaching out to snare them.

Adam said, 'Let her fall off a point.' He saw Captain Bosanquet with one of his corporals positioned by the boat-tier. If she drove aground they would need every boat, perhaps to try and kedge her free again. But men in fear of their lives would see the boats as their only security, their link with the invisible *Halcyon*.

He looked at the masthead pendant again. *How many times?* Holding steady. If the wind backed again they would not weather the next island, with its headland jutting out like a giant horn. *If, if, if.*

He heard the big forecourse flap noisily, and felt the deck heel very slightly.

Jago muttered, 'Just stow that, matey!' Adam had not realised that he was at his side.

'An' a quarter six!'

Adam released his breath very slowly. Slightly deeper here. He had seen the splash of the lead hitting the water, but his mind had rejected it, as if afraid of what it might reveal.

'Deck there! *Boats ahead!*' From his lofty perch Sullivan could very likely see over, if not beyond, the outthrust headland, and on to the next leg of the channel.

Bosanquet snapped, 'Put your men in position, Corporal!'

His best shots, although his chosen marksmen were with the landing party.

Adam said, 'Over here, boy!' He swung Napier round like a puppet and pointed him towards the bows. Then he laid the telescope on his shoulder. 'Breathe easily.' Surely the boy was not afraid of him? With the ship in real danger of being wrecked, perhaps overrun by Algerines, it was impossible. He steadied the shoulder, and said quietly, 'This will show them, eh?'

He saw the leading cutter spring into focus, the oars rising and falling to a fast, desperate stroke. Another cutter was close astern, and the third appeared to be stopped, its oars in confusion. A man was hanging over the gunwale, others were trying to drag him from the looms. They had been fired on, the sound muffled by *Unrivalled*'s shipboard noises. One officer, *Halcyon*'s second lieutenant, a seaman tying a bandage around his arm.

Even at this distance Adam could see Colpoys' disbelief, when he turned and saw *Unrivalled* filling the channel.

And then he saw the chebeck. She must have used her sweeps to cut past the wreckage and overhaul the three cutters. The great, triangular sails were filling, pushing the chebeck over while her sweeps rose and froze in perfect unison. No wonder unarmed merchantmen were terrified of the Barbary pirates.

243

Adam gritted his teeth, and felt the boy stiffen as the leadsman's chant came aft to remind them of their own peril.

'By th' mark seven!'

He said sharply, 'Stand to your guns, Mr Massie! Bow-chasers, then the smashers!'

He saw Massie look aloft. A split second only, but it said everything. If *Unrivalled* lost a spar, let alone a mast, they would never see open water again.

Adam rubbed his eye and laid his hand on the boy's shoulder again. It was madness, but it reminded him of the instant she had raised her hand to strike him, and he had gripped her wrist with such force that it must have shocked her.

He said, 'Still, now!' and winced as a bow-chaser banged out from the forecastle, the recoil jerking the planks even here at his feet.

He tried again, and then said, 'Over yonder, boy. *You* look. Tell me.'

He thrust the long signals telescope into his hands, and tensed as another shot cracked out from forward. From a corner of his eye he saw one of the cutters passing abeam, suddenly dark in *Unrivalled*'s shadow, men standing to yell and cheer when moments earlier they had been facing death.

There were more shots now, heavy muskets, and the sharper, answering crack of the marines' weapons.

He felt something thud into the packed hammocks, heard the screech of metal as a ball ricocheted from one of the quarter-deck nine-pounders. Men were crouching, peering through open ports, waiting for the first sight of the chebeck, waiting for the order as they had been taught, had had hammered into them day after day.

But Adam did not move an inch. He could not. He had to know.

Then Napier said in a remarkably steady voice, 'It's them, sir! On the headland! Four of them!' The significance of what he had said seemed to reach him and he twisted round, the telescope forgotten. 'Mr Galbraith is safe, sir!'

Then Massie's whistle shrilled and the first great carronade lurched inboard on its slide, the noise matched only by the crash of its massive ball as it exploded into the chebeck's quarter. Timber, spars, oars and fragments of men flew in all directions, but the chebeck came on.

Massie gauged the range, his whistle to his lips. After one shot from the 'smasher', many men were too deaf to hear a shouted order.

The second carronade belched fire, and the ball must have exploded deep within the slender hull.

Adam called, 'As you bear!' He gripped the boy's shoulder. 'I want them to *know*, to feel what it's like!'

There was more firing in the far distance, like thunder on the hills: *Halcyon* in pursuit of the third chebeck, her captain perhaps believing that his consort had been wrecked.

'By th' mark . . .' The rest was lost in the crash of gunfire as Massie strode aft, pausing only to watch each eighteen-pounder fling itself inboard and pour a murderous charge into the stricken chebeck. There were still a few figures waving weapons and firing across the littered water. Even when the final charge smashed into the capsizing hull Adam imagined he could still hear their demented fury.

'By the mark fifteen!'

Adam saw the lead splash down again, could picture the seabed suddenly sliding away into depths of darkness.

'We will heave to directly, Mr Cristie.' He raised his voice; even that was an effort. 'Mr Wynter, stand by to retrieve those boats. Inform the surgeon. I want him on deck when they come aboard.'

He stared at the headland, misty now with drifting smoke.

'I'll take the gig, sir.' It was Jago. 'Fetch Mr Galbraith.'

Adam said, 'I'd be obliged.' He looked away as men hurried past him. 'And, thank you.'

Jago hesitated by the ladder and looked over his shoulder. The captain was standing quite still as orders were shouted and, with her sails in disorder, his ship came slowly round into the wind.

He had kept his word. Jago could hear the boats pulling towards the ship, their crews exhausted but still able to cheer.

He heard the sailing master say quietly to his mate, 'Not a choice I would have cared to make, Mr Woodthorpe.'

Jago shook his head. *Not yours to make, was it?*

As if to put a seal on it, the leadsman, forgotten in the forechains, yelled, *'No bottom, sir!'*

They were through.

16

In Good Hands

The letter lay on the cabin table, held down by the knife Adam
had used to open it, its flap moving slightly in a faint breeze
from the stern windows, the broken seal shining in the sunlight
like droplets of blood. He tried to think it through rationally,
as he had taught himself to do with most things.

Unrivalled had anchored that morning, with *Halcyon* entering harbour close astern. A moment of triumph, a lingering
excitement after the short, savage encounter with the chebecks
and the sheer pleasure of greeting a filthy but grinning
Galbraith, his shirt scorched almost from his back, and his
equally dirty but jubilant companions.

Adam had taken his report ashore, only to be told that
Bethune was neither at his headquarters nor aboard his flagship
Montrose. He had boarded one of the squadron's brigs, and
with Sir Lewis Bazeley had gone to examine potential sites
for new defences in Malta and the offshore islands.

He had already noticed that the courier schooner *Gertrude*
was in harbour, and she was preparing to weigh and make sail
again by the time he had returned to *Unrivalled*. As was the
way of fleet couriers.

He had been expecting a letter from Catherine, hoping for
one. It was stupid of him and he knew it. She would be
recovering from her loss, and would need time to decide what
she must do in the immediate future and with the rest of her
life. But he had hoped, all the same.

Instead, there had been this letter. The same neat, round
handwriting which had followed him from ship to ship, from

247

despair to hope. Always warm, as she had been ever since that first day when he had arrived exhausted at the Roxby house after walking all the way from Penzance. From his mother's deathbed.

Aunt Nancy, Richard Bolitho's youngest sister, was the last person from whom he had been expecting to hear, and yet in his heart he knew there was none better suited to this task.

He walked to the stern windows and stared across at *Halcyon*, swinging to her cable and surrounded by harbour craft, with scarlet coats on her gangways to deter unwanted visitors. He had sent Captain Christie a copy of his report. *Halcyon* had done well, and between them they had lost only four men.

He looked at the letter again, as if his mind were refusing to lose itself in matters concerning the ship and the squadron. That other world seemed very close: rugged cliffs, treacherous rocks, and in contrast rolling hillside pastures and great, empty moors. A county which had produced many fine sailors, probably more than any other part of England. He could see Falmouth in his thoughts . . . the people, the quality of strength in its seamen and fisherfolk.

Where Belinda, whose hand had once rested on his cuff as he had led her up the aisle to marry Falmouth's most famous son, had been killed. Thrown from a horse. *Killed instantly*, Nancy had written. And yet he could not come to terms with it. Perhaps he had never really known Belinda, or been close enough to understand what had destroyed his uncle's marriage; she had always been beautiful, proud, but distant. She had been at the old house, and Adam could guess why, although the family lawyer had touched only in passing on it. Not wishing to trouble a King's officer, *fighting for his country's rights*.

And there was his cousin, Elizabeth. She would be about twelve or thirteen by now. She would stay with Nancy until things were 'more settled'. Adam could almost hear her saying the words.

Nancy had also written to Catherine. The mare given to her by his uncle was now stabled at the Roxby house. Adam had known instantly that Belinda had been riding Tamara at the time of the accident.

The letter ended, *'You must take good care of yourself,*

dear Adam. Here is your home, nobody can ever deny you that.'

The ink was smudged, and he knew she had been crying as she wrote, doubtless angry with herself for giving into it. A sailor's daughter, and the sister of one of England's finest sea officers, she had had plenty of experience of separation and despair. And now that her husband was dead she was alone once again. Elizabeth would be a blessing to her. He picked up the letter, and smiled. *As you were to me.*

Catherine was in London. He wondered if she was alone, and was surprised by how much it could hurt him. Absurd . . . He glanced at the skylight, hearing voices, Jago's carrying easily as he called out to the gig's crew. Vivid memories: the leadsman's chant, the closeness of danger on all sides, Massie and Wynter, and the boy who would rather risk death than take refuge below when the iron began to fly.

And he thought of Falmouth again. The house. The grave portraits, the sea always out there, waiting for the next Bolitho.

He turned almost guiltily as someone rapped at the door. It was Bellairs, who was assisting Wynter as officer of the watch.

'Yes?'

Bellairs glanced around the cabin. His examination was in orders, here in Malta. The next step, or the humiliation of failure.

'Mr Wynter's respects, sir, and a new midshipman has come aboard to join.' He did not blink, although he must have been recalling his own time as a young gentleman.

'Ask Mr Galbraith . . .' He held up his hand. '*No.* I'll see him now.'

Bellairs hurried away, mystified that his captain, who had just inflicted a crushing defeat on some Algerine pirates, should concern himself with such trivialities.

Adam walked to one of the eighteen-pounders which shared his quarters and touched the black breech. Remembering; how could he forget? Anxious, worried, even defiant because he had imagined that his first captain, his uncle, would find fault or cause to dismiss him on that day which was so important to him.

He heard the marine sentry say, 'Go in, *sir.*' Guarded, yet to be proved. A midshipman was neither fish nor fowl.

He saw the newcomer standing by the screen door, his hat beneath his arm.

'Come over here where I can see you!' Again the assault of memory. They were the very words his uncle had used.

When he looked again, the youth was in the centre of the cabin, directly beneath the open skylight. Older than he had expected, about fifteen. With experience he could be very useful.

He took the envelope and slit it with the knife he had used earlier, feeling the midshipman's eyes watching every move. *As I did.* All those years ago.

He was not new, but had been appointed from another frigate, the *Vanoc*, which had been temporarily paid off for a complete overhaul. His name was Richard Deighton. Adam raised his eyes, and saw the youth look away from him.

'Your captain speaks well of you.' A young, roundish face, dark brown hair. He would be fifteen next month, and was tall for his years. Serious features. Troubled.

The name was familiar. 'Your father was a serving officer?' It was not a question. He could see it all more clearly than the chebecks of only three days ago.

The youth said, 'Captain Henry Deighton.' No pride, no defiance.

That was it.

'Commodore Deighton hoisted his broad pendant above my ship, *Valkyrie*, when I was with the Halifax squadron.' So easily said.

The midshipman clenched one fist against his breeches. 'The rank of commodore was never confirmed, sir.'

'I see.' He walked around the table, hearing Jago's voice again. He had been there too on that day when Commodore Deighton had been shot down, it was thought by a Yankee sharpshooter. Except that after the sea burial the surgeon, rather the worse for drink, had told Adam that the angle of entry and the wound were all wrong, and that Deighton had been killed by someone in *Valkyrie*'s own company.

The matter had ended there. Deighton had already been put over the side, with the boy John Whitmarsh and others.

But the faces always returned; there was no escape. The family, they called it.

'Did you ask for *Unrivalled*?'

The midshipman lifted his eyes again. 'Aye, sir. I always hoped, wanted . . .' His voice trailed away.

Bellairs was back. 'Gig's alongside, sir.' He glanced at the new midshipman, but only briefly.

Adam said, 'Take Mr Deighton into your charge, if you please. The first lieutenant will attend to the formalities.'

Then he smiled. 'Welcome aboard, Mr Deighton. You are in good hands.'

As the door closed he took out the letter once more.

It was like seeing yourself again . . . something you should never forget.

He picked up his hat and went out into the sunshine.

Captain Victor Forbes leaned back in Bethune's fine chair and raised a glass.

'I'm glad you chose to come ashore, Adam. I've been reading through your report, Christie's too, and I've made a few notes for the vice-admiral to read on his return.'

Adam sat opposite him, the cognac and the easy use of his first name driving some of his doubts away. The flag captain was obviously making the most of Bethune's absence, although it was apparent from the occasional pause in mid-sentence to listen that, like most serving captains, he was ill at ease away from his ship.

Forbes added, 'I still believe that raids on known anchorages, though damn useful and good for our people's morale, will never solve the whole problem. Like hornets, destroy the nest. Time enough later to catch the stragglers.'

Adam agreed and tried to recall how many glasses he had drunk as Forbes peered at the bottle and shook it against the fading sunlight. 'I'd have given anything to be there with you.' Then he grinned. 'But with any luck *Montrose* will be a private ship again quite soon!'

'You're leaving the squadron?'

Forbes shook his head. 'No. But we are being reinforced by two third-rates, and about time too. Sir Graham Bethune will likely shift his flag to one of them. A damn nice fellow,' he grinned again, 'for an admiral, that is. But I believe he is eager to leave, to get back to a stone frigate, the Admiralty again, most likely. I'll not be sorry. Like you, I prefer to be free of flag officers, good or bad.'

Adam recalled Bethune's restlessness, his sense of displacement even in a world he had once known so well. And there was a wife to consider.

Forbes changed tack. 'I hear that you've got a new midshipman, a replacement for the one who was killed. Deighton – I knew his father, y' know. We were lieutenants together in the old *Resolution* for a year or so. Didn't know him all that well, of course . . .' He hesitated and peered at Adam as though making a decision. 'But when I read the account of your fight with the Yankee *Defender*, in the *Gazette* I think it was, I was a little surprised. He never really struck me as being in the death-or-glory mould, one who would fall in battle like that. His son must be proud of him.' He sat back and smiled. Like a cat, Adam thought, waiting to see which way the mouse would run.

'He was killed by a single shot. It is common enough.'

Forbes exclaimed, 'Thoughtless of me! Your uncle . . . I should have kept my damn mouth shut.'

Adam shrugged, remembering when Keen had left Halifax to return to England for promotion and high command at Plymouth. And to marry again . . . Deighton was to remain as commodore in charge until otherwise decided. He could remember Keen's words to him, like a warning. Or a threat.

'Be patient with him. He is not like us. Not like *you*.'

He said, 'How is Sir Graham getting along with his visitor?'

Forbes gave him the grin again, obviously glad of the change of subject.

'They both know about wine, anyway!'

Adam smiled. 'Claret, of course.'

A servant appeared with another bottle but Forbes waved him away.

He said, 'I shall be dining with the army tonight. Don't want to let our end down!'

Adam prepared to depart. It had been a friendly, informal discussion, but he had been a flag captain himself, and a flag lieutenant to his uncle. Both roles had taught him to sift fact from gossip, truth from rumour, and in this brief meeting he

252

had learned that a new admiral was about to be appointed, and that Bethune would be leaving. The new flag would decide all future operations, as so ordered by the Admiralty. An aggressive demonstration of sea power might deter the Dey from any further attacks on shipping, or from offering refuge to any pirate or turncoat who offered his services in return for sanctuary.

Forbes had made a point of not mentioning Lady Bolitho's death, although it was no doubt common knowledge in a place like this. Adam himself had said nothing about it; it was private, if not personal. Belinda was dead. *I never knew her.* But was it so simple?

Forbes frowned as a shadow moved restlessly beneath the door.

'Not like a ship, Adam. Too many callers, always wanting things. I'd never make an admiral in a thousand years!'

Adam left, cynically amused. He could see Forbes as precisely that.

Outside he paused to study the copper sky. It was a fine, warm evening, and in England the summer was over. It would be the first Christmas without war. And without his uncle.

Forbes had also avoided mentioning Bazeley's lovely young wife. He wondered if she had fared any better aboard the brig, with its cramped quarters and limited comforts. After an Indiaman and then *Unrivalled*, a brig would seem like a work-boat. Eyes watching her every move, men deprived of a woman's touch, the sound of a woman's voice.

He had told Jago to return to the ship, saying that he would take a duty boat from the jetty. He grinned in the shadows. He had been expecting Forbes to ask him to stay. Instead, he would return to his own, remote cabin.

Something moved in a doorway, and his hand was on the hilt of his sword in a second, unconsciously.

'Who is there?'

The action and strain had cost him more than he would have believed.

It was a woman. Not a beggar or a thief.

'Captain Bolitho. It *is* you!'

He turned in a patch of golden light and recognised Lady Bazeley's companion.

'I did not know you were here, ma'am. I thought you would be with Sir Lewis and his lady.'

The woman stood very still, and he felt the intensity of her eyes, although her features remained hidden in shadow.

She said, 'We did not go. Her ladyship was unwell. It seemed the safest thing to do.'

He heard footsteps, measured, precise, and relaxed again. It was the marine sentry at the gates, pacing his post, his mind doubtless far removed from this place.

The woman touched his arm, and then withdrew her hand just as quickly, like an unwilling conspirator.

'My lady would like to see you before you leave, sir. We saw you earlier in the day. And then you came back.' She hesitated. 'It is safe, if you will allow me to lead.'

Adam looked back, but there was only silence. Forbes must have known that the women had stayed behind, but had made a point of not mentioning that either.

Was she really unwell, or was she merely bored, needing to be amused? *At my expense.*

He said, 'Lead on, ma'am.' Perhaps she wanted to remind him of his awkward advances, his clumsiness. He thought of the leadsman's cry. *No bottom!* What it had meant, after the risk he had taken for what Lovatt would have called a gesture, a conceit.

The woman walked swiftly ahead of him, untroubled by the rough paving where he guessed guns had stood in the past when Malta had been in constant fear of attack. Perhaps she was used to running errands for her mistress. He recognised the same parapet as before, but knew it was at the opposite side of the rambling building, in shadow now, the old embrasures touched with colour from the melting light.

And the view was the same. When he had held her, and the invisible orchestra had offered its private gift of music. Ships anchored as before, some already displaying lights, topmasts clinging to the last copper glow, flags limp, barely moving.

And then he saw her, her gown pale against the dull stone, the fan open in her hand.

She said, 'So you came, Captain. You honour us.'

He moved closer and took the hand she offered him.

'I thought you were away, m' lady. Otherwise –'

'Ah, that word again.' She did not flinch as he kissed her hand. 'I heard there was fighting. That *you* were fighting.'

It sounded like an accusation, but he said nothing. Nor did he release her hand.

She said in the same level tone, 'But you are safe. I heard you laugh just now. Recognised it. Enjoying some of Sir Graham's cognac in his absence, yes?'

He smiled. 'Something like that. And you, I hear you were unwell?'

She tossed her head, and he saw her hair fall loose across one shoulder.

'I am well enough, thank you.' She withdrew her hand slowly and deliberately, then turned slightly away, towards the ships and the harbour.

She said, 'I was concerned, about you, *for* you. Is that so strange?'

'When we last met –'

She shook her head again. 'No. Do not speak of it! There were so many things I wanted to say, to share, to explain. I could not even manage that unaided.'

There was a catch in her voice, more from anger than despair.

'I showed you arrogance when I wanted only to thank you for helping me as you did. There has been no word of it, so I knew you had said nothing.' She held up the fan to silence him. 'Others would, and well you know it!'

He said, 'Because I cared. I still do. You are another man's wife, and I know what harm this might cause. To both of us.'

She did not seem to hear him. 'I know that people talk behind my back. Giving myself to a much older man, because of power, because of wealth. I am not so young that I do not understand how they think.'

He said abruptly, 'Walk with me.' He took her hand again, expecting her to resist, to turn on him, but she did neither. 'Like old friends, you see?'

She held his arm and fell into step beside him. Only by the parapet could the sounds of the harbour and a nearby street reach them.

She said, 'I spoke with your Captain Forbes. He told me of

255

you and your family.' He felt her turn to look at him. 'Your uncle. I knew some of it. I guessed some of it, too, when I heard you speak that night with such conviction, and when you were talking with your men and did not know I was there.' He felt the pressure of her hand on his arm. 'And then you helped me.'

'When you were sick.'

She laughed softly. 'I was drunk, like some dockside slut!' She quickened her pace, and he could sense her mind moving, exploring it again. 'He came to me that night, did you know? He is like that. He cannot believe that I need to be myself on occasion, a person – not some *thing* to arouse his passion!'

He said, 'I think you should stop, m' lady. I came here because I wanted to see you. Even if you had spat in my face, I would have come.'

She stopped by the parapet once more and stared at the anchored vessels. Almost to herself, she murmured, 'Your world, Adam. Something I can never share.' She turned. 'I did not marry from choice, or out of greed, for myself.'

Without realising what he was doing, he put his fingers to her lips.

'There is no need to tell me. I am not proud of some of the things I have done, or what I might have done, if my life had been different. So let this be a secret between us.'

Gently, firmly, she pulled his hand away.

'My father was a fine man, but when my mother died of fever he seemed to fall apart. Sir Lewis, as he now is, was his junior partner, a man of ambition. He was quick to come to his assistance.' She touched the buttons on his coat. 'And he taught him how to enjoy himself again.' She laughed, a small, bitter sound on the still air. 'Introduced him to others who would help to expand the business, the only thing he had left to care about. Gambling, drink . . . he would not listen to a word against Lewis. He could not see the ground opening beneath his feet. There were debts, broken contracts with government commissions, with the military as well as the navy. In the end,' she gave a little shrug, and Adam felt it like a blow, 'prison was the only reality. We would have been left like beggars. My two brothers also work for the business. I was given little choice. No choice at all.'

256

He hardly dared to speak, afraid to break the moment.

'So he asked you to marry him, and then all the debts would be made good, and the business restored.'

'You know my husband,' she said. 'What do *you* believe?'

'I believe I should go. Leave here without delay.' He felt her move as though she too would go, but he did not release her. 'I know I have no right, and others would condemn me . . .'

She said softly, 'But?' Only one word.

'That night, aboard my ship, I wanted you.' He pulled her closer, feeling her warmth, her nearness. Her awareness. 'I still do.'

She leaned against him, her face in his shirt, perhaps giving herself time to recognise the danger, and the folly.

She said, 'You have not been fed by the gallant Captain Forbes. I can at least do something about that.' She tried to laugh. 'I can smell the cognac, so I was right about the pair of you!'

But when he held her again she was shivering.

'We will go inside . . . then you can tell me all about yourself.' She could not continue. 'Come, now. Quickly. Banish all doubts!' She paused only to look at the harbour. 'All that can wait, this once.'

Even though he had never set foot in the place before, he knew it was the same. Here Catherine had spent her last night with her Richard, in these rooms which Avery had found so difficult to describe, and of which Bethune had carefully avoided speaking, as if it was too painful even for him.

He walked to a window and eased the shutter aside very slightly and looked down into the courtyard, dark now but for the reflected glow from a copper dusk.

He heard the sentry at the gates stamp his feet, and the clink of metal as he shifted his musket, yawning at the dragging hours.

There were no lights in the windows opposite. Forbes had gone to dine with the army; the staff had probably been left to do as they pleased until Bethune's return.

He felt his muscles contract. Voices now, very low, the sound of glasses. And when he closed the shutter and turned he saw her facing him from the other side of the room, her

257

eyes very clear in the glow of candles which must have been arranged here earlier.

She said, 'A little wine, Adam. It is as cool as can be expected. Some food can be sent for later.'

She watched him cross the room, and turned slightly so that the piece of silver at her breast shone suddenly like a flame. She wore a plain white gown which covered her from her throat to her feet, now bare on the marble floor.

He put his hands on her arms, and said, 'You kept it. I thought you'd thrown it away.'

He touched the small silver sword and felt her stiffen as she answered, 'I am wearing it for you. How could I not wear it?'

He lowered his mouth to her shoulder and kissed it, feeling the smoothness of her skin beneath the gown.

'The *wine*.' She pressed him away. 'While it's cool.'

He brought the glasses from the table and held one to her lips, and they looked at one another over the rims, all pretence gone, all reason scattered.

She did not resist or speak as he kissed her shoulder again, and each breast in turn until she gasped softly and put her arms around him, holding him there, her head moving from side to side as if she could no longer contain herself.

He stood, and held her at arm's length, seeing the darker patches on the silk, where he had kissed and roused the points of her breasts.

There was a tall mirror on the wall and he turned her towards it, his hands around her waist, seeing the reflection of her eyes in the glass, then deliberately he unclipped the little sword, and opened and removed the gown. He looked over her shoulder, his face in her hair as he watched with her, as if they were onlookers, strangers. Exploring her body, feeling every response like his own, until she twisted round in his grip and said, 'Kiss me. Kiss me.'

He lifted her as he had the night aboard *Unrivalled*, holding her tightly as they kissed again. And again. He laid her on the broad bed and threw off his coat, and the old sword slid unnoticed to a rug by his feet.

She propped herself on one elbow, and said, '*No!* Come to me now!'

258

He knelt beside her, his mind and reason gone as she struggled to free him from his clothes, pulling him down to kiss her mouth once more until they were breathless.

He gazed at her, hungry for her, the hair disordered across the pillows, the hands, suddenly strong, gripping his shoulders, one moment holding him away and then drawing him down to her body, her skin hot and damp as if with fever.

He felt her nails breaking his skin as he came against her, and she moved still further, arching her body until they were almost joined. Then she opened her eyes, and whispered, '*I yield*!' and gave a small, soft cry as he found and entered her.

It was like falling, or being carried along by an endless, unbroken wave.

Even when they lay exhausted she would not release him. They clung to one another, breathless, drained by the intensity of their congress, their need.

Hours later, after they had explored every intimacy, she sat on the bed, her knees drawn up to her chin as she watched him pulling on his breeches and shirt.

'A King's officer. To everyone else but me.' She reached out impetuously and touched him again, held him, while he bent to kiss her. She had found and touched the old wound and had kissed the jagged scar, her passion roused again. *No secrets, Adam* . . .

When he looked again she was dressed in the thin robe, the silver clasp in place, as if the rest had been a wild dream.

A chapel bell was ringing tunelessly; someone was already awake. She opened the door, and he saw that fresh candles had been brought to light the stairs. Hilda, ensuring that nothing would go amiss.

He held her, feeling the supple limbs through the silk, wanting her again in spite of the risks.

She said, 'No regrets.' She was still looking after him when he reached the courtyard.

Her voice seemed to hang in the warm air. *No regrets* . . .

The guard at the gate was being changed, and a corporal was reading out the standing orders, too tired or too bored to see the naval officer striding past.

He paused in a deserted alley, which he thought was the

one where he had purchased the little silver sword. He could still feel her, enclosing him, guiding him, taking him.

He might never see her again; if he did, she might laugh at his desire. Somehow he knew that she would not.

He thought he heard the creak of oars, the guardboat, and quickened his pace.

But regrets? It was far too late for them now.

17

The Family

Adam Bolitho sat at his table, a pen poised over his personal log, the sun through the stern windows warming his shoulder. Another day at anchor, and the ship around him was quietly alive with normal working sounds, and the occasional shouted order.

He stared at the date at the top of the page. *30th September 1815.* So much had happened, and yet at moments like these it was as if time had been frozen.

He thought of his conversation with Captain Forbes earlier in the evening he had ended in the room above the courtyard. That, too, was like a dream. But Forbes had been right in what he had told him, or rather what he had not told him. It had broken over the squadron just two days ago when Bethune had returned from his inspection of coastal defences with Sir Lewis Bazeley. It was no longer a rumour, but a fact. Bethune was leaving as soon as he was relieved. And that was today.

The two third-rates of which Forbes had also spoken had already been sighted by the lookout post ashore.

Adam laid down the pen and recalled his last meeting with Bethune, who had seemed pleased at the prospect of a new position at the Admiralty as assistant to the Third Sea Lord, with all the promise of advancement it would carry for him. But he had been on edge, evasive, although Adam had not known why. And then, with all the other captains and commanders of the squadron, he had partly understood the reason. The new flagship was *Frobisher*, which had been Richard Bolitho's own, and now it was returning to Malta where so much had begun and ended.

The other arrival would be the eighty-gun *Prince Rupert*, which Adam had seen and boarded at Gibraltar. The big two-decker was no longer Rear-Admiral Marlow's flagship, although Pym was still in command, and he had heard the flurry of speculation as to why the new flag officer, a senior admiral, should hoist his flag over the smaller of the two ships.

He was convinced that Bethune, better than anyone, would know the answers. Lord Rhodes had been Controller at the Admiralty when Bethune had been there, and those who understood or were interested in such matters had been convinced that Rhodes had been put forward for First Lord, supported by no less than the Prince Regent. Then the appointment had been suspended, quashed, and now it was obvious that Rhodes had been given the Mediterranean station as an honourable demotion. Rhodes would not need reminding that Lord Collingwood, Nelson's friend and his second-in-command at Trafalgar, had been given the same command. For some reason Collingwood had neither been promoted to admiral nor allowed to return home, even though illness had forced him to apply many times for relief. He had died at sea, five long years after leading the Lee Division against the combined fleets of France and Spain.

And now *Frobisher* was here again. Different faces perhaps, but the same ship. New compared to most ships of the line, she would be about nine years old now, French-built, and taken as a prize on passage to Brest some five years back. He turned it over in his mind warily, like a hunter looking for traps. James Tyacke had been his uncle's flag captain, and his predecessor had been a Captain Oliphant, a cousin of Lord Rhodes, a favour which perhaps had misfired. In one of her letters Catherine had mentioned meeting Rhodes just prior to the choice of flagship, and it had been obvious that she had disliked him. It could be that Rhodes had chosen *Frobisher* merely because she was the better ship. He considered Bethune's uncharacteristic evasiveness and doubted it.

There was a tap at the door and Galbraith peered in at him.

'The flagship has been sighted, sir.'

Adam nodded. Not *new* flagship; Galbraith would know his captain's thoughts about *Frobisher*, and how he would feel when he was summoned aboard for the first time. The memories, and the ghosts.

Galbraith said, 'I have made certain that all hands will be properly turned out. Yards will be manned, and we will cheer-ship if necessary.' He smiled. 'I understand that Admiral Lord Rhodes will expect it. Two or three of the older hands have served under him.'

Adam closed his log. That said it all. It was a long time since Rhodes had walked the deck of his own flagship; he would be looking for flaws, if only to prove he had forgotten nothing. Galbraith watched him impassively, recognising the signs.

'Our new lieutenant has settled into his rank quite well, sir. Though I fear Mr Bellairs will need a larger hat if he continues in this fashion!'

But there was no malice in the comment, and Adam knew he was as pleased as most of the others when Bellairs had returned from his promotional examination with his *scrap of parchment*, as the old timers called it. An extra lieutenant. That would not be tolerated, beneficial though it might be for running the ship.

Adam leaned back slightly. 'There will be an opening in the squadron, or perhaps within the fleet before long.' He saw Galbraith stiffen. It was the moment he had been hoping for, what every lieutenant dreamed of. 'You held a command before you came to *Unrivalled*. Your experience and example did much to iron out the wrinkles, so to speak, before we were all put to the test. Perhaps we did not always agree about certain matters.' He smiled suddenly, the strain and the tension dropping away like the years. 'But as your commanding officer I, of course, always have the advantage of being right!'

Galbraith said, 'I am well content here, sir . . .'

Adam held up his hand. 'Never say that. Never even think it. My uncle once described a command, especially a first one, as *the most coveted gift*. I have never forgotten it. Nor must you.'

They both looked at the glittering water beyond the anchored vessels astern as the first crash of cannon fire rolled across the harbour. The response, gun by gun, from the battery wall seemed even louder.

Adam said, 'We'll go up, shall we?'

He clipped on the old sword, then he said, 'Mr Bellairs will have no sword as yet.' He gestured to his own curved hanger in its rack. 'He may have that one if he chooses to wait until his parents do him the honour!'

He touched the sword at his hip. So many times. So many hands. And he was reminded of the note Catherine had written for him, and had left with the sword at Falmouth.

The sword outwore its scabbard. Wear it with pride, as he always wanted.

Frobisher was back. And *he* would know.

Vice-Admiral Sir Graham Bethune winced as the Royal Marine guard of honour slammed to attention once more, a cloud of pipeclay floating over their leather hats like smoke while the band struck up a lively march. The ceremony was almost finished. Bethune could not recall how many he had witnessed or participated in since he had entered the navy. Probably thousands. He tried to relax his muscles. Why, then, was he so disturbed, even agitated, when this was opening new doors to his own future?

He glanced at the man for whose benefit this ceremony had been mounted. His successor: to him it might seem the end of everything, rather than a fresh challenge.

Admiral Lord Rhodes was shaking hands with the governor's representative, but it was impossible to tell what he was thinking. Rhodes had been at the Admiralty when Bethune had been appointed there, and for a good many years before that, and they had met occasionally, but Bethune had never really known him. His elevation to First Lord had been taken for granted, until the day Sillitoe had burst unannounced into the office and had demanded to speak with Rhodes. Bethune had learned only then that he had been appointed the Prince Regent's Inspector-General.

It had been Rhodes' cousin, once *Frobisher*'s captain, who had attempted to rape Catherine. *Because I allowed her to go home unescorted.* He thought of Adam's face when he had mentioned Rhodes' particular interest in Sir Richard Bolitho's flagship. He had been ashamed that he could conceal the full truth, but it would have helped no one, least of all Catherine, and he had to consider what old hatreds might do to his own future, as well as Adam's.

But the much-used code of conduct failed to afford him any comfort. It seemed in this instance merely a device which placed expediency before honour and friendship.

He studied his successor once more. Rhodes was tall and heavily built, and had once been handsome. His face was dominated by a strong, beaked nose which made his eyes appear small by comparison, but the eyes, overshadowed though they were, missed nothing. The band was comprised of soldiers borrowed at short notice from the garrison commander, a friend of Captain Forbes; the frigates carried Royal Marine drummers and fifers but they had not yet paraded together. Rhodes had commented on the music, a military quick march, which he thought inappropriate.

The walls had been lined with people watching the ceremony, and Bethune had found himself wondering how long it would take news of Rhodes' appointment to reach the Dey of Algiers.

He walked across the dusty jetty as the guard was dismissed and the onlookers began to disperse. He saw Sir Lewis Bazeley standing in the shade of a clump of sun-dried trees; how would he get along with Rhodes, if he stayed in Malta? An energetic man, eager, Bethune had thought, to impress on younger men what he could do, although Bethune could not imagine him having anything in common with the girl he had married. He had never known if Lady Bazeley had really been in ill health when she had declined to accompany them in the brig. He had thought about Adam's presence here during that time, but Forbes had said nothing to him on the subject, and he was, after all, his flag captain.

And finally, he considered England, the grey skies and chill breezes of October. He smiled. It would be wonderful.

Rhodes strode over to join him. 'Smart turn-out, Sir Graham. Standards – they count more than ever, eh?'

Bethune said, 'I shall show you the temporary headquarters building, m' lord. I have sent for a carriage.'

Rhodes grinned. 'Not a bit of it, we'll walk. I can see the great barn of a place from here!' He gestured to his flag lieutenant. 'Tell the others!'

Bethune sighed. Another Bazeley, or so it seemed.

By the time they had gone halfway Rhodes was breathing heavily, and his face was blotched with sweat, but he had never stopped firing questions. About the six frigates in the squadron, and the expectations of getting more. About the many smaller craft, brigs, schooners and cutters which were the eyes and ears of the man whose flag flew in command.

They paused in deep, refreshing shadow while Rhodes turned to stare at the anchored men-of-war, shimmering in haze above their reflections.

'And *Unrivalled*'s one of them, is she?' He looked at Bethune, his eyes like black olives. 'Bolitho, what's he like?'

'A good captain, m' lord. Successful as well as experienced. What the navy is going to need more than ever now.'

'Ambitious, then?' He looked at the ships again. 'He's done well, I'll give him that. Father a traitor, mother a whore. He's done *very* well, I'd say!' He laughed and strode on.

Bethune contained his fury, at Rhodes and with himself. When he reached the Admiralty perhaps he could discover some way to transfer Adam. But not without *Unrivalled*. She was all he had.

Rhodes had stopped once more, his breathless retinue filling the street.

'And who is *that*, sir?'

Bethune saw a flash of colour on the balcony as Lady Bazeley withdrew into the shadows.

'Sir Lewis Bazeley's wife, m' lord. I explained –'

Rhodes grunted, 'Women in their place, that's one thing.' Again the short, barking laugh Bethune had often heard in London. 'But I'll not have them lifting their skirts to my staff!'

Bethune said nothing. But if it came to drawing a card, his own money would be on Bazeley rather than Rhodes.

And then he knew he was glad to be leaving Malta.

Luke Jago bowed his legs slightly and peered at *Halcyon*'s stout anchor cable to gauge the distance as the gig swept beneath her tapering jib boom, then glanced at the stroke oar and over the heads of the crew, easing the tiller-bar until the flagship appeared to be pinioned on the stemhead. They were a good boat's crew, and he would make certain they stayed that way.

He saw the captain's bright epaulettes catch the sunlight as he leaned over to gaze at the anchored seventy-four.

Professional interest? It was more than that and Jago knew it. Felt it. There were plenty of other boats arriving and leaving *at God's command*.

Vice-Admiral Bethune at least had seemed human enough, and had obviously got on well with the captain. Now he had gone. Jago had seen Captain Bolitho and the first lieutenant watching the courier brig as she had made sail, with the vice-admiral her only passenger. Most senior officers would have expected something grander than a brig, he thought. Bethune must have been that eager to get away.

And now there was Lord Rhodes, a true bastard to all accounts. More trouble.

Jago looked at the midshipman sitting below him. The new one, Deighton. Very quiet, so far, not like his father had been. He wondered if the boy had any idea of the truth. *Killed in action, for King and Country.* His lip almost curled with contempt. Deighton had been scared rotten even before the ball had marked him down.

The flagship was towering over them now, masts and spars black against a clear blue sky. Every piece of canvas in place, paintwork shining like glass.

A ship, any ship, could look very different in the eyes of those who saw her. Jago knew from hard experience how it could be. To the terrified landsman, snatched from his daily life by the hated press gang, the ship was a thing of overwhelming terror and threat, where only the strong and the cunning survived. To a midshipman boarding his first vessel she would appear awesome, forbidding, but the light of excitement was already kindled, ready to be encouraged or snuffed out.

He looked at the captain's shoulders, squared now as if to meet an adversary. To him, she would seem different again.

He saw him shade his eyes and raise his head, knew what he was looking for, and what it meant to him. Today. Now. The Cross of St George lifting and rippling from *Frobisher*'s mainmast truck: the admiral's flag, where his uncle's had been flying when they had shot him down.

He had died bravely, they said. Without complaint. Jago found he could accept it, especially when he looked at his own captain.

'Bows!' He did not even have to raise his voice. Other coxswains were here, watching, and there were several, grander launches with coloured canopies over their sternsheets.

Jago swore silently. He had almost misjudged the final approach to *Frobisher*'s main chains, where white-gloved sideboys were waiting to assist their betters to the entry port.

'*Oars!*' He counted seconds. '*Up!*'

The gig came to rest alongside perfectly. *So you could crack an egg between them*, as old coxswains boasted.

But it had been close. Jago had seen the canopied launches. It usually meant that women would be present, officers' wives maybe, or those of the governor's staff. But there was only one who troubled him, and he could see her now, half-naked, her gown soaked with spray and worse. And the captain holding her. Not scornful, or making a meal of it like some, *most*, would have done.

Adam got to his feet, one hand automatically adjusting his sword. For only an instant their eyes met, then Jago said formally, 'We shall be waitin', sir.'

Adam nodded, and looked at the midshipman. 'Listen and learn, Mr Deighton. *Your* choice, remember?'

The midshipman removed his hat as Adam reached for the hand ropes. They heard the twitter of calls and the bark of commands, then he asked quietly, 'You were there too, weren't you? When my father . . .'

Jago answered sharply, 'Aye, sir. A lot of us was there that day. Now take the tiller an' cast off the gig, can you manage that?'

The youth dropped his lashes. It was as if Jago had told him what he had not dared to ask.

Above their heads, as the gig cast off to make way for another visitor, Adam replaced his hat and shook the hand of *Frobisher*'s captain, a lantern-jawed Scot named Duncan Ogilvie. He was well over six feet tall, and it was hard to imagine him living comfortably in any ship smaller than this.

'You must allow the admiral a few minutes to bid farewell to an early visitor.' He gestured vaguely with his head. 'Commodore from the Dutch frigate yonder.'

Adam had watched her anchor and had felt the old uneasiness at the sight of her flag amongst the squadron's ships. The flag of a once respected enemy, but an enemy for all that. It would take even stronger determination when the French ships began to appear. He turned to say something, but the other captain was already greeting a new arrival, and his eyes were moving swiftly beyond him to yet another boat heading for the chains.

Adam had been a flag captain twice, with his uncle and with Valentine Keen. It was never an easy appointment. To be Rhodes' flag captain would be impossible.

A harassed lieutenant eventually found him and escorted him aft to the great cabin. Even with all the screens removed and furniture kept to a minimum, the whole of the admiral's quarters was packed with uniforms, red and scarlet, and the blue and white of sea officers. And women. Bare shoulders, bold glances from the younger ones, something like disdain from the not so young.

The lieutenant called out Adam's name and ship, and a marine orderly appeared as if by magic with a tray of glasses.

'Better take the red wine, sir. T' other's not much good.' Then, as an afterthought, he murmured, 'Corporal Figg, sir. Me brother's one o' your Royals!' He hurried away, wine slopping unheeded over his sleeve.

Adam smiled. The family again.

'Ah, there you are, Bolitho!' It sounded like *at last*. Rhodes waited for him to push through the crowd, his head bowed between the deck beams. He was almost as tall as his flag captain.

Rhodes said loudly, 'I don't suppose you've had the pleasure of meeting Captain Bolitho? Commands one of my frigates.'

And there she was, smiling a little as she stepped from behind the admiral's considerable bulk. She was all in blue, her hair piled above her ears, the luminous skin of throat and shoulders as he remembered.

She said, 'On the contrary, Lord Rhodes, we know one

269

another quite well,' and offered her hand deliberately, unaware or indifferent to the eyes upon them.

An officer was speaking urgently to the admiral, and Rhodes had turned away, obviously angered by the interruption.

As Adam raised the hand to his lips, she added softly, 'I should have said, *very well*.'

They stood by the stern windows, watching their reflections in the thickened glass. They did not touch, but Adam could feel her as if she was pressed against him.

She said, 'We shall be leaving Malta very soon.' She turned as if to follow another reflection, but the figure melted away and was lost in the throng.

Then she moved slightly, with one hand raised. 'Look at me.'

Adam saw the little silver sword at her breast. There were so many things he wanted to say, needed to ask, but he could sense the urgency, the hopeless finality. Of a dream.

She said, 'You look wonderful.' Her free hand moved and withdrew. As if she had been about to touch him, had forgotten where they were. 'The bruise? Is it gone?'

Their eyes met, and he felt the irresistible thrill of danger as she murmured, 'My mother said when I was a child and I hurt myself, *I'll kiss it better, Rozanne*.' She looked away. 'It was so beautiful, all of it.' Her lip quivered. 'I shall not spoil it now.'

'You couldn't spoil anything . . .' He lingered over the name. 'Rozanne.'

He heard Rhodes' voice again, and Bazeley's, and their laughter. She raised her chin, and said steadily, 'You see, *Captain*, I love you!'

Bazeley said loudly, 'Here she is!' and, as they turned, 'Captain Bolitho. More adventures, I hear!' He took his wife's arm. 'That's a sailor's life! Not for me, I'm afraid. I like to build things, not knock 'em down.'

Rhodes' eyes were on Bazeley's hand around her bare arm. 'Sometimes we have to do one before we can afford the other, Sir Lewis!'

Bazeley grinned broadly. 'There, what did I tell you?' He made a show of dragging out his watch. 'I must make our excuses, m' lord. I have to see some people.' He looked at

270

Adam. 'I wish you well.' He did not offer his hand, or remove it from her arm.

A lieutenant was waiting anxiously. 'I have summoned your boat, Sir Lewis.'

Bazeley nodded, dismissing him. 'Given the backing of Parliament, we shall see Malta turned into a fortress. It makes me feel humble to be offered the task, huge though it is!'

They moved away into the crowd, but when Bazeley paused to speak with a senior army officer and clasp him ostentatiously around the shoulders, Rozanne turned and looked directly at Adam.

No words. Just the hand on the little silver sword, pressed against her breast. Nothing more was needed.

Rhodes was saying thickly, 'If *he's* humble, then I'm the bloody Iron Duke!'

Adam realised that Captain Forbes had joined him, and was holding two glasses, one of which he offered.

Forbes said, 'Quite a gathering,' and sighed. 'And ours is a private ship again, for better or worse.' Then he murmured, 'I heard before you joined the squadron that you were not afraid to take a risk, if you considered it justified.' His eyes shifted to the admiral. '*Now*, I understand.'

When Adam looked again, she had gone.

Catherine Somervell turned away from the low stone wall and watched the coachman and groom adjusting the harness, and quieting the two horses which had just been led from the stables. A smart carriage, but it was strange not to see the familiar crest on its door. This one was Roxby's. She smiled sadly, reminiscently. *The King of Cornwall*, as he had been known, affectionately for the most part, although not, perhaps, to those who had appeared before him in his capacity as magistrate.

She saw Roxby's widow, Nancy, giving a parcel to the coachman and emphasising something with a gesture. Food for the journey. Like Grace Ferguson at the old Bolitho house, Nancy always seemed to think she was not getting enough to eat.

She turned her back on the drive and the house and gazed at the nearest hillside. Smooth and green, and yet the sea lay just beyond it. Lying in wait . . .

She had stayed for a single night here with Richard's youngest sister. Now she would return to Plymouth, where Sillitoe was waiting. She had had mixed emotions about meeting Valentine Keen again, but she need not have worried; he and his wife had made her more than welcome, and Sillitoe also. There had been no questions or hints, not even the revival of old memories. Keen would never change, and his second marriage was obviously a success. Gilia was exactly what he needed, and Catherine knew simply by talking to her that Keen was still unaware of Adam's love for Zenoria.

Coming back to the old house below Pendennis Castle had been very hard for her. So many familiar faces, obviously delighted to see her again: Bryan and Grace, Young Matthew, so many of them. And one other. Daniel Yovell, Richard's secretary, had moved back into his little cottage and Bryan Ferguson had signed him on as his deputy, with obvious relief. One of *the little crew*, as Richard used to call them. There had been no time to visit Fallowfield, and she still did not know if she was relieved or saddened by it. Seeing Allday again so soon might have been more than she could bear. With Keen and the others it was difficult enough; she thought Allday would have broken down her last defences.

Nancy joined her by the wall, wrapped in a thick shawl.

'There'll be an early winter, I think.' Catherine felt the eyes on her, full of affection and anxiety. 'If only you could stay a while longer. But if there's anything you need, you have only to write and let me know.' She slipped an arm around her waist, like a young girl again. The girl who had been in love with a midshipman, the young Richard Bolitho's best friend.

'We have many things to do before we sail for Spain, Nancy. I have so enjoyed being here with you.'

They stood in silence for a moment.

'You mustn't worry about Tamara. She'll be well exercised and cared for, until . . .' She broke off. 'You know what I mean.'

Catherine said deliberately, 'I am not living at Chelsea now, Nancy. I am staying at Lord Sillitoe's house in Chiswick.' She had started; she could not stop. 'I have never felt the same about the Chelsea house since that night.' She felt Nancy's grip tighten around her waist. 'Sometimes of late I have seen men watching the house, or imagined I have. Waiting for a chance to see *that woman*.'

Nancy asked softly, 'Shall you marry this Sillitoe? It is obvious to me that he adores you, and rightly so. Remember, I did not marry Roxby for love, but it grew to something even stronger. I still miss him.'

They turned away from the wall and faced the carriage. It was time.

Catherine said, 'He gave up his appointment to the Prince Regent because of me. I shall not destroy his life as well with another scandal.' She inclined her head, as if someone had spoken to her. 'I shall tell you, you of all people.'

There were faces at the upper windows, servants looking out as *that woman* prepared to leave their ordered world. And Elizabeth would be here tomorrow. Another challenge, for both of them. Nancy had sent her to Bodmin with her governess to arrange for some more appropriate clothing and to see something of the town.

Growing up fast, Nancy had said. A withdrawn, demure child who had been too long in the company of older people. She had told Catherine about the day following the girl's arrival. It had been hard to tell how she had been affected by her mother's untimely death, and even now she was still not sure.

But on that day Nancy had taken her down to one of the beaches where Catherine had so often walked with Richard. Some children had been standing in the shallows, hunting for shells, Nancy thought. Elizabeth had remarked on their bare feet. *Had the children no shoes? Were they too poor to own them?*

She had said, 'My word, when I think what *we* used to do at her age!'

Catherine turned and embraced her with great feeling.

'I shall never forget your kindness, and your love. I have always known why Richard cared so much for you.'

The door was open, a gloved hand was held out to support her wrist, Nancy was crying, and suddenly the wheels were moving.

Out on to the road, which ran in the other direction to the old grey house. Where she had waited, and hoped, for the sound of his voice.

When she looked again, the hillside had moved out to hide the house and the small figure who was still waving.

She sat back against the soft leather and stared at the parcel wrapped in its spotless napkin. His old boat cloak was folded beside it, which she had always worn when the wind was blowing coldly off the Bay. There were scissors in the pocket, and she had found one rose still alive and blooming in that familiar garden.

But she had been unable to cut it. And was glad. It was a part of her. It belonged there.

The last rose.

Unis Allday knotted the ties of a fresh apron behind her back and gave herself a critical glance in the parlour glass. The first customers would be arriving soon, most likely buyers and auctioneers on their way to market in Falmouth, and it would be busy at the Old Hyperion inn. She checked each item in her mind, as she did every day. Deliveries of meat and fowl, ale from the brewery.

She walked to the door of the Long Room. Rugs brushed clean of the mud from farm workers' boots, shining mugs and fashionable glasses for the salesmen, and a fire burning in the grate even though it was only October.

A carter had told her that fishermen had reported heavy mist around Rosemullion Head. They were all talking of an early winter.

Little Kate was out walking with Nessa, the new servant at the inn, a tall, dark woman who rarely smiled but had drawn many an admiring glance nevertheless. Not least from Unis's brother, the other John. She was younger than he, but Unis thought she would be good for him; it would be a new beginning for both of them. Nessa had fallen for a soldier from the garrison at Truro; it was a familiar enough tale. She had carried and lost his child, and her lover had been posted with unseemly haste to the West Indies.

Nessa's parents were good chapel people, well known in Falmouth for their strict Christian beliefs. They had turned their daughter out of the house without hesitation.

Unis had taken her into the inn and she had settled down,

perhaps grateful for Unis's trust, and her own sturdy interpretation of Christian charity.

The door from the stable yard swung open and John Allday strode into the parlour.

She knew instantly that something was wrong with him, her man, her love. She also thought she knew what it was.

Allday said heavily, 'I just seen Toby the cooper's mate. He told me Lady Catherine was up at the house. Yesterday, he said.' It sounded like an accusation.

She faced him; she had been right. 'I did hear something about it.' She put a hand on his sleeve; it looked very small and neat on his massive arm.

'You never said?'

She regarded him calmly. 'And well you knows why, John. You're coming to terms with things. So let you think of her, too. Poor lamb, she's got more'n enough to carry.'

Allday smiled fondly. Small, neat and pretty. His Unis. But woe betide anyone who tried to take advantage of her. She was strong. *Stronger than me in many ways.*

They walked to the window together. The place had been in debt when she had bought it. Now it was prospering and looked pleased with itself. One of the ostlers was doing his usual trick with a potato, making it disappear in mid-air and then holding out both tightly clenched fists and letting little Kate choose the one where it was hidden. The child was thinking about it now, her face screwed up with concentration, while Unis's brother stood nearby, watching the dark-haired Nessa.

The child tapped a fist, and it was of course empty, and she screamed with delight and frustration. It never failed.

'We've done well, John.' And they were widening the lane across Greenacre Farm; coaches would be stopping here soon. People had laughed at old Perrow when the plan had been made public, but they would be laughing on the other sides of their faces before long. The wily squire would charge a toll for every coach that crossed his land.

Allday said, '*You've* done well, lass.'

It was there again, the old sense of loss. Like when he had told her about Captain Tyacke calling at Falmouth in his new command.

She heard her brother's wooden leg thudding across the

floor, and wondered what Nessa thought about that, or if she had even guessed his feelings for her.

He said, 'Someone asking for you, John.'

Allday came out of his thoughts. 'Me? Who is it?'

He grinned. 'Didn't offer, John.' He added, 'Odd-looking cove. Knows *you* right enough.'

Allday opened the other door and stared past the fire. There were two people in the room already, a black dog snoozing between them.

For a moment he thought he was mistaken. The wrong surroundings. The wrong background.

Then he strode across the room and grasped the newcomer around his narrow shoulders.

'*Tom!* In God's name, Tom Ozzard! Where in *hell* have you been hiding?'

'Oh, here and there. Up home in London, mostly.'

'Well, I'll be double-damned! You skipped off the ship the minute we was paid off. Not a word out of you. What are you doing here?'

Ozzard had not changed in one way. He was as curt and abrupt as ever, the pointed features unsmiling.

He said, 'Thought you'd have a corner where I could pipe down before moving on.'

Moving on. Up home in London. Ozzard had no home.

'*Course* you can stay, you old bugger!'

Unis observed this from the doorway, seeing all things which her beloved John did not see, or want to see. The split shoes, and the threadbare coat with its missing button, the fading hair tied back with a piece of worn ribbon. But this man was part of a world which she could only share at a distance, the life which had taken one husband and had given her another, this big, shambling man who was so glad to see one of its ghosts return. He had spoken often of Ozzard, Sir Richard's personal servant. Like Ferguson, joined now by Yovell up at the house, he was part of the little crew.

She said gently, 'I've some stew on the fire. Maybe you've not eaten yet.'

Ozzard stared at her with eyes which were almost hostile. 'I haven't come because I need anything!'

Allday said quietly, 'Easy, Tom. You're among friends

276

here,' and frowned as voices echoed from the yard. The first of the road labourers were arriving.

Unis was aware of two things. That Ozzard was wary, even distrustful of women, and that her John's pleasure was changing to distress.

She said, 'Come into the parlour. That lot are too noisy for greeting old friends.'

Ozzard sat silently at the table, staring around the room until his eyes came to rest on the model of *Hyperion* in its place of honour.

Allday wanted to talk, if only to reassure him, but was afraid to break something so tentative, so fragile.

Unis was stirring the pot in the kitchen, but her mind was elsewhere.

She said over her shoulder, 'Of course, you being used to Sir Richard an' the likes of other naval gentlemen, you'll know all about wines an' that like.'

Ozzard said suspiciously, 'More than some, yes.'

'I was thinking. With the trade improving on this road, you could be a help to us. To me. There's a room over the tack store. You'd be more'n welcome until you want to move on again.'

She sensed Allday's pleasure and added casually, 'I can't vouch for the money though.'

She had to say something, she thought. Anything. She had noticed the torn cuffs and broken, dirty nails. But he was one of the men who had been with her John and Sir Richard in battles she dared not even begin to imagine.

She came over with the bowl and said, 'Game stew. Get that inside you, an' think about what I said.'

Ozzard bowed his head and blindly picked up the spoon. Then he broke.

'I've got nowhere else,' was all he said.

Much later, when they were alone together, and the inn was quiet until the new day, Allday held her in his arms and murmured, 'How did you know, Unis love?'

She pulled his shaggy head down to her breast. 'Cause I knows *you*, John Allday. An' that's no error!'

She could taste the rum in his kiss, and she was content.

18

Of One Company

'Heave, lads! Heave away!'

With both of *Unrivalled*'s capstans fully manned and every available seaman putting his weight on the bars, the cable was barely moving. Adam Bolitho stood by the quarterdeck rail, his hands clasped beneath his coattails, watching the strange light and the low, scudding clouds. The harbour walls, like the waterfront buildings, seemed to glow with a dull yellow texture, and although it was morning it seemed more like sunset.

The wind had risen slightly, hot against his face, and he tasted grit between his teeth, as if they were already standing off some desert shore. He heard Midshipman Sandell shout impatiently, 'Start that man! Put some weight on the bars there!'

And, instantly, Galbraith's curt, 'Belay that! The cable's moving at last!' He sounded impatient, frustrated, perhaps because of the time wasted here in Malta since Admiral Lord Rhodes had hoisted his flag, which had been followed by this sudden order to get the ships under way.

Clank. The iron pawl of the capstan dropped into position. *Clank*, and then the next one.

Someone said, 'Flagship's cable is shortening, sir!'

Galbraith retorted, 'They have six hundred idle hands to play with!'

Adam looked forward where Massie was peering through the beakhead to watch the bar-taut cable. All of *Unrivalled*'s tonnage and the pressure of wind, set against muscle and sweat.

278

Clank. Clank. As if to a signal he heard the scrape of a violin and then the shantyman's quavery voice. So many times. Leaving harbour. For the sailor the future was always unknown, like the next horizon.

> When first I went to sea as a lad . . .
> *Heave, me bullies, heave!*
> A fine new knife was all I had!
> *Heave, me bullies, heave!*

Adam relaxed slightly. To sea again. But this time under the Flag. The fleet's apron strings, as he had heard other frigate captains describe it.

> And I've sailed for fifty years an' three
> *Heave, lads, heave!*

It was coming in faster now, the capstans turning like human wheels.

> To the coasts of gold and ivory!

Midshipman Sandell hurried past, pointing out something to the new member, Midshipman Deighton.

He had heard Jago remark, 'Look at 'im, will you? Cocking his chest like a half-pay admiral!'

Another memory. What Allday had often said to describe some upstart.

He thought of Admiral Rhodes' hurried conference aboard the flagship. He had received news of another unwarranted attack on some innocent fishermen. A battery had fired on the vessels, and then chebecks had appeared as if from nowhere and had captured or massacred the luckless crews. One of the squadron's armed schooners had been nearby and had attempted to offer assistance, only to be driven off herself. It had been a close thing, to all accounts.

Rhodes had been beside himself with anger. *An example must be made*, before the weather changed yet again. He would delay no longer; all available ships must be ready to sail.

The squadron had been reinforced by a bomb vessel named *Atlas*. She had sailed at first light with *Matchless* as escort.

Adam knew from experience that bomb vessels were difficult at the best of times, being clumsy and unhandy sailers. To use just one such craft without waiting for promised reinforcements would be asking for trouble, no matter how experienced her company might be.

At the captains' conference aboard *Frobisher* he had said as much. Rhodes had turned on him instantly, as if he had been waiting for the chance.

'Of *course*, Captain Bolitho. I almost forgot! A frigate captain of your style and record would condemn the more controlled approach.'

Only Captain Bouverie of *Matchless* had laughed. The others had waited in silence.

Rhodes had continued, 'No daring cutting-out, or some hand-to-hand skirmish with undisciplined renegades, so *you* consider this is not a useful undertaking!'

'I resent that, my lord.' The words had hung in the air, while Rhodes had made a point of studying one of his charts. 'To break the Dey's hold over the Algerine pirates, as he chooses to call them when it suits his purpose, a fleet action will be required.'

Rhodes had shrugged. 'Knowledge is not necessarily wisdom, Captain Bolitho. I trust you will remember it.' He had looked pointedly at the others. 'All of you.'

The shantyman's reedy voice broke into his thoughts again.

And now at the end of a lucky life!

Massie yelled from the forecastle, 'Anchor's hove short, sir!'

Adam nodded, satisfied. 'Loose the heads'ls!' He stared up at the braced yards. 'Hands aloft and loose tops'ls!'

Midshipman Cousens, who had not lowered his telescope and was still watching the flagship, shouted, 'Signal from Flag, sir! *General . . . Make haste!*'

Adam saw the wind feeling its way into the loosely brailed topsails. It was easy to contain your anger when the enemy was so obvious.

The shantyman ended with a flourish, 'Well, still I've got that same old knife!'

'Anchor's aweigh, sir!'

Adam walked to the opposite side to watch the land sliding away, as more men released from the capstan bars hurried to add their weight to the braces, to haul the yards round and capture the wind.

He took a telescope from its rack and trained it on the ancient battlements, and the gaping embrasures where cannon had once dominated the harbour. Where they had held one another. And had loved, impossible though it was to believe.

Galbraith had found him on deck during the morning watch, and had probably imagined he had risen early to see the bomb vessel and the weed-encrusted *Matchless* clearing the harbour.

Or had he guessed that he had been watching the third ship making an early departure, tall and somehow invulnerable with her spreading canvas. A merchantman, the *Aranmore*, bound for Southampton. Had she also been on deck to watch the anchored men-of-war, he wondered? Had she already forgotten, or locked it away, another hidden secret?

He said, 'Take station on the Flag, Mr Galbraith, and lay her on the starboard tack once we are clear.' He tried to smile, to lighten it. 'As ordered, remember?'

He paced to the compass box and back again. And then there was Catherine's letter. Perhaps it would have been better to have sailed earlier, before the latest courier had anchored. *My dear Adam . . .*

What, after all, had he expected? She had nobody to care for her, to protect her from malicious gossip and worse.

He raised the glass again and waited for the image to focus on the first patch of windblown water. *Frobisher*. Much as she had been when she had quit Malta with his uncle's flag at the main. He had felt it when he had walked her deck, sensed it in the watching faces, though few, if any, could have been aboard on that fatal day.

He lowered the glass and looked at his own ship, the seamen flaking down lines and securing halliards. In spite of everything, he had seen the bond grow and strengthen. They were one company.

Perhaps he was wrong about Rhodes, and a show of force was all that it needed. But in his heart he knew it was something else. Unsaid, like that which Bethune had left behind, as dangerous as *Unrivalled*'s shadow on the seabed when they had entered the shallows.

He saw Napier coming aft with something on a covered tray. The boy who had trusted him enough to come and tell him of Lady Bazeley's plight. He laid his palm briefly on the polished wood of the ladder where she had been lying helpless.

He should be able to accept it. Instead, he was behaving like some moonstruck youth.

He heard Cristie give a little cough, waiting to make his report, course to steer, estimated time of arrival. Then the purser would come: provisions and fresh water, and this time, no doubt with Forbes' influence, some welcome casks of beer from the army.

'Signal from Flag, sir!' Midshipman Cousens sounded subdued. '*Make more sail!*'

'Acknowledge.' Adam turned away and saw Midshipman Deighton speaking with the newly minted lieutenant, Bellairs. It gave him time to think, to recall Forbes' words on board *Frobisher*. *Not afraid to take a risk if you thought it justified.*

He said, 'Be patient, Mr Cousens. I fear you will be much in demand until we sight an enemy!'

Those around him laughed, and others who were out of earshot paused in their work as if to share it.

Adam looked through the great web of spars and rigging. Perhaps Rhodes was watching *Unrivalled* at this very moment.

Aloud he said, 'I'll see you damned, *my lord*!'

Bellairs watched the captain walk to the companion way and then gave his attention to the new midshipman again. It was hard to believe that he had been one himself, and so recently given his commission. It would make his parents in Bristol very proud.

The war was over, but for the navy the fighting was never very far away. Like this new challenge, the Algerine pirates. He found violent death more acceptable than the prospect of life as one of those he had seen left wounded and hopelessly crippled.

He touched the fine, curved hanger at his side. He had been astounded when the first lieutenant had told him of the captain's offer.

He suddenly realised what Midshipman Deighton had been asking him about the ship and her young captain.

He said simply, '*I'd* follow him to the cannon's mouth.'

He touched the hanger again and grinned. A King's officer.

Midshipman Cousens lowered the big signals telescope and dashed spray from his tanned features with his sleeve.

'Boat's casting off from the flagship now, sir!'

Lieutenant Galbraith crossed to the nettings and stared at the lively, broken water, the crests dirty yellow in the strange glare. The weather had worsened almost as soon as they had left Malta, wind whipping the sea into serried ranks of angry waves, spray pouring from sails and rigging alike as if they were fighting through a tropical rainstorm. If the wind did not ease, the ships would be scattered overnight. As they had been last night, and they had struggled to reform to the admiral's satisfaction.

As Cristie had often said, the Mediterranean could never be trusted, especially when you needed perfect conditions.

He saw the cutter staggering clear of *Frobisher*'s glistening side; it was a wonder that it had not capsized in its first crossing. To use the gig had been out of the question. A cutter was heavier and had the extra brawn to carry her through this kind of sea.

He had been both doubtful and anxious when Captain Bolitho had told him he was going across to the flagship to see Rhodes in person, after three signals to the admiral requesting an audience. Each had been denied without explanation, as was any admiral's right. But it was also the right of any captain to see his flag officer, if he was prepared to risk reprimand for wasting the great man's time.

With his own coxswain at the tiller Bolitho had headed away, his boat cloak black with spray before they had covered a few yards. It would not have been the first time a captain had been marooned aboard a flagship because of bad weather. Suppose it had happened now? The captain would have had to endure the sight of his own command hove to under storm canvas, and another man's voice at the quarterdeck rail. *Mine.*

He watched the cutter lifting, porpoising slightly before riding the next trough of dark water, the oars rising and dipping, holding the hull under control. At other times he could scarcely see more than the bowed heads and shoulders of the boat's crew, as if they were already going under.

Galbraith felt only relief. He had heard the rumours about Bolitho's disagreement with the admiral at the last conference, the hostility and the sarcasm, as if Rhodes were trying to goad him into something which would be used against him. It was something personal, and therefore dangerous, even to others who might be tempted to take sides in the matter.

The cutter plunged into a trough and then lifted her stem again like a leaping porpoise. Even without a glass he could see the grin on the captain's face, stronger than any words or code of discipline. He had seen it at first hand in action, when these same men had doubted their own ability to fight and win, had seen how some of them had touched his arm when he had passed amongst them. The victors.

He called sharply, 'Stand by to receive the captain!'

But the boatswain and his party were already there. Like himself, they had been waiting with their blocks and tackles, perhaps without even knowing why.

He saw a small figure in a plain blue coat, drenched through like the rest of them: Ritzen, the purser's clerk. A quiet, thoughtful man, and an unlikely one to spark off a chain of events which might end in a court martial, or worse. But Ritzen was different from the others around him. He was Dutch, and had signed on with the King's navy when he had been rescued by an English sloop after being washed overboard in a storm and left for dead by his own captain.

Ritzen had been ashore in Malta with Tregillis, the purser, buying fruit from local traders rather than spend a small fortune at the authorised suppliers. He had fallen in with some seamen from the Dutch frigate *Triton* which had called briefly at the island. Her captain, a commodore, had paid a visit to Lord Rhodes.

Galbraith could recall the moment exactly, after another long day of sail and gun drill, and a seemingly endless stream of signals, mostly, it appeared, directed at *Unrivalled*.

Everyone knew it was wrong, unfair, but who would dare to say as much? Galbraith had gone to the great cabin, where he had found the captain in his chair, some letters open on his lap, and a goblet of cognac quivering beside him to each thud of the tiller head.

Despair, resignation, anger: it had been all and none of them.

After reporting the state of the ship and the preparations for station-keeping overnight, Galbraith had told him about the purser's clerk. Ritzen had overheard that the Dutch frigate was on passage to Algiers, her sale already approved and encouraged by the Dutch government. It had been like seeing someone coming alive again, a door to freedom opening, when moments earlier there had been only a captive.

'I knew there was something strange when I heard it aboard *Frobisher*!' Adam had gone from the chair to the salt-stained stern windows in two strides, the dark hair falling over his forehead, the weight of command momentarily forgotten. 'A commodore in charge of a single frigate! That alone should have told me, if nobody else was prepared to!'

Perhaps Rhodes had forgotten, or thought it no one else's business. Maybe Bethune's records had not been examined. Galbraith thought it unlikely, and when he had seen the light in the captain's eyes he knew it for certain.

'I shall see the admiral . . .' He must have seen the doubt in Galbraith's face. To risk another confrontation, and all on the word of the purser's clerk, seemed reckless if not downright dangerous. But there had been no such doubt in Bolitho's voice. 'Such intelligence is valuable beyond measure, Leigh! To *any* sea officer, time and distance are the true enemies. This man spoke out, and I intend that his words should be heard!'

He had stared at the leaping spectres of spray breaking across the thick glass, and it had been then that Galbraith had seen the locket on the table beside the goblet. The beautiful face and high cheekbones, the naked shoulders. He had never laid eyes on her, but he had known that it was Catherine Somervell. *That woman*, who had scorned society and won the hearts of the fleet, and of the nation.

Galbraith stood back from the dripping hammock nettings. He was soaked to the skin, but he had felt nothing. He suppressed a shiver, but it was not cold or fear. It was something far stronger.

'After you have secured the cutter, Mr Partridge, pass my compliments to the purser and have a double tot issued to the boat's crew.' He saw the little clerk staring up at him. 'And also for Ritzen.'

And, as suddenly as he had departed, the captain was here on the streaming deck with his gasping, triumphant oarsmen.

He shook his cocked hat and tossed it to his servant.

'All officers and warrant ranks aft in ten minutes, if you please.' The dark eyes were everywhere, even as he pushed the dripping hair from his face. 'But I must speak first with you.'

Galbraith waited, remembering the moment when Bazeley's wife had offered her hand to be kissed. The notion had touched him then: how right they had looked together. He had wanted to laugh at his own stupidity. Now, he was not so sure.

Then Adam spoke quietly, so softly that he could have been talking to himself. Or to the ship, Galbraith thought.

'I pray to God for a fair wind tomorrow.' He touched his lieutenant's arm, and Galbraith knew the gesture was unconscious. 'For then we must fight, and only He can help us.'

Lieutenant Massie looked around the crowded cabin, his swarthy features expressionless.

'All present, sir.'

Adam said, 'Sit where you can, *if* you can.' It gave him more time to think, to assemble what he would say.

The cabin was full; even the junior warrant officers were present, some of them staring around as if they expected to discover something different in this most sacred part of their ship.

Adam could feel the hull moving heavily beneath him, but steadier now, the wind holding her over, all sounds muffled by distance.

He could picture Galbraith moving about the quarterdeck overhead, and recalled his face when he had outlined the possibilities of action, as he had to Lord Rhodes.

286

Now Galbraith was on watch, the only officer absent from the cabin.

The two Royal Marine officers, a bright patch of colour, the midshipmen in their own whispering group, and young Bellairs standing with Lieutenant Wynter and Cristie, the taciturn sailing master. The surgeon was present also, dwarfing the scrawy figure of Tregillis the purser. Despite the lack of space the other warrant officers, the backbone of any fighting ship, managed to keep apart. Stranace the gunner stood with his friend the carpenter, 'Old Blane' as he was known, although he was not yet forty. Neither of them could work out a course or compass bearing on a chart, and like most professional sailors they were content to leave such matters to those trained for it. But lay them alongside an enemy ship and they would keep the guns firing, and repair the damage from every murderous broadside. And the master's mates: they would keep the ship under command, knowing they were prime targets for any enemy marksman. The flag and the cause were incidental when it came to surviving the first deadly embrace.

He knew without looking that his clerk, Usher, was at the table, ready to record this rare meeting, with a handkerchief balled in one fist to muffle the cough which was slowly killing him.

The only missing face was that of George Avery. Even as Adam had outlined his convictions to Admiral Rhodes he had thought of Avery, as if he had been speaking for him.

So many times they had talked together, about his service with Sir Richard, his friendship with Catherine. Galbraith had touched upon it too, only a few moments ago in this same cabin.

I think he knew he was going to die, sir. I think he had given up the will to live.

He glanced along the cabin's side. The big eighteen-pounders were held firmly behind their sealed ports, but dragging at the stout breeching ropes with the sway of the deck. As if they were restless, eager.

But instead he saw *Frobisher*'s stern cabin, the great ship riding almost disdainfully across the broken water. Where his uncle had sat and dreamed; had believed, perhaps, that a hand was reaching out at last.

287

The surprising part had been the admiral's frowning silence while he had explained the reason for his visit.

Avery again . . . How he had described their meeting with Mehmet Pasha, the Dey's governor and commander-in-chief in Algiers. Face to face, with no ships to support them but for the smaller twenty-eight gun frigate *Halcyon*. She was out there now, riding out the same weather, with the same young captain who had served under James Tyacke as a midshipman, in this very sea at the Battle of the Nile.

Avery had forgotten nothing, and had filled a notebook with facts of every kind, from the barbarous cruelties he had witnessed, not so far from where they had cut out *La Fortune*, a thousand years ago, or so it felt, even to the names of ships moored there, and the Spanish mercenary, Captain Martinez, who had changed sides too many times for his own good. This command would be his last, one way or the other. Adam seemed to hear Lovatt's despairing voice while he lay dying, here, just beyond the screen of his sleeping quarters. Where he had held the boy Napier circled in his arm, to make himself believe he was the son who had turned away from him.

He licked dry lips, aware of the silence, the intent, watching faces, barely able to accept that he had been talking to these men for several minutes. Even the shipboard noises seemed muted, so that the scrape of Usher's pen seemed loud in the stillness.

He said, 'I believe we shall fight. The main attack will be carried out by the flagship and *Prince Rupert*, and at the right moment by the bomb vessel *Atlas*. Perhaps this is merely a gesture, one worth risking ships and lives. It is not my place to judge.' He held the bitterness at bay, like an enemy. '*Unrivalled*'s place will be up to wind'rd. Ours is the fastest vessel, and apart from the two liners the best armed.' He smiled, as he had done in the cutter to give his oarsmen heart for the return pull. 'I do not need to add, *the best ship*!'

Rhodes would have his way. The bombardment would be carried out without delay after yet another reported attack on helpless fishermen and the murder of their crews. It might make a fitting beginning to the admiral's appointment.

He thought of the Dutch frigate again. Expedience, greed, who could say? The great minds who planned such transactions never had to face the brutal consequences of close action. Maybe the Dutch government had fresh plans for expansion overseas. They already held territories in the West and East Indies, so why not Africa, where rulers like the Dey could obstruct even the strongest moves of empire?

Such deals were left to men like Bazeley . . . his mind faltered for a second . . . and Sillitoe. He saw Lieutenant Wynter watching him fixedly. Or *his* father in the House of Commons and those like him.

'The Dutch frigate *Triton*, or whatever she may now be called, is a powerful vessel . . .'

He heard Rhodes again, his confidence and bluster returning like a strong squall.

'They would not dare! I could blow that ship out of the water!'

He continued, 'I know not what to expect. I merely wanted to share it with you.' He paused, and saw O'Beirne glance around as if he expected to see a newcomer in the cabin. 'For we are of one company.'

He had already seen the doubt on Massie's dark countenance. He knew the chart, the notes in Cristie's log, and now he knew *Unrivalled*'s holding station, well up to windward. Rhodes could not have made it plainer.

'Be content to watch the flank for a change!'

Even the flag captain had warned him openly before he had climbed down to the pitching cutter.

'You've made an enemy there, Bolitho! You sail too close to the wind!'

He would, of course, deny any such remark at a court martial.

They were filing out of the cabin now, and Usher bowed his head in a fit of coughing.

O'Beirne was the last to leave, as Adam had known he would be. They faced one another, like two men meeting unexpectedly in a lane or on some busy street.

O'Beirne said, 'I am glad I wear a sword only for the adornment, sir. I consider myself a fair man and a competent surgeon.' He tried to smile. 'But command? I can only watch at a distance, and be thankful!'

The surgeon walked out into the daylight, and was surprised

to see the planking steaming in the warm wind as if the very ship were burning. There was so much he had wanted to say, to share. And now it was too late. Before sailing from England he had met *Frobisher*'s previous surgeon, Paul Lefroy; they had known one another for years. He smiled sadly. Lefroy was completely bald now, his head like polished mahogany. A good doctor, and a firm friend. He had been with Sir Richard Bolitho when he had died. O'Beirne had pictured it in his friend's words, just as he had seen some of it in his youthful captain's face, and he glanced aft now as if he expected to see him.

Lefroy had said, 'When he died, I felt I had lost a part of myself.'

He shook his head. For a ship's surgeon, even after several glasses of rum, that was indeed something.

But for some reason the levity did not help. The image remained.

Napier, the captain's servant, watched O'Beirne leave, and knew his captain would be alone, perhaps needing a drink, or simply to talk, as he did sometimes. Perhaps the captain did not understand what it meant to him. The boy who had wanted to go to sea, to become someone.

And now he was.

He touched his pocket and felt the broken watch, its guard punched in two by a musket ball, where the little mermaid had been engraved.

The captain had seemed surprised when he had asked if he could keep it, instead of pitching it outboard.

He turned as he heard the sound of a grindstone and the rasp of steel. The gunner was back, too, supervising the sharpening of cutlasses and the deadly boarding axes.

He found that he could face it. Accept it.

He touched the broken watch again and smiled gravely. He was no longer alone.

Joseph Sullivan, the seaman who had taken part in the Battle of Trafalgar and who was *Unrivalled*'s most experienced lookout, paused in his climb to the crosstrees and glanced down at the ship. It took some men years to become used to the height from the deck, the quivering shrouds and treacherous rigging;

some never did. Others were never afforded the chance. Falls were common, and even if the unfortunate lookout fell into the sea it was unlikely that he would recover. If the ship hove to in time.

Sullivan was completely at ease working aloft, and always had been. He looked briefly into the fighting top he had just passed, where some Royal Marines were occupied with a swivel gun and checking their arms and powder. Marines were always busy, he thought.

Sullivan took the weight on his bare soles, so hardened and calloused over the years that he scarcely felt the tarred ratlines, and linked an arm through the shrouds.

The ship had been up and about since before first light, as he had known she would be. He could still taste the rum on his tongue, the pork in his belly. It was a hard life, but he was as content as any true sailor could be.

He peered up at the black shrouds, the big main topsail filling and emptying while the wind tried to make up its mind. No need to hurry. It was too dark to see more than a few yards. He shifted the knife which he carried across his spine like most seamen, where it could not snare anything, but could be drawn in a second.

He smiled. Like the Jack in the shantyman's song when they had weighed anchor, he thought. Sullivan had been in the navy for as long as he could remember. Good ships and foul ones. Fair captains and tyrants. Like the shanty. The old knife was about the only possession he still owned from those first days at sea.

He could smell smoke and grease and heard a splash alongside. The galley fire had been doused; the ship was cleared for action. He sighed. From what he had heard, *Unrivalled* would be well out of it when the guns started to roar. He thought of the captain's face. He was feeling it. He grinned. A real goer, like his uncle to all accounts. But a man. Not afraid to stop and ask one of his men what he was doing, or how he felt. Rare, then.

He began the final climb, pleased that he was not breathless like some half his age. He saw the masthead pendant streaming away to leeward towards the larboard bow. Lifting, then curling again, undecided. He grinned again. Like the bloody admiral.

He reached his position in the crosstrees and hooked his leg around a stay. The wind was steady enough, from the north-east, but the bluster had gone out of it. That would mean that overnight the other ships would have drifted off their stations.

A bombardment, they said. He rubbed his chin doubtfully. It was to be hoped that the admiral knew what he was about. A two-decker made a fine target. It only needed some heated shot to upset the best-laid plans.

He shaded his eyes as the first sunlight played across the sails and braced yards; it was a view which never failed to stir him. People you knew, moving about the deck like ants, and other, isolated scarlet coats like those in the maintop. Marks of discipline, like the blue and white uniforms on the quarterdeck and down by the foremast at the first division of eighteen-pounders. His eyes crinkled as he recalled his captain climbing up to join him. No fuss, no swagger. He had just sat here with him. Not too many could say that.

He could see the coloured bunting scattered over the deck by the flag lockers. Signals to be made and answered, once *Frobisher* was in sight. He could see some of the others now, the bigger *Prince Rupert*, sails apparently limp and useless, and a frigate just off her starboard quarter. That would be *Montrose*, although she was well off station.

He felt the mast shiver, shrouds murmuring as the wind pressed into the topsails again. *Unrivalled* was standing well up to windward, while nearer the coast the whole squadron might become becalmed.

He stared beyond the larboard bow again, but the coast was still little more than a shapeless blur. There could be a mist, too.

He turned his head as a cloud of sea birds took off suddenly from the water and circled angrily over the ship. The spirits of dead Jacks, they said. Surely, he thought, they could find something better to come back as?

He laughed and began to whistle softly to himself. Whistling was forbidden on board a man-of-war, because it could be mistaken for the pipe of a boatswain's call. *They* said. It was more likely because some old admiral in the past had said as much.

That was another part of it. The freedom. Up here, you were your own man. Experience taught you the shades and colours of the sea that governed your life. The depths and the shoals, the sandbars and the deeps. Like when young Captain Bolitho had taken her right through that narrow strait . . . Even Sullivan had felt uneasy about that.

He peered down again and saw one of the midshipmen training his telescope, adjusting it for a new day. And he remembered the captain's surprise, that time when he had proved his skill as a lookout.

He glanced at his arm, the tattoos of ships and places he could scarcely remember. They all swore that they hated it, but what else was there? Perhaps when *Unrivalled* eventually paid off . . . He shook his head, dismissing it. How many times had he said that?

He looked up again and the whistle died on his lips. For only a moment longer he held on to the view, the wheeling gulls, the pale deck far below, the men who were his companions from choice or otherwise.

He held one hand to his mouth, surprised that he had been caught out.

'Deck thar! Sail on th' starboard bow!'

He was too old a hand to consider pride. He was, after all, a good lookout.

293

19

'Trust Me . . .'

Joshua Cristie, the master, watched his captain stride from the chart to the compass box, and said, 'Wind's still holdin' steady from the nor'-east, sir.'

Adam Bolitho stared at the great span of hardening canvas, the masthead pendant reaching out towards the bow like a lance.

He said, 'Make to Flag. *Sail in sight to the west.*' He paused long enough to see Midshipman Cousens and his signals party bending double to fasten the flags into order for hoisting, and caught sight of Bellairs turning from the rail, his eyes anxious, as if he were concerned that someone else was carrying out what had been his duty before his examination for lieutenant.

He forgot them as he raised a telescope and levelled it on the flagship. The other ships were badly scattered, and *Frobisher*'s yards seemed to be a mass of signals as Rhodes tried to muster his command.

It was not long before Cousens shouted, 'Acknowledged, sir!' But it felt like an age. Then Cousens called again, '*Disregard, Remain on station.*'

Adam turned away. 'God damn him!'

Galbraith joined him. 'Shall I send Bellairs aloft, sir? Sullivan's a good hand, but . . .'

Adam looked at him. 'There is a ship, right enough, and we both know which one she is!'

He swung round again as a rocket exploded like a small star against the dusty shoreline. The bomb vessel was moving into position between the flagship and the old fortifications.

294

Rhodes' *show of strength.* Adam knew that anger was blunting his judgment, but he could not help it. If Algiers had any doubts before, they would be gone now.

Even if it was the Dutch frigate, one such ship could do little against Rhodes' array of force.

He thought of the response to his signal. Like a slap in the face, which would soon be known to every man here today. It was cheap. And it was dangerous.

He saw Napier standing by the companion hatch and said, 'Here, take my coat and hat.' He saw Galbraith open his mouth as if to protest, then close it again. Perhaps he was embarrassed to see his own captain making a fool of himself, or maybe he felt it as a slight on his ability that he had not been consulted.

If I am wrong, my friend, it is better for you to know nothing.

Jago was here too, but took his sword and tucked it under his arm without comment.

Adam strode to the shrouds, where he turned and looked back at Galbraith.

'Trust me.' That was all.

Then he was climbing the ratlines, his boots slipping on the taut cordage, his hands and arms grazed by rigging he did not even feel. As he drew level with the maintop the marines stared at him with surprise, then some of them grinned, and one even gave a cheeky wave. Perhaps the man whose brother was a corporal in the flagship.

On and on, higher and higher, until his heart was pounding at his ribs like a fist.

He took Sullivan's hard hand for the last heave up on to the crosstrees, and gasped, 'Where away?'

Sullivan pointed without hesitation, and might even have smiled as Adam dragged out the small telescope which could easily be slung over one shoulder.

The light was still poor, high though he was above the tilting deck, but the other ship was a frigate right enough. Standing away, with all plain sail set and filling to the fresh north-easterly.

He swung the glass to larboard and studied the scattered ships. The two liners were on course again, *Frobisher* in the lead, with *Matchless* and *Montrose* standing well away on either quarter. And, far away, her masts and topsails shimmering in haze, was *Halcyon*, the admiral's 'eyes', leading the squadron.

Then he saw the bomb vessel *Atlas* and found time to pity her commander as he sweated to work his ship into a position from which he could fire. From here it was all a sand-coloured blur, with only the slow-moving ships making sense. Adam had been aboard a bomb vessel during the campaign against the Americans, and *Atlas* seemed little improved. Bluff-bowed, and very heavily constructed for her hundred feet in length; bombs were always hard to handle. Apart from two immensely heavy mortars, they also carried a formidable armament of twenty-four pounder carronades as well as small weapons to fight off boarders. But the mortars were their reason for being. Each was thirteen inches in diameter and fired a massive shot, which, because of its high trajectory, would fall directly on top of its target before exploding. Adam felt his own ship riding over again to the wind. They could keep their bomb vessels . . .

Sullivan said, almost patiently, 'I reckon that when the light clears a bit we'll see the other ship, sir.'

Adam allowed the glass to fall on to its sling and stared at him.

'I saw the frigate. Surely there's no other.'

Sullivan gazed beyond his shoulder. 'She's there, sir. A big 'un.' He looked directly into his eyes. Not the captain, but a visitor to his world. 'But I reckon you already knew that, sir?'

Adam gazed down at the deck. The upturned faces. Waiting . . .

'There could only be one. The merchantman that left Malta when *Atlas* sailed. *Aranmore*.'

Sullivan nodded slowly. 'Might well be, sir.'

Adam reached across and touched his leg. 'A prize indeed.'

He knew Sullivan was leaning over to watch him descend. Even the marines in the fighting top remained quiet and unsmiling as he clambered down past the barricade and its swivel gun, the daisy-cutter, as the sailors called them. Perhaps they saw it in his face, even as he felt it like a tightening grip around his heart.

Galbraith hurried to meet him, barely able to drag his eyes away from the tar-stained shirt and the blood soaking through one knee of his breeches.

'I think the frigate is chasing *Aranmore*, Leigh.' He leaned on the chart, his scarred hands taking the weight.

Galbraith said, 'Suppose you're wrong, sir?'

Cristie forced a grin, and said, 'There was only one man who was never wrong, Mr Galbraith, an' they crucified *him*!'

Adam lingered on the warning, and knew what it must have cost Galbraith to say it.

'But if I'm not? If the Algerines capture *Aranmore*,' he hesitated, loathing it, 'it will make Lord Rhodes a laughing-stock. The hostages could be used for bargaining, and so much for "a show of strength".'

Galbraith nodded, understanding. Experience, instinct; he did not know how it came about. And he was ashamed that he was glad the choice was not his. Nor probably ever would be.

He watched the captain's face as he beckoned to Midshipman Cousens. Outwardly calm again, his voice unhurried, thinking aloud while he held out one arm to allow his coxswain to clip the old sword into position.

'Make to Flag, Mr Cousens. *Enemy in sight to the west, steering west-by-south*.' He saw Cristie acknowledge it. '*In pursuit of . . .*' He smiled at the youth's frowing features. 'Spell it out. *Aranmore*.'

It took physical effort to take and raise the spare telescope. The next few hours would be vital. He heard the flags squeaking aloft and in his mind saw them breaking out at the yard and, across that mile or so of lively water, another signals midshipman like Cousens reading the signal, as someone else wrote it down on a slate.

Cousens' brow was furrowed in concentration. 'From Flag, sir. *Acknowledged*.' He sounded rather subdued. 'Flag's calling up *Halcyon*, sir.'

Adam snapped, 'No use! *Halcyon*'s too far downwind – it will take her a whole watch to close with them!'

Cousens confirmed it. '*Chase*, sir.'

Galbraith was beside him again. 'They might run for it when they see *Halcyon*, sir.'

'I think not. The man in command will lose his head if he fails this time. And he will know it!'

He looked back at the signals party.

'Anything, Mr Cousens?'

Sullivan's voice broke the spell, '*Deck thar!* Frigate's opened fire, sir!'

He heard the distant thuds, bow-chasers, he thought, testing the range, hoping for a crippling shot.

Cousens shouted, 'Signal *Chase* is still flying, sir!'

Adam walked to the compass, the helmsmen gazing past him as if he was invisible, the big double-wheel moving slightly this way or that, each sail filled and fighting the rudder.

He said, 'Then acknowledge it, Mr Cousens.' And swung away, as if he might see in the boy's eyes the folly of his own decision. 'Get the hands aloft, Mr Galbraith! T'gallants and royals!' He grinned, the strain and doubt recoiling like beaten enemies. 'The stuns'ls too, when we may!' He strode over to Cristie and his mates. 'How so?'

'West-by-north, sir.' The master gave a wintry smile, as if the madness was infectious. 'It'll give 'er room to run down on the bugger!'

'Stand by, on the quarterdeck! Man the braces there!'

Another squall moaned through the stays and shrouds, and the canvas cracked as if it would tear itself from the yards as the helm went over.

'Flag is repeating our number, sir!' Cousens' words were almost drowned by the distant reverberating crash of mortars. The bombardment had begun.

Galbraith shook his head. 'Hoist another ensign, Mr Cousens,' and attempted to smile, to share what the captain was doing. 'That will be duty enough for you today!'

He watched the seamen running from one task to the next, not one tripping over a gun tackle or snatching up the wrong line or halliard. All the training and the hard knocks had paid off. It was insanity, and he could feel it driving away his reserve and his concern at the captain's deliberate misinterpretation of the admiral's signal. He had even found time to note it and sign the log, so that no one else could be officially blamed.

Galbraith saw Napier handing his captain a clean shirt, laughing at something he said as he pulled it over his unruly hair. The sunlight was stronger now, enough to shine briefly on the locket the captain was wearing, the one he had seen in the cabin with the letters.

He felt a sudden chill as the boy handed Captain Bolitho his coat, not the one he had been wearing when he had first appeared on deck, if he had ever left it, but the gold-laced dress uniform coat with the bright epaulettes. A ready target for any marksman. Madness again, but Galbraith could imagine him wearing no other this day.

'West-by-north, sir! Steady she goes!'

Adam looked along his ship, hearing the intermittent crash of gunfire. *Halcyon* was under fire already, long-range shots, like the ones laid on *Aranmore*.

He thought of Avery, his comments concerning the infamous Captain Martinez, and touched the locket beneath the clean shirt, and said aloud, 'You were right, George, and nobody saw it. The face in the crowd.'

He turned to see the other ensign breaking to the wind, seeming to trail on the dark horizon as the ship heeled over, knowing that his mind must be empty now of everything which might weaken his resolve. But a memory of his uncle came, as he had seen him all those other times.

'So let's be about it, then!'

Luke Jago stood by the mainmast's great trunk and looked along the frigate's maindeck. So many times; different ships and in all weathers, but always the same pattern. The whole larboard battery of eighteen-pounders had been run in, hauled up the tilting deck by their sweating crews, held in position by their taut tackles and ready for loading. Each crew was standing by with the tools of their trade, rammers and sponges, handspikes and charges, while every gun captain had already selected a perfect ball from his shot garland for the first, perhaps vital broadside. Around and at the foot of every mast the boarding pikes had been freed from their lashings, ready to snatch up and spit anyone brave or stupid enough to attempt to board them. The weapons chests were empty, and each man had armed himself with cutlass or axe with no more uncertainty than a farm-hand selecting a pitchfork.

He could sense the new midshipman watching him, breathing hard in his efforts to keep up with the captain's coxswain. Jago had wondered why the captain had given him the task of nursing Commodore Deighton's son. One day he would be an officer like Massie or so many others he had known, quick to forget past favours, and the secret skills which only true seamen knew and could pass on.

He felt the deck jerk to the double crash of the bomb's two mortars. Even at this distance, the ships were barely visible through the haze and dust, and yet the mortars' recoil seemed to rebound from the very seabed.

He had heard some of the men joking about the captain's reading of the flagship's signal. They would be putting bets on it too, if he had made a serious mistake. He loosened the cutlass in his belt, swearing quietly. Captain Bolitho would be a marked man anyway, as far as the admiral was concerned.

He said to the midshipman, 'You'll be needed to pass messages between the forrard guns, under Mr Massie,' he jerked his thumb in the direction of the quarterdeck, 'an' the cap'n. And if *he* falls, to th' next in command aft.'

He saw the boy blink, but he showed no fear. And he listened. He glanced at Midshipman Sandell by the empty boat-tier, even now snapping at some luckless seaman. He'd be no bloody loss to anyone.

He said, 'An' remember, Mr Deighton, always *walk*, never run. That only makes the lads jumpy.' He grinned at Deighton's seriousness. 'Stops you bein' a target too!'

Then, seeing his expression, he touched the midshipman's arm. 'Forget I said that. It just came out.'

He stared at his own scarred hand on the boy's sleeve. *Let him think what he damn well likes. He'll not care a straw for a common seaman.* But it would not hold.

He said, 'Now we'll carry on aft.'

Deighton said, 'It seems so empty without the boats on deck.'

'Never you mind them. We'll pick 'em up afore sunset.'

Deighton said softly, 'Do you believe that, really?'

Jago nodded to Campbell, who was leaning on a handspike near his gun. Like most of the crews he had stripped to the waist, his scarred back a living testimony to his strength.

Jago sighed. Or stupidity. It was not long since he had done the same, his defiance of the authority which had wrongly punished him, leaving him scarred until the day he dropped.

The boy was murmuring, 'I've never been in a real sea fight before.'

Jago knew that Deighton had transferred from the old *Vanoc*, a frigate said to be so infested with rot that she was as ripe as a pear, with only her copper holding her together.

He looked up at the towering masts and their bulging pyramids of canvas. From down here, the topgallant masts appeared to be bending like whips to the mounting pressure.

It was there again. Pride. Something he had all but taken an oath against. But she was flying through the water, spray bursting through the beakhead and drenching the figurehead's naked shoulders, a veritable sea nymph. He saw *Halcyon*, so much closer now, heeling over at a steep angle from *Unrivalled*'s bow. A well-handled ship, he conceded. But no match for the big Dutchman.

And the lookouts had reported that the merchantman *Aranmore* was somewhere ahead. Victim or prize, it depended on which side you took.

Jago thought of the girl he had helped to carry below. He stared at the poop, the officers' figures leaning over to the sloping deck as if they were nailed to it to hold them in position. And now she was out there with her bullyboy of a husband and God alone knew how many other important passengers. Jago had seen the captain's face that night, and again when he had gone ashore to see her, even if he had not intended to meet her or it had been a complete accident. Jago thought otherwise. He shaded his eyes and saw the captain standing with one hand on the quarterdeck rail. By that same ladder.

And why not? As smart as paint, she was. He smiled crookedly. And she knew it, what's more.

The sound of cannon fire across the sea's face, and for an instant Jago imagined that the wind had changed direction.

Sullivan's voice cut through the boom of canvas and the groan of straining cordage. 'Deck thar! *Halcyon*'s under fire!'

Jago ran to the side and stood on a gun truck to get a better view. *Halcyon* was as before, cutting through the water, her ensigns very white against the hazy sky, their scarlet crosses like blood. Then there was a sudden groan, and her foretopmast and spars began to topple; the sea and wind muffled the sound, and yet he seemed to hear it clearly, the slithering tangle of masts and rigging, snapping cordage and torn canvas, and then the complete mass plunging over the lee bow, flinging up spectres of spray. There would be men there, too, some killed in the fall, others dragged over the side by broken shrouds and stays, dying even as he watched, while others ran to hack the debris away. There was never time for pity.

Within minutes the fallen foretopmast was dragging *Halcyon* around like a giant sea anchor, and her guns were pointing impotently at open water.

'Stand by to wear ship!' That was the first lieutenant, voice distorted by his speaking trumpet. *'Pipe the hands to the braces!'*

Jago waited, feeling the ship's response to wind and rudder. The afterguard tramping past those same officers, hauling at the mizzen braces while *Unrivalled* altered course to windward, as close as she'd come, some of the sails already whipping and cracking in protest until more hands brought them under control.

Midshipman Deighton called, 'What are we doing?'

Jago watched the tapering bowsprit and jib boom, the enemy frigate clearly visible for the first time, as if sliding downwind to larboard. Captain Bolitho was going to try and overreach the enemy, to claw into the wind and then run down on them, much as he had heard the dour sailing master describe.

But all he said was, 'We're going to fight. So be ready!' Then, together, they climbed the ladder to the quarterdeck.

Adam Bolitho looked only briefly at the scene on the quarterdeck. The marines, their boots skidding on the wet planking while they secured the braces again before snatching up their muskets and running back to their stations. Four men on the wheel now, one of Cristie's mates adding his weight to the fight against wind and rudder.

He glanced up at the masthead pendant, almost hidden by the wildly cracking canvas. The wind was still steady, from the north-east, but from aft he could believe it was almost directly abeam. The ship lay hard over, and his eyes stung as a shaft of sunlight found them for the first time.

And the enemy was still firing at *Halcyon*. There was no smoke to betray the shots, the wind was too strong, but he could see the other frigate's sails pockmarked with holes, and great, raw gashes along her engaged side; the enemy was trying to rid himself of one foe before dealing with the real threat from *Unrivalled*. He fought back the anger. Rhodes was so intent on humiliating him that he had been blind to the true danger. Dutch-built frigates were heavier, and could take a lot of punishment. *Halcyon* could not even close the range and hit back. He saw her main-topmast reel drunkenly now in a tangle of black cordage, like something trapped in a net, before crashing down across her gangway.

He took a telescope from its rack and trained it on the other frigate. Magnified in the powerful glass, he could see terrible damage, could feel her pain, and knew he was thinking of his beloved *Anemone* in her last fight against odds. When he had been badly wounded, and unable to prevent her colours being struck to the American.

He heard Cristie yell, 'As close as she'll come, sir! Nor'-west-by-west!'

He realised that Midshipman Deighton was beside him at the rail, and said, 'Take a good look, Mr Deighton. That is a ship to be proud of.' He lowered the glass, but not before he had seen the tiny threads of scarlet running down *Halcyon*'s tumblehome from the forward scuppers, as if the ship and not her people was bleeding to death. But an ensign was still flying, and from what he had heard of her captain another would be in readiness to bend on if it was shot away.

What sort of men were they about to fight?

He had heard one of the master's mates ask Cristie the same question.

He had answered harshly, 'The scum of a dozen waterfronts, gallows-bait the lot of 'em! But they'll fight right enough. Pirates, deserters, mutineers, they've no choice left any more!'

More shots found their mark in *Halcyon*. Her steering had been carried away, or perhaps there were only dead men at her wheel now. She was drifting, but occasionally a single gun would fire at her attacker, despite the range.

Adam said, 'You may load and run out now.' The gun captains would know. Single shots this time; an overloaded eighteen-pounder would be useless. He watched the sea boiling away from the lee side, the one thing he had dreaded about holding the wind-gage. Maximum elevation for the first broadside. And after that . . .

He found that he was holding the locket through his spray-soaked shirt. At least she was free of the worry and the strain at every separation.

And I have nobody to grieve for me.

'Sir!' It was Galbraith, reaching out as if to drag him from his sudden despair.

'What is it?'

Galbraith could not seem to find the words immediately. '*Halcyon*, sir! They're cheering!' He fell silent, as if shocked at his own emotion. '*Cheering us!*'

Adam stared across the wind-torn water at the battered, defiant ship, and faintly, above the shipboard sounds and the squeal of gun trucks, he heard it. The hand reaching out again. The lifeline.

He shouted, 'As you bear, Mr Massie! On the uproll!'

It was too far, but the other frigate was changing tack. Preparing to fight, and, if possible, to board on their own terms.

'*Fire!*'

Adam gripped young Deighton's arm and felt him jump as if he had been shot.

'Go forrard to the carronades. Remind them *not to fire* until ordered!' He shook him gently. 'Can you do that?'

Surprisingly, the youth smiled, for the first time.

'Aye, ready, sir!'

He hurried down the ladder and walked purposefully forward, not even faltering when, gun by gun, the larboard battery recoiled from their open ports. Adam heard muffled shouts and felt the impact of a heavy ball smashing into the side, and thought of O'Beirne below in his domain, his glittering instruments laid out with the same care as these gun captains took with theirs.

'*Sponge out! Reload!* Move yerself, that man!'

'Take in the courses, Mr Galbraith.' Adam leaned over the rail and saw the spare hands running to obey the call. With the big courses brailed up and loosely furled it was like being stripped naked, with the ship open from forecastle to taffrail.

And there was the enemy. In mid-tack, sails all in disarray, some ports empty, others with their guns already run out for the next encounter.

'*Ready*, sir!'

Every gun captain was staring aft with raised fist, the gun crews barely flinching as another mass of iron slammed into the lower hull. They were on a converging tack, like a great arrowhead painted on the sea. Two ships, all else unimportant, and even *Halcyon*'s brave defiance forgotten. The other ship was beginning to lean to the wind on the opposite tack, but just for a minute she would be bows-on, unable to lay a single gun on *Unrivalled*. A minute, maybe less.

Adam found that his sword was in his hand, and that he was standing away from the rail, and yet he remembered neither.

'As you bear, lads!' How could a minute last so long?

He thought he heard the far-off rumble of heavy guns. Rhodes was still bombarding the fortifications, as timeless as those ancient ramparts in Malta where the invisible orchestra had played for them and they had taken, one from the other. Without question.

The sword sliced down, like glass in the sunlight.

'*Fire!*'

Gun by gun, each hurling itself inboard to be manhandled and reloaded without a second to fumble or consider.

He saw holes appear in the other ship's foresail and jib, and long fragments of gilded woodwork blasted from the ornate beakhead. But she was swinging through the wind; they would be alongside and mad for revenge. The boarding nets would merely delay the inevitable.

He heard Napier shout; it was more like a scream. '*Foremast*, sir!'

Adam had seen some of *Unrivalled*'s shots cutting through the water beyond the target. It was too difficult for them to lay their guns with any hope of accuracy.

It was impossible, but the enemy's whole foremast was going over the side, as if severed by some great, invisible axe.

Shots hammered into the deck and he saw two marines fall

305

from the hammock nettings. He heard the bang of swivels from the tops and knew that Bosanquet's men were following their orders, their marksmen already firing down into the mass of figures scrambling through and over the fallen mast to reach the point of collision. But Bosanquet would never know. He lay with one immaculate leg bent under him, his face destroyed by a splintered ball which had come through one of the gunports.

Luxmore, his second-in-command, was already down there with his own party, bayonets gleaming in the smoky light, all mercy gone as the first boarders leaped wildly across the narrow gap of water only to be hacked down or impaled. Closer and closer, until *Unrivalled*'s long jib boom, its canvas in rags, was pointing directly at the enemy's forecastle.

Adam sliced the air with his sword again. Had the carronade crews understood? Had Deighton managed to reach them or had he, too, been killed? But Deighton was here beside him, and he shook himself, feeling the despair falling away.

It was more a sensation than a sound; the carronades were almost touching the other ship when they belched smoke and lurched inboard on their slides.

Adam yelled, 'To me, *Unrivalled*!' Then he ran along the gangway, hearing the shots, feeling some of them crack into wood and metal and flesh. The nets hung in shreds, and the massed boarding party was blasted into a pile of bloody gruel. Men were running to follow him, and he saw Campbell wielding a boarding axe, hacking down anyone who tried to prevent *Unrivalled*'s people from boarding.

And all the while, through the bang of muskets and the clash of steel in the hand-to-hand fighting, and the screams and pleas which went unheard in any language, he could think only of one fact which stood out above all else. Pirates, corsairs, mercenaries, the names by which the enemy were known meant nothing. Somehow he knew that the man who had offered shelter to the French frigates in the event of Napoleon's escape from Elba was here *in this ship*. It was all that counted. Martinez, indirectly or otherwise, had killed Richard Bolitho, as surely as if he had aimed the weapon.

Someone lunged at him with a sword and he heard Jago

shout, 'Down *you* go, you bastard!' The man fell over some broken timber to be crushed between the two hulls.

His arm felt like lead and throbbed with pain, and there was blood on his hand, his own or another's he neither knew nor cared.

They were halfway along the unfamiliar deck, some of the enemy still putting up a fierce resistance, but many falling as his marines directed a swivel gun from the ship's gangway.

Massie was down, his hands like claws across his stomach as he fell. Adam saw Lieutenant Wynter stoop to help him, and Massie's angry rejection, shaking his head as if to urge him back into the fight. Then the blood came and it did not stop. Massie had had his way, and had remained quite alone to the end.

He heard Galbraith shouting above the din, and saw more men climbing over the fallen rigging to join the first boarders and their own captain. There was cheering too, and he wondered how they could find the strength. He hacked a sword aside and felt the pain tear his muscles as the point grated against the man's ribs before the blade found its mark, choking the scream before it had begun. It seemed to take all his strength to tug it free. Somehow he had dragged himself up a ladder, where smaller groups of figures were locked in what he knew was the final resistance.

Jago gasped, 'I can see smoke, sir! Fire below, by my guess!'

Adam gripped a stanchion and gulped at the air. 'Get our wounded across to the ship! Leave *nobody*!'

Jago peered at him. How did he know it was over? Men were still fighting, or chasing some of the defenders, hacking them down.

Adam wiped his face with his sleeve and almost laughed. It was his best uniform, the one he had been wearing when he had gone to her room. Madness. A wild dream. He gripped his sword even more tightly, knowing that if he allowed himself to laugh he would be unable to stop it.

He heard someone gasp and swung round to see Napier on one knee, a wood splinter protruding from his thigh like a bloody quill.

'Here, my lad, you're coming with me!' Then, as he bent

307

to give the boy his arm, he saw Martinez, crouching behind a raised hatch, a pistol in one hand. It had to be him; but how could he be so sure? It was only a glimpse, too quick for him to see the dark eyes widen with shocked disbelief as he had stared first at the slim figure in a post-captain's soiled coat, and then, instantly, at the old sword. Something like recognition, something he had never forgotten.

And it was too late. Adam could not reach him with his sword, and if Martinez fired now he would surely kill the boy he had lifted from this stained and fought-over planking.

Martinez said thickly, *'Bo-lye-tho.'* And took careful aim.

But the shot seemed louder, or came from a different bearing. It was the marine corporal Bloxham, Bosanquet's crack shot. He stepped carefully over a corpse and kicked the unfired pistol across the deck.

He said, "Ere, sir, I'll take the lad from you,' and grinned, the strain slipping from his features. 'But I'll just reload old Bess 'ere first, to be on the safe side!'

Adam touched his arm, and walked across to look at the dead man. He heard the sudden wave of frantic cheering. The fight was over.

My men. And they had won the day, because of a trust which few could explain. Until the next time. Now he must go and face these same men, and share it with them before the pain of loss intruded.

He gazed along the disputed deck, with its bloody scars of battle. Soon only the dead and the poor wretches who had fled below would remain.

He saw his own ship angled away from the bows, suddenly clear in the fresh sunlight, her wounds hidden by drifting smoke, and only then did he know what had held him here. He looked down into the dead face, frozen at the instant of impact. As he had sworn to do.

Perhaps he had expected elation, or a sense of revenge. There was nothing.

He heard voices calling out and knew they would come to find him, interrupting this moment which he could share with only one.

He let his sword arm fall to his side and turned once more

to look at his ship, and smiled a little, as if he had heard someone speak.

'Thank you, Uncle.'

The Most Coveted Gift.

**Order further Alexander Kent titles
from your local bookshop, or have them delivered
direct to your door by Bookpost**

☐	**Relentless Pursuit**	0 09 941488 0	£5.99
☐	**Man of War**	0 09 943628 0	£6.99
☐	**Form Line of Battle**	0 09 908850 9	£5.99
☐	**Cross of St George**	0 09 942166 6	£5.99
☐	**Enemy in Sight**	0 09 905520 1	£5.99
☐	**Success to the Brave**	0 09 936370 4	£5.99
☐	**Passage to Mutiny**	0 09 914160 4	£5.99

Free post and packing
Overseas customers allow £2 per paperback

Phone: 01624 677237

Post: Random House Books
c/o Bookpost, PO Box 29, Douglas, Isle of Man IM99 1BQ

Fax: 01624 670923

email: bookshop@enterprise.net

Cheques (payable to Bookpost) and credit cards accepted

Prices and availability subject to change without notice.
Allow 28 days for delivery.
When placing your order, please state if you do not wish to receive any
additional information.

www.randomhouse.co.uk/arrowbooks

arrow books